Dear Reader,

Thank you for choosing to celebrate more than a decade of award-winning romance with Arabesque. In recognition of its ten-year anniversary, Arabesque launched a special collector's series in 2004 honoring the authors who pioneered African-American romance. With a unique 3-in-1 book format, each anthology features the most beloved works of the Arabesque imprint.

Intriguing, intense and sensuous, this special collector's series was launched with *First Touch,* which included three of Arabesque's first published novels written by Sandra Kitt, Francis Ray and Eboni Snoe. It was followed by *Hideaway Saga,* three novels from award-winning author Rochelle Alers; the third in the series, *Falcon Saga,* by Francis Ray; and concluded with Brenda Jackson's *Madaris Saga.*

In 2005 we continued the series with Donna Hill's *Courageous Hearts,* Felicia Mason's *Seductive Hearts,* Bette Ford's *Passionate Hearts* and, in November, Shirley Hailstock's *Magnetic Hearts.*

This year we are continuing the series with collections from Arabesque authors Angela Benson, Lynn Emery, Monica Jackson and Gwynne Forster. The book you are holding—*Unforgettable Passion*—includes three sizzling romances from Gwynne Forster: *Sealed with a Kiss, Against All Odds* and *Ecstasy.*

We hope you enjoy these romances and please give us your feedback at our Web site, at www.kimanipress.com.

Sincerely,

Evette Porter
Arabesque Editor
Kimani Press

# GWYNNE FORSTER

## UNFORGETTABLE PASSION

ARABESQUE®

UNFORGETTABLE PASSION

An Arabesque novel published by Kimani Press 2006

Copyright © 2006 by Gwendolyn Johnson Acsadi

ISBN-13: 978-1-58314-724-5
ISBN-10:    1-58314-724-1

The publisher acknowledges the copyright holder of the individual works as follows:

SEALED WITH A KISS
Copyright © 2006 by Gwendolyn Johnson Acsadi

AGAINST ALL ODDS
Copyright © 2006 by Gwendolyn Johnson Acsadi

ECSTASY
Copyright © 2006 by Gwendolyn Johnson Acsadi

www.kimanipress.com

**Printed in U.S.A.**

# CONTENTS

# SEALED WITH A KISS

# Chapter 1

She burrowed deeper into her pillow, hoping to silence the persistent ringing in her ear. Finally, she gave up trying to sleep and reached for the phone.

"It's six-thirty in the morning. Would whoever you are please go back to sleep?"

"Gal, I want you to come over here right away. There's something I ought to tell you." Naomi sighed and sat up in bed. The Reverend Judd Logan's commands did not perturb Naomi. She had dealt with her paternal grandfather's whims and orders since she was seven years old, when he became her guardian and she went to live with him. She tumbled out of bed, her eyes still heavy with sleep, and groped for the bathroom. She hadn't asked him whether it was urgent: of course it was. To him, everything was urgent. And you never knew what to expect when you received his summons, but you could be certain that you were supposed to treat it as if it came from a court of law. She smiled despite herself. She was twenty-nine years old, but she was still a child as far as he was concerned. However, because she loved him, she didn't have trouble with that. After all, there was nearly a seventy-year difference in their ages. Thoughts of his age gave her a moment of anxiety; his call really could be urgent. She dressed hurriedly, remembering to take a light jacket. Early mornings in October were sometimes chilly.

The drive from her condominium in Bethesda, Maryland, across Washington to Alexandria, Virginia, were her grandfather lived, took half an hour even at that time of morning. She parked her gray Taurus in front of her grandfather's imposing Tudor-style home and rang the doorbell before letting herself in. Judd Logan didn't like surprises. If you handed him one, he lectured you for an hour.

She entered the foyer dragging her feet, wondering at her sudden feeling of apprehension. The spacious vestibule had been her favorite childhood haunt, because her grandfather had put a console piano there for her and always placed little gifts and surprises on it. She would look up from her practice and notice him listening raptly, though he never told her that he enjoyed her playing. The piano remained, but it held no attraction; her childhood had ended abruptly when she was sixteen.

She found him in his study, writing his memoirs, and walked over to hug him, but he dusted her off with a gruff "Not now, gal, wait until I finish this sentence." How typical of him to shun affection, she thought; not once in the nearly twenty-two years since she had gone to live with him had he ever made a gesture toward her that she could confuse with true emotional warmth. She knew that he locked his feelings inside, but she wished he would learn a little something about affection before he left this earth. At times, she'd give anything for a hug from him—or from just about anybody. For some odd reason, this was one of those times.

With a sigh, she sat down, perusing the snow-white curly hair that framed his dark, barely lined face and the piercing hazel-brown eyes that seemed to reflect a knowledge of all the ages gone by.

"What's this about, Grandpa? You seemed a little agitated."

He turned his writing pad upside down, drew a deep breath, and plunged in without preliminaries. "I've had two letters from them and yesterday I finally got a phone call. It's about the baby."

She jerked forward. "The baby? *What* baby? Who called you?"

The old man looked at her, and a sense of dread invaded her as she saw his pity and realized it was for her. "Yours, gal. I tried back then to spare you this. I thought that since the adoption papers were sealed by law, no one would ever know. But they found me, and that means they can find you, too. The adoptive mother says that the child wants to find its birth mother." She saw him wince and knew that the lifelessness that she felt was mirrored in her face.

"Grandpa, I've lived as a single woman with no children, and I've worked to help young girls avoid experiencing what I went through. I'm a role model. How can I explain this?" She pushed back the temptation to scream. "I knew I shouldn't have given in to their pressure, their browbeating. The counselor at the clinic made me feel that if I didn't give the baby up for adoption, it wouldn't have a chance at a normal, happy life. They said a child born to a teenager starts life with two strikes against it. I was made to feel selfish and incompetent when I held out against them. But they finally convinced me, and I gave in. It didn't help that I was depressed, and Chuck didn't answer my letters. Grandpa, I've been sorry every day since I signed that paper. They didn't even let me see the baby, said it was best to avoid any bonding. I wish you hadn't let me do it."

He stood and braced his back with both hands. "No point in going over that now, gal; we've got to deal with this last letter. Take my advice and let well enough alone. Don't turn your life upside down; you'll regret it."

Naomi looked off into space, reliving those days when all that she loved had disintegrated around her. She spoke softly, forcing words from her mouth. "I've spent the last thirteen years trying to pretend that it never happened, but you know, Grandpa, it has still influenced every move and colored every decision that I've made."

"I know, Naomi gal. But where would you be now if you had kept that child and been disgraced?" She looked around them indulgently at the replicas of bygone eras. Judd's 1925 degree from the Yale University School of Divinity, framed in gold leaf, hung on the wall. Doilies that her grandmother had crocheted more than sixty years earlier rested on the backs of overstuffed velvet chairs. And on the floor lay the Persian carpet that the old man's congregation had given him on his fortieth birthday. She smiled in sympathetic understanding.

"Grandpa, out-of-wedlock motherhood is not the burden for a woman that it was in your day. I tried to tell you that."

He shook his snow-white head. "They wanted to reach the child's biological father, too, but, well…"

"Yes." She interrupted him gently. "I remember believing that Chuck had deserted me, and he'd drowned surfing off Honolulu. I didn't know. I'll never understand that, either, you know; he was a champion swimmer. I've wondered if he was as unhappy as I was and if it made him careless."

"I'd feel better about this whole thing, gal, if you'd just find yourself a nice young man and get married. You ought to be married; I won't live forever."

She stared at him, nearly laughing. Wasn't it typical of him to bring that up? He could weave it into a technical discussion of the pyramids of Egypt. She broke off her incredulous glare; he didn't accept reprimands, either spoken or silent. "Get married? I've stayed away from men. Who would accept my having a baby, giving it up for adoption, and never bothering to tell its father? What man do you think is going to accept all that? Anyway, I'm happy just as I am, and I have no intention of offering myself to anybody for approval."

The old man straightened up and ran a hand across his still remarkably handsome face, now nearly black from age. "A man who loves you will understand and accept it, Naomi. One who loves you, gal," he said softly. The sentiment seemed too much for him, and he reverted to type. "You have to watch yourself. You're moving up in that school board and working with that foundation for girls. You're out to change the world, and you don't need this on your neck." She opened her mouth to speak and thought better of it. Judd had managed things for her since she was a child; she was a woman now.

"You let me handle this thing, gal, it's best you not get involved." She didn't care if he mistook her silence for compliance. She had learned long ago not to argue, but she would do whatever she wanted to.

It seemed to her that the drive back to her studio on upper Connecticut Avenue in Washington took hours longer than usual; a jackknifed truck, a two-car accident, rubber necking, and the weather slowed her progress. The day was becoming one big conspiracy against her peace of mind. "Am I getting paranoid?" she asked herself, attempting to inject humor into something that wasn't funny. Having to assume the role of mother nearly fourteen years after the fact was downright hilarious—if you were listening to a stand-up comic. She would not fall apart; she was doggoned if she would, and to prove it, she hummed every aria from *La Traviata* that she could remember.

She didn't get much done that day, because she spent part of it listless and unable to concentrate and the rest optimistically shuffling harebrained schemes to locate her child. She had to adjust to a different world, one that wasn't real, and the effort was taking a toll. She couldn't summon her usual enthusiasm during her tutoring session that evening and could hardly wait to get home. But tomorrow would be different, she vowed. "I'm not going to keel over because of this."

At home that evening, she curled up in her favorite chair, intent on relaxing with a cup of tea and soothing music, determined to get a handle on things. "I'm going to find something to laugh about at least once an hour," she swore. As she searched the dial on her radio, a deep, beautifully sonorous male voice caught her attention, sending shock waves through her and raising goose bumps on her forearms. Well, he might have a bedroom voice, she quickly decided, but his ideas were a different matter. "Educated career women, including our African American women, put jobs before children and family, and that is a primary factor in family breakups and youthful delinquency," he stated with complete confidence.

How could anyone with enough prestige to be a panelist on that program make such a claim? He was crediting women with too much responsibility for some of the world's worst problems.

She rarely allowed herself to become furious about anything; anger crippled a person. But she *had* to tell him off. After trying repeatedly to telephone the radio station and getting a busy signal, she noted the station's call letters and flipped off the radio. Meade, they'd called him. She would write him and urge him into the twentieth century.

Her immense relief at being able to concentrate on something impersonal, to feel her natural inclination to mischief surface, restored her sense of well-being. She embraced the blessed diversion and wholeheartedly went about giving Mr. Meade his comeuppance. But as she walked briskly, almost skipping to her desk, she admitted to herself that the basis for her outrage was more than intellectual. His comments had come bruisingly close to an implied indictment of her, even if she didn't deserve it. She shrugged it off and began the letter.

"Mr. Meade," she wrote, "I don't know by what right you're an authority on the family—and I doubt from your comments tonight in the program *Capitol Life* that you are—but you most certainly are not an authority on women. If a great many American women, and especially African American women, didn't work outside the home, their families would starve. Would that bother you? And if you tried being a tiny bit more masculine, maybe the women with whom you associate might be 'less aggressive,' as you put it, softer and more feminine. Don't you think we women have a big enough load without you dumping all that on us? Be a pal and give us a break, please. And don't forget, Mr. Meade, even *squash* have fathers. Please be a good sport and don't answer this note. Most sincerely, Naomi Logan." She addressed it to him in care of the program and the station.

That should take care of him, she decided, already dismissing the incident. But within a week, she had his blunt reply: "Dear Ms. Logan, if you had listened to everything I said and had understood it, you might not have accused me so unfairly. From the content of your letter, it would appear that you've got some guilt you need to work through. Or are you apologizing for being a career woman? If the shoe fits, wear it. The lack of a reply would be much appreciated. Yours, Rufus Meade."

Naomi hadn't planned to pursue her argument with Rufus Meade; it was enough that she'd told him what she thought of his ideas and that her letter had annoyed him. A glance at her watch told her that the weekly radio program *Capitol Life* was about to begin. Curious as to whether he was a regular panelist, she tuned in. He wasn't a regular, she learned, but had been invited back because of the clamor that his statement the previous week had caused.

The moderator introduced Rufus, who lost no time in defending his position. "Eighty percent of those who wrote or called protesting my remarks were women; most of the men thought I didn't go far enough. Has any of you asked the children in these street gangs where their mothers are when they get home from school—provided they're in school—what they do after school, when they last had a home-cooked meal, whether their parents know where they are? I have. Their mothers aren't home, so they don't know where their children are or what they're doing. With nobody to control them, the children hang out in the street, and that is how we lose them. Children need parental guidance. When it was the norm in this society for mothers to remain at home, we had fewer social problems—less delinquency and fewer divorces. One protestor wrote me that even squash have fathers. Yes, they do. And they also have mothers who stick with them until they're old enough to fend for themselves. In fact, the mothers die nurturing their little ones' development."

Naomi rubbed her fingers together in frustration. A sensible person would ignore the man and his archaic ideas. She flipped off the radio in the middle of one of his sentences. Wednesday's mail brought another note from him.

"Dear Ms. Logan, I hope you tuned in to *Capitol Life* Sunday night. Some of my remarks were for your benefit. Of course, if you have a closed mind, I was merely throwing chaff to a gusty wind. Can't say I didn't try, though. Yours, RM."

Excitement coursed through her as she read his note. She knew that not answering would be the best way to get the better of him. He wanted her to be annoyed, and if he didn't hear from her, he would assume that she had lost interest. But she couldn't resist the temptation, and she bet he was counting on that.

Her reply read, "Dear Mr. Meade, next time you're on the air, I'd appreciate your explaining what a two-month-old squash does when it no longer needs its mother and fends for itself. (Something tells me it gets eaten.) You didn't really mean to equate the maturity of a squash with achievement of adulthood in humans, did you? I'd try to straighten that out, if I were you. Don't bother to write. I'll keep tuning in to *Capitol Life*. Well, hang in there. Yours, NL."

She only had to wait four days for his answer. "Dear Ms. Logan, you have deliberately misunderstood me. I stand by my position that as long as women guarded the home rather than the office and the Mack truck, juvenile crime and divorce were less frequent occurrences. You are not seriously concerned with these urgent problems, so I will not waste time writing you again. I'm assuming you're a career woman, and my advice is to stick with your career; at least you'll have that. Yours, RM."

Naomi curved her mouth into a long, slow grin. She always enjoyed bedeviling straitlaced, overly serious people, though she acknowledged to herself that her cheekiness was a camouflage. It enabled her to cover her vulnerability and to shrug off problems, and besides, she loved her wicked side. Rufus Meade's words told her that he was easily provoked and had a short fuse, and she planned to light it; never would she forgo such a tantalizing challenge.

Curled up on her downy sofa, she wrote with relish: "Dear Mr. Meade, I've probably been unfair to you. You remind me so much of my grandfather, who was born just before the turn of the century. If you're also a nonagenarian, my sincere apologies. For what it's worth, I am not a 'career woman.' I am a woman who works at a job for which I am well trained. The alternative at present would be to marry a male chauvinist in exchange for my keep, or to take to the streets, since food, clothing, and shelter carry a price tag. But considering your concern for the fate of the family, I don't think you'd approve of the latter. But then, it isn't terribly different from the former, now, is it? Sorry, but I have to go; the Saturday afternoon Metropolitan Opera performance is just beginning, and I'm a sucker for *La Traviata*. Till next time. Naomi Logan." After addressing it to him, she mailed it and hurried back to listen to the opera.

Several days later, engrossed in her work, Naomi laid aside her paintbrush and easel and reluctantly lifted the phone receiver. In a voice meant to discourage the caller, she muttered, "Yes?"

There was a brief silence, and then a deep male voice responded. "Miss Logan, please."

She sat down, crossed her knee, and kicked off her right shoe. That voice could only belong to *him*. She had heard it only twice, but she would never forget it. It was a voice that commanded respect, that proclaimed its owner to be clever, authoritative, and manly, and, if you weren't annoyed by its message, it was sensually beautiful.

"Speaking," she said almost reluctantly, as if sensing the hand of fate. There was more silence. "I'm hanging up in thirty seconds," she snapped. "Why are you calling?"

His reply was tinged with what struck her as a grudging laugh. "Miss Logan, this is Rufus Meade. It seems that your spoken language is as caustic as your letters."

Her world suddenly brightened; she'd made him angry enough to call her. She tucked a little of her wild hair behind her ear and laughed. Many people had told her that her laughter sounded like bells clinking in the breeze. "I thought I had apologized for being disrespectful," she said softly, with an affected sweetness. "If Grandpa knew how I'd behaved toward an older person, he'd raise the devil."

"At the expense of being rude," he replied tightly. "I doubt that there's a ninety-year-old man on the face of this earth who is my equal, and if you're less than eighty, I'm prepared to demonstrate it."

Oh ho, she thought, and howled with laughter, hoping to infuriate him further. "My, my. Our ego's been pricked, and we've got a short temper, too."

"And less patience, madam. You're brimming with self-confidence, aren't you, Ms. Logan?" She assured him that she was. Up to then, his conversation had suggested to her that he didn't hold her in high regard, so his next words surprised her.

"Taking a swipe at me in person should be much more gratifying than having to settle for snide remarks via the mail and over the phone, so why don't you have lunch with me?"

She laughed again, turning the screw and enjoying it. "You couldn't be serious. Why would you think I'd enjoy the company of a man who prefers bimbos to women who can spell? No, thank you."

She sighed, concerned that she might have overdone it and realized that she had indeed when he replied in a deadly soft voice. "I hope you enjoy your own company, Ms. Logan. Sorry to have troubled you."

He hung up before she could reply, and a sense of disappointment washed over her, a peculiar feeling that warmth she hadn't realized she felt was suddenly lacking. It was strange and indefinable. She didn't welcome close male friendship because she couldn't afford them, and she had not been courting Rufus's interest. She had just been having fun, she reasoned, and he wasn't going to have the last word.

She got out her pen and paper and wrote: "Dear Rufus, how could one man have so many quirks? Bimbos, short temper, heavyweight ego, and heaven forbid, spoilsport. You need help, dear. Yours faithfully, Naomi."

Naomi hadn't heard from Rufus in three days, and she was glad; their conversation had left her with a sense of foreboding. She arrived home feeling exhausted from a two-hour argument with her fellow board members of One Last Chance that the foundation, which she had cofounded to aid girls with problems, would overstretch itself if it extended its facilities to boys. In the Washington, D.C., area, she had insisted, boys had the Police Athletic League for support, but for many girls, especially African American girls, there was only One Last Chance. And she knew its importance. How different her life might have been if the foundation had been there for her thirteen years ago, when she had been sixteen and forced to deal with the shattering aftermath of a misplaced trust.

She refreshed herself with a warm shower, dressed quickly in a dusty rose cowl-necked sweater and navy pants, and rushed to her best friend Marva's wedding rehearsal. Dusty rose reminded her of the roses that her mother had so carefully tended and that still flourished around the house on Queens Chapel Terrace, where she had lived with her parents. She couldn't recall those days well, but she thought she remembered her mother working in her garden on clear, sunny mornings during spring and summer. She regularly resisted the temptation to pass the house and look at the roses. She'd never seen any others that color, her favorite. It was why she had chosen a dress of that shade to wear as maid of honor at Marva's wedding.

Marva was her closest friend, though in Naomi's view they were exact opposites. The women's one priority was the permanent attainment of an eligible man. Marriage wasn't for her, but as maid of honor, she had to stand in for the bride—as close to the real thing as she would ever get. At times, she desperately longed for a man's love and for children—lots of them. But she could not risk the disclosure that an intimate relationship with a man would ultimately require, and to make certain that she was never tempted, she kept men at a distance.

Naomi knew that men found her attractive, and she had learned how to put them off with empty, meaningless patter. It wasn't that she didn't like any of them; she did. She wanted to kick herself when the groom's best man caught her scrutinizing him, a deeply bronzed six footer with a thin black mustache, good looks, and just the right amount of panache. She figured that her furtive glances had plumped his ego, because he immediately asked her out when the rehearsal was over. She deftly discouraged him, and it was becoming easier, she realized, when he backed off after just a tiny sample of her dazzling double-talk.

I'll pay for it, she thought, as she mused over the evening during her drive home. Whenever she misrepresented herself as frivolous or callous to a man whom she could have liked, she became depressed afterward. Already she felt a bit down. But she walked into her apartment determined to dispel it. The day had been a long one that she wouldn't soon forget. "Keep it light girl," she reminded herself, as she changed her clothes. To make certain that she did, she put on a jazz cassette and brightened her mood, dancing until she was soaked with perspiration and too exhausted to move. Then she showered, donned her old clothes, and settled down to work.

She took pride in her work, designing logos, labels, and stationery for large corporations and other businesses, and she was happiest when she produced an elegant, imaginative design. Her considerable skill and novel approaches made her much sought after, and she earned a good living. She was glad that a new ice-cream manufacturer liked a logo that she'd produced, though the company wanted a cow in the middle of it. A cow! She stared at the paper and watched the paint drying on her brush, but not one idea emerged. Why couldn't she dispel that strange something that welled up in her every time she thought of Rufus? It had been a week since her last provocative note to him, and she wondered whether he would answer. It was dangerous, she knew, to let her mind dwell on him, but his voice had a seductive, almost hypnotic effect on her. Where he was concerned, her mind did as it pleased. Tremors danced through her whenever she recalled his deep voice and lilting speech. Voices weren't supposed to have that effect, she told herself. But his was a powerful drug. Was he young? Old? Short? She tried without success to banish him from her thoughts. While she hummed softly and struggled to fit the cow into the ice cream logo, an impatient ringing of her doorbell and then a knock on the door startled her. Why hadn't the doorman announced the visitor, she wondered, as she peeped through the viewer and saw a man there.

"May I help you?" She couldn't see all of him. Tall, she guessed.

"I hope so. I'm looking for Naomi Logan." Her first reaction was a silent, "My God it's *him!*" Her palms suddenly became damp, and tiny shivers of anticipation rushed through her. She would never forget that voice. But she refused him the satisfaction of knowing that she remembered it. She'd written him on her personal stationery, but he'd sent his letter to her through the station; she didn't have a clue as to where he lived. She struggled to calm herself.

"Who is it, please?" Could that steady voice be hers?

"I'm Rufus Meade, and I'd like to see Miss Logan, if I may."

"I ought to leave him standing there," she grumbled to herself, but she knew that neither her sense of decency nor her curiosity would allow her to do it, and she opened the door.

Rufus Meade stood in the doorway staring at the woman who had vexed him beyond reason. She wasn't at all what he had expected. Around twenty-nine, he surmised, and by any measure, beautiful. Tall and slim, but deliciously curved. He let his gaze feast on her smooth dark skin, eyes the color of dark walnut, and long, thick curly black tresses that seemed to fly all over the place. God, he hadn't counted on this. Something just short of a full-blown desire burned in the pit of his belly. He recognized it as more than a simple craving for her; he wanted to know her totally, completely, and in every intimate way possible.

Naomi borrowed from her years of practice at shoving her emotions aside and pulled herself together first. If there was such a thing as an eviscerating, brain-damaging clap of thunder, she had just experienced it. Grasping the doorknob for support, she shifted her glance from his intense gaze, took in the rest of him, and then risked looking back into those strangely unsettling fawnlike eyes. And she had thought his voice a narcotic. Add that to the rest of him and…Lord! He was lethal! If she had any sense, she'd slam the door shut.

'You're Rufus Meade?" she asked. Trying unsuccessfully to appear calm, she knitted her brow and worried her bottom lip. She could see that he was uncomfortable, even slightly awed, as if he, too, was having a new and not particularly agreeable experience. But he shrugged his left shoulder, winked at her, and took control of the situation.

"Yes, I'm Rufus Meade, and don't tell me you're Naomi Logan."

She laughed, forgetting her paint-smeared jeans and T-shirt and her bare feet. "Since you don't look anywhere near ninety, I want to see some identification." He pulled out his driver's license and handed it to her, nodding in approval as he did so.

"I see you're a fast thinker. Can't be too careful these days."

Unable to resist needling him, she gave him her sweetest smile. "Do you think a bimbo would have thought to do that?" It was the kind of repartee that she used as a screen to hide her interest in a man or to dampen his, like crossing water to throw an animal off one's trail.

His silence gave her a very uneasy feeling. What if he was dangerous? She didn't know a thing about him. She tried to view him with the crust caused by his physical attractiveness removed from her eyes. Clearly he was a most unlikely candidate for ridicule; nothing about him suggested it. A strapping, virile male of about thirty-four, he was good-looking, with smooth dark skin and large fawnlike eyes, a lean face, clean shaven and apparently well mannered. She backed up a step. The man took up a lot of psychological space and had an aura of steely strength. He was also at least six feet four, and he wore clothes like a model. So much for that, she concluded silently; all I learned is that I like what I see.

His demeanor was that of a self-possessed man. Why, then, did he behave as if he wanted to eat nails? She was tempted to ask him, but she doubted his mood would tolerate the impertinence. He leaned against her door, hands in his pockets, and swept his gaze over her.

"Miss Logan, your tongue is tart enough to make a saint turn in his halo. Are you going to ask me in, or are you partial to non-agenarians?"

There was something to be said for his ability to toss out a sally, she decided, stepping back and grinning. "Touché. Come on in." She noticed that he walked in slowly, as if it wouldn't have surprised him to find a booby trap of some kind, and quickly summed up his surroundings. After casually scanning the elegant but sparsely furnished foyer and the intensely personal living room, he glanced at her. "Some of your choices surprise me, Naomi." He pointed to a reproduction of a Remington sculpture. "That would represent masculine taste."

"I bought it because that man is free, because he looks as if he just burst out of a place he hadn't wanted to be." He quirked his left eyebrow and didn't comment, but she could see he had more questions.

"The Elizabeth Catlett sculpture," she explained, when his glance rested on it, "was the first sculpture that I had even seen by an African American woman; I bought it with my first paycheck. I don't know how familiar you are with art, but along with music, it's what I like best. These are also the works of African Americans. That painting," she pointed to an oil by the art historian James Porter, "was given to me by me grandpa for my college graduation. And the reproduction of the painting by William H. Johnson is...well, the little girl reminded me of myself at that age."

Rufus observed the work closely, as if trying to determine whether there was anything in that painting of a wide-eyed little black girl alone with a fly swatter and a doll carriage that would tell him exactly who Naomi Logan was.

While he scrutinized the Artis Lane lithograph portrait of Rosa Parks that both painter and subject had signed, Naomi let her gaze roam brazenly over him. What on earth is wrong with me, she asked herself when she realized, after scanning his long, powerful legs, that her imagination was moving into forbidden territory. She had never ogled a man, never been tempted. Not until now. She disciplined her thoughts and tried to focus on his questions. Her heartbeat accelerated as if she'd run for miles when he moved to the opposite end of the room, paused before a group of original oils, turned to her, and smiled. It softened his face and lit up his remarkable eyes. She knew that she gaped. What in heaven's name was happening to her?

"So you're an artist? Somehow, I pictured you as a disciplinarian of some sort." He stared intently at the painting of her mother entitled "From My Memories" and turned to look at her.

"Isn't this a self-portrait? I don't have any technical knowledge of art, but I have a feeling that this is good." She opened her mouth to speak until she saw him casually raising his left hand to the back of his head, exposing the tiny black curls at his wrist. She stared at it; it was just a hand, for God's sake. Embarrassed, she quickly steadied herself and managed to respond to his compliment.

"No. That's the way I remember my mother. Have a seat while I get us some coffee. Or would you prefer juice, or a soft drink?" She had to put some distance between them, and separate rooms was the best she could do.

He didn't sit. "Coffee's fine," he told her, trailing her into the kitchen. She turned and bumped into him, and excitement coursed through her when he quickly settled her with a slight touch on her arm. Her skin felt hot where his finger had been, and she knew that he could see a fine sheen of perspiration on her face. Reluctantly, she looked up, saw the tough man in him searing her with his hot, mesmerizing eyes, and felt her heart skid out of place. He made her feel things that she hadn't known could be felt, and all of a sudden, she wanted him out of there. The entire apartment seemed too small with him in it, making her much too aware of him. The letters had been fun, and she had enjoyed joshing with him over the phone, but he had a powerful personality and an intimidating physique. At her height, she wasn't accustomed to being made to feel small and helpless. And she had never experienced such a powerful sexual pull toward a man. But, she noticed, he seemed to have his emotions under lock and key.

He leaned over her drawing board seemingly to get a better view of the sketches there. "Are you a commercial artist, or do you teach art somewhere?"

"I'm a commercial artist if by that you mean work on contract."

Rufus looked at her quizzically. "Did you want to be some other kind of artist?"

Naomi took the coffee and started toward the living room. She had a few questions of her own, and one of them had to do with why he was here. "I wanted to be an artist. Period." She passed him a cup of coffee, cream, and sugar. He accepted only the coffee.

"Why did you come here, Rufus?" If he was uncomfortable, only he knew it. He rested his left ankle on his right knee, took a few sips of coffee, and placed the cup and saucer on the table beside his chair. His grin disconcerted her; it didn't seem to reach his eyes.

It wasn't a hostile question, but she hadn't meant it as friendly, either. She watched as he assessed her coolly. "You certainly couldn't have put it more bluntly if you tried. Whatever happened to that gnawing wit of yours? I came here on impulse. That last hot little note of yours made me so mad that neither a letter nor a phone call would do. You made me furious, Naomi, and if I think about it much, I'll get angry all over again." She leaned back in the thickly cushioned chair, thinking absently that he had an oversupply of charisma, when his handsome brown face suddenly shifted into a fierce scowl.

She wasn't impressed. "What cooled you off?"

He shrugged first one shoulder, then the other one. "You are so damned irreverent that you made the whole thing seem foolish. One look at you, standing there ready to take me on, demanding to see my ID with your door already wide open—well, my reaction was that I was being a jackass when I let you pull my leg. You've been having fun at my expense."

It didn't seem wise to laugh. "It was your fault."

He stiffened. "How do you figure that any of this is my fault, lady?" This time, she couldn't restrain the laughter.

"Temper, temper. If you didn't have such a short fuse and if you talked about things you know, especially on a radio broadcast, none of this would have happened."

He stood. "I'm leaving. Never in my life have I lost my temper with a woman, or even approached it, and I'm not going to allow you to provoke me into making an exception with you. You're the most exasperating…"

Her full-throated laughter, like tiny tinkling temple bells, halted his attack. He gave her a long, heated stare.

She shivered, disconcerted by his compelling gaze. With that fleeting desire-laden look, he kindled something within her, something that had fought to surface since she'd opened her door. She walked with him to her foyer, where indirect lights cast a pale, ethereal glow over them, and stood with her hand on the doorknob. She knew he realized she was deliberately prolonging his departure, and she was a little ashamed, but she didn't open the door. It was unfathomable. A minute earlier, she had wanted him to leave; now, she was hindering his departure. Less certain of herself than she had been earlier, she fished for words that would give her a feeling of ease. "I meant to ask how you became an expert on the family, but, well, maybe another time."

Rufus lifted an eyebrow in surprise. He hadn't thought she'd be interested in seeing him again. Despite himself, he couldn't resist a slow and thorough perusal of her. He wanted to…no. He wasn't that crazy. Her unexpected feminine softness, the dancing mischief in her big brown eyes, and the glow on her bare lips were not going to seduce him into putting his mouth on her. He stepped back, remembering her question.

"I'm a journalist, and I've recently had a book published that deals with delinquent behavior and the family's role in it. You may have heard of it: *Keys to Delinquent Behavior in the Nineties.*"

"Of course I know it; that book's been a bestseller for months. I hadn't noticed the author's name and didn't associate it with you. I haven't read it, but I may." She offered her hand. "I'm glad to have met you, Rufus; it's been interesting."

He drew himself up to his full height and pretended not to see her hand. He wasn't used to getting the brush-off and wasn't going to be the victim of one tonight. He jammed his hands in his pockets and assumed a casual stance.

"You make it seem so...so final." He hated his undisciplined reaction to her. Her warm, seductive voice, her sepia beauty, and her light, airy laughter made his spine tingle. He had really summoned her up incorrectly. She was far from the graying, disillusioned spinster that he had pictured. He wanted to see what she looked like; well, he had seen, and he had better move on.

"Couldn't we have dinner some evening?" He smiled inwardly; so much for his advice to himself.

He could see that she was immediately on guard. "I'm sorry, but my evenings are pretty much taken up." She tucked thick, curly hair behind her left ear. "Perhaps we'll run into each other. Goodbye."

He wasn't easily fooled, but he could be this time, he cautioned himself, and looked at her for a long while, testing her sincerity and attempting to gauge the extent of his attraction to her. Chemistry so strong as what he felt wasn't usually one-sided; he'd thought at first that she reciprocated it, but now, neither her face nor her posture told him anything. She's either a consummate actress or definitely not interested in me, he decided as he turned the doorknob. "Goodbye, Naomi." He strode out the door and down the corridor without a backward glance.

Naomi watched him until he entered the elevator, a man in complete control, and hugged herself, fighting the unreasonable feeling that he had deserted her, chilled her with his leaving; that he had let his warmth steal into her and then, miser-like, withdrawn it, leaving her cold. What on earth have I done to myself, she wondered plaintively.

\* \* \*

Rufus drove home slowly, puzzled at what had just transpired. Everything about Naomi jolted him. He didn't mislead himself; he knew that his cool departure from her apartment belied his unsettled emotions. What had he thought she would be like? Older, certainly, but definitely not a barefoot, paint-spattered witch. She'd had a strong impact on him, and he didn't like it. He had his life in order, and he was not going to permit this wild attraction to disturb it. She had everything that made a woman interesting, starting with a mind that would keep a man alert and his brain humming. Honorable, too. And, Lord, she was luscious! Tempting. A real, honest-to-God black beauty.

He entered his house through the garage door that opened into the kitchen and made his way upstairs. All was quiet, so he undressed, sprawled out in the king-sized bed that easily accommodated his six feet four and a half inches, and faced the fact that he wanted Naomi. It occurred to him from her total disregard for his celebrity status that Naomi didn't know who he was. She found him attractive for himself and not for his bank account, as Etta Mae and so many others had, and it was refreshing. If she didn't want to acknowledge the attraction, fine with him; neither did he. If there were only himself to consider, he reasoned, he would probably pursue a relationship with Naomi, though definitely not for the long term. It had been his personal experience that the children of career women didn't get their share of maternal attention. That meant that he could not and would not have one in his life.

# Chapter 2

Several afternoons later, Naomi left a meeting of the district school board disheartened and determined that the schools in her community were going to produce better qualified students. She had a few strong allies, and the name Logan commanded attention and respect. She vowed there would be changes. She remembered her school days as pleasant, carefree times when schools weren't a battlefield and learning was fun. A challenge. When she taught high school, she made friends with her pupils, challenged them to accomplish more than they thought they could, and was rewarded with their determination to learn, even to go beyond her. She smiled at the pleasant memory, suddenly wondering if Bryan Lister was still flirting with his female teachers, hoping now to improve his university grades.

Oh, there would be changes, beginning with an overhaul of that haphazard tutoring program, even if, God forbid, she had to run for election as president of the board. She ducked into a Chinese carry-out to buy her dinner. As she left the tiny hovel, she noticed a woman trying to shush a recalcitrant young teenaged boy who obviously preferred to be somewhere else and expressed his wishes rudely.

She got into her car and started to her studio, a small but cheerfully decorated loft, the place where her creative juices usually began flowing as soon as she entered. Sitting at her drawing board, attempting to work, she felt the memory of that scene in which mother and son were so painfully at odds persist. The boy could have been hers. Maybe not; maybe she'd had a girl. What kind of parents did her child have? Would it swear at them, as that boy had? How ironic, that she devoted so much of her life to helping children and had no idea what her own child endured. She sighed deeply, releasing the frustration. She would deal with that, but she wasn't yet ready. It was still a new and bruising thing. It had been bad enough to remember constantly that she had a child somewhere whom she would never see and about whose welfare she didn't know, but this…she couldn't help remembering…

She had stood by the open window; tears cascading silently down her satin-smooth cheeks, looking out at the bright moonlit night, deep in thought. The trees swayed gently, and the prize roses in her grandfather's perfectly kept garden gave a sweet pungency to the early summer night. But she neither saw the night's beauty nor smelled the fragrant blossoms. She saw a motorcycle roaring wildly into the distance, carrying her young heart with it. And it was the fumes from the machine's exhaust, not the scented rose blooms surrounding the house, that she would remember forever. He hadn't so much as glanced toward her bedroom window as he'd sped away.

She heard her bedroom door open but didn't turn around, merely stood quietly, staring into the distance. She knew he was there and that no matter what she said or how much she pleaded, he would have his way; he always had his way.

"Get your things packed, young lady, you're leaving here tonight. And you needn't bother trying to call him, either, because I've already warned him that if he goes near you, if he so much as speaks to you again, I'll have him jailed for possessing carnal knowledge of a minor."

"But, Grandpa…"

"Don't give me any sass, young lady. You're a child, sixteen years old, and I don't plan to let that boy do any more damage than he's already done. Get your things together." She should have been used to his tendency to steamroller her and everybody else, but this time there was no fight in her.

"Did you at least tell him…" He didn't let her finish, and it was just as well. She knew the answer.

"Of course not."

She fought back the tears; the least sign of weakness would only make it worse. "You didn't give me a chance to tell him," she said resignedly, "so he doesn't know."

She looked at the old man then, tall and erect, still agile and crafty for his years. A testimonial to temperance and healthful living. With barely any gray hair, he was an extremely handsome example of his African American heritage and smattering of Native American genes. She thought of how much like him she looked and brought her shoulders forward, begging him with her eyes.

"But, Grandpa. Please! You can't do this. He didn't take advantage of me. We love each other, and we want to…"

"Don't tell me what I can't do. I'm your legal guardian. That boy's nineteen and I can have him put away. You're not going to blacken the name of Logan; it's a name that stands for something in this community. You'll do as I say. And what you haven't packed in the next hour, you won't be taking."

She got into the backseat of the luxurious Cadillac that the First Golgotha Baptist Church had given her grandfather when he'd retired after forty-five years as its pastor. "Where are we going?" she asked him sullenly, not caring if she displeased him.

"You'll find out when you get there," he mumbled.

"I thought you'd stopped driving at night."

"I'm driving tonight, but it's not a problem; the moon's shining. And kindly stop crying, Naomi. I've always told you that crying shows a lack of self-control."

She bristled. Did he even love her? If he did, why couldn't he ever give her concrete evidence of it? She made one last try. "You have no right to do this, Grandpa. I love him, and he loves me, and no matter what you make me do now, when I'm grown, Chuck and I will get together."

She heard the gruffness in his aged voice and the sadness that seemed to darken it. Maybe there was hope…

"I'm doing what's best for you, and someday you'll see that for yourself. You know nothing of love, Naomi. That boy didn't fight very hard for you, gal. Seems to me I gave him a good reason to run off when I warned him to stay away from you. It's a moot point, anyway; his folks are sending him to the University of Hawaii, and you can't get much farther away from Washington, D.C., and still be in the United States. This is the end of it and I know it, so I'm not letting you offer yourself up as a sacrificial lamb on the altar of love. I've lived more than three-quarters of a century, long enough to know how outright stupid that would be."

Her tears dropped silently until she fell asleep. When they had arrived at their destination, she got out of the car and walked into the building without even glancing back at her grandfather. Two months later, tired of resisting the pressure, she listlessly signed the papers put in front of her without reading them.

Naomi sat at the drawing board in her studio without attempting to work and tried once more to reconcile herself to her grandfather's incredible news. If they'd found him, they would easily find her. Did she want to be found? Or did she want to find the child and its family? But who would she look for? I've had a few hassles in my life, she thought, but this! She answered the phone automatically.

"Logan Logos and Labels. May I help you?"

"Yes," the deep, sonorous male voice replied. "You certainly may. Have dinner with me tonight." Of course, Rufus meant the invitation as an apology for his abrupt departure from her home, she decided. She searched for a suitable clever remark and drew a blank as thoughts of her child crowded out Rufus's face. Her throat closed and words wouldn't come out. To her disgust, she began to cry.

"Naomi? Naomi? Are you there?"

She hung up and let the tears have their day, tears that had been waiting for release since her grandfather had signed her into the clinic and walked away over thirteen years ago. She got up after a time threw water on her face, and went back to her drawing board, hoping for the relief that she always found in her work. Then she laughed at herself. Solitary tears were stupid; crying made sense only if someone was there to pat you on the back. She looked at her worrisome design and shrugged elaborately. It would be about as easy to get that ridiculous cow into the ice-cream logo without changing the concept as it would be to get her life straightened out, tantamount to getting pie from the sky. She sat up straighter. Mmmm. *Pie in the sky.* Not a bad idea. In twenty minutes, she'd sketched a new ice-cream logo, an oval disc containing a cow snoozing beneath a shade tree and dreaming of a three-flavors dish of ice cream. Why didn't I think of that before, she asked herself, humming happily, while she cleaned her brushes and tidied her drawing board. She held the logo up to a lamp, admiring it. Nothing gave her as much satisfaction as finishing a job that she knew was a sure winner.

Her euphoria was short-lived as she heard the simultaneous staccato ring of the doorbell and rattle of the knob. She opened the door and stared in dismay.

"Is anything the matter? Are you all right?" Rufus asked her, pushing a twin stroller into the room, apparently oblivious to the astonishment that he must have seen mirrored on her face.

She said the first thing that came to mind and regretted it. "You didn't tell me that you are married," she accused waspishly.

She put her hands on her hips and frowned at him. She usually took her time getting annoyed, but she wasn't her normal self when it came to Rufus Meade. She took a calming deep breath and asked, him, "Whose are these?" pointing a long brown finger toward the stroller.

One of the twins answered, "Daddy look." He reached toward the ten-by-fourteen color sketch for the ice-cream logo. "Ice cream, Daddy. Can we have some ice cream?"

Rufus shook his head. "Maybe later, Preston." He turned to her and shrugged nonchalantly, but Naomi didn't care if her exasperation at that ridiculous scene was apparent.

"What was happening with you when I called, Naomi? You

sounded as if…look, I came over here because I thought something was wrong and that maybe I could help, but whatever it
was evidently didn't last long."

Still not quite back to normal, and fighting her wild emotions,
she figured it wasn't a time for niceties and asked him, "Where
is their mother?"

This time, it was the other twin who answered. "Our mommy
lives in Paris."

"She likes it there," Preston added. "It's pretty."

Rufus glanced from the boy to Naomi. "Since you're alright,
we'll be leaving." He wasn't himself around her. Her impact on
him was even greater than when he'd first seen her. Tonight,
when he'd faced her standing in her door with that half-shocked,
half-scared look on her face, her shirt and jeans splattered with
paint, hair a mess and no makeup, he had been moved by her
open vulnerability. It tugged at something deep-seated, elicited
his protective instinct. He admitted to himself that fear for her
safety hadn't been his sole reason for rushing over there; he was
eager to see her again and had seized the opportunity.

Her softly restraining hand on his arm sent a charge of energy
through him, momentarily startling him. "I'm sorry, Rufus.
About your wife, I mean. I had no idea that…"

"Don't worry about it," he told her, mentally pushing back the
sexual tension in which her nearness threatened to entrap him.
Expressions of sympathy for his status as a single father made
him uncomfortable. He regretted the divorce for his sons' sake,
but Etta Mae had never been much of a wife and hadn't planned
to be a mother. She wanted to work in the top fashion houses of
Paris and Milan and, when offered the chance, she said a hurried
goodbye and took it. Neither her marriage nor her three-week-
old twin sons had the drawing power of a couturier's runway.
She hadn't contested the divorce or his award of full custody;
she had wanted only her freedom.

He watched the strange, silent interplay between Naomi and
Preston, who appeared fascinated with the logo. His preoccu-

pation with it seemed to intrigue her, and she smiled at the boy and glanced shyly at Rufus.

"Do you min if I give them some i-c-e c-r-e-a-m?" She spelled it out. "I have those three flavors in the freezer." He eased back the lapels of his Scottish tweed jacket, exposing a broad chest in a beige silk Armani shirt, shoved a hand in each pants pocket, and tried to understand the softness he saw in her. He couldn't believe that she liked children; if she did, she'd have some. She probably preferred her work.

"Sure, why not?" he replied, carefully sheltering his thoughts. "It'll save me the trouble of taking them to an ice-cream parlor where they'll want everything they see."

"Do they have to stay in that thing?" She nodded toward the stroller.

"You may be brave," he told her, displaying considerable amusement, "but I don't believe you're that brave." His eyes were pools of mirth.

"What are you talking about?" She tried to settle herself, to get her mind off the virile heat that emanated from him. She had never before reacted so strongly to a man, and she disliked being susceptible to him.

His suddenly huskier voice indicated that he read her thoughts and knew her feelings. "Preston can destroy this place in half an hour if he really puts himself to it," he explained, "but with Sheldon to help him, you'd think a hurricane had been through here. We're all better off with them strapped in that stroller."

"If you say so." She knelt unsteadily in front of the stroller and addressed the twin who'd pointed toward the logo. "What's your name?" A miniature Rufus right down to his studied gaze, she decided.

"Preston," he told her with more aplomb that she'd have expected of a child of his age, and pointed to his twin. "He's Sheldon."

"How old are you?" she asked his identical twin brother.

"Three, almost four," they told her in perfect unison, each holding up three fingers.

Naomi looked first at one boy and then the other, then at
Rufus. "How do you know the difference?"

"Their personalities are different." He looked down at them,
his face aglow with tenderness, and his voice full of pride.

She introduced herself to the boys and then began serving the
ice-cream. On a hunch, she took four of the plastic banana-shaped
bowls that she'd bought for use in the logo and filled them with
a scoop each of the chocolate, vanilla, and strawberry flavors.

Rufus nodded approvingly. "Well, you've just dealt successfully with Preston; he'd have demanded that it look exactly like
that painting. Sheldon wouldn't care as long as it was ice cream."

Naomi watched Rufus unstrap his sons, place one on each
knee, and help them feed themselves while trying to eat his own
ice-cream. Her eyes misted, and she tried to stifle her desire to
hold one of the children. She knew a strange, unfamiliar
yearning as she saw how gently he handled them. How he carefully wiped their hands, mouths, and the front of their clothes
when they had finished and, over their squirming objections,
playfully strapped them into the stroller.

"Do they wiggle because it's a kid thing, or just to test your
mettle?"

He laughed aloud, a full-throated release as he reached down
to rebutton Sheldon's jacket. She would have bet that he didn't
know how; it was the first evidence she'd had that his handsome
face could shape itself into such a brilliant smile, one that
involved his eyes and mouth, his whole face. He had a single
dimple, and she was a pushover for a dimple. The glow of his
smile made her feel as if he had wrapped her in a ray of early
morning sunlight, warming her.

"Both, I guess," he finally answered.

He turned to her. "That was very nice, Naomi. Thank you.
Before I leave, I want you to tell me why you hung up when I
called you. Didn't you know that I would have to send the police
or come over here myself and find out whether you were in
trouble? I brought my boys because I don't leave them alone and
I couldn't get a sitter quickly."

"Don't you have a housekeeper, nursemaid, or someone who takes care of them for you?"

Rufus stood abruptly, all friendliness gone from his suddenly stony face. "My children are my responsibility, and it is I, not a parental substitute, who takes care of them. I do not want my children's outlook on life to be that of their nanny or the house-keeper. And I will not have my boys pining for me to get home and disappointed when I get there too tired even to hug them. My boys come before my career and everything else, and I don't leave them unless I have no choice." He turned to leave, and both boys raised their arms to her. Not caring what their father thought, she quickly took the opportunity to hug them and hold their warm little bodies. His expression softened slightly, against his will, she thought, as he opened the door and pushed the stroller through it. "It was a mistake to come here. Goodbye, Naomi." As the door closed, she heard Preston, or maybe it was Sheldon, say, "Goodbye, Noomie."

Naomi began cleaning the kitchen, deep in thought. Did they have low tolerance for each other, or was it something else? She had never known anyone more capable of destroying her calm, not even Judd. And there was no doubt that she automatically pushed his buttons. The less she saw of him, the better, she told herself, fully aware that he was the first man for whom she'd ever had a deep, feminine ache. "I don't know much," she said aloud, "but I know enough to leave him alone."

Naomi parked her car on Fourth Street below Howard University and walked up Florida Avenue to One Last Chance. She chided herself for spending so much time thinking about Rufus, all the while giving herself excuses for doing so. She had just been defending herself with the thought that being the father of those delightful boys probably added to Rufus's manliness. He was so masculine. Even his little boys had strong masculine traits.

Rufus had made her intensely aware of herself as a woman. An incomplete woman. A woman who could not dare to dream of what she wanted most; to have the love and devotion of a man

she loved and with whom she could share her secrets and not be
harshly judged. A home. And children. Maybe she could have
it with…oh, God, there was so much at stake. Forget it, she told
herself; he would break her heart.

She increased her pace. It seemed like forever since the foundation's board members had argued heatedly about the wisdom
of locating One Last Chance's headquarters in an area that was
becoming increasingly more blighted. But placing it near those
who needed the services had been the right decision. She walked
swiftly, partly because it was her natural gait, but mainly because
she loved her work with the young girls, whom she tutored in
English and math. She welcomed the crisp, mid-October
evenings that were so refreshing after the dreaded heat and
humidity of the Washington summers. Invigorating energy
coursed through her as the cool air greeted her face, and she accelerated her stride. Not even the gathering dusk and the barely
camouflaged grimness of the neighborhood daunted her.

Inside OLC, as the girls called it, her spirits soared as she
passed a group playing checkers in the lounge, glimpsed a
crowded typing class, and walked by the little rooms where experienced educators patiently tutored their charges. She reached
the nurse's station on the way to her own little cubicle, noticed
the closed door, and couldn't help worrying about the plight of
the girl inside.

Linda was half an hour late, and Naomi was becoming concerned about her. The girl lacked the enthusiasm that she had
shown when they'd begun the tutoring sessions, and she was
always tired, too worn-out for a fifteen-year-old. When she did
arrive, she didn't apologize for her tardiness, but Naomi didn't
dwell on that.

"Do you have brothers and sisters?" Naomi asked her, attempting to understand the girl's problems.

"Five of them," Linda responded listlessly.

"Tell me what you do at home, Linda, and why you come to
One Last Chance. Speak carefully, because this is our diction
lesson for today." Already becoming a fatalist, Naomi thought

sadly, when the girl opened her mouth to object, but closed it without speaking and shrugged indifferently.

"At home, I cook, clean, and take care of my mama's children. I study at the drugstore where I work after school and weekends, but I have to be careful not to get caught. I come here for the company, so I can hear people talk good English and see what you're supposed to wear and how you're supposed to act. I can get by without the tutoring."

"Do you enjoy the tutoring, Linda?"

"Yeah. It makes my grades better, but I just like to be around you. You treat me like I'm the same as you."

"But you are the same."

"No, I'm not. You got choices, and I don't have any yet." She smiled then. "But I'm going to have them. I'm going to be able to decide what I want. I'm going to learn to type and use computers. That way, I'll always be able to get a good job, and I'll be able to work my way through college." She paused and looked down at her hands. "I'm not ever going to have any children, and I'm never going on welfare and have people snooping around to check on me. It's humiliating."

Good for you, Naomi thought, but she needed to correct her about one thing.

"I'm sure that motherhood has many wonderful rewards," she told her. "When you fall in love and get married, you may change your mind."

Indicating what she thought of that advice, Linda pulled on one of her many braids and rolled her eyes disdainfully. "Not me," she objected, slumping down in the straight-backed chair. "All I have to do is look at my mama and then look at you. There's never going to be a man smart enough to con me into having a baby. After taking care of all my mama's babies, I'd have to be touched in the head to have one."

Naomi didn't like the trend of the conversation. "You'll see things differently when you're older," she responded, thinking that she would have to teach Linda that life was more enjoyable if you laughed at it sometimes.

"Really?" the girl asked skeptically. "I see you don't have any kids." Linda opened her book, effectively ending the discussion. Shocked, and unable to find any other way to get the privacy she needed, Naomi lowered her eyes.

They completed the literature assignment, and as Naomi reflected on Linda's above-average intelligence, the girl suddenly produced a drawing.

"What do you think of this?" she asked, almost defensively.

Naomi scrutinized it and regarded the girl whose face was haunted with expectancy. "You've got good technique, and this piece shows imagination. I like it."

Linda looked up and smiled wistfully. "I love to paint most of all. It's one thing nobody can tell me is good or bad, because I always manage to paint exactly what I feel." As if she had disclosed something that she thought too intimate to tell another person, Linda quickly left the room.

Naomi watched her leave. Crazy about painting and forced to study literature. It was almost like seeing her own youth in someone else, except that she had had all the advantages of upper-middle-class life that Linda lacked. She understood now that her strong attraction to Chuck had partly been escape from loneliness. He had fulfilled her need for the loving affection that she missed at home, and he'd made her feel wanted. Cherished. God forbid that because of a desolate life, Linda should follow in her footsteps, she mused, getting up to replace her teaching aids in the cabinet that held her supplies.

Rufus stole silently away from the open door and, deep in thought, made his way slowly up to the president's office. He was a board member of Urban Alliance and stopped by One Last Chance to discuss with its president participation in the Alliance's annual fund-raising gala. He hadn't known of Naomi's association with OLC and was surprised to find her there. Certainly, he would not have expected to witness her gently nurturing that young girl. She had empathized totally with the girl, whose background was probably the exact opposite of her own, holding him nearly spellbound. He mounted the creaky spiral staircase whose once-regal Royal Bokhara runners were now threadbare, thinking that perhaps he had misjudged Naomi again. He had gotten the impression from her letters that career and independence were what she cherished most and that, like his ex-wife, she thought of little else and wouldn't take the time to nurture another human being.

Maybe she was different from what she represented herself to be. She was tender and solicitous with his boys, who were immediately charmed by her. Captivated was more like it. Not because of the ice cream, either; they ate ice cream just about every day. No. It was more. He couldn't define it any more than he could figure out why she'd had such a powerful impact on him, why she was constantly in his thoughts.

She was brash and a little cynical. But she was also soft and giving. He remembered his sudden need to get out of her apartment, away from her; he had never had difficulty controlling his libido until he'd met that woman. He grinned. She affected his temper that way, too.

He sat listening to Maude Frazier outline her plans for One Last Chance's contribution to the gala, aware that her words held no interest for him; his mind was on Naomi Logan. In an abrupt decision, he politely told Maude goodbye and loped down the stairs in hopes of seeing Naomi before she left. He was relieved to find her in the basement laundry room. And what a sight! Without the combs and pins, her hair was a wild, thick frizz, and her slacks and shirt were wet in front. He leaned against the laundry room door and watched her dash around the room folding laundry and coping with an overflowing washing machine.

"Want some help?"

She dropped a clean tablecloth back into the sudsy water, braced her hands on her hips, and stood glaring at him.

"See what you made me do? You frightened me." He observed her closely, but with pretended casualness. Was she trembling?

"Sorry. Anything I can do to make up for it?"

"You can help me fold these things, and you can wipe that cocky grin off of your face." She hated being caught off guard; he didn't blame her. It put you at a disadvantage.

She was obviously wary of him, and he wanted to put her at ease, so he spread his hands palms upward in a gesture of defenselessness. "I'm innocent of whatever it is you're planning to hang me for, Naomi. Now, if you'll show me how you want these things folded, I'll help you." She did, and they worked in companionable silence.

Rufus carefully hid his inner feelings, controlling the heady excitement of being with her, but he wouldn't bet that he'd be able to hold it back for long. He wouldn't put a penny on it. She zonked him.

His impatient nature wouldn't allow him to wait longer before probing. "I'm surprised to see you here."

"And why would that be? Why do you think I don't care about people?" she asked him, a bit sharply.

Didn't she know that her defensiveness was bound to make him suspicious? He was a journalist, after all. He shrugged and decided not to accept the challenge. He wanted to know her, not fence with her. "Did I say that, Naomi? I've seen softness in you." *And I want to know whether it's real.*

"Humph. Me? A career woman?" Her glance must have detected the tenderness, the protectiveness that he felt, because she reacted almost as if he'd kissed her. Her lowered eyes and the sensual sound of her sucking in her breath sent his blood rushing through his veins.

Rufus quickly cooled his rising ardor. He sensed her nervousness but didn't comment on it, as he weighed her consistent refusal to carry on a serious conversation with him. When she finally looked directly at him, he spoke. "You treat everything I say with equal amounts of disdain."

"Be fair. Aren't you exaggerating?" He was sure that his words had stung her, though that was not what he had intended.

"Not by much, I'm not," he answered, running the fingers of

his left hand through his hair and furrowing his brow. "Do you volunteer here often?" He switched topics in the hope of avoiding a confrontation and making peace between them. "You seemed to have unusually good rapport with the girl whom you were tutoring. Most kids in these programs don't relate well to their tutors and mentors. How do you manage it?"

He found her inability to disguise her pleasure at his compliment intriguing; it meant that she valued his opinion. If he let her have the psychological distance that she seemed to want, maybe she would open up.

"You saw us?" He nodded. "It isn't difficul; she's hungry for attention and for a role model, and I really like her." They were leaning against the washing machines, and he appraised her with a thoroughness that embarrassed her.

"Is she one of the girls sent here from Juvenile Court? What had she done?"

Naomi's eyes snapped in warning, and her tone was sharp. "Linda found her way here on her own. She had the intelligence to realize that she needed help. I doubt she'll ever become a delinquent."

Her fierce protectiveness of the girl puzzled Rufus; his reporter's instincts told him that something important lay behind it, but he didn't consider it timely to pursue the matter. He looked at the pile of laundry that they'd folded and sorted. "Well, that's finished. Anything else?"

"No. That's it. I've got to get home and deal with my work." When he didn't respond, she looked up, and he had the satisfaction of seeing guilt mirrored in her eyes. Guilt for having been provocative again without cause. He altered his censorious appraisal of her, relaxing his face, letting the warmth within him flow out to her, and her expressive eyes told him that she responded to what he felt. She should have moved, but she didn't, and he reached for her, involuntarily, but quickly withdrew his hand. He looked into the distance, then glanced back at Naomi, who remained inches from him, standing in a way that told him she wouldn't mind if he touched her. He didn't want to leave her, he realized, but he had little choice unless he found a casual way to keep her with him.

"I promised to attend a lecture on the family over at Howard, and I'd invite you to join me if your clothes were dry." He thought for a second. "Well, you can keep you coat on. Think your work can wait an hour or so?" She smiled, and he sensed an inner warmth in her that he hadn't previously detected. He'd always thought her beautiful, but that smile made her beauty ethereal.

He took her hand. "Come on. Say yes." She nodded, and he clasped her hand, soft and delicate, in his. At that moment, he knew he felt more for her than he wanted to or than was sensible and made a mental note to back off.

# Chapter 3

They left the lecture in a playful mood. "Okay, I agree that he wasn't a genius," Rufus declared, "but he did make some good points." His changing facial expressions fascinated her. Naomi watched a grin drift over his face slowly, like a pleasant idea dawning, and walked closer to him. She was not inclined to give the lecturer as much credit as he did, though, and they joked about the man's shortcomings.

Arm in arm, they crossed the street to where two boys in their mid-teens stood beneath the streetlight. One cocked his head, gave them a hard look as they approached, and then ran up to Rufus.

"I don't believe it, man. Look who this is! How ya doin', Mr. Meade?" Naomi watched while Rufus autographed the boys' shirts, since they had nothing else on which he could write, answered their questions, and gave them reasons why they shouldn't hang out in the streets. The happy youths thanked him and promised to take his advice.

"Right on, man!" one said, as the two ambled toward what Naomi and Rufus both hoped was home. He's a kind and gentle man, she decided. And not merely with his own children. What other celebrity with his stature, a best-selling author, would stand on a street corner at nine at night and give autographs to two street urchins? She frowned. And when had boys like those begun to read books on delinquency? Maybe they knew his journalistic writings, but she didn't think so. No doubt there was something about him that she didn't know.

At her car, he told Naomi, "I've enjoyed being with you

tonight, Naomi. I enjoyed it a lot." He paused, making up his mind, remembering his earlier vow to back off. She was a heady lure, a magnet, and he wasn't going to get mired in her quicksand. He took his time deciding to walk away, all the while searching her face intently. Then he held the door for her. "Goodnight Naomi, I hope we meet again soon."

Naomi drove away feeling as if he had dangled her from a long pole, gotten tired, and dropped her. She had learned one thing that evening, though: she wasn't merely attracted to him; Rufus Meade was a man whom she could genuinely like, even care for. And therein lay the danger! But she knew he had not forgiven her for suggesting that he hire a woman to care for his boys. If he had, he would have kissed her goodnight, she reasoned, because every move he made said it was what he wanted. And she had wanted him to do it. She had better watch herself.

She entered her apartment and didn't stop until she reached her bedroom. At least I'm consistent, she joked to herself, looking around the dusty rose room, as she pulled off her dusty rose sweater and reached for her gown of the same color. She stretched out on a chaise lounge and thought about the evening with Rufus.

She could hardly believe that he had invited her to the lecture of that she had so readily agreed to go. She hadn't said yes voluntarily; she had been drugged by his charisma. He was smoldering fire, and if she didn't stay away from him, she would be badly burned. Her tinkling laughter broke the silence. All of a sudden, she understood moths.

Rufus took his minivan swiftly up Georgia Avenue, across Military Road, and north on Connecticut Avenue to Chevy Chase and home. His sister, Jewel, greeted him at his front door.

"Who on earth is Noomie? Preston and Sheldon have been telling me stories about her: she's a fairy; she makes ice cream; she has a pink nose; she lives in Thessa; and you are angry with her."

Rufus frowned. "She doesn't have a pink nose, and she lives

in Bethesda. Except for that, they're right." He had already
learned that when you have small children, you have few secrets.

Jewel put her hands on her hips and wrinkled her nose affectionately. "Anything else?" He knew she always became suspicious when he didn't satisfy her curiosity. Still, he was
uncomfortable with the discussion.

"Not that I know of. Thanks for staying with my boys, Jewel;
I hate for them to sleep away from home, and if you didn't sit
here with them, I wouldn't have a choice." He walked her to her
car. "I'll call Jeff and tell him you're on your way so he can
watch for you. Don't forget to call me. You know when you
babysit for me at night, I'm always uneasy until I know you're
safely in your house."

She hugged him affectionately. "Rufus, you are such a wor-
rywart. You know I'll be all right. Look…"

"Go on, say it."

"No. I shouldn't interfere in your life."

He opened her car door. "Of course I worry about you, Jewel.
I look after you because you're my sister. Heck. I can't remember
a time when I wasn't looking out for you. But I'd be equally concerned for the safety of any other woman leaving me and traveling alone this time of night—though that rarely happens."

Jewel grabbed the chance. "Does that include Noomie? Or do
you plan to keep her a secret forever?"

"Her name is Naomi, and there isn't much to tell. She has
pros and she has cons and right now, I'm shuffling that deck,
so to speak."

"Which side was winning when you left her tonight?"

Jewel understood him better than anyone else ever had, so he
wasn't surprised at her blunt question. She always said that pus-
syfooting around got you nowhere with him. Still, he didn't like
being transparent, not even to her. "You're saying I was with her
tonight?" He looked down at his sister, a beautiful, happy wife
and mother, and grinned when he felt her grasp his arm lightly.
Jewel always liked to touch when she talked. Naomi was a
toucher, too.

"Yes, you were. There's a softness about you that says you wish you were with her now."

He leaned against her dark blue Mercedes coupe and folded his arms against his broad chest. "I think it best that I don't discuss her just now, Jewel; I don't know where our relationship is going or if it's going anywhere at all." He looked off into the distance. He didn't want to talk about Naomi; he was too full of her.

"Rufus," Jewel began apologetically, as if wary of breaching is privacy. "Are you beginning to care for this woman? If you are, give her a chance, a real chance. There must be a reason why the boys are so taken with her, talking about her almost nonstop."

"I'd rather not go into this, Jewel." He didn't want to legitimize Naomi as the woman in his life by discussing her with his sister. He knew Naomi wasn't like Etta Mae. And he knew that his loveless marriage with his ex-wife wouldn't have worked even if she hadn't wanted a career as a high-fashion model. She had never committed herself to the marriage, and when the twins were born, she didn't commit to them. Only to her career. He hadn't discouraged her; she needed the spotlight, and he had wanted her to be happy. But how could she have left her three-week-old babies and gone on an overseas modeling assignment? And she'd stayed there.

Jewel's grip tightened on his arm. "This is part of your problem, honey. Don't compare her with Etta Mae, whom you still refuse to talk about; it hurts you, so you bury it all inside, where it simmers and festers and gets bigger than it really is. She isn't evil; she just has tunnel vision. Try to stop reopening those wounds; you'll never be happy till you do. Let it go, Rufus."

He moved away, turned, and voiced what he had never before mentioned to her. "What about Mama? She wasn't there for us, either."

Jewel shook him gently. "But she took whatever jobs she could get, and that meant traveling. She once told me that she didn't have a choice."

It was as if he hadn't heard her. "She made a living, but she was never home, and in the end, she didn't come back. When I knew that she wasn't coming back, that she had gone down in that plane, I thought I would die, too. She was going to write a book on cocoa. Cocoa, for God's sake!"

His sister's startled look told him she hadn't realized that after sixteen years he was still in such turmoil about their mother. "Rufus listen to me. You've forgotten something very important. Papa had been an invalid since before I was born, and Mama had to support us. Etta Mae worked because she wanted to. That's a big difference."

The only evidence he gave of his inner conflict was the involuntary twitch of a jaw muscle. "Maybe I shouldn't have voiced my feelings. But I used to cry myself to sleep when I was little, because I missed her. You didn't feel so alone, because you had me. When you were born, I swore I'd take care of you. Mama had a hard life: a breadwinner, a young woman married in name only and forced to be away from her children. Jewel, I don't want a woman I love to be caught up in that kind of conflict, and if I married while my boys are little, well…"

He disliked speaking of his personal feelings, but his love for his sister forced him to continue to try and make her understand the choices he made. "Preston and Sheldon are my life. I left my job at the *Journal* to work at home as a freelancer because they needed me, and I wanted to be there for them. I remember what it was like to be left with a succession of maids, babysitters, and cleaning women to whom I was just a job. And my boys are not going to live like that. Jewel, I can't expect a woman to put my children before her own interests; their own mother didn't do it."

He put an arm around his sister's shoulder. "Naomi has a career and she's devoted to it. She's also very good at what she does, and she deserves every opportunity to reach the top of her field." He paused, then spoke as if to himself. "And I'll be the first to applaud her when she gets there."

He opened the car door. "Enough reminiscing. It's getting late."

Jewel started the motor. "At least you're thinking about her. That's all I want, Rufus, that you'll find someone who truly cares for you and whom you can love in return. When that happens, you'll forget about these other concerns."

Rufus looked in on his boys, got a can of ginger ale from the kitchen, and went to his study. But after an hour, still looking at a blank page, he conceded defeat. He couldn't afford to become involved with Naomi. She was a complicated mixture of sweetness, charm, sexiness, simple decency, and fear. He enjoyed her fun and intelligence and, most of the time, loved being with her. Her cynical wit didn't fool him, and didn't matter much. He knew it was a screen, a defense. And he couldn't dismiss his hunch that there was a connection between Naomi and that girl at OLC, or that Naomi saw one.

He answered the telephone on the first ring, hoping it was the woman in his thoughts.

"Rufus, this is Jewel. I want you to think hard about this. What can be so unacceptable about Naomi if Preston and Sheldon are crazy in love with her? You know they aren't friendly with strangers; in fact, they shy away from people they don't know well. Talk, Rufus. It might help."

He hesitated, understanding that his response to her could become his answer to himself. He knew with certainty only that he wanted Naomi, but he wasn't foolish enough to let his libido decide anything for him. He thought for a moment and answered her as best he could.

"I'm not sure I know the answer, or even that she's as important to me as you seem to think. She has some strangely contradictory traits, and this bothers me. But worry not, Sis; I'm on top of it." He hung up, walked over to his bedroom window, and let the moonlight stream over him.

She's got a hook in me, he admitted. I'll swear I'm not going to have anything more to do with her, but when I'm with her I don't want to leave her; when I see her, I want to hold her. But I've got my boys, and they come first.

He stripped and went to bed, but sleep eluded him. One thing was sure: if he didn't have the boys, he'd be on his way to Bethesda, and the devil take the morrow.

Naomi unlocked her studio, threw her shoulder bag on her desk and opened the window a few inches. The sent of strong coffee wafted up from a nearby cafeteria, but she resisted retracing her steps to get some and settled for a cup of instant. She had barely slept the night before. Rufus had weighted the temptation of kissing her against the harm of doing it, and harm had won out. It wasn't flattering no matter how you sliced it, especially since she had wanted that kiss. When had she last kissed a man, felt strong masculine arms around her? She knew she was being inconsistent, wanting Rufus while swearing never to get involved. Keeping the vow had been easy…until she'd first heard his voice. When she saw him, it was hopeless. She sipped the bland-tasting coffee slowly.

Images of him loving her and then walking away from her when he learned her secret had kept her tossing in bed all night. She'd finished reading his first book, *The Family at Risk,* and had been appalled at some of his conclusions: the family in American society had lost its usefulness as a source of nurturing, health care, education, and economic, social, and psychological support for the young. Spouses, he complained, had separate credit cards, separate bank accounts, and separate goals. Oneness was out of fashion. Homemaking as an occupation invited scorn, and women avoided it if they could. He claimed that the family lost its focal point when women went to work, and without them as its core, the family had no unity. She hadn't realized how strongly he believed that women had a disproportionate responsibility for the country's social ills. He wouldn't accept her past, she knew, so she'd put him behind her.

She laughed at herself. She didn't have such a big problem, just a simple matter of forgetting about Rufus. But what red-blooded woman would want to do *that?* It was useless to remain there staring at the stark white walls. "I'm going home and put on the most chic fall outfit in my closet," she declared, "and then I'm going to lunch at the Willard Hotel."

The maître d' gave her a choice table with a clear view of the entrance. The low drone of voices and the posh room where lights flickered from dozens of crystal chandeliers offered the perfect setting for a trip into the past, but she savored her drink and resisted the temptation; wool gathering slowed down your life, she told herself. Suddenly, she felt the cool vintage wine halt its slow trickle down her throat, almost choking her, and heated tremors stole through her as Rufus walked toward her. But her excitement quickly dissolved into angst when his hand steadied the attractive woman who preceded him. He wasn't alone.

The sight of the handsome couple deeply engrossed in serious conversation stung her, and she lowered her eyes to shield her reaction. She looked at the grilled salmon and green salad when the waiter brought it, and pushed it aside. She just wanted to get out of there. Aware that she had ruined the day for the little maître d', she apologized, paid with her credit card, and stood to leave. A glance told her that Rufus was still there, still absorbed in his companion and their conversation. She took a deep breath, wrapped herself in dignity, and with her head high, marched past his table without looking his way.

The furious pace of her heartbeat alarmed her, and she decided it would be foolish to drive. Dinosaurs. This was a good time to see them. But on her way to the Smithsonian Institute, the crisp air and gentle wind lured her to the Tidal Basin, and she walked along the river, deep in thought. Why was she upset at seeing Rufus with another woman? There wasn't anything between her and him, and there couldn't be anything between them. Not ever. She took a few pieces of tissue from her purse, spread them out, and sat down. She could no longer deny that he was becoming important to her, so she braced her back against a tree and contemplated what to do about it.

"Even if you wanted to be alone, you didn't have to pick such a deserted place. Are you looking for trouble?"

By the time Rufus ended the question, she was on her feet, trembling with feminine awareness at the unexpected sound of his voice. "Don't you know you shouldn't frighten a person like that?" she huffed, not in annoyance, but in pulsing anticipation. "It's downright sadistic, the way you suddenly appear. Where did you leave your date?" She blanched, realizing that she had given herself away, but pretended aloofness. She didn't want him to know that seeing him with an attractive woman had affected her.

He cocked an eyebrow. "I helped Miss Hunt get a taxi, and she went back to her office."

"Why are you telling me that?" she asked, as if he hadn't merely answered her question. "It isn't my concern."

"I didn't suggest otherwise. Are you okay?"

"Of course, I'm okay," she managed to reply, and turned her back so that her quivering lips wouldn't betray her. "How did you get here?" It was barely a whisper.

"I followed you. When you passed my table immediately after your lunch was served, you seemed distressed. I wanted to be sure you were all right."

He walked around her in order to face her. "I was surprised to see you lunching alone in that posh place. I only go there because Angela, my agent, loves to be seen there. She says it's good for her image.

Intense relief washed through her, and she gasped from the joy of it. Her mind told her to move back, to remember who she was and that she had reasons to avoid a deeper involvement with him, but her mind and heart were not in sync, she learned.

Oblivious to the squirrels that were busily hoarding for the winter, the blackbirds chirping around them, and the wind whistling through the trees, she stood with her gaze locked into his, shaken by her unbridled response to him. She was barely aware of the dry leaves swirling around them and the wind's accelerated velocity as they continued to devour each other with the heat in their eyes, neither of them speaking or moving. Feeling chill-like tremors, she rubbed her arms briskly, letting her gaze shift to his lips.

His sharp intake of breath as he opened his arms thrilled her, and she walked into them, her body alive with hot anticipation. He had lost his war with himself, and she gloried in his defeat. She felt him sink slowly to the turf, clasping her tightly. He lay with her above him, protecting her from the hard ground. She knew, when he immediately helped her to her feet without even kissing her, that their environment alone had stopped him. Blatant desire still radiated from him. She didn't remember ever having encountered such awesome self-control.

"Chicken sandwiches and ginger ale taste about the same as grilled salmon and salad," she told him, when they finished.

"Something like that occurred to me, too." He smiled.

They stood at the curb, near her parked car, neither speaking nor touching, just looking at each other. She hadn't noticed that he'd shortened his sideburns or that he had a tiny brown mole beside his left ear. And in the sunlight, she could see for the first time that his fawnlike eyes were rimmed with a curious shade of brownish green. Beautiful. A lurch of excitement pitched wildly in her chest. *Back off, girl, before you can't!* Without a word, she turned blindly toward her car, but he grabbed her hand, detaining her, and forced her to look at him. Then he brushed her cheek tenderly with the back of his closed fist and let her go.

She drove slowly. She could stay away from him, she thought, if he wasn't so charismatic. So handsome. So sexy. So honorable. And oh, God, so tender and loving with his kids. He was a chauvinist, maybe—she was becoming less positive of that—had a trigger-fast temper, and was unreasonable sometimes. But he made her feel protected, and he was the epitome of man. *Man!* That was the only word for him and, if she were honest, she'd admit that she wanted everything he could give a woman—his consuming fire, his drugging power and heady masculine strength—just once in her life. But most of all, she wanted the tenderness of which she knew he was capable. Naomi laughed at herself. Who was she kidding? Well, her grandpa had always preached that thinking didn't cost you anything; it was not thinking that was expensive.

She mused over that as she drove, deciding that in her case, both could cost a lot. Once with him would never be enough, she conceded, wondering how he was handling their…encounter.

Rufus steered into his garage and forced himself to get out of his car. He walked around the garden in back of the house, sat on a stone bench, absently turned the hose on, and filled the birdbath. Why couldn't he leave her alone? It had taken every ounce of will he could gather to stop what he'd started down by the Tidal Basin. He couldn't pinpoint what had triggered it, and he wondered how he managed to appear so calm afterward when he actually felt as if he would explode. And why had he felt obligated to ease her mind about Angela? He'd never even kissed her, thought he'd just come pretty close to it. Besides, he and Naomi spent most of their time together fighting. He had been discussing a three-book deal with Angela when Naomi had passed their table; one look at her face, and he knew she'd seen them. He had immediately terminated the discussion and followed her. Get a grip on it, son! He noticed two squirrels frolicking in the barbecue pit, walked over to the patio, and got some of the peanuts that he stored there for his little friends. He went to the pit, got down on his haunches, and waited until they saw him and raced over to take their food from his hand.

Why couldn't he leave her alone? Nothing could come of it. The question plagued him. And another thing. Good Lord! She was jealous of Angela. Jealous! How the devil was he going to stay away from her if she reciprocated what he felt? They didn't even like each other. Scratch that, he amended; only fools lied to themselves. He went up to his room, changed his clothes, and went to get his boys from Jewel's house.

Naomi sat at her drawing board that afternoon and wondered whether she could do a full day's work in two hours. She was way off schedule, and she didn't have one useful idea. "Oh, hang Rufus," she called out in frustration. "Why am I bothered, anyway? Why, for heaven's sake, am I torturing myself?" She dialed Marva, who answered on the first ring. Naomi always found it disconcerting that Marva's telephone rarely rang a second or third time. She would almost believe her friend just sat beside the phone waiting for a call, but Marva was too impatient.

"Are you going to One Last Chance this afternoon?" she asked her. "I think we ought to firm up the plans for our contributions to the Urban Alliance gala. If we don't get a bigger share of the pot this time, OLC will be in financial difficulty."

"I know," Marva breathed, sounding bored, "but it'll all work out. You ought to be concentrating on who's going to take you and what you're going to wear." Suddenly, Marva seemed more serious than usual. "Someday, Naomi, you're going to tell me why a twenty-nine-year-old woman who looks like you would swear off men. Honey, I couldn't understand that even if you were eighty. Don't you ever want somebody to hold you? I mean *really* hold you?"

Caught off guard, Naomi clutched the telephone cord and answered candidly. "To tell the truth, I do. Terribly, sometimes, but I've been that route once, and once is enough for me." Well, it was a half-truth, but she knew she owed her friend a reasonable answer, and she would never breathe the whole truth to anyone.

She changed the subject. "Guess what happened while you were gone, Marva."

"Tell me."

"Well, Le Ciel Perfumes saw the ad I did for Fragrant Soaps and gave me an exclusive five-year contract. I get all their business. Girl, I'm in the big time now. Can you believe it? I talked to them as if I could barely fit them into my tight program. Then I hung up, screamed, and danced a jig."

"You actually screamed? Wish I'd been there."

"But, Marva, that's what every commercial artist dreams of, a sponsor. I treated myself to a new music system. My feet have hardly touched the ground since I signed that contract."

"Go, girl. I knew you had it in you. We'll get together for some Moët and Chandon; just name the hour."

On an impulse and as casually as she could, she asked Marva,

"You know so many people in this town, do you happen to know Rufus Meade?"

"Cat Meade? Is there anybody in the District of Columbia who doesn't know him or know about him?"

"I didn't know him until recently, and I didn't realize you read books on crime and delinquency, Marva," she needled gently.

"Of course I don't; I hate unpleasantness, especially when it's criminal. What does this have to do with Cat Meade? Cat was the leading NFL wide receiver for five straight years. Didn't you ever watch the 'Skins?"

"Oh, come on, girl. You know I can't stand violence, and those guys are always knocking each other down."

Marva laughed. Naomi loved to hear the big, lusty laugh that her friend delighted in giving full rein.

"Now I understand your real problem," Marva told her. "You haven't been looking at all those cute little buns in those skin-tight stretch pants."

"You're hopeless," Naomi sighed. "What about Meade? Did he quit because he was injured, or does he still play?"

"From what I heard, he stopped because he'd made enough money to be secure financially, and he'd always wanted to be a writer. He's a very prominent print journalist, and he's well respected, or so I hear. Why? Are you interested in him?"

In for a penny; in for a pound. "He's got something, as we used to say in our days at Howard U, but he and I are like oil and water. And it's just as well, because I think we also basically distrust each other. He doesn't care much for career women, and I was raised by a male chauvinist, so a little of that type goes a long way with me. Grandpa's antics stick in my craw so badly that I'm afraid I accuse Rufus unfairly sometimes. Why do you call him 'Cat'? That's an odd name for a guy as big as he is."

Marva's sigh was impatient and much affected. "When are you going to learn that things don't have to be what they seem? They called him Cat, because the only living thing that seemed able to outrun him were a thoroughbred horse and cheetah, and he moved down the field like a lithe young panther. My mouth used to water just watching him." The latter was properly supported by another deep sigh, Naomi noted.

"I hope you've gotten over that," she replied dryly.

"Oh, I have; he's not running anymore," Marva deadpanned. "And besides, it's my honey who makes my mouth water these days." She paused. "Naomi, I've only met Cat a few times at social functions, and I doubt that he'd even remember me. Of course, any woman with warm blood would remember him. Go for it, kid."

"You're joking. The man's a chauvinist." She told her about his statement when he'd appeared on *Capitol Life,* supporting her disdain, but she could see that Marva wasn't impressed.

"Naomi, honey," she crooned in her slow Texas drawl, "why are you so browned off? If isn't like you to let anybody get to you like this. Lots of guys think like that; the point is to change him...or to find one who doesn't."

"Never mind," Naomi told her, "I should have known you wouldn't find it in your great big heart to criticize a live and breathing man."

She assured herself that she wouldn't be calling him Cat. "I don't care how fast he was or is." They'd been having a pleasant few minutes together the night he'd brought the boys to her apartment, and she had asked him a simple, reasonable question. After all, a working journalist couldn't take twin toddlers on assignment, so who kept them while he worked? But he was supersensitive about it. That one question was all it had taken to set him off. Then, down at the Tidal Basin, he'd nearly kissed her. She should never have let him touch her. Why the heck wasn't he consistent? The torment she felt as a result of that almost kiss just wouldn't leave her. She hoped he was at least a little bit miserable. What she wouldn't give to be secure in a man's love! *His* love? She didn't let herself answer.

Naomi's contemplations of the day's events as she dressed hurriedly that evening for an emergency board meeting at OLC was interrupted by the telephone. Linda's voice triggered a case of mild anxiety in her; the girls at OLC were not allowed to call their tutors at home.

"What is it, Linda?"

The unsteadiness in the girl's voice told her that there might be a serious problem.

"I hated to call you at home, but I didn't know what else to do. My mama says I can't go on the retreat. I won a scholarship, and it won't cost anything, but she says I can't go."

Naomi sat down. Maude Frazier and OLC would wait. "Did she say why?"

"Yes. She said I'll do more good here at home helping her and working in the drugstore than I will wasting two weeks with a gang of kids drawing pictures. She said she never wants to see another piece of crayon. What will I do?"

Naomi pushed back her disappointment; how would the girl ever make it with so little support? "I'll speak with your principal. Don't worry too much. We have two months in which to work out a strategy and get your mother's approval, but I'm sure the principal can handle this. Why didn't you tell me that you won a scholarship? How many were there?"

"One. I didn't tell you, because I figured Mama wouldn't want me to go." Naomi beamed, her face wreathed in smiles. She wished that she could have been with Linda to give her a hug. She doubted the girl received much affection; she certainly didn't get the approval and encouragement that her talent deserved.

"Just one scholarship for the entire junior high school, and you won it? I'm proud of you, Linda, and I'm going to do everything possible to help you get those two weeks of training. I'll see you in a couple of days?" The conversation was over, but it had an almost paralyzing effect on Naomi. What was her own child going through? Were its parents loving and understanding? Did they encourage it? *It!* God how awful! She didn't even know whether she'd had a girl or a boy.

She hurriedly put on a slim skirted, above the knee dusty rose silk suit with a silk cowl necked blouse of matching color, found some navy accessories, and left home having barely glanced at herself in a mirror. She knew that color always set off her rich brown skin, and when she wore lipstick of matching color, her only makeup, as she did now, the effect was simple elegance. She arrived precisely on time and was not surprised when, at the minute she seated herself at the long oval table, Maude Frazier, the board's president and arbiter of social class among the African American locals, lowered the gavel. "Now that we're all here, let us begin our work."

Naomi considered Maude's philosophy, that if you weren't early, you were late, autocratic, and unreasonable. One morning, either in this life or the next, Maude was going to wake up and discover that she really wasn't the English queen. Naomi got immense pleasure from the thought.

Maude's announcement that they had a guest brought Naomi's gaze around the table until she found Rufus Meade sitting there looking directly at her. Her reaction at seeing him unexpectedly was the same as always. Tension gathered within her and her heartbeat accelerated when he dipped his head ever so slightly in a greeting and let his lush mouth curve in a half smile. She knew the minute he responded to the fire that she couldn't suppress, that the tension pulsing between them was a sleeping volcano ready to erupt. She felt her heart flutter madly and shifted nervously in her chair as Maude opened the discussion.

She would not have anticipated that the talks would become so heated. The meeting ended, and she realized from Rufus's facial expression that he was furious with her. She believed her argument—that One Last Chance existed to be a buffer between distressed girls and the cruelty of society—was the correct one. And she was amazed when Rufus took the position that what she really wanted was for the foundation to be a shelter for delinquents. She hoped he wasn't a poor looser; several board members sided with him, but the majority supported her.

She was wrong, and he would straighten her out, he vowed, forcing himself to remain calm while, oblivious to onlookers, he ushered her to the elevator and on to the little office where she tutored. "I know there are special circumstances, but we have to be very careful when we're deciding what they are."

"I'm already familiar with your brand of compassion," she told him, with what he recognized as exaggerated sweetness; "it doesn't extend to females. It does cover cute little replicas of yourself, naturally, but it amazes me that you allowed your perfect self close enough to a woman to beget them. I don't suppose it was the result of artificial insemination, was it?" He wanted to singe her mouth with his when she looked at him expectantly, as if deserving a serious, friendly answer, though she knew she'd irked him.

He surprised himself and figured that he probably shocked her as well when he broke up laughing. When he could stop, he looked down at her and, in a playful mode, shook his head from side to side, his single dimple on full display. "Naomi, I refuse to believe that you are so naive as to issue me that kind of challenge. Don't you know better than to tell a man to his face that you doubt his virility? Are you nuts?"

Her intent regard amused Rufus. If she had been aware of the look of fascinated admiration on her smiling face, ten to one she would have banished it immediately. Her answer riled him. He wondered whether her attention had strayed when she asked provocatively, "How far off was I?"

Abruptly, he stopped smiling, forgot caution, and felt his face settle into a harsh mask. He pulled her close to him and absorbed her trembling as he lowered his head and brushed her mouth with his lips. He drew back to look at her, to gauge her reaction, but fire raced through him when she braced her hands against his chest in a weak, symbolic protest and whimpered, and he knew he had to taste her. Her soft, supple body offered no resistance, and as he sensed the giving of her trust, a warm, unfamiliar feeling of connection with someone special gripped him. She burrowed into him, giving herself over to him, pulling at something inside him. Something he didn't want to release.

He fitted her head into one of his big hands and gently stroked

her back with the other, trying to temper their rapidly escalat-
ing passion. But her gentle movements quickened his need. He
nearly bent over in anguish when she wiggled closer, caught up
in her own passion. Capitulating at last and in spite of himself,
he captured her eager mouth in an explosive giving of himself,
his body shuddering and his blood zinging through his throbbing veins.

He sensed a change in her then—a feminine response to his
own burgeoning need—and altered the kiss to a sweet, gentle
one, easing the pressure before asking for entrance with the tip
of his tongue. Her parted lips took him in, and he felt her tremble
from the pleasure of his kiss as she wrapped her arms around his
neck in sensual enjoyment. He didn't wonder that she returned
his kiss so ardently, that she was caressing his arms, shoulders,
and neck, that she was loving him right back. His only thought
was that she felt so good in his arms, tasted so good, responded
to him hotly and passionately, that she fitted him, that she
belonged right where she was. He didn't remember ever having
had such a passionate response from a woman nor even having
had one excite him as she did. He wanted her and he was going
to have her even if she was… He jerked his head up and looked
down into her passion-filled eyes. Not in a million years. *Never!*
He told himself as he put her gently but firmly away from him.

Naomi grasped her middle to steady herself. He had to know
that it was good to her, she surmised. Like nothing she had ever
felt. Did he know that her body burned from his kiss? She had
waited so long for it. Forever, it seemed. Nearly all her life.
Those strong, muscular arms holding her, soothing her; the
heady masculine smell of him tantalizing her; and the possessive way that he held her were more than she could have resisted.
More than she wanted to resist. And she needed to be held,
needed what he had given her, needed *him.* Her eyes closed in
frustration. What was it with him?

"Look," she heard him say, as he brushed his fingers across
the back of his corded neck, apparently struggling both for

words and for composure, "I'm sorry about that. You made me mad as the devil, and I got carried away. My apologies."

She reeled from his blunt rejection, but only momentarily. With more than thirteen years of practice at putting up her guard, she slipped it easily into place. "Looks as if I was right, after all, Mr. Meade," she bluffed, covering her discomfort. "You've got a problem." She whirled around and left him standing there. He would never know what it had cost her.

# Chapter 4

An hour later, still puzzled over Rufus's behavior, Naomi forced herself to answer her doorbell. Tomorrow, she was going to speak to the doorman about not buzzing her to ask whether she wanted to receive visitors. What was the point in having such an expensive place if it didn't guarantee her security and privacy? She knew very well that if it was Rufus, the young doorman would be so awed that he wouldn't dare insult him by asking his name and announcing him, as house rules required. With a tepid smile, she cracked the door open and saw him standing there, the epitome of strength and virility. She tried to curb her response to him, a reaction so strong that blood seemed to rush to her head. And that annoyed her. Her next impulse was to close the door with a bang, but she wasn't so irritated that she wanted to hurt him.

"May I come in, Naomi? Not once when I've stood at this door have you willingly invited me in."

Feeling trapped by her attraction to him, and hoping that a clever retort would put her in command, she gave him what she hoped was a withering look.

"What do you want, Meade? You've already gotten yourself off the hook with an apology, so why are you standing here?" She spoke in a low, measured tone, trying to keep her voice steady.

Rufus was silent for a minute, trying to gauge her real feelings, which he had learned were probably different from what she let him see. Her gentle tone belied her sharp words, and he welcomed it. He watched her bottom lip quiver while she shifted her weight from one foot to the other, trying not to respond to what he knew she saw in his eyes. His gaze traveled slowly over her, caressing her, cataloging her treasures—flat belly, rounded hips, wild hair, long legs, a full, generous mouth, and more. He wanted her badly enough to steal her. Badly enough to forget everything else and go for her. But he hadn't come to her apartment for that. Telling himself to get with it, he reined in his passion and assumed a casual stance.

He cleared his throat, impatient with his physical reaction to her. "Naomi, it must be clear to you that we have to reach some kind of understanding. We have to work together for the next month, and if we can't cooperate, that gala will be a disaster. So ease up, will you?"

He was taken aback by her forced, humorless smile. And her words. "Why don't you level with yourself? You didn't come over here tonight to make it easier for us to work together. You're here for two reasons; your testosterone is acting up; and you're feeling guilty about the way you behaved back there at OLC. Well, you can go home, wherever that is. Your boys will be 'pining' for you."

Rufus could see that she wanted to take back the words as soon as they escaped her lips. Weeks earlier, those revealing remarks had slipped out of his mouth before he could stop them—childhood hurts that remained solidly etched in his memory—and she had thrown them back at him. He knew that she saw pain in his eyes, that his reaction to her barb aroused her compassion. He regretted having exposed himself to her when he alluded to his unhappy childhood, and she could bet he wouldn't make that mistake again. He hated pity. To cover her own insecurity, her own vulnerability, she had used it against him. But she reached out to him then with her heart as well as her hand, and he looked first into her eyes, softer than he had ever seen them, and then at her extended hand, grasped it, and walked in. Into her house and into her arms.

He breathed deeply, savoring the union, as they held each other without the intrusion of the passion and one-upmanship that had marked their brief relationship. When he felt himself begin to stir against her, he moved away.

"Naomi, if you'd put on more clothes, maybe we can talk this thing out."

Her embarrassment at having greeted him in her short silk dressing gown was too obvious to conceal, and he noticed that she didn't try, but expected him to understand that she had forgotten she was skimpily dressed. It was a small measure of trust, but it was something, and he welcomed it.

"All right. I'll be back in a minute. There's a bar; help yourself to a drink." She left him in the living room and returned within minutes dressed, as promised. He liked that.

"Didn't you find anything you'd like to drink?"

"I don't drink anything stronger than an occasional glass of wine at dinner. Thanks anyway." She looked great no matter what she was wearing, he observed, and told her so. "You're really something to look at, you know that? My common sense almost deserted me when I saw you standing there in that red jersey robe, with that thick black curly hair hanging around your shoulders. Dark women look great in pinks and reds."

She sat down and kicked off her shoes, and he could see that his compliments made her nervous. She did not want an involvement with him any more than he wanted one with her. He grinned. In their case, want didn't count for much.

"Thank you," she replied briskly, "but there isn't anything to talk out, as you put it. I am not looking for a romantic involvement with you or anyone else, not now or ever, so we shouldn't have any difficulty working together."

Rufus glanced at her shoeless feet as she tucked them beneath her. A free spirit would do that, he figured. But she had caged that side of her, he guessed, and she had done it years earlier. He leaned back in the sofa and appraised her slowly and thoroughly until she suddenly squirmed. What a maze of contradictions she was! If she thought so little of romantic involvement and marriage for herself, why had she championed it for her young charge at OLC? The thought perturbed him; her adamant disavowal of interest in men didn't ring true. He noted that the shoes were back on her feet.

Rufus leaned forward. "Sorry about that," he apologized, referring to his blatant perusal of her. "But I can't believe you know so little about what happens when a man and a woman get their hooks in each other. So I have to assume that either you're being dishonest with yourself or you just don't care to level with me. That kiss you gave me, Naomi, almost made me erupt; I'm still reeling from it. You were right when you said that's why I'm here."

"You're making too much of this," she told him, obviously uneasy with the drift of the conversation.

Her attempt to minimize it annoyed him. "When you kiss a man like that, giving him everything he's asking for and letting him know that you're loving what he's doing to you, you're either consenting or making demands of your own or you've gone too far."

He ignored the outrage that he saw in her reproachful eyes and went on. "You and I want each other, Naomi. Don't doubt it for a minute; we want to make love to each other. I confess that making love with you was one of the first thoughts I had when I met you. But I told myself then, and I'm telling you now, that I don't intend to do one thing about it. You and I would be poison together."

Naomi was a worthy adversary, he recalled at once. "Of course you aren't going to do anything about it," she purred, "because *I* won't let you. As for me wanting you, let me tell you how much weight you can put on that. I saw a beautiful pair of green leather slippers in Garfinkel's not long ago, and I wanted them badly. They were the perfect complement to something I had just bought. I took a taxi all the way back up here to Bethesda at a cost of twenty dollars, got my credit card, taxied back, and would you believe those shoes were gone? You know what I did? I shrugged my shoulders and bought a pair of royal blue ones that didn't match a thing I owned. When I left the store, I was perfectly happy. Nothing gets the better of me, Rufus. Believe me, *nothing!*" He disliked her facetious grin. "So you're right; there's no need to make a big deal out of it," she went on, her quivering lips belying her tough words. "You'll find another one—darker or lighter, taller or shorter, but with the same basic equipment—and you'll be just as happy."

He shook his head in amazement. "I don't believe you said that." His blood pounded in his ears when she crossed her knees and let her right shoe slip off as she did so, revealing a flawless size nine foot with its perfectly shaped red toenails. His couldn't take his eyes from her.

He swore softly. "You'd drive me insane if I spent much time around you. Stop acting," he growled in a velvet soft voice. "You're as vulnerable to me as I am to you." He told himself to cool off. "We have to have a meeting Tuesday or Wednesday. Which would you prefer?"

"Neither." His impatient glance provoked a hesitant explanation. "I tutor at One Last Chance in the afternoon of both days this week, and I can't disappoint this girl; she has a lot of problems, and she's known very little caring. The night you saw her with me, she showed me an excellent drawing that she had done with crayons; it was wonderful. She just needs guidance."

"Then you believe she has talent for art?"

"Yes, but I'm not tutoring her in art. I'm helping her with math and English."

"What's the girl's name?" He wondered if now was the time. Her feelings for this girl aroused his curiosity and his suspicions, too, he realized.

"Linda."

Rufus hesitated, aware of a primitive protectiveness toward her, fearful of hurting her. "Naomi. If I'm wrong here, tell me. I get the impression that you have a special connection with this girl, that you have deeper feelings for her than for the others at OLC. And my instincts say that your concern for her has a personal basis." He watched as she readied herself to divert him.

"Really, Rufus, what could have made you think such a thing?"

"I realize that you were tutoring her in English, but I didn't know that you were qualified to teach math as well. What level?"

"She's in her last year of junior high. I taught those subjects in high school for four years."

"Why did you give it up?" Naomi was a complex person, he was beginning to understand, and the more he saw of her, the more he wanted to see. He leaned back against the deeply cushioned brown velvet sofa, watching her intently.

"I never wanted to teach, but Grandpa would pay for my education only if I studied to be a teacher. Teaching is the proper work for girls of my class, he told me a thousand times. I did as he wanted, same as everybody else always does, and I taught until I'd saved enough money to study for a degree in fine art. He hasn't forgiven me for it, but, well, he's done some things that I haven't been able to forgive him for." He nodded, letting her know that he sympathized with her, then lifted his wrists and glanced at his watch.

"I've got to get home; I told Jewel I'd be there by nine." He hesitated to leave. "How did you get involved with One Last Chance?"

He pondered the reasons she might have for taking so much time to answer. "I saw the need for it. I'm one of its founders. Who's Jewel?" On to another topic, was she? The tactic neither fooled nor amused him.

From Naomi's reaction, he realized that his grin had been mocking rather than disarming, as he had intended. "Jewel's my baby sister. Why? Are you jealous?" He couldn't resist the taunt; it was the second bit of concrete evidence she'd given him that her interest was more than casual and his attraction for her more than physical. Yet he doubted that she would ever own up to it.

Her studied smirk as she slanted her head, tipped up her nose, and peered at him had all the arrogance that any crowned European could have mustered. It was admirable. What a gal!

"Well?" he baited.

"Put all your money on it," she bantered, with a brief pause that he knew was for effect, "and then see your lawyer about filing for bankruptcy." He smiled, enjoying the teasing.

"You'd be fun if you'd just forget about sex," she told him, referring to his comment about their heated kiss.

He knew she meant to provoke him, but instead of indulging her, he quipped: "Forget about sex?" Sweetheart, that is one thing I'll remember even after I'm buried."

His seductive wink, a mesmerizing slow sweep of his left eye, was aimed to strip her of any pretense about her feelings. And for the moment, it did. He held his breath when she dusted a speck of lint from the lapel of his jacket, pushed the handkerchief further down in his breast pocket, and rubbed a speck of nothing from his chin. The expression in her eyes nearly unglued him, but he kept his countenance and satisfied himself with a brush of his fingers across her cheek. He was unprepared for the warmth that quickly enveloped them and for the sweet, mutual contentment that they had not previously experienced together. Wordlessly, they walked to her door and stood there looking at each other, comfortable with the tension, with their desire in check. Simultaneously they reached out to each other, but didn't touch and withdrew as one, as if it had been choreographed. He sucked in his breath and left without a word.

The rooms appeared to have grown larger after he left her, and her beloved apartment seemed cold and unfriendly. Her footsteps echoed along the short, tiled hallway. Strange, but she had never noticed that before. A restlessness suffused her. She reached for the telephone, then dropped her hand. So this was loneliness. This was what it was like to miss a man. She had to stop it now. Maybe it was already too late. She didn't think she had the strength to face exposure, certainly not his rejection. Rufus already meant too much to her, had too prominent a place in her life, and she couldn't bear his scorn if he ever knew about her past. One Last Chance was important to her, but if she couldn't get Rufus out of her life any other way, she would have no choice but to leave it, to walk away from the most satisfying thing in her world other than her work. He was right; she had wanted him desperately. She still did. But if she walked away from him, away from the sweet and terrible hunger that he stirred in her, away from the promise of love in his arms... She went to bed trying not to think about Rufus and fell asleep imagining the ultimate joy that he could give her.

The next morning Naomi got up at six-thirty, unable to sleep longer, and phoned her grandfather.

"Why are you calling so early, gal? I thought you artist types worked at night and slept most of the day."

She ignored his attempted reprimand for having abandoned teaching for art. "Grandpa, I think we ought to look up those people who want to find me and get it over with; I can't stand this uncertainty. A month ago, I had a quiet life and was contented, all things considered. It's like a death sentence must be; maybe the waiting and not knowing is worse than the actual execution."

"Don't you be foolish, gal," he roared into the phone. "They may give up or I may find a way to discourage them."

"But where does that leave me? Did I have a girl, a boy, twins? And are the adoptive parents loving, abusive, rich, dirt poor? What about my feelings, Grandpa? This is becoming un-bearable." She thought about Rufus and how devoted he was to his boys. He put them before everybody and everything, includ-ing his career. She recalled his painful allusion to his childhood when, after "pining" all day for someone, no doubt his mother, that someone had gotten home too tired to give him the love he needed. What would he think of her? She heard Judd's insistent voice.

"What was that, Grandpa?"

"Where's your mind, Naomi?" She imagined that he was rolling his eyes upward, expressing his frustration. "I said that I tried to spare you as best I could. But if you're going to be foolish and go looking for trouble, I'd better hire a lawyer. Never could tell you a thing."

"So the lawyer can tell you that we don't have any options? This is something that has to be done on a personal basis." She hated discussing it with him. Her grandfather would soon be ninety-five; he'd been born the last day of the nineteenth century, and she tried never to argue with him. Not only because he'd

taken her in and made a home for her when her father had re-
married to a woman who didn't want a stepchild around, and had
become her legal guardian when her father had died, but because
she cared for him and didn't like to upset him. He's the product
of anther era, she reminded herself, a time when a man did what
he thought best for his family and expected them to accept it as
he knew they would.

"We've got a problem, so we'll get legal advice," she heard
him say in his usual authoritarian fashion. The sisters and
brothers of the First Golgotha Baptist Church didn't get out of
line with their pastor, and forty-five years of such near idolatry
had spoiled Judd Logan. "These hotshot lawyers are worthless,"
he continued, "but you need them sometimes."

"There's no point in asking you not to, Grandpa, because
you always do whatever you like. I don't need a lawyer; I need
to meet my child's adoptive parents and ask them to let me see
my child. If they want to reach me after all this time, there's a
good reason." She wouldn't say more about it then; it would
take him a while to accept the idea, if he ever did. "I have to
go over to One Last Chance, Grandpa. One of the girls is
meeting me there at nine." She didn't say goodbye, because she
knew he'd have a comment then or later. Twirling the phone
cord, she waited.

"I want you to listen to me, gal. Don't rush into anything. And
I wish you'd stay away from those places like Florida Avenue,"
he complained. "What kind of people do you meet over there?
I'm sure Maude Frazier doesn't waste time around there. It's not
proper for an unmarried girl of your class to hang around those
people." Naomi grinned, stifling a giggle as she did so. The old
man was on a roll. He loved to preach, and it didn't matter
whether he had an audience of one hundred or one.

"Grandpa, you're talking about seventy years ago." Reminding herself that there was a generation between them and enough
years in age for a two-generation gap, she let it pass.

"We're never going to agree on certain things," she told him
gently. "You tried to save people's souls. Well, when I'm at One

Last Chance, I'm trying to help people mend their lives. There must be a connection there somewhere." She told him goodbye and hung up.

Half an hour after arriving at OLC, Naomi looked at her watch. Linda was late. She knew that the girl wouldn't offer an excuse, and when she arrived, she didn't. Linda had missed several sessions, and Naomi had been tempted to speak with her mother but had refrained for fear of causing trouble.

"I spoke with your principal. Has he told your mother the consequences of your not going to the retreat and completing your art project?"

Linda's eyes widened. "You mean he's going to tell my mama I'll be in trouble if I don't go? Boy, that's super cool! Tell me to tell her I can't go to the retreat unless I have my hair done."

Naomi laughed. "Linda, we tell the truth to the extent possible. The principal won't be lying. That retreat is important to you; your career decisions may hinge on it."

She knew that Linda admired her, but she was stunned when the girl suddenly told her, "I wish I could be like you, Naomi. I wish I was you."

Naomi tugged at her chin with a thumb and forefinger. "My dear, if you knew everything there is to know, you might not want to be in my shoes at all."

Linda stared directly at her. "With you, I'd take my chances." Shaking her head, Naomi looked at Linda and remembered herself fourteen years before. If you got what you prayed for, she thought with wise hindsight, it could ruin your life.

She went home and began designing invitations for the Urban Alliance gala. There weren't enough sponsors, she decided. Rufus would know what to do about it. She got his number and telephoned him. She was taken aback when his initial response to her call was unfriendly; he was deep into his current manuscript, *Subculture of the American Juvenile,* he explained, and hadn't wanted to be disturbed. But he'd immediately become warm and agreeable.

"Give me an hour, and I can get over there," he stated, as if confident that she would accept his offer. She couldn't help smiling. To begin the day with Judd Logan and end it with Rufus Meade would tax a saint—that is, unless the saint was slightly sweet on Rufus, her conscience whispered.

She pushed the thought aside and asked him, "How far away are you, Rufus?"

"Fifteen minutes. Just over in Chevy Chase. Why? You need something that'll melt? Or maybe something that'll melt you? Hmm?" He laughed, but she refused to join in his merriment. She wished he'd be consistent and stop the sexual teasing, since they had both sworn not to get involved.

"Are you bringing the boys? Should I dash out and get some ice-cream?"

He answered gruffly, yet seemed touched. "Thanks, no. They're over at Jewel's house, playing with their cousins. I'll see you shortly."

Naomi hung up and leaned against the edge of her kitchen table. Rufus claimed that he would not permit anything to happen between them, and that was fine with her, because she couldn't afford it. But his behavior didn't always suit his words. He teased her, and though he didn't telephone her, when they spoke, he took every opportunity to make her aware of him as a man. A desirable man. She shook her head in wonder, but her bewilderment was fleeting; she spun on her heels and headed for her bedroom.

"Two can play this game," she told herself, as she remembered how elegant he'd been when he'd come to her house, even when he'd had the twins with him. "If he's a phony," she muttered, "we'll both know it soon." She reached into her closet for her silk knit "Sherman tank," a sleeveless cowl-necked magnet for males, dismissed caution, and shimmied into it.

# Chapter 5

To her chagrin, Rufus arrived wearing a long-sleeved sport shirt with black jeans under a light overcoat. His dreamy eyes took her in from head to foot, apparently appreciating the svelte curves revealed by her burnt orange knit tube dress. His grin didn't reach his eyes, she noticed. Leaning against the wall with his arms folded across his broad chest, he told her without a trace of a smile and in deadly earnest, "Don't you play with fire, honey. I wouldn't want you to get singed."

She had an awful feeling of defeat, but only temporarily, because she knew that her sharp mind rarely deserted her. She pushed one of the kitchen chairs toward him, hopefully gave him a level stare, and asked in what she had cultivated as her sweetest voice, "You wouldn't be the culprit, would you?" A bystander would have thought that she was seriously seeking valuable information. "You usually back off when things warm up. So I don't have to worry about you, do I?" But she quickly realized that Rufus was not in a joshing mood. She saw his body stiffen and his muscles tense and thought of a big cat about to spring.

He rounded the table. "You like to tease, do you? Well..." She headed him off, sensing something subtly different about him. It wasn't the annoyance; she'd seen him practically furious. It was the steel, a street kind of steel that a man reserves for his true adversary.

She gulped. "I'm not teasing you, I've never..."

"I'm not asking you; I'm telling you. You didn't wear that hot little number all day long, now, did you? And I'll bet you weren't wearing it when you called me."

She backed up a little. Where was that suave, genteel man with the iron control? This Rufus seemed to be itching for friction, to need it. But she was doggoned if she'd let him intimidate her.

"Your reputation doesn't include being a bully, so be yourself and sit back down."

His steely, yet strangely gentle fingers sent fiery ripples spiraling down her arm. "Don't play with me, Naomi. You poured yourself into that thing to get my attention." He grinned, and she realized for the first time that his grin did not necessarily signify amusement. "You've got my attention. I told you that I had no intention of pursuing this…this whatever-you-want-to-call-it between us, and you assumed that I meant I wouldn't take you to bed. That shows how much you know about what goes on between a man and a woman."

He was right. She knew very little about it, but enough that she sensed the danger of her galloping attraction to him. She scoffed at him, pretending amusement.

"You do fancy yourself, don't you? Well, I want you to understand something, Mr. Meade: I don't knuckle under for *any* man."

She watched with frank fascination while Rufus walked away from her, turned, and placed his hands on his hips. "Naomi, only a fool would wrap himself in a red sheet and go out to meet a thousand-pound bull. I don't fancy myself; but baby, you *do* fancy me." Then he added in a dangerously soft voice, "I'd rescue you from a burning building, Naomi, but if you push me another fraction of an inch, I'll have that dress off of you in a split second. And before you can bat one of your big eyes, you'll be begging for mercy. Believe it!"

Tiny shivers skittered from her head to her toes and a rapidly spiraling heat suffused her as she imagined what he would be like if she dared him. She stared in rapt attention at his hypnotic face, taking in his serious manner, thrilled at the temptation of him standing before her, tense and flagrantly male, excited in a way that she had never been before. She didn't wonder or even care what he thought as she stood there looking at him, trembling. Time had no meaning as her gaze traveled up his long, lean frame, pausing briefly on his powerful chest and strong corded neck and reluctantly coming to rest in the turbulent pools of fire that his eyes had become. Vaguely, she realized she needed to compose herself, but a feeling of helplessness nearly overcame her. She rimmed her lips with the tip of her tongue and, with what sense she had left, turned to leave the room.

Rufus narrowed his eyes at what was one of the most lush examples of honest feminine need he'd ever seen. He reached for her, and she moved to him without caution or care, like a moth to a glowing flame, nail to magnet. He gathered her to him with stunning force, and as if it was what she needed, she moved up on tiptoe, curled her arms around his neck, and let her long artist's fingers weave through the tight black curls at the base of his head. He brushed her lips briefly, molded them softly to his, and held her head while he took his pleasure. Dimly, he realized that she was out of her league when she felt him growing against her and sagged in his arms.

Gently he lifted her and pressed his closed lips to her breast, hating that offending dress that separated him from her flesh. "Rufus. Oh, Rufus." Was she begging him for more, or pleading for mercy? He couldn't tell which, but he knew he was rapidly reaching the point where he'd need awesome self-control. He lowered her to her feet, held her away from him, and looked at her. She was as shaken as he, and his behavior annoyed him, because he didn't want to mislead her or hurt her. And he didn't trust himself to have an affair with her, after that kiss, which had been even more powerful, more punishing that the other that they had shared, he wouldn't count on his ability to keep his head straight. He moved away from her, certain from the look of her that she wanted him even closer. And he was pretty sure now that her experience with men had been minimal. But what was he supposed to do while she stood there, apparently absentminded, rubbing the spot where his lips had been? He swore softly and pulled her to him again.

"I want you, Naomi." He spoke in low guttural tones, the quiver in his voice a sure sign—if she had known it—that he could be putty in her hands. But she didn't know it, he discovered, and she replied with the volley of an ingénue.

"Please let me go. That doesn't flatter me, Rufus. I told you, it's not going to happen now or ever." If she had been a hot poker in his bare hand, he could hardly have put her away from him more quickly. He had almost made a fool of himself over her, and she'd turned him off, just like that. How could a woman go up in smoke in a man's arms one minute and arrogantly tell him to get lost the next?

He wiped his mouth symbolically with the back of his hand and allowed her to witness one of his indecipherable grins. "Better stop playing it so close to the edge with me; the next time you behave the way you did tonight, we may both regret it. And Naomi," he chided gently, almost affectionately, "you deserve better than you asked for just then, and I should have given you better than you got. But I'm human; try to remember that, will you?" There's something about her that's different, he thought, but couldn't name it. Shrugging it off, he reached both hands toward the ceiling and grabbed fists full of air, stretching his big frame like the great cats for which he'd been nicknamed.

Naomi admitted to herself that her passionate exchange with Rufus was a humbling experience, and she had the guilty feeling that she'd brought some of it on herself. She knew how she looked in that dress, but she didn't intend to worry about it. His last remark convinced her that he really was very likeable, that she could trust him with herself anyplace and at any time. Frankly observing him, she could almost pinpoint the second that he decided to change the tenor of the conversation.

"All right, let's get started," he directed. "I'm sure some of the fraternities would be glad to join this; I can get my frat to go along and you might contact your sorority."

"What's yours?" she asked. "I'm a Delta." She shook with laughter at his stunned disbelief that they belonged to brother-sister Greek letter societies. Her Delta to his Omega. Stranger things had happened, she reminded him, hinting that at last they had found common ground.

He feigned innocence. "You're joking! What do you mean, 'at last'? What kind of ground was that we found when we were setting each other on fire a minute ago? As an English teacher, you should take a page from Shakespeare, 'to thine own self be true.'"

She had backed away from involvements, from attachments that she would have liked to pursue, because she didn't trust a man to love and accept her as she was. And she paid for it in loneliness. Even now, she chose craftily not to reply to his message but to the package in which he wrapped it. "Mr. Meade," she queried, "where is it written that you're not a man unless you mention sex at least once in every sentence?"

"Who mentioned sex? I was talking about whatever it is between us that draws us together, no matter how much we swear we don't want it. I know what I'm backing away from, Naomi, and I know why. But do you?"

She wouldn't have dared to tell him that she was backing away from what she thought she wanted, but hadn't previously *known* she needed; the love of a strong, tender man. A man like him. And she couldn't tell him that it was fear of his rejection, his scorn, that wouldn't let her reveal herself, the self she knew he would like, that he might even love. Nor could she tell him that, if she were true to herself, he might even become hers for a little while— before her world caved in. And never could she utter the words that would tell him what he was coming to mean to her.

A frivolous reply that would hide her feelings was on the tip of her tongue. But his question was too threatening, too intimate for a trivial answer, and she heard herself say, "I've been backing away so long that I do it without thinking." She must have made him speechless; he was quiet for a long time. When he did speak, it was to suggest that they get something to eat. Relieved, she nodded in agreement. "Sounds good to me."

Naomi rarely sat in the front seat of a car when she wasn't driving; when she did, she tended to be uncomfortable. But not with Rufus at the wheel. She turned to him. "Driving a car is an ego trip for a lot of men, but not for you; you're very careful."

She wouldn't have thought that such a simple statement would please him so much. But his face showed genuine pleasure. "Life's a fragile thing, Naomi, and I don't risk mine or anyone else's, if I can help it. Besides, I'm all that the boys have."

There was a silent minute while he seemed to test her interest, and then he added, "Those little rascals are my life; I can't imagine it without them. They're not quite four yet, but I feel as if I've always had them. I have to leave them sometimes, like tonight, and when I get back home the way they greet me…Naomi, they make me feel like I'm king of the world." The dreamy smile on his face told Naomi that he was speaking not only to her, but to himself as well, that he was counting his blessings. She was silent for so long that he apologized.

"You'll have to pardon me for going on about my boys; I forget that they're not as precious to other people as they are to me."

He couldn't be serious. She never tired of seeing or hearing of love between children and their parents. If there was anything more precious, she hadn't heard of it. "Don't apologize. I was thinking how fortunate they are, how fortunate any child would be to have a parent who loved it like that. It's something about which I know little or nothing, but I recognized it when I saw you with them, and I sensed that they know it, too." Her own words jolted her. They told of her youthful needs, but they might also describe the needs of the child she had borne but never seen. She didn't know, but God she hoped not! Her left hand clutched her chest.

"What is it, Naomi? Are you okay?" At her continued silence, he said, "No, I guess you aren't. Did you grow up without parents?"

She had, she told him. "My grandfather gave me a lovely home and anything that I needed, and he took good care of me. But, Rufus, he was forty-one when my father was born, and he's almost Victorian in his thinking. He thinks that any show of emotion is a sign of weakness. Can you imagine a little seven-year-old girl dealing with that? I think he loves me, but not on the basis of anything he's ever said."

"Was he harsh with you?"

She had always found it difficult to talk about the little pricks and hurts that she kept locked deep inside. Although his calm protective mien tempted her to pour out everything, she quickly threw up her guard. She knew she was hedging, and she suspected that he did, too.

"Not really. The problem was that he made mistakes, mistakes that hurt, but he never seemed to question his decisions nor his actions. He's given me some tough rows to hoe, but I love him, Rufus. I love him, because he's always meant well, and as you said, I'm all he has." He turned off Wisconsin onto M Street and parked.

"Where are you going?"

"I'm surprised you didn't ask earlier," he needled. "You independent gals usually want to be in on every decision no matter what it is." He pulled off his overcoat, reached in the back seat, got a suit jacked out of a dry cleaner's bag, and slipped it on. If you wanted service at the Brasserie, you had to wear a jacket.

"More often than you would imagine, our escorts turn out to be men of little minds," she explained patiently, tongue in cheek, "and we've learned to express our opinions in the interest of self-preservation." He put his overcoat on while he walked around the vehicle to the passenger door.

She accepted his hand he offered to help her out of the minivan and jumped when he gave her a delicate little squeeze for the sheer sport of it. She supposed that she looked a little startled, because he explained to her as patiently as she had explained to him: "Excuse me, but that remark of yours closed down my little mind. Temporarily, of course."

Naomi bubbled with laughter and lightheartedness, unable to remember being so happy. She turned around and skipped backward to keep up with his long strides, joy zinging through her, proud and even a little reckless as they ambled along, teasing and bantering. The brisk night air invigorated her, and the low hum of familiar city sounds lulled her into a carefree mood. How could one man change her world so drastically, so completely? They walked into the crowded Italian Brasserie, overlooking the

Chesapeake and Ohio Canal, and were seated facing the narrow stream. Soft lights, reflected from the restaurant, danced on the water, and she wished that Rufus would hold her hand. Walking in there with him was an experience she wouldn't forget. She was unprepared for the smiles, stares, and waves that greeted him as they entered, giving her a sense of how famous he really was.

"I don't believe I know any of them," he told her in response to her question. "I played football some years ago, and I guess some people are nice enough to remember. But those days are behind me, Naomi, and I rarely look back on them. I'm grateful for the success I had, though, because it allows me to write, which is what I love to do best, on my own terms. I gather you aren't a football fan."

"No, I guess not. The roughness makes me nervous. I've often wondered how the families of those players can tolerate seeing their loved ones banged around like that. Some of those big guys seem to try to kill the ball carriers. I just can't watch it." He's really modest, she thought. When had she last been in the company of anyone who showed such humility?

Rufus had been studying her intently. "Naomi, that tells me you aren't as hard-boiled as you'd like me to think." He handed her a menu. "Everything's good here," he explained, before she could respond, "but what they do to broiled stuffed mushrooms is sinful." The waiter mixed their orders with those of another table, and Rufus gave him a gentle reprimand, alluding to his greater attention to Naomi than to their orders. Not that he blamed the man, he secretly admitted.

Surprised, Naomi opened her mouth to speak and thought better of it. Rufus was treating the handsome waiter to a lesson in the meaning of male territorial rights: *Don't get on my turf* was the message on his fierce countenance. Of course, Rufus wouldn't allow another man in his yard, she figured; he was too possessive for that. But he wasn't consistent, and that made her edgy; she was beginning to accumulate a lot of questions about him. He had sworn that he wouldn't become involved with her, but he acted as if he had a claim, a right to tell another man to stay away from her.

Or maybe he was just demanding that the waiter show him proper respect. Enigma, thy name is man, she thought.

Rufus smiled as if nothing had happened. "I'm sure your thoughts are worth far more than a penny, so I won't offer to buy. Where were you just then?"

"I was feeling bad for the poor waiter. You probably could have shriveled rock with the look you gave him."

"I'm sorry if you were made uncomfortable, Naomi." But not sorry that he'd reprimanded the waiter, she noted. Talk about self-possession; he had it.

"You haven't made me uncomfortable," she corrected. "It's just that every time we meet or talk, you show me another facet of your personality. Riding in a Model-T Ford must have been something like that: bumpy and full of surprises." When he merely shrugged a shoulder and didn't comment, she decided that he didn't bother with self-analysis. Strong, but unpretentious. She liked that. They finished their meal in companionable silence.

"The dinner was lovely," she told him later, digging into her purse. "How much is the bill?"

Rufus reached for his wallet. "This isn't a dutch treat, Naomi. I do not, repeat, *do not* go dutch with females, be they eight or eighty, sweetheart, wife, or sister."

She gave him what she hoped was her most angelic plastic smile. "For your sake, I'm glad your rule isn't etched in stone, because I pay my own way."

Rufus frowned, a muscle twitching in his jaw, and she could see that he was giving his hot temper a stern lecture.

"Naomi, almost every time we've ever been together, our partings have been less than friendly. This time, could we please avoid that?"

She refused to back down. "Of course, we can, dear," she agreed pleasantly, stressing the "dear." "It's very simple; try being less of a chauvinist, and we'll leave here like two peas in a pod."

The deepening of his frown into a fierce scowl delighted her; his temper was going to be his undoing.

"Naomi, you give me a royal pain in the...in the neck." His long, labored sigh bespoke total exasperation with her.

Not caring that she'd gotten his goat, she told him, "Well, at least you can sit down. After I've been haggling with *you,* I usually have to stand up for a while."

He stared, scowling, before his frown dissolved into a hearty laugh, and he reached over and squeezed her hand affectionately. Then he handed her the check. "Here. Pay the whole damned thing."

Rufus fought to come to terms with the lightheartedness that he felt when they stepped out of the restaurant holding hands; neither of them behaved as if it was strange. The early November wind had become stronger and more biting, and after they'd taken a few steps, he tucked their joined hands into his left overcoat pocket. And they didn't seem to find that incongruous with their professed intentions not to become involved with each other, either. Rufus shook his head in wonder. He disliked the fact that she made him happy, and if he had an ounce of sense, he'd put her in a cab and send her home. He glanced down and savored her serene smile. Oh, what the heck!

"Let's stop by Saloon and listen to some jazz," he suggested. "Carter is there, and they have great ribs. Maybe I'll get some of their barbecued ribs to take home. It's just down the street. I remember that you like opera; *La Traviata,* wasn't it? I hope I'm right in assuming that you also like jazz. I like opera, too, but it's never made me want to dance or hug anybody." Not that he needed any added inducements to snuggle up with her. She was as potent a lure as a man could tolerate. And he was rambling, he realized to his disgust, something he never did. Another indication that he should put some distance between them.

Naomi laughed in that joyous way that always made him want to squeeze her to him. So much for his admonition to himself. "You can't resist needling me, can you? I love jazz, and I don't want to shock you, but I also love country music. As for the ribs, well, I'm afraid you can keep those. They're fattening."

He tugged her closer. "Wouldn't shock *me;* I like country music, too. But in my book, no ribs, no soul." Still holding her hand in his pocket, he squeezed it gently. He wasn't overloaded with soul himself, but she didn't have to know it. "And as for needling," he told her, "lady, you've got that down to a very fine art."

They reached the club quickly and found a table in the rear. An attractive waitress walked over with a bottle of ginger ale and a glass of ice for Rufus, spoke to him, and asked Naomi what she would have. Naomi ordered the same.

"I see you come here often. Do you come just to listen to jazz, or for more personal reasons?"

He watched her above hands clasped in pyramid fashion and decided not to growl at her. What was it about the woman that made him want to walk away from her one minute and love her the next?

"Naomi," he began, as patiently as he could, "if I had anything going with a woman who worked in this place, I wouldn't be so insensitive as to entertain you or any other woman here. You said you don't want us to be more than friends. Buddies was the way you put it I think." He threw his head back and rolled his eyes skyward, indicating what he thought of that likelihood.

"Exactly," she said, head high and nose up. That particular affection was becoming familiar to him; she was covering up her real feelings.

Careful here, Rufus told himself, but he wanted to take advantage of the opening that she had unwittingly given him. He said softly, "Sometimes I sense that your razor-sharp tongue hides a lot of pain."

When she stiffened, he quickly added, "Try to ward me off, if you ever anticipate that what I'm about to do or say will add to that pain. Promise me that." For a brief, poignant moment, she relaxed her guard, revealing hurt that he had already begun to suspect was an essential part of her. And he received a thorough shock; for the first time, he couldn't throw off his vulnerability to her. He had to accept his feelings. He wanted to take her and leave, but that, he knew, would be the wrong move.

"Have I offended you?" Her silence weighed heavily on him.

"Of course not," she answered him. "You just surprised me, that's all." When the waitress brought another round of drinks, he noticed the way in which Naomi looked at her and figured that her stare duplicated the one he had thrown at their waiter. Both of them saw the similarity and appreciated the humor of it. They sat in rapt attention while Benny Carter's soulful saxophone gave a memorable rendition of Duke Ellington's *Solitude*. She drifted into the past, and Rufus took her left hand in both of his, bringing her back to him.

Naomi struggled to hide the jitters that overcame her when Rufus parked and started around to the passenger side of the car. I don't want any of his mind-blowing kisses tonight, she told herself. They make a wreck out of me. She knew he'd be annoyed, but before he could reach the door, she opened it.

"I had a great time. Thanks," she offered, attempting to dismiss him.

"Naomi," he began, in a tone that suggested mild amusement. "You know that I'm going to see you safely to your door, don't you? So you are going to save your breath about how often you get there on your own, now, aren't you?"

She pretended at first to be speechless. "You've been associating with liberated women, haven't you?" She bit her tongue; it was stupid to bait him when he was being so gracious.

He ignored the taunt and held her hand as they entered the elegant lobby; she would have withdrawn it if she could have forced herself to do so, but she knew he wouldn't have permitted it if she'd tried. When they reached her door, he tipped her chin up with a strong but gentle index finger.

"Now you may tell me how much you enjoyed the evening." She had learned that his facial expressions did not always reflect his mood. His lips were laughing, but when she looked into his eyes, she saw that they were serious with sensual longing. She suddenly lost her capacity for either pointed innuendos or meaningless banter.

He prodded her. "Cat stole your tongue?"

She stunned him with her loaded reply. "No. Cat *wants* my tongue." His cool, off-putting response didn't alter the fact of his genuine surprise, she noted, when his eyes darkened with suspicion.

"You know what my nickname is?"

She nodded and worried her bottom lip. "Yes. Marva, my best friend, told me one day last week. Until then, I hadn't even known you'd played football. She said you ran like a lithe young panther." With each word, she moved closer to him. Unconsciously. Tremors streaked through her as she stared at the dark desire in his mesmerizing eyes. Her every nerve tingled with exhilaration, drowning her in a pool of sensuality, when his long fingers caressed the back of her head, wound themselves through her thick, tight curls, and slowly pulled her to him. She parted her lips before he bent his head.

When his mouth finally touched hers, they both moaned aloud from the intensity of what they felt; more than desire; far more. Naomi turned toward the door, whether to invite him in or to escape, she didn't know. But he stopped her, and she shivered as his strong arms pulled her to him. His firm lips brushed hers softly and then kissed her with such tenderness, such gentle sweetness, that she couldn't bear it and sagged against him. The moisture from her eyes touched his mouth, and she trembled when his lips kissed the tears from her face. She rested her head against his strong shoulders and held him. She couldn't disregard her awareness of him; it was too powerful. Sniffling softly, she relaxed in his warm protectiveness while he stroked her arms.

"I can't leave you if I've made you feel bad, Naomi. Why are you crying? Are you afraid of something? Certainly not of me."

"I'm not afraid of you, Rufus. I'm not." She sniffled and snuggled closer.

"Then you're afraid of yourself." She tried to move out of his arms, but he held her there. "You're afraid, because you want me, and for once, you're not in control." She twisted restlessly, and he let her go. "Don't ever let that bother you, Naomi; I would never take what a woman doesn't want me to have. And

I don't mean sex alone. I won't accept anything that she gives grudgingly, nothing unless the feeling is mutual. And *that,* my lovely lady, is definitely written in stone." He tipped an imaginary hat, gave her a brilliant smile, and left her standing there.

She watched him go, telling herself she was relieved. Inside her apartment, she undressed and tried to find oblivion in sleep. Hours later, she got up, showered and went back to bed. She needed Rufus, but she also needed to know her child. A sixteen-year-old isn't capable of making decisions for a lifetime; they pressured me, but I'm the one who has lived with it and agonized over it for over thirteen years. I won't be cheated like this; I deserve to see my child. But once she walked through that door, she knew she could say goodbye to everything that meant anything to her—the board of education, OLC, the twins, Linda…what would Linda say if she knew? And Rufus. After reading his current bestseller, in which he listed the causes of juvenile delinquency and placed mothers' behavior at the top of the list, she knew he'd never accept her past.

Rufus sat up in bed before sunrise and tried to reconcile himself to the emotional charge that had taken possession of them the night before. But no matter how he rationalized it, he faced a no-win situation; either capitulate and take it all the way, or let it go. What a choice! He was exactly where he'd been since the first time he'd laid eyes on her. He thought back to the smooth way in which she had used his nickname. If she knew it, she must also have known who he was. He hadn't thought that her responses to him were calculated, but acting was an honored profession, and he had met many woman who excelled at it. Especially Etta Mae, whose deceit in pretending to have been taking the Pill had ordained their marriage. So, why not Naomi?

He got up and went downstairs to his state-of-the-art kitchen, looked around, and wondered why he needed all those gadgets. He had reluctantly given in to the boys' tearful plea to spend the night with their cousins, so he didn't have to cook breakfast. He squeezed a glass of orange juice, drank it, and glimpsed the fresh fruit bowl on the table as he was leaving. He loved apples and thought they were better snacks than nuts and candy. He selected the largest red apple, polished it, and prepared to relish the tart sweetness. Then he bit into it and frowned. Beautiful and crunchy on the outside. Spoiled on the inside. He threw it into the garbage disposal. Was there a message in that somewhere?

Several mornings later, Naomi skimmed the report of the community school board's monthly meeting, slammed it down on her desk, got up, and paced the floor. Just a lot of loose talk. Unless they got better officers, there wouldn't be any improvement. She walked over to her desk and telephoned Judd.

"Grandpa, I'm going to try for president of my community school board."

"Now, you watch what you're doing, gal. You don't want to get in the public eye with this thing about the baby hanging over you. You could be asking for trouble. It's all right to be on the board, but being its president is too public. 'Course, I know you'll do whatever you want."

His reaction surprised her. She had thought he would be pleased, that he would support anything that enhanced the Logan name. Well, her mind was made up.

"Don't worry, Grandpa, it's just a local board, and it seldom makes news," she told him, vowing not to let it dampen her spirits. "There have to be some changes in those schools, and I'm going to see to it."

A few hours later, as she walked down the steps of the Martin Luther King, Jr., Memorial Library on G Street, where she'd traced the school board's record over the past decade and a half, she thought she heard her name. She heard it again, less faint than before, but it seemed to come from far away. She turned her back to the street to lessen the bite of the wind and saw Rufus and his boys ambling toward her. He restrained the children when they tried to run to her, preventing them from tumbling down the concrete steps. She opened her arms to them when they reached the sidewalk, and the little boys rushed to her, covered her face with kisses, and delighted in the love she returned.

Awed by their reception, she looked up into Rufus's sultry gaze and drank deeply of the warmth and affection she saw there. "Hi."

"Hi. They're obviously glad to see you. I'm surprised they recognized you from that distance. They've been returning library books. I let them do it themselves, and they've made friends with some of the librarians. It's a big adventure and one of their favorite outings. What brings you down here?" She told him about the school board and her decision to seek its presidency.

"Grandpa doesn't think much of the idea, but I'm going ahead with it." Still hunkered down, she continued holding the boys in her arms.

"I think it's a great idea. I can introduce you to a good publicist who'll get you free television interviews, guest shots on panel shows, newspaper coverage, the whole shebang. He's been disgusted with your school board for years, so he might not charge you. I'll do a story on you for the *Journal;* how about it?"

Her eyes widened in alarm, and she released the boys almost absentmindedly, rubbing her coat sleeves nervously. He reached down and helped her to her feet.

"What is it, Naomi? Don't you want any help? You'll certainly need it." His eyes narrowed quizzically.

"Y-yes, thank you. I...I just hadn't thought that far ahead. I'll let you know when I'm ready." She knew he'd think her wishy-washy, but she couldn't help remembering her grandfather's warning.

He looked closely at her. "If you feel you can make a difference, don't let anybody discourage you."

"Daddy's going to buy us hot chocolate, Noomie. You want some?" She looked at Sheldon, who regarded her expectantly, and hesitated. Finally, she told him she had to get back to her studio. Then she hugged the children, straightened up, and looked into Rufus's cool gaze. Shaken, she told them goodbye and went on her way, aware that her behavior baffled Rufus. She hadn't considered the necessity of a publicity campaign; cold fear clutched her heart at the thought of it. But she'd find a way, she promised herself. After all, she had nearly six months in which to make a move.

Rufus watched her until she was out of sight. The more he saw of her, the more of a puzzle she seemed. Was she reluctant to accept his help, or was it something else? As soon as he'd offered it, her enthusiasm for the idea had seemed to wane. What was behind it? He wanted to give her the benefit of the doubt, but she hadn't made it easy.

With the date of the gala rapidly approaching Rufus began laying out plans for a media blitz publicizing it. He would represent the Alliance, but they'd get more mileage, he decided, if Naomi spoke for OLC, and other organizations also had their own spokespersons. He hadn't seen her in over a week, not since that morning at the library. He had wanted to see her, and not calling her had tested his resolve, but he had desisted. She was far enough inside him as it was. He didn't want to think about her right then; if he did, the morning would be shot, as far as his work was concerned.

He worked on his manuscript until ten o'clock, gave his boys a mid-morning snack, and then telephoned Naomi to ask whether she'd be willing to make a few appearances on local television shows to promote the gala. There was a spot available that evening at seven-thirty.

Naomi agreed to his suggestion, but after hanging up, she began to worry that whoever was looking for her would be able to put a face with her name and would easily find her through her connection with One Last Chance. She wasn't sure she was ready for that yet and fretted about it for hours. She knew that she intended to see her child, to explain why she had given it up for adoption; it would take the United States Marines to prevent it, but she hadn't thought beyond that. The shock of having to face it after trying for so many years to forget it was only now beginning to wear off. Finally, she called Rufus, forced herself to be pleasant, even a little jocular, and gave him a weak excuse.

Then she redesigned the gala program to make it impossible for anyone to trace her through it.

Thirteen years. Nearly half her life had been fraught with fear. For over thirteen years, she had let fear of being exposed about something over which she had had almost no control circumscribe her life. And because of that fear, she lived without love, without a family, without real intimacy with anyone. But she hadn't had an idea of what she'd missed. Now she could imagine how it could be with Rufus if there were no barriers between them. Walking away from him might prove to be the most difficult thing she'd ever done, as hard as learning that she could at last see her child, a child who called someone else "Mother" and who would surely judge her harshly. But she could deal with it. She would. She *had* to! She wasn't so naive that she didn't know how uniquely suited she and Rufus were, but she knew that it couldn't happen. One day soon, she was going to sit down and deal with it, all of it, and fear wouldn't figure in her decisions. Lost in her thoughts, conjuring up her future, Naomi answered the phone, but the sound of his voice sent her heart racing.

"Hi." It was low and suggestive, though she was sure that after their last encounter, he hadn't meant it to be. "Look. I've got a problem, Naomi. Jewel isn't home, and I don't know whether she'll be able to keep my boys for me. Could you tell me where you'll be around three o'clock? If I haven't been able to make an arrangement for them by then, I'm afraid you'll have to go to the station."

"I'll be here," she promised grudgingly. She telephoned Marva. "I can't make rehearsals tonight. Can you reschedule it? Rufus said I may have to appear on WMAL this evening to publicize the gala, and I probably won't get out of there until after nine. I'm sorry, Marva." Marva changed the dates and advised Naomi that after leaving the station she should spend the evening with Rufus.

Rufus called Jewel, and she used the occasion to tell him that it was time he got a live-in nanny for the boys. "You can well afford it, and you won't have to sacrifice your career and your social life while you baby-sit."

Rufus didn't want to be vexed with his sister. She had made the point numerous times over the past three years, but in this instance it really annoyed him. It was one of her more subtle hints that Naomi would be a welcome sister-in-law, and they hadn't even met.

"Jewel, I'm not going over this with you again. If you have to go to a PTA meeting, keeping my boys is out of the question. I'll work it out."

"You could get married, you know," she shot at him. "It's time you forgave Etta Mae; you've been divorced for more than three years, and she's still ruining your life because you insist on seeing something of her in every woman you meet. Give it up, Rufus; you're hurting yourself."

His long, deep sigh was that of a man whose patience had been exceeded. He knew that his sister was right; forgiving and letting go had always been difficult for him. He chose to reply to only part of her comment.

"I want a companion for myself, Jewel, and if I ever remarry, it will be to a woman who can be a mother for my sons. Find me that woman, and maybe I'll take your advice. Well-informed, brainy career women make great companions, but in my book, they're not the best wives and mothers because they're never home; nor should anybody expect them to be. And the woman who's likely to stay home all the time, keep house, and live for her family alone might be good for the boys and is probably what today's family needs, but she'd bore the hell out of me. Believe me, single is better."

"I've got a career, and I'm a good wife and mother."

"Yes, you are. You're committed to your children and your husband, and he's committed to you. The two of you are a team, and that's what a marriage should be. But your kind of marriage is not common."

"Thanks for the confidence; you should be eager to get what Jeff and I have. If you don't know a good woman when you see one, talk to my husband and get a few pointers," she admonished him. He hung up thinking about what she'd said and about what he wanted. He wanted Naomi, and no amount of advice from Jewel's husband or anyone else would change that.

She answered after the first ring. "I'm afraid you'll have to go on tonight," he informed her without a trace of regret. "I've already told the station's program director that one of us would be there. So how about it?"

"I'm sorry, but I just can't. Bring the boys over here, and I'll keep them for you." Why was she stammering, and what had happened to her normal poise? He jerked the telephone cord impatiently, alert to a possibly hidden reason for her refusal.

"I thought you said you'd be busy. If you're busy, how can you take care of my boys?"

"I'm expecting a business call," she told him, digging a deeper hole for herself.

"At night? At home? Are you leveling with me?" He was openly suspicious of her motives now.

"Okay, I'm a poor liar. I just hate speaking in public without notes and without enough time to prepare myself. I'm uncomfortable with it." She was talking rapidly in a high-pitched voice that told him she had lost her composure.

He couldn't buy it. "As fast as you are with the repartee? You want me to believe that? Look, if you don't want to do it, just say so. I'll go if you're still willing to take care of my boys for a couple of hours. I'm due at the station at seven o'clock, so we'll be over at six."

He sat for a long time, pondering her strange behavior. Not for one second would he believe that she'd be nervous speaking about anything so dear to her as One Last Chance. She was a high school teacher, for Pete's sake, trained for impromptu speaking. She was lying. Period. He thought of the way he felt about her, how that feeling was growing with each day, and experienced a tinge of apprehension. His coach had once said that one could excuse a blind man for getting into a hole, but not a man with sight. "I can see," he reminded himself.

* * *

Naomi watched Rufus take the greatest of care unstrapping the boys and removing their coats. He hugged them so many times before leaving that she thought she might cry, and to her surprise, the twins waved him off without a tear. She had fortified herself with plastic building blocks, an electrical musical keyboard, and a pair of walkie-talkies that worked. Once they discovered the walkie-talkies, she had no problem with discipline, because Preston sat in the foyer and talked to Sheldon, who remained in the kitchen. Rufus called just before air time and asked to speak with them, but she vetoed the idea.

"I've got a good system going here, and it's working perfectly. The sound of your voice will definitely disturb the peace, so no, you can't speak with them."

"I can't speak with my boys?"

"You got it." She knew that she'd shocked him, but figured that after thinking it over, he'd see the logic. If he didn't, well, she had a full plate dealing with her thoughts of her own child. Afraid of being exposed on the one hand, and on the other, wishing she had it with her. He'd soon be with his boys.

Rufus expected to find Naomi and the boys in total chaos, but when he arrived, he saw the three of them sitting at the kitchen table, laughing and eating. "What on earth did you give them, laughing gas?" He had worried that his boys would wear Naomi out and that she wouldn't be able to control them, and he relaxed visibly. He didn't want to put a damper on their fun, but he was too relieved to be jocular. Leaving the station, he had fought a thrill of anticipation of seeing Naomi with his children. He could barely wait to get back to her. The incredible scene that greeted him gave him hope—something that for years had remained beyond his reach—but he tried to squelch the feeling that rose in him. If he wasn't careful, he'd do something that he would regret for a very long time.

"Laughing gas? Of course not," she objected, affecting what he knew was her favorite pose, that of pretended detachment.

"These boys know their roots; I gave them southern fried chicken and buttermilk biscuits."

"This time of night."

She didn't get a chance to tell him that they'd fallen asleep and had awakened hungry. Preston intervened, "And we got a surprise. We saw you on television, Daddy, and Noomie said you were talking to the people."

"Yes," Sheldon intoned, "and we had a nap after it."

He forced himself to look at Naomi, though he didn't want to, didn't want her to see what he was feeling. How had she persuaded his two little hellions to behave civilly? He saw the softness in her and responded to it. And that vexed him. Where was his resolve of just that morning? He didn't want to care for her, didn't even want to like her, but she was likable and he cared; he couldn't deny it. And he would no longer deny that she would probably be lovable if he was ever foolish enough to drop his guard and let himself do the unthinkable.

"Want a biscuit, Daddy?" Preston inquired, reaching toward his father.

"Yes. Don't you want to join us? I've got some string beans, too, but the boys didn't want any, so we struck a bargain, and they're drinking milk instead." She worried her bottom lip and looked at him expectantly. "But maybe you don't like soul food."

Rufus forced a light smile. It was the best he could manage; with every new move, she crawled deeper inside of him. "Sure, I like soul food," he said, pulling up a chair. Sheldon reminded Naomi that she had also promised them ice-cream.

"All we want," he added.

Naomi seemed to know when she was being taken. "Sheldon," she admonished him, "good little boys always tell the truth."

Rufus's eyes rounded in astonishment. "They're dressed identically. How do you know which is which?"

"Same way you do. As you said, their personalities differ."

He tried to reconcile the soft and gentle woman before him— the one who patiently tended his boys, loving and teasing them—with her other strong, clever, and elusive self. If this was the real Naomi, or if her two selves had their proper places in her life, there was a chance that he could have with her what he'd yearned for but hadn't wanted to admit. He needed a woman he loved in his life, his home, and his bed, one who loved him and needed him and loved his children. But she had told him repeatedly that she didn't intend to become involved. Well, he had said the same, but maybe…

# Chapter 6

The phone rang once. "Hi." Rufus leaned back against the headboard of his king-sized bed and waited for more of her soothing voice. But she didn't say more, so he plunged in.

"I didn't realize you'd be in bed so early. It's only about eleven o'clock. I didn't thank you properly for taking care of my boys, and I…well, thank you. They seemed to have enjoyed the experience."

"Me, too." She wasn't forthcoming, and it was unlike what he'd come to expect of her. He marveled at the pure feminine spice of her voice; every time he heard it, he felt as if she was toying with him. Deliberately and carelessly seducing him. He searched for something banal to say, something that would guarantee that their conversation didn't become too personal.

"What would you have done if it had been Maude Frazier calling you?"

"If I can greet you with 'hi,' it'll do for Maude." So she was waiting him out; it was a trait of hers that he admired; patience. She didn't mind silence, and lulls in conversation didn't make her nervous. Since he called, she seemed to imply, he should do the talking.

"What did you think of my interview? Think it was a good advertisement for the gala?"

She apologized and congratulated him on a very professional performance. "I'm ashamed that I didn't mention it when you were here. You did yourself proud, Rufus, but I don't suppose you're asking me for praise." Her voice seemed more distant, as if she had moved further from the phone. "I'm told that your mere entrance into a football stadium brought thunderous roars from your fans. You must be sick of adulation."

He let that pass. She was right; he didn't give a hoot for praise. Never had. "It hadn't occurred to me that you would let my boys watch. It's the first time they've seen me on television. I thank you for that."

She knew that he could have thanked her before leaving her apartment; in fact he had, so she waited for the real reason why he'd called. Probably to interrogate her some more about her refusal to do the television interview, she surmised. Suddenly apprehensive, tendrils of fear began to snake down her back, and she attempted to disconcert him.

"Rufus, what happened to the boys' mother?" She hadn't realized that the question was on her mind, and his long silence told her that he didn't welcome it.

His succinct reply confirmed it. "She didn't care for marriage, motherhood, or domesticity in any form, so she left."

"Did you love her?" She tried to sound as if his answer was unimportant.

"I married Etta Mae because I'd made her pregnant. She wanted glamour, so she got a man whom she thought would give it to her quickly. She got pregnant by pretending that she was taking the pill, though as she later told me, she had never taken a birth control Pill in her life. But she knew I would marry her if she carried my child. I was sick of the spotlight, and I wanted a home. I committed myself to the marriage and to her." His deep sigh was the only evidence he gave of the pain his explanation must have caused him. "We might have made a go of it," he continued, "but her priority was to be more famous and more sought after than Iman or Naomi Campbell. Nothing was going to prevent her being the top African American model in the country, even the top model. Etta Mae is driven. Driven to escape everything that plagued her as a child. Her mother brought her here from Alabama when she was ten. She told me she suffered verbal abuse and ridicule from her schoolmates, because she was poor and different, and that she'd sworn she'd best them all. I suspect she has. Did I love her? No. Etta Mae isn't lovable, Naomi, but she gave me my sons."

His words weren't comforting. The more she learned of his life, the more certain she was that he would never accept her. His attitudes about wives and mothers were deep-seated, a reaction to unmet needs, to what he had been deprived of and what he had seen his sons denied. She doubted whether she would be able to combat that successfully even if she didn't have the load she carried.

"I'm sorry, Rufus. It was none of my business." She wished she hadn't asked. The less she knew about him, the less the like-lihood of her becoming more deeply involved.

Surely she doesn't think I called her to talk about myself, he thought peevishly. "Naomi, I need to know something." She wouldn't welcome his questions, but he didn't intend to let that stop him. He craved her and he knew it was foolish. His head told him that she wasn't for him, but the rest of him didn't agree with his mind. He wanted her and that meant he had to under-stand her, if he could. Getting a grasp of who she really was and what motivated her would either cure him or sink him, and he didn't believe she could pull him under.

"Have you ever appeared on television?" She acknowledged that she had. "Then what frightened you off tonight? You're a competent, self-possessed woman; I can't imagine your being shy about speaking in public. This has me perplexed."

"I already told you. I wouldn't have been comfortable with it. If I hadn't thought you'd be tired, I'd have called to tell you that I redesigned the program for the gala and that as soon as we can get full sponsor approval, I'll…"

So *that* was her game. Did she think she could spin him around like a top? "I didn't call to talk about that, and I don't intend to. If the reason you backed off tonight is none of my business, save us some time and just say so."

"It isn't. Any of your business, I mean."

He knew that his sharp tone had hurt, but she deserved it. As sensitive as she was, she must have realized that he needed more from her than she gave and that what he needed was deep and personal. Well, hell! What should he expect from a woman raised by a grandparent more than three times her age, and a Baptist minister, to boot? If she didn't know when a warm, feminine response to a man was the only acceptable one and the only one that could bring him to heel, it probably wasn't her fault. He asked himself why he was quizzing her and why he was trying to understand her when he was going to force himself not to give another hoot about her.

"Thanks for keeping my boys, Naomi. Good night." He said it as smoothly as he could, without preamble and with exaggerated politeness, and hung up. If she wanted a completely impersonal relationship with him, he wasn't about to care, he told himself.

But he was dissatisfied and dialed back immediately. She meant something to him, even if he didn't want her to. "Naomi, it's my business to observe and to be sensitive to what is not ordinary in people and in situations. A journalist finds a newsworthy story not in the commonplace, but in the exceptional, in what is unique. I'm good at that, Naomi, and in my book, you just do not add up." He expected a snide remark or a red herring, but he got neither.

"I'm sorry if I've disappointed you, Rufus, but I'm getting along as best I can right now. If you want to be a friend, you'll just have to try to accept me as I am. I can't make myself over for everybody I meet."

"Look, I don't know exactly why, but I need to understand you, and I'm trying. There's something going on here." His treacherous mind suddenly pictured her in her burnt orange dress, and he could smell her, taste her, feel her against him, warm and wildly aroused. She was more woman that he'd ever held, and he was man enough to want what he knew was there. But he wasn't fool enough to walk into a hornet's nest.

"Naomi, how do I fit into your life? Don't answer now; think about it carefully, because I intend to ask you again."

"All right, I'll think about it," she promised. "And if it seems that we're at cross purposes, we'll just have to wave each other goodbye."

She hung up the phone, went to her closet, and took out the dusty rose evening gown that she was to wear as Marva's maid of honor. She hooked the hanger over the door. She wondered if the two of them would remain friends after Marva married. She took a quick shower and crawled into bed. Marva was getting her man; for the first time, not having one of her own gave Naomi a sense of rootlessness.

Hours later, Naomi got out of bed, unable to sleep. She was less certain that she could remain unscathed by what was beginning to develop into a heady, deeply moving entanglement with Rufus. Even their "good night" had been too tender for a man and woman who professed to be casual friends. "I've written my last letter of protest," she declared aloud in frustration. "Not to any public official, entertainer, community leader nor—God forbid—panelist, will I ever again write one single letter of the alphabet." She told herself that she would not allow him to get next to her, then cursed her inability to kill the feeling for him that was steadily growing stronger within her. She thought about how it had hurt her to hold his wonderful, lovable little boys, to take care of them, and to be solely responsible for their well being, remembering all the while that loving and frolicking with her own child had been cruelly denied her. What could she do? What *should* she do? She had made a life for herself, had achieved stature in the community and enjoyed the respect of friends and business associates. But she wanted to know her child. She wrapped her arms around her middle and paced her kitchen floor.

She noticed the daylight and opened the blinds. The breaking day on a clear morning was usually guaranteed to raise her spirits, but on that particular morning, it failed to lift her mood. She had swum in darker waters, faced equally stymieing dilemmas, but none had involved a man who'd affected her as Rufus did. She put the coffee mug to her lips and held it there, images of him flitting through her mind. She had to deal with it. "I'm doomed," she declared when he didn't answer her ten o'clock phone call. She had intended to tell him it was best that they go their separate ways. Now, she'd have to work up the courage. Again.

Morose and having difficulty shedding it, Naomi stepped into the limousine that would carry her to Marva's wedding. The crowd waiting outside All Souls Church created an aura of excitement, but she barely managed to smile as she walked into the sanctuary. The service began, and she started slowly up the aisle. She wasn't jealous of her friend, but she had to acknowledge her longing for marriage and her own family. The bright camera lights annoyed her, but she tried to force a smile as she felt a dampness on her cheek. After the ceremony, she had to smile through the reception and escaped at the first opportunity.

Rufus saw Naomi nearly every day during the next three weeks, but always in connection with their responsibilities for the Urban Alliance gala. He deliberately engineered their meetings. He got the sense that she'd prefer to have him out of her thoughts, her life, maybe even out of her dreams, and he suspected that he'd broken through barriers that she had carefully erected, something her other suitors probably hadn't managed.

As they left OLC together by chance one evening, he decided to corner her. "You promised to let me know what you want from me, but you can't seem to decide. I find that odd for a woman with your talent for self-expression. Care to enlighten me?" When she didn't reply, he spoke in as cold a voice as he could muster. "Then maybe you won't mind explaining this. Did you know that your friend's wedding would draw the television cameras?"

"No, I didn't. I learned that the wedding was being televised when the lights shone in my face as I walked up the aisle." Her voice seemed strained. Why would such an impersonal question make her uneasy? He knew she would think him merciless if he probed further, but she intrigued him. Maybe if he stripped her of her superficial armor, he thought ruthlessly, she would no longer interest him.

"It was reported on the evening news. You outshone the bride, Naomi." He stopped walking. "Tell me. Didn't you know the bride always throws her bouquet to her maid of honor? And are you aware that all of Washington was watching when your friend threw the flowers straight to you, almost hitting you in the face, and you ducked? In fact, if you hadn't ducked, they'd have landed in your eyes. Why did you do that? I've hardly been able to think of anything else since I saw it. What were you thinking about to do such a thing?"

She walked on, speaking to him over her shoulder. "Weddings are emotionally charged occasions; everyone involved is uptight. Be a hero and switch to another topic."

He detained her with a hand on her arm. "Do you think so little of me, Naomi, that you refuse to do me the courtesy of being honest? Something else that I observed from that short clip were your tears when you were walking to the altar ahead of the bride. Why were you crying?"

"Rufus. Please! Why do you think you're entitled to see my bare soul?" She began to walk away from him. "Can't you drop it?"

He stood with legs wide apart and his right hand in his pocket, while his left thumb pressed beneath his jaw and his index finger tapped his left cheek. "No, Naomi. I can't. I can't. I remember telling you that you don't add up." Her steps faltered then, and he grasped her elbow in support, secretly reveling in the feel of her, in being close to her after so many days. He went on.

"You're wicked, fun, and witty, but I'm beginning to realize that you're unhappy. Oh, you cover it nicely, but I notice everything about you. You're a puzzle, and for me, puzzles are meant to be solved." She was far more to him than a puzzle, but he knew her well enough now to pretend otherwise.

"Puzzles entice you until you've solved them," she countered, "and then you probably lose interest. I'm not a puzzle, Rufus, so please don't give me your undivided attention." He was like a bloodhound, on the scent of something and unwilling to back away without his prize. Of late, he'd been delving too deeply and getting just a little too close. How could she tell him that her tears as she walked up that aisle were for what she longed for but could never have—a mutual love, a home, and children? She had to be more careful.

They reached her car and he leaned against the door, skillfully blocking her access. "It's early. How about stopping for coffee?" She would have sworn that he didn't expect her to accept, and her first impulse was to refuse. But that wouldn't be shrewd; he would know at once that he had made her uneasy.

"Okay," she agreed reluctantly. "Someplace not too far, if you don't mind."

He suggested Louella's Kitchen on upper Georgia Avenue. At the door, he stopped her with a firm hand on her arm.

"Naomi, I'm not up to battling with you over your inalienable right to pay fifty cents for your own coffee. So, do we go in, or not?"

She shrugged her shoulders. "Fine with me. I always offer because some guys can't afford it, some don't want to afford it, and a few want something for nothing. So I got in the habit of playing it safe."

"Does that mean you're not going to hassle with me about it?"

She tilted her chin upward and grinned. "I don't hassle, though with you, it's hard to resist. I'm not a feminist, unless that means standing up for my rights any and every time somebody attempts to abrogate them."

He held the door for her and caressed her playfully on the cheek as she passed him. What man could resist her? She was physically beautiful with her flawless, dark tan complexion and enormous dark brown eyes, and man that he was, he was drawn to her feminine attributes. But for him, her spunk and character, the character she tried to hide, were far greater assets. He smiled inwardly; she'd never believe that.

Louella greeted them warmly and gave them a back table nestled in a romantic little nook. "Do you want your cappuccino with a dusting of cinnamon, hon?" she asked Rufus, "or do you want it plain tonight?"

His affectionate regard rested briefly on her time-worn, but unwrinkled, brown cheek before he pressed a kiss to her forehead and sat down. "Cinnamon, please. Lou, have you met Naomi Logan?" His love for Louella was unqualified, he realized; she had been a mother figure during his late teens, guiding him through attempts to achieve manhood.

Louella took Naomi's extended hand. "No, Rufus, but I saw her on television in that wedding the other Saturday." She looked at Naomi. "Honey, that bride had a lot of courage to let you be her maid of honor. She looked great, but you were really something."

"Thanks," she told the woman, "but it was the dress; dusty rose is my best color."

"Pshaw." Louella dismissed Naomi's modest reply. "Go away from here, girl. You'd better enjoy it now while you got it; youth is fleeting, and when it's gone, fifty face lifts won't make you look like you look now. By the time I realized I was good-looking, it was too late to take advantage of it; too late for a lot of things. When I woke up, I was fifty years old, with three restaurants and an award-winning house. But I'm by myself on those trips abroad and expensive cruises, and I haven't got a single heir." She looked steadily at Naomi. "I hope you're smarter than I was. One great thing about Rufus: he *knows* what's important in this life. Don't you, hon?" She gave his shoulder a squeeze and trudged on back to the kitchen.

Naomi inclined her head in Louella's direction. "I could have missed that lecture. Is she always so candid?"

He leaned against the wall and fingered his jaw, deliberately disarming her with apparent nonchalance. "Lou's one of the most respected restaurateurs around, but sometimes I think she'd exchange it for a couple of kids and a husband or even a live-in sweetheart." He was certain that she didn't want him to resurrect the subject of the wedding. But she was relaxed, and now was as good a time as any; you could wait weeks to catch Naomi off guard.

"Why do you dislike the idea of marriage, Naomi? Have you been married?" And why was she squirming? He had yet to see her lose her cool, seemingly unflappable façade; she didn't even let herself get angry enough to lose her temper. But underneath that polished exterior was a warm, passionate woman. A sensitive woman. And he vowed to see more of that woman and less of the one that she seemed to want him to see.

"Why is that so difficult to answer?" he prodded mercilessly. "You either have been or you haven't."

She recovered quickly, he noticed. "It just brought back some bad, best forgotten memories." She was hedging. Not lying, maybe, but he didn't think she was telling the whole truth either.

"Well, have you? Yes or no?"

"I haven't been married," she replied softly, "and I don't plan to be." She paused. "You're probably not interested, but if you are, I don't intend to have an affair, either."

That didn't ring true, coming from a woman who could melt into a man as quickly and as completely as she, with only a couple of kisses for a starter.

He regarded her with seeming casualness. "You're a mass of conflicts. You're liquid fire in your responsiveness to men—at least to me—and don't dispute it, because I *know* it. And I agree that you wouldn't settle for a casual affair; but don't expect me to believe that you don't want marriage. If you're counting on a life of celibacy, honey, you're in for a big surprise."

She watched his sensuous lips part to reveal perfect white teeth as he gave her a slow, mesmerizing grin. "You tempt me to go over the line, Naomi, and I don't think you want that. But I'm just a man, and it isn't clever of you to continue attacking my ego, especially like now, declaring to me that I'm never going to be your lover. This isn't the first time you've done that." The grin disappeared, and his face was as hard as steel. Like an accomplished actor, she thought, fascinated.

"Better let it be the last time, Naomi." The grin was back in place, unsettling her and annoying her almost to the point of anger.

She refused him the satisfaction of seeing how his words affected her. She wouldn't have elected to live without a loving mate, but she hadn't been allowed a choice. She attempted to hide her feelings behind what she hoped was a blank facial expression and to respond in a voice whose steadiness belied her inner turmoil. But her mouth twisted slightly and she shook her head as if denying something unpleasant.

"If you knew me better, you would know that nobody dictates to me. Judd Logan can testify to that, and I'd bet that he's even dictated to the Lord on occasion. We can always discuss things, Rufus, but don't dare me and don't tell me how to behave; neither will get you anywhere." She thrust her head up, convincing herself; she didn't need him to remind her that he had only to take her in his arms and she would willingly dance to whatever tune he played.

Louella brought their cappuccino and slices of her prize-winning caramel cake. "The cake's on the house," she informed them. "And my great grandmother is supposed to have said that this recipe is the only good thing to come out of nearly two hundred and fifty years of slavery. I figured I had to do something to make the two of you smile, and my cake's guaranteed to do that."

Rufus flashed a grin. "I've been smiling, Lou."

She shook her head. "You've been grinning, and most of the time that means nothing. It's just a mask you put on to hide your real feelings." She looked at Naomi, who was observing them keenly. "Don't let him get away with it. He's not as tough as he seems."

"You seem to know him very well," Naomi prompted. But she failed to get the reply that she wanted and rephrased the question.

"How long have you known each other?"

"Since Rufus was a freshman in college. He worked his way through school in my first restaurant, starting as a busboy, but I promoted him after a week; he must have been the youngest maître d' in the country." She smiled, and Naomi sensed the woman's deep affection for Rufus. "He never gets too important to drop by and see me a couple of times a month. I'm real proud of him."

Rufus reflected on those days when life had been hard for a struggling young orphaned boy who had a younger sister to care for; but it hadn't been complicated. There had been no fame or notoriety to make him question every woman's motives; no heartbreaking, loveless marriage; and no consuming interest in a woman with whom he wasn't sure he wanted a liaison, whom he didn't understand, and who seemed unable to trust him enough to let him know her.

What a difference an hour could make, Rufus thought, as they walked back to his car, each obviously preoccupied with personal thoughts. The psychological distance between them widened during the drive to Naomi's apartment. He could feel her sliding away, closing her protective shield around her. He said nothing when, apparently lost in thought, she waited until he walked around the car to open the door for her. That was out of character for her.

They reached her apartment door and he spoke first. "Most of the time, I enjoy being with you a lot, Naomi." He didn't think it necessary to tell her that tonight hadn't been one of those times. "You're stimulating, compassionate, lovely, intelligent. And you're a real woman; in fact, I'm not even sure you know how much of a female you are. I don't know what I want out of this relationship, but I do know that I can't stand superficial relationships, and I hate conflict. That's what my marriage was—endless conflicts, maneuvers, and challenges. Always a jostling for advantage. Etta Mae thought only of herself, never of *us*. And when I stopped letting her maneuver me and demanded that she treat our marriage as a partnership, our war began in earnest. I'm too old, too weary, and too contented to go that route again. You're holding back something, and it's definitely not a small thing. I readily admit that you're entitled to your privacy, so let's...let's give each other some space; you seem to want it, and I...well, I bow to your wish."

He had the impression that she had carefully digested every word he'd said. Her cynical laugh held just enough of a tinkle, just enough merriment, to rattle him. He stared in a detached awe, as she raised her chin, dropped her head slightly to one side, and smoothly derided everything that had happened between them since the day they'd met.

"Rufus, you sound as if we're ending a love affair, when there hasn't been anything between us to end. Lighten up, honey. As my grandpa likes to say, Franklin D. Roosevelt died and to everybody's surprise, the world kept right on turning. We can both be replaced. Next year, you won't remember that you ever knew me. And I…" She shrugged and let it hang, blew him a kiss, and turned to open her door.

Arms of steel spun her around. "I'm surprised somebody hasn't blunted that sharp tongue of yours. I've told you that I will not permit you to banish me with the wave of your hand as if I'm of no consequence. No other woman has ever tried it, not even Etta Mae, and she was a master of games and feminine shenanigans. I fire you up as no other man ever has, and I can do it at will."

Her tantalizing face-saving smile gave him the impression that she thought she was being indulgent, something that he refused to tolerate. He was already simmering from the effect that her laughter, her flowery, sexy scent, and her beloved feminine presence had been having on him since they'd left OLC. His temper and his libido blazed in response, and he reached behind her, turned the key that she'd just inserted in the lock, pushed the door with his foot, and pulled her inside. The words she would have uttered died inside of his mouth.

She knew he intended it to be a punishing kiss, an expression of his frustration and anger, but to her it was simply his kiss, his passion, and she surrendered to it. He barely touched her and she curled into him, turning his fire into a tender ravishment that electrified her, inflamed her as he'd said he would. She had been so hungry for his touch, so starved for the feeling of protection, of the wonderful masculine strength that she always found in his arms, that she forgot about his anger. Almost simultaneously with his touch; her arms went around his strong corded neck and her lips parted for his kiss. She forgot about caution and her decision to preserve a distance between them. Driven by her need for him, she melted into him, moaning her pleasure, as he deepened the kiss and raised her passion to the level of his own. He brought a hand to her hips, and held her tight against him, but she tried to nestle even closer and stilled his dancing tongue while she feasted on it.

His shudder made her aware of his need for relief, of relief in her, but she was lost in the emotional fog that he had draped around her and was oblivious to the warning. He slipped his hand inside her coat and caressed her breast through the sweater. She knew only that she wanted, needed more of what he was giving her, and, barely conscious of her actions, she pressed his hand more firmly to her. Naked awareness possessed her and she moaned his name. Was she falling, or had the world spun off axis? Her fingers dug into his shoulders, claiming him for her anchor.

"Rufus. Oh, Rufus!" The words were barely intelligible.

"Naomi, I can't stand any more. Take me to your bed, or send me home," he whispered in a voice husky and thickened with desire, as he put her gently from him. She stood trembling before him, disoriented, wanting him. "Do you want me? We can't go on like this; we're driving each other crazy. Tell me!" His overwhelming need must have pushed him beyond thought of what making love with her might do to them both. She gazed up at him and into eyes that glistened with passion and with a tenderness, a softness that nearly took her breath away.

"Tell me," he repeated patiently.

She shifted her eyes from his consuming gaze, wanting desperately to embrace what she saw there, knowing that she could not. "I want you," she told him softly, swallowing the lump that thickened her throat. "I don't remember ever having had this feeling before—what I feel with you, I mean. But I can't, and I'm sorry I let it get out of hand. At least you proved your point."

From his slow, deep breaths, she sensed that he was attempting to bring his passion under control. "I don't care about points." He shifted his stance and seemed more relaxed. "Neither of us is the winner here, Naomi." He spoke in a voice so low that she strained to understand.

"I'm sorry, Rufus. Good night." *Dear God, make him leave. Please don't let him see me tremble like this.*

She would have expected that after such an experience, a man would leave abruptly and in anger, so she watched him warily. But he took her hand and walked into the kitchen, opened the refrigerator, poured them each a glass of orange juice, and gently stroked her back while they sipped in silence. Apparently satisfied that she had settled down, he held her tenderly, then kissed her on her forehead and left.

After half an hour, she managed to move from the spot in which he'd left her and lock her front door. How could he be so caring and loving after she had thoughtlessly led him on? And why did he persist with his sweetness and gentleness when he knew she wasn't what he needed? If she let herself believe in him, if she weakened and began to hope, she would be courting disaster, wouldn't she? She wanted to trust him and what he represented, and in spite of her sense of foreboding, she began to hope. She crawled into bed, but instead of sleep, her mind was filled with the memory of his kisses, of the way he had stood with her in her kitchen, calming and stroking her. Protecting her.

"God, don't let me need him," she pleaded.

For Rufus, there was no sleep that night. He didn't bother to go to bed, but sat in a deep lounge chair in the boys' room and thought about his life and about Naomi. He had never been affected by a woman as he was by her; she responded to him eagerly, wholeheartedly, even joyously, and withheld nothing. He was momentarily amused by the thought that it was always he who put out the fire; she never seemed to think beyond what she was feeling. God, but she was sweet, and he wanted that sweetness for himself alone. When she was in his arms, he felt as if he could slay dragons single-handedly. He didn't know when he had begun to need her, but he had.

By daybreak, he had decided that he was going to have her no matter the cost; beyond that, he refused even to guess. He stroked his jaw and sipped from the warm can of ginger ale that he'd gotten out of the refrigerator hours earlier. Naomi was a maze of conflicts, but he was beginning to wonder if the inconsistencies he saw in her were deep-seated. He thought not. After he'd let her provoke him with that burnt orange dress, he'd noticed something different about her, but he hadn't been able to put his finger on it. Now, it came to him; Naomi had discovered feminine power that night. She didn't discover how to use it, but she found out that she had it. He shook his head in wonder. At age twenty-nine? And in spite of her strong attraction to him, she was unusually shy of involvement. But hadn't he told her he didn't want any emotional attachments? And she wasn't as he had first thought, a tunnel-vision person who focused on work and nothing else. Oh, she needed her work, all right, just as he needed his, but she found time to work hard for One Last Chance and to help others. He nodded slowly, having found a piece of the puzzle: Naomi *needed* to help others. That kind of woman usually wanted a nest, but Naomi swore that she didn't. He didn't believe her.

The following morning, Naomi received another early-morning summons from Judd. As usual, his request was urgent, but this time she sensed in his manner a deep concern. Whatever it was, she'd face it. How many more shocks could Judd give her, she wondered, dressing hurriedly. She filled a bag with the chocolate fudge brownies she'd made the previous morning and was soon on her way. Her grandfather loved chocolate and was always pleased when she made brownies for him. She walked into the sedate Tudor house and found him sitting in his study with a man he introduced as his lawyer. The situation had escalated beyond the old man's control, she learned; the child through its mother had retained a private investigator. She knew that the adoption papers were sealed by law, but it appeared that nothing prevented the principals from obtaining information by other legal means.

She discovered that the private investigator had begun his search at the few private clinics in the area that also served as halfway houses and found that only one of those currently operating had ever had an African American client and that had taken place only two years earlier. Records of a defunct clinic showed that there had been one in the year in which Naomi's child was born, and interviews with two former workers had identified Judd, a prominent and highly visible clergyman, as the person who had brought her there. She felt intense pleasure at the fate of the owners of that clinic, who, she learned, had been forced to close when the unusually large number of babies they'd placed in adoption had come to the notice of public officials. The old man seemed to have switched his interest to the right power play. She expressed strong disagreement.

"I didn't create this situation," she informed the two of them acidly, "and I'm not going to let it destroy me. If I have to pay a penalty, I'll pay it. There are such things as decency and duty, Grandpa. At least, that's what you've been preaching to me, and to anybody else who would listen, all these years."

She watched dispassionately as he huffed and shifted in his chair, indicating that he was losing patience with her. He peered at her over his glasses. "I appreciate what you're saying, but if you do something hasty, gal, you'll regret it as long as you live."

Her best bet was to switch tactics, she figured. Judd had his own system of logic. "Now, Grandpa, don't get your dander up," she chided the old man, "there may be a legitimate reason why they're looking for me after all this time. Can't you see that? And it isn't the standing of the name Logan in the community that's important here"—a reference to his argument when he'd bullied her into going to that clinic fourteen years earlier—"there may be a child's well-being at stake, and that child is my flesh and blood." She paused. "Your flesh and blood, too, Grandpa. Didn't you stop to think of that?" She grabbed her bag and left hurriedly, unwilling to let her grandfather see her break down.

Naomi turned the key in the ignition and backed slowly out of the driveway. Nervous and scared, she contemplated her next move. She couldn't remember ever before having had the feeling that she was all alone, on her own, as she was now. Judd Logan had made up his mind, and he had never learned how to reverse himself. It was one thing to defy him when her actions concerned only her, but this was a bigger issue, one that involved a number of people, probably far more than she knew. The bright sunshine reflecting off clean, new snow was blinding, and she lowered the visor. Behind it, she glimpsed the magazine picture of Mary McLeod Bethune that she kept there. Its framed twin hung in her studio. She had clipped the pictures while at the clinic awaiting the birth of her child, and whenever she needed inspiration, she looked at one of them.

She thought of the hurdles over which her idol had climbed. Mary Bethune was an African American, a child of slaves, an educator who had worked throughout the first half of the century to improve education standards among her people in the South. That such a woman had in 1904 founded a college that still flourished after ninety years had inspired her to help create One Last Chance. She had cofounded it to help young girls who were experiencing what she had faced. An unmarried pregnant girl would be advised sympathetically of her options and of the short- and long-term consequences of her decision. And she would receive the nurturing and support that she needed.

She glanced briefly at the picture. "I'm not facing the odds that you did, Mary, old girl," she said aloud. She took a shortcut toward Rock Creek Parkway, oblivious to the scenic beauty created by the unusual late-autumn snow. A bullhorn called out her license plate number got her attention, and she pulled over. She accepted the ticket for speeding and drove into a filling station to try and steady her nerves. What else could happen in one morning?

She noticed a telephone booth, and without even considering what she did, she dug in her purse, found a quarter, and dialed.

"Meade." His voice thrilled her, comforted her; he wasn't in that filling station with her, but he was there, and that was something. She opened her mouth but couldn't make a sound.

"Naomi?" His voice held impatience. "What is it? Why are you calling?"

"Rufus. I...I don't know why I called. I saw this telephone booth and I...I just called you. It's been such an awful morning. I'm sorry I bothered you."

"You aren't bothering me." She hadn't even wondered how he'd known that it was she who'd called. Her one thought was that he was there and she needed his strength. The tremors in her voice had been uncontrollable, and he had heard them, she realized, heard and known that she had reached out to him in distress.

"Where are you?"

She told him.

He was silent for a while. "Why not go home and get into something warm and casual, and the boys and I will pick you up in about an hour. I promised to take them sledding in the park, and it's best when the snow's still fresh. Would you like that?"

"Yes. Yes. I'd love that. It would be wonderful. See you later." He didn't hang up, so she waited.

"Are you all right? Can you drive home?" Naomi assured him that she could. She felt better for having spoken with him, even as her common sense cautioned her that she was courting heartache. Of all the men she'd met, this was the one man who was least forgiving by nature and who would not accept the explanation that she would someday have to give him if she didn't stop now. And what about him? For the first time, she considered how he might be affected if he grew to care for her, learned her secrets, and felt betrayed. *I care too much,* she admitted.

Rufus watched his children's faces light up when Naomi opened the door. Their joy at seeing her and her pleasure at their excited greetings touched him, and he knew he had done the right thing in inviting her to join them.

"Where's your sled?" Preston asked her, in a mild reprimand.

"You can ride mine, Noomie," Sheldon declared protectively, chiding his brother.

"She can ride mine, too," Preston was quick to add. She hugged them and got hugs in return.

When she finally looked up at Rufus, he fought to remove all but a tolerant expression from his face.

"Hi. Thanks for inviting me to go along. The children are so nice to be with."

His raised eyebrow was his response. He disliked small talk, considering it too strong a challenge to one's honesty. "I'm glad to see you with a bloom on your face. What happened?" He had promised himself to keep things between them impersonal, but when she'd called needing him, he hadn't remembered it. His only thought had been to shelter her.

"I called you just after I got a ticket for speeding at eighty miles an hour on the Shirley Highway and the Washington Boulevard." She had told him the truth, he conceded, but he wasn't fool enough to believe she had given him the whole story.

"I don't have to ask where you'd been. Does your grandfather upset you like that very often?" Getting a traffic ticket wasn't what had upset her, what he wanted to know was why she'd been so distressed that she hadn't known how fast she was driving.

She grabbed the straw he'd given her. "He's a genius at it." More evasion, he knew, but he hadn't expected anything different. Not yet. Just give me time, he promised himself, and I'll get behind all of it. Didn't she remember that he was a journalist, a good one, and that collecting facts was his business? All he needed were a few sharp clues, and she had already unwittingly given him several. He'd get it; she could be sure of that.

Rock Creek Park was deserted. It was eerily beautiful, Naomi thought, gazing into the distance. The unusually early snow had preceded a blast of cold that left icicles hanging from branches, and snow-crusted evergreens and pines lent color to the white forest. They gamboled in the snow, pulling the sleds as the boys giggled and screamed with pleasure, throwing snowballs and building snow figures. She watched Rufus's handsome face crease in a slow grin when he noticed one of hers.

"Pretty clever," he told her in a voice laced with humor. "I'm not sure I've seen a snow girl before. How'd you get that skirt on her?"

She rubbed her nose and fought the sniffles. "With my nail file. Where there's a will, there's a way. Try it sometime."

He sauntered over to her and rubbed snow on her forehead. "You can't stand peace, can you? It just kills you to be surrounded with so much contentment, doesn't it?" The warm, alluring eyes that could so easily seduce her sparkled with mischief. "I'm glad you're the only female chauvinist I know. Personally, I mean. And sometimes I wonder how the devil I let that happen." He got out of the way quickly as if anticipating the snowball that he knew would be heading his way. She hadn't enjoyed a genuine snow fight in years; the boys loved it, too, she noticed.

Rufus turned to his boys. "Why aren't you defending *me?* You always take sides with me against your aunt Jewel."

"We have to help Noomi," Preston answered, as Sheldon nodded in agreement.

Rufus regarding his offending offspring, puzzled by their deep affection for Naomi, as he began to pack them into his car with the intention of driving Naomi home. But Preston had other ideas.

"Noomie, we have a snowman in our back garden; you wanna see it?"

"Yes," Sheldon urged, "and our daddy says we're having chili for lunch. Aunt Jewel made it. You want some?" Rufus restrained his inclination to squelch the idea. Having Naomi for a house-guest was not in his plans; the entire afternoon had been too cozy, and he didn't want her to misinterpret it. As it was, the course of their mutual attraction, or whatever you'd call it that was happening between them, seemed to be self-propelled.

"Our daddy can't cook chili," Preston added. Rufus had the impression that she didn't want to look at him for approval, but that she couldn't help it. She wanted to go, and she wanted him to invite her; that was obvious. But why? She's more mixed up about this than I am, he thought. I know what I want; I just don't know for how long.

"You're welcome to come," he said, almost reluctantly, silently weighing the consequences. "There's more than enough." Ashamed of the lack of enthusiasm in his voice, he smiled and looped an arm around her shoulder. "We'd love your company, Naomi."

"All right, if you're sure." She looked at him steadily, and he had the feeling she was trying to see beyond his words.

"I'm sure. If I weren't, I wouldn't have said a word." And he was sure. It might not be the right thing, but he wanted it. Her uncertainty showed in the way she worried her bottom lip and in her forced, shaky smile. He hated that he'd made her insecure and squeezed her to him a little. He glanced down at the two identical pairs of eyes that were watching them intently and winked, reassuring his boys.

"Could we drop by my place first? If I drive, you and the boys won't have to bring me home."

He nodded, understanding that she wanted the freedom to leave at will if she found herself uncomfortable. "All right. Then you can follow us home."

He waited until she'd started her engine before heading toward the highway. He didn't feel as though he was merely driving home with a guest, but rather that he had opened a door and entered a place from which there was no exit.

# Chapter 7

A strange, almost otherworldly sensation came over her as she parked and looked at Rufus's home—a large, sand-colored modern brick house nestled in wooded surroundings. She had never been there, never seen it, but it was familiar, welcoming. It seemed to beckon her. She had to quell an unsettling desire to run to it, to be enveloped in its shelter. She started toward it, trying without success to focus on the pristine white snow that banked the long, curving walkway like a painter's border for a fairyland scene. Her heart began to beat rapidly, to gallop like a runaway horse. She walked faster, and when she reached the front door, he opened it and smiled. The boys rushed to greet her as if they had been separated from her for days rather than minutes. She fought the urge to weep; this wasn't her family, her home, and it never would be.

Naomi walked through a large foyer to the living room, observing its high ceiling, large windows, and massive stone fireplace. She admired the Persian carpets scattered about the floor and found it oddly comforting that there was nothing chrome to be seen. It was a room for daily living that proclaimed its owner's simplicity and self-confidence. She was tempted to ask him why his sofa wasn't bordered by matching end tables and lamps, until she realized that the room was intentionally unique. Groupings of a small table and two or three chairs were scattered about the large room; a leather recliner beside which stood a small writing table faced a picture window and garden. And there didn't seem to be a bar. A curved staircase led to the second floor, and African sculptures and tapestries decorated its adjoining wall.

Rufus made a fire in the great stone fireplace. "Entertain Naomi for me," he told Preston and Sheldon. He held the kindling in front of him, disbelieving, as he watched them walk on either side of her, each holding her hand as they led her through the house and down to their own little padded world in the basement. He found them there later, head to head. She had her arms around the boys, who were trying with minimum success to explain their video game to her. He watched them unnoticed as an unfamiliar constriction settled in his chest and knew it wasn't caused by a physical ailment, but by what she made him feel. He shrugged off his alarm at the sight of her cuddling his sons and their eager response to it and thought of quicksand.

Back off, buddy, he admonished himself; you're not planning anything permanent here. But she looked up then, vulnerable, with eyes wide and suspiciously shiny, and he stopped himself just before he gathered the three of them into his arms. His grin was meant to be deceptive; she had almost caught him in a raw moment.

"Ready? For lunch?" Both boys jumped out of Naomi's arms and ran to him for the cleaning ritual. To her astonishment, he told them a little tale about each body part that he washed while they bounced and giggled with pleasure. Still sitting on the floor, she wrapped her arms around her drawn-up knees and spoke as though perplexed.

"You're not really a chauvinist, are you? How could you be, when you get so much enjoyment out of giving your boys the kind of care and affection that children usually get from their mothers?" She seemed embarrassed at having voiced her thoughts. He had suspected that some of her brashness was a cover for shyness, and now he was certain of it.

"I'd better be a chauvinist," he joked, "otherwise, you'll lose interest in me. If you discovered I was an egalitarian, you couldn't fight with me; you'd lose the inspiration for your sharpest wit and sarcasm; you wouldn't resent me any longer; and you wouldn't have a need to change me. So don't get any fancy notions about me; I'm the biggest chauvinist you're ever going to meet."

He put a boy in each arm and nodded to her. "Come on, woman, the food is getting cold." After paying proper homage to the chili, Naomi brought out the bag of brownies that she had forgotten to give her grandfather and further cemented the bond between herself and her three hosts.

Warmth suffused Rufus as he furtively watched the interplay between Naomi and his sons. He reclined in his big chair in the living room while they huddled on the floor before the fire. Each time she indicated that she should leave, one of his boys found an excuse to detain her, and she readily acquiesced.

Finally, she told him, "If I don't leave here, you'll be serving me dinner." Without making it obvious, he had been weighing and judging her every act, gesture, and word all afternoon and had found her more puzzling than ever.

"Do you want to go?"

"No," she answered, "but I'm going before I abuse your hospitality."

Preston and Sheldon demanded and got their share of goodbye kisses, using more delaying tactics in the process. Rufus watched with a sense of wonder. What was it about her? His children had always been retiring with everyone except Jewel and her family.

"Since you're being so generous with your kisses, maybe I can have one, too?" He couldn't help it; it was foolish, but he felt excluded from something important, something good.

She told him with what was obviously mock sincerity, "the boys made me a snow girl out back, turned cartwheels for me, and climbed into my lap while I sang them some songs. If you do that or better, you'll get some kisses, too."

A tiny frown creased his brow, and he shoved his itchy fingers deep into the pockets of his slacks. "You want a demonstration of some of my…er, abilities? Is that what you're asking me for? That's hardly fair, Naomi. I could be hauled into court by corrupting the morals of minors. You could, too, for that matter," he deadpanned.

"Your mind's always in the same rut," she informed him, as

she reached up to kiss him. He didn't let her off until he'd exacted a small price, grabbing her shoulder and letting her feel the force of his tongue for a split second. She reeled slightly, to his immense satisfaction.

"I owe you one for that, Meade," she said, digging into her shoulder bag for her car keys.

Rufus put his hands back in his pockets, where they'd be safely out of trouble. "I'm looking forward to collecting," he retorted smoothly. "I'd tail you home, but I don't want to take the boys out again." They stood in the foyer, exchanging light banter, the boys clinging to her hands; then she hugged them goodbye again. He wished she wasn't leaving him, then wished he could retrieve the thought. He shrugged. The hell with it; he felt good. He walked her to her car, kissed her quickly, and opened the door for her. It was the first time that their kiss hadn't been the product of fire-hot desire, the first time that they both had felt the need to join in ways that transcended the physical.

"I enjoyed this time with you," he told her, and meant it. He wasn't in the habit of lying to himself; she had touched him. How he'd deal with it was going to be a problem.

Naomi let herself into her condominium, walked slowly down the hallway to the kitchen, and put on a kettle of water. Deep in thought, she stood there until the water boiled, made tea, and sat down to drink it. She didn't pretend that she wasn't emotionally shaken; getting to know the little boys and observing the loving relationship between them and their father had unsettled and disturbed her. She knew she could love those boys with all her heart, and she knew just as certainly that they could love her. What kind of mother would she have been, she wondered. And what kind of mother did her own child have? Her eyes burned with tears that she didn't dare shed for what she had lost. Crying was useless. She had let her grandfather run her life when she'd been helpless to oppose him, but she wasn't helpless now. She understood that her grandfather would have felt humiliated if her pregnancy had been public knowledge. After all, he had preached sexual responsibility to his parishioners. And though he hadn't told her to give the baby up for adoption, he hadn't told her not to do it, and he had certainly facilitated it.

She stood by the telephone and glanced at her watch. Four o'clock. Her mind made up, she would face whatever came with her head up. She picked up the phone, dialed, and set fate into motion. Judd's lawyer answered on the first ring.

"You'd better think this thing through before you make any contact, but it's up to you. What are you planning?"

"I don't know. I only know that I can't bear to go on like this."

"I'm Reverend Logan's lawyer," he reminded her, "and if you're planning to do something against his wishes, I couldn't advise you. It would be unethical."

"I'm not asking for advice. What I want is accurate information. Can you at least give me that? Have you met the family? Is the child a boy or a girl? Are they in some kind of difficulty?" She knew she sounded desperate.

"The child is a boy. He's healthy, intelligent, and not a problem in any sense, as far as I know. I can't tell you more."

When she could get her breath, she tried to thank him. "When will you confer with the family again?"

"I have an appointment at their home Monday morning at ten-thirty. You may call me around noon if you have any questions."

She had a son. But he wasn't really hers, she reminded herself. Monday morning. It was Saturday, so she'd better get busy.

At ten-thirty Monday morning, Naomi parked on a side street off Georgia Avenue in Silver Spring, Maryland, a Washington suburb. She was unrecognizable in a reddish-brown wig of long straight hair and bangs, and contact lenses that changed her irises from dark brown to gray. The car she drove was a rented dark blue Mustang. She had followed the lawyer, as she supposed he'd figured she would, but she'd kept well behind him in case he hadn't counted on her little maneuver. She sat there in the cold until noon, long after the lawyer had left, unable to leave the scene. How many times had she passed that modest red brick ranch-style house on her way to visit Marva, five blocks away? She wrote down the address, turned the key in the ignition, then turned it off. Impulsively, she got out of the car and walked the half block to the house. She didn't see anyone. The boy should have been in school, so she didn't expect to see him.

I just can't ring the bell and introduce myself, she thought, but I can't leave here not knowing anything more. Then she saw the name plate on the lawn: Hopkins. It was something. She hurried back to her rented car and quickly drove away. She couldn't have said why, but she felt more at peace than at any time since she'd learned that her child's family was searching for her and that she could see him; she had a link to him.

Later that afternoon, the telephone rang just as Naomi was about to leave her workshop. "Logan Logos and Labels. May I help you?" It was her automatic phone greeting when she was in the shop.

"You could be more enthusiastic about it," came the bubbly response.

"Marva! Girl, have I ever missed you! How was the honeymoon?"

"What do you mean, how *was* it?" Marva drawled. "It's just started. Honey, you'd better get busy. What this man does to me! Well, I just never even dreamed that anybody could remain just barely conscious all the time and be deliriously happy about it. Love somebody, Naomi; I swear it'll make you a better person. How's Cat?"

"Who? Oh, you mean Rufus. All right, the last time I saw him, which, before you ask, was Saturday. Please don't pressure me about him, Marva. He's nice and I like him, I guess, but we're really oil and water."

"Are you going to the gala with him?" Naomi didn't want to think about the gala and the television cameras that would be all over the place. Whatever happened in regard to her future relationship with her child, she wanted to be the one who maneuvered it. An accidental meeting could be painful.

"I'm going alone, and I'm going to sit at the sponsors' table." She said it almost belligerently.

"Why don't you come along with Elijah and me? Lije has a really nice friend who could join us, and he's tall, too."

"Marva, please. I don't want to have blind dates with any more of Lije's friends. I hate blind dates, and if I wanted a man to take me, finding one wouldn't be difficult. I'm going alone."

"*Jet* magazine will just love that."

"I don't care. I'm not going to run my life according to what people might think." She almost laughed. That was exactly what she'd been doing for Judd's sake.

Marva tried again. "Well, at least wear something really sexy, and be sure it's either dusty rose or burnt orange. Stay out of black. You and I are going to have a talk about your social attitude, honey, and I'm going to make you spill all. I know you think I'm frivolous, but my degree in psychology didn't leave me totally stupid about human behavior. If you're smart, you'll call Cat and ask him to go with you to the gala. Oil and water! Humph! It's probably more like flint and steel. See you at the gala."

A glance at her watch reminded Naomi that Linda was developing a habit of arriving late for her tutoring. She hoped the girl would be more responsive than she'd been at her two previous classes. Naomi had the feeling that Linda wanted her to lose patience, to stop the sessions. The girl arrived breathless and flushed, but not apologetic. She handed Naomi a tablet of her drawings.

"What do you think of these?"

Naomi flipped the pages slowly, astonished at the talent displayed there. "I think you have great potential. Do you mind if I keep these?

Linda's pleasure at the request was obvious in her broad smile and diffident manner. "I did them for you."

Naomi thanked her and decided to have copies made and to circulate them among several universities in the hope of getting a scholarship for her young charge.

The following evening, Naomi checked her appearance in the full-length mirror attached to her closet door. She'd had her hair straightened to make it manageable and styled into an elaborate French twist. Her dress was an off-the-shoulder lavender-pink sheath slit above the left knee, and the diamond studs in her ears were her only jewelry. Her fur-lined black silk evening cape matched the silk evening bag; and her black silk pumps were plain except for their rhinestone buckles. She sprayed some Fendi perfume in strategic places, closed her door, and went down to the lobby to await her taxi.

Maude Frazier had placed her right in front of Rufus at the narrow end of the oval-shaped sponsors' table. It hadn't occurred to Naomi that he'd be sitting near her. When she arrived, he stood, nodded politely, and walked around the table to assist her in sitting. She hadn't seen nor spoken with him since the afternoon she'd spent at his home, but that might have been because she'd deliberately erased the messages on her answering machine before listening to them. Desire knotted her insides when she looked at him. Why did she respond to him the way she did? He was tall, elegant, and drop-dead handsome; the sight of him nearly took away her breath.

"You look lovely, Naomi. Where's your date?"

"He let me out of the house all by my little self tonight, just to see if I could be trusted not to get lost," she taunted, wearing one of her sugary-sweet, plastic smiles. He had an urge to shake her. It was unreasonable, but so was she.

"Try to discipline your tart little tongue for tonight, so that your tablemates can enjoy the evening, *darling*." He spoke to her ears only and drew the word out to make certain that it annoyed her. He'd called her every evening that week, and she hadn't answered her phone or returned the messages he'd left on her answering machine.

"Who's the little femme fatale sitting on your right and throwing darts at me? Poor thing; put her at ease and tell her there's nothing between us." He tried not to react; she might feel reckless, but he didn't.

He inclined his head toward the younger woman seated next to his chair. "She's smart enough to know there's nothing between us. And why do you care, anyway? You took yourself out of the picture." *And left me here in limbo!* He had had a week of emotional upheaval, half eager to see her and half dreading what seeing her would do to him. And she'd walked in looking like a queen, wrapped securely in her protective witch armor. He went back to his seat.

The young woman seated beside Rufus laid claim to his attention most of the evening, but to Naomi's delight, she didn't always get it, and he either sat out the dances or partnered another woman, never asking Naomi. It embarrassed her that Marva's husband was her most frequent dance partner, and she knew that was a result of Marva's prompting. Finally, the orchestra leader announced the last dance. *Jitterbug Waltz,* a slow, sensuous, heat-provoking jazz piece. She wasn't looking when he left his chair, but she knew instinctively that the fingers that brushed her bare shoulders were his.

"Dance with me, Naomi." It wasn't a question. Everyone at the table looked at them. It was the last dance, and he was asking Naomi to share it with him.

Slowly, she rose to her feet, her three-inch heels making her only a few inches shorter than he. "A gentleman dances the last dance with the woman he brought." She didn't try to hide the bitterness she felt. All evening she had ached to be in his arms, to glide across the floor with him, and all evening he had looked elsewhere for his partners.

He brought her a trifle closer. "If I had brought a woman here, I would be dancing with her right now." She missed a step. "I came alone, Naomi."

"But…"

"I met Maude's niece here tonight. You should have guessed that she wasn't with me." He changed the subject. "You look beautiful. You're always beautiful, but tonight you're lovelier than ever." He pulled her to him and rocked her to the pulsating rhythmic beat with a voluptuous tilt of his hips.

"Move with me," he whispered in a low, sultry voice.

"Rufus. I…" She couldn't muster another word. He danced lightly on his feet and moved them with a slow, enthralling glide that sent her heart racing. Thoughtlessly, she moved closer to him, and he welcomed her, clasping her possessively to him as their dance turned into one of riveting desire.

"You're mine right now," he whispered, as his lips gazed her ear, and she shivered against him. He barely moved, merely let their bodies angle this way and that to the beat of the all consuming rhythm.

Rufus knew the minute she remembered where she was and that she had slid her hands up the lapels of his navy tuxedo and rested her head snugly under his chin. As usual, she had let her senses take over.

"Rufus, please! We're in a public place." She tried to move away from him, but he held her and danced a lovers' dance with her.

"Would you make love with me right now if we weren't in a public place? If we were in the privacy of your bedroom? Would you? Tell me." It wasn't a taunt; he whispered it sweetly, lovingly, softly. She didn't answer, but tried to put a little space between them; he wouldn't allow it. His warm fingers stealthily traced the cut of her gown to her lower back and caressed the flesh revealed there, and he felt her capitulate and let him have his way. He had gotten the only reward he figured he'd get; he'd robbed her of her will to resist him, had scrambled her wits.

At last the music ended; the dance was over, and he watched fascinated as she stood facing him, looking at him, drinking him in, seemingly immobile. Then, like the changing seasons, her eyes slowly lost their soft, besotted look and assumed a glare of murderous intent.

"How dare you do that to me on a public dance floor?" She kept her trembling voice low, and he realized that Naomi was angry. For the first time since he'd known her, she was angry. He rethought it: she was mad, and he had best remain silent. He understood, too, that while she was mad at him, she was more furious with herself, and that put him in the mood to placate her.

Back stiff and head high, she walked back to their table, collected her purse, and bade their fellow guests good-night. Then she turned to Rufus and spoke to him between tightly clenched teeth.

"You come with me; I've got a few things to say to you." She began walking, all but ordering him to follow her.

"All right," he told her, when they reached the entrance to the ballroom, "I'll walk you to your car."

He figured she'd like to destroy him with that withering look and pretended he didn't see it.

"I didn't drive tonight. How could I, with this dress on?"

Rufus shrugged elaborately. "Good point. I still haven't figured out how you got into it. May I have your cloakroom ticket?" She gave it to him, along with two one-dollar bills for the tip. He looked first at the money and then at her, started to speak, and clamped his mouth shut. If she was going to explode, she'd do it without any more help from him.

The porter brought his car to the front. Naomi looked first at the silver gray Town Car and then at Rufus. "I should have known that a minivan wouldn't satisfy you." He said nothing, but merely took her arm and walked toward his car. She was upset, and he suspected it was much more than their dance that had ticked her off.

"Why do you think I'm getting into that thing with you?" she asked him, in a tone that was only a little less peevish than it had been earlier.

He sighed patiently. "Be reasonable, Naomi. You said you wanted to speak to me, but you don't have your car, and it's cold out here. I don't discuss private matters in taxis, because I don't want to read about it the next day. What's the alternative?"

"Oh, all right," she huffed. He opened the door and assisted her into the passenger's seat.

"Why are we going in here?" she queried, somewhat ungraciously, when he parked in front of an exclusive late-night supper club.

Rufus turned, put his right arm on the back of her seat, and looked at her. "My patience isn't endless, Naomi, and you've already tested what little forbearance I have. We can go to my place, but one of my boys would awaken and disturb us; I left a sitter with them. We could go to your place, but in my current mood, I couldn't guarantee that I wouldn't be in your bed with you five minutes after we got there. So this is it." He was well aware that she didn't disagree with his reasoning, and it didn't brighten his mood: knowing that she acknowledged an inability to resist him was more temptation than he wanted.

He asked for and got a table in a corner far from the piano-playing chanteuse, whose songs all sounded the same. It surprised him that Naomi was still so mad, but there was no mistaking it. Slow to anger and slow to yield it, he mused.

"Lighten up, Naomi; nothing that happened could have been as bad as you're making it out to be." She pursed her lips and glared at him.

"All right. All right. Spill it," he urged, conceding himself to the right to a little anger.

Annoyance surged through her, enlivening her. "You had no right to seduce me on that dance floor. No gentleman would have done what you did to me out there. You practically made love to me right out there in front of all those people," she fumed. "You don't respect me, and now everybody knows it." It poured out of her, but not a word described what she actually felt; words couldn't have described it. A wintry desolation had beset her, saturating her consciousness with a deep need for the shelter of his arms, for the solace of his whole self. Apprehensive of her feelings, she took refuge in her annoyance, grasping at straws.

"Shut up, Naomi." It was gently said, without vocal inflection.

"What?" She lowered her voice. "What do you mean, telling me to shut up?"

"Naomi," he drawled, giving her the impression that he was drawing on his last reserve of patience. "'Shut up' is exactly what I mean. I'm the one who got seduced on that dance floor. Me! I was dancing normally, just as I always do, and then you stepped into me." She opened her mouth to protest, but his look suggested that silence would be prudent.

"That's right. You just tucked your little tush under and moved right into me. What do you think I'm made of, huh? And another thing. If you weren't susceptible, you wouldn't have reacted the way you did. That's mostly what this is about, isn't it. You're scared of what you felt. And you're scared of something else, too, Naomi, but that's another story, isn't it?"

She leaned back in the richly upholstered chair and glared at him. "So what happened out there was all my doing, eh? Big, six-foot-four-inch man got snowed by a female who doesn't know that"—she flicked a finger—"about the art of seduction. Get real, Rufus."

Laughter deep and warm rippled from his throat as he glanced at his watch. Their waiter seemed to have taken a break. "Honey, you don't have to know anything about the art of seduction; you just do what comes naturally. Uninhibited, that's you. No *wonder* you try to hold yourself aloof. You're scared of what you might do if you really let yourself go." He drained his glass and stood. "You're enjoying this conversation because it's cooling you off, but it's heating me up, and I've finished with it. If I offended you, I apologize. But, lady, I'm not one bit sorry for anything that happened on that dance floor."

He winked as he reached for her hand, disconcerting her. "I'd do it again if I had the chance, and I'd bet my Rolex that you would, too."

"Not with you, I wouldn't," she threw at him hating his obvious amusement, his cocky grin.

"I don't believe you," he countered, his face as somber as she'd ever seen it.

They walked out of the supper club, and her pride in being with Rufus overrode her anger. He had complemented his navy tuxedo with a ruffled pale gray silk shirt and pale gray on navy accessories, and the combination offset his dark good looks. Tall and elegant, he was the picture of male power. I'm not vain, she thought, but right now I'm glad I'm not bad-looking.

They reached her door. "Rufus, could we please not have the kind of scene we had when you last brought me home?" She sounded so prim that she annoyed herself. "I want to avoid it."

"I'm not stopping you," he teased. "You have my permission to avoid it." His charismatic smile enveloped her, but she resisted the temptation to forgive and turned toward her door.

"Naomi, how can you stay angry so long? With me, it's over in minutes."

"And a good thing, too, or you'd be angry all the time. Any little thing ticks you off." His censoring frown challenged her statement. "Well, a lot of things do," she amended.

He moved closer, and she'd have stepped back if there'd been anyplace to go. "If you didn't play a part in what happened to us during that dance and if you're not susceptible to me, as you claim, I'd like to be sure of it. Kiss me, Naomi. I won't move, I promise, and there's no music here."

He leaned toward her, and with the closed door for support, braced his hands on either side of her. "Kiss me, baby." Her heart thundered widely at the suggestiveness in his low, husky words. "Put your arms around me and kiss me," he cajoled silkily. His voice had become thick and slurred. She stared into his eyes mesmerized, and then let her glance drift to his sensuous lips. When he parted them ever so slightly, she sucked in her breath and succumbed to his tempting maleness. He closed in on her, his hands still braced against the wall, and his mouth devoured her as she grasped him to her and clung.

Desperate now, she whimpered. "Hold me. Please hold me." But he didn't touch her until her knees buckled. Then he held her with his left arm, took her key, and opened the door.

"Good night, Naomi."

She barely noticed his short, rapid intake of breath and the look of longing in his eyes, but focused on what she felt. What she needed. "Good...*what?*"

It registered that he was actually leaving her. "I hate you, Rufus. I do. I hate you, and I'm never going anywhere else with you. *Never.*" She hissed it at him, trembling with frustration.

She calmed herself, allowed her good sense to surface, and with reason restored, no longer felt rejected. If he had crossed that threshold, she'd have had some confessing to do, come morning. And she wouldn't have known where to start and certainly not how to end it. She didn't know the end. She did know that Rufus had proved his point incontestably. She not only wanted him; she needed him.

"I know how you feel," he muttered, as he walked away, equally frustrated, but determined to leave her. Gently, and at considerable expense to his shattered emotions, he had pushed her inside her door and left. If the day ever came when she could look him in the eye and say she wanted him and would have no regrets, he'd stay. Not before.

# Chapter 8

Rufus received the Reverend Judd Logan's seven-thirty a.m. phone call with astonishment. He had written exactly one paragraph of the thoughts he'd collected and didn't want to be disturbed. But Judd didn't so much invite as command him to his home in Alexandria for breakfast that morning, not even hinting at what had prompted the invitation. Curious, Rufus agreed to go, but mainly because he figured he might learn something about the mystery that he sensed surrounding Naomi. He took his boys to Jewel's house and left them with her husband, a dentist. Jeff's afternoon office hours enabled him to keep the children while Jewel taught, and she relieved him at three o'clock.

Judd's cook, who seemed nearly as old as his employer, led Rufus to the study. Something out of an old movie, he thought, only grudgingly amused, as he looked around at the antique furniture, heavy velvet drapes, and ecru lace curtains. His working day was shot, his deadline was now almost unattainable, and his boys were off their schedule. Judd Logan stood, his stature belying his great age.

"I see you made it. Just have a seat; breakfast will be served in here in a minute." Rufus remembered Naomi having said that Judd seldom bothered to thank anybody for anything, certainly not for obeying one of his unreasonable commands. So he remained standing, raised an eyebrow, and left the expression of incredulity on his face so long that the old man took a hint and said, "I'm glad to meet you."

The breakfast was consumed and the crafty old man still had

spoken only of the weather and of similarly mundane things. Rufus tired quickly and demanded, "What may I do for you, sir? I'm sure you know that Chevy Chase isn't just across the street from you. I'm a busy man."

Judd gazed at Rufus intently, obviously appraising him. "So you're Cat Meade."

"I used to be. Yes."

"Well, who are you now?" The old man's sharp eyes bored into Rufus, sizing him up. Rufus was accustomed to power plays; he had learned to be a master at them when he negotiated his football contracts, and bluffing was fifty percent of it. He didn't take up the challenge.

"I gave that up five years ago. I never intended to make football my life's work; I'm a journalist and a published author. What exactly do you want with me?" He wanted to be respectful to Naomi's grandfather, but the man rankled him, and what's more, didn't seem to mind that he did.

"What are your intentions with regard to my granddaughter?" Rufus sucked in his breath and stared wide-eyed at his host. Was this man serious? It was on the tip of his tongue to tell Judd Logan that he'd had a driver's license for nearly twenty years and didn't take kindly to having his behavior questioned. Then he laughed.

"You couldn't be serious! I thought Naomi might be stretching the truth with some of the things she told me about you. You're way off, Reverend Logan; your granddaughter and I are not on the best of terms. In fact, we're barely speaking now." He didn't add that he'd merely assumed it from Naomi's mood when they'd parted the night before.

Judd appeared irritated. "Are you telling me that you dance like that with a woman you're hardly speaking to? In my days, no decent woman would have permitted you to dance with her that way, and no gentleman would have attempted it."

Rufus sighed. "Maybe that's because cold showers hadn't been invented," he muttered under his breath.

Judd's hearing proved to be fine. "What? I'm serious here.

The whole of Washington and every town near it saw that show you two put on," he stormed.

"What do you mean?"

"My God, boy, didn't you know the television stations had their cameras there? African Americans of our status have to set a good example. Everybody expects more from us."

Rufus wasn't impressed with that reasoning; he leaned forward. "Of course, I didn't know that our dance was being televised." Though if he had, it wouldn't have made one iota of difference once he had her in his arms. "There's no point in being upset about this, Reverend; I haven't compromised her, and I won't. As for that dance, Naomi already gave me the devil about it."

The old man peered at him. "You can't make me believe you're not interested in each other. You're the one man I've met who could turn her head. And if she doesn't turn yours after what I saw last night, I want to know what you're made of."

Rufus sat back in the generously overstuffed chair, getting more comfortable, and gave the man one of his intentionally in-decipherable grins. "I came here out of respect, but this is really none of your business, sir." He stood.

Judd looked up at Rufus and released a long, tired breath. "I'm living on borrowed time, son. I'll be ninety-five in a few weeks, and I'm all she has. I'd hate to have to leave her all alone. She's so fragile." He'd spoken almost as if to himself. "I hope I haven't caused any hard feelings." He stood tall and straight, for all his ninety-four years.

"None whatever, sir."

"Well, at least I got to meet one of my favorite football players. It was good of you to come."

"It was my pleasure." Rufus stepped toward the foyer and turned, surprised, when the old man's thin fingers grasped his arm.

"I don't care what you said. My Naomi wants you. It's been more than fourteen years since she let herself get as close to a man as she was to you last night. And I know that for a fact."

Rufus opened his mouth to speak and closed it, at a loss for words, not certain that he wanted that information and positive that within its core lay the key to her character.

"I know she acts tough, son. She learned a long time ago to harden herself to life; she had to. But that toughness is just a front; deep down, she's very fragile. My Naomi spends a lot of time hurting. You're strong, just what she needs. Well, goodbye." They parted with a friendly handshake.

Rufus drove toward Washington, pondering Judd Logan's revealing words. He had known almost from their first meeting that Naomi's flippancy was a shield, and he had begun to realize that her insistence that marriage was not for her was nothing more than pretense, her solution to a problem that she had found no other way to handle. He suspected the real Naomi was the woman who cared that a young slum girl needed a role model, who responded to him without ego or inhibition, who gave herself to him totally in every kiss or caress. The real Naomi, he surmised, was the woman in whom his sons had immediately sensed warmth and tenderness; they had been drawn to it. That kind of woman needed a nest and knew it.

He stopped downtown at Garfinkel's to buy long-sleeved T-shirts for Preston and Sheldon. They outgrew their clothes so rapidly that he bought them a size larger than they needed. As he left the store, a thought occurred to him, as he headed back toward the shoe department.

Tired, cold and discouraged, Naomi let herself into her studio, questioning the wisdom of what she'd decided to do. She pulled off the wig and threw it in her desk drawer, stored the contact lenses, and sat down at her drawing table. She had wasted an hour sitting in a cold, rented car, and no one had entered or left that house. But she was doggoned if she would let it get her down. She took out her sketchpad, closed her eyes, and tried to imagine how the design should look. She'd finished the ad campaign for the ice-cream company, but the parent firm had engaged her to design new paper milk cartons. No, she thought, green wouldn't work for milk.

She reached for the phone after its first ring. "Logan Logos and Labels. May I help you?"

"Hi. So you're finally there. Most people are in their office between three and four, Naomi. Do you always take a late lunch?"

She had completely forgotten lunch. "I work when I'm getting results, Rufus." It wasn't a lie, and her whereabouts were not his affair. She told him, "As a writer, I'm sure you've had experience with that. Did you call to apologize?"

If Rufus hadn't remembered his conversation with Judd, he might have interpreted her words as a mild reprimand or even rudeness. He did neither, but inquired, "Should I?" He couldn't' believe she was still annoyed because he'd given her that blistering kiss and left her without explanation. Surely she understood why he'd had to get away from her and fast.

"Why did you call?" She hoped her voice didn't reflect her wariness. She wanted to see him, to be with him, but while she'd waited in front of her son's home, she'd decided to put Rufus out of her complicated life once and for all. She was going to focus on finding a way to know her son and his adoptive parents and managing it without her grandfather's interference.

Her brusqueness apparently didn't discourage him. "I called because you're the only woman I'm kissing these days, and my energy is low. Thought I'd get a little sugar."

Naomi laughed. Drat him; he knew how to get next to her. "Well, here goes a kiss right through the wire. Now, hang up, and let me work."

He didn't let her off. "You complain about Judd, but you're certainly his granddaughter."

"*Whatever* do you mean? Of course, I'm his granddaughter. My father was his only son."

"I mean you've either inherited or copied his bluntness and directness, and I have to tell you, it looks better on him than it does on you."

"How do you know so much about him?" She felt the skin crawl on the back of her neck. What had the old man been up to now?

"He wrecked my day with a summons out to Alexandria this morning to explain my intentions toward you."

Naomi let out a mild shriek. "He *what?* Oh, my goodness. He must have seen us on television last night. I saw the cameramen, but then I forgot about them. This is none of his business."

Rufus chuckled softly. "I told him precisely that, but I could have saved my breath."

"You told him it was none of his business?" she asked, in frank admiration. "I wish I'd been there."

"He took it like a man, sweetheart," he told her, and she sensed his sincerity in the endearment. "I liked him. I liked him a lot. I want to see you, Naomi, but I don't want to leave my boys with a sitter again tonight. Could you come over about six and have supper with us? I don't like to feed my boys too late. I'll take them and get some fried chicken and other stuff, maybe some rice and gravy from one of the takeouts just off Connecticut Avenue. Would you like anything special?"

He'd just assumed that she'd accept, and she was tempted to refuse him, to stick to her resolve not to see him again. But she had missed Preston and Sheldon, and the thought of being with them even for a little while raised her spirits from where they'd dropped while she'd sat in that cold car, watching a house in Silver Spring.

"I guess not, but I could bring something, too. See you at six." She hung up, stared at the phone, and thought of the reasons why she should call him back and tell him that she had changed her mind. But she knew she wouldn't do it; an hour and a half was already too long to wait. Her heartbeat accelerated at the thought that she would soon be with him.

"What's in the bag, Noomie?" Preston asked her, pulling at her shopping bag. Rufus watched his sons greet Naomi, dancing happily and plastering wet kisses all over her face, and his anxiety about his relationship with her increased with each passing second.

He and Naomi set the table, put the food, including what she'd brought, in serving dishes, and placed it on the table. Her reaction to his heated look showed her pleasure at his obvious approval.

"You actually cooked greens and baked sweet potatoes? Do you know how crazy I am about collards and sweet potatoes with fried chicken? Did Jewel tell you?"

Her shy smile told him that his comment pleased her. "I've never spoken with Jewel. I just thought it would be nice to have it."

Four little fawnlike eyes gazed up at them. Rufus looked down at his children and had a ridiculous urge to search them. There were times when they seemed to have special knowledge enabling them to sense any change in his emotions. He dismissed the thought, glanced back at Naomi, and caught her struggling to replace with nonchalance the passion he'd glimpsed in her. He flicked an index finger beneath her chin.

"I want to kiss you, and I'm going to."

"But the children…"

"They already got theirs," he said, heedless of his previous concern. "Now, I want mine." He touched her lips with his own in a brief, sweet kiss, intending to make it chaste. And he would have if he hadn't sensed in her response a need as strong and compelling as his own. What had come over her? He stared at her in amazement. She had moved away when he'd attempted to deepen the kiss, the first time she'd broken his kiss. He looked down at his boys; she'd shown concern for them in a situation where she'd never shown any for herself. Had he been completely wrong about her? He sat down at the table, said grace, and began to eat, but his mind was not on the food.

Naomi watched Preston and Sheldon indulgently as they devoured the greens, sweet potatoes, and fried chicken. Sheldon indicated that he'd like to have it again. "That was good, Noomie. You coming back tomorrow?"

She saw Rufus's back stiffen. "No, Sheldon. But I'll come see you some other time. All right?" She pulled an apple pie out of the other bag and earned the undying gratitude of all three Meade males.

The boys had been put to bed over their strong objections.

"They're usually more cooperative than they were tonight," he told her, stretching his long legs out in front of him as the flames flickered in the great stone fireplace. "They know I get more work done when they cooperate, and they take pride in contributing to what I do. I show them how much I've written, but lately, Preston has taken it upon himself to criticize my progress." Rufus smiled. "He doesn't think much of five or six pages for half a day's work. Thank God, Sheldon is kinder and fattens my ego every time Preston takes me down a peg."

Contentment warmed her as she watched him, captivated by the love in his eyes. She stored in her memory the honeyed tone of his voice as he talked about his precious children.

"I'd give anything to have grown up surrounded by that kind of love," she said wistfully. "And I hope I get to experience it just once." She leaned back and sipped her cool coffee. Rufus remained silent, as if comprehending that her words were to herself, that she had not meant to share such private thoughts.

"Grandpa tries; he always has, but he and I are the products of two vastly different eras. I try to remember that."

His penetrating and compassionate look aroused her need to feel his arms like steel bands around her, but she glanced away. Sometimes, she thought, *he seems to be looking into my very soul.* As if realizing that she was reaching for something deeply personal and beyond his means to provide, he leaned toward her slowly, seeming to fear disturbing her.

"Naomi, will you come over here, sit beside me, and lay your head on my shoulder?" He spoke in a low, gentle voice, as if trying not to break her mood.

"What?" He smiled and held out his hand. But she had snapped out of it.

"Why can't you come over here?"

"I didn't want to seem threatening and you...I was just being a friend."

Naomi looked at Rufus with new eyes. Was there a chance that he had enough room in his heart to love one more person? To love that person just half as much as he loved his boys? She quickly shifted her thoughts from that dangerous path. "I'd better be going; I have a few things to do at home."

He had been looking at her, and she supposed that her need was mirrored in her eyes. "Don't run away, Naomi. You don't need to be alone just now, and I'm here. Lean on me. Just this once, let me take the weight of what it is that burdens you."

She wished she could put out everything, that she could just open up and let it out. Let go of the awesome weight that had been suffocating her for nearly half her life. If he loved her, she might have a chance finally to live a normal life, to love a man and let him love her, because only a man who loved her deeply would understand and accept. Rufus wasn't that man; he was judgmental and unforgiving. She was never going to meet one who would willingly share her awful burden, and she wouldn't risk exposing herself to rejection and maybe even scorn for something over which she'd been too young to control. She glanced up, saw him watching her, and plastered a bright smile on her face.

"Really, Rufus, you're imagining things. I've got to produce a draft design for a milk carton, that's all."

Discouraged by her refusal to trust him, he stood and helped her to her feet. The backs of his fingers scraped through his short, curly hair, and he began to speak slowly, his tone grim.

"Stop fooling yourself, Naomi. Until you admit the importance of whatever it is that you fear, your life won't be what it could be, what it should be. If you face it, you'll move mountains to straighten it out. And you'll find the strength to do it. I know. Come on; I'll walk you to your car."

He'd sworn to himself that he would have her, but he wondered now if the price wouldn't be higher than what he was willing to pay. She carried a lot of emotional baggage, maybe too much. Yet he couldn't help wanting to protect her, to banish the gnawing anxiety that he sometimes sensed in her. But neither could pretend to be undisturbed by her attempt to belittle what they felt for each other.

She gloried in the security of his hand holding hers as they'd walked, but he hadn't kissed her good night, and she went to bed empty and lonely. Her conflicting feelings—her need for Rufus and her longing to know her son—gave her a feeling of hope-lessness. Why did it have to be one or the other? And why had she let herself begin to yearn for the love that she knew Rufus was capable of giving? A love that she hadn't known existed until she had seen him with his children. And she wanted the gentleness that she knew he possessed. But somehow, she had to know her son. Maybe, if she could see him, talk with him just once. She didn't want to hurt him or his family in any way. Thinking of that made her question whether she shouldn't stay away. Confused and uncertain, she wondered if she was ready for a clean break from Rufus, giving up One Last Chance, and possibly inviting ruinous public exposure. It was nearly daybreak when she finally fell asleep.

Several evenings later, the One Last Chance board of direc-tors nominated Naomi as its delegate to the National Urban Alliance convention in New Orleans. She had never been there, hadn't been a convention delegate, and had no idea what was expected of her. She fretted about it, then tucked in her pride and called Rufus, who was an NUA officer.

"I'll call you back in a few minutes," he told her. She decided he'd made a power move, but she couldn't blame him. Her behavior with him had been anything but consistent.

He returned the call after half an hour. "Your call surprised me; how may I help you?" She winced at his coolness and forced herself to assume a casual demeanor as she told him of her board's decision, but she wouldn't let him see how his coolness had affected her.

"I've got a lot of material here that might help you. I'll sort through it and bring it over tomorrow night after my own board meeting, if you'd like." His tone was impersonal.

"What about the boys?" She wanted him to bring them, even as she savored the idea of being alone.

"Jewel keeps them overnight when I have a late meeting or another engagement."

You mean when you stay out all night, she thought, feeling a cold tightness in her chest.

"Tomorrow night is fine with me. Thanks, Rufus." She didn't know how to hang up and just held the receiver and said nothing. He, too, seemed unable to break contact. Nervous and ill at ease, Naomi resorted to flippancy, thought it lacked her usual bite.

"Just think, if you'd been as reluctant to hang up on me once before, we probably never would have met."

"I didn't hang up on you." He paused briefly. "Did I?"

"Yes, you did. When your Ivan-the-Terrible temper roared out of control, you said a few cutting words and hung up."

Rufus chuckled, but his deep voice sounded more like a growl. "I've got better manners than that, lady."

"I know. That's one reason why we got acquainted."

"What's another one?" He considered why he enjoyed needling her; a twenty-minute conversation with Naomi when she was at her devilish best could brighten his life for days.

"Your ego's big enough, Meade." She was sorry as soon as she'd said it.

"There ought to be a law against suppressing compliments."

"Well, there isn't," she giggled. "Let's count to ten and hang up."

Rufus laughed. "The last time I did anything like that, I was in junior high. See you tomorrow night. One…"

Rufus left his desk, walked to the window, and looked out at the bare trees. There was something calming about winter scenes; nature was at rest, but you knew that new life would soon emerge. Would it happen to him? When Naomi had telephoned him, rather than talk with her then, he had elected to call her back, giving himself time to get his emotions under control. The sound of her voice had sent his heart racing. Bringing the material to her was a ploy; he could have told her what she needed to know by phone. But he had held his breath while he waited for her answer.

* * *

He spent the better part of the next day prowling through his house, eager for the night when he would see Naomi. Around three o'clock, exasperated with himself, he packed the boys in the minivan and drove to Louella's. Lou let them in the tradesman's entrance at the back. He sat on a high stool and helped her clean string beans for the dinner crowd, while the boys watched *Sesame Street.*

"What's wrong, hon? Why aren't you working?" He should have known that she wouldn't let him escape her motherly interrogation, but he felt too raw for a discussion of his feelings.

"I thought I'd bring my boys over to see you."

"Not in the middle of a workday. How's Naomi?"

He laughed. Trust her to cut to the chase. "You old fox. She's fine, as far as I know, and she's driving me crazy." Louella sat down beside him and wiped her hands on her checkered apron.

"If it doesn't come easy, hon, just let it go."

He pulled at his chin and looked into the distance. "I can't.

Louella draped an arm loosely around his broad shoulders. "But from what you told me, she's everything you don't want. So what's the problem?"

"The problem, Lou, is that she is also everything I do want. *Everything.*"

Louella sucked in her breath, got up and padded over to the sink. "Then you'll just have to decide whether you'll be more miserable with her or without her." He stood and began putting on the boys' coats.

"I don't have to decide. I know."

The camaraderie that Naomi and Rufus had shared by phone the previous evening didn't seem to ease their discomfort when Naomi opened the door. It was like the first time. Excitement coursed through her when she looked at him. They stood there, caught up in unwelcome longing. The clock that had belonged to her mother chimed nine times; by the ninth, his face had formed what she recognized as a forced smile.

"Usually, when someone opens a door to me, I'm told to come in, and that's what I do. But every time I come here, I wonder if you're going to let me in." He walked in without waiting longer for an invitation, raised his free hand as if to caress her cheek, but quickly withdrew it.

"Have a seat." She put her trembling hands behind her. Why had she agreed to this meeting when she knew that being alone with him in her home might be a disastrous move? He remained standing, looking at her intently, the only sound the ticking of the clock.

"Please, sit," she repeated. His response was a half smile. "After you." He gave her the folders, explained the registration procedure and how to get the best rooms, told her of the more interesting committee appointments, and cautioned her about the political maneuvering.

After thirty minutes, he rose to leave, tired of the strain that being with her imposed on him. She had been careful not to dress provocatively, but his desire wouldn't have been less feverish if she'd been wearing sackcloth. He didn't have to see her in sexy clothes to desire her; he just *did.*

"I'd better be going." She didn't respond, but her look of disappointment told him that she didn't want him to leave. He looked at her mass of thick, curly hair hanging around her shoulders, and the way her navy slacks and mauve-pink sweater outlined her tall, slim body and shook his head.

"Why couldn't you be somebody else?" He hadn't meant to say it, but she'd spoken simultaneously and hadn't understood.

"I wish you'd brought the boys; I'd love to see them. They're really special." She was trying to prolong his stay, and both of them knew it.

Rufus wondered how much truth there was in her statement. If only he could… "They ask about you," he heard himself say, though he hadn't planned to tell her. "It's odd, because they hardly ever ask about Jewel, and they know her so much better." He shook his head slowly. "I can't believe they'll be four on

Thursday." He leaned against the wall, and his voice became softer, deeper, almost musical. "They want me to keep their birthday until Christmas and let Santa Claus bring it."

Naomi laughed that joyous liquid laugh that always made his spine tingle. "I'll bet that was Preston's idea."

He creased his forehead, wondering how she knew. "Yes, it was. I'm surprised at how well you understand their personalities and the interplay between them. My brother-in-law has such a problem with their identities that it's their greatest pleasure to play tricks on him. Jewel's the one who tells them about Santa Claus." He straightened up, began to pace, and stopped right in front of her.

"Don't you?" she asked in a shaky voice, betraying to him her struggle not to lose her composure. She clasped her arms where they joined her shoulders and looked at him through half lowered lashes, but he reined in the desire that threatened to erupt. His gaze remained steady, probing, but he answered her as if there was no tension between them. As if he hadn't jammed his hands into his pockets to keep them off her.

"I don't lie to my boys. Not ever. When they ask, I tell them, 'that's what people say.'" He hesitated. "Well, I've got to be going." But he didn't move. He stood still right in front of her, a breath away, looking deeply into her wide, revealing eyes. He knew she was in a turmoil that matched his own. Her eyes adored him, and he stared at her in wonder, mesmerized. Was she as soft and as sweet as she sometimes seemed? Like right now?

"Naomi, I…Naomi!"

"Rufus!" She was in his arms, sobbing his name. And she wilted when his lips found hers in a kiss that was almost feral in its consuming power. Drugging. Humbling. When he finally eased his lips from hers and looked into her dazed eyes, he knew there was a decision to be made, and made soon. Where were they going?

"We can't be platonic friends, Naomi. It isn't possible."

"I know."

"So I guess I'll see you in New Orleans." He still held her to him.

"Who'll keep the children? Jewel?" He detected a hopeful-
ness in her voice and wondered at it. Did she think he'd leave
his boys with a casual friend? He smiled inwardly. Or did she
think him a philanderer? He grazed her cheek softly with the
knuckle of his right hand.

"Yes. I know she'll take good care of them."

Her pensive manner didn't fit with her soft sexiness of
moments earlier, and her next words told him why. "Do you
mind if I see them for a few minutes Thanksgiving Day, since
it's their birthday?"

Rufus released her, shrugging first his left shoulder and then
his right, uncertain as to how he should respond. A glance at her
face told him that a negative reply would crush her. "Of course.
Just call first; we might be over at Jewel's house."

Jewel Meade Lewis answered Rufus's phone. "Happy
Thanksgiving. Who's calling?"

A chill went through Naomi. He had told her that she was the
only woman he was kissing, but maybe he'd been joking. If not,
then maybe he had lied, though that seemed out of character.
Well, what did she care? She didn't doubt that Rufus wanted her,
and wanted her badly. Let this woman, whoever she was, do the
worrying. Nobody intimidated Judd Logan's granddaughter.

"This is Naomi Logan. I want to speak with Mr. Meade,
please." She made her voice sweet and seductive, almost a purr.

"Naomi! How nice to speak with you. I've been wanting to
meet you. The twins talk about you constantly, but my brother
is too tight lipped to satisfy my curiosity. Come on over. We'll
wait for you, then we're going over to my place. How long will
it take you?"

A steamroller—that's what she was, Naomi thought. But she
felt too relieved to resent it and agreed to get over to Rufus's
house in twenty minutes.

Rufus opened the door, and the twins were right behind him.
He looked at the two huge, gaily wrapped boxes and the single
small one before glancing inquiringly at Naomi.

"Don't worry, it won't hurt them." The boys greeted her warmly, and she discovered a kindred soul in Jewel. Her gifts of giant pandas and a videogame featuring them enchanted Preston and Sheldon.

"Come and have dinner with us, Naomi. Can you stay?" His eyes beseeched her.

"I'd love to," she replied, attempting to hide the eagerness in her voice, "but it depends on what my grandpa is doing." A call revealed that Judd was being fêted by the sisters of his church and had wanted her to join them. But when he learned that she would be with Rufus, he seemed happy to excuse her. She wondered whether his eagerness to pawn her off on a man hadn't helped to cement her vow to remain unattached. His domineering behavior could also have been a factor. If Judd had been different—less obstinate, more loving and tender—would she be more willing to risk loving a man, to believe that a man's love for her could be so powerful that he would trust her with his happiness? That he would overlook her liabilities?

Naomi wouldn't soon forget her dinner with the Lewises and the Meades. She liked Rufus's sister. Jewel took her in hand immediately and effortlessly made her feel like a family member, as if she belonged. She looked around at the large Duncan Phyfe table laden with food, the country curtains, and the homey touches that gave the room its lived-in character. She noticed that although the table was formally set, neither Jewel, Jeff, nor Jeff's parents had bothered to dress. Rufus, too, wore casual attire. The twins and their two cousins, aged six and four, each said a line of grace. The dinner was a traditional one of corn chowder, roast turkey, baked ham, stewed turnip greens, candied sweet potatoes, boiled tiny white onions, a dish of raw vegetables, buttermilk biscuits, and pumpkin pie.

She entered eagerly into the camaraderie that flowed among them during the meal. Many different levels and kinds of love flowered in the small group, and the knowledge of it thrilled her. The children talked among themselves, the adults to each other,

Sealed with a Kiss

and above it all, a state-of-the-art sound system reproduced the voices of Marian Anderson and Paul Robeson singing spiritu- als, folk tunes, and operatic songs while at the peak of their vocal powers. Judd had always preached that you weren't supposed to talk while eating; a mistake she concluded.

Exclaiming that the meal was an example of the best in Southern cooking, Naomi asked Jewel, "Were you born in the South?"

"No. We were born here, in the District. Our mother was born in North Carolina and our father was from Virginia. But Mom wasn't much of a cook, Southern or otherwise." Naomi detected a preference for another topic in Rufus's change of expression. Jewel must have noticed it.

"Come on, big bro," she chided, "don't be a stick in the mud."

"What's a stick in the mud?" Preston asked.

"It's a real sweet man who gets his wires crossed," Naomi answered, without giving the matter much thought.

Jeff, Jewel's husband hooted. "Looks to me like things have evened out. There's another sharp-edged tongue at this table today." The bantering continued through desert, and Rufus gradually rejoined the fun, but Naomi knew that her question had cast a temporary pall over the gathering: Rufus had seemed pained by the reference to his mother.

Rufus left his children with Jewel while he drove Naomi back to his house to get her car. She was nervous and a little anxious about being alone with him; each time they were together, her attraction to him became stronger, less man- ageable. And she was weakening in her ability to focus on his certain reaction to the factors in her past that he would never accept. *But I like being with him.*

At the expense of displeasing him, she risked mentioning his mother. "I'm sorry about your mother, Rufus. And I'm sorry for some of the things I said in those notes I wrote to you before we met. I...Rufus, what happened to your mother?"

That she'd brought it up, knowing how he would react, sent a strong message to him: her action wasn't motivated by curiosity. He looked straight ahead into the clear, starlit night, his mood deeply pensive. For a long while, he said nothing. But Naomi didn't fidget or appear anxious. She simply waited, and her calm soothed him. Comforted him. A woman with enough patience to let a man weigh his words carefully before he uttered them was to be prized, he marveled, and wondered how she had developed it.

He told himself not to resent her question, that she had spoken to him of his mother because she felt something for him and needed to know him. He pushed aside a rising annoyance; Naomi was asking of him what she refused to give.

"Naomi, my mother was in a two-engine jet prop plane between Kumasi and Accra in Ghana, and it crashed." He closed his eyes and his lips tightened. How could the pain be so severe after sixteen years?

"At first, I got angry with her for risking her life to get some ridiculous chocolate recipes for a book on cocoa. And then I cried. I still can't forget how I missed her when I was little, because she had to work to take care of our invalid father, Jewel, and me. And I missed her when I got my degree, when I was named Super Bowl MVP, when my children were born, and when my marriage broke up. I wanted Mama to share my glory, and when Etta Mae left, I needed Mama to help me understand why I didn't hurt, why I couldn't make myself care."

He glanced down at the woman beside him. "Well, you wanted to know. I won't apologize for spilling it; once I started, I couldn't stop."

Naomi moved closer to him and settled for a hand on his right arm. He let her console him that way, though she said nothing, and he was glad; words were not what he needed.

After a while, he continued. "My memories of my father prior to his accident aren't very clear. I do know that he became an invalid shortly before Jewel was born. I was seven then. Mama once said that when Papa was healthy, he was a man among men and that she would love him forever. As an adult, I understand why she was away so much, but as a child, it hurt and I resented it."

Naomi squeezed his hand and spoke softly. "Jewel seems to have come to terms with this."

It amazed him that Naomi could get such a keen understanding of people after having been around them only briefly. His sons. His sister. He wondered if she understood him, too. "You're very perceptive." He looked to his left, as a speed demon drove by. "None of this affected her as it did me, mostly because Jewel had me from birth. And I told myself when she was born that I would take care of her, protect her from loneliness. And I have. Still, Jewel makes certain that she doesn't duplicate Mama's life; she has an old-fashioned profession and old-fashioned attitudes about home. Even her house is old-fashioned. It's Jeff who's modern. He shares the housework and child care with her. They're happy because they're a team. They think of each other and of their children before they consider themselves. Jewel is a devoted wife and mother, and last year she received the PTA's annual award as outstanding teacher. I'm proud of her." Naomi moved closer to him so that their bodies touched and, deeply affected, he accepted the gesture for what it was.

"Jewel is very likeable." While he drove through the night, she searched his facial expression as though trying to gauge his mood.

He shrugged. "Most people think so. She also likes to try to run my life, even though I'm seven years her senior."

"You shouldn't begrudge her the effort; I'm sure she just tries out of habit."

"What does that mean?" He wasn't certain of the implication.

"I'm trying to think of the kind of person who could tell you what to do, and when and how to do it." She explained. "Nobody comes to mind, except perhaps your football coach, and I'll bet you gave him a hard time. Nope. I don't think anybody could run your life; you wouldn't stand for it, and Jewel knows it."

He relaxed his bruising grip on the steering wheel, relieved that she hadn't reacted with one of witticisms. Why had it been so important to him that her comment not be flippant?

"I'm not so difficult, Naomi, and I don't think I'm overly sensitive. But I've had some experiences that I don't intend to have again. And I'm going to do everything within my power to see that my boys are spared what I went through. I used to sit up until all hours and wait for Etta Mae to come home. I would have met her after work, but she never knew what time the crew would finish the shoot. If she got a coveted assignment, she was happy only until she heard that another model had gotten a better one. It was an obsession; nothing else and no one else mattered. In the end, it destroyed our marriage." He eased up on the accelerator and took the car slowly up Hillandale Road on a meander through Little Falls Park and the beautiful surrounding neighborhood.

She wanted to get still closer to him. It was the first time he'd spoken to her that way, and she felt a new kinship with him. Finally, unable to resist, she pressed herself against him, and, as if warmed by her gentle caring, he turned into Wellington Drive and stopped the car.

"Why are you stopping?" She knew that if she commented on his disturbing revelations, he would withdraw and the mood would be destroyed.

Rufus turned to her. "I'm leaving you in your lobby tonight, because if I get past that, I'll be in trouble." He didn't soften it with a smile.

"I'll keep you out of trouble; trust me." She wished she could believe that, but she failed to convince even herself.

"Yeah, I know, Just as you always do." His voice held a hint of amusement, enough to remind her exactly how little immunity to her he had. He braced his right elbow on the backrest and rested his head in his hand.

"I've never had such a puzzling relationship with anyone, female or male. You and I have a great deal in common. We like each other…well, most of the time we do, and we want each other. *All* the time, I'd say. You know, there are times, Naomi, when I feel in my gut that you're right for me, that something really good could develop between us. But there are other times when I doubt that, when I'm positive I don't know you at all, that something important about you is hidden somewhere. And that it's hidden intentionally."

She had been looking at him, listening intently, and getting the uncomfortable feeling that she had already lost her way. She was going to hurt and hurt badly no matter what she did.

"But I don't..." she said aloud, and stopped.

"Don't what? Don't hide what matters most?"

She shook her head and tried to divert him. "You've said a lot in those few words, Rufus; I'll have to consider what you've said. I want to give you honest answers, but you want me to think about things that I've been unwilling to address."

He rested his arm lightly around her shoulders. "Am I ever going to know who you are, Naomi?"

She raised her left hand to his face, acting innocently, motivated purely by her need to touch him, to show him some tenderness, to communicate the deeply compassionate nature that she so rarely allowed him to see. He looked down at her as she caressed his jaw with featherlike touches. "It seems we've both had difficult lives," she said, almost in a whisper, seducing herself with the intimate gesture of stroking his face. "If I get all the answers and if we're still friends when that happens, I'll share those answers with you."

"I want to believe you. Why don't you try trusting me? I won't disappoint you. Believe me, I know how it feels, Naomi, when someone you care for lets you down, when you find that you can't depend on that person." She'd seen him wicked, serious, angry, and in other moods, but he had not previously allowed her to see him in a state of such heartrending vulnerability. Suddenly, his carefully sheltered need was exposed and she could see the man who'd missed out on the strong parental attentiveness that he'd craved as a child, and who had seen his dreams of his own happy family and graceful home dissolve into bitterness.

She didn't think; her arms stole around his neck. She leaned toward him, and without the least hesitation, he met her with an urgent, hungry kiss, crushing her to him. Everything that had gone on between them throughout the afternoon and into the evening had been leading up to that moment, when his stifled groan told her how much he needed her. Instinctively, she drew him closer to her, kissed his stubbly cheek, his closed eyelids, his chin. She couldn't say the words, knew even in her passion that she had better not say them, but her every gesture said, *I adore you.*

They sat silently, entwined in each other's arms, buried in their separate thoughts. Finally, he reached into the back seat and got a beautifully wrapped rectangular package.

"Open this after you get home," he suggested, almost diffidently she thought. "I hope it'll be okay."

She looked from him to the gift and started to speak, but he shushed her.

"Please accept it, Naomi. If it isn't all right, I'd like you to exchange it for something that is." She took it graciously, her heart pounding; what was the meaning of it?

Naomi hated to think of Marva as her mentor, but she admitted that she turned to her friend whenever she had a serious problem, even though she invariably ignored Marva's advice. She drained her coffee cup and glanced around her friend's new kitchen. Marva had been observing her closely, adding little to what had passed for a conversation between them, and Naomi knew Marva had noticed that she lacked her usual verve.

"How are things between you and Cat?"

"The same. And why to you always call him 'Cat'? I don't like that name; it's not him. Cats are stealthy."

Marva chuckled and, embarrassed, Naomi shifted her glance as she realized she was being protective of Rufus.

"You're getting to be too sensitive," Marva told her, in a voice laden with censorship. "You don't seem willing to match wits and just do girl talk anymore. Why won't you talk?" She propped her chin up. "You like him a lot; you know that, don't you?"

"Yes. I know it. It's time I got back to work; I'm not at leisure, like you are." She quickly collected her handbag and the portfolio that she had brought along in order to test Marva's reaction to her ad campaign layout.

Marva laid a hand on her arm. "You're not yourself, Naomi, or at least, not the person I think I've known. I've realized for a long time that you have secrets, important ones, but I thought you'd come to terms with whatever those secrets were about. Lately, there seems to be something tearing at you; everything is forced. Your smiles, your laughter, even your humor is forced. Your smiles, your laughter, even your humor is forced, and it's been more and more noticeable since the gala. Get on top of it before you drown in it. You won't talk to me; can't you confide in Cat?"

Marva was only five foot three and had to reach up to put her arm around Naomi's shoulder. "I was certain that after the way the two of you danced that night, you'd have become very close by now. Let him love you, honey," she drawled. "It'll change your whole world; your big problems will get smaller; work will be easier; even the stars will be brighter. Believe me." Her laugh was rich, throaty, and knowing. "And that's just for starters."

"Thanks, Marva. But Rufus is only part of the problem. I'll call you." She wanted to get out of there; nothing was as simple as Marva claimed. She had a husband whom she adored to share her problems and to hold her at night. When a load got too heavy, she could just hand part of it to him. I can't look forward to that, she reminded herself as she started her car, with Rufus or any other man. *And if the stars don't get brighter, that'll just be my tough luck.* She drove to her studio and buried herself in her work; it didn't help.

Naomi got home late that evening, out of sorts and hungry. She went into her bedroom to change and saw the present from Rufus that so far she hadn't had the courage to open. She made coffee, heated the rolls and roasted Cornish hen she had brought in, and sat down to eat with the beautifully wrapped box beside her plate.

I'm being silly, she told herself, and opened the box with shaky fingers to find a pair of green leather dress shoes that were remarkably similar to the ones she'd told him about. How had he guessed that she wore size 9B? And why had he done it? She thought about it for several minutes and decided that he had wanted to make up for something missing in her life; the shoes were merely a symbol. She slipped them on. They were a good fit and matched the green Chinese silk dress. Her heart lurched as she looked at them. She longed to telephone him, but decided against it, fearful that her raw emotions would betray her. Instead, she wrote him a thank-you note and signed it, "Love, Naomi."

Three evenings later, Rufus walked out of the OLC building and into its back parking lot, a place that he disliked, especially at night. With the simple act of walking through a door, he was transported from a progressive environment to the profusion of crying children and blaring radios and televisions that emanated from the neighboring apartment buildings. He walked swiftly over the buckled pavement and stopped, all his senses alert. With the help of the overhead lightbulbs that shone from the unshaded apartment windows, he could see in the twilight three figures in animated discussion a few feet from his car, and he was certain Naomi was one of them. He moved stealthily closer and leaned against the wooden fence that bordered the lot, ready to defend her if necessary. His eyes became accustomed to the near darkness, and he recognized first Linda and than a young man. Their words drifted to him.

"Naomi, I'm not doing anything wrong. What's wrong about my going to a party?"

"You're going against your mother's orders, Linda, that's what's wrong. You're getting involved with the wrong crowd, and this man is too old for you. And why do you need an overnight bag just to go to a party? When you find yourself in trouble, you'll regret this night as long as you live. I know what I'm talking about. Look around you. Isn't this the environment that you're trying so hard to escape? Well, it's the one you're headed toward, if you go through with this. I know you're hungry for love, Linda, but you won't find it tonight. Wise up, honey, before it's too late."

Would Linda go off with that man and leave Naomi standing there after she'd pleaded with her? And where was the man's common sense? Linda was a minor. He made a quick decision, rounded two cars, and stepped between Linda and her friend.

"You'd better be careful, fellow. This girl is fifteen, and you're at least twenty. Don't you know that if you touch her, you could get a jail sentence? What's your name?"

"My name is Rodney Hall, Mr. Meade," the man told him, surprising Rufus that he was recognizable under the dim lights. "And Linda told me she was eighteen. I don't hang out with underage girls; that stupid I'm not. Linda's real nice, and I like her, but I sure thought she was older. Looks like I'm in your debt, man." He turned to Linda. "Stay out of trouble, kid, it's rough out here in the streets." Rufus watched Rodney walk away, hands in his pockets, his shoulders hunched. Better to be disappointed, he thought, sympathizing with the man, than to face a jail term.

Rufus had some questions to ask Naomi. Her involvement with Linda was personal, he'd swear to it. She identified with the girl as though they were mother and daughter. His conviction about the strength of their tie deepened when Naomi attempted to embrace Linda and the girl responded by turning away, seeming to sulk.

He sensed Naomi's disappointment in Linda and thought, unhappily, that she'd have preferred that he hadn't witnessed that scene, which seemed to have left her shaken. But he had, and he wasn't leaving that lot until she did.

"Hello, Naomi. Linda. It's just six-thirty. Would the two of you join me for a soda or coffee? I can't suggest dinner, because I have to get my boys in about forty minutes." Both declined. He turned to Linda and winced when he saw tears streaming down her face. She must have been deeply hurt or embarrassed, for she dropped her head and turned her back to him.

He walked around to face her. "Rodney may be a nice guy,

Linda; I don't know. Whether he is or not, you shouldn't have deceived him. Don't lie to a man about your age. You could ruin his life, and you'll almost certainly ruin yours if you settle for a one-night stand." He regarded her intently.

He didn't like the silent treatment he was receiving from Naomi, who was behaving as if he wasn't there, as if she resented his interference. He walked over to her and reached for her arm, but she backed away, almost stumbling over the uneven pavement.

"I'll see you to your car, Naomi." What had he done to make her behave as if he was poison? He reached for her hand. "I take it you're driving Linda home, so you two come on. I'm not leaving you here in this back lot in the dark, Naomi, and you know it," he growled. After she drove off, he got into his minivan and sat there, letting the motor idle. He'd just been given a clue to who Naomi was, and he didn't know what to do with it. Maybe he should have asked Linda whether she and Naomi were related. Naomi hadn't seemed like herself. She hadn't wanted him to touch her, and she'd barely said a word to him. He was more puzzled than ever.

An hour and a half later, Naomi sat down to a cold supper of fried chicken, baked sweet potato, and milk. She had driven Linda to her home at North Capital and P Street. Not the worst neighborhood, but close, and waited until the girl was inside her door. Had she herself been that naive fourteen years ago, looking for love in the wrong place? She thought back to the scene in the OLC lot. To leave the lot, you either went back into OLC or through the gate and into the dark alley. If Linda had gone through that gate with Rodney, there'd have been no turning back. Naomi marveled that such a gifted, intelligent girl had given no thought to the consequences. Was the need for love so powerful? Did she need Rufus like that, and did it explain her attachment to Chuck?

She answered the phone after its fourth ring. "Hello. I'm busy; may I call you back?"

"In that case, why didn't you just let your answering machine say that for you? If my boys weren't in bed, I'd invite myself over. Could you call a taxi and come over here? That way, I can at least be responsible for your transportation. How about it?" She thrilled at the sound of his deep, masculine voice, but she couldn't talk with him or see him, not when she felt so raw. She'd been through the wringer once tonight, and she wasn't going to subject herself to Rufus's inquisition. She didn't know how much of herself she had exposed to Linda, nor what he had heard. But Rufus was like a master agent; nothing escaped him, and he always got what he went after. She stalled.

"Well, what about it?"

"I'm eating dinner. I'm tired, and I'm going to bed. If you called about Linda, I saw her safely to her door."

"I didn't call about Linda; I called about you."

She leaned her left hip against the table and contemplated the probable effect of telling him that she didn't want to see him anymore. None, she decided. "Rufus, we'll have to discuss me some other time. I'm going to turn in." *Don't lie to a man, Linda.* She hadn't lied to Rufus, but she hadn't told him the truth, either, and she felt as though she was caught in her own trap. He had wanted to protect her when they were in the OLC lot, but she couldn't allow it. If she ever began to depend on him…

"There's no point in trying to run from your problems, sweetheart," he said, getting her attention. "Like the man in Samarra, when you get there, whatever's chasing you will be waiting."

"I don't want to see you tonight, Rufus, and I took Philosophy 101 almost twelve years ago."

"You told Linda to wise up. You wise up! *You* send a man a note and sign it, 'Love,' and the next time you see him, you behave as if he's a leper. And you accused me of being inconsistent. Maybe we'll run into each other in New Orleans. Good night, Naomi."

She replaced the receiver and threw out the rest of her dinner. There were times when he made her truly happy. And then, like now, she could be miserable because of him. She wished she'd never seen him, and she wished she didn't have to go to that convention in New Orleans.

# Chapter 9

When she arrived at the registration desk of the conference hotel in New Orleans, Naomi saw that Rufus had just checked in and was deep in conversation with an attractive blond clerk. Of course, the little blonde doesn't care that fifteen or twenty of us are waiting in line to register, Naomi thought crossly. He hadn't noticed *her,* and it was just as well, she figured; her feelings for him just then were anything but friendly. Distasteful was more like it. She recognized the sensation as one of jealousy and soothed herself with the thought that jealousy was as natural and spontaneous as yawning. She laughed softly at herself, but loudly enough for Rufus to hear from a distance of five feet and turn toward her. Sweet, feminine triumph flowed though her when he immediately smiled at her, the pretty registration clerk evidently forgotten.

He greeted her with a captivating smile. "Hi. We should have taken the same flight."

Still slightly miffed at the pleasure he seemed to have been getting from his conversation with the pretty clerk, she replied grumpily, "Why didn't we?"

"Good question. Probably because if you'd wanted us to travel together, you'd have answered the messages I left on your machine yesterday morning." He shoved his luggage aside, and a middle-aged woman immediately sat on it, nodding an apology toward him.

A delicious little quiver darted through her chest. At least he'd called. "It wasn't deliberate," she explained. "That machine has been giving me problems. I didn't get your message." Then, feigning disinterest, she slipped into her old pattern of behaving differently from the way she felt. "Don't let me keep you from your little blond friend over there."

He laughed heartily, and she knew he recognized her annoyance as a cover for jealousy and that it pleased him. "You could have called me and suggested we fly together," he reprimanded. "It isn't etched in stone, as you like to say, that between the two of us, I make all the calls."

She didn't want to give up her annoyance; it was a good defense against the fevered turmoil into which seeing him had plunged her. She couldn't seem to move her eyes from his full bottom lip that always looked inviting—hard and tender at the same time. He raised his hand to rake his fingers over his hair, and her gaze fell upon his strong, tapered fingers, those pleasure giving digits. She could almost feel them stroking her. Her glance rested on his face, and she had an urge to run, because she knew he'd read her thoughts.

He winked, and her recovery was swift. "I'm glad to know that a nineteenth-century guy thinks it's okay for a woman to invite a man to join her on an out-of-town trip," she told him, falling back on flippancy.

"I thought we'd gotten well beyond the stage where you cover your real feelings with sarcasm," he told her, as a grim look settled over his face. "Say what you really mean, what you feel, Naomi, even if it embarrasses you. At least you'll know you were honest."

"I've never been dishonest with you, Rufus." She tried to look past him in an effort to hide from the accuracy of his assessment. "I may not tell you everything you want to know, but I don't lie to you." He stood before her, self-possessed and comfortable with himself, his tall, sinewy bulk blocking out everything and everybody else from her vision, the same way thoughts of him had begun to crowd other people and things from her mind.

He's taking over my life without even trying or wanting to. Why should I be defensive, she asked herself, looked up into his shadowed gaze, and was stunned by what she saw. He regarded her with a look that seemed to say he adored her soft sepia beauty, and she quickly shifted her eyes from his. When she glanced back at him, she was solemn. "Talk's easy done; it takes money to buy land, my grandpa always says. You try facing your personal problems head on and being honest about them even when it might knock you from your pedestal. Try it, I'm going up to my room now; maybe I'll see you later this evening."

Naomi started past the huge marble columns to the elevator and stopped when she heard a man exclaim, "Cat Meade! It's been years, man. What's happening? How's the old clavicle? Still holding together?" And while she waited for the glass elevator to arrive, another and still another old friend greeted him joyously. One of them inquired, "How you doing, man? Who was that fox I saw you talking with just now?" Naomi didn't hear Rufus's reply, but she managed to get a good look at the hopeful smiles of several women and the bright welcome of others who stood in the ornate reception area waiting to register. It was Cat Meade's world, and it seemed as if everyone around wanted to be a part of it. She could have been proud, but he hadn't given her the right to take a personal interest in him. Nor had she decided that she wanted that right.

When she reached her room, the phone was ringing. She let it ring. Her gaze took in the soothing beige and blue decor, and satisfied with the room, she began to unpack. The phone rang and she relented; who but Rufus would be calling her? She knew, too, the reason for his call. With his bulldog tenacity, he must certainly be a great journalist. She tried to remember what she might have said to set his curiosity juices flowing.

"Hello."

"Naomi, could we get together either in your room or mine for a few minutes? I want to talk with you, and we won't have any privacy in the hotel's public areas. Say, twenty minutes?"

"Twenty minutes suits me. We can talk here, and I'll order some coffee and a couple of sandwiches. Is that all right?"

He agreed, and she ordered the food, unpacked, and sat on the edge of her bed waiting for him. Naomi knew she had to solve her dilemma, and soon; the effect was crippling her and maybe others as well. What did she feel for Rufus? She wasn't ready to name it, but she admitted that she couldn't even contemplate not having him in her life. She had avoided involvements successfully for over thirteen years. No longer; Rufus had changed that. And there was her son. Before she'd known that her child's adoptive parents were trying to find her, she'd hidden her experience of motherhood. But she knew now that she could see him, and wouldn't rest until she did. Maybe she could even get to know him and explain that she hadn't wanted to give him up, that she'd been pressured, that she'd been a child herself.

She had to know ether he or his family needed her. That meant breaking all ties with Rufus and his children, because Rufus would see in her every fault that he'd found with his wife and his mother, and he would coldly scorn her. She was probably going to damage beyond repair the reputation and credibility that she had worked so hard to establish. Leaving One Last Chance would be one of the most onerous and prophetic penalties of all. Well, she rationalized, she would still have her work; commercial artists needn't be identified. *If only she was sure that she was ready to face it all.* From royalty to servitude in a single step; in matters relating to the morals of women, the African American upper and upper-middle classes in Washington, D.C., were unforgiving. Naomi sighed. Well, so be it.

She answered his soft knock. One look at him and she knew the conference wasn't on his mind. He didn't waste a minute. "What are you facing that can knock you off your pedestal, Naomi?" The precision with which she had described her dilemma registered with her then, and her own carelessness and the accuracy with which he had divined the meaning of her words shocked her.

"I was talking about you, not me. You're the one with the public acclaim and adulation," she bluffed.

"But I don't have any personal secrets that could knock me

off my pedestal. Your words. So what were you talking about if not something pertaining to yourself?"

He paced the richly carpeted floor. "Sometimes, Naomi, when you're in my arms, you electrify me; you wipe out every pain—real or imagined—that I've ever had. Sometimes, when you're so giving—the way you were Thanksgiving night—I feel as if I'm just beginning to know what life is about. At other times, like now, you make me feel hollow inside, because you're not being straight with me. I know you feel something for me, and it's deep. But you're afraid to trust me with your feelings, your secrets, or your pain."

He grinned unexpectedly. "Have it your way, sweetheart; you're not indebted to me. You can say what you want and do as you damned please. See you around." The grin hadn't covered the dismal expression she'd seen on his face and been powerless to wipe away.

The doorbell rang and she rushed up the three steps leading to the foyer to answer it, thinking that he might have had a change of heart and returned, but it was the bellboy, wheeling in a linen-covered table on which were two elegant place settings, two carafes of coffee, two sandwiches, the standard pickles, and a bill for forty-one dollars, tax included. She paid the bill and sent him away, along with the overpriced fare.

She stood in the middle of the richly decorated room, at a loss, looked around, and saw the package of materials that Rufus had so carefully assembled for her. She could...her shoulders drooped; she could do what? She wished she had been better schooled in the ways, wants, and needs of the modern male. Nonagenarians? She could give a seminar on those. Naomi laughed at herself. She could be miserable, or she could telephone Rufus and talk with him. Anything, just as long as she had contact with him.

While she dialed, a niggling voice demanded: why are you doing this? Either you walk away cleanly or you take a chance, trust him, and tell him everything.

"Meade." Was he really as impatient as he sounded? She drew in her breath and identified herself.

"Why did you call me, Naomi?"

Truth. Tell him the truth, her common sense preached. "I just wanted to talk."

"*What?* I just left you. What changed your mood? That is, if it's changed."

"Rufus, I've…I've avoided entanglements since I was…well, most of my adult life. I've avoided them because I can't commit to a lasting relationship, and I have wanted to avoid hurting anyone or getting hurt. You sneaked up on me." His silence cut her.

"Actually, I was calling to ask if we could go to the dinner dance together, unless you're going with someone else." He still hadn't responded. "Well, if you'd rather not talk…I'm sorry I disturbed you. But you did say that I had a right to invite you out, even across state lines, and this is just a matter of getting on the elevator and going downstairs."

"Cut it out, Naomi," he growled. "For just this once, if you're hurting, for God's sake, let it show. If you need me, damn it, tell me! *Tell me!*"

She uttered a deep, labored sigh and whispered, "I need you."

"I'll be right there."

She hung up and had to fight the tears. *Oh my Lord! I love him. I love him.*

He had been coasting, taking it as it came, because she had become important to him, and he couldn't will himself to walk out of her life and stay out. Not until ten minutes ago. He had meant what he said. But because he cared, he would open his ears and his heart and listen to her.

He stepped into the room with arms open, and she melted into them eagerly and expectantly. But he didn't intend to precipitate a torrent of desire between them. He wanted them to understand each other, to communicate at a meaningful level, so he crushed her to him and quickly stepped away.

Her discomfort was evident, and he understood the emptiness, the yearning for completion that her demeanor communicated to him, because he also felt it. When she tried by gesture and stance to deny it, throwing her head back and smiling a forced, vacant smile, he shook her shoulders gently.

"It's okay to need, Naomi, and it's okay to need *me*." She leaned toward him, but he stepped away, determined that they should speak with clear heads. He had never attempted to bring about a meaningful understanding between them because he hadn't decided that it was what he wanted. And his indecision stemmed partly from her deliberate efforts to prevent him from knowing her real self by throwing up screen after screen whenever he got close. But he was no longer going to accept any shamming from her—not if he recognized it. And he was going to find out what they meant to each other and why she could burn up in his arms and then downplay the relationship whenever it suited her.

She looked at him openly, letting him see that she hurt. "You say it's all right for me to need you, but you don't mean it deep down, and it's just as well. You and I *both* know that I'm not what you need; I've got a career that I love, and you can't tolerate that."

A note of censure laced his voice, irritation evident, as it usually was when anyone second-guessed him, but he pushed his annoyance aside. "Shouldn't you leave that to me? I'm more than capable of deciding who and what I need and what I can tolerate." He leaned against the door and stuffed his hands in his pants pockets, out of reach of temptation. "And let's get this straight: I never said I couldn't tolerate career women. What I said, in effect, was that women who place their careers *before their children and their family* risk impairing the welfare of their family, and especially their children. If you had listened to the entire program, and if you had read my books all the way through and with an open mind, you'd know that I also empha-size the man's role in family disorganization and adolescent de-linquency. So stop misquoting me. And let's get back to the subject." She seemed to relax, and he gained the impression that she was considerably relieved by his explanation.

Her eyes held an expression of longing as she gazed at him. "Rufus, I'm trying to tell you that I don't have anything more to give." He regarded her intently, sensing that insecurity was at the root of her insistence on their incompatibility. If she'd allow their relationship to follow its natural course, she'd discover that they had plenty in common. He didn't have much hope for that, but he had to persevere for his own sake.

"I know you feel that way," he told her, "and you may even be right, but sharing changes things."

"What do you want, Rufus?"

Was he having a hearing problem? She couldn't possibly be serious. "I want you, Naomi. Beyond that, I don't know. And I won't know until you give us a chance, until you let me know who you are. You took a big step when you called me, and also when you told me that you have problems that complicate your life, limit your options."

"I said that?"

"In effect, you definitely did. And you told me that you need me; as long as you do, Naomi, I'll be here for you." Etta Mae hadn't needed him, but for all her posturing and clever tongue, Naomi did, and so did his boys. And they could rely on him as long as he had breath and strength.

He watched Naomi carefully, already sensitive to every change in her. "Don't close yourself off from me, Naomi; I'm not going to hurt you. And promise me you'll stop concealing your emotions behind clever comments. Why do you do that, anyway?"

He stifled the desire that coursed through him when she raised her left hand and brushed aside the unruly hair that nearly hid her left eye. "Is that what I'm doing? Well, you met my grandfather. Can you imagine being indoctrinated by him from the age of seven, when he was already seventy-three? At least twice a day he told me to control myself, that tears were unacceptable, and that you didn't let other people see any weakness in you. He even discouraged my showing him any weakness."

He nodded. "Yeah. I guess he would do that; he was too old

for such responsibility." Mention of Judd reminded him of their torrid dance at the gala.

"Do you really want me to accompany you to the dinner dance?" He gazed quizzically at her, purposefully mischievous, his white teeth framing a deliberately roguish grin. "I shouldn't think you'd be willing to risk dancing in public with me again."

"Why not? I may even repay you. I think I'm entitled to that, don't you?"

"Depends. I'll look forward to it." He draped an arm loosely around her shoulders.

She snuggled closer. "Depends on what?"

"As with most risks in this life," he explained solemnly, "whether you should gamble depends on your willingness to live with the consequences." He felt her tremble and held her to him. Then he noticed the quiver of her lower lip and was puzzled as to why she should be nervous. What was it? He had a driving desire to protect her. But from what?

"Sometimes, we have little choice." Her voice seemed small and came to him as if from a considerable distance.

He shushed her. "When you're ready to tell me everything, to trust me, Naomi, we'll work through whatever it is together. Don't dribble it out; I don't think I could handle that."

She leaned closer, as if unconsciously borrowing his strength. "I don't understand, Rufus. Why are you bothering? A smart man wouldn't invest any of himself in me when he's been warned that a serious relationship is out of the question."

"I've already invested a lot of myself in you, and whether or not you admit it, we've been in a serious relationship almost from the time we met. I finish whatever I start, and I've started something with you. I don't fish often, Naomi; I've never cared much for the sport. But when I do catch a fish, believe me, I don't throw it back into the water." He glanced at his watch. "I'd rather not leave you right now. It's poor strategy to walk out of a negotiation when it's going your way, but I'm chair of a committee that's meeting in twelve minutes."

"Is this going your way?"

"It's going *our* way, Naomi. You're talking to me and you're listening with more than your ears." He squeezed her to him, lifted her chin, and searched her eyes. She glanced shyly away, but what he had seen satisfied him.

"You have something to give me, Naomi, something that's real, and I want it." He kissed her then, quickly, gently, and possessively.

"You can't just ignore what I've been telling you, Rufus: I'm not for you; I can't be. *I just can't!*" But he sensed a wavering of her resolve, as he held her firmly but tenderly by the shoulders and let his gaze roam over her lovely coffee-colored face and her long, curly black tresses before seeking her eyes. It was her eyes that had first captivated him. Dark eyes. Large, wistful eyes that spoke silently of her innocence, her pain, and her longing. Eyes filled with mischief. Eyes that sometimes said, "I hurt." And eyes that could grow dark and sultry with hot desire. He had a sudden impulse to take her and go somewhere, anywhere, where he could have her to himself, but it was a fleeting urge; he was not ready to make a total commitment to her, though he was far from certain that he never would be. She had become more important to him than he would have thought possible even a week earlier.

Naomi lowered her eyes under his intense appraisal, and he was glad that she seemed to misunderstand his mood. "There's no place for us to go, Rufus; I think we ought to stop seeing each other." He didn't have to be clairvoyant to know that those words had caused her pain. But she laid back her shoulders, raised her chin, and smiled tremulously. God! He admired her!

He quirked his left eyebrow and summoned what he considered his made-to-order noncommittal grin. "You know, it never occurred to me that you might be daft, Naomi." The grin swiftly vanished, and he projected a serious, almost severe mien.

"Can that idea, sweetheart. Don't even dream it. I'll meet you in the coffee shop at eight o'clock." He tipped her chin up with his right index finger and studied her, trying to see beyond what she was showing. Then he tangled his fingers in her thick hair, gave her a quick kiss, and left her standing there, speechless.

\* \* \*

After a while, she moved, dreamlike, to the balcony and stood fingering the glossy green leaves of the magnolia tree that thrived there in a large wooden tub. Restless, she stroked the satin-smooth wooden arm of the swing as if it had human properties, as if it were Rufus, then sat down and stared at the floor. She needed to get rid of the load she was carrying, to talk to somebody. But to whom? Rufus had said he'd be there for her. She put her flat palms on her knees and tapped her fingers. She wanted to believe he'd open his heart to her and give her a place that she'd never had, a place where she could leave her anxieties, her heart's wounds, and her inner turmoil, but she didn't think any such man existed. Besides, Rufus couldn't even contemplate what a mess her life was.

She thought of the prizes at stake and wanted to take a chance. Then she remembered the penalties. She hadn't ever let anything beat her down, and she wouldn't now; she had made her choice, and she'd stay with it. She had to know her son.

# Chapter 10

She needed nerves of steel to walk into that huge, crowded banquet hall with Rufus Meade. The commotion he'd caused at the registration desk should have warned her, but she had foolishly asked him to accompany her. Too late, she told herself. All I can do is look my best. And she did. When he greeted her with a sharp catch of his breath and a nod of approval, she was satisfied that her efforts had produced the effect she'd wanted. Rufus insisted on holding hands with her as they entered the hall, but she tried to hold back, claiming, "People will think we're a couple, Rufus."

He acted as if he couldn't care less; he was a man at ease with the choice he'd made. "Fine with me. I don't let what people might think dictate my behavior, Naomi. I believe in pleasing myself whenever I can." She looked first at him, handsome and elegant, and then at the admiring looks that they received, and she couldn't help being proud and squeezed his hand almost involuntarily.

He looked down at her. "When a man has a woman like you, he wants every other man to know it." She bit her tongue. He has said that she should stop covering up her emotions, so she didn't joke about it and she wouldn't ask him what he meant.

Instead, she winked at him and drawled, "We women like to show off when we're with a great looking guy, too." She laughed disdainfully. "We're being just a little too polite for my taste, Rufus. You look terrific, and I'm enjoying the jealous stares these women are giving me." Rufus grinned, and she could see that her comment pleased him.

\* \* \*

The fresh fruit cup, chicken à la king poured over flaky pastry shells, green peas, and potato croquettes had been pushed around her plate, and the tricolored three-layer coconut cake had been rejected. Naomi sipped her black coffee and consoled herself with the thought that at least she would lose some weight. The speeches that were somehow the same every year no matter what the occasion or who delivered them were over. People— mostly women showing off their expensive gowns—were table-hopping in order to be seen, and the band members had begun taking their seats on the bandstand.

All through their forgettable standard banquet meal, Rufus had quietly watched Naomi, responding to her rare remark and wondering how she could let long stretches of time pass without saying a word or seeming bored. She didn't feel compelled to talk. He admired that in her and hoped it meant she was com-fortable with him. She slanted him a sly smile, and he felt it from his toes to his fingertips. He reached for her hand.

The band swung into its third number, and he squeezed her fingers. "Dance with me?" She moved with him in a slow waltz until he switched to a sensuous one-step, sending her heart into a wild flutter, and she danced a little away from him.

He nudged her closer. "I thought you'd planned on getting revenge. You won't get it dancing a mile away."

Her nose lifted in disdain. "It wouldn't be in good taste to bring you to your knees right here in front of all these people, especially since most of them are your fans."

Rufus angled his head to one side and drawled provoca-tively, "Say what you mean. You're afraid of falling into the trap you were going to set for me. Go ahead, lady; work your magic." He grinned at her and goaded, "I'm immune." He wasn't and knew it, but what the heck? He got a thrill just from looking at her; if she wanted to do her thing that ought to be something to watch.

The band began a livelier number, and behind Rufus, Naomi saw a couple spinning and gyrating in the earthiest, sexiest dance she had ever seen on a dance floor. It would serve him right, she decided, and took up the challenge.

"Wait until the band plays something earthier," she promised daringly.

He pulled her a little closer, held her there, and taunted, "It'll be my pleasure." As they walked back to their table, a light, carefree mood enveloped her. She hadn't known that their sexual teasing could be so much fun. Happiness. It was wonderful.

The music began, and she leaned toward him. A frisson of fire shot through him at the gentle squeeze of her delicate fingers around his wrist and the provocative glint in her eyes.

"This one."

Surprised, he rose and held out his hand. So she wants to dance a cha-cha, he mused, and swung into the seductive rhythm. He relished moving to the hot, pulsating beat, dancing it off time, taking one step for every two beats of the drummer's stick. Heat suffused him in response to her seductive movements, the slow, tantalizing undulations of her hips, and the provocative invitations of her hands as she tossed her head from side to side in wild abandon.

Caught up in the storm of passion that she ignited, mesmerized by her frankly sexual gestures, he suddenly ceased to tease, and his mood for it deserted him. Blood roared in his head when she gazed at him dreamily, obviously half drunk on him and the music. Her words were almost slurred.

"Had enough?"

His lower lip dropped. The she-devil! "Yeah!" he gripped her to him, wanting her to feel his strength, to revel in his maleness. He took control of the dance, placing her left arm on his shoulder and her right hand around his neck. He held her to him and moved in a sensual step, the cha-cha forgotten.

Rufus came slowly out of his trance when he recognized a tap on his shoulder and glanced around to a man who was asking to dance with Naomi. He scowled ferally; some of those movers and shakers belong to another era. Let the guy find his own woman.

"Man, you must have left your mind back there in your chemistry lab," he threw over his shoulder. Then he looked down at the woman in his arms. "You want to dance with this guy?"

She moved closer. "What guy?" When a second man wanted to dance with Naomi, Rufus glared at him and stopped dancing. Then, without a word, he led her from the dance floor and out of the hall.

Standing with him in the anteroom, she folded her arms and grinned mischievously. "Aren't you supposed to yield when a man taps you on the shoulder?"

"You're putting me on." He couldn't appreciate humor right then. "Some of my fraternity brothers have a weird sense of humor. Yesterday afternoon, Watkins expressed a lot of interest in…what was that he called you. Yeah. 'That little fox,' I believe he said. Then he had the temerity to try busting up my dance. I've seen the day when I'd have made him pay for that stupidity." Rufus laughed inwardly. He saw no need to tell her about the times during his university days when he had cheerfully done the same to Watkins.

"Which one was Watkins?" she teased. His eyes must have reflected his murderous feelings, because she winced.

"You don't need to know. Would you like to go to Corky's and dance? Or to the Maple Leaf? There're a lot of live jazz spots on Oak Street. Or we could go to Preservation Hall and listen to some Dixieland." He let his hand caress her shoulder. "Tell me what you'd like."

"I'm hungry. Let's go around to the cocktail lounge and have some wine or something. Maybe they'll serve hors d'oeuvres with the drinks. That dinner was awful."

Rufus grimaced. "Make that 'something.' I had a glass of wine with dinner. Besides, there's an old Ashanti proverb that says, 'When the cock is drunk, he forgets about the hawk.' And with all these hawks here tonight and half of the wives back at home, I need my wits." She drank white wine and he sipped Perrier while the cocktail pianist plodded along.

He wanted to please her, but he'd had as much as he could tolerate. "Want to go to Preservation Hall?" he asked hopefully.

"This brother needs to go back to music school." She got a light stole and they took a taxi to St. Peter Street, but when they stepped out of the car, Rufus glanced around at the revelers, music makers, and crowds of onlookers, and the idea of a hot, noisy, and smoke-filled room held no appeal.

He took her hand. "Let's walk a bit. It's a pleasant night, or it would be, if we could get out of this crowd."

"Okay. The next time I'm here, I want to go down to the levee. Maybe some warm summer night. The Mississippi should be prettier at night in the moonlight, when you can't see how muddy the water is."

"It isn't summer, but it's balmy and the moon is shining. We could get a taxi and go down there now. What do you say?"

"How'll we get back?"

His arm slinked possessively around her waist as he hailed a passing taxi. "I'll have the taxi wait."

"Where you want to go ain't exactly across the street," the driver explained. He turned up his radio, and they heard a great rendition of *Jelly Roll Blues* as the taxi sped toward the levee. At the river, Rufus faced the water and Naomi stood with her back to him, enveloped in his arms. Her conscience pricked her; she wasn't leading Rufus on, she told herself. She just wanted to be with him, to push aside even for a little while the problems that plagued her. She fought the temptation to worry about her future; this was her night, and she was going to be happy. As if reminding herself to enjoy the moment, she began to sing softly *As Time Goes By* in a rich throaty alto.

Rufus didn't speak until she'd finished. "You have a lovely voice."

"Of course I have," she threw out. "Don't you know that all black folk are supposed to be able to sing?" They both laughed, but Rufus cut his laughter short, and she knew immediately that it was because she had done it again.

"Naomi," he asked grimly, "couldn't you simply have said thanks? Was it necessary to belittle the compliment, to pretend

that it was inconsequential? Stop shielding yourself from me."
He tightened his arms around her in a protective gesture, and she
rested comfortably against him as they communicated in a way
that didn't require speech. The silence enveloped them, a full
moon brightened the sky, and a fresh breeze swirled around
them. Heaven must be something like this, she thought, as the
voice of a nightingale pierced the night.

They didn't speak for a long time, and she savored his
nearness, relished his strong arms around her, and had to fight
the urge to face him and lose herself in him.

"Have you ever been in love, Naomi?" Immediately she
wished she hadn't mentioned wanting to see the levee by moonlight. The scent of anything approximating a mystery piqued his
interest, and there was no stopping him until he had the answer.
She tried to think of a way of distracting him. But the full moon,
fresh southern breeze, and mournful saxophone coming from a
barely lit vessel that moved eerily and slowly downstream practically guaranteed that his mind would not waver from her.

"Have you?" Emotion colored his low, husky tone. "Look at
me. I asked whether you've ever been in love." He took her face
in his palms and gazed into her eyes, but with the sweetest, most
loving expression she had ever seen on a man's face. She trembled
with sensuous anticipation and excitement at his powerful,
wordless communication. She should move, but she couldn't. She
should remind him that nothing could ever come of their relationship, but she couldn't part her lips. His slow smile lit his eyes,
transformed his mouth, and made his handsome face glow.

"You still haven't answered me. Don't you know?" He
removed the scarf that had begun to dangle from her shoulder and
draped it snugly, but attractively, around her neck, taking the
same care with her as he did with his boys. Her heart constricted
at his gentle gesture. Why was the forbidden always so desirable?"

It would have been easy to reply with a quip, but she knew
he didn't want that and wouldn't accept it. And she didn't want

to respond that way, so she took a deep breath and decided to trust him with the truth.

"I don't know the answer, Rufus, and I wouldn't want to…well, I just can't say." She wasn't going to lie, and if she said yes, he would want to know who. She couldn't tell him that she loved him; maybe she never would.

He pulled her to his side. With her nonchalant façade and outward calm, only someone close to her would ever guess she was so vulnerable. He pulled her closer, wanting to shield her from whatever it was that she seemed to do constant battle with. He had the cool Louisiana breeze in his face and a sweet woman in his arms and he was… *Damn!* He was out of his mind! Or was he fooling himself? Maybe. But he had to know her, what she felt, what hurt her, what made her happy, who she had loved, and what he had to do to make her want him, and everything and everybody else be damned.

Why did she resist answering even the simplest question? He had to persist. He'd do it gently, but he'd get it. He was on the verge of falling for her against his good judgment and his repeated advice to himself, and it worried him. But if she had loved once, maybe he could teach her to love again. "Did you care deeply for him?"

Her answer was a startled stare, the look of a deer caught in the rays of high-powered headlights. He didn't need the words.

"Whoever he was, he was a fool not to have kept you with him forever."

She relaxed, and her sigh of relief was so powerful that he felt it. "I did care," she said in a guarded tone. "Or at least, I thought so then."

"What happened to make you question it?" He had the disquieting feeling that she was hedging, and he was certain that she didn't want to talk about it.

She looked into the distance, and after a moment, spoke as one who carried a tremendous load. "Time and age." *And you.* The light in her eyes dimmed, and she leaned toward him unsteadily.

"Sweetheart, what is it? I told you that I'm here for you, and

I meant it." She didn't answer, but raised her parted lips to his. She's what I want, what I need, he thought, when she clasped him to her, asking for more, taking him with her into a torrent of desire. When he was finally able to, he stepped back from her, shaking his head from side to side, running his fingers through the tight curls at its base. At some other time, he might have been amused, but there was nothing humorous about what he felt and the dilemma in which it placed him.

"Naomi, I'd bet there isn't another woman on this earth who starts the kind of fire that you do and never gives a thought about what will happen once it gets going. Honey, I'm in trouble here."

"What does that mean?" She snuggled close to him; talk about fires was clearly of minor interest.

"It means," he explained indulgently, "that I'm human, and one day we're going to exceed my capacity for control."

She chuckled, obviously unconcerned, and teased, "If you lose it, we'll work something out."

His eyebrows arched upward. *"What?"* She continually astonished him; surely she wasn't that innocent.

She seemed to throw away all caution. "Now, now! Don't get your dander up. You told me to trust you, and that's what I'm doing."

"Naomi, I am trying to have a serious discussion with you. Would you please not joke?" Sometimes he thought she might be playing a game. She couldn't be as naive as she seemed, could she? It was near the end of the twentieth century, for heaven's sake; how could such a beautiful woman insulate herself to the point that she knew practically noting about men? *And why would she do it?*

Her voice came to him as if from a distance, disturbing his worrisome thoughts. "You're right, I guess. But I already told you that I haven't had too much practice with this kind of thing. Give me time."

He was about to probe dangerously deep when he remembered Judd Logan's words: *"It's been almost fourteen years since she let herself get as close to a man as she was to you last night. And I know that for a fact."* Naomi forestalled any comment that he might have made by drifting into a soft hum of Duke Ellington's *Solitude.* As she had no doubt hoped, he let the matter of his self-control drop. And there, beneath the Louisiana moon, he opened he jacket of his tuxedo, got as much of her in it as he could, wrapped her close, and began a slow one-step on the bank of the Mississippi.

He disliked ambivalence in himself. After such an evening with a woman, he'd have expected them to spend the rest of the night together. And he was tempted, almost eager for it. But he needed more from her than what he was certain would be mind-shattering sex. He wanted total communication, all of her. The problem was that he didn't know for how long, only that he needed it. When had he come so far, and how? When she was soft and loving, like now, he never wanted to leave her.

She commented on the eeriness of a dingy lit barge that chugged down the river with the help of a ghostly tugboat. A hoarse horn warning an approaching vessel had broken the night silence and their mood. He looked down at her comfortably settled in his arms, but seemingly oblivious to her effect on him, and he wondered how he made her feel. His mood changed, and she eased out of his arms.

"Maybe we should be getting back. That taxi driver probably thinks we've decided to spend the night." She stumbled. "There goes my shoe heel." He checked, saw that it was broken, lifted her, and began walking toward the taxi.

He held her closer when she shifted in his arms and demanded that he put her down. "I may need help, as you impressed upon me on more than one occasion," he reminded her, "but at least I know how to accept it when I get it. You've got to learn how to accept help—and compliments, too—graciously. I'm not putting you down. You can't walk if one shoe has a three-inch heel and the other is flat." He opened the door and put her in the taxi.

"You're attentive, and I like that, but I don't want to be suf-focated," she mumbled grumpily. He sensed that she was distancing herself, putting her emotional barrier back in place, and he was getting tired of it.

It was best to tell her good night in the hotel lobby. He wanted to spend the night with her, but he didn't want to have to pick his way through her minefield of personal conflicts. And he had a choice of that or settling for physical release, something he rejected. Both of them deserved better. Rather than deal with the heat he knew would consume them if he walked her to her door, he'd just look up some old buddies. At the elevator, his kissed her quickly and left her.

He changed his ticket so that they could fly back to Washington together. Even after the two-hour flight, she was still withdrawn. He instructed the taxi driver to take her home first. At her door, he told her that he would be away for a week or ten days.

"I have to go to Lagos, Nigeria, to get material for a magazine piece that I agreed to write. I could have refused, but not without some backlash. I won't see you again before I leave, but I'll call you."

Her surprise was evident. He knew that her mental wheels were busily turning and that she would reach the wrong conclusion: he hadn't hinted about it during three days in New Orleans, when they had been together almost constantly, nor during their flight back to Washington.

Her response wasn't what he'd expected. "What about Sheldon and Preston? Will they stay with Jewel?" He shook his head in dismay. Why in the name of God did she cling so tenaciously to her rigid self-control?

"Yes. Of course." He leaned casually against the door. "She takes good care of them, but...I don't know. I hate to leave them again so soon, especially to go out of the country. I like to be here for them if they need me." His voice trailed off.

"When will you leave?"

He studied her carefully. Did it matter to her? She was behaving as if their relationship was entirely impersonal.

"Day after tomorrow. I have to get back before Christmas." He continued to look at her for a good while and would have walked away, but she stepped closer, grazed his lips slightly and quickly with her own, and whispered, "Come back safe—and soon." He kissed her then, turned, and left. But a keen sense of dissatisfaction enveloped him. His own feelings were more ambivalent than they had been the night before, while they'd held each other on the bank of the Mississippi. He knew that was partly due to Naomi's coolness. She was baffling. Their relationship was baffling. He was convinced that it was in his best interest to stay away from her, but he didn't seem able to; he was drawn to her, and the pull was unlike anything he had experienced with any other woman. But she would swear that there could be nothing between them, and in less than five minutes, she could be in his arms, heating him up until he wanted to explode. And you're no better, his conscience nagged at him. Maybe by the time he got back from Nigeria, it would be out of his system. He laughed derisively; there wasn't much hope for that.

Naomi unpacked, put her soiled things in the laundry, and went to the refrigerator to see what she could find for dinner. Was there another like him? A man, a quintessential male who enjoyed nurturing his small boys, who fretted about leaving them in good care only for a week? Didn't he see in his own dilemma what his mother must have faced countless times?

"I'm not going to think about Rufus," she told herself adamantly. She wasn't sorry that she had gone to New Orleans, nor that they had gotten close to each other while there. But she wished she hadn't let him know that she cared for him. She hadn't been able to help herself. When he had indicated that he was fed up and left her, she'd thought she'd never be with him again and had weakened. And she *had* needed him. Then he'd walked back into her hotel room with his arms open and gathered her to him, and she had felt for the first time since her mother's death that someone cared for her and wanted to protect her.

He claimed that his shoulders were big enough for whatever burden she was carrying and that together they could work through any problem she had. All she had to do was open up her soul to him, tell him about her mistakes, what hurt her, the dilemma she faced. He didn't want much—just for her to lay her heart on the line and give him proof positive that she wasn't what he thought, so he could turn his back and crush her heart. I'd rather have a broken heart and his respect than to have his scorn *as well as* a broken heart, she told herself. I was right all along; there's no place for him in my life.

# Chapter 11

Sleep didn't come easily for Naomi that night. The decision she'd reached was a troublesome one, but it was time to put order into her life. She got out of bed before sunrise and waited impatiently until she could telephone Judd's lawyer. He didn't welcome her call nor the information that she had followed him and had been policing the Hopkins house. But she got what she wanted from him: the boy did not attend school out of town, but worked after school and on weekends. Sitting in front of the house, waiting for him to come home from school, had been a waste of time.

She switched tactics and began morning surveillance. On the second day, she saw him just as she drove up. Her heart pounded painfully as she watched him jump off the porch onto the walkway and breeze away on his in-line skates with his book satchel on his back. He was tall for his age, as she'd expected he'd be, and had his hair cut in the style of a Mohawk warrior. She couldn't see his facial features, except for the café-au-lait complexion that he'd inherited from his father, along with towering height; but she didn't doubt he was hers. She couldn't doubt it; every molecule in her body had reacted to him. She tried without success to steady her hands on the steering wheel, and for an hour, she sat there trying to summon enough calm to drive home.

Her spirits lifted when she found in her mailbox letters from chairs of fine arts departments at three universities, each asking for more information about Linda. The girl's sketches had impressed them, and their carefully worded letters allowed Naomi to hope that Linda would get the training her talent warranted.

Naomi's attempts to work proved a waste of time. Disconcerted, she intermittently pondered what to do about her son or sat catatonic-like, stunned by the proof that she had a child almost as tall as she was. She noticed the flashing red button on her answering machine and played her messages back without really listening to them—until Rufus's voice pierced her dim consciousness. "I'm sorry you weren't able to return my call last evening and that you had to leave home so early this morning. I'm on my way to Washington National Airport. Take care." She replayed it three times. No goodbye. No "See you when I get back." Nothing. A bottomless, piercing ache dulled her insides, and she knew that its only cures—her son and the man she loved—were out of her reach. She swallowed the bitterness, stood up, and looked around her. Her bedroom appeared to be the same; so did her hands when she glanced at them. But nothing was the same, and it never would be again. The whole world had changed. She had a boy who was at least five feet eight inches, and she had never touched him. She took a deep breath and steadied herself. "I'll be damned if I'll cry."

Two mornings after that, Naomi stood by a window in her studio, painting a winter scene from a photograph that she had taken in Rock Creek Park the previous winter. Realizing that she had absentmindedly juxtaposed on the scene of pristine white snow and evergreen shrubs the shadowed silhouettes of a man and two small boys, she put her brush aside and threw the canvas into the wastebasket. "Just like I'm messing up my life." She answered the telephone reluctantly to hear Jewel ask the unthinkable and the impossible.

"I can't do that, Jewel," she pleaded. "I can't keep Rufus's boys. He'd never forgive you. Things aren't good between us, and they aren't going to get any better." But she finally acceded to Jewel's request. With her husband hospitalized for a ruptured appendix, Rufus's sister couldn't care for her own children, and since the boys wanted to stay with her, she reasoned, she couldn't refuse. Jewel couldn't leave them with a stranger. She lost the battle with her conscience and her heart.

"I don't have room enough here, Jewel, so you'll have to let me stay at Rufus's house with them. He won't like it," she warned again.

She had her telephone calls transferred, got some crayons and a small sketchpad for the children to use, packed a few personal things, and left. At the elevator, she stopped and considered taking her work with her, thought better of the idea, and continued on her way. She was unprepared for the boys' joyous reception; they danced, laughed, and smothered her with hugs and kisses. She knelt and held them in her arms, her heart lighter with the feeling that she was no longer so alone and that the horrible ache that had plagued her all morning had dulled and become almost bearable. She closed her eyes and hugged them to her.

Naomi looked up, embarrassed, to find Jewel watching them and knew the conclusion that Rufus's sister had reached. But she couldn't hide her feelings for the children. Jewel gave her the keys to Rufus's cars and the money he'd left with her and went home.

Naomi packed the happy boys into the back seat of her car, strapped them in, and went grocery shopping. Rufus had obviously taught them to be helpful, because they advised her on brand names, the color of grapes—they always bought green ones—and the size, shape, and color of the milk container, among other things. She didn't believe Sheldon's claim that Rufus always bought them a big bag of candy and ignored it.

She couldn't remember a happier time in her life. She devoted her days to the children, discovering that they loved to draw and to sing, helped them make welcome-home drawings for their father, and plastered them all along the wall for him to see as he climbed the stairs. Rufus's grill was too heavy for her to move out of the garage, so she put together a makeshift one and they roasted hot dogs on the back terrace.

The days passed swiftly, and she realized she didn't want her time with the little boys to end, didn't want to return to her own life, with its web of secrets, uncertainty, and heartbreak. But Rufus was to return the next day, so in the evening she cooked what she knew he liked, got the house in order, gave the boys their bath, and helped them into their pajamas. She read them a story that she had written and illustrated for them. It was about two little boys, their daddy, and a fawn that had wandered lost into their garden. The boys loved the story and had demanded it each night after that.

She had slept every night in Rufus's big bed, rationalizing that she should be near the boys, who had the adjoining room, rather than at the end of the hall, in the guestroom. She loved to read in bed and was enjoying a historical romance when a powerful clap of thunder seemed to shake the house. A brilliant bolt of lightning followed. Thunderstorms made her nervous, but there was no time to indulge in fear. At the second and even louder burst of thunder, both boys came running into the room and tumbled into the bed on each side of her. She got out of bed and turned on all the upstairs lights so that the lightning flashes wouldn't seem so ominous, then crawled back into bed between the twins and decided it was as good a time as any to teach them *Jingle Bells.*

Rufus said a prayer of thanks as the big jet rolled to a stop at Washington National Airport. The trip had been twice as long as scheduled and fraught with peril and near disaster; at one point, he'd wondered if he'd ever get home. An attempted hijacking at an airport in Africa had been tragically foiled; at Heathrow Airport in London, the plane had landed in a heavy rainstorm; and the flight from there to Washington had been diverted to Philadelphia due to the storms hovering over the lower half of the eastern seaboard. It had taken hours to get a plane out of Philadelphia. More than once during the ordeal he had thought of his mother, whose life had been ended while she was on a business trip only a few hundred miles from Lagos. He got through customs quickly, hailed a taxi, and decided to go directly home to get the minivan. Glancing at his watch, he saw that it was eight-thirty, but he wanted to see his boys and he wanted them home with him. Anxiety gnawed at him when he saw that every room on the second floor of his house was brightly lit. No one was supposed to be there.

He unlocked his front door and opened it carefully. Nothing seemed amiss. The storm might have caused a short circuit or something similar; at least, he hoped that explained it. He set his luggage in the foyer and moved carefully into the hallway, where he could see the staircase and the light in the upstairs hall.

Halfway up the stairs, he simultaneously noticed the childish drawings and clay figures and heard the singing. He bounded up the remaining steps three at a time. They didn't hear him, and he stood unnoticed at his bedroom door and took in the incredible scene. Preston and Sheldon sang lustily at the tops of their little voices, laughing and jumping around Naomi, hugging and teasing her, and she was adoring them, showing them in numerous tender ways that she loved them. He heard her patiently explain to Sheldon that the word was jingle and dingle, then watched her take his little face into the palms of her hands and tell him that he was smart and wonderful and that she "loved him to pieces." Preston sat in her lap, and she cuddled him playfully, and then the boys knocked her backward and the three of them laughed hysterically.

His heart swelled in his chest until he almost burst with joy. Could he be dreaming? It was his house, his bed, his boys, and Naomi. He clutched at his chest as if to stop his heart's wild pound, as if to control the dizzying delirium that sped through him. He loved her. Right there, he knew that he loved her totally, profoundly, and irrevocably. He thought of his reservations about her, his convictions about independent women, his sworn resolve to put her out of his life. None of it mattered. Even his suspicions were unimportant. He loved! For the first time in his life, he loved! He pushed away from the door, his only thought being to get to them and to her and to get them into his arms. Naomi and his sons saw him and welcomed him with shrieks of joy. He gathered them to him and held them, and the boys began talking excitedly, but Naomi only gasped her amazement at his unexpected presence, clearly overwhelmed.

She struggled to detach herself from the aura of unbridled joy that permeated the room. He had so much love to give, and he showered it on his boys. She longed to be a part of it, to belong to them, but she had made her decision and she would abide by it. She watched enviously as he hugged and teased his boys, giving himself to them without reservation. Nearly an hour elapsed before he calmed them and got them to sleep.

"No reading tonight," he told them. "It's already two hours past your bedtime." They didn't want to cooperate, but sleep soon claimed them, and he finally turned his attention to her. She remained in the middle of his bed wearing her cotton ski pajamas, too shocked to be embarrassed. He hadn't been angry, but happy...and almost lighthearted. She got up slowly and reached for her robe, which she'd thrown across the foot of his bed.

"Where are you going?" His voice was low and husky, almost a growl. And there was a tinge of belligerence, too. She looked up at him, wonder if his earlier pleasantness had been a sham.

"I'm going home. Now that you're here, there's no need for me to stay." She backed away a step, almost bumping into a bookcase, when he walked over and stopped right before her. He brushed her cheek with the thumb of his left hand and searched her eyes, and her heart began a furious pounding in her chest. She stifled a sob and turned quickly away. Her heart wanted her to stay with him always, but her head admonished her to remember her son and her vow that he would be a part of her life.

His hand rested lightly on her shoulder. "What happened? I left the boys at Jewel's house." She told him.

"Jeff's recovering from an operation for a ruptured appendix, and Jewel is taking care of him. He's been very sick, but he's coming along nicely. Their kids are with Jeff's parents, and I agreed to keep your boys." He nodded. She hated that he'd found her in his bed wearing dreary, unfeminine pajamas, and that because she hadn't been expecting him, she'd been uninhibited in her welcome. She wasn't certain whether he was pleased to find her there with his boys, and he seemed to sense that.

He took her hand, walked over to the bed, and sat down. "I hope you realize," he said in a warm, reassuring voice, "that if my boys couldn't have remained with Jewel, you're the *only* person I'd have wanted them to be with. They love you, and you love them. I can't tell you how much I appreciate what you've done." She wanted to go home. She didn't want his appreciation; she couldn't let him thank her for the happiness she'd had with his children. She spoke dispassionately, in a detached voice.

"It was my pleasure, Rufus. Please don't take that away by thanking me. I'm glad you're home safe. Now I have to go."

He looked at her and thought of the way she'd been in the middle of his big bed, gamboling with his sons. Thought of the nights when he had tossed in that same bed, wanting her so badly that it pained him. Thought about how much he loved and needed her, needed to love her, to give himself to her. Desire flared in him, but he had promised himself that he wouldn't touch her unless and until she assured him that she wanted him and would never regret holding him in her body. He tried to cool the heat that invaded his loins, but the fire intensified.

"Don't go, Naomi. Stay here...with me. Please stay." He didn't attempt to hide the low shimmer of his voice or the pleading tone that sprang from the pit of his gut. She reached out to caress his face, and the feel of her silky fingers gently soothing him was more than he could bear; he grasped wrist and pulled her to him. "I need you. *Naomi, I need you!*"

She gazed at him as though disbelieving her ears, as if she was afraid to hear his words, afraid that he might be serious.

She glanced up, intending to tell him that she was definitely leaving, and gasped at the naked, vulnerable look of longing on his face. The temptation was so great; she could go home and have all her worries greet her when she got there, or she could stay with him and...and then what? She stood, determined to be sensible.

Then she thought back fourteen years, when she hadn't said no; back more than thirteen, when she'd writhed in pain as a consequence; and back ten days earlier, when she'd thought he was gone from her life forever.

She shook her head to blot out the confusion she felt, but then he said, "Oh, sweetheart, I can't make it like this," and pulled her to him. He swallowed her protest into his mouth, and she trembled against him as his tongue brushed her lips, begging for entrance into the sweet haven of her mouth. She opened to him, and when he thrust into her deeply and possessively, she whimpered and capitulated, pulling his tongue into her mouth and sucking it voraciously until his whole body quivered. She felt him hard against her and held him closer, and when he spread his legs, she moved quickly into the cradle he'd made for her.

Remembering that she never gave a thought to the consequences once her libido got possession of her, he warned her huskily, "Sweetheart, if you're going to stop me, please do it now." If she heard him, she didn't make it evident, but reached up and pulled his head down, captured his mouth, and took what she seemed to need.

"Naomi, for God's sake. Think about what you're doing. I want you. I want the sweet warmth of your body, and I want it badly. I need it. I need *you!*" She brought both hands to his buttocks and pressed him tightly to her. Close to exploding, he pulled up her pajama top and tossed it across the room, picked her up, and fastened his mouth on her nipple. Her uninhibited cry of passion excited and thrilled him, and he lay her on the bed and stood looking down at her, getting himself under control for what was to come. For the pleasure that they would give to each other.

She gazed up at him, silently, searchingly. How could he make her feel as if she were half a person, needing him and him alone for completion? He turned away, and she sat up quickly, suddenly self-conscious and wary.

"Oh, no you don't," she exploded. "You don't do this to me again. You started it, and you're going to finish it…if you can, that is."

Rufus turned toward her, plainly shocked. "You really thought I was going to walk out of here, away from you? And even if I had intended it, don't you know how to make sure that I don't leave this room if you don't want me to?"

She shook her head, embarrassed. Now he knew that she'd had practically no experience. "Where were you going?"

"To hang my jacket on the back of that chair." He pitched the jacket toward the leather-covered wing chair, walked back, and stood in front of her. Gazing deeply into her eyes, he kicked off his shoes, methodically removed his shirt, belt, and pants, letting them fall, and reached for his shorts. Her lips parted, seemingly of their own accord, and her eyes widened. With trembling fingers, she stilled his hand. She had never seen a nude man, and she hadn't dreamed that the male body could be so beautiful and enticing. In a dreamlike state, she licked her lips, reached for his shorts, and began slowly to peel them off him. He jumped to full readiness, and as if charmed by a beautiful snake, she leaned forward and quickly kissed him. His groan sent a hot ache to the seat of her passion, but she slid away when he reached for her and stood to gaze at his male beauty.

"Naomi, love, for God's sake." Her frank, open adoration of his maleness seemed to make him proud and to excite him almost beyond control. Looking at him, tendrils of heat snaked through her, and she reached for the headboard to steady herself as arousal weakened her.

"Baby, come here to me." She didn't move. And it wasn't fear that held her rooted in the spot, but riveting, searing passion. She tried to raise her lead-heavy arms, but they remained dangling at her side. "Come here," he growled unsteadily. "If you want me, sweetheart, come to me." She took one shaky step, and he reached out and pulled her into his arms, into the first skin-to-skin embrace that she'd ever experienced. Her erect nipples caressed his hard chest, his full arousal pressed against her belly, and she responded like a leaf in a violent wind, trembling un-controllably. She felt him hold her closer to steady her and then, enthralled by his nearness and his tenderness, she only sensed his fingers grip the elastic top of her pajama bottoms and ease them below her hips, dropping them to the floor. At first, she gasped at the sudden intimacy of their total nakedness, but when he shifted his hips and undulated against her, she eagerly returned the suggestion, lifted her arms to his powerful shoulders and her gaze to the shimmering love in his fawnlike eyes, and gave herself to him.

Her responsiveness had always excited him, and it was balm to his ego that she seemed to think of nothing but him and her feelings whenever he touched her. But her action now told him that she had always held something back, or perhaps what she felt now was different, more powerful; he only knew that she was different. It was as if she was no longer *in* a hurricane, but had *become* the hurricane. He lifted her, removed the pajamas from her ankles, and lay her in his bed. Then he leaned over her and brushed her lips in a kiss that was merely a promise.

"I'm going to lock the door," he told her, remembering how she had reacted earlier when he had turned away. "The boys walk in here whenever they like. You're the only woman who's ever been in this bed, and I don't want them to grow up too fast."

In seconds he was back. "Are you sure?" She nodded. "Tell me that you will never be sorry. Say the words, Naomi."

She raised her arms to him in a gesture instinctive to every woman, welcoming him to her. "I'll never be sorry. It's what I've wanted and needed since the first minute I saw you."

"You're sure?" he asked one final time. "Tell me now."

She gazed at the tender, loving smile that glowed on his face, leaned forward, and pulled him down to her. She might be sorry for a lot of things, she thought, but never this; it would probably have to last her for life. "I've never been more certain of anything. Come to me, now." He climbed into bed and clasped her to him, molding their bodies from shoulder to knee. She felt him strong and hard at the portal of her passion and tried to urge his entrance, but he refused to relinquish control.

"You're not ready for me, love. Just relax; we've got plenty of time." Her breath quickened and her eyelids fluttered closed with the weight of passion at the light brush of his lips and the gentle stroke of his fingers on the inside of her bare arms. Heat surged through her and she felt herself sinking deeper into a spi-raling rush of desire as his big hand feathered down her hip and teased the inside of her thigh. She thrashed about as passion overcame her, and fissions of fire burned her wherever the dancing, stroking electric rods that his fingers had become singed her. Unashamedly frantic for his possession, her undu-lating thighs trapped his hand between them, signaling her readi-ness for more. He put his left hand beneath her head, covered her mouth with his in a hard, passionate kiss, and found the core of her with his talented fingers.

The intrusion caused her to jerk upward, but her deep sigh of pleasure immediately followed, and she gave herself up to his double assault on her senses. With his bold tongue, he let her know what he planned for her, all the while stroking her to full passion, driving her to frenzied madness, out of her senses. Oh, Lord, where was her anchor? She was a rudderless boat tossing in a raging storm far from shore. She grabbed his hips.

"Rufus, please."

"Please what? Tell me what you want, love. I want to please you."

"I want to please you, too, and make you feel like I feel. Help me." She damned her innocence, her lack of experience, because deep in her heart she wanted to bind him to her and she didn't know how. He stroked her faster, and she lifted her hips, frantic for completion.

He took her hand and closed her fingers around him. "You are pleasing me, and you will. Just relax, love, we'll get there; I promise." A wave of exquisite pleasure washed over her, and her nerves tingled as if wired to electric current when he bent his head to her breast and suckled her slowly and rhythmically while his fingers worked their magic. She cried out and pulled him over her.

"Rufus," she moaned. "Oh, darling, please. I need you."

And she did, he realized, as the warm love liquid flowed over his fingers and she spread her legs in eager anticipation. He thrust into her, but she winced visibly, muffling a cry, and he paused and looked down at her searchingly, trying to curb his passion.

"What happened?" he asked urgently. "Did I hurt you? Talk to me, Naomi. Is this your first time?"

She shook her head. "No, there was one other time, but that was a long, long time ago. I'm all right." Fourteen years ago? he almost asked, and caught himself. He didn't doubt that any such question would have ended it immediately, so he banished the thought and kissed her, holding himself back with difficulty; his control tested to the limit by the loving clutch of her velvet warmth.

He knew that she feared he might end it because he'd hurt her and watched her carefully. She smiled and held him tightly to her while her body adjusted to him.

"Love me, Rufus," she pleaded. "I think I'll die if you don't." Then she reached down and stroked his buttocks lovingly. He trembled in her slim arms, gathered her to him, and began to move. Strong. Possessive. With every powerful stroke, he branded her. You're mine, he told her wordlessly, and I'm claiming what's mine. Instinctively, she wrapped her long, silken legs around his waist and let him lead her.

He wanted to give her everything, to wipe out whatever had been hurting her for fourteen years. He put his hand between them, stroking her, adding the pressure until she begged him for relief. His heart raced joyously and his body shook when he felt her sweet quivers as she tightened around him. With all the control he could muster, he quickened his pace and drove masterfully within her. Stunned by the intensity of her passion, he raised his head and looked down into her emotion-charged face as she cried out his name over and over and fell apart in his arms. Never before had a woman given herself to him so completely, relinquishing all sense of self. It shattered him, and helplessly he gave her the essence of himself in a thunderous release.

Still lying above her, locked within her, he gazed down into her face, looking for some sign that she felt for him what his heart held for her. But he wasn't going to press it; he didn't need to make another mistake. And he hoped to hell that love didn't turn a man into a fool, because if it did, he was ripe for it. He nudged her nose gently with his, wanting to see into her tightly closed eyes.

"Look at me, baby." He tried unsuccessfully to control his gruff, unsteady voice.

Slowly, she opened her eyes and risked looking into his beloved face, risked exposing her heart and soul to him. She wanted to tell him that she loved him, that he was air and breath to her, but if he then asked for a commitment, no matter how small, she wouldn't be able to follow through. She'd done it up this time; not having him was going to be living hell, but she wasn't sorry. She had known the consequences, so she locked her feelings in her bursting heart and merely smiled at him.

"Any regrets?" he asked her hoarsely, with the urgency of one awaiting sentencing. Naomi looked at him and frowned.

"How could I regret it? I feel as if I've just come alive." Then she realized that he was also asking something more.

"It was wonderful," she added quickly. "I never dreamed that a person could feel like that, I…I hope it wasn't one-sided." She eyed him anxiously.

Rufus laughed. "Sweetheart, I have never felt that way before in my life, either. Ah, baby, that was pure soul mating, and it will only get better." He separated from her and reached out to gather her to his side. She was leaving the bed.

"Where are you going?" His voice was calm, she noted, but he was not. She wouldn't let that deter her; she couldn't yield to her feelings.

"Home," she answered casually. As soon as he'd alluded to a future relationship between them, she'd questioned the wisdom of what she'd done. After the cherished way he'd made her feel, she couldn't expose herself, and she couldn't risk a deeper involvement with him without telling him everything; it would be unfair. She had to go, and she had to go right then, before she weakened and crawled back into his arms, back to his warm, strong body that she already craved again—feverishly. "I have to be getting home," she emphasized, wondering how her voice could be so strong.

Rufus couldn't believe what he was seeing and hearing. He lay there with both hands locked behind his head, fear coiling in the pit of his belly. "Let me get this straight," he said slowly in a low, controlled voice. "You make love to me the way you did just now, rocking me out of my senses, then coolly tell me that it was wonderful and you've got to get home. Just like that. As if I was…as if what we did here was just a quick…" He bit his tongue and said it: "Just a quick lay."

Naomi didn't answer him. He jumped off the bed and grabbed her shoulders, feeling them stiffen at his touch when only minutes earlier everything about her, all of her, had been soft and supple, in complete submission.

"Talk to me, Naomi. Is what you had here with me a one-night stand? Something that means so little to you that you can shut me out and just walk off?" He started to squeeze her shoulders in a quest for warmth, for any kind of reaction, but he dropped his hands instead. She still hadn't spoken, and from the set of her chin, and her closed expression, he could see that she was determined to leave. He went into the bathroom to control his temper and to deal with his anguish. Who was she? What was she, and why had he thought that because he'd fallen in love with her she'd be different?

When he came out, she was walking slowly down the spiraling stairs with her small bag. He slipped quickly into a pair of jeans and his shoes, grabbed his short shearling coat, and caught her at his front door. "What will I tell my sons, Naomi? That you've finished with them? That you've taught them to love you, but you're sorry if they mistook what you felt for them as love? What about that? And what about me? Why in God's name did you get into that bed with me?"

She reached for the doorknob, and he could see her lips quivering in spite of her obvious effort to control her emotions. He stopped her.

"Look at me, woman. I am not just so much refuse that you can accumulate and discard at will. You felt something for me, felt it deep down, and you'll never convince me otherwise. What is this all about? Look at me!"

He forced her chin up and looked into her eyes. "*My God!* What is it?" He shuddered. What in heaven's name could be responsible for her ashen face and the gut-searing anguish that he saw mirrored in her eyes before she snatched the door open and slipped away?

He stood silent, arms akimbo, while the noise from her car engine faded until he could no longer hear it. Twenty minutes. Just twenty short minutes earlier, he'd had it all. The woman he loved, who loved his children, and who had thrashed wildly and helplessly in passion beneath him, his name spilling over and over from her trembling lips. She had no control, had been totally at his mercy, and he knew it. Gone!

"Daddy, I had a bad dream." Rufus turned to see Sheldon at the top of the stairs, rubbing the sleep out of his eyes. He mounted the steps slowly, taking in the drawings and clay sculptures that were his children's presents to him. And he could see Naomi's loving hand in it as she'd taught his sons to write, "I love you, Daddy"; "Welcome home, Daddy"; and "Kisses, Daddy." Wearily, he took Sheldon back to his bed and soothed him until he fell asleep.

He sat for a long time near his children's beds, thinking about Naomi and the strange way in which she had behaved. Try as he might, he couldn't be angry with her, because he couldn't forget the tortured look in her eyes when she'd left him. He was certain that some demon was riding hard on her; she hurt, and hurt badly. He wondered…what was it Judd had said? *My Naomi spends a lot of time hurting.* He couldn't let her go. He loved her. Oh, God, how he loved her! To have known at last what it meant to share his body with a woman whom he loved…he swore softly. Naomi cared deeply for him, or she wouldn't have made love with him after fourteen years of abstinence. And for her, abstinence had definitely been by her choice.

He walked slowly down the winding stairs to his office. Reminders of her were everywhere. He dialed her number and got a busy signal, not even her answering machine, he thought in frustration. After repeated attempts, he decided that she'd disconnected her phone. And disconnected him from her.

Naomi hardly remembered how she got home. She threw her bag into the hall closet and made it to her bed by willpower alone. Disconsolate. Shattered. She hadn't known that she could hurt so badly, and she had hurt him, too. She had wanted to make it right, to tell him that it was killing her to leave him, but she knew that if she offered a single word in her defense, all that pained her, every wish and every secret, would flow out of her in an unbridled torrent. She wanted him to call her, to tell her that he could forgive anything, but the phone didn't ring and she wondered why she had even hoped it would. Hours later, she showered and got ready for bed. Looking in the mirror, she laughed mockingly at her ashen face and haggard eyes.

"Rufus, you're not only the lover that women dream of, you're a magician," she said aloud. "I haven't fallen apart like this since Grandpa left me at that private clinic all those years ago." She went to the kitchen, got some ice, and held it to her forehead. She climbed into bed, reminding herself that she'd never let anybody or anything demoralize her. I might lose it all, she told herself, but not without a good fight. As she dozed off, she remembered that she had transferred her calls to Rufus's number and that if he did call her, he would only get a busy signal from his own number. Seven-thirty the next morning found her knocking on Judd Logan's front door.

# Chapter 12

Judd was obviously taken aback by Naomi's sudden appearance; she hadn't rung the bell as was required, she wasn't smiling, and she'd barely murmured a greeting. As though sensing that something was wrong, he clung anxiously to his usual manners and routine.

"You've forgotten what I taught you, Naomi gal; you should've rung the bell and announced your presence. Sit down over there and I'll have Calvin bring us some breakfast."

Naomi looked at her grandfather, who seemed visibly older each time she saw him. I've got to do this, she reminded herself.

"Tell me everything you know about that clinic and my child, Grandpa."

He shifted in his chair, uncomfortable, she realized; a man unused to being held accountable, too proud and too virtuous to lie.

"I've told you the situation, Naomi." She reminded him that the records were sealed and demanded to know more about how the family had located her. Judd admitted that he wasn't infallible; the clinic guard had recognized him when he'd brought Naomi, and everyone at the clinic knew her first name. It hadn't been difficult for the family's detective to locate her.

"I'm sorry, Naomi gal."

She smothered the pity that she felt for the old man. "I don't want sorry, Grandpa. What I need is a solution. I'm in love with someone, and I have to get my life straightened out. I don't know what, if anything will come of it because from now on, my son comes first with me. But I have to give myself a chance with this man."

The distant gleam that lit his old eyes told her that it was what he had waited years to hear. She didn't let his apparent indifference lull her into unwariness; Judd was an expert at controlling and hiding his feelings.

"You marrying him?" he asked casually, as if it were of minor importance.

"He hasn't asked," she cautioned, "but if he does and if I decide I want that, I can't go to him living a lie and worrying about being found out. I want the woman's telephone number."

"But suppose they're after extortion money?"

"Grandpa, they can do that now," she pointed out, "but if we cooperate, make an offer, maybe she'll let me see my boy."

"Don't think of him that way, gal; it'll only cause you pain."

Naomi reached for the black coffee that the cook had placed on a small antique table beside her chair. "I saw him. Don't look so shocked. I just followed your lawyer and identified the house. One morning when I was parked there, I saw him, and I'll never forget the feeling that I had, watching him skate down the street with his books strapped to his back. I've got to meet him, Grandpa, I've go to."

She imagined that as usual, Judd would weigh the gains and losses before making a move, a trait that had made him a champion chess player; he would want to know what was at stake.

"Who've you fallen in love with, Naomi? Is he good enough for you, gal?"

"After that trick you pulled, summoning him out here as if he were a teenager and demanding to know his intentions, I shouldn't tell you a thing."

The sedate Reverend Judd Logan whooped for joy. "Cat Meade? You're in love with Cat Meade. I knew it. I just knew it," he exclaimed gleefully. "I told him you wouldn't dance like that with him if he wasn't special to you."

She gave him what she hoped was a withering look. "You were out of line, Grandpa."

She sat forward, amazed at the transformation in him. Humility. "Anything I've ever done, gal, was because I love you and want the best for you." She stared open-mouthed as he went on. "Cat Meade, huh? Now, *there's* a real man; not a bit like most of these young fellows today. He's strong, Naomi, and if he gives himself to you, he'll be there for you always. He'll never leave you."

She lowered her head to prevent his seeing her loss of composure. "Grandpa, that's the first time you ever said you love me; all these years, it's what I've wanted most to hear you say. I didn't know you did." She had to struggle to control her trembling voice. Maybe if he had showed her that he loved her, she wouldn't have needed so badly to find love with Chuck. Maybe...

"How could you not know, Naomi gal?" His voice was weak, suddenly old. "You were all I had. But after Hazel left me, my heart just sort of constricted. I loved her so; I still do. One reason why the thought of dying doesn't bother me is because I know she's waiting for me. I kept you away from me because I didn't want you to hurt so badly when I have to leave you, not the way I suffered when your grandma went." She saw a tear roll down his age-roughened face. "I loved her in a way that I've never had the words to express."

She walked over to him and hugged him tightly to her. "I wish I could know a love like that, but I don't hope for it, Grandpa. I'm carrying too much baggage."

He wiped his eyes. "Now, gal, I've taught you not to be negative; think on the good side. You'll find it, and you'll find it with Cat Meade. I've been watching people for almost a hundred years, and I watched him; he's a good man. And he cares for you, or he wouldn't have come out here when I asked him to. I'd die real happy, gal, if I could leave you with him."

Naomi felt a warmth that she hadn't known before and wondered if her son was seeking what she had just been given— the gift of parental love. "Grandpa, I hope you're with me in this, but if you aren't, I'll have to go it alone. And I'm not doing this for Rufus; I'm doing it for myself."

He nodded slowly. "All right, I'll call my lawyer and get the information you need."

Naomi drove into the garage beneath her condominium building, turned off the motor, and sat there. On the way home, she had tried to take her mind off the changes in her life during the preceding twenty-four hours. Now, her mind and heart were flooded. She thought of Rufus, the all-consuming power and passion with which he'd made love to her, and the unbelievable joy she'd known in his arms. She shivered when her mind focused on their parting and the chasm that she'd had no choice but to put between them. She thought of her grandfather's loneliness, of the forty years during which he'd silently and stoically mourned the loss of such a powerful love, and she rejoiced in the healing knowledge that he deeply loved her, his only grandchild. It gave her a measure of peace that she couldn't deny, in spite of her emotional turmoil about her son. About Rufus.

She opened her apartment door to hear Jewel's voice on her answering machine. Preston had fallen down the basement steps and injured himself and Rufus was with him at Children's Hospital. Sheldon was with Jewel.

Naomi didn't question the rightness of it; she went immediately to the hospital and found Rufus in the waiting room, his long legs spread out in front of him and his forearms resting on his thighs. His surprise was obvious, and she could see that he tempered his pleasure at her having come to him.

"I'm rather surprised to see you. I suppose Jewel called you." He didn't want her to think that he had asked his sister to notify her, and she understood his message.

"Do you have any news?" He moved over so that she could sit beside him on the leather sofa.

"Nothing yet, but I suspect he might have dislocated his shoulder; he was in terrible pain. It's the first time he's deliberately done what I told him not to do. Both of them seemed to resent my working this morning. I know it's because I've been away so much recently, only three days between my New Orleans and West African trips. I shouldn't have taken that assignment." He dropped his head into his hands.

She put a hand lightly on his arm. "You couldn't have guessed what he would do, so don't blame yourself." She soothed him before quickly changing the subject. "You didn't tell me whether you were satisfied with your trip."

No, he thought. I fell head over heels in love with you and couldn't think of anything but you and how much I wanted you. Aloud he said, "I didn't bring back the story that I went for. The real story isn't the children in the street, though there certainly are some. I got a different story, one that my eyes wouldn't let me leave without, and I checked it with short trips to three adjacent countries. Poverty, armed conflict, disease, and drought are at the bottom of just about everything that happens over there, including the problem of street children. And that's my story. I got it in personal interviews with real people about the problems in their daily lives. I feel real good about it."

"I know it may not mean anything to you," she told him, "but I'm so proud of you."

Rufus looked down at her, his mouth twisted in disbelief, almost angry. "Why shouldn't it mean something to me?" he asked scornfully. "Do you think I made love to you without caring what you think of me?" He noticed the look of horror on her face and told himself to calm down. "Thanks." It was grudgingly offered. "My publisher is making it the lead article, but he wants it next week, and I'm not going to abandon Preston for the sake of it."

"Are you going back to investigative journalism?" she asked, giving herself time to think.

Rufus sighed deeply, indicating his impatience with the question. "Naomi, Preston almost broke his neck with me right there in the house. I'm not leaving them again until they're old enough to play college basketball."

"Go ahead and write your story. I'll stay with them while you work."

He couldn't keep the bitterness out of his voice. "Are you sure you can handle being around me for any amount of time? I work all hours, night and day." Rufus regarded her intently, pushing back the rising desire. He had made soul-shattering love with her, the most electrifying experience of his life, but he didn't know her. He watched her squirm uncomfortably under his blatant scrutiny.

"Do you want me to leave?"

He didn't spare her. "When I wanted you to stay, you wouldn't. And I wanted it badly. Now, you may suit yourself. If you stay, stay for Preston, because if you stay for me, be prepared to explain yourself. By that, I mean, lay all your cards on the table."

She rose to leave, and he would have let her if he hadn't glimpsed again that grim, desolate look in her eyes, the same look she'd had the night before, when she'd left his house. He couldn't bear to see her in pain; she was his first love, his only love, and his only thought then was to comfort and protect her. He stood quickly and pulled her gently into his arms. When he looked around, seeking privacy for them, he saw none, so he just held her to him, stroking her back slowly, trying to soothe her.

"What is so awful and so powerful," he began softly, "that it rules your life? When we met, you were laughing at life. What's happened to make you so unhappy? I know that you care for me; why can't you open up to me?"

She shook her head slowly—in denial, he thought.

"Oh, yes. You care, and I know it. You were in my arms, and I was inside your body. Remember?" He didn't need her answer; the quickening of her body and her accelerated breathing were enough. He gazed down at her, cursing his powerful, uncontrollable response to her nearness.

"That's the whole point, isn't it?" he asked bitterly. "You either want to forget it or you've dismissed it. *Why are you here, Naomi?*"

She raised troubled eyes to his, but she laid her shoulders back in graceful dignity and told him, "I thought you might need me. That's all. If you do, just let me know and I'll be there."

The doctor came in at that moment and settled the matter. Preston had a dislocated shoulder, a mild concussion, and bruises on an arm and leg. He would have to remain still and absolutely quiet.

Naomi's eyes pleaded with Rufus. "Let me help. Let me be with him while you work; I need to be with him, Rufus." He was torn between his need to protect her, comfort her, and bind her to him and his fear that his children would become more deeply attached to her. She was asking him to let her care for his son; he could not have denied her anything.

Naomi tried to make herself invisible to Rufus, spending her time with Preston and Sheldon. She had taken the guest bedroom, explaining to Rufus that unless and until she was able to sort out some personal problems they should avoid intimacies. He had accepted it, because it was what he felt, but both of them suffered and were unable to hide it.

Rufus finished the article at about ten-thirty one night and couldn't resist sharing his excitement with Naomi. He brought it to her in the living room, where she sat illustrating a story for the boys.

"It's finished, all printed out and ready to go."

Still holding her brushes, she glanced up at him, taking in the lines of exhaustion in his haggard face. "What's finished?" Her heart was in her throat. Did this mean she had to leave? That she had to put the four glorious, idyllic days behind her and tackle the most difficult situation she would probably ever face?

"My story—I'd like you to read it." She put aside the illustrations, took the story from him, and began to read. By the time she finished, her face was bathed in warm tears; tears for the subjects of his interviews, for the magnitude of the problems that the people faced, and tears of joy for Rufus.

"It is a masterpiece," she whispered in awe. "I never imagined that your writing was so forceful, so powerful. I feel as if I know

those people, as if I've been a part of their lives. It's wonderful."
She walked over to him.

"Congratulations!" Her hand delicately grazed his cheek, and
she reached up and kissed him fleetingly. But he must have been
hungry, for the moment she touched him, he became full aroused
and brought her to him. His man's scent, the feel of him, sent
tremors through her, and her eyes glazed over as desire gripped
her. The devil with her good intentions; he was hers to take, and
she meant to have him. Right there. Right then. And as if to make
certain that she didn't change her mind, she made the most
brazen gesture of her life, found him, and with exquisite,
dazzling efficiency let him know that she remembered well what
he had taught her only a week earlier. He uttered a tortured
groan, the cry of a wounded animal, clamped his open mouth
upon her parted lips, and surrendered to his passion.

Rufus gripped her tightly as she moved against him, but he
wouldn't be rushed; gently and tenderly, he cherished her, wor-
shipping her with sweet, fleeting kisses. She squeezed him to
her, silently asking for more, but he refused to let the demands
of his throbbing desire override his love for her.

"Noomie! Noomie, Preston is crying," Sheldon called from
upstairs. She froze, and within seconds, was racing up the stairs.

He stood where she'd left him, immobilized in the helpless
clutch of passion. His first thought was that if she'd wanted him
as badly as she'd pretended, she couldn't have forgotten him in
a second. Then he grimaced in self-disgust. Get a grip on
yourself, man, he told himself, she responded the way you
should have. She wanted him, all right, he acknowledged, and
there was no better evidence of her feelings for his boys than the
fact that she placed their needs above her own, above his.

He got down on his haunches, took a few deep breaths to get
his passion under control, and raced up the stairs.

"What happened?"

"Preston rolled over on his shoulder," she told Rufus, still
holding the boy, soothing him. Sheldon stood by with his little
hand on her thigh, anxiously watching Preston.

"Is he going to be okay, Noomie?" She hugged the child and gave him the answer that he needed.

Rufus had remained in the doorway, watching Naomi love his sons. It occurred to him that Sheldon hadn't called him, but Naomi, and suddenly he knew what he wanted, and he also knew that he stood a very real chance of never getting it. He swore softly. Why can't she let me love her, protect her? he wondered. Even if she's committed murder, even if she's a fugitive, there would have to be good reasons. Can't she see that I'm here for her? She sang both boys to sleep and then went into the guestroom and began to pack.

She had been in his home for four days and nights and had scrupulously avoided any intimacy with him until he'd gone to her with his finished article. He knew he could write, but her reverential tone when she appraised his work had heightened his sense of self, had been balm for his ego. She'd sat there reading his article, swinging her foot and alternately frowning, shaking her head and finally crying. Knowing that he'd moved her so deeply made him feel invincible, all-powerful.

"Leaving? Tonight?"

She looked at him and smiled weakly. "You don't need me anymore, so I'd better catch up on things at home."

Rufus paced the room, fingering the evening stubble on his cheeks. He stopped and watched her. "I won't argue with the last part of that sentence, but the first part is open to question." He considered what good reasons she might have for rushing off. "How did your client like the logo you designed for their new perfume line?"

"I didn't finish it," she said, barely loudly enough to be heard.

"But you had a deadline, didn't you?" Then he realized what she'd done. "You gave up that lucrative contract to...?" She turned away from him and continued packing.

With the swiftness that had made him king of NFL wide receivers for five straight years, he was beside her. "Naomi, look at me. *Look at me!*" She shivered as he carefully forced her chin up, wanting to make her see in his eyes the overwhelming need he felt to hold her, to love her.

Naomi didn't expect love from Rufus and didn't see it brimming in his eyes. She grabbed her coat and bag.

"Let's be in touch." She avoided his eyes and walked toward the stairs. He caught her and loped down with her.

"The boys will want to see you Christmas; I hope you'll be able to make time for them." What about you? her heart screamed.

"I want to see them, too. If it's all right, I'll come over for a while." She had to get out of there. Away from the stilted conversation that had no place between lovers; away from the man who possessed her heart and from whom she never wanted to be separated. She turned toward the door.

"Naomi, don't leave like this. Half an hour ago, you were making love to me; in seconds, we'd have been on that carpet."

No. She couldn't leave him again without an explanation—something. "I know. Rufus, please. Someday you'll understand. It isn't you; it's me, and I'm trying not to do any more damage than I already have. When I know where I'm going, I'll tell you whatever you want to know. Everything."

He looked off, stuck his hands in his pockets, and gave his expensive Persian carpet a good kick. "Just tell me this. Is there a man involved?"

She hesitated for a second; technically, there was a male involved. "No. There's no man. I couldn't have made love with you if there had been."

He relaxed visibly. "That's what I thought. All right. I'll try to be patient, but I can't stay in limbo indefinitely, so do whatever it is you have to do. And thanks, Naomi. Your being here these days has meant everything to me."

She got home and looked at her watch. Too late to call her grandfather, so she'd have to wait until morning. She took a shower and prepared for bed, feeling even lonelier than when she'd been passing time in that clinic. She slept fitfully, awakened early, and phoned Judd. Resigned, he gave her what she wanted, and at eight o'clock precisely, she telephoned Rosalie Hopkins.

# Chapter 13

Naomi's hand hung heavily over the phone. If she took that step, she could never undo it. She couldn't banish her anxiety, the certainty that she was shadow-boxing with fate, and she withdrew her hand. Her mind wandered back to those moments out of time when Rufus lay above her, completely vulnerable to her, the light in his eyes telling her that she was precious to him. No, she shouldn't focus on that; she'd heard that you couldn't rely on what men said and did in the heat of passion. But she couldn't forget how Preston and Sheldon had tugged at her hands and clothes, kissing and hugging her at will, behaving as though they owned her. And she remembered the tears in her grandfather's old eyes when he spoke so touchingly of his beloved Hazel and his abiding love for her after forty years.

Could she have that with Rufus? Not unless she took this first step—and maybe never. With or without him, she had to know her son. For half her life, she had let fear control her, cause her to pass up the pleasures that belonged only to the young, make her brittle when it was against her nature. Not anymore. Somewhere she had read, "It is better to light a candle than to curse the darkness." She squared her shoulders, punched the numbers, and waited.

"Hopkins residence, Rosalie Hopkins speaking." Naomi shuddered, feeling as though the bottom had dropped out of her stomach.

"This is Naomi Logan. I understand you've been trying to reach me. Mind if I ask why?" The woman's gratitude for having received the call was unmistakable.

"Miss Logan," Rosalie Hopkins began, "my son has become adamant about meeting his birth parents. He's a good boy, but he's become so obsessed with it that it's affected his behavior at home, his school grades, even his interest in school. So I decided to take a chance before it's too late and I lose him to the streets."

The woman's perfectly natural reference to the boy as her son cut Naomi to the quick, but she fought off the pain. "Where is your husband, Mrs. Hopkins?" The woman told her that she was a widow, but that her son's identity crisis hadn't begun until one of his classmates, who was also adopted, had met his biological father and seen himself in the man. Father and son had since become very close.

"So my Aaron got the idea that he was missing something, and he can't seem to think of anything else."

Naomi didn't know what she'd expected, but it wasn't this. She sucked in her breath; it was no longer a matter of "the boy" or "the child"; her son had a name—Aaron. She wanted to repeat it until it became a part of her. She brought her mind back to the conversation.

"Mrs. Hopkins, I'm sure your private investigator told you about Aaron's father."

"Please call me Rosalie. Yes, he did. I'm sorry, Naomi; that must have been terrible for you. After we found out, Aaron was more anxious than ever to see you. I want you to know that if for any reason you don't want to meet us, I'll just drop it, because I don't want to interfere with your life. But our PI said you weren't married, so I thought I'd try."

At noon the next day, Naomi sat at a corner table in a restaurant near her studio, waiting for Rosalie Hopkins. Her sudden desire to get on with the meeting was in sharp contrast to the feelings of dread and fear that had dogged her earlier. She'd gained courage and strength from her determination to swallow whatever medicine she got without complaining. She was going to see her son, and that was worth whatever price she had to pay, even the price of losing Rufus. Her heart pounded furiously when she thought of him. She had promised to tell him the truth, and she would, no matter the cost; he deserved to hear it.

She liked the woman on sight. About forty, she surmised, intelligent and friendly. She learned that her son's adoptive mother worked as a head operating-room nurse and that before she'd been widowed, she'd had a happy marriage. To Naomi's surprise and barely suppressed terror, Rosalie suggested she bring Aaron to meet Naomi Sunday afternoon. Two days. Just two short days.

Naomi viewed her apparent calm as a new kind of hysteria. It started Sunday morning, when she began a minute-by-minute countdown while she waited for them. Fourteen years of consternation: concern about exposure and social censure; apprehension at getting close to a man who liked her or who she might have liked; and once she learned of the possibility of meeting her son, worry about her future relationship with him. Now she would see him, but she was afraid he would hate her.

Tentacles of painful uneasiness flashed throughout her body as the sharp, staccato peals of the doorbell startled and unnerved her. Calm down, girl, she warned herself, as she walked unsteadily to the door, rested her hand on the knob, uttered a prayer, and made herself open it. A powerful surge of happiness rocked her and her heart raced in her chest when she looked into her son's face for the first time. He was tall and handsome, and except for his light complexion, his features proclaimed his Logan genes. She saw in him her large, wide-set brown eyes, thick, curly hair, beautifully shaped mouth, and strong chin. Nearly breathless with emotion, she grasped the door for support and summoned her natural calm as an indescribable joy threatened to overwhelm her.

Rosalie spoke first. "Naomi, this is Aaron." Naomi didn't move her gaze from her son's face; when she opened her mouth to speak, no words came. Rosalie stepped forward, ushering them into the apartment, draped her arm around Aaron's waist, and gave him a light nudge. But he made no outward response, merely gazed at the woman who'd given him birth.

"I think it would be best if I left the two of you alone," Rosalie said, and stepped around to Aaron's side. "Remember what I told you. This is what you wanted, but if you find you've made a mistake, you'll still have learned something. I'll be at home, so call me if you need me." He nodded without taking his gaze from Naomi. Rosalie inclined her head to Naomi, her expression one of sympathy. "I don't know how to thank you, Naomi. We'll be in touch." Naomi looked toward Rosalie as she walked out and closed the door. She struggled to control the wild skittering of her nerves now that she was alone with her son.

Aaron began to fidget, and she realized that her reaction to seeing him had made him uneasy. Her struggle to smile was rewarded when he seemed to relax and tossed off a nod of his head.

"I'm glad you're here, Aaron." Somehow, a simple hello was too banal greeting, too far removed from her fierce urge to wrap him in her arms, to hold him to her heart. To lay claim to her right as his mother. But she had no right. She fell back on the control that she had drilled into herself for fourteen years. He walked in and looked around with pretended casualness. He was neither hostile nor friendly, she decided, just a nervous adolescent who was facing a major crisis and feigning nonchalance. What an actor, she thought, mildly amused.

He glanced slowly around, seeming to take in everything. Then he stopped and looked at her as if seeing her for the first time. They silently appraised each other.

"So how's everything?" It was a stunt she might have pulled at about his age. But she was going to start their relationship right. She was the adult, and she knew that no matter how tempting it might be to court his goodwill, she had to set the tone of their relationship. She felt older than her years, but she strove to reply in a motherly manner.

"Not so good, Aaron. Not with me and not with you. So I'll get us a couple of sodas, and we'll sit down and talk. I'm going to answer any question that you have about me, no matter how badly it hurts, and I hope you're prepared to do the same.

"Why should it hurt?" She was surprised that his voice had already changed. Somehow, it made talking with him more difficult; almost as if she was dealing with a man rather than a child.

She stared at him in amazement; he had a lot of chutzpa, but so did she. "Is that a serious question, or are you being fresh?"

Aaron cocked his head to one side, looked hard at the woman who'd given him birth, and must have decided to back down. She was slightly unnerved by his laconic reply.

"Fresh. Where do you want to sit?" She decided that it was best to be informal and told him to walk with her to the kitchen. Walking ahead of him, she wondered why she wasn't nervous. He pulled out two kitchen chairs, plopped down in one, and put his feet, legs crossed, in the other.

Naomi recognized the challenge. Her work at OLC had prepared her for any stunt a teenager could conceive of. She walked over and placed a hand lightly on his shoulder, tempering discipline with tenderness.

"Your feet belong on the floor, Aaron. Which one of us is going to put them there?" he put them on the floor and looked up at her to see what effect he'd gotten. Satisfied that she was unimpressed, he apologized. She gave him a Coke and got a ginger ale for herself.

"Got any ice-cream?"

She smiled, remembering her first meeting with Preston and Sheldon. "Vanilla. Would you like some?"

"Could you put it in a big glass? I'd like to make a shake with it." Spiraling warmth seeped through her, commencing a process of healing that had long been denied her. Even that little piece of information about him was precious. He finished it quickly, and she made another one in the blender and, to his delight, topped it with a slice of candied ginger.

When were they going to get down to business? She was afraid to ask why he wanted to meet her; after all, it was natural that he would. She was considering her next move when the telephone rang.

"He's right here," she told her grandfather, for once, thankful for his interference. "Maybe he'd like to speak with you. I'll ask him."

Aaron was beside her before she could ask him. "Who is it? Who do I want to speak with?"

She took a deep breath, looked steadily into eyes that were identical to hers, and told him, "Your great-grandfather."

His mouth hung open and his eyes became enormous in an astonishingly close resemblance to her father when he had been surprised. "My *what?*" She repeated it.

"That's your grandfather?" She nodded.

"How old is he?" She told him that Judd would be ninety-five within a few weeks.

"Well, I'll be…" He caught himself and reached for the phone, still wearing a stunned expression on his youthful, handsome face. She didn't know whether to laugh or cry.

"Hi ya, Gramps. Where? Alexandria? Come on! That's across the world, man." A long pause ensued.

"Uh…" He frowned, as though displeased. "Uh…no, sir. Sorry, sir. I'll ask her, sir. Me, too. Goodbye, sir." She didn't need to have heard the other side of the conversation; Judd was Judd, and Aaron had needed exactly what his great-grandfather had given him—a good verbal spanking.

Aaron hung up and looked anxiously at Naomi. "Guess I blew that, didn't I? He's strict, huh?" She risked laying a hand on his shoulder and her heart fluttered with joy as she realized he didn't mind if she touched him.

"He was strict with me, too," she explained, "but he loves me. He raised me from the time I was seven so for most of my life, there's only been Grandpa and me."

Aaron digested her words—thoroughly, it seemed—and Naomi began to realize that he wasn't as frivolous as he had at first appeared, though he certainly had her talent for flippancy.

"You didn't have any brothers or sisters?" She shook her head. "You got any other children?" She closed her eyes briefly in a prayer of thanks: he had acknowledged that he was her child. Again, she shook her head.

"So how come you're not married? You're real pretty."

Naomi took her son by the hand and walked toward the living room, where she could face him while she spoke. She needed to know his reaction to her every word. But Aaron must have sensed that he was about to hear what he came for, because he began to drag his feet, walking almost as if she was pulling him. And in a sense, she was. She was pulling them both, because they were both scared. He backed up.

"Where are you going?"

"I forgot my shake."

Naomi took his hand, hurting for him and for herself; she had to pay the piper, and this young boy had to deal with the secrets he had unsealed and the painful wounds he'd opened.

"You've already finished your soda. Come on. I know this won't be easy for either of us. Sit down, Aaron." He sat across from her, dropped his head for a moment, and when he raised it, his eyes blazed with defiance. The intensity of his emotion stunned her and she stared, riveted by his hostility, and the honesty with which he expressed it. She admired him for it.

"Okay, why aren't you married?"

What on earth was he thinking? "I loved your father, Aaron," she told him, earning his smile and relieving the tension. She related truthfully what had happened, careful not to turn him against Judd.

"I haven't married," she want on, "because I didn't believe that a man would understand and accept what I've just told you, so I discouraged men who liked me and avoided a man if I began to like him until…"

"Until what?" He leaned forward, eyes narrowed, as if waiting to pounce.

"We'll get to that later. Right now, I have to finish this." She told him what her life had been like from the time she knew she'd conceived him. "A little over two months ago," she explained, "I learned that you wanted to find your birth parents. Until then, I hadn't known whether I'd had a girl or a boy. I hadn't been allowed to see my baby, because the counselors at the clinic believed that if I bonded with you, I wouldn't give you up. I wasn't even awake during the birth. I didn't want the adoption, but I couldn't hold out against their logic that it was best for the baby.

"About the time I learned that Rosalie was looking for me, I met a man who slipped through the wall I'd built around me, even as this news about you tore me into shreds." She told him of wanting to see him; to get to know him; to learn whether he was loved, well cared for, and happy; and of her certainty that the man with whom she was falling in love—the first to touch her in fourteen years—would not accept her having given a child up for adoption.

She flinched at the scorn in his voice when he interrupted her. "But you just said you didn't want to give me up for adoption."

"And I didn't. But how could I prove it to him? Besides, my friend suffered personally from parental inattentiveness, and so have his little twin sons. He's bitter about parents who don't take care of their children."

Aaron leaned back against the sofa, obviously drinking in her every word and gesture. "Is he in love with you?"

"I don't know," she confessed painfully. "I know he cares, but he hasn't said he loves me." The low quiver in her voice betrayed her growing distress, and she struggled to control it.

The boy's ability to wait patiently for her words, to sit quietly and think, to mull over what she'd said before responding, unnerved her. How was it possible that he had her personality when he had lived for over thirteen years without ever having seen her? The eerie quality of it made her shudder.

He rested his left elbow on the back of the sofa, propped the back of his head up with his hand, and told her sympathetically, "Looks to me like you should just tell him. If he can't handle it, find yourself a guy who can." He could have been speaking to a child. "Do you like his kids?" She nodded.

The diffidence was gone, along with his nervousness. She knew with certainty then that he was old beyond his years, and as he sat there coolly sizing her up, she felt pride in him, pride tinged with a little gnawing fear. Was he capable of harsh revenge?

Aaron crossed his right knee and began swinging his foot. "You planning to tell him about me, or you just going to chicken out and pretend that me and him don't exist?" This child had a man's mind, Naomi realized, and tried to imagine the kind of life he'd had. It didn't seem as though he'd spent much of it being a child.

"I promised him that he and I would have a frank talk, and I keep my promises." Had she gotten through to him, made him understand the circumstances of his birth well enough to forgive her and at least like her?

He didn't keep her in suspense. "I listened to what you said, but I can't buy it. You didn't say anybody forced you to have me adopted, so you agreed to it—right?"

"You have to believe me. I've told you things that no one else, not even Grandpa, know, because it's important to me for you to understand that I wouldn't have given you up if even one person at that clinic had supported my wanting to keep you. Everyone was against it, and my grandpa refused to interfere. Can you imagine how I feel when I think that I missed your first steps, first words, first day in school? I don't know whether you had all your shots, if your teeth are strong and healthy, if you're left-handed or right-handed..." Her tears began to flow in torrents, cascading down her face and onto her dress.

He jerked up and dashed over to her. "I'm left-handed. Please, don't cry. For God's sake, stop it! Look, I didn't mean to upset you." She tried to calm herself but couldn't; instead, her sobbing intensified. Aaron responded as if he'd never seen anyone hurt so badly. Clearly shaken to the core, he flopped down on the arm of her chair, pulled her into his young arms, and held her until she became quiet.

After a time, he stood. "I'd better call my mom."

She reached behind her, got a portable phone, and handed it to him. They had been together for little more than an hour, but in that time, her world had changed. Her son had put his arms around her, commiserated with her, tried to soothe her. It was sweet. And it had the bitterness of gall. She would love Rufus forever but she would never regret having made her choice— putting him out of her life and reaching out to her son. The seeds of love for her child had germinated within her heart and taken root. She would no sooner disown his existence or trade him for another love than she would sever her hands from her arms. She closed her eyes and leaned back.

"She's having a hard time of it," Naomi heard Aaron tell Rosalie Hopkins. "I think I'll stick around till she gets her act together. Yah, she *is* nice." Slowly placing the phone in its cradle, seemingly deep in thought, he looked warily at Naomi.

"You got anything here to eat? My mom says I eat her out of house and home. Say…" He paused for a long while, contemplating his next words, she thought, sensing his mood change. "What do you want me to call you?"

There was one name he would never call her, so it didn't matter. "Whatever you like." But she realized from that question that he wasn't planning to make it a one-time visit and breathed more easily.

He joined her in the kitchen, and she fought to cope with the intense emotion that swirled within her, first catapulting her into euphoria and then jerking her back to humbling reality. He could decide that having seen her was all he wanted, or…please, God, she didn't want to be just a curiosity to him. She quickly banished the idea and concentrated on the joy of cooking for her child.

She fried a chicken, baked some sweet potatoes in the microwave, warmed up leftover collard greens and buttermilk biscuits, and had a mid-afternoon meal with her son. He no longer seemed nervous or anxious, and she was grateful that he didn't appear to be censorious. She knew that the acute pain he'd witnessed in her had softened him, forcing him to empathize with her. But she needed his acceptance, not his pity and not the barrier that he had erected between them. It was like a thin veil, but it was there.

"Hey, uh…this is good stuff. My mom can't cook worth a…she can't cook." He put his fork down and looked at her, his eyes piercing in their intensity. "You don't cook like this just for you. Does that guy live here with you?" Before she could reply, he answered his question. "I guess he doesn't if he's got two little kids. How old are they?" She told him.

"What do they call you?"

"Noomie. It's easier for them to pronounce."

He bit into a chicken leg, savored it, finished chewing his mouthful, and said, "Noomie, huh? I like that. Think that's what I'll call you. So where'd you go to school, Noomie?" She wondered if her heart would burst.

"Howard University and Columbia University," she told him, pleased that he was interested. She couldn't imagine why he was astonished to learn that she had studied fine art and was an artist.

"I can't believe this; that's what I'm planning to study. I guess I got that from you, huh? Did you do all this stuff here and in the living room?" She showed him the paintings that were hers and learned that he played the guitar and sang in the boys' choir at school, and that painting and drawing were his special hobbies.

He thanked her for the meal and stood to leave, but she needed something else; she had to know what he thought of her, how he felt about her. Maybe it was unfair to ask him after one short visit, but the ache that permeated her body, the dread in her heart, overrode logical thought. She walked on unsteady legs to the door with him, paused before opening it, and saw at once that she'd made him edgy. I won't back down now, she told herself, squarely facing his searching look.

"Aaron, do you think you can tell me where I stand with you?" She learned then that he was blunt and honest.

"I think we can get on, but the rest...well, I don't know. I'm still not sure about that part where you were pressured into giving me up."

She reached deep into herself for the composure that she needed. Had any woman ever had such a conversation with a child to whom she had given birth?

"I don't have any proof, Aaron, so whether you believe me will depend on your faith in me." After an awkward moment, she succumbed to her deep yearning, pulled him into her arms, hugged him, and released him. She smiled at the cocky thumbs-up sign he gave her as he left her standing in the doorway watching him walk to the elevator. He hadn't believed what she needed most to have him accept, and it hadn't even occurred to her that he would find that terrible truth implausible. Pain stabbed her chest; he had barely tolerated her hug.

"Oh, Rufus," she moaned softly, "I need you. If you only knew how I need you." She closed the door, changed into an old jogging suit, and began to clean her apartment. It didn't help; if Aaron didn't believe her, neither would Rufus. What could she tell him? Maybe she shouldn't tell him anything. But he had said that no matter what troubled her, they would work through it together. Maybe he believed; she was less sure.

# Chapter 14

How could she have held her son in her arms the night before and yet look no different this morning? She moved away from the mirror and dressed hurriedly, anxious to get into the Christmas spirit. She hadn't worn a cap in the shower, and her hair was frizzly and unmanageable. I don't care, she told herself, as she tied it back with a small silk scarf, I'm going to be happy, and I'm not going to worry about my hair or Aaron or Rufus.

But as soon as she got caught up in the crowd of shoppers, she had an overwhelming desire to talk with someone with whom she could open up and tell all—the things that hurt her and the joy that flowed inside of her. Rufus. She needed him desperately. If screaming would have brought him to her right then, she'd have stood there in the middle of F Street and done exactly that.

In the fourteen years since that fateful day when she'd grown up summarily, her studies, her work, and the music that she loved had been her companions. Not even Marva had been her confidant. Today, she was unaccountably, woefully lonely. The city wasn't a place for a person alone. But was any place? She finally brought presents for Judd and Marva, as usual, found a child's guitar for each of the twins, and got an old-fashioned gold-plated fountain pen for Rufus. She ruminated about buying a gift for Aaron, uncertain as to how such a gesture from her would be accepted, and realized that that was the source of her forlorn mood. She didn't even know what her child would enjoy. Refusing to indulge further in self-pity, she called Rosalie for advice.

"Do you mind if I give Aaron a small Christmas present?" Rosalie didn't.

"I think that's a wonderful idea, and I suspect Aaron would be disappointed if he didn't get something from you." There was a pause. "Thank you for asking me about it, Naomi," she said, and offered a few ideas. Naomi completed her shopping and rushed home to wrap the gifts. As she absently caressed her gift to Aaron, she considered the probable effect of changing her position on several amendments that the OLC board proposed to attach to the foundation's constitution. She couldn't continue to oppose boys' use of the foundation's services; she had a boy of her own.

She took her seat at the OLC monthly board meeting that evening with five minutes to spare and earned a reproving frown from Maude, who called it to order immediately as a reprimand.

Maude announced that she had invited Rufus Meade to join the board and asked for a vote. As Naomi expected, it was unanimous in his favor.

"Would someone go to my office and ask Mr. Meade to join us?" She looked directly at Naomi, who ignored her and left the task to another board member. Rufus walked into the room, took the seat that Maude had left vacant beside her, and looked around. The sensation that her heart had stopped beating flustered her. She was never prepared for the powerful aura of masculinity that enveloped him everywhere and all the time. Her face burned, and she wondered if everyone present could tell that she had been in his bed and that he had made love to her until she had practically flown out of her body in ecstasy. She caught her breath and pinned her gaze to the table, certain that she was giving herself away, but finally, unable to resist, she *had* to look at him.

She gasped audibly. Rufus's gaze was locked on her, soft, tender, scintillating, and she realized with a shock that he didn't care who knew what he was thinking and feeling. She glanced quickly at Maude, who fixed her eyes alternately on Naomi and Rufus. The rogue, Naomi thought, when she could collect her wits. He's doing this deliberately.

But Rufus wasn't playing a game; he didn't play about serious matters, and he had become serious about Naomi. Gone was his uncertainty. He no longer equivocated about what he wanted from her. He had fallen in love with her, and he knew it was forever. She could use whatever ruse she chose, but he was going to get her and he wouldn't be satisfied until she loved him as hopelessly as he loved her. It was the main reason why he'd suggested to Maude that he would be interested in joining OLC's board; it allowed him to see Naomi while he waited for her to keep her promise. He had known that Maude would be delighted and he meant to work hard for the foundation, but his purpose in being there was Naomi Logan and he didn't plan to let either her or himself forget that. He tuned out the boring drone of Maude's monotonous voice and toyed with the notion that maybe he could reach Naomi by mental telepathy.

"A leading national magazine wants to run a cover story on OLC," Maude said. "I realize that you have refused newspaper and television interviews, but this one is very important to us, Naomi. Would you consider it?" Naomi would, she advised the board. Rufus stopped wool gathering and put his mind on the meeting. So Naomi had made a practice of avoiding publicity; it hadn't just been the occasion when he'd substituted for her on local television.

"…And we have to admit boys into our programs," Judge Kitrell, the eldest board member, declared. "If we don't, we'll lose financial support of some of our most dependable donors. I think we ought to take a vote."

Rufus watched in stupefaction while Naomi let it pass without saying a word. He remembered the finesse with which she had successfully fought the move six weeks earlier. Something of immense importance had happened with Naomi, he decided, and reckoned that she didn't plan to tell him about it.

Oh, but I'll find out, he silently vowed.

He blocked her way as she was leaving the boardroom. "Tell me that you weren't planning to leave without speaking to me," he chided gently. Rufus knew it wasn't a fair statement; Naomi had spoken to him, but they had been in a circle with three other board members. He wanted a more personal greeting, and he didn't doubt that she understood as much.

"How are Preston and Sheldon? Has Preston's shoulder healed?" She knows I don't want an impersonal conversation any more than she does, he told himself, but she isn't ready for a serious discussion; maybe she never will be ready.

"Children's bodies heal rapidly, Naomi, but it takes their hearts and minds a bit longer." He stopped to make certain that his blow struck its mark. "Sheldon wants me to teach him how to use the telephone, and he wants your number. I'm going to give him the number and teach him how to use it. Then he can telephone you whenever he likes. If you object, take it up with Sheldon."

"The last time I saw Sheldon, he was four years old, not quite old enough to run his life. I presume that hasn't changed."

"Not to my knowledge. One thing has changed, though; instead of asking for you two or three times a day, your name is almost every other word, and they talk constantly. What are you planning to do about your little friends, Naomi?"

She stared at the faded green in the frayed Persian carpet that covered the hall floor and was reminded of the shoes that Rufus had bought her. Probably an impulsive, impersonal act, she thought irritably. Be fair, she admonished herself. He wouldn't do that or much else on impulse, and damming him wouldn't make her life more bearable. She looked up at him and her breath caught in her throat when she saw the bitterness etched in his face. Oh, God. She shouldn't have joked about Sheldon's age; now he would think that after allowing the boys to care for her, she was callously deserting them.

She paused beside her car, not wanting the evening to end without her having so much as held his hand, but she couldn't think of a way to bridge the chasm that separated them. "I'm still planning to see the boys Christmas day, if it's all right." She opened her car door.

"What's the hurry? It's only nine; let's go up to Louella's for a while. You drive; I'll follow you, but don't speed, Naomi." She wrinkled her nose at him flirtatiously.

Louella greeted them with what Naomi took to be an innuendo. "I'm glad to see you two still together." She glanced at Naomi. "Is he taking good care of you, honey?" Flustered, Naomi dropped her gaze. Apparently attuned to her, sensing her discomfort, Rufus put his arm around her in a protective gesture. Louella waddled off to get their drinks—ginger ale for Rufus and white wine for Naomi—and Rufus grinned wickedly and teased the woman encircled within his powerful arm.

"You're an open book, sweetheart. Lou wasn't saying what you were thinking, but believe me, by now you're both thinking the same thing. Baby, people cannot look at us and know what we've been doing."

"We aren't. I mean, there was just that one time, so you shouldn't put it that way." He was making her nervous. She did not want to be reminded of that night, what he had done to her, and how he had made her feel, but she *was* reminded of it, and when he slid his leg against hers beneath their table, she swooned. Rufus exposed his beautiful white teeth in a mesmerizing grin, forcing her to confess that he had achieved his goal.

Captivated, she tried to hide it with a frown. "All right! I know you're here, Rufus. Now, will you please get off of my case." He howled with laughter.

"Never, baby. Believe me, I mean never."

Louella brought their drinks and a cup of coffee for herself and took a seat opposite them.

"I enjoyed seeing your boys, Rufus. Bring them by again sometime soon, and I'll fill them full of ice-cream free of charge. How are they?" Naomi imagined that Louella could recall some interesting experiences with Preston and his passion for ice-cream.

"I think they're in mourning these days; apart from that, they're fine. Hellions, but fine."

"What or who are they mourning?" Louella inquired. Rufus

showed his teeth in what passed for a grin, but his glacier-like eyes told the two women that the grin was plastic and the little metaphor about his sons' mourning shouldn't be taken lightly. Intuitively, Naomi knew Louella would discern that she was the source of the hurt that Rufus made no attempt to hide.

Louella sipped her coffee and leaned back. "Would you mind explaining yourself, hon? You writers have a way of making things clear by saying something other than what you mean."

Naomi didn't expect him to pull punches. Louella was more mother than friend to him, and he wouldn't mislead her or lie to her. "Naomi taught my boys how to express themselves with crayons and pencils," he told Louella, while his gaze scorched the woman beside him. "Now, they've got my house littered with drawings of her, and each one shows her either walking away or hiding from them. At least, they tell me that's what they've drawn. They've used up three pads of drawing paper in the last two days, and every sheet is taped to the wall along my staircase. Another one of Naomi's ideas. If that isn't enough, every other word is 'Noomie.' Noomie this and Noomie that. Sheldon doesn't even want me to read to him at night; he wants his Noomie. It's sending me up the wall."

Naomi shifted uncomfortably. She knew Rufus felt this more deeply than his words suggested; that it wasn't something she would be able to explain away.

"Tell them that I'll spend Christmas Day with them." It was weak balm for a searing pain, and she knew it, but what else could she do? She had to affect conciliation with Aaron, and no matter how much she loved Rufus and the twins, Aaron had to have priority. He deserved it. And until she understood him, what he wanted from her, and how he felt about Rosalie, she would be there for him no matter what. It would be unfair to encourage the boys to become more deeply attached to her. And Rufus. Well, she would face that when she had to.

She glanced at Rufus and shivered from the tremors that his hot, desire-filled gaze sent snaking down her spine. He might be annoyed with her because the boys needed her and she wasn't there for them, but he wanted her. Not that that meant much; she knew that Rufus put his boys before himself, and that he wouldn't let his libido interfere with their welfare.

Louella intervened in the long silence that followed Naomi's weak recompense. "Use the phone, honey. Kids love to get phone calls. 'Course, you could solve that another way, but I'm not one to meddle in other people's personal affairs." She drained her coffee cup, patted Naomi's shoulder, and went back to her customers.

"Have they really been asking about me? I just left there four days ago. I didn't think…"

"Four days are like four years to a child that age. Don't you know that?" He waved a hand in dismissal. "This is my problem; I created it, and I have to deal with it." He checked the time. "Naomi, I've got to relieve the sitter. Her husband will be there for her by ten." She considered letting him leave without her and decided not to test his patience or his temper. They would still have plenty of time for a leisurely talk, if he didn't intend to trail her home.

He parked in front of her building, and she drove into her garage. Raw nerves unsettled her as she walked into her building with the gentle guidance of his hand at her back. He was quiet and unreadable, and her nerves scattered wildly when they reached her door and he opened his hand for her key.

"Rufus?" He took a step closer.

"Give me your key, Naomi." His woodsy cologne and masculine scent tantalized hers, and his heat surrounded her, weakening her and seducing her, drawing perspiration from the pores of her thighs. Dazed, she handed it to him. He unlocked the door, walked in with her already in his arms, kicked the door closed, and bent to her.

"I need to nourish my soul. Open your mouth for me."

"Rufus…" She couldn't give in to him. She wouldn't. There was too much as stake: for her son, his children, Rufus himself. He was her world, but she had to push that aside. "Rufus, please. I don't want this."

"No, you don't. That's why you're holding me as if your life depends on it. Kiss me. Open your mouth and kiss me. Sweet woman, I need you." She whimpered and gave him kiss for kiss, twirling her tongue around his. Frantic to have all of him, she took his tongue into her mouth and held it captive there, feasting on it. She protested when he stepped away, separating them. But his heated, feral gaze warned her that he'd had as much as he could take. Then, in a gesture that contradicted his untamed look, he caressed her porcelain-smooth cheek with the backs of his fingers. Lovingly. Possessively. "Is that what you want from me right now? Do you want to make love with me?"

She nodded. "But I can't. I promised myself that I wouldn't go any further with you until I...until I got some things straightened out."

He wiped perspiration from his forehead with the back of his hand, braced his back against the door, and stoked the fire in her as he stroked her shoulders and then pulled her toward him.

"You've already gotten some things straightened out, I think," he told her bluntly. "When are you planning to tell me about it?" What had to be a startled look in her eyes must have told him he had guessed correctly, and she attempted to take a step backward, but his powerful arms gently but firmly imprisoned her.

"When?" he persisted. What did he know, and how had he known it? she wondered. She was at a loss only briefly; the stakes were too high to allow herself to be sidetracked.

"When I have something to tell you, I will. You promised to wait patiently and I'm depending on you to keep that promise."

"I've been keeping it," he griped, "but we didn't discuss the duration of my patience, and believe me, it's petering out. Of course, you could say that's tough, but what about my boys? I know that you aren't their mother and that you aren't obligated to them in any way. This is what I wanted to avoid, but I didn't, and it's my fault, not yours, that they're hooked on you. No woman, not even their aunt Jewel, has ever given them the love that you have. They feel it, Naomi. And I feel it." She turned her face into his shoulder and groped for equilibrium.

"At tonight's board meeting, you did nothing to prevent boys' gaining access to OLC. I was present once when you defeated it single-handedly. Why did you change your position? And another thing. In the past, you've apparently refused all requests for interviews either from print journalists or video reporters. Now, all of a sudden, you don't mind. Maybe when I know the reason for these switches in concern, I'll know everything that I need to know. Right?" The word "right" was on the tip of her tongue, but her presence of mind saved her.

"I don't see anything so strange about it," she demurred. "If eleven members want boys in OLC, the one member opposed should accede. And as for that business about the interviews, I'm starting my New Year's resolution early."

Rufus pushed away from the door and put his hand on the knob, signaling his departure. "When you pass a mirror, try to avoid looking at it; you might get a shock."

"Whatever do you mean?" She knew precisely what he had in mind, but she wanted the satisfaction of forcing him to say it.

Rufus chuckled humorlessly. "I like your nose, Naomi; I'd hate to see it start growing. What time are you coming to my place Christmas Day? Try to make it early. My boys will be unmanageable until you get there."

She looked at his hand turning the doorknob and then glanced up at his deliberately expressionless face. He couldn't leave her; in the four days since she'd seen him, her world had spun out of control. Without his presence and support, she'd had to face one of the most challenging ordeals that could confront a woman. And she'd needed him so badly that the pain of his absence had seemed physical. Need propelled her to him, and she reached up and pulled his mouth down to hers. She plowed into him, heedless of her vow to stay away, guaranteeing that it was he who was seduced. She chucked her inhibitions and made love to him as if she knew it would be the last time. Her soft hands held his face, and she kissed him until they were both breathless, until she was limp and he was strong and hard against her.

He didn't seek compliance; her traitorous body gave him his

answer. He picked her up, carried her into her bedroom, and in a minute's time, had her clothes off and was stripping himself. She lifted her arms to him in invitation, impatient for him to join her, to unite them. But he coaxed, teased and tantalized her until she begged him for relief.

"Rufus, please…"

"Don't call me 'Rufus' when I'm with you like this; I want to hear something sweet and loving." Tremors shook her as he bent to her breast and toyed with her sensitive nipple until she lay helplessly open to his ministrations.

"Please, I…"

"Please, who?" he demanded, dropping his hand to the inside of her thigh and dragging his fingers slowly upward, mercilessly, until she writhed beneath him in frantic anticipation.

"Please, love…" It erupted from her like lava from a volcano as his devilish fingers found their mark.

Later, when they lay sated, holding each other, her stillness told him she was already searching for words of denial. She attempted to move out of his arm, but anticipating her action, he pulled her back to him, nudged her neck, and bent over her. He wanted a clear view of her expressive eyes.

"Don't tell me your sorry, Naomi, and that you didn't mean for this to happen. I don't want to hear it. We needed this; we needed each other. And it ought to tell you something. There is nothing commonplace about what we feel for each other, and it isn't going to go away." If he had been wearing his thinking cap and hadn't let his heart rule him, he'd have taken her to bed four nights ago, when she'd packed her things and left his house. But he loved her, and because he couldn't bear to be the source of her discomfort, even indirectly, he had allowed her to call the shots.

"It isn't going away because you have decreed otherwise," she replied. "When we first met, you didn't want anything to do with me; in fact…boy, this is funny. The merest suggestion of intimacy between us and both of us swore that we didn't want it; we were practically insulting to each other. Me, I was hoodwinked. What happened to you? Did you follow my suggestion and get help?"

She had resorted to humor. Desperate humor, he decided. And why? Minutes earlier, locked in his arms, she had been as honest as a woman could be. Another one of her screens. Irrefutable evidence that he had gotten too close. Well, he wasn't going to make it easy for her.

"Naomi, I had begun to think that you'd given up that sly trick of using wit and sarcasm to cover your true feelings. Don't you dare trivialize what we just experienced. I suppose you figure that if you knock it down, it won't mean so much to you. Well, don't believe it." He pulled her body tightly up to his, letting her feel the need that surged in him. And he gloated with pure masculine pride when he felt the heat rise in her as he rotated his hips and she rocked beneath him, silently demanding his penetration.

"It means more to me than you could ever imagine, but it shouldn't have happened, Rufus. I told you when we were in New Orleans that I don't have anything to offer."

"And I told *you* that you *do* have something to offer me, and that I want it. I was prepared to leave here tonight. Why didn't you let me go? You knew what would happen if you so much as put your hand on me, and you went far beyond that. Why did you keep me here?" She squirmed beneath him, but he didn't ease up. He had too much riding on her acceptance of what for him was a forgone conclusion: she was his. He would do whatever he had to in order to make her acquiesce. He sensed her nervousness and knew it was because she didn't want to share her secrets with him, but he'd get those, too, he swore to himself. His pulse quickened as he gazed down at her.

"Why?" he persisted.

"I didn't think about it. I didn't weight the pros and cons. You needed me; you told me so, and I could feel it myself. It was powerful, like some kind of opiate." He sucked in his breath and let his gaze travel over her, seductively, possessively, until she sighed deeply and buried her face in his shoulder.

"I needed you, too, and something in me just reached out to

you," she mumbled. "I had no control over it. I just couldn't bear to see you leave like that, and I needed you to stay. Am I making myself clear? It was both." It was clear to him, but he wondered if she understood it. It was time he let her know the man in whose arms she snuggled.

"Why, Naomi?" He held her close, feathering kisses over her face, neck, and shoulders. Maybe he wasn't giving her a fair chance, but he didn't really give a damn about fairness right then. He needed to know where he stood with her; his future and that of his children were bound up with her.

"Why, baby?" he persisted, in a voice that he intended to sound sultry and seductive, running his tongue around the rim of her ear and nibbling on her shoulder. "Come on. Tell me. Why can't you bear to see me hurt?" He put an arm around her shoulders and a hand under her buttocks, parted her legs with his knee, and let her feel the hard power of him poised at her portal of love, just out of reach.

"Rufus, I…"

"Didn't I ask you not to call me 'Rufus' when I'm with you like this? Didn't I? Now, tell me why you need me and why you couldn't deny me. Baby, open up to me." He hoped that by now, her senses were full of him. If not, I'll give her more, he vowed silently, as he felt her tremble with excitement and frustration from the feel of his warm, silken steel flesh so close, yet not a part of her. He teased and tantalized her until he felt her frantic movements signaling her desperation to feel the heat, passion, and protection of his male power. He was playing trump cards and didn't care if she knew it.

"Tell me why, baby."

"I…oh, honey, please. I can't bear it any more. I need you. Oh, God, Rufus, I love you so. I love you. *I love you!*" A shudder of relief escaped him as he entered her with a powerful surge of his body, cherishing her and loving her until their passion consumed them and left them spent.

A long while later, Rufus watched her steadily as he buttoned his shirt and secured his cufflinks. "Your mental wheels are busily turning again. Don't tell me you've found some more negative things to say about what's going on between us." His stance became aggressive, but he didn't allow his face to tell her anything.

"But, Rufus, nothing has changed."

He bent over her, grasped both her shoulders, and looked intently into her eyes. "Really, Ms. Logan? You told me that you love me, and, baby, you told very convincingly. I already knew it, but I had to make certain that you did. Now, as soon as you can trust me, *everything will change.*"

Half and hour later, having told the sitter good night and checked on his boys, he walked into his bedroom, fighting an uneasy feeling. "Everything will change," he'd told her, but she had denied it quickly and forcibly. Maybe he had misjudged her after all. She had secrets; he was certain of that. But did she erect barriers between them for some more compelling reason? Like her career? Was success driving her, as it had Etta Mae and his mother? He didn't want to believe he was so gullible, that his feelings for her had caused him to drop his guard completely, to accept her unconditionally, knowing what his bitter experience had taught him. His instincts cautioned him to be fair: after all, hadn't she deliberately risked and lost a lucrative account in order to take care of Preston while he worked? And what did that prove? That she felt guilty for having ignored the boys, even though she knew that they yearned to see her? Hell! How was he to know? He stretched out on his back, both hands beneath his head.

He had been in an emotional vortex, a sexual hurricane. Her passion had filled his nostrils with lush female scent, bruising his senses, robbing him of his very self. He could still taste her warm, sweet flesh and hear her moans of total surrender as they spun together into an otherworld, possessed by each other…it had been the sweetest torture he'd ever known. He loved her and wanted her, but he was definitely going to be more careful. Until he got some answers, he intended to pull back, but not so she'd know it.

*"Everything will change!"* Three days later, Naomi still pondered those words. What had she done? Her life was in total

chaos. She couldn't even conceive of a solution, but she had let her resolve waver and had broken down and told him that she loved him. She couldn't even claim to have been in the grip of ecstasy. But telling him had felt so good, a powerful, cleansing release, a mental catharsis such as a guilty person must feel confessing a crime. How would she feel if she told him everything? Could a man change to the extent that he seemed to have done? She remembered that he hadn't mentioned love, though he'd forced her to confess. Maybe he believed in her; maybe not. She couldn't afford to risk it; she had set her course, and she would stay with it.

Shaking her head as if to deny existence of the dilemma, she walked up the steps of the red brick ranch house on Pershing Street in Silver Spring. The gaily decorated Christmas tree with its whimsical lights in the shapes of musical instruments greeted her through the picture window, giving the house a semblance of gaiety, a Christmas Eve welcome of its own. And it comforted her to know that Aaron lived in a home where the holidays were a time for caring.

Rosalie Hopkins opened the door and greeted her as she would a sister. She had a keen sense of disappointment that Aaron was at work that afternoon; she wanted to see him in his own environment, to know how he and his adoptive mother related to each other. There was so much she needed to learn, so much she had to know before she could begin to have peace about Aaron and herself. They entered the living room and she glanced at the wall unit that housed an elaborate music system.

"Who's the music buff? You or Aaron?"

"I am," Rosalie explained. "This is company for me when Aaron is occupied with his books, paints, guitar, and you-name-it downstairs in his private kingdom."

"He doesn't watch television?"

Rosalie seemed proud when she answered. "Rarely. He says it's a stupid waste of time. And I'm glad. It offers too much of what he shouldn't know and too little of what he should. Anyway, he's not a passive person. Have a seat. I'll be right back." She hadn't planned to visit, but Rosalie made tea and invited her to stay. Her gaze took in the warm, attractive room, it's well maintained appearance and the tasteful but simple furnishings. She saw nothing flashy; a child raised in this environment by such a woman as Rosalie would have garnered a worthwhile system of values. Rosalie returned with the tea and they talked for a few minutes, exchanging meaningless banalities. Then, abruptly, Rosalie rose, as if having arrived at a decision, and took her first to Aaron's room and then to his basement hideout.

Naomi touched his little league trophies and pennants and his first guitar and looked through his sketches and drawings, all neatly organized by subject matter and date. She gazed in wonder at his glee club photographs, dozens that chronicled his growth from about age six onward. Rosalie walked over to his desk and showed her a watercolor portrait under which was written, "Noomie." She struggled to hold back the tears, and when they came, Rosalie comforted her.

"I hope we can be close friends, Naomi," the older woman said hesitantly. "Aaron didn't tell me much, but he seems content, and that's about all I can ask, since you've been together only once. I do know that he hasn't been restless." Her smile was that of a mother having fond thoughts of a child, Naomi realized.

"He seemed more concerned about me and how I feel about his seeing you," Rosalie continued. "I'll be honest with you. I want his happiness, and I want him to grow to become a fine man, but no matter what, he'll always be my son. And I'll fight for that with my last breath."

She took the woman's hands into her own and reassured her as best she could. "You have nothing to fear from me, Rosalie; I'm only grateful that you are a compassionate person and that you seem to understand what I'm feeling. You've been more than gracious to me, and you've offered me your friendship; I won't abuse it. Another woman might have refused to let Aaron meet me, and I would never have known him."

Naomi looked with affection at the woman beside her whose

name would never be included in Maude Frazier's social register, but who possessed more honorable traits than most of the socialites she knew. Her glance fell upon a tank of tropical fish nestled in a recessed cove in the hallway.

"What an odd assortment of tropical fish."

"My husband brought them to me from Honolulu. He always brought us something when he returned from his trips. Those Thai temple bells hanging from the ceiling along the hallway and down the stairs to the basement were his gifts to Aaron. My son likes to run his hand along them as he walks. He says he gets a different tune each time."

This home has been filled with love, she thought. Love between a man and wife and between them and Aaron. There was just one more thing.

"Rosalie, does Aaron ever go to church?"

Rosalie shrugged. "He always has, but since none of his friends go, he's become stubborn about it. I've decided not to make it an issue between us." Naomi laughed. She had behaved in the same way, but a lot of good it had done her. Just wait until Judd lowers the boom on him, she thought. She was happy...or she would have been.

Suddenly she wanted to tell this stranger about Rufus and her fear that he would find her contemptible if she told him about Aaron. She sensed that this woman had suffered and would understand and not scorn her. I can't dump on her, she thought; it would make sense. She handed her two packages; one containing a small bottle of perfume, and the other an artist's palette and brushes for Aaron, wished her and Aaron merry Christmas, and continued her rounds.

Her next stop was Marva's house, but she realized that though she loved Marva, she had no interest in visiting with her friend. She was sick of shielding her emotions from her closest friend, of living a double life. Judd and Aaron knew her secrets, and with them she was free. But she needed to be with Rufus, unfettered by fears of exposure. She needed to feel his arms around her. To bare her soul to him, confessing everything, and then to have him cherish her. But it wouldn't happen, and she had made up her mind to accept that. The more involved she became with Aaron, the more willing she was to sacrifice everything—Rufus included—for her son.

Naomi drove downtown to North Capital and P Street and parked in front of Linda's house. Walking slowly up the walk, she wondered whether she was doing the right thing, whether Linda would think her visit an invasion of privacy. The front door opened before she'd reached it, and Linda stood with it ajar, waiting. Naomi knew at once that the girl didn't want her to go inside. She handed Linda a beautifully wrapped package containing a book of reproductions of the paintings of Matisee and William H. Johnson. Linda eagerly tore open the package, stared at its contents, and gasped. She looked up at Naomi with glistening eyes and grasped her in a joyous, enthusiastic hug, her first gesture of affection toward her mentor. Startled, Naomi recovered quickly and pulled the girl to her in a motherly embrace.

"I'm going to keep this forever," Linda promised. Naomi wished her merry Christmas, swallowed the lump in her throat, turned, and left.

# Chapter 15

Naomi opened the windows, turned up the radio, and let the crisp winter air flow in while the music swirled around her. She loved the English Christmas carols and hummed along as they filled her living room. How long had it been since she had welcomed Christmas morning? Years. This one wasn't perfect, not by a mile. She didn't have Rufus, and her son didn't belong to her, but Aaron was a part of her life and she knew that if she needed Rufus, he'd be there for her. Right now, she wasn't asking for more. She snipped the needle ends from the holly leaves and made a bouquet of holly and Santa Claus with his reindeers that she tied on her gifts to Preston and Sheldon. Then she wrapped her grandfather's gift— Klopshc's 1901 *Red Letter New Testament* that she'd found in a used bookstore, added Rufus's gift to the pile, and quickly dressed.

She looked in the mirror. Why hadn't she been born in a culture where men wore their hair long and women wore theirs short? She got her long, thick tresses into an attractive twist just as she heard a playful jingle of the doorbell. Who could that be? Her heart pounded furiously when she saw Aaron standing there, smiling shyly. She stepped aside, took his hand, and pulled him into the foyer. That seemed to amuse him; his sheepish grin tugged at her heart as he awkwardly handed her two attractively wrapped packages.

"We thought we'd give you these." He handed her the gifts. "My mom and me, I mean." She thanked him, risked putting an arm loosely around his shoulders, and walked with him into the living room.

"How come you only got this little tree? Couldn't you find a bigger one? It's nice, but…" His voice drifted off.

"There's only me, so I don't put myself out much when it comes to celebrations." He clearly didn't think much of it and didn't try to hide his disdain. He was blunt, too, she remembered, and figured he hadn't learned to misrepresent himself; she hoped he never would. He walked around the tree, pushed his hands into the pockets of his jeans, and shrugged.

"It's too little. Next year, I'll get you a big one. Well, maybe I oughta go. My mom's relatives are coming for dinner, and I have to help her. Uh…Noomie, my…er…your grandfather called me. He said I have to go out there and see him. Are you going to his house today?" She nodded, unable to believe her ears. He was planning on being a part of her life, and he wanted to meet Judd.

"If you're going this morning, can I bum a ride? I can't stay but a few minutes; my mom needs help with the dinner and stuff. But I promised him I'd go. What time you gonna leave?"

"I'll phone Grandpa, and we'll go right away." His quick glance and nonchalant shrug might have amused her, if she hadn't understood adolescent insecurity. He was nervous about meeting the old man. She drove past Bethesda's beautiful residential neighborhood, wishing that it was night and she could share with her son the elegant colorful Christmas decorations for which the area was so famous.

Aaron looked at Naomi, apparently surprised, when she parked in front of Judd's house, cradled her head in her arms, and leaned on the steering wheel.

"Uh, what's the matter, Noomie? You're not scared to go in with me, are you? I mean, you're not sorry you brought me, are you?" Her head snapped up sharply at his words, his misinterpretation of her action.

She patted his knee affectionately. "Aaron, I never dreamed I'd have the pleasure of bringing you to my grandpa. Do you know what it means to be so happy that you're a nervous wreck? I hardly realized I was driving, and that's dangerous. Sorry I brought you here? Honey, you're smarter than that—I'm sure of it."

His grin, brilliant and sincere, warmed her from head to the soles of her feet. "Just checking. Mom said I shouldn't do anything to upset you." Naomi looked at her child, a cocky, lovable boy, and understood the implication of his questions: he was insecure about her. He had really been asking her whether she was ashamed of him. She reached in the back seat for her handbag, squeezed his shoulder, placed her hand on the door, and paused.

"Aaron, I'm proud of you. You're a wonderful boy, and I know Grandpa will be proud of you, too." The astonishment and pleasure in his young face told her that her words had been precisely what he needed.

Judd opened the door before she rang the bell. "Well, well. Come in. Come in. Let me look at you. Come here. Come here." Judd feasted his eyes on the boy as he moved closer.

"I never thought I'd live to see my great-grandchild. Merry Christmas, son." Naomi stood with her back to the door, transfixed, as Judd put an arm around the boy, and the two went into Judd's study. Her grandpa hadn't said a word to her. Just then, he looked back at her.

"Merry Christmas, gal. Thanks for bringing him to me."

"Merry Christmas, Grandpa." She could barely get the words out.

The strange peace, the sense of right, of once more being a part of a family, was almost more than she could bear. If she had ever doubted that she had done the right thing, the tears that she saw in her grandfather's eyes erased that uncertainty. She wanted to remind Judd that they had no claim on the boy, that he shouldn't become too attached to him. But she said nothing. Christmas was a day of joy, and she hadn't the heart to cast a shadow over her grandfather's happiness. She didn't want to remember it herself, but experience had made her a realist.

Remembering how important it had been for her and Aaron to have privacy when they met, Naomi remained in the foyer and watched from there as the old man showed Aaron a picture of his maternal great-grandmother, his maternal grandparents, and his own mother as a child. The boy's questions indicated a keen interest in his roots, causing Naomi to wonder if anything other than identity had motivated him to locate her. A glance at her watch told her it was safe to assume that the twins had become uncontrollable and Rufus close to furious. Judd released them after getting Aaron's promise of another visit soon.

When Aaron got out of Naomi's car at his home in Silver Spring, she thought he looked at her as if there was something he wanted to say. So she smiled and waited, and when he only shrugged, thanked her for taking him to visit Judd, and ran into the house, she felt let down. What had she expected of him? She turned the Taurus toward the East West Highway, Chevy Chase, and Rufus. Rufus. She'd see him soon. Soon she'd be with him. Nothing would happen; he wouldn't even kiss her, but she'd see him. She'd be able to touch him. She eased off the accelerator; not point in getting a ticket. And no point in getting herself wound up over Rufus, because nothing had changed.

To leave her own child and spend Christmas day loving children who were not her own, even though she did love them, wasn't a thought that made her feel like dancing. And if she let her mind dwell on spending Christmas with the man she loved while not sharing it with him as lovers would, she might scream like a banshee. She laughed: that would be so far out of character that she'd voluntarily commit herself for mental observation. She slowed down as snowflakes dusted her windshield. Thank God for Judd. She could finally appreciate his favorite sermon: if you concentrated on your blessings, what you didn't have would seem less important. Well, old girl, she told herself, when you lay an egg, you challenge an ostrich, don't you.

Her heart soared as she glanced up at Rufus's sprawling house; in minutes she would see the man and his wonderful little boys. Common sense told her to calm herself, to walk carefully over the slick stones, but her feet seemed to take wing. The door opened before she reached it and the boys bounded out, almost knocking her down in their excitement and adulation. Tears of joy brimmed her eyes, but she refused to shed them. The children jumped into her arms, ignoring the beautifully wrapped packages, covering her face with kisses.

"Merry Christmas, Noomie," they cried in unison. "Merry, merry Christmas. We love you to pieces," they told her. She had told them that when she'd kept them while Rufus was in Nigeria. She put the packages on the floor just inside the door and hugged them feverishly, delighted that they remembered.

"I love you to pieces, too. Merry Christmas." She didn't want to release them; their love and warmth filled a void, an aching emptiness. They laughed excitedly, but only she knew what their love meant to her.

When she could no longer postpone it, she straightened slowly, letting her gaze travel upward as she did so, past his powerful jean clad thighs and his flat belly and up to the tight curls visible from his open-collared T-shirt. The familiar pangs of desire gripped her, and she forced herself to shift her glance to a neutral object. But it landed instead on his hard, masculine biceps, and shivers rocked her as the vivid memory of them strong around her, holding her, seemed almost real.

Like a caged animal who'd just lost its battle for freedom, she looked unwillingly into his face, then quickly freed herself from his fierce, knowing look. But his strong, irresistible pull would not release her, and she admitted surrender and allowed her gaze to settle on his fiery eyes. She couldn't remember the torment of the past few days nor the pleasure of that morning with Judd and Aaron. Her five senses were focused on Rufus. The rumble of the passing car could have been the beat of his heart; the rising wind, his breath; even the odor of pine and bayberry that wafted toward her became his own scent. She took a deep, labored breath and rimmed her full lips with the tip of her tongue, mesmerized.

His eyes darkened to a glistening mahogany, his breathing quickened, and she didn't have to be told that under different circumstances, he'd have had her in his bed within minutes. The warmth of his hand when he touched her shoulder reached her through her clothing, and she leaned into him as he steadied her and quickly but tenderly pulled her into his arms. "Merry Christmas, sweetheart." She struggled to speak, but emotion muffled her words, and she could only cling to him.

In his strong arms, where she needed to be, peace and contentment flowed over her, chasing away the tension and the desire. The twins pranced around her like little magpies. Rufus squeezed her to him and released her—reluctantly, she realized—and she wrapped her arms around herself. She tingled from his warm smile, from the sweetness that she felt coming from him. She could almost dance for joy. The boys had become still and were silently gazing up at them. Then, as if on cue, they each took one of her hands and led her into the living room.

"Look at our tree, Noomie," Preston urged, as Rufus placed her gifts beneath it. She did look at it. Hundreds of little twinkling reindeer shaped lights danced on the nine-foot spruce; red and white candy canes, mistletoe, angels, and cherubs hung from its dark green branches; icicles, gilded pine cones, and red holly berries decorated its needles. "We did it with our daddy," Sheldon volunteered. Her gaze moved from the tree to the three of them, and beyond them to the crackling fire that warmed the great stone hearth. Carols filled the air. She had to struggle hard to contain her feelings. Opting for the safety of wit, she made herself smile and ask Rufus, "Is it all right if I bawl? Bawling is kind of like house-cleaning; you have to do it once in a while."

Rufus watched her fight the tears, and understood what she hadn't wanted him to see: as a youth, she hadn't had a family Christmas with all the frills. He draped an arm casually around her shoulders, wanting to share whatever she felt. She was made of stern stuff, he discovered, when she brightened up, swung around, and kissed him on the cheek. Before he could react, she gave the boys similar treatment.

"There," she announced cheerfully. "Thanks for letting me see your beautiful decorations. I love the tree. Now, I'd better get going; I don't want to interfere with your plans for the day."

"You can't go!" Sheldon screamed, and began to cry. Startled at his son's unusual outburst, Rufus snapped his head around. But Preston's quiet fury, with tears rolling silently down his little cheeks, was the real shocker. Rufus looked down at his son. He was going to have to cool down Preston's temper. He'd had enough personal experience with a quick temper to know how much trouble one could cause. He smiled inwardly. If he didn't have a quick temper, he'd never have met Naomi, and look what he'd have missed.

"She isn't leaving, boys. I'll make us a hot drink, and we can read some Christmas stories." His boys trusted him, but both looked at Naomi for confirmation. She smiled agreement, and he suspected that she didn't want to go, that she'd been polite when she'd said she had to leave. They sat by the fire and drank hot mulled cranberry juice while he read them classic Christmas stories.

"Now *you* read one," he suggested to Naomi.

"I'd rather tell one, if you don't mind." He nodded, and she told the story of three kings and the first Christmas. "And that's why we give gifts at Christmas," she told the boys. Rufus watched them nod to her as if in complete understanding. She began to fidget uncomfortably, and he figured he'd better make a move.

"Stay and have dinner with us, Naomi, unless you already have an invitation." Her deeply drawn breath warned him that she was about to decline.

"Don't worry," he told her, a genuine grin creasing his face. "I'm having it catered, so it'll be edible. Might even taste good." He winked. "Well, what do you say?" She looked longingly at the children, and he could see that she wanted to share their day, and the fleeting flicker of pain in her eyes told him that she might not want to leave him, either. If she loved him, as she'd said, surely she would want to spend Christmas with him.

"Cat got your tongue?" he asked her provocatively, deliberately reminding her of sweet moments they'd shared weeks earlier. He got the impression from her quickly raised brows that he'd surprised her. But he knew well that she could give as good as she got.

"You already know the answer to that one," she joshed.

"Well? We all want you to stay. Will you?" He wasn't going to beg her, and he wasn't going to ask her any more. He wanted to spend the holiday with her and his boys, but if it wasn't important to her, she could go whenever she wanted to. He shoved his hands in the pockets of his jeans and assumed an air of indifference.

"Rufus, I'd love to spend the whole day with you and the boys, but I promised my grandpa that we'd go out to dinner. I can't let him eat alone on Christmas day." He watched her lean against the back of the soft leather sofa, twisting her hands. Yes, she wanted to stay.

"Grandpa can eat with us, too," Preston explained excitedly.

"Can he, Noomie? Can he?" Sheldon pressed her. Rufus had already headed for the telephone. He laughed when Judd Logan answered on the fourth ring, because he knew that the telephone was right beside Judd's chair.

"Merry Christmas, Reverend Logan. This is Rufus Meade. Naomi is here with my boys and me, and we want her to stay for dinner. She says the two of you are going out. Now, why should you go to a restaurant when I'm having a big turkey over here that won't taste good unless Naomi eats some of it? Be over here in a couple of hours." Rufus had to dig into himself to contain his amusement. He knew that both Naomi and Judd were probably staring with their mouths open at his audacity.

"You're big on temerity, aren't you, boy?" he heard Judd say, after clearing his throat loudly. Rufus leaned around a broad column from which dangled the boys' collection of miniature crystal airplanes, got a look at the shock on Naomi's face and allowed himself a joyous belly laugh.

"Just taking a leaf from your book, sir. Well, what do you say? We'd love to have you, and you can meet my boys."

"Meet your boys, huh? I didn't know you had any. If my Naomi wants me to, I'll get over there. Where do you live?"

Rufus stood at the door with his boys, waiting to greet the Revered Judd Logan, as he got out of a big limousine that Rufus had ordered for him and walked unbowed up the winding stone walk. Rufus thought of his own father, how he'd have loved Preston and Sheldon, and gave silent thanks for Judd Logan. Kids needed grandparents, and for today, Judd would do just fine. Wondering about Naomi's decision to stay in the living room, he opened the door and extended his hand just as the boys ducked beneath his arms and gave the old man what was probably the best greeting.

"Hi, Grandpa," they said in unison. "Merry Christmas." Rufus shook his head in wonder. That ninety-four-year-old man didn't even see his proffered hand, but bent nimbly to the twins' level and exclaimed, "My heavens, you're twins. And good-looking ones, too." The boys dragged Judd into the house, and the old man hadn't so much as greeted him. Rufus stood at the door, his left hand absently rubbing the back of his neck. What was it about the Logans? They charmed his boys without even trying. He took Naomi to the kitchen with him, explaining that he wanted to fix Judd some mulled cranberry juice.

"He hasn't said a word to me, Naomi. What do you think he's up to?" He figured from her deep frown that she was as perplexed as he. After a moment she responded.

"My grandpa doesn't hold grudges, so he's not sore because you were smart with him. Anyway, he probably admired you for that. I think he's besotted with the boys. Right now they've got him down in their basement empire. I hope he's got sense enough to stay off their trampoline, but you don't rate with them unless you bounce around that thing."

"What about me? What do I have to bounce around on to rate with you?" He felt her tense slightly, but he didn't care; a man had to make hay while the sun was shining. He set the bottle of cranberry juice on the table without taking his eyes from hers and moved toward her. "What do I have to do, Naomi?" She backed away, and he moved slowly and surely to her until her back touched the wall. His heart skipped a beat at the suddenly accelerated pace of her breathing and the telltale quiver of her lower lip. Even as he reached for her, she came to meet him, her lips already parted in anticipation of what she knew he'd give her.

He used what strength he could muster and resisted kissing her. "I'm hungry for you, sweetheart, but I can't stand the punishment of a couple of kisses. I can't have what I need from you, so I'll just content myself with the fact that you're here with me and my boys. That's more than I'd hoped for, so I'll just wait." He'd always loved her smooth, delicate skin, dark like perfectly caramelized brown sugar. He let the backs of his fingers gently graze her cheeks. "Ah, Naomi, it isn't written anywhere that a person has to be perfect. You love me with all my shortcomings. Why can't you open up and…" He almost said, *Let me love you.* Maybe the problem was both of them, not just Naomi. He saw in her turbulent brown eyes a need as great as his own and eased away from her.

"You said you'd just wait, Rufus. Wait for what?" He grinned one of those grins that he'd come to realize unsettled her.

"You're kidding. Right?"

She shook her head. "I want to know." He rested his hip against the marble countertop and folded his arms. "We can take this up another time, if you'd like. In fact, I want us to do just that. But today's Christmas, and it feels good having you here. Judd, too, though he hasn't bothered to acknowledge my presence. Let's avoid deep talk, okay? Soul splitting conversation is bad for the digestion." He whirled her around and kissed her hard and quickly on her eager lips. Then he took a tray with the pitcher of cranberry juice and five mugs into the living room, let the caterers in, and called Judd and the boys upstairs. After teasing Judd about ignoring him, he served the drinks and announced that Judd would tell them some stories.

He liked the twinkle in the old man's eyes when he said, "Rufus—I expect I can call you that, since you got so familiar with *me* this morning—I see you like to play hardball. I practically ordered you to my house, and now you've commanded me to yours. We're even."

Rufus laughed. "I stand corrected, sir." He looked at his boys, each comfortably ensconced on one side of Judd, drinking in his every word. Rufus was happier than he ever remembered being, and pretty soon he was going to be even happier, he promised himself.

But for Naomi, while the day was far more than she'd expected, it was less than it could have been. She was sure Judd was happier than he'd been since he'd lost her grandmother. The years had seemed to fall away from him when he'd looked at Aaron. At least she'd given him that much. She'd hung back when Rufus and the boys had gone to the door to greet him, because to stand there with them would have been too much like a happy couple and their children greeting a guest. Too much like the scenarios of her dreams. And there was Aaron. She was thankful for the beginnings of a relationship with him, but she couldn't help wanting them to be together for Christmas dinner. She caught Judd watching her furtively and scolded herself for wanting it all. Four out of five wasn't bad; in fact, it was a pretty high percentage. But why couldn't she be with Rufus and the twins every day, all the time, forever? She closed her eyes tightly, calming herself. She wanted so badly to tell him, but she wouldn't be able to bear his contempt. Why should he judge her less harshly than he did his own mother?

Naomi realized that Judd was telling the boys a story about her one Christmas when she was a little girl. Embarrassed, she glanced quickly at Rufus and had to struggle to hide the excitement that surged through her as his heated gaze devoured her. She shook her head slowly, clearing her mind, trying to relieve the tension. Rufus grinned deliberately, and she laughed, grateful to him for undoing the damage he'd just caused. They both looked at Judd, whose knowing wink told them that their secret wasn't that anymore.

Rufus stood and extended a hand to Naomi. "Come on, everybody, let's open the gifts. I promised the boys we'd do it before dinner. They got some teasers this morning so they'd settle down. Sorry, we don't have presents for you, Judd."

"Your company is all the present I need. Being here is gift enough." Rufus grazed his jaw with his forefinger, deep in thought. Older people had no business living by themselves, not even when they were as independent as Judd Logan. No wonder the old man was so imperious; he needed companions.

"I hope you won't make this your last visit." He didn't doubt that his statement pleased Naomi's grandfather, who sat with an arm around each boy. They opened gifts and enjoyed the miracle of children at Christmas. Mr. Ernest, the caterer, announced that dinner was served, and Rufus reached for Naomi's hand.

"What kind of impression are you trying to give my grandpa?" she hissed, earning one of his wicked grins.

"He's grown, has been for years. It's been decades since anybody fooled Judd Logan, so I'm not depriving myself of the pleasure of holding your hand, thinking that he doesn't know what's going on with us. Come on. And I want you to sit opposite me at my table." They walked down the long hall toward the dining room ahead of Judd and the boys, holding hands.

"The two of you have so much in common that it's eerie," she told him, and he hoped her pout was pretense. "He's a Capricorn, born December thirty-first. What about you?"

Rufus laughed heartily and squeezed her hand. "Naomi, you won't believe this; my birthday is January second. I'm a Capricorn, but I'm not bossy, like Judd. No way." She looked skyward, as though invoking heavenly powers to deal with such blasphemy. Judd said grace, and Rufus told himself he had better start taking the boys to Sunday school.

Preston and Sheldon didn't want Judd to leave, but he soothed them by getting their promise to visit him. Rufus watched the limousine as it turned the corner carrying Judd Logan to Alexandria. If he ever got Naomi to marry him, could they make Judd a part of their family? If you've been head of your own house for seventy years, you're not likely to accept another man in that position. Well, he could build a guest cottage out near the little brook. He walked back into the living room; such thoughts were premature. He'd learned during his football playing days never to try running with a ball before he'd caught it. Still, when he told the old man his intentions about Naomi, Judd happily gave his blessings, along with a warning that getting her wouldn't be easy. Judd hadn't disagreed when he'd said that Naomi seemed weighted down with personal problems, and he hadn't seemed surprised that she refused to share them with him. "Get her to trust you deep down," Judd had said. "That's the key, son." He knew it was going to be tough, though he didn't understand why. And if she knew he'd spoken to Judd about them while she was out of the room, she'd be furious.

The boys didn't want to go to sleep. It wasn't just the day's excitement, he knew; they were afraid that when they woke up, Naomi wouldn't be there. She pulled a chair up between their beds, lowered the lamp, and sang softly to them, lulling them. Her soft, sultry voice soothed the boys, whose eyelids soon became heavy; but it didn't soothe him. His emotions splintered like ancient shards at the sights of her loving his children, nurturing them in a way that was new to them and that they seemed to love. As she kissed each of them goodnight, he had to restrain a powerful urge to reach for her and hold her to him. But they no longer had chaperons, and he wasn't going to the brink with her tonight. If he touched her, she'd go up in flames, though nothing would have changed. And nothing would until she put her cards on the table. He was in this for the long haul, to win, and he was smart enough to realize that each time he gave her a chance to tell him no, saying no to him became easier for her. He rested a hand lightly on her shoulder.

"They're asleep. Let's go down and get something to drink." He took her hand and walked down the curved stairs with her, reflecting on her unusual quietness throughout the day.

"You haven't been very talkative, today, Naomi. Was it because of Judd's presence, or did something happen to make you so quiet and pensive?" He put the coffee on and set a tray, remembering to add pieces of the coconut cake that was Louella's present to him and his boys. They went into the living room and sat on the loveseat at a right angle to the fireplace.

\* \* \*

Naomi smiled at Rufus's perceptiveness. "I've been awed, to tell the truth. I don't remember having spent such a wonderful Christmas with my grandpa. He seemed so much at home here. And he was happy. Are you really going to let the boys visit him?"

Rufus sipped his coffee and looked at her, rather sternly, she thought. "Naomi, if I told him I'd take the boys to visit him, that's what I'll do. I keep my word. And beside, you don't think Preston and Sheldon would let me forget that promise, do you? Why did you change the subject?" His voice lowered, and she sensed anxiety in him. "I really want to know whether you've been happy here today." She got the impression that he cared deeply about her answer.

She crossed her right leg and swung her foot, playing for time. For composure. She didn't want him to know how the day had affected her, what joining their families for the festive occasion had meant to her. With effort, she told him in a casual voice, "Rufus, I don't remember a day in my life that was happier than this one." Then, not wanting to sound overly sentimental, she joshed, "As a host, you're a class act, though the boys are already giving you a run for your money."

His smile was humorless. "Have you forgotten your promise not to cover your real feelings with clever repartee?" How could she forget it? By agreeing to that, she'd let him take away her props, leaving her vulnerable, without defense, against his powerful attraction for her. She was suddenly aware of the heat that emanated from him, of his strength and solid manliness. Quickly, she jumped up.

"I'd better go. It's seven-thirty, and I have to get up early tomorrow." She started toward the hallway, and he followed. She was glad he didn't attempt to persuade her to stay longer.

"And my grandpa will call me no later than six-thirty in the morning to give me his views on you and the boys," she went on. "I'm as sure of that as I am of my name." She reached for the doorknob, but his hard, masculine hand covered hers, halting her.

"When will I see you again, Naomi?" His heated gaze sent

her pulse skidding rapidly, and she opened her mouth to give him a day, then thought of Aaron and turned away.

"We'd better leave things as they were, Rufus. I told you that if I ever get things together, I'll come to you, and we'll talk." The fire that she saw in his eyes suddenly became impersonal, and she knew he was about to lose a battle with his temper. She struggled not to panic when he suddenly closed the distance between them, towered over her, and pulled her into his arms.

"Have you ever seen a puppet as big as I am? One that you can dangle according to your whims, huh? Have you?" His words and tone sounded agreeable, but she knew by the fiery daggers in his eyes and the involuntary twitch of his jaw that he was spitting mad.

"Do I at least get a kiss for Christmas?" In his arms, under his spell, feeling his strength, she didn't have the energy or the desire to speak. He had only to lock his heady gaze on her to scramble her brain. He didn't wait for her reply, and she met his mouth with parted lips. She had expected his kiss to be an avalanche, a roaring fire. It wasn't, and she shuddered at its tender possessiveness and clung to him, saturated with need.

His eyes didn't betray his feelings, and she barely had control of hers. "What…what is it, Rufus? I thought you were furious with me, but you…you can't kiss me like this if you're angry—can you?"

"I hate to end Christmas Day like this, Naomi, especially since I don't remember being happier. But I'm tired of this. I'm almost thirty-five years old, and I didn't make out like this when I was nineteen. I'm serious about us, Naomi. I've told you that often enough, so I assume you know it and that when you're ready, you'll do something about it. When you *do* get around to it, I may still be serious, but there's a chance that I may not be. I hope you haven't mistaken passion for love, because there's an important difference." He walked her to her car. "Drive carefully, and don't play your cards too close to your chest. Oh, and call me so I'll know you're home safe."

Uneasiness stole over her when he walked away before she

turned the key in the ignition. Was he preparing himself psychologically to stop feeling protective toward her? She pulled out of his driveway slowly, telling herself it was what she wanted, but she no longer believed that. She drove past the beautiful homes, festively decorated and welcoming, with shades up and blinds open. Many families were still at their dinner tables. She thought back on the day, and happiness surged through her. She'd had a real family Christmas, and she had shared the morning with Aaron.

Nobody's life was perfect; you changed what you could, and what you couldn't change, you accepted. Some people didn't, and that's why psychiatrists were rich. She laughed. They weren't getting a shot at her. She glanced at her small tree as she walked into her living room; it hadn't seemed so puny until Aaron had scoffed at it. The memory prompted a smile; he'd promised to get her a big one next year. She reached for the phone to call Rufus and stopped. What right did he have to judge her feelings for him when he hadn't once told her what he felt?

And how could he demand that she pour out her insides to him when he hadn't ever given her a solid reason for doing so? Maybe she wasn't the only one having a problem with trust. She kicked off her shoes and reached for the phone. Maybe he didn't reciprocate what she felt.

"Hi. I'm home. Thanks for a special Christmas. Kiss the boys for me. 'Bye." She hadn't given him a chance to do more than greet her. The phone rang, just as she'd expected.

"Goodnight, Naomi." Furious, was he? Her spirits soared at the thought of Rufus battling his temper, knowing that he'd overreacted to her little mischief. "If I'm not careful, I'll go absolutely nuts over that guy, and then where will I be?"

# Chapter 16

Naomi crawled out of bed, dragged herself into the kitchen and got a cup of instant coffee. Then she put on a pot of real coffee and waited for her grandfather's telephone call. Judd was as predictable as night and day, so she wouldn't have to wait long. She lifted the receiver on the first ring.

"Good morning, Grandpa. How are you this morning?"

"I'm surprised you're up so early after your late night, gal." She wanted to correct him about that, but he didn't pause. "I see you've finally got smart and found yourself a good man. You'd better latch on to him, gal; You don't find men like him often these days. And he's got two nice boys there. I want you to bring those boys out here, and I want my great-grandson to come over here and spend some time with me. That's a fine boy; you can see the Logan genes in him. Are you working today?" Naomi sighed. She should have known that having Judd with her at Rufus's home was going to cost her something.

"We'll see, Grandpa. It wouldn't hurt you to have a friendly talk with Rosalie Hopkins about Aaron. Don't forget, she's his mother." It hurt deep in her soul to say it, but she had to accept it. And Judd Logan had to do the same. "She and I are on good terms, Grandpa, so please don't upset her."

"What do you take me for, gal? Now, you bring those boys out here."

Naomi spread her bed linen across the chairs on her balcony to freshen up in the crisp, dry air. She raced back into the kitchen to the telephone and was disappointed to discover that it was Marva. Why had she hoped Rufus would call her?

They exchanged pleasantries and season's greetings before Marva asked her, "Are you going to the town meeting tomorrow night? The topic is teenage behavior, and Cat Meade's book is being discussed. I'd like to go, but Lije says he's sick of the subject."

"I'll call you later and let you know." Naomi sat on the kitchen stool long after their conversation was over. What was she to think? She'd spent eight hours with Rufus yesterday and he hadn't mentioned it. She'd show him. She'd go.

She and Marva arrived early and found seats in the front row of the small auditorium. Radio and television cameras, cords, lights, and other trappings of the trade alerted them to the significance of the occasion, as did the presence of some local leaders. How could she experience so many emotions simultaneously, she wondered, after the program began. Exhilarating pride in the man, in his dignity and bearing brought her shoulders upright. He was different, apart from other men. She knew a keen delight in the smooth, knowledgeable way in which he answered audience questions, but she was furious at some of the things he said. She couldn't wait to tell him off. To think that she'd almost been willing to believe him capable of understanding and accepting her. But no, he was standing by what he'd written in that book. She rushed out at the end, before the applause died down, heedless of Marva's difficulty in keeping up with her.

"Naomi, for goodness' sake, what's the matter with you? Why are you so mad at him? I thought he was wonderful." Naomi slowed enough to let Marva catch up. She put an arm around her friend's shoulder, and they walked swiftly through the shadowy parking lot until she spotted Rufus's minivan. There was no sense in trying to explain the point to Marva. And besides, she wanted to hold on to her anger until Rufus got there.

As if sensing that the issue was a personal one between them, Marva gave Naomi an excuse when they saw Rufus coming toward them still some distance away, and went to find her car.

"Hello, Naomi. I was surprised to see you here tonight." She continued to lean against the driver's door, blocking his way.

"I'll bet you were. Probably as surprised as I was to learn about this from someone other than you."

She smiled, hoping to unsettle him. "Honest, Rufus, your views are outdated. If you backed into the twentieth century, just think how many people you could bring along with you. You've got a lot of fans." She grinned more broadly. "You going to give it a try?"

"That ploy won't work," he growled. "You're not ringing my bell tonight, sweetheart. I knew when I saw you in the audience that you'd be spoiling for a fight the first chance you got. I'm tired, and I didn't have time to get any dinner, so would you please let me get in my car?" She didn't move. A light shone almost directly above them, letting her see his face clearly. To her dismay, he wasn't angry, or even slightly annoyed, and she sighed deeply, feeling the fight go out of her. He must have detected it, because his face creased into a gentle smile.

"I know you're touchy about anything related to motherhood and the family, just as I am, so let's bury it for now, shall we? Come, let's get something to eat; I'll drive you back here later to get your car."

She stared at him, horror evidently showing on her face. "What is it, Naomi? Did you forget something?" Her laughter rang out in the quiet darkness, echoing back from the adjoining alleys. Marva and her matchmaking, she'd deal with her friend properly.

"I didn't forget anything, but Marva's forgot that she drove me here, and she's gone home." She moved from the door.

"My good fortune. Give Marva my thanks." A glance at his face told her that his joviality was real; he seemed to be glad that she was with him.

Truth. Maybe that would be her New Year's resolution. "I'd enjoy a light meal with you, Rufus." He opened the door and almost bodily put her into the van, then seated himself and looked down at her.

"Can you tell me why we stood out there nearly twenty minutes? This is the coldest night of the year." His broad, electric smile was all the warmth she needed, but she didn't plan to take the truth that far. His heat reached her through her coat when his arm grazed her leg as he shifted gears. She wouldn't move closer to him, but she knew she should make herself move away. She did neither and soon felt him do it again, deliberately this time, and with a little more pressure. Then her glance caught him observing her out of the corner of his eyes. She tried to think of a clever remark but could only sputter and finally double up with laughter.

"Go on. Press your luck, Meade."

He laughed with her. "Terrible, aren't I? Want to go to Maison Blanche?"

She shook her head. What kind of a mood was he in?

He shrugged elaborately. "Why not?"

"It's too rich for my taste this time of night. I couldn't eat a five-course meal. What do you say to Twenty-One Feral? Great lobster, and the potato-crusted salmon is to die for."

He turned onto L Street. "Sounds good to me." They were shown to a table not far from the pianist, who played a haunting blues. For a while, Naomi hummed along softly.

"Why did you stop? I enjoy your voice, even when you're only humming." He reached across the table and tucked a bit of hair behind an ear. Her heartbeat accelerated at the tender gesture, and she bowed her head. Warm sensations whispered within her at the touch of his index finger gently stroking her chin, a silent entreaty for her to look at him. Her glance swept upward almost of its own volition, as if she had no will of her own.

"Why?" he repeated, his warm, fawnlike eyes sending her intimate messages and daring her to give him back the same. She wanted to be angry with him for twirling her around as if she was a top, unraveling her just when she thought she had it all together.

"Why?" he persisted, even though they both knew her answer was of little importance.

"I'm not in the mood for the blues," she finally replied. "Blues can rip your insides out, just tear you up." His eyes widened in astonishment, but he let it pass.

"Are you in the mood for me?" Lightning-like thrills warmed

her as the heat in his seductive gaze matched his words. Hadn't something similar happened the night before last, Christmas night?

"You aren't deliberately toying with me, are you, Rufus? Let's just resist that sort of thing tonight, okay?" But as the cool wine trickled down her throat and his seductive gaze commanded her submission, she ceased struggling against him. She didn't care if he was provocative; feeling his caress and being able to touch him was what mattered. Still, it might be best to get onto a different topic.

"My grandpa called and ordered me to bring Preston and Sheldon to see him. He also had a few nice things to say about you."

Rufus laughed. She liked his laugh, as opposed to some of his grins. When he laughed, he meant it. "Naomi, Judd called me before seven yesterday morning, and ordered *me* to bring the boys to see him. I told him I'd take them this weekend, and I intend to beat him at a few games of chess while I'm there."

Her eyebrows went up at his last statement. "Even though my grandpa is ninety-four, Rufus, he's a wizard at chess."

He must not have heard her. "I'm looking forward with pleasure to beating him." Their dinner arrived. A shrimp salad for her and grilled salmon steak with boiled potatoes and asparagus for Rufus. Naomi declined dessert, but Rufus helped himself to a heavy serving of chocolate cake with raspberry ice-cream. She wondered where he'd put it.

Between sips of espresso, Rufus prodded Naomi about her reaction to his talk earlier that evening. "Why did you get upset about my mentioning Rosie the Riveter? Everybody knows the American family hasn't been the same since the Second World War. I gave five factors that I thought were responsible for changes in the family, but you latched on to that one. Naomi, what is behind this? It's almost as if…why are you so passionate about it?" If only she wouldn't resort to wit, if she'd just talk to him, let him understand her. He needed to understand her, to know her, really *know* her. "Naomi, what is it?" He watched disappointed as she put a hand under her chin, propped her elbow on the table, and smiled wanly.

"I'd like to know what's behind *your* stubbornness about this, Rufus." Shaking his head in frustration, he signaled the waiter and ordered them additional cups of espresso. They had so much in common. And their attraction for each other was so powerful that he knew it might one day bring him to his knees. But not yet.

He watched the flickering candle flame in the hurricane lamp that lit their table. "You know, from time to time there's a barrier between us that I just can't figure out. We'll be on the same wavelength, singing the same tune, and suddenly you'll put up an impenetrable wall between us. I suspect it leads right back to what we're talking about now. To what my book is about."

He slid his left hand slowly down her soft right cheek, touching the silk he knew he'd find there, gently caressing the warmth that he suddenly needed. A shudder plowed through him, catching him unawares, when she sucked in her breath and lowered her eyes.

He took her hand, turned it over, and examined her long, tapered fingers, brushed the back with the tips of his own, and looked at her steadily. "I guess we can't discuss it. We're not talking about conditions in our community or anywhere else, for that matter; we're talking about ourselves, Naomi, and I don't think we'll ever agree. If we do, I suspect that'll be the day we both begin to live, really live. We need each other, but neither one of us is willing to settle for half a loaf. And neither of us should. Let's go."

Naomi raced anxiously to her front door the next morning, hoping that the caller was Rufus. She'd had a sleepless night with dreams and visions of her and Rufus at opposite ends of every-thing—buildings, streets, and poles, even a canoe. It was symbolic, she knew, but her flesh prickled at the memory of the eerie happenings in her dream. Shaking her head as if to clear her mind of all unpleasantness, she reached for the knob. Maybe their relationship wouldn't have stood a chance even if Aaron hadn't existed. Aaron...thoughts of him warmed her, and she smiled inwardly. Would she ever get used to having a thirteen-year-old child? Good heavens, he'd be fourteen tomorrow, she remembered. Shock riveted through her when she opened the door and saw Aaron standing there with a worried look, biting his bottom lip.

"Hi, I, uh...I hope I'm not disturbing anything." He looked at her, hopefully, she thought, and then kicked at the carpet. "My mom told me I could visit you anytime you don't mind. She said I ought to call or we oughta make an arrangement or something, but I figured if you were busy I'd just go on back home. I mean, it isn't like you were expecting all of a sudden to have me hanging around. My mom had to go to work, so...look, I'm sorry I bothered you."

She put an arm around his shoulder and pulled him through the door. Seeing his relief, she figured it wouldn't hurt to give him a hug. That seemed to relax him. Still holding his hand, she walked on back to the kitchen, where she had been testing designs for a sportswear logo.

"I'm glad you came, Aaron. Can I safely assume that you're hungry?"

He grinned broadly and settled more comfortably in the straight-backed chair. "Always. What you can't assume is that I'm not hungry. What are you going to cook?" She wondered what he'd do if she hugged him breathless.

"It's still breakfast time, so why don't I make us an old-fashioned country breakfast? You know—biscuits, sausage, grits, eggs, and fried apples. You can have hot chocolate." He wrinkled his nose in apparent disdain.

"What would you prefer, s—Aaron?" What would he do when she finally slipped up and called him "son?"

He crossed his left ankle over his right knee and smiled indulgently, knocking her breath away. "Coffee. Noomie, I'm too old to be drinking hot chocolate. That's kids' stuff." She laughed, and Aaron sat upright, staring at her.

"What's the matter?" What had she done to make him look so serious? Only a moment earlier he had been jocular, laughing at her.

"You've got a real pretty laugh. It reminds me of those temple bells my dad brought me from Asia. I never heard anybody laugh like that. Real nice." She hoped the smile that she'd tried to force on her face actually made it. He wouldn't understand tears of joy, she knew, as she fought to control her emotions.

When she could, she turned away from the stove and faced him. "My grandpa says that when he hears me laugh, it's like hearing my mother laugh. He says she loved to laugh. I don't remember her. What's in the bag, Aaron?"

"My skates. I didn't wear them 'cause I caught a ride with one of the neighbors. I also brought along the Christmas present you gave me. It's real cool. I was wondering if you'd give me a few lessons—you know, brushstrokes and mixing paints, stuff like that. I paint, but I haven't had any lessons." He moved slightly so that she could set his place at the table.

"Aaron." She sat across the table from him. It was time to put him straight about a few things. "I want you to visit me whenever you like, as long as it's all right with Rosalie. And I'll be happy to teach you anything I know, so don't be apologetic about asking. Rosalie showed me some of your watercolors, and I thought they were impressive." He drew his shoulders up and sat erect, evidently pleased by her compliment. "I'm glad you like to paint," she told him, patting his hand before turning to take the biscuits from the oven. "It's what I like to do best. If you have any problems with math or English, I can help you with that, too. I once taught both subjects to high school students. And if you need help with anything else, just ask me. If I can, okay; if not, we'll find someone who can."

She couldn't hide her amusement at the sight of his eyes getting bigger when she placed the food on the table. He glanced at her from the corner of his eyes.

"I'm not triplets, Noomie. You of all people ought to know that." Laughter spilled from her lips. When she could calm herself, she noticed an expression on his face that proclaimed he'd witnessed the unusual. At her inquiring look, he explained.

"I'm not used to this laugh of yours yet. Too bad you can't sell it." He bit into a biscuit and gave her a thumbs-up sign.

\* \* \*

She taught him the basics about mixing his paints and showed him some of the differences between brush techniques with oils and with watercolors. Laughter bubbled within her when he joked derisively at his mistakes and with his hand, patted himself on the back when he'd look at her, wink, and say, "I did good, right?" The third time he looked at his watch, she had the gloomy feeling that he was tiring of her company. Feeling stomach pangs, she looked at her watch.

"Are you hungry, Aaron?" His sheepish grin was answer enough, but he confirmed it.

"Well, I could use a hot dog or something. It's one-thirty already. Do you think we could drop in on my…your grandfather for a couple of minutes today or tomorrow? I'm not in school this week."

"He'll like that. I'll check and see which day is best for him. When we go, ask him what he wants you to call him." She pursed her lips. "I'm sure the two of you can work something out." They finished eating and she packed a bag of biscuits for Rosalie.

"What's wrong with your feet?" She saw him looking down at them with a worried expression.

"I'm a mess, and I promised my mom I'd try to be a little more tidy. She's a neat freak. I've got paint of every color on my shoes. No wonder you're barefooted." She showed him the laundry room where he could wash his sneakers and took the opportunity to phone her grandfather.

"As far as I'm concerned, he can come over here and stay. About today, I'm not so sure. Depends on how much Rufus knows," he told her. Taken aback by his reference to Rufus, she asked him what he meant and whether Rufus was there.

"No, but he will be shortly with those little boys of his." She knew from the tone of his voice that he was withholding his censure.

"I haven't told him anything, Grandpa, and I don't want you to tell him." She could have added that he wasn't always right. She hadn't yet made him eat crow for advising her not to get in touch with Aaron; when she disobeyed him, look how he acted. You'd think he'd spent his life looking for the boy. He rapped out at her, getting her attention.

"Where are your ears, gal? I said, what do you take me for? It's not my business, but you'd better hurry up and tell him about it before this balloon pops right in your face. You listen to me, gal. I've lived a long time. That's a good man; you mind what you do." She told him she'd bring Aaron for lunch the next day and hung up. This time she had to admit Judd was right.

She leaned against the edge of the kitchen sink, waiting for Aaron to return from the laundry room. Rosalie had done a wonderful job raising the boy. He had good manners and good habits. And there was much of herself in him. She'd have to be careful not to go overboard, she reminded herself, because his mother was Rosalie Hopkins, a good, decent woman. Would she have been as generous if their roles had been reversed? She didn't think so; she doubted many women would have been and she was going to do whatever she could to make certain Rosalie never regretted what she'd done.

Aaron walked into the apartment in his stocking feet, holding his clean white sneakers high over his head. "I oughta get going, Noomie. I've got a few chores to do at home if we're going to Alexandria. Won't take me but half an hour." She explained that they'd be going the following day and noticed an involuntary twitch of his jaw. Was she about to learn something else about him?

"What's the matter? The old man doesn't want my company today, or you don't feel like taking me?" His humorless smile didn't fool her; he felt rejected. And his hard penetrating stare seemed out of character for the light-hearted boy with whom she'd spent the last four hours, but she sensed that it was part of him, that he could be harsh. He wasn't an easy one, and she'd better not forget it.

"Aaron," she told him in a soft voice, "Grandpa has company this afternoon. He said he'd rather you came tomorrow, when he can spend all his time with you. In fact, he said he wouldn't care if you went over there and stayed with him."

"He said that?" His face brightened immediately, and he didn't seem to need an answer, but treated her statement like a self-evident truth. He sat down and began pulling on his sneakers, and she sighed deeply. What a turnabout!

"Before I go, you want to tell me what you do for a living? I know you're an artist, but how do you make money doing this?" After explaining her work to him, she put on her coat and boots and informed him that she was driving him home. He didn't need to know that she was afraid for him to skake on the highways at the height of the rush hour.

"Phone your mom and tell her we're leaving. I don't want her to worry."

"She's still at work, but I'll phone her." He did, and when they got in the car, he looked at the bag in her hand.

"I sure hope you put some of those biscuits in there."

She patted his hand, aware that she no longer felt as if by touching him she violated his privacy. "There's nothing here but biscuits, and you're going to tell Rosalie that I sent them to her." She put her arm across the back of the seat and looked at him.

"On your honor?" He grinned sheepishly, and she supposed that his little mannerisms would always pull at her heartstrings. She'd just have to get used to not hugging him at such times. He wouldn't have liked it at his age if he had been living with her all his life.

"I'm wai...ting." She sang the word.

"Okay, but you sure drive a nasty bargain. Why don't you just give me a couple of them now? That'll hold me."

She tossed him the bag. I'm a pushover, she thought, as she drove. Aaron tuned to a rock station, and her mind drifted to Rufus. What would he and Judd talk about? If only she could share with him her feelings about the morning she'd spent with Aaron. She couldn't judge whether she and her child had made any progress toward real friendship, because he had so quickly shown suspiciousness of her. She had never felt so helpless, but there was nothing she could do but wait; it was all up to Aaron. She glanced at him sitting there, seemingly without a care—his head resting on the back of the seat, his fingers tapping his knees to the sounds of rock—and looked quickly away. She had the urge to throw caution aside, tell Rufus everything, and pray that he'd take her in his arms and keep her there.

"Are you in a hurry all of a sudden, Noomie? Sixty is kinda fast in the city."

She took her foot off the accelerator. "Sorry. My mind wandered." She parked in front of the house, and her spirits soared when Aaron patted her shoulder and teased, "Thanks. You'd better get your pilot's license if you're planning to continue flying. See you tomorrow."

She stopped by a bakery and ordered a cake, bought some oils and other supplies, locked herself in her studio, and turned on the answering machine. Hours later, the burning in her stomach reminded her that she hadn't eaten dinner, and a glance toward the window informed her that it was dark and snowing. The telephone had rung several times, but the caller had hung up as soon as her message had begun. Satisfied with her logo design for a record company's new label, she prepared to leave. The telephone rang again, and moments later, she heard his hypnotic voice.

"Did you call me earlier?"

"Three times. I hate those infernal machines. You promised a magazine interview for OLC, and I'm thinking it would be more impressive if the story covered spokesperson for several of our foundations. I've spoken with an editor of *African Americans Today,* and she would like, say, five separate stories in the same issue. I'd write the overview, and you would be the lead. What do you say?"

He had the ability to burst her balloon without trying. Her heart had thumped wildly at the sound of his voice, at the chance that he'd missed her or just wanted to talk with her. But no— he'd called to talk business. She glanced over at her drawing board at the sketches of which she had been so proud, that had made her feel like skipping instead of walking to her car, and wondered how she'd let his impersonal manner suck away her good mood so easily.

"Could we talk about this some other time, Rufus? I've just realized it's snowing, and I'd better get home. I don't know what condition the streets are in." She thought she heard him sigh, but she wasn't sure.

"Wait there a few minutes while I step outside and check the weather. Stay there until I get back to you." He hung up before she could tell him she didn't want his on-again, off-again caring. She shouldn't have answered, she told herself, knowing that after she heard his voice, hardly anything could have prevented her from lifting the receiver.

She sat down at her drawing board to wait for his call and busied herself developing ideas for a cosmetics ad. At the knock on her door, she looked at her watch; almost twenty minutes had passed. She should have realized that he'd come. She opened the door to him and the blast of cold air that still swirled around him. She hadn't seen him in knickers before. The thick Scottish tweeds and knee-high leather boots suited him. With the heavy parka, they gave him the look of a rugged outdoorsman. He walked in without waiting for an invitation, and she gave full rein to the laughter that bubbled in her when she noticed the snow-flakes sticking to the tiny black curls on one side of his head.

He lifted his brow quizzically. "I amuse you?" It was diffi-cult at times to know whether he was serious.

"I didn't realize you'd come here. The weather must be terrible. Who's with Preston and Sheldon?"

He shrugged and unzipped his parka. "I left them with a sitter, a young boy who lives across the street. They had a great time with Judd this afternoon. I think they're ready to adopt your grandfather; they're crazy about him." He tilted his head to one side and narrowed his eyes slightly. Here it comes, she thought.

"I can't imagine why you were surprised to see me. You must have known I wouldn't let you drive in this blizzard if I could prevent it. I'll drive you home. Don't worry—I'll get your car to you tomorrow morning."

She frowned, nodding hesitantly. She was taking Aaron to visit Judd tomorrow and she wouldn't consider postponing their visit; it would be the first of her son's birthdays that she'd spend with him, and she'd already seen how quickly he could become suspicious of her.

"But I'll need the car by eleven."

"Then I'll have it here by eleven." She had to fight to hold down the panic; what if Rufus found Aaron at her apartment? But she breathed a sigh of relief when it occurred to her that she could phone Aaron and tell him she'd pick him up. Letting the breath out of her lungs slowly, she mustered a little enthusiasm and agreed to his suggestion.

At her apartment door, he asked whether she planned to invite him in for coffee. "I haven't even had dinner yet, so you'd have a long wait for coffee," she hedged. She suspected that coffee wasn't his goal, but how could she deny him something so simple after his generous gesture, going out for her and driving her home?

"Ask me in anyway, and give me a chance to warm up before going back out there in that blizzard." She tried to ignore the coolness of his grin, the clear evidence that something displeased him. He walked in behind her, unzipping his parka as he did so.

"Don't be so melodramatic," she threw over her shoulder. "It's just a little snow." But she sensed before the words were out that he wasn't in a mood for humor.

"This place always looks so warm and inviting. Like you." He stood looking down at her, his eyes and facial expression unreadable.

She placed her hands on her hips, stood with arms slightly akimbo, and gazed up at him. Bravado seemed the best way to handle Rufus right then. "Rufus, I'm going to eat my dinner and you're going to drink a cup of instant coffee and then go home."

The message in his eyes carried the precision of words. "Want to bet?" they asked her, as he took a few steps closer, almost but not quite crowding her. She wouldn't let him see how he affected her and stifled the tremors that threatened to unbalance her.

"Don't start anything that we aren't going to finish. It's bad for my nerves." She laughed. "And we're as far apart tonight as we were last night. Nothing's change. You know that."

"Nothing's changed because you won't trust me; you won't share what's inside you, eating at you."

She looked past him to the refrigerator. "And *that's* because you've never shown me a good reason."

"Then you admit there's something." He moved closer but she backed up a step and looked at him steadily, neither confirming nor denying it.

He took his parka from the back of the chair, put it on and started toward the hallway. "I don't really like instant coffee. Your car will be here in front of your door at nine."

Another evening gone sour, she thought, as he reached out and dusted her cheek with the back of his hand. "Goodnight, Naomi." It seemed that lately their partings always left them further apart than when they'd gotten together. She warmed some leftovers in the microwave for dinner. Later, she called Aaron and told him she'd stop by for him at noon. Rosalie had enjoyed the biscuits. "You can send some more any time; they were delicious," Rosalie told her, and added, "Next time, stop in and visit for a while. You'll be welcome."

Rufus drove slowly. Considering his state of mind, he'd be smart to walk. Something about his driving her home had made her fearful, or at least sufficiently concerned to hesitate. It was understandable that she might not want him to go home with her, their libidos were almost certain to flare up if they were alone together. He knew he should wait until she straightened out whatever was bothering her, but he was increasingly doubtful that she ever would. Walking away no longer seemed an option for him; he loved her and needed her, and if she didn't come to him soon, he was going to force the issue. Failure wasn't something he was familiar with. He laughed at himself. He'd come full circle—from disliking her to letting her get into his blood. Then, he'd fallen in love with her, and if he knew anything at all, he knew this was for keeps. His mother would have loved her, too, he reflected.

\* \* \*

Naomi and Aaron found Judd pacing the floor when they arrived shortly after noon, worried that the storm would interfere with their visit. After the most elaborate lunch she'd ever known Calvin to prepare, Naomi brought out Aaron's birthday cake. She wouldn't have thought that a person's smile could bring her so much pleasure. But there was more to come. Happiness flooded her when Aaron leaned over a chair that was between them, wiped the chocolate crumbs from his mouth with the back of his hand, and kissed her on the cheek. She had to try hard not to overreact. To her surprise, Aaron didn't want to leave, not even when she reminded him repeatedly of the slippery streets and encroaching darkness.

At the door, she heard her grandfather tell Aaron, "You can stop calling me sir and call me Grandpa. Won't hurt you one bit to do that." She watched Aaron closely for any sign of resentment, but didn't see any.

The boy looked at Judd in the eye and told him, "I know who you are, sir. If that's what you want me to call you, it's all right with me. Uh, s—I mean, Grandpa, my mom said she'd like to meet you. Maybe you could call her sometimes." He looked from one to the other. "Thanks for the birthday lunch and especially for the cake. Chocolate's my favorite." Naomi bit her lip. It had been on the tip of her tongue to say that Rufus also loved chocolate cake.

Aaron arrived the next afternoon, as agreed, for another painting lesson. His talent and swift mind impressed her. She realized as they worked that Aaron wouldn't hesitate to ask her any questions that came to his mind. She hoped it was become he felt comfortable with her. Maybe she could ask him about something that had been bothering her.

"Aaron, how did you feel about your adoptive father?"

"I loved him," he told her. "He was great, really great. We were real close, and I still miss him. But I always felt something wasn't right. I didn't look like anybody. I'm a lighter complexion than my mom and dad, and my hair's like yours, wild and woolly. Theirs was softer and, you know, tame. Most of my friends looked a lot like one or both of their parents. Now, you…" He put the scraper aside and looked directly at her. "I look like you. Just like you. It's eerie as…it's eerie. You must look like your dad, 'cause both of us look like Grandpa."

The telephone rang, and she reached for the extension on the kitchen wall.

"Hello."

"It's Sheldon, Noomie."

"Sheldon? Darling, where are you? Home?" She remembered that Rufus had said he was going to teach the boy how to dial her number. They talked for a few minutes.

"I have to go now, Noomie. I'm supposed to stay in my room because I've been bad. We miss you, Noomie, and we want you to come see us." She told the child that she missed him and Preston, too. He hung up and she suspected that he'd been caught outside his room. She went back to her drawing board, distracted. What had they been talking about before that call?

"What's the problem, Noomie?" Who was that?"

She told him, adding cryptically, "The problem is that I can't have my cake and eat it, too."

"Yeah, wouldn't that be a blast?" he quipped. Then, as if sensing an undercurrent of emotion in her, he queried, "Is Sheldon the son of that man you told me you love? Remember the day we met? You told me that." He looked steadily at her, seeming to grow older by the second. "You said the guy had four-year-old twins." He touched his head with his forefinger. "I've got a memory like an elephant, Noomie; I never forget anything." She knew her silence whetted his appetite for more information, and because she didn't have any answers, he'd draw his own conclusion, indicting her.

"Why can't you go see the kid? Seems to me if he likes you so much he called you, you've been spending some quality time with him. Is it because of me you don't see them anymore?" She had promised him that she'd answer truthfully any questions he had about her.

She leaned back and rested her elbows on the drawing board. If she was going to keep his respect, she had to appear to be in control. "I don't see them as much as I did, because their father and I are not so close anymore." She watched his eyebrows shoot up and braced herself for more quizzing. He didn't disappoint her.

"Did he drop you?" She shook her head, an amused smile playing around her lips.

"I didn't think so. You didn't tell him about me, did you? You'd rather drop him. Look, if you're ashamed of me, just pretend I don't exist. I don't need to hang around here, and I can get to Alexandria by myself." Her mind raced as she searched frantically for words that would reassure him, prevent a break in their relationship. He reached for his jacket, and she grabbed his hand.

"Aaron, no man is worth losing you again." He stared at her long and hard, as if trying to see inside her, and she had to reach deep within for the strength to withstand his scrutiny without flinching. Suddenly, he shrugged nonchalantly, as if none of it mattered.

"Whatever. I'd better be going; my mom likes for me to be home before dark." He zipped up his jacket, slanted his head, and asked her, "Do you still love this guy?" She nodded. He looked at his feet, then directly into her eyes. "I'm not sure I like this. I'll see you in a couple of days." He gave her his thumbs-up sign and left, and she wondered if she was going to lose both of them.

# Chapter 17

**R**ufus turned off his computer. He should punish Sheldon for having disobeyed him, but he sympathized with the child. Sheldon and Preston loved Naomi and missed her as much as he did. Preston translated his hurt into anger, but Sheldon's temperament was different, and he suffered more. He had tried to protect his boys from what they were experiencing with Naomi, but an hour after they'd met her, it was too late. They feel for her as instantaneously as he did. Naomi seemed to have a way with the Meade males.

He walked upstairs, opened the door to the boys' room, and found them huddled together on Preston's bed, whispering. He watched as Preston patted Sheldon on the back, seemingly comforting him. Rufus closed the door softly, went back to his office, and phoned Naomi. Sheldon didn't need punishment; it was Naomi who needed it. He greeted her, skipped the preliminaries, and told her he knew about Sheldon's call and what he had just witnessed.

"Give me a ring when you find a solution to this." He told her goodbye and hung up. By now she was hurting, and he was sorry, but he had to play the hand that had been dealt him. He loved her. He wanted her. But if he played by the rules, he'd never get her.

Naomi's hand rested on the phone long after she'd hung up. She'd thought when she'd established contact with Aaron that she'd begun to straighten out her life. But had she? Instead, she'd precipitated new relationships and situations that had taken on a life and momentum of their own, that were all tied up together, and that would someday have to be straightened out. "I'll cry tomorrow," she quoted, as she put on a jazz album to change her mood.

At nine the following evening, Naomi conceded defeat, locked the door of her little cubicle at OLC, and headed for her car. Her steps echoed thought the empty building, accentuating her aloneness. Tutoring was usually suspended during the holiday school recess, but Linda had agreed to meet her with a report on the retreat. She couldn't imagine why the girl hadn't come, had kept her waiting there on a blustery cold night in a barely heated building. She'd have thought Linda would be anxious to share with her what she'd learned about art and painting at the retreat.

She telephoned Linda the next day at the drugstore where the girl worked part-time and asked for an explanation. She didn't mind that Linda was unapologetic, but her indifference hurt. She explained carelessly that her mother had kept her at home and, as if she had become distrustful of Naomi, asked, "Why are you so interested, anyway?"

You couldn't beat teenagers for bluntness, Naomi thought, re-membering her conversation with Aaron the day before, nor for cruelty. "Linda, I see in you myself as I was at your age, and I understand you. I know where you're headed and why, and I just want to be sure that you don't get there. I'm going to speak with your mother."

She called the woman immediately and was sorry she hadn't done it earlier. Linda's mother seemed to appreciate the call and promised to encourage and support her daughter. They agreed that Linda would help her mother after work, that Naomi would tutor the girl at her apartment on Saturday mornings, and that they would stay in touch. If only her other problems could be solved so easily.

She dressed and went to buy a present for Judd's ninety-fifth birthday and one for Rufus's thirty-fifth. Aaron hadn't called her, and she decided not to pressure him. Her eyes widened and she couldn't utter a sound when he opened Judd's door just as she reached for the knob.

"Well, what a surprise. I guess you weren't joking when you said you could find your way to Alexandria." She heard the hurt in her voice and didn't try to conceal it. Something akin to embarrassment flickered in his brown eyes, but he didn't give quarter.

"Today's Grandpa's birthday. I thought I'd come out and let him beat me at chess. You coming in, or are you planning to stay out there in the cold?" Before she could react to that series of questions, he released another at bullet speed. "You want to let me carry that for you, or do you want to just give me, er, the devil for getting smart at you when I left your place?" She succumbed to his charm, fully aware that he'd turned it on to ease things for himself.

"You said you'd see me in a couple of days. What happened?" she chided.

"I've been sorting things out," he told her casually. She supposed her uneasiness showed, because he explained, "I decided to talk to Grandpa and I feel a little better about it. Have you been to see Sheldon and his brother yet?" Looking up at him, she shook her head and could have sworn that he'd grown a few inches in the last three days.

His mouth curved almost cynically. "You have to get your act together, Noomie. Talk to the guy. You won't have any less than you've got now." As if to soften the blows of his words, he stroked her cheek with the backs of his fingers, and she had to fight back the tears. Rufus often did that, usually when he was leaving.

To complicate things, Rufus called to wish Judd a happy birthday, and the boys also talked with him, filling the old man's day with happiness and giving her a feeling of aloneness. She marveled at Aaron's silence as she drove him home. Like her, he didn't feel compelled to talk unless he had something to say. But as she swung off Georgia Avenue onto his street, he turned to her.

"You'd feel better if you talked to them. Happy New Year, Noomi." He bounced out of the car and up the steps, turned, and waved.

She usually spent New Year's Eve alone, so she didn't mind it. But she made some double fudge brownies in case she got into a blue funk. The sinfully delicious treats would cure most any ailment, or at least take your mind off it. She ate her dinner and had just settled down to watch the holiday festivities on television when the doorbell rang.

Her heart leaped in her chest when she opened the door and saw Rufus and his boys. She knelt and gathered the children into her arms, showering them with kisses, barely aware of the happy tears that streaked her cheeks. The boys hugged and kissed her, dancing excitedly, lavishing her with love. At last, she stood and looked into Rufus's eyes. If only he'd take her in his arms, if only he'd hold her and kiss her, as the boys had done. She dropped her gaze, unwilling to let him see what was in her heart.

Rufus looked down at Naomi, at the sweetness of her expression and the warmth in her smiling, tear sparkled eyes that nearly took his breath away. "We came to wish you a happy New Year."

When she glanced around, he figured she was looking for the boys. He knew they'd followed their noses and had gone looking for brownies, the fragrance of which enveloped the apartment.

"Come in. I always forget to ask you in." He stepped inside, noticing that she didn't step back to make it possible and guessed that she wanted him closer. He wasn't ready to accommodate her. Preston and Sheldon had wanted to see her and had tormented him until he'd brought them. He had wanted to see her, too, but unlike four-year-olds, he regulated his desires; they didn't regulate him. She looked up at him, seeming to beseech him, but he wasn't about to spend the rest of the night—and probably a lot longer—aching for her.

"I'm so glad you came and that you brought the boys. I don't think anything could make me happier."

His lips tightened with disdain. "Nothing? Why don't I believe you? Oh, I know you think you're telling the truth, but if nothing would make you happier, sweetheart, you'd find yourself with us more often. Maybe constantly." He grinned. "Right?"

She took his hand. "Come, let's see what the boys are into. I don't want them to open the oven." They found the boys on their knees, peering at the glass oven door. When she would have rushed toward them, he restrained her. "They won't get closer, and they wouldn't touch it even if it were cold." She put the brownies on the balcony to cool and made hot chocolate.

Rufus sat at the table, holding his empty coffee cup and looking over at Sheldon, who stood beside Naomi with an arm around her and his head resting in her lap. Then he looked down at Preston who, in an unusual gesture, had taken the same position with him. He had to do something. Couldn't she see that they all belonged together?

He stood abruptly. "They're getting sleepy, so we'd better be going." At the door, he gazed at her, letting her see everything he felt; love, loneliness, need. Her quick intake of breath told him that she'd seen what he'd wanted her to see. She lowered her head, and he swiftly pulled her to him, teased her lips apart, and thrust his tongue between them, taking from her what he needed and making sure that her night would be as lonely as his. He wanted to hold her to him forever, but she stepped away, clearly shaken, gasping. He winked at her, lifted the boys into his arms and left.

The new year is only two days old, Naomi thought, and my life is in a bigger mess than ever. How had she gotten herself into such a predicament? Linda was coming for her Saturday morning tutoring session, and Aaron had decided he wanted to visit. Moreover, he refused to accept her reasons for asking him to come in the afternoon and chose instead to take it as a rejection. When she explained that Linda was a fifteen-year-old teenager who needed her help, he had curtly informed her that if she'd rather help Linda, it was fine with him; and if she didn't want her friends to meet him, he didn't care to meet them. It hadn't occurred to her that he'd see it that way.

Her wait that afternoon for Aaron was fruitless, and she realized belatedly that he hadn't promised her he'd come. Dispirited, she called Marva in hopes that a good chat with her friend would lift her mood. They talked about everything but what bothered her, and she hung up feeling worse than before she'd called. She couldn't settle into her work, and when she found herself pacing the floor, she followed her heart and telephoned Rufus.

Rufus allowed their conversation to stall after an exchange of pleasantries. He wasn't going to engage in small talk with Naomi when there were so many important things they needed to discuss. Besides, he hated small talk. "Why did you call me, Naomi? You couldn't be interested in my views on the weather. I'm a journalist, not a meteorologist."

"I just wanted to talk, Rufus. Haven't you ever just needed to talk?"

"Give me some credit, Naomi, and level with me. I know you didn't call me at ten-thirty at night to talk about nothing. I thought that when we were in New Orleans, we progressed to the point where you could admit needing me. And later, we got to the point where you lay in my arms with me deep inside you and told me you love me." Softness colored his voice, and he had to clear his throat when it clogged with emotion. "What happened since then, Naomi? You promised me you would tell me what this is all about as soon as you knew. I have a feeling that you know, and that you've made up your mind that I'm expendable. But for one, your heart refuses to follow your mind, and you're in trouble." She offered no comment when he paused. "How am I doing so far?" he asked with pretended jocularity.

"*I—I* think I'd better hang up, Rufus. This isn't helping. Kiss the boys for me. Goodnight."

His hand automatically replaced the receiver, but he still heard the quiet tears in her voice when she'd asked him to kiss the boys for her.

As soon as she hung up, Naomi jumped up. How could she have forgotten that it was Rufus's thirty-fifth birthday? She hadn't even arranged to give his birthday present. She removed the receiver and punched in his telephone number. She'd given her relationship with Aaron the highest priority and had removed everything and everyone else from her central thoughts. But even the slightest problem, no matter how inconsequential, turned her mind to Rufus and her need of him. She got a busy signal, hung up, and dialed again. Maybe it was the feeling she had in his arms, after he made love to her, that bound her irrevocably to him. When he folded her to him and held her, she soared, secure in the knowledge that he'd keep her safe no matter what, even in the eye of a hurricane. She heard his magnificent voice and sighed. "Happy birthday, Rufus."

Naomi rubbed furiously at the finish on her Shaker rocking chair, one of the few things of her mother's that she'd kept. She sat on the floor in front of the chair, looking at it, but seeing her life. Shiny in places, paint bare in some, and coming apart in others. The doorbell rang, and she looked at her watch, wondering which of four or five people she'd find there at ten o'clock in the morning. Aaron.

Wide-eyed with amazement, she took the bird of paradise he handed her and opened her arms to him, trying without success to control the trembling of her body as he hugged her back. He was trying to make up for yesterday, she knew, though there'd been no need for that. But they'd just passed a milestone. Maybe it was a good omen.

"I was out of line, yesterday, Noomie. I don't know what got into me. I mean, just because this girl—uh, Linda—is a kid doesn't mean you like her better than me. Does it?" Her heart raced in her chest at his admission that he wanted to be important to her. She held his hand as they walked down the hallway to the kitchen.

"No. And in your heart, you know that. Thanks for the flower; when it dries, I'm going to press it in the back of the family Bible." She gave him a half dozen brownies and a mug of coffee.

A sheepish grin softened his face as he bit off a piece of brownie. "You are, huh? I'd better go. My mom's got me painting my bathroom. Say, this is terrific. I'll take the rest of this with me." He looked down at the rocking chair. "That thing needs a lot of work. Leave it till the next time I come over. I refinished a couple of things for my mom. She liked what I did. Look, I gotta split." She walked with him to the door, rested her hand on the knob, and waited. It was his move. His kiss on her cheek washed away a lot of the pain she'd felt the night before.

"Oh, Noomie. My school is having its annual parents' day program tomorrow night. The boys sit with their fathers and the girls with their mothers. They're having some big shot guest speak, but I didn't get his name. Grandpa agreed to sit with me. My mom said you could go along with her if you want to. She said be at our house by seven o'clock. You coming?" She nodded, too full to speak. She managed to grin at his familiar thumbs-up sign, closed the door, and went to finish her coffee.

Naomi leaned against the door, speechless. She knew that her grandfather was taken with Aaron, but she found it hard to believe that he'd go so far as to publicly acknowledge him. She went into the living room, picked up the portable phone, and dialed.

"Grandpa, did you tell Aaron that you're going to sit with him at his school's program tomorrow night? Won't that be the same as announcing that he's my son?" The old man cleared his throat. His reticence made her wary; she had never known him to be reluctant to express his views.

"Naomi, gal, we have to face this now. We've turned a corner, and there's no going back. Aaron wanted to go to church with me last Sunday, and I had to postpone it. I'm a minister of the gospel, gal, and I have to do what's right. I've thought about it, worried about it, and prayed about it, and I have to do this. I've been kept here for a purpose, to support my great-grandchild, maybe. I don't know. You took a stand and did what you felt you had to do. I admired your for it, even though I opposed it, and I'm glad you did it. Now, I have to do what I know is right. We'll face whatever comes together, Naomi gal. Just take my advice and do what I've been telling you. Talk to Rufus before it's too late." She'd barely hung up when the doorbell rang. She put the flower in a bud vase and placed it on the table in the foyer as she went to open the door.

* * *

Rufus felt a tightening in his stomach as the doorknob turned. He didn't know what he'd hoped to accomplish with this spur of the moment visit, but he couldn't stay away. He had to see her. She had been hurting when she'd called him last night, and it was a deep hurt. The startled look on her face when she'd opened the door and seen him standing there had quickly changed to welcoming warmth, and he knew she was glad to see him. She opened the door wider and stood back to let him in. He stopped before her. Close. Reading her eyes and the slight quiver of her lips. Oh, God, he needed this woman so badly.

"Ah, Naomi, come here to me, sweetheart." Miraculously, she stood wrapped in his arms, sobbing his name against his lips. A shudder ricocheted through him as her soft, warm body and roaming lips inflamed him. He picked her up and set her bodily away from him; he'd warned himself before leaving home that making love with her wouldn't solve their problems, would only exacerbate them. She tried to move back into his arms, but he restrained her gently.

"Hold on, sweetheart, we need to talk. How about some coffee?" They walked back to the kitchen, and she gave him a mug of coffee.

"Why did you call me last night, Naomi?" He waited until she sat down and deliberately faced her across the table. He had to see her eyes and the movements of her mouth: Naomi had spent so much time covering up her feelings that you needed a microscope to figure out what was going on with her.

"Are you going to tell me why you called me? Naomi, if I start making love to you, I can get you to tell me anything, but that's not what I want for us. Beside, it's a form of blackmail. You're so articulate, witty, and wicked when it suits you, why won't you talk to me? Are you willing to drop this? If you are, tell me. It won't kill me."

Naomi had been sipping her coffee, seeming to weigh his every word. She remembered Judd's advice of minutes earlier, but she couldn't banish her fear that if she told him everything, he would scorn her. "Rufus, why do you think I had a hidden motive for calling you?"

"I didn't come here for that, Naomi." How could she look so calm, knowing that she was skirting the truth?

She straightened up and looked directly into his eyes. Maybe she was going to level with him at last. She spoke softly, seeming to measure her words carefully.

"There's noting else I can tell you now, Rufus. I'm glad you came over here this morning, more than you could guess. And knowing that you'd have been there for me last night if I'd had a problem makes me happy."

He placed his cup on the table and stood. "That's it." Bitterness laced his voice. "That's all you've prepared to say to me?" She nodded. His hand touched his forehead in a mocking military salute.

"Stay there, honey. I can let myself out."

She got up slowly and put the few dishes in the dishwasher. She hadn't been able to deal with Rufus's questions; her mind had been on her narrow escape. If he had arrived five minutes earlier, he'd have found Aaron there. She tried to dismiss the feeling that she stood at a precipice, about to tumble into disaster.

Rufus stepped briskly up to the lectern. Next to writing, his greatest pleasure was in talking to young people, especially teenagers. As usual, before he began to speak, he let his gaze sweep his audience as he took its pulse. Why was Naomi there? If she wanted to see him, she knew where he lived. But this wasn't the time to think about Naomi, he told himself, and got down to the business at hand. He smiled appreciatively at the waves of applause that greeted him at the end of his twenty-minute talk. Reaching down for the small case that he'd brought with him, he stepped across the rostrum to the boys and girls who stood with their parents. He knew that the older boys weren't shaking hands with the speaker, but with Cat Meade, the former NFL wide receiver. Nonetheless, he hoped his message would have an impact on their lives. He handed each a key ring, a small

gold-plated replica of a house, on the back of which was in-
scribed, *"Best wishes, Rufus Meade."*

He reached for the hand extended to him and looked into
Judd Logan's face. "What are you…" His glance shifted to the
right and the boy beside Judd. He managed to exchange greetings with them, finish his round, smile at everyone, and get off
the stage. He had to find her.

As if she'd known he'd come, she remained seated, right
where she'd been all evening, open and vulnerable. He walked
up to her, knowing that if he said a word, he'd regret it. The
people around them were just a faceless mass of human flesh;
there was only Naomi, the woman he loved beyond all reason.
The woman who thought so little of his capacity for caring and
understanding that she couldn't tell him she had a teenaged son.
If that boy wasn't hers, there was no such things as genes. He
stared at her for minutes and said nothing. Talking would have
been useful yesterday or that morning, but not now. He shook
his head sadly, not caring that his disappointment showed,
nodded to the startled woman beside her, and walked away.

Home at last, away from the fuss and adulation that he hated,
away from the scene of his shocking discovery. At the door to
his sons' bedroom, watching their peaceful sleep, he gave thanks
for the one constant in his life: his love for his sons and theirs
for him. Why couldn't she have trusted him? Why hadn't she
realized that he'd have climbed mountains for her, and that he'd
have made her problems his own, that all he asked in return was
her trust, her faith in him? He walked to the window, drawn there
by the howling winter wind, and looked out at the desolate,
leafless trees, eerie shapes beneath the dark, cloudy skies. He'd
never felt so disheartened, nor so alone.

He'd had clues, but they hadn't fit any pattern. At last he
understood Naomi's protectiveness toward Linda and her sudden
refusal to block the admittance of boys to OLC. Still, something
didn't fit. If the boy was hers, where had he been? Naomi had
said she was an only child, so that boy had to be her son. And

the age fit the bits and pieces of information he'd gotten from her and Judd. *It's been over fourteen years since she let herself get as close to a man as she was to you last night. And I know that for a fact,* Judd had told him. That boy had to be about fourteen. He walked out of the room and closed the door. Something wasn't right, and he had to decide whether he cared enough to find out what was beneath it all. He wondered what she was thinking right then, whether she realized what she'd done.

Naomi looked up at the inquiring faces of Aaron and Rosalie and into the knowing eyes of her grandfather. "Come on, Naomi gal, we're the last ones here." His withered fingers grasped her shoulders, urging her to get up, and his old eyes softened with sympathy. She trailed them outside, hardly aware of her surroundings. At her car, Judd stopped her. "No point in crying over spilled milk, gal. You didn't tell him, and now he knows. Either find a way to patch it up, or forget him and get on with your life. Neither course is going to be easy. If I'd known this would happen, I'd still have sat with Aaron. It was past time for you to level with Rufus; you hadn't any right to let him care for you while you kept him in the dark about something like this. I kept your secret, but you know I didn't like doing it. I begged you just yesterday to talk to him. You're going to have to make the first move, and you'd better make it soon."

Naomi turned at the touch of Aaron's hand on hers. "I'll be over tomorrow morning, Noomie." She nodded. Ten minutes later, she walked into her apartment, too numb to do more than pull off her clothes and get into bed. She hadn't misinterpreted the cool disapproval in Rufus's eyes; he had condemned her without giving her a chance to explain. She had been right not to confide in him; he didn't care enough. And she'd have to straighten Judd out. She'd told Rufus many times that there couldn't be anything between them, so she couldn't be accused of leading him on.

She answered her door at eight-fifteen the next morning to find a very solemn Aaron standing there. He walked past her quickly, as if to avoid a greeting.

"If you didn't eat breakfast yet, I'll eat with you. All I did was get up, put my clothes on, and leave. My mom dropped me off." She wondered about his nervous chatter; it was unlike him. She put together a hearty breakfast and sat down with him.

"What's on your mind, Aaron?" She didn't plan to let him disturb her equilibrium, no matter what he said or did. Rufus had given her enough to deal with.

He chewed his bacon deliberately, swallowed it, and sipped some coffee. "What is Cat Meade to you, Naomi?" She hadn't expected his question to be so direct. Unfazed, she looked into her son's steely, accusing gaze. She no longer had a reason for evasiveness and secrecy; she could be herself.

"I love him, Aaron."

"I see. So he's the one. And you didn't tell him about me. He found out on his own last night, because I'm the spitting image of you and I was with Grandpa. Why didn't you tell him?"

"I didn't think I could handle it if he scorned me for having a child that was given up for adoption. He doesn't know that part yet, and he still judged me harshly, without hearing me out."

"Come on, Noomie. The guy got a shock. Do you think it would've been worse if you'd sat down and talked to him?" He sipped the last of his coffee, and she watched his young face sadden.

"I should have stayed out of your life. If I hadn't pushed my mom so hard to find you, you'd probably be married to the guy by now. But I'm not really sorry, Noomie, because now that I know you, I understand myself better. I guess I shouldn't have stuck so close to you and Grandpa, though. My mom says it's natural for me to like being around you, since you don't mind. But I'll disappear, if it'll make things better between you and Mr. Meade." He looked at her expectantly, and she hurt for him. He had chosen to take responsibility for the mess she'd made.

"Aaron, Rufus can't replace you in my life, any more than you can take his place. Try to understand that you aren't part of any solution to my problem with Rufus. And meeting you was my decision; a decision I have never regretted. Nor will I ever. You come here as often as you like and as long as Rosalie doesn't mind." He seemed more relaxed, and she hoped she'd put his mind at ease.

Later, he stood at her door, about to leave, more pensive than she remembered having seen him and without his usual swagger. "I hope you make up with him, Noomie. I like him a lot. Us guys in my class think he's a saint; he's practically our guardian angel. Sometime you can tell me how you met him." She laughed at the memory, and Aaron smiled broadly, as if glad to see the change in her. He left, but forgot his thumbs-up sign. If only he'd forget about her and Rufus; she knew she had to do just that. From Rufus's behavior last night, it was over between them.

Rufus sat in his office with Sheldon on his knee and Preston between his legs leaning against him and listened to Dick Jenkins drone on and on. He didn't usually discuss business with his boys hanging onto him, but Dick had dragged the appointment out for three hours. He had switched on the answering machine and didn't answer the phone, but when he heard, "I'm Aaron Hopkins. I met you last night," he picked up the receiver.

"Hello, Aaron. I can't speak with you right now. Give me your number, and I'll call you in five minutes." That should get rid of Jenkins.

"Aaron, this is Rufus Meade." The boy wanted to come and see him. He wasn't going to discuss Naomi with anyone, but he'd listen to Aaron, he decided. He opened the door an hour later to the handsome boy who looked so much like the woman he loved.

"Come in, Aaron." He noticed the boy's reticence and draped an arm loosely around his shoulder.

"Thanks for letting me come. Where are the twins?" He hadn't expected that Naomi would have told the boy about him and his children.

"They're about to have a nap." He poured two glasses of ginger ale and sat down, motioning to Aaron to do the same. "What can I do for you?" He watched Aaron take a deep breath, as if preparing himself for an ordeal.

"I'm fourteen, and I'm very reliable. So if you need a sitter sometime, or maybe someone to run errands or something, I'd be glad to do it without charge. Reverend Logan could give you a reference." He wondered what had given the boy such a guilt complex, but he wouldn't pry.

"Thanks, I appreciate the offer, and I may call on you, but I'll pay you the going rate. Never offer charity where none is needed, son. I hear my boys running around upstairs. Come, I'll introduce you." Sometime later, he dressed the boys for their trip to the library, listening to their chatter about their new friends, Grandpa and Aaron. What had prompted Aaron to seek him out? He remembered seeing him in the school gym, a bright, inquisitive kid, but the boy had never said a word to him. And he sensed Aaron's protectiveness toward Naomi. But why? Strange, that he'd never seen evidence of him in her apartment.

Rufus arrived at the *Journal* the next morning, a few minutes early for his appointment with Hector Shaw, its editor-in-chief. He'd left the boys with Jewel's husband, but he had been tempted to ask Aaron to stay with them. Hector rushed in at precisely nine o'clock.

"Sorry, Cat, but there was an accident, and I had to make a detour. Let's check the police headquarters and see if we can find out anything. There appeared to be several cars involved." He picked up the receiver, dialed and got down to business. It was routine, a part of the job.

"How old is he? Did you get his name? How do you spell that? Thanks."

He hung up and turned to Rufus. "A bad accident, but no fatalities. Routine stuff. A kid on in-line skates. They took him to the hospital center. I'll put Joyce on it. She'll get the human interest aspect. Those skates are dangerous." He puffed on his stale pipe.

Rufus saw nothing routine about a kid getting hit. An odd sensation pricked the back of his neck. "How old is the boy?"

"Early teens. Why?"

Rufus knew that he only pulled at his chin when he was disturbed. He resisted doing it, but for some reason, he had an unaccountable edginess. "What is the boy's name?"

Hector checked his notepad. "Hopkins."

Rufus turned on his heel with the speed for which he was famous. "I'll speak with you later on. Right now I've got to get to that hospital," he called over his shoulder.

He found Naomi and Rosalie huddled together in the waiting room, frightened. "I'm Rufus Meade," he told Rosalie. Naomi's tear-streaked face and sad, reddened eyes clutched at his heart as she looked at him. "Rufus, this is my friend Rosalie Hopkins. We don't have any news yet. A car side-swiped him, and two other cars collided to avoid hitting him. He's in surgery. How did you know about this?"

"I was at the *Journal*." His mind raced, searching for a logical explanation of the relationship between the two women and Aaron. Hours later, a doctor informed them that Aaron had suffered internal injuries and a sprained knee, but would recover fully within a few weeks. He advised them to go home; the boy was in intensive care and wouldn't be allowed visitors for twenty-four hours. Naomi had said she was an only child and that she'd never married. Rosalie and Aaron had the same last name, but Aaron resembled Naomi, not Rosalie. Somewhere in there lay Naomi's reason for secrecy, he'd bet on that.

Naomi walked zombie-like into her bedroom and sat on the bed. Rufus had insisted on bringing her home, and she was grateful. The chill in her chest had nearly disappeared when she saw him coming toward her in the hospital, confident but concerned. "I think you should undress and try to sleep," he advised her. "I'll phone Judd. Then I'll run over to Jewel's to look after my boys, but I'll come back and see that you get dinner."

She tried to keep the weariness out of her voice so that he wouldn't think she was asking for his sympathy. "I don't expect that from you, Rufus, though I do thank you for being there today. It meant more to me than you could imagine. But I'll be all right."

His gaze seared her, and she shifted nervously under its impact. "I said I'll be back here. Give me your keys, and I'll let myself in." She gave them to him, wondering why he'd bother.

She awakened at his urging two hours later to a lobster dinner complete with white wine and chocolate mousse for dessert. He had set her kitchen table for two, adding candles and three calla lilies he'd brought her. He reached across the table, took her hand in his, and said grace, then proceeded to eat as though it was their daily routine. She loved lobster, but salty tears impaired its taste.

He spoke for the first time. Lovingly. Compassionately. "Don't worry, Naomi. The doctor said he'll be okay, and that there won't be any aftereffects."

She brushed away the tears and forced a smile. "If I'd known you could cook like this, I'd have asked you to marry me. With this kind of talent, I'd take a chance."

He looked steadily at her. "I'm glad you feel like joking, even if it's at my expense. And incidentally, if I can cook like this, why would I want a wife?"

She laughed; he could give as good as he got, though she figured he felt about as much like teasing as she did. She looked at him. *Oh, Lord. He wasn't joking.*

"I'm sorry." Poor recompense, she knew, but it was what she felt. They finished the meal, and he insisted on straightening up the kitchen. She took the flowers from the table and thanked him for them. He only nodded, and she realized too late that he wasn't a man to diminish his standard of behavior no matter what anyone else did. He would be gracious and considerate even if he wanted to throttle her. She walked out of the kitchen slowly, dispirited; from the way he acted, she could be a woman he'd just met.

She put the flowers beside her bed and crawled under the covers. "Life begins tomorrow," she told herself, "and if I can't have him, I'll just get along without him."

Her heartbeat accelerated wildly at the sound of his soft

knock. "Yes?" Emotion clogged her throat, nearly strangling her. Was he asking to come in? He couldn't be!

"If you need me, Naomi, I'll be in your guestroom. I've just spoken with the doctor at the hospital. Aaron is comfortable and not in any danger. Goodnight."

"Goodnight, Rufus. And th-thank you."

Hours later, she turned on the light, unable to sleep. Was this how Rufus felt when she refused to tell him what kept them apart? When she got downstairs the next morning, Rufus had already left.

Each morning she joined Rosalie in Aaron's hospital room and sat there with her most of the day. And she watched the door impatiently every afternoon until Rufus arrived. She and Rosalie noticed that Aaron was brighter and more responsive during Rufus's visits. And Naomi became increasingly conscious of the bond that had begun to form between her and the woman who had nurtured her son. She gasped in astonishment at Rosalie's suggestion that Aaron recuperate at her apartment, explaining that she had lost two weeks' pay and couldn't afford to lose more.

Naomi remembered that Rosalie was a nurse and would have been the more logical choice as caregiver for Aaron. Her common sense told her that Rosalie's financial circumstances must be more modest than she had thought, and the knowledge saddened her. But she gloried in the chance to care for Aaron and to help him stay abreast of his schoolwork. She expected that Rosalie would be attentive to Aaron, visiting him daily. But she could not have imagined that Rufus would care for them and nurture them as he did, calling in advance for her shopping list, even cooking on occasion. She looked forward to his daily visits and especially to those times when he brought the boys with him. But the deep, aching need that spread through her each time she saw him remained unappeased when he left. How could he be so impersonal? Friendly. Caring. Considerate. And still so detached. She'd catch him looking at her and see the hot desire in his eyes immediately turn to cool disinterest. Chills coursed through her as she thought of him sitting beside her in Aaron's room or passing within inches of her, always with a smile that barely reached his lips and always avoiding touching her. He hadn't made a semblance of an overture toward her since that awful night, and she knew he wouldn't.

Judd visited Aaron nearly every day, and one afternoon, he followed Naomi into the living room. "He's giving you a hard time, isn't he, gal?"

"Oh, Grandpa, I made a terrible mistake. I just know it. He is completely unselfish and caring. I believe he might have understood if I'd given him a chance. He quietly takes care of us; if we need anything, we don't have to ask him, he just seems to sense it."

"You're being foolish not to tell him what's in your heart, gal."

"I can't, Grandpa. All those times he gave me the chance, I didn't take it. If he'd given me even a little sign, I'd go for it. But he keeps me at a distance."

Judd raised one eyebrow. "In my days, if a man cared for a girl, she could get him to do just about anything short of dishonoring himself. What's the matter with you young people?" Shaking his head, he left her standing there and went to the kitchen where Rufus was changing a recessed light bulb in the ceiling.

Rufus looked down from his perch on a ladder. He'd been expecting Judd to corner him for an inquisition. The old man looked up and squinted. "You're good about letting my Naomi depend on you, boy, but you're still giving her a hard time. I want to know exactly why you're here every day."

Rufus grinned. He cared a lot for Naomi's grandfather, but he wasn't going to let him treat him like a child. "You're meddling again. But I suppose it's too late to stop you; you've made a lifelong career of telling people what to do. Naomi is mine, Judd, and I am going to take care of her. And if you're smart, you'll refrain from tattling."

He watched Judd walk away with a pretended indifference, but he knew that his words had pleased the old man. Let Naomi figure out for herself the mistake she'd made with him. She was ready for a reconciliation, but he wasn't. He needed her. His body ached for her, and he missed her weird humor, and their warm camaraderie. But for the first time in his life, he appreciated the virtue of patience. He wasn't giving an inch until she came to him, opened her heart to him, and let him know that she trusted him completely and needed him.

# Chapter 18

Naomi opened the door for Rufus, mumbled, "Hello," and left him to trail her as she walked back to her room. "Why didn't you let yourself in?" she threw at him over her shoulder, and blanched at his smooth retort.

"I was reminding myself that I don't really live here." She'd asked for that, but being with him constantly while he treated her like a discarded shoe was wearing on her. Nothing seemed to ruffle him.

She turned to him, tossing her head arrogantly. "Have no fear. *I* hadn't forgotten it." He grinned, and tremors shot through her as she stared at the dancing lights in his eyes and felt his blatant masculinity leap at her. But as quickly as he'd turned on the charm, he extinguished it, reminding her that they were still at odds.

"I'd like to take Aaron over to my place this afternoon, give him a change of scenery for a while. And he thinks he'd like to try using my on-line computer service, make friends with some fellows his age in Texas, California, or wherever." He paused, and her hair crackled with electricity as he eyed her knowingly, like a man going in for the kill. "Whose permission do I get? Yours, or Rosalie's?" She turned away, uncertain as to her next move.

"I'm too tired to go right now, Mr. Meade," Aaron called from his room, letting them know he'd heard their conversation.

She fought against the tension that churned within her as Rufus's mouth curved in a mocking grin. "He's very protective of you. I wonder how he got so tired this early in the day while lying in bed. Preston could have thought up a better one than that."

Naomi sucked in a deep breath. How had it come to this? She tried to hide her vulnerability to him and lowered her eyes to prevent his seeing what she knew they mirrored. When she looked up at him, her heart pounded furiously at the pain in his eyes, the pain of a tortured person. Her hand went out to him of its own volition; taken unawares, he grasped it and clung to it for a moment. Then she watched unhappily as a curtain of indifference seemed to descend over him. Wordlessly, he turned and went into Aaron's room.

She went into her own room, closed the door, and telephoned Rosalie. "What shall I tell Rufus? If Aaron wants to go with him, do you mind?" She waited anxiously for Rosalie's answer, for this clue to their future relationship, for the first evidence she'd have of how far Rosalie would allow her tie with Aaron to go.

"Naomi, when Aaron is with you, he's responsible to you. If it's a question of policy, of course I must be consulted, but ordinarily, you decide. As time goes on and we get to know each other better, it'll be easier." Naomi wondered at her long pause before she continued in the same gentle voice. "I am definitely not suggesting that we share parenting; that wouldn't make sense. But I want Aaron to have a good, healthy relationship with you, and that means obeying and respecting you. So far, our relationship has been good for all of us. I'll be over after work."

Naomi paced the floor. She'd have to find out what Aaron wanted; then she'd speak with Rufus. He had deliberately put her on the spot, indirectly challenging her to explain the relationship between Rosalie, Aaron and herself, though she was certain he'd figured it out.

She found Aaron alone, pensive and anxious for her. He raised up and braced himself on his right elbow. "Noomie, I don't want you and Mr. Meade to be mad at each other because of me. I called my mom, and she said I can suit myself if you agree, so why don't you tell him I'll go to his place after lunch? I like him, Noomie, and I want to see those little rascals of his." He took her hand in his. "You have to make up with him. Promise."

Joy swelled within her. He cared for her, wanted her to be happy. She looked at her son, shook her head at the changes in him, and asked him a question that Rufus had once asked her. "I promise, but whatever happened to your gnawing wit? You've gotten so serious lately."

He placed his hand under his chin, knitted his eyebrows, and pretended to be an old sage. "We're dealing with serious stuff here, Noomie." Her musical laughter filled the room, and he laughed with her.

"I could use a good laugh." She glanced up as Rufus entered the room. Did his eyes always sparkle like diamonds, and did she feel seduced every time she saw him smile? Emotion muffled her words as he walked toward her, carelessly self-possessed. Her hand clutched her throat as she forced herself to speak calmly.

"Aaron wants to go with you, and there's no reason why he can't."

"None?" he asked sardonically.

Aaron heaved himself up in bed. "Mr. Meade, if Noomie says it's okay, it's okay." The both stared at Aaron; the testiness in his voice was unmistakable.

Rufus grimaced slightly. The boy could be touchy. "I'll be ready when you are, son."

Rufus observed that Aaron was unusually quiet. He had a right to be irritated; blood was thicker than water, he'd always been told. The boy knew he'd been putting pressure on Naomi, and he suspected Aaron knew why. He admired her strength, her old-fashioned grit. Strong men would have fallen under what she'd endured during the past month: his discovery of her secret; Aaron's near-fatal accident; her peculiar arrangement with Aaron and Rosalie; having a man she loved so close every day and so detached. He doubted that he'd have borne it all as gracefully. She was vulnerable and raw on the inside, and he was half mad with her for refusing to relent and talk to him. Lord, how he wanted to comfort her, hold her, love her. He sighed deeply. Stubborn woman!

\* \* \*

Naomi used her afternoon of freedom to visit Marva. She needed to talk to someone who would give her the blunt truth. Judd had already voiced his thoughts, but he seemed to have taken out a life membership in the Rufus Meade for everything club and was biased. She knew immediately that she wouldn't be able to speak candidly with her friend. She found Marva knitting booties and unable or unwilling to consider any topic other than her marvelous pregnancy, as she called it. She left Marva, disappointed.

A letter in her mailbox gave Naomi cause for celebration. She telephoned Linda at home to tell her that if she maintained a B average until she finished high school, she'd have her choice of at least three universities with a full scholarship. Linda's screams and confessions of love must have attracted her mother's suspicion, because Linda's mother took the phone and inquired, with some hostility, as to the caller's identity. To Naomi's amusement, the woman's reaction to the news was identical to her daughter's. She couldn't hold back the tears that streaked her cheeks and colored her voice; Linda had a chance at a fruitful, happy life. It was up to her, and Naomi didn't doubt she'd seize the opportunity. Naomi had a sense of triumph, of having finished a difficult task, when Linda's mother invited her to have a meal with them. It had not been easy, but she'd made a friend.

She sat in a leather chair in her living room, sipped mint tea, and contemplated the changes in her life over the past half year. Her euphoria at Linda's good news disappeared. She hadn't known she'd felt so alone until Rosalie arrived.

"Why are you sitting here without lights, Naomi? Are you all right?" Maybe it was the concern with which she spoke, or even the quiet, compassionate way she had of talking. She seemed to invite confidence. A floodgate sprang open and within seconds, Naomi found herself pouring out her soul to this stranger who'd become her friend. She omitted nothing.

"What'll I do, Rosalie? I love him with every fiber of my being. He is my world, my life. I thought I could get him out of

my mind and out of my heart, but now I know I can't. I love
Aaron, and I need Rufus. I made a terrible mistake."

Rosalie walked over to the sofa, sat beside Naomi, and put
her arms around the mother of her adopted son. "You carried a
terrible load for a long time, Naomi, and because of unfounded
fear, you kept it all inside. Just when the load got bigger, you
found someone with whom you could share it, but you couldn't
let go of the fear. You couldn't trust. Rufus hasn't been here for
you night and day since Aaron got hurt just because he doesn't
have anything else to do. Have you asked yourself why? My
mother used to tell me that 'pride goes before destruction and a
haughty stumble before a fall.'"

Her deep-set brown eyes misted, and for a moment, she
seemed to be reliving a treasured experience. "I wouldn't let
pride keep me out of the arms of a man like Rufus Meade." She
went on. "Stuff your pride, Naomi. Let him know you have faith
in him, that you trust him. It's all you need to do."

Naomi watched Rosalie's suddenly brilliant smile. "Now I
know we're friends; you've never told that to anyone else. Well,
I've always wanted a sister, and you'll do nicely."

"No, I haven't," Naomi, confirmed. "And now that I know
what I've missed, never having had a sister, I'm definitely going
to cherish the one I've got now. Let me get you some more
coffee." They talked about their lives and familiarized themselves with each other until Rufus brought Aaron back.

"Will you stay for dinner? It's not much, but there's fried
chicken." She wanted him to stay, and she couldn't keep the note
of hope out of her voice. His leaving would have been easier to
accept if he'd shown any reluctance, but he hadn't.

"I promised Preston and Sheldon I'd be right back. We'll
have to do this again soon, Aaron; my boys and I enjoyed having
you with us." He nodded to Rosalie and Naomi. "Goodnight. I
can let myself out."

Rosalie had gone home, and Naomi sat by Aaron's bed, listening to his excited account of his afternoon with the Meade

family. "He's a great guy, Noomie, Cat Meade practically walks on water."

He slanted his head in a sly grin. "Of course, you do, too—walk on water, I mean." Her eyes widened, and he patted her hand. "Don't get a big head now." She watched as his light olive toned face suddenly curled into a deep frown, his youthful expression becoming serious and strained. "What you told me about when I was born…you know…that stuff about the pressure those people put on you. I believe you. Now that I know you, I can't imagine that you'd willingly have given me up for adoption. I love my mom, Noomie; she's my mom. But I've got a real special place in here for you, too." He pointed to his heart. "I'm lucky my mom is the kind of person she is; otherwise I wouldn't know you."

He used the corner of the sheet to wipe away his mother's tears. "I'm going to try and be a son to you. I promise."

His words warmed her as would a brilliant light, and comforted her, completing the catharsis that had begun with her confession to Rosalie. "I didn't even pray for this, Aaron, because I didn't think it possible for you to love me; I was just hoping you'd like me enough to be with me sometime. You…you're my heart; you're precious to me, and I care deeply for Rosalie, too." She sniffled a few times and had to fight off her emotions. A woman's tears made a man uncomfortable, and sensing that, like most of them, Aaron had low tolerance for heavy emotional scenes, she rose. "I'll get us some ginger ale, or would you rather have a Coke with a couple of scoops of vanilla ice-cream?"

He rewarded the suggestion with a broad grin and his thumbs-up sign. "Noomie," he called after her. "You, my mom, and me are straight. Now all you have to do is get it together with Mr. Meade."

Rufus entered his house through the garage door and rubbed his arms vigorously. Washington wasn't usually so rough in winter, but the entire East Coast was in the clutches of a cold wave. He called a taxi for the sitter, sent her home, and ran upstairs to let his boys know he'd returned. He went back downstairs and made hot chocolate for the three of them, got a tray, and stopped. He could have stayed and had supper with Naomi. She had wanted it so badly, and her wordless entreaty had nearly made him lose his resolve. But if he allowed himself to weaken, all would be lost and she'd never open up to him. Unless she came to him, she wouldn't know that he didn't want to judge her, only to have her complete trust.

He rubbed the back of his neck. Being around her constantly, looking at her, and brushing against her for almost four long weeks had tested his self-control, tried him to the limits of his willpower. But he was damned if he'd give in. He swallowed the saliva that had suddenly accumulated in his mouth. Memories of her woman's scent in the heat of passion assaulted his olfactory senses, and he could feel again her long, silky legs rubbing against his, caressing him as she writhed uninhibitedly beneath him. His blood rushed through his body, telling him how long it had been since he'd loved her. Something had to happen; their standoff had to end, and soon. He picked up the tray and slowly climbed the stairs, deep in thought.

Naomi telephoned her grandfather early the next morning. He wasn't going to like what she had to say, but as he'd said, there was no going back.

"Naomi gal, you can't let well enough alone, can you? Why would you walk into that pit of snakes and present them with the ammunition they'll use to kill your chances? If you take Aaron with you to that school board meeting, you'll never be elected board president. You can find another way to let him know what he means to you."

She had expected him to react that way, but she had to make certain that Aaron would never again think her ashamed of him. She told Judd as much.

"All right, gal. I think you might regret it, but being president of that bunch of snipers is nothing compared to what Aaron means to us. If you'd listened to me, I would never have known my great-grandson. You go on and do what you have to do. You always did, and I'm proud of you."

"Thanks, Grandpa. Aaron loves us, and we've got to show him it's mutual. His last name is Hopkins, but he's family, and he accepts that. I'll let you know what happens at the board meeting."

She brought Aaron's breakfast to him and sat beside him with her own tray. "Noomie, I can eat at the table. You're spoiling me."

Her gaze swept lovingly over his handsome face. "I'm making up for lost time. Besides, I think you're wrong. Rufus told me the doctor said you shouldn't move around too much for another week yet."

As if he'd been waiting for that cue, he placed his tray beside him on the bed, put both hands behind his head, and leaned against the headboard. "You know, Noomie, I think Mr. Meade must be crazy about you. The radio said it was eight degrees and icy outside, and he drove all the way over here to bring you a bottle of milk and a carton of eggs that we could have done without. 'Course, I'm glad he threw in the ice-cream and Coke."

She knew he noticed the clatter of her cup and saucer as she placed them with trembling fingers on the table beside her. Her throat constricted in pain as she forced out her words.

"If he's crazy about me, you and he are the only ones who know it."

Aaron leaned toward her. "I'm a kid, Noomie, but somebody half my age would pick up on that. I've seen him looking at you, just as I've seen you looking at him. You mean he's never told you anything about how he feels?"

"Never, Aaron, and I don't want you to talk to me about it. There was a time when I might have been able to straighten it out, but it's too late now. At first, we didn't like what we saw in each other; then we got close, but I couldn't tell him about my life, so I kept a barrier between us. He figured it all out for himself that night, and I guess he couldn't accept it. Don't think badly of him, Aaron; this mess is my fault. I knew better than to get involved with him."

He seemed restless and his expression turned hard. "Does Mr. Meade know you love him? I mean, did you ever tell him?"

She looked down at her hands, remembering that night. He

had pushed her over the edge, controlling her senses, igniting her, blackmailing her with her wanton hunger for his possession. Then his body had consumed hers with blazing tongues of fire as he'd driven her to mind-shattering ecstasy. Tremors colored her voice. "Once, I told him."

"And you still do." There was no question in his voice. "So how is this your fault? Why must you be the one to fix it? Let him sweat; only a fool would pass up a woman who looks like you, Noomie. And Mr. Meade is not a fool." He let out a long breath, as one who is disgusted. "Sometimes I wonder why adults think they know everything." Naomi took the remains of their breakfast to the kitchen, straightened up the room, and got dressed. She'd stopped wondering why Aaron's thinking so often belied his age; Rosalie had told Naomi that she and her husband hadn't shielded the boy, but had included him in all but the most private aspect of their lives. She tapped on his door, opened it, and leaned in. "I'm going to the supermarket; I should be back in about an hour." She grinned when he folded his fist and stuck his thumb up.

Cold fear knotted Naomi's stomach as she walked through the quiet house and up the stairs to Aaron's room. Intuition and the eerie silence told her that she was alone in the house. The door to Aaron's room stood ajar, the bed made, the room empty. She started to knock on the door of his bathroom, glimpsed the sheet of paper pinned to his pillow, and knew that he was gone. But why? He could barely walk without support. She picked up the paper and for the first time read his careless script.

> Dear Noomie, I know it's not right to leave like this, but I think it's time I went back to my mom. I can look after myself now. Thanks for everything. And don't worry. I'm taking a taxi. I'll call you.
> Love Aaron.

She had to fight the hysteria that welled up in her. What had caused him to leave so suddenly? He'd said he loved her and would be a son to her, and then he'd left, walked out on his word. She couldn't lose him; she *couldn't*. She couldn't find Rosalie's number at work. Wringing her hands in despair, she fought the urge to call her grandfather. She didn't know whether he could stand the jolt; Aaron had come to mean everything to him.

*Oh, Rufus. I need you so!* Her feet propelled her to the telephone beside Aaron's bed as if of their own volition. He answered on the first ring. "Rufus, it's me, Naomi. I went to the supermarket, and when I got back, Aaron had gone. His note said he was going home." She tried to control the trembling in her voice. "I can't lose him, Rufus. I can't lose him. I can't…"

He interrupted her gently. "Settle down, Naomi. It will be all right. Just wait until Rosalie gets home and we can get to the bottom of this. I'm surprised the boy didn't tell you he intended to go; he's always so straightforward."

She wiped her nose with her sleeve and took a deep breath. "That's why I'm worried. Something's wrong."

"Nothing's wrong, Naomi." His voice came to her strong and confident. She knew he had no more information that she did, but his convincing assurance restored her hope. "I'll call you back in an hour or so," he told her. "Don't worry about it, now. Aaron is a good boy, and he's very responsible."

Rufus had registered his boys in a morning preschool program, and he'd already learned that there were benefits for him as well as for the boys. He could leave home suddenly without getting a sitter. He drew his parka on over his cashmere sweater, got into his Town Car, took the East West Highway, and within ten minutes was knocking on the door of the red brick house on Pershing Street.

The surprised look on the boy's face when he opened the door and saw him might have been comical if he hadn't noticed that Aaron was withdrawn, almost unfriendly. "May I come in, Aaron?"

"Sure, Mr. Meade. How did you know where I live?"

What an actor! This kid was mad as the devil about something, but he obviously didn't intend to show it. "I've driven Rosalie home several times. Aaron, Naomi is terribly upset about your leaving her like this." He walked into the living room and sat down. "She's nearly hysterical with worry."

"What's it to you? What do you care how upset she is?"

He could see that the boy would love to slug him. Whatever the problem, he was in the middle of it. "Aaron, this attitude is not one bit helpful. If you've got something to say to me, say it. I'd have thought our relationship merited honesty on both our parts." He watched the boy as the anger left him, and he dropped his head. Rufus waited. Aaron sat in the chair across from him, spread his legs, rested a hand on each knee, and observed him steadily, as if making up his mind. Suddenly, he leaned back.

"Mr. Meade, do you know what Noomie is to me?"

Rufus's eyebrows shot up. He hadn't expected this turn of conversation. "I'd have to be blind not to know. Why?"

Aaron slanted his head to the side in a gesture so reminiscent of Naomi that Rufus shifted uncomfortably at the vision he suddenly had of her. "If I hadn't pushed my mom so hard to find Noomie, you'd probably be married to her by now. She doesn't know how you feel about her, but I do."

Rufus sat forward, a frown furrowing his brow. "What are you talking about? Who is…Aaron, I don't need to hear this from you; I need to hear it from Naomi."

"If you needed to hear it from her, why didn't you ask her right out, Mr. Meade? Can't you see she's been miserable? I know I'm the reason you two can't get together. I hate to see her hurt; she's been hurt enough. If you loved her, you'd talk to her. She said you'd never told her whether you…how you felt about her, but she told *you*. You don't deserve her. I left this morning because if I'm not there, you won't go there every afternoon, and she won't have to be around you." He shrugged. "I just can't figure it out. You'd do anything on earth for her except tell her how you feel. I sure hope I don't grow up to be that stupid!"

Rufus laughed. "Stupid" wasn't one of the names he'd acquired, but maybe it was appropriate in this instance. Aaron's demeanor suggested that if there was anything comical about the matter, he hadn't registered it.

Rufus rose, walked over to Aaron, and extended his hand. "I'll put it right…if she'll let me. Thanks a lot. I'll let myself out." He smiled at the boy's knowing grin and thumbs-up sign. Had it been twenty-one years since he was that age? And had he been that self-assured? He looked at his watch. He didn't have enough time for a visit with Naomi before picking up his boys. He got in his car and dialed her on his cellular phone.

"Naomi, this if Rufus. I've just left Aaron. He's fine, and you've nothing to worry about, believe me. I think he was just matchmaking," he told her cryptically, then added, "I'd like to come over tonight around eight-thirty, if it's okay with you." She agreed, and he hung up. If he was lucky, she'd be wearing that burnt orange dress.

He parked in front of the private day-care center and sat there, pensive. Aaron's words burned his mind, forcing him to see his own role in his volatile relationship with Naomi. He got the boys, drove home, and packed an overnight bag for them. He didn't like them to sleep away from home, but he had to straighten out the issues between him and Naomi, even if it took all night. He left his boys with Jewel and went home.

Naomi took a long, scented bath, tamed her hair into a French twist, and dressed carefully. It might be her last chance with Rufus, and she wanted to look her best. He'd said that dark women look good in pinks and reds, so she donned a lavender pink bra and bikini panties of silk lace that left her practically nude, looked over the pink corner of her closet, selected a wool crêpe dress of the same color, and slipped into it. She decided against pantyhose and wore garters instead. It was frankly a come-on, but she couldn't worry about that; this was war.

When her bell rang at exactly eight-thirty, she moved effortlessly and languidly toward the door, hot anticipation already beginning to steam within her. The frank appreciation in his sensuous gaze told her that the effort she'd made to please him had paid off. She took the beautiful crystal vase of red roses he handed her and stood back to let him enter. Then she placed the vase on the table, took his overcoat, and breathed a prayer of thanks that she'd had the foresight to dress well. He was the epitome of elegance.

He looked down at her as they entered the living room, but the warm anticipation she'd felt knowing she'd see him soon began to dissipate; his eyes were not smiling, but distant and wary. She sat on the sofa and nervous quivers knifed through her when he sat close beside her. He hated both pretense and small talk, so she knew he'd go straight to the point.

Rufus glanced at her as she sat patiently, hands folded in her lap, waiting for him to speak. "I'm a man on a high wire, Naomi; if I make one false step, I'll cripple myself for life. I went to see Aaron, to find out why he left you, but I learned far more than that. The boy is so perceptive and so blunt." He sensed her anxiety and suspected that she was nervous in anticipation of what Aaron might have told him.

"I had no right to ask of you what I couldn't give you in return, Naomi."

She gaped at him. "What do you mean?"

He ran his left hand over his tight, well groomed curls and took a deep breath. Attitudes he'd developed through his life had to be discarded; he'd thought he'd done it, but he realized now that he hadn't. "I asked you to trust me, to share with me what I now realize was the most personal of information. And I accused you of not trusting me, of being secretive and evasive. But you were justified; I've never given you a reason to trust me."

She squirmed beside him. "How can you say that? I've never met anyone more trustworthy than you. Rufus, please don't take responsibility for this…this situation. No one could have been a better friend than you've been these past few weeks." He smiled; she couldn't ever refer to their relationship as the mess that it was.

"I haven't given you the basis for the level of trust you needed and deserved. Oh, I know I came here and helped you and Aaron, did things for you for purely selfish reasons. I had to be with you, and I couldn't allow you to be without anything you wanted or needed." His glance swept over her profile. She was so beautiful, so elegant, and right now, she was so vulnerable. "And haven't you done the same for me," he asked her softly. "What I'm saying is that I self-righteously demanded that you bare your soul to me. I even pressured you into telling me that you loved me and reminded you of it on more than one occasion."

He turned sideways to look fully into her face and saw the tears that glistened unshed in her wide brown eyes. "Baby, don't cry. Don't. I can't stand it." Her lips quivered as her gaze shifted to his face. She lowered her eyes quickly, but he had seen the need in them, the simmering want, had seen her emotionally naked. There was so much that the wanted to say, had to say, but the fire-hot desire that suddenly blazed in his body muffled his words, extinguished every thought but that she wanted him. With a gut-wrenching sigh, he pulled her into his arms, and she reached for him, her lips parted and waiting for the thrust of his tongue.

Naomi opened up to him, a flower offering nectar and receiving life-giving pollination. She grasped the back of his head and held him to her. Hungry. Starving. She gave, and he took. She took, and he gave. He pulled away slightly, and she could see the fine sheen of moisture around his forehead that desire had wrung from him. If he walked away from her tonight, she couldn't bear it. It would be over, and she wouldn't allow it to end. She gazed drunkenly into his mesmerizing eyes, his beloved face. Why didn't he say something? Well, she thought recklessly, when the world didn't turn the way you were going, you walked the other way. Her hand reached out and cupped his chin, but his only reactions were the flicker of passion in his eyes and the slight quiver of his full bottom lip. She could hear the silence that surrounded them, silence so pregnant with the tension of desire that it spoke with a voice of its own. A groan escaped her soft lips, and she clung to him.

"Don't...don't leave me tonight." She wanted to beg him to never leave her. His passion filled eyes drilled her as he seemed to look deeply within her, questioning her desire for him.

"I need you, Rufus. I'm not ashamed of it. I ache for you."

"Oh, God. Naomi, sweetheart, I need you, too. I'm hungry for you, out of my mind with it. All these weeks without you." Heated sensation streaked through her as his sweet mouth found her waiting, hungry lips. Jolts of fiery craving claimed her and she capitulated completely, her head lolling against his breast, her body limp with desire. He took her up in his arms and into her bedroom

He settled her on her feet beside the bed where he'd last loved her, faced her, and found her zipper with his fingers. She stepped away as the dress fell to her feet, and his breath was momentarily lost in anticipation of ecstasy as hot desire shot through him. She had dressed for him, had planned for them to make love. His gaze roamed slowly from her feet, moved up her long, shapely legs, and rested on the vee that cradled her sweet, moist tunnel, her citadel of love. Then it meandered slowly up to her full breasts, bare to his hot gaze except for the tiny scrap of nothing that caressed her nipples. She was beautiful. Intoxicating. How had he stayed away from her, denied himself the fulfillment that he needed so badly, that in his entire life he had found only within her arms? He shuddered violently with the fierceness of his arousal. Breath hissed through his teeth when her hand found his hard flesh and caressed him lovingly through his slacks. Shaking with desire, he picked her up, lay her gently on the bed, removed her intimate garments, and quickly stripped himself. His gaze drifted up and down the reclining body of his *naked maja,* a smile playing around his lips, unable to believe that she was his.

Desire gripped her and her body trembled in anticipation as she stared rhapsodically at the virile man who stood over her, powerful and beautiful in his nudity, his proud sex ready and eager for her. Her tongue slowly rimmed her slightly parted lips and her arms opened to him as her body took control of her mind. She gloried in her womanhood when he fell trembling into her waiting arms. His weight upon her heightened her need, fueled her impatience for his possession. She heard his softly murmured words of assurance, telling her of her beauty and that he adored her. He wrapped her to him and tension curled in the pit of her belly as his strong, hard legs brushed her and her nipples tingled against his chest. She felt the full measure of his hot, steely flesh against her belly and cried out in want.

Somewhere in the distance she heard a loud crash and twisted her body up to his. "It's all right, baby. Just the clock falling to the floor." Tremors swept her as his mouth covered hers tenderly, hotly, in a mind-drugging kiss, as if to rekindle her rushing passion. She strained against him in shameless supplication, but the continued his assault on her senses, curling his tongue around her nipple and pulling it slowly into his warm mouth, punishing her senses as he suckled her voraciously.

"Rufus, please…"

"Didn't I ask you not to call me Rufus when we're together like this? Tell me what you want. Tell me."

"Rufus, darling. I…oh God, honey, I'll die. Please, get in me." She felt his smile as he kissed her belly.

"We've got all night, sweetheart. Just give yourself to me."

Dizzying currents of heat danced through her body as his fingers strummed it, stroked it, played it skillfully like a priceless lyre, and she cried out, writhing and undulating beneath him. Desperate for consummation, her desire at fever pitch, she spread her legs and took his hard, silken flesh into her soft hands. He raised his head and looked down into her face with love-lit eyes. Then he pressed gently against her, but she grasped his tight buttocks and thrust upward, sending a rush of air from him and a loud moan from her lips.

Her body quickly attuned itself to him, and she met his powerful thrust as their bodies moved in perfect unison. Soon the tide of ecstasy began to course through her and she tried to hold it back, to stay with him.

"Let it go, baby. Let it happen. Give yourself to me. I'll be with you all the way."

The waves of ecstasy began at her feet and spiraled through

her body, settling in her core and gripping the man she held within her. She cried out from the sweet torture of it as he buckled above and they flew together, their passion undimmed, free.

Shaken beyond words, Rufus looked down at the woman whose body encased him and kissed her tenderly and lovingly. Then, without releasing himself, he turned on his side, bringing her with him.

"I love you, Naomi." He felt her body stiffen. "I have for a long time. I realized it the night I got back home from Nigeria, and I should have told you then, before we made love, because I knew." He held her closer when he felt the tremors of her emotional reaction.

"I realize now that I didn't tell you because I didn't trust you not to exploit it, and because I couldn't see you in the setting I envisaged for my boys and myself, even though I told myself otherwise. Yet I asked you to trust me. I was wrong in every way, and I know it. You're what I want and what I need."

"Oh, Rufus, there's so much you don't know." He turned to her and kissed her soft brown cheek.

"Not as much as you may think. And before you tell me I want to say something, and it's important. Whatever happened to you in the past, Naomi, can't be undone, and it's not what matters. What the past has made of you is what counts with me. I just want to know if you still love me."

"Oh, yes. I think I started loving you the minute I saw you. I'd watch you with Preston and Sheldon, how you loved them and how secure they were in your love. I knew you had a great capacity for love, and I wanted you to love me. I pushed you away because I thought because of your past experiences with your wife and mother, you'd reject me when you found out about Aaron."

She told him about her son, beginning with the day she'd learned of her pregnancy. "Once I knew he wanted to find me, I had to see him. And then I had to choose between the two of you. I couldn't let Aaron get away from me a second time."

Quietly, he thought over what she'd told him. She'd be a wonderful companion and lover, wife and mother. He had misjudged her badly, but she'd helped by misleading him. Judd was right; pain had to have been her constant companion. But not anymore; he'd see to that, if she'd let him. She began to squirm, to move away from him, and he tightened his hold.

"From now on, we trust each other. We could have spared ourselves a lot of sleepless nights and heartache if we'd believed in each other."

He rolled her over on her back and let her feel him growing within her. "If you'll marry me, I'll be a happy man, Preston and Sheldon will be delirious, Judd will be out of his mind, and Aaron will get off of my case. What about you?"

She sucked in her breath as his gaze consumed her and his intoxicating virility fired her womanhood. I'll be ecstatic."

# AGAINST ALL ODDS

# Chapter 1

Melissa Grant hung up the phone. Anxious. Her graceful brown fingers strummed her desk. She'd had to expand her business in order to stay ahead of her competition, but months would pass before she got the results that she anticipated. Until then her financial status would be precarious at best. Her banker knew that and—because her first loan hadn't been fully paid—had denied her request for a second one. Now she stood a good chance of losing her business. She knew when she came to New York that she could expect tough competition, but she had worked hard and established one of the top executive search firms, and she'd done it in less than five years. She had taken stock of her resources and decided that she had three alternatives, all of them unattractive. She could put her personal funds into her MTG Executive Search firm—something she'd been taught in business school never to do; she could borrow the money from her father; or she could take the lucrative Hayes/Roundtree account. Bankruptcy was preferable to discussing a loan with her father, Rafer Grant, and only trouble could come from any kind of involvement with a Roundtree. Adam Roundtree's executive assistant, Jason Court, had called her with a request that she find a manager for "Leather and Hides," the division of Hayes/Roundtree Enterprises, Inc., that tanned leather and made leather goods. She noticed the light on her phone.

"MTG." She leaned back in her desk chair, twirling a slingshot that she won in a charity raffle. "Hello, Mr. Court. I'm not sure I'm the person you want for this job. I don't know a thing about leather."

"In other words, you don't want the contract," he said as

though surprised. "Adam wants MTG. He thinks your firm is the best, and Adam is used to having the best. Think it over. I can raise the fee by twenty percent, but no more."

Melissa hung up and buzzed her secretary for the Roundtree file.

"Here you are." Kelly put the folder on Melissa's desk. "I thought you said you wouldn't take that job for all the bullion in Fort Knox."

"That was yesterday. The bank just refused my request for a loan." She scanned the few pages. "This must be a mistake." She checked the figure on the last page. "He's offering more money than I ever dreamed of asking for a search. I can find a manager who'll suit him—I don't doubt that, but the consequences could be...explosive. Probably hell to pay."

Kelly frowned. "I don't get it."

"Someday when we have a few hours to throw away, I'll tell you about it." Melissa weighed the pros and cons. If she took the contract, she would no longer have a financial problem and, when she listed a firm on the New York Stock Exchange as one of her clients, her ability to attract fat accounts would be guaranteed. She looked over the papers, corrected the fee, initialed it, and signed the contract without giving herself a chance to change her mind. Her signature was unreadable, and she didn't doubt that Adam Roundtree would inscribe his name beneath hers. But when he found out...when they all found out! Talk about dancing with the devil!

She walked over to her bookcase, scanned a shelf of business and reference books, and selected a volume of an encyclopedia with the intention of learning about leather tanning. The afternoon sun glared in her face, and she lowered the blinds, wondering absently why Adam Roundtree worked for Jenkins and Tillman, a New York real estate firm, rather than with his family's Hayes/Roundtree Enterprises. Had he left northern Maryland and come to New York to escape his parents as she had? From what she'd heard of him, she doubted it. Men of his reputation didn't run from anything or anybody. She put the book in her briefcase, sat down, and lifted the receiver.

"Would you please send this signed contract to Jason Court at Jenkins and Tillman?" she asked her secretary. "Get a messenger, and mark the envelope confidential. I'll be leaving in a minute." She pushed her tight curls away from her olive-toned face and completed her final task of the day.

Melissa walked out of her office, two blocks from Wall Street, and into the sweltering early July heat, her discomfort intensified by the high humidity for which New York City was famous. She didn't wait long for a taxi, sat back and took a deep breath, grateful that she'd escaped the rush hour madness. Ten minutes later, getting a taxi within a mile of Wall Street would be impossible.

Adam Roundtree sat in his New York office reviewing reports from Hayes/Roundtree Enterprises, Inc. The Maryland-based company belonged to his family, handed down to them by his maternal grandfather. Jacob Hayes hadn't believed that his gas field would produce indefinitely, and it hadn't, but he'd lived modestly and ploughed his money into a hosiery and a fabric mill, the leather business, and the newspaper. His foresight had enabled him to pass considerable wealth to his children and grandchildren. Adam appreciated his social station and the wealth that he'd inherited, but he wanted his own kingdom, wanted to build his own legacy for his children—that is, if he ever had any. His father's recent death meant that he had to take an active interest in the family business, including management of the leather factory, which his father had skillfully nurtured. His mother possessed a sharp mind, but his grandfather had thought it improper for a young woman to work, and she'd never used her university education. His younger brother, Wayne, a journalist, had his hands full running the newspaper. No help there. So the onus was on him. It would mean working two demanding jobs, but he'd do it.

He summoned Jason Court for a progress report on the search for a manager of the Leather and Hides division. Adam had just gained full partnership in what was now Jenkins, Roundtree, and Tillman, and he had worked hard for it. He didn't see how he could manage a leather tanning and manufacturing business located in Frederick, Maryland, from his office opposite the World Trade Center in New York.

"Come in, Jason, and have a seat. What have you got for me?"

"I have a contract with MTG for your signature." Adam slapped his right knuckle into the open palm of his left hand.

"Nothing else?" If Jason felt pressured, he didn't show it.

"I got the contract by messenger twenty minutes ago." He handed it to Adam, who didn't even glance at the papers but fixed his concentration on the man opposite him.

"How much time did you allow? A week ought to be more than enough for a firm that knows its business. I need that position filled yesterday. Make that clear." He signed the contract and handed it back. "Thanks, Jason." Adam watched his executive assistant as he left the room. The man was his perfect complement; he liked working with him. A sharp mind and a cool head. But he didn't like doing business by mail with an anonymous nonhuman entity, because he wanted to know with whom he was dealing, see him, size him up, and know what to expect. He called his secretary.

"Olivia, would you arrange a meeting here with the president of MTG tomorrow morning, if possible? I don't like dealing with a faceless company." He walked around to Jason's office, next door to his own.

"Tell me something about this fellow who heads up MTG. I've asked Olivia to have him come over here tomorrow morning, and I need a line on him."

He watched Jason lean back in his chair with a half smile playing around his mouth.

"Adam, the president of MTG is a woman."

"A woman?" He quickly veiled his astonishment; no one was going to accuse him of bias against women or any other group.

"Yeah. And she's a no-nonsense person and a good-looking sister, to boot. She's feminine, but she's the epitome of efficiency, a thorough pro. I figured the fact that she wears a skirt wouldn't bother you."

"It doesn't. I take it from your reference to the sisterhood that she's African-American." Jason nodded. "Well, all I want is for her to bring me a first-class manager."

"She will."

"She'd better."

When Olivia opened his office door, Adam stood. The tall, light-skinned woman approached him slowly and confidently, the epitome of self-possession. Cool, laid-back, and elegant, she didn't smile as she made her way, seeming to saunter, across his vast office to where he stood. Stunned. Poleaxed. She stopped a few feet from him and, flabbergasted as he was, he could nonetheless detect a complete change in her—could see the catch in her breath, the slight droop of her bottom lip, the acceleration of her breathing, and the widening of her incredible eyes just before she lowered them in what was most certainly embarrassment. Woman. She was certainly that. He managed to erase the appreciative expression from his face just as she looked up, her professional demeanor restored, and offered her hand.

"I'm Melissa Grant. It's good to meet you."

His eyebrow quirked, and then a frown stole over his face as he walked to the leather sofa and offered her a seat. She took the chair beside the sofa. Amused, he told her, "The name Grant is anathema to my family."

"As Roundtree is to mine," she coolly shot back.

If he had needed a damper for the desire that she'd aroused in him the second she walked through his door, she'd just provided it. Ordinarily he didn't mind getting a fast fever for a woman, stranger or not; he didn't have to do anything about it. An unexpected sexual hunger assured him that he had the virility a man his age ought to possess, but he didn't like this powerful assault on his senses, the jab in his middle that he'd just gotten in response to Melissa Grant. He wouldn't have liked it if her name hadn't been Grant. Making sure of his ground, he asked her, with seeming casualness, "You're not by chance related to the Frederick, Maryland, Grants, are you?"

"I'm Rafer Grant's daughter, and my mother is Emily Morris Grant. I assume you're Jacob Hayes's grandson."

He had to admire the proud lift of her head, the way in which she fixed her gaze on him, and he didn't doubt her message: if her being a Grant was bothersome, it was his problem, not hers. His desire ebbed and, in spite of himself, his mind went back to his fifteenth year and to Rafer Grant's beautiful and voluptuous sister, Louise, and the way in which she'd flaunted his youthful vulnerability. The memory wasn't a pleasant one, and he brought himself back to the present and to the business at hand. What he felt right then wasn't desire but annoyance at himself.

Assuming his usual posture with a business associate, he pinned her with an unwavering gaze. "What have you managed so far?" He knew his tone was curt, brusque; he made it so deliberately. He wouldn't give her the satisfaction of knowing that she'd gotten to him so easily.

"What do you mean?"

He detected a testiness in her voice. If she had a temper, he'd probably know it soon. "I mean, what have you come up with so far?" He imagined that those were storm clouds forming in her eyes, but he didn't have to imagine that her excessively deep breath bespoke exasperation. He repeated the remark and leaned back to observe the fireworks.

Her cool response disappointed him. "Mr. Roundtree." She punctuated his name with a slow turn of her body toward him and paused while she seemed to weight her next words. "Mr. Roundtree, I signed that contract less than twenty-four hours ago. If I were a magician, I'd be in a circus or perhaps in the White House where miracles are expected. You couldn't be serious, because the contract gives me one month." He was accustomed to women who smiled at him at least occasionally, but not this one. Just as Jason had said, she was all business, and he had just made a tactical error. He'd practically demanded what he hadn't put in the contract, solid evidence that he'd let his emotional response to her interfere with his professionalism, something he'd never done before. He wouldn't do it again, he promised himself, resenting his slip.

He nearly gasped as she stood abruptly, preparing to leave. Nobody terminated an interview with him. Nobody. And neither would she. He stood and began walking toward his office door, but she stopped before reaching it and held out her business card.

"I'm giving you this in case you feel you need to speak with me in person again. My office is as close to you as yours is to me. Otherwise…" She pointed to the telephone. "This has been most informative. Good-bye."

His gaze lingered on her departing back Was this more evidence of Grant contemptuousness for a Roundtree? Or was she telling him that he'd been out of order in requesting that she come to his office for a business meeting rather than suggesting lunch at a neutral place? If the lady disliked his having called rank on her, she had good cause. He should have invited her to lunch.

Adam answered his intercom. "Yes, Olivia. Well, get DiCampino to translate those papers. She claims to know Italian."

"She's out today."

"Really? This is the third time this week. Get a replacement."

He heard Olivia's deep sigh. "Adam, I think Maria is pregnant, and the love of her life is unprepared to honor that fact."

"Well, hell, Olivia." He knew his secretary was waiting for him to pounce on the subject of males who mistreat females, and he didn't keep her waiting. "A man shouldn't impregnate a woman if he's unprepared to make a commitment to her and to their child. He's obligated to marry her. Deliver me from these modern-day Johnny Appleseeds. It's one thing to leave a legacy of apple trees, but it's something else to produce a bunch of fatherless kids. Find out what she needs and let me know." He knew without seeing her that his secretary's face bore a smile.

"Yes, sir. But I can tell you now that she's going to need shelter pretty soon, because her father has threatened to kill her. He says it's an affront to the Blessed Virgin for a good Catholic girl to get pregnant out of wedlock."

He threaded his fingers. "Well, get her a place, and whatever else she needs. And tell her that if the guy doesn't marry her before she begins to show, she should stay away from him."

"Yes, sir. I figured you'd help her."

"Did you, now?" He switched off the intercom and turned on his closed-circuit television. He needed a quote on cowhide futures. He'd thought his life was in order and his career in advance of where he hoped to be at this stage of his life. When his father passed away unexpectedly six weeks earlier, all of that changed. He was the elder son, and he had a responsibility to his family but, in truth, he didn't want to leave his firm. Leather and Hides had always been the most profitable unit of Hayes/Roundtree Enterprises, and it was in trouble and didn't have a manager. He didn't believe in promoting the person who had been on the job longest—he went after the best man, even if he was an outsider, and he wanted the best product. His thoughts went to Melissa Grant. She had impressed him with her professional manner. He smiled. Professional after she recovered from the surprise they both received when they met. He wondered what his family would think of Ms. Grant.

*What had she done?* Melissa sat back in her desk chair and tried to imagine the possible fallout from her signature on that contract when Adam's family found out about it, not to speak of her father's behavior when he learned of her reaction to Adam Roundtree's blatant, blistering masculinity. He haunted her thoughts, as he had done since she first looked at him. A big man. Self-possessed. And he was very tall, very dark, and very handsome. Thinking of him unsettled her, and she recalled that her entire molecular system had danced a jig when she laid eyes on him. But he was like the fruit in the Garden of Eden—one taste guaranteed a fall from Grace. Until today, as far as she knew, the Grants and Roundtrees and the Morrises and Hayeses before them hadn't communicated by mouth or letter in her lifetime or her parents' lifetime. Yet three generations of them had lived continuously within twenty miles of each other. And if today was an indication, their contact now wasn't likely to be pleasant. They had been the bitterest of enemies since Moses Morris, her maternal grandfather, accused Jacob Hayes, Adam's maternal grandfather, of cheating him out of a fortune nearly seventy years earlier. Whether she did it to assuage a sense of guilt, she didn't know, because she didn't examine her motive as she lifted the receiver and dialed her mother.

"Why are you calling in the middle of the day, dear?" Emily Grant asked her daughter. "Is anything wrong?"

"No," Melissa said, groping for a plausible explanation. "I haven't answered your letter, and I thought I'd better make up for that before I forgot it. How's Daddy?" Her mother's heavy sigh did not surprise her.

"Same as always. I'll tell him you asked." The voice suddenly lacked its soft, southern lilt. "I know you're busy, dear, but come home when you can. And take care of yourself. You hear?"

Melissa hung up, feeling no better than before she'd made the call.

Melissa arrived at her apartment building that evening just as her friend, Ilona, reached it. She had met Ilona—a blond, vivacious, and engaging Hungarian with a flair for wit, conversation, and romance...and who admitted to fifty years—in the mail room just off the lobby. Until she'd met her, Melissa had never known anyone who kept a salon. You could always meet an assortment of artists, musicians, singers, dancers, and writers in Ilona's bachelor apartment. Most were Europeans; all of them were interesting.

"Melissa, darling," Ilona said in her strong accent, "come with me for a coffee for a few minutes." Ilona drank hot espresso even on the hottest day.

"Okay, but only for a couple of minutes." They rode the crowded elevator in silence and didn't speak until they were inside Ilona's place.

"What's with you, darling?" Ilona called everybody "darling."

"Who is the man?" Laughter tumbled from Melissa's throat, the first genuine merriment she'd felt since signing that contract.

"With you, it's always a man, Ilona. This time, you guessed right." She recounted her meeting that morning with Adam Roundtree.

"I don't understand," Ilona said.

"If I had passed up that contract, I might have had to declare bankruptcy. Now…well…Ilona, Adam Roundtree didn't know who I was, but when he found out, I could see the light dimming in his eyes. You see, back in the 1920s his grandfather and my grandfather pooled their money to prospect some unproductive Kentucky oil fields for natural gas. For some reason, my grandfather pulled out, and six months later, Jacob Hayes brought in gas. My grandfather claimed that the gas field belonged to both of them, but he lost the court case. The townspeople gossiped, and years later Adam's mother sued my family for slander and won an apology. It's a mess. As far as I know, the Hayes-Roundtree clan and my folks hadn't spoken in seventy years— until today when I met Adam Roundtree. You can't mention their names in my father's house."

"And how do you feel about all this?"

"I don't carry grudges." Her weak smile must have reflected her grim mood; for once, Ilona had no clever response. Ilona brought their espresso coffee and some frozen homemade chocolates, explaining that she hadn't made them and that she never cooked.

"If I had been wearing my glasses this morning, I'd have been better prepared for what I saw when I got close to Adam." She thought that glasses didn't become her and wore them only when absolutely necessary. Her laughter floated through the apartment. "The truth is that if I could have seen him, I wouldn't have been foolish enough to get that close to him." She rose to leave, but Ilona detained her.

"Darling, what are you going to do about this man?"

Melissa shrugged. "Avoid him as much as possible."

"I'm sorry you feel that way," she said, "but I'd never give up on that man."

"I'd like to see more of him but, knowing what I know, that wouldn't be smart. I'd better go."

Melissa left Ilona and went home to get her dinner and review some contracts. Her face heated as she remembered what she'd felt when she got a good look at Adam. He'd made her feel... Recalling it embarrassed her. His smooth sepia skin invited her touch, and when she'd looked into his warm brown eyes, eyes that had a natural twinkle, she sensed herself being lulled into a receptive mood, receptive to anything he might suggest or do. Although twenty-eight, she had never experienced such a reaction to a man. His big frame had towered over her five feet eight inches, but she hadn't been intimidated. Power. Flagrant maleness. He exuded both. Adam Roundtree was handsome... and dangerous. His eyes continued to twinkle, she recalled, even when his tone became cool.

Melissa arrived early at her office, drank a cup of tasteless machine coffee, and settled into her work. At about eight thirty, she answered her secretary's buzz.

"Yes, Kelly."

"Mr. Roundtree insists that he won't speak with anyone but you, and that if you refuse to talk to him, he'll void the contract. He says he knows other executive search firms; he's serious."

Melissa remembered Jason Court's deference to his boss. Void their contract? "Just let him try it," she told Kelly. "Put him on." She let him wait a second, but not so long as to seem rude. "How may I help you, Mr. Roundtree?"

"My name is Adam, Melissa, and you may help me by assuring me that you don't palm off your clients on your assistants. I'm paying enough to be able to speak with you directly. You left my office before I had an opportunity to tell you what you can trade off. I know what the contract says, but we may have to give a little, because I can't wait for a manager until you've checked every guy who's been close to a cow. Could we meet somewhere for lunch tomorrow, say around one thirty?"

"Does that mean I can check every gal who's been near a pig

or an alligator?" she asked, alluding to other sources of leather. She heard him snort, but before he could answer, she agreed to meet him. "One o'clock would be better for me, and I like a light lunch. How about Thompson's?" He had to compromise, she figured. And why couldn't he discuss it right then? Adam's voice interrupted her thoughts.

"Alright. Thompson's at one. And Melissa, leave your armor in your office."

"Will do. And you leave your tough guy personality in yours."

"See you tomorrow." He hung up, and she thought she heard him make a noise. It couldn't have been a laugh. Maybe he had a hidden soft side, but if he did, she didn't want to be exposed to it—what she'd seen of him was more beguiling than she cared to deal with.

Melissa walked into her co-op apartment in Lincoln Towers, three blocks from Lincoln Center for the Performing Arts, closed the door, and thanked God for the cool, refreshing air. She got a glass of orange juice from the refrigerator, took it into the living room and drank it while she watched the six o'clock news. After a few minutes her mind wandered to Adam Roundtree, and she switched off the television. She disliked driven, overachieving, corporate males. Gilbert Lewis had been one, a man with a time-table for everything. After "X" number of dinners, movies, and taxi rides, you either went to bed with him, or you were off of his list. She had told him to get lost when he gave her his stock ultimatum. She had stupidly fallen for him, and his attitude had hurt, but she'd kept her integrity. And now there was Adam Roundtree, a man whose impact on her when she met him was far more profound than any emotion Gilbert Lewis or any other man had ever induced.

Melissa wouldn't have admitted that she dressed with special care that morning, had the red linen dress that she wore only when she wanted to make an impression not been proof. If her parents knew she planned to have lunch with Adam Roundtree, they'd have conniptions. She'd never been able to please her father, and her mother only said and did that which pleased her husband. She stared at herself in the mirror and saw her mother's grayish brown eyes and her father's mulatto coloring—the result of generations of mulatto inbreeding—and prayed that that was as much like them as she'd ever be. One thing was certain—if her business went under, she would consider it to have been due to her own shortcomings, not the fault of some imagined enemy that could be conveniently blamed the way her father always blamed the Hayeses and Roundtrees for his succession of failures. She let her curly hair hang down around her shoulders in spite of the summer heat, picked up her briefcase, and went to work.

She arrived at Thompson's promptly at one to find Adam leaning casually against the cashier's counter at the entrance to the restaurant. Punctuality fitted what she'd seen of his personality, and it was a trait she admired. His piercing gaze and that twinkle in his eyes fascinated her, and she realized she'd better get used to him—and quick—or he'd be laughing at her. She shook his hand and greeted him with seeming casualness, but the feel of his big hand splayed in the middle of her back as he steered her to their table was a test she could have happily forgone.

Melissa's heavy lashes shot upward, and she gasped in surprise at the dozen yellow roses on their table. She glanced quickly at Adam, opened the attached note, and read: "My apologies for not having done this Tuesday rather than ask you to come to my office. Forgiven? Adam."

Unable to associate the man with the soft gesture, she merely stared at him.

"Well?"

Melissa glanced downward to avoid his piercing gaze with its suggestive twinkle, certain that he discerned the flutter in her chest.

"Thanks. It's a lovely gesture."

Immediately he replaced his diffidence with his usual businesslike mien.

"Well, did you bring it?"

"Did I bring what?" she asked. His tone was jocular, but she wasn't certain that it depicted his mood. She suspected that, with him, what you saw and even what you thought you heard might mislead you.

"Did you bring your armor?" She wanted to glare at him but didn't trust herself to look straight into his eyes long enough to make it effective.

"It's always close by," she told him with studied sweetness, "but I'm not wearing it out of deference to your sensitive, gentle self." He laughed. The dancing glints in his eyes matched both his softened face and the smile that framed his even white teeth, and hot sparks shot through her, his transformation very nearly electrifying her. He broke it off at once, and she had the feeling that laughing wasn't something that he did often.

"When did you last laugh?" She watched him quirk an eyebrow and then frown.

"Not recently. What made you ask?"

She narrowed her eyes, squinting to get a good look, and shrugged her shoulder. "You didn't seem comfortable doing it." He laughed again, and she realized that he surprised himself when he did it.

Melissa controlled the urge to laugh along with him, reminding herself that she couldn't afford to be captivated by his mercurial personality—they were there to discuss business. *Her* business. He sat erect suddenly, all semblance of good humor banished. She needn't have been concerned, she told herself, because he had his own techniques for keeping people at a distance. And right then, his method was to serve his charm in small doses.

"Why did you need to see me in person?" she asked him. Did the twinkle in his eyes become brighter, or was she mistaken? She wished she could look somewhere else.

"My father managed Leather and Hides in his own way, ignoring the latest techniques and machinery. He made a good product, the best, but he's gone now, and he didn't leave a manual. I need a manager who can deal with that, who can make the business a state-of-the-art operation without sacrificing the quality that my father achieved. And I want an increase in productivity. We need to work together if I'm going to get what I'm looking for."

"What are you willing to give up?"

He listed several traits that she considered minor.

"Okay. Now I'd like to eat my salad." She looked down at her food and began to eat, but she knew he was glaring at her.

"Melissa, do I automatically ring your bell, or are you planning to carry on this ridiculous family feud?"

"I could ask you that."

"You ring something, alright, but I'd hardly call it a bell. As for the rest, I chart my own course. I alone decide what I think and how I act, and my criteria for judging people don't include reference to their forebears."

"I can buy that. But with all their weaknesses, parents and siblings are very important, and it isn't easy or comfortable to turn one's back on them." She could have kicked herself for that statement—after all, her thoughts about her family were not his business. "Why are you staring at me?" she asked him.

He seemed momentarily perplexed. "I didn't realize I was. My common sense tells me I'd never forget a woman like you, but there's something... Do you get the impression that we've met before...under unusual circumstances?"

"No. To my knowledge, I saw you yesterday for the first time. Why do you think we met somewhere else?"

"Just a feeling I have. When you were speaking softly about your family, your voice reminded me of someone and something special. Forget it. It's probably just my imagination. Well, I've enjoyed our lunch, Melissa. Are you going to take my calls, or will I have to use blackmail again?"

She didn't look at him. With that teasing tone, she could imagine the expression in his eyes. "Blackmail. But try something more original next time." They both laughed, and she realized she liked him.

Adam told Melissa good-bye and walked briskly toward his office. In spite of the heat he didn't want to go inside. He had a strange and uncomfortable feeling that something important was about to occur. It was like smelling a storm in the scent of the wind. Melissa Grant did not fit a mold, at least not one with which he was familiar. She wasn't beautiful, but something about her grabbed him, embedded itself in him. He'd often wondered if he would ever feel for a woman what he'd felt the first time he saw her, wondered whether there would ever be a graceful, intelligent woman who'd bring him to heel. He had an irritating certainty that she could. She'd made him laugh, too, not once but three times, and it had felt good. The loud horn blast of a red Ford alerted him to the changing traffic light, and he stepped back to the curb and waited under the blazing sun. Melissa respected him, he reflected, but she wasn't afraid of him, and he didn't know many men about whom he could say that. But she was a professional associate, and she was a Grant.

Several days later at their regular Monday morning conference, Adam questioned Jason Court about Melissa. He wanted to know what progress she'd made, but he had other queries, too.

"Jason, why did you choose MTG for this search? I'm not displeased, just interested." He had to know exactly what Melissa's relationship was to Jason, and he scrutinized the man for any shred of evidence that he had a personal interest in her.

"MTG placed me in this job, Adam. I presume since you've just met her that my predecessor negotiated the terms. Anyway, she impressed me with her efficiency and manners. She's thorough. She's competent. If you answer all of her questions truthfully, you won't have a secret when she's through with you."

"Oh, I don't doubt that." So there was nothing personal between them. Good. He recalled her reaction to him when they met; if any other man was interested in Melissa Grant, he was out of luck.

Adam watched Jason tilt his head to one side, as if making certain of his words, before he said, "She's not bad on the eyes, but she's nearsighted as all hell. Man, she can't see a thing from a distance of five feet, and when she does wear glasses, they're on top of her head instead of on her eyes." Adam couldn't control the laughter that erupted from his chest. His head went back, and he laughed aloud, causing Jason to gape at him, apparently stunned.

"What's so funny, Adam? That's the first time I've heard you laugh in the four years I've been working for you."

Adam stood, effectively terminating the meeting. "You don't want to know, Jason. Believe me, you don't." He went to his office, closed the door, and enjoyed a good laugh. The morning she'd come to his office, Melissa hadn't seen him clearly until she was close enough to touch him, and what she saw must have sent her hormones into a tailspin. At least it was mutual.

The flashing phone lights brought him out of his heretofore unheard-of indulgence in reverie. "Roundtree." He'd hoped it was Melissa calling to say that she had found a prospect, but it was his younger brother, Wayne.

"I've engaged a search firm to find a head for Leather and Hides, Wayne. Yes, I know you're not keen on headhunters, but it's the most efficient way to get the kind of person we want." He didn't mention that he'd hired Melissa Grant to do the job; time enough when the bimonthly report circulated. He wasn't ready to take on Wayne and his mother, especially his mother, about dealing with a Grant or a Morris. Mary Hayes Roundtree would go to her grave despising the Morrises and Grants. Such a waste of emotion! He got up from his desk and began to pace. Wayne was asking a lot of him. The telephone cord reached its limit and halted Adam's pacing.

"You're suggesting that I leave my firm here in New York and spend three months in Frederick reorganizing Hayes/Roundtree Enterprises? But I've just been made full partner, Wayne—this is hardly the time to amble off for a few months leave of absence. I know you have your hands full with the paper, but I'll have to give this some thought and get back to you."

A leave of absence. He could do it, though he disliked leaving his department in the hands of another person, even Jason Court. But what choice did he have? Wayne wouldn't suggest it if there was a way around it. His brother couldn't continue to manage both the leather factory and the newspaper. He needed that manager. He walked around to Jason's office, thinking of the fallout when their families learned of that contract.

That question plagued Melissa as she prepared and ate a light supper and mused over the day's events. The telephone ended her reverie, and one of her father's demands greeted her hello, shattering her good mood.

"Daddy, I know you think my business is child's play, but it has supported me well for five years, and I've never asked you for help. Can't you at least credit me with that?" Wrong tactic, she knew at once: independence was precisely what he sought to deny her. "I can't leave my business and go back home. And I don't want to."

"Your mother needs you," he replied, emphasizing the words this time as if to say, "You wouldn't dare disobey me."

Scoffing, she ignored his words. She didn't wonder that her brother, Schyler, had taken a job overseas to avoid the emasculating effects of their father's dominance, overprotectiveness, and indulgence.

"Daddy, I'm running a business here. I hire three people full time. I can't close my business like that—" she snapped her finger "—and leave them and my clients stranded. I have contracts to fulfill."

"But your mother's been feeling poorly, and I want you to come home. You don't have to work—I'll take care of you. You come home."

"Don't my responsibilities mean anything to you, Father?" Melissa wanted to kick herself—he knew she always called him Father when he managed to make her feel like a small child.

His answer didn't surprise her. "What's an employment agency? Anybody can run that. You come home where you belong." Why had she expected anything different? He could as well hire a companion for her mother, and if she went home, he probably wouldn't even realize she was there. And if her mother needed anyone, it was her husband, the man who ignored her at home but played the besotted husband in public.

Her father hadn't wanted a girl and had ignored her, but he doted on her brother, and her mother seemed to love whatever and whomever her father loved, because she hadn't the will to confront or defy her domineering husband. Resentment coursed through her. No matter what she did, her father wasn't satisfied with her. And now he demanded that she give up the life she'd made for herself. For as long as she could remember, she had done everything she could to please him, but whenever he needed something he imposed on her, never on his precious Schyler.

"I'll go down and see Mother," she told him, "but I'll have to come back." He hung up, and she knew he was furious, but for once she didn't care. Immediately shame and remorse overcame her for having thought unkindly about her family. Family was important—Rafer Grant held that premise sacred and had taught her to do the same. She mulled over her father's suggestion; perhaps moving back to Maryland might not be such a bad idea. She could care for her mother, and computers and fax machines would enable her to run her business from there. She'd also have lower overhead, and she'd be away from the temptation of Adam Roundtree.

# Chapter 2

Several days later, frustrated by the poor caliber of the applicants she'd contacted, Melissa answered the phone without waiting for her secretary to screen the call.

"MTG."

"Melissa? Adam. You must have guessed that it was me. Otherwise you wouldn't have picked up, right?" What had come over him? She'd had the impression that he didn't joke much, but that if he did, his words had an important, second meaning.

"Well?"

His voice carried a tantalizing urgency that challenged her to open up to him, but the very idea put her on guard, and she shifted in her chair. He had to be thirty-four or -five and couldn't have reached that age without knowing his effect on people, especially women. Well, if he wanted to play cat and mouse, fine with her, but she was not going to be the mouse.

"Sure thing," she bantered. "Didn't you know that I'm a psychic?" She wasn't, but let him think about *that*.

"You disillusion me. I thought you answered because you're on my wavelength, but I've been wrong a few times. How are you getting along?"

"Just fine."

"You have some good prospects? That's great."

"I don't have any prospects, but I'm just fine." Silence greeted her delicate laugh. "Adam, what happened to that sense of humor you had a minute ago? Don't tell me that it only operates at somebody else's expense?" Before he could reply, she asked him, "You wanted something?"

"I told you. I want to know how you're getting along with the search."

"Adam, when I have a candidate, I'll contact Jason Court."

"Are you saying you prefer speaking with Court?"

Melissa's sigh, long and deep, was intended to warn him of her exasperation. "I'm assuming that you're too busy to deal with so insignificant a matter as a head hunt." Where was her brain? How could she have told him that he was paying her an exorbitant fee for an insignificant service?

Adam's thoughts must have parallelled hers, because he spoke in clipped tones. "I didn't realize you thought so little of the service you provide." Did his voice reflect bitterness? She wasn't sure.

"I'm sorry, Adam. It wasn't my intention to imply that I don't take your needs seriously."

"Now you see why I dislike discussing business on the telephone. If I had been looking at you, I wouldn't have mistaken your intent. Have lunch with me, and let's straighten this out."

"Adam, I don't see that there's anything to straighten out. Anyway, you probably won't enjoy lunch with me. I don't care much for power executives and two-hour lunches."

He spoke more slowly, and his tone suggested that he didn't like what she'd said. Why did the worst in her always seem to come out when she talked to him? She reckoned that, no matter how much the corporate giant he was, he had feelings, and she didn't want to hurt him.

"I take it you don't care for executive men. Why?"

"It isn't that I dislike them—I understand them."

He winced, and she had no trouble figuring out what he'd thought of that. Not much.

"I wasn't aware that we were all alike," he replied with pronounced sarcasm. Then he asked her, "Melissa, when you signed our contract, did you know I was a member of the Hayes-Roundtree family in Beaver Ridge, Maryland?"

"Yes, I knew." She'd been expecting the question and had

wondered why he hadn't asked earlier. That was one thing she had decided she liked about him—he didn't waste time speculating if he could get the facts. "I run a business, Adam, and I try to give my clients good service. If I think I can find them the kind of employee they want, I take the job. I don't hold one person responsible for what another did." The words had barely left her mouth when she realized her mistake.

His low, icy tone confirmed it. "Moses Morris's accusation was false and unconscionable, and that was proved in court."

"I'm sorry I alluded to that. I'd rather not discuss it. As far as I'm concerned, the matter was over seventy years ago."

"No. You won't state where you stand on that issue, though you know it's important. You'll evade it just like you walked out of my office without completing our discussions the day I met you. Avoid the heat, lady. That way you can stay calm, unruffled, unscathed, and above it all."

She couldn't tell from his voice whether she had angered him or saddened him, but she wouldn't let him browbeat her. "You're very clever to have learned so much about me in the…let's see, two and a half hours that you've been in my presence. The arrogance of it boggles my mind, Adam. Well, let me tell you that I hurt as badly as the next Joe or Jane, and I bleed when I get cut, just like you do."

"Look, I didn't mean to— Melissa, this was a friendly call. I wanted to get to know you. I… We'll talk another time."

Her gaze lingered on the telephone after she hung up, annoyed with herself for having revealed such an intimacy to Adam. She could hardly believe that he'd been so accurate. She'd gotten out of his office that morning to preserve her professionalism, but for reasons other than he'd said. His effect on her had been mesmerizing, and she'd had no choice but to flee or lose her poise. She couldn't allow him to regard her as just so much fluff—she headed a flourishing business, and she wanted that fact impressed on him.

Adam replaced the receiver with more care than usual and stared at the blank wall facing his desk. He didn't want to feel compassion for Melissa; she'd made a solid enough impression on him as it was. It was one thing to want her, but if he also began to care about her feelings, he'd be in trouble. He had close women friends, but he didn't allow himself to become emotionally involved with them. One woman had taught him to need her, to yearn for her, but foolish boy that he'd been, he had believed her seductive lies and gone back for more. Her full breast and ripe brown nipples were the first he'd ever seen. She had guided his lips to them while she stroked him, and he'd gone crazy. How could he have known that she only wanted to humiliate him? After nineteen years her vicious laughter still rang in his ears. *Not again.* Yet his life lacked something vital: a loving woman with whom he could share everything, the deepest desire of his soul; a home warm with a woman's touch, devoid of the chrome and black leather sofas that decorators loved. And children. He shook his head. Just so much wishful thinking.

He left work late, grabbed a hot dog from his friend, who sold them at a corner pushcart, and made his way to the Metropolitan Museum of Art. He enjoyed the concerts there. People went because they appreciated the music, not because it was the chic thing to do, and they didn't applaud halfway through a piece. At intermission he strolled out to the hallway for a stretch and a look at the crowd. Was he seeing correctly? He wouldn't have thought that Melissa would attend a concert alone. Maybe she was waiting for someone. He watched her, undetected, and saw that she didn't have a date. Just as he decided to speak to her, she looked directly at him, surprise mirrored in her eyes, and flashed him a cool smile.

Melissa watched Adam walk toward her, a gazelle in slow motion, and resisted the urge to smile. He must collect women the way squirrels gather nuts, she mused. She told herself not to be captivated by his dark good looks, his blatant masculinity, but she sucked in her breath as he neared her and wished that she'd taken off her distance glasses at the beginning of intermission.

She couldn't hide her surprise at seeing him there alone. What had happened to the New York City women that such a man as Adam Roundtree attended concerts by himself? She decided not to comment on it, not to rile him, since he seemed more relaxed, less formal than previously, though she sensed a tightness about him. Her heart lurched in her chest as his slow, captivating smile spread over his handsome ebony face. She wasn't a shy person, but she had to break eye contact with him in order to control her reaction. When her glance found him again, he had nearly reached her, and she had to steel herself against the impact of his nearness. *What was wrong with her?*

Adam held out his hand to her, and she took it, but they didn't shake—though that was what he seemed to have intended. Instead he held her hand, and they looked at each other. His gaze burned her until her nervous fingers reached for the top button of her blouse. What is it about him? she asked herself. He spoke first.

"The auditorium is barely half full. Why don't we sit together for the remainder of the concert?" She didn't want to sit with him, and she didn't want him holding her hand. Tremors ploughed through her when he touched her. She eased her fingers from his—feeling as though he'd just branded her—opened her mouth to refuse, and had half turned from him when another familiar voice caught her attention. Gilbert Lewis sauntered toward them.

"Yo, Melissa. I saw you sitting by yourself. I'm going for a drink, mind if I join you?" The man glanced up at Adam. "Or are you busy?" She wondered if he would have suggested it had she been alone.

"Excuse me, Gilbert. I'm with Mr. Roundtree." She watched Gilbert Lewis walk away and thought how long she'd waited for that small measure of revenge. Small, but priceless. If a man saw a woman with Adam Roundtree, he knew he didn't have an iota of a chance. The lights blinked, signaling the end of intermission, and Adam touched her elbow to guide her to their seats. She stepped away, but he trapped her.

"Have a good look at me, Melissa, so that you won't try this trick with me again. I'm not accustomed to being used, Melissa, because nobody dares it. If you didn't want that man's company, you could have told him so. You said you're with me—and lady—*you are with me.* Let's get our seats before the music begins." He walked them to their seats. Chastened, she explained.

"Adam, if you knew how much that scene meant to me, you wouldn't grumble."

His tone softened. "Are you going to tell me?"

She laughed. "You're a hard man, aren't you? Not an inch do you give."

His shrug didn't fool her that time, because his eyes denied the motion. "If it suits you to think that, I wouldn't consider disabusing you of the idea." At least he smiled, she noted with satisfaction. They took their seats, and she turned to him as the curtain opened. "You realize, of course, that if I didn't want to sit with you, I'd be over there somewhere, don't you?" She nodded toward some empty seats across the aisle. He patted her hand, and his words surprised her.

"I should think so. If you were the type to allow yourself to be steamrollered, you'd be less interesting."

They stepped out of the great stone building, J. Pierpont Morgan's grand gift to the city, and into the sweltering night. Several men removed their jackets, but not Adam. Her glance shifted to him, cool and apparently unaffected. She wondered how he did it. She had the impression that he didn't allow anything, including the weather, to interfere with his adherence to the standards he'd set for himself.

The swaying trees along the edge of Central Park provided a welcomed, if warm, breeze as they walked down Fifth Avenue, but as though they had slipped into private worlds, neither spoke until they reached the corner and waited for the light to change.

"It's early yet," Adam observed. "Let's stop somewhere for a drink." If he hadn't been staring down at her, she reasoned, saying no would have been easier. But a smile played around his lips almost as if he harbored a delicious secret—she didn't doubt that he did—and the twinkle in his eyes dared her to be reckless.

She voiced a thought that tempered her momentary foolhardiness. "Adam, if anybody in Beaver Ridge or Frederick saw us walking together, they'd be certain the world was coming to an end."

"Why?" he asked, taking her arm as they crossed the street, "we're not holding hands." She was grateful that he wasn't looking at her and couldn't see her embarrassment, but she needn't have worried, she realized, because his thoughts were elsewhere.

"Melissa, why did you agree to find a manager for me if you knew who I was?"

"What happened between our grandfathers was unfortunate, Adam, and it is one legacy that I don't intend to pass on to my children. I've never been able to hate anyone, and I'm glad, because hatred is as crippling as any disease. Believe me—I've seen enough of it. Anyway, why shouldn't I have taken your business?" she hedged, unwilling to lie. His large retainer had been her salvation. "I operate a service that you needed and for which you were willing to pay." She looked up at him and added, "It's tempting to walk through the park, but that wouldn't be safe even with you. How much over six feet are you, Adam?"

"Four inches. How much under it are you?"

"Four inches." He stopped walking and looked down at her. "How much under thirty are you?"

"Two years." Her lips curled into a smile. "How much over it are you?"

"Four years." He grasped her hand and threaded her fingers with his own.

Each time she was with him, he exposed a little more of himself, she realized. His wry wit and unexpected teasing appealed to her—she liked him a lot. Pure feminine satisfaction enveloped her. Here was a man who was strong and self-reliant, sure of himself, who didn't need to blame others for his failures, if he had any. She shook her head as though to clear it. Adam Roundtree could easily become an addiction. And she knew that part of his appeal was his contrast with her father. Adam was direct, fair, but her father tended to be manipulative, at least with her. Adam was a defender, but for all his accomplishments, Rafer Grant was a user.

"Where are we going for this drink? We're walking toward my place, but we could go over to Madison and find a café or bar. There's no reason to go further out of your way."

"Stop worrying, Melissa. I recognize your status as my equal—well, almost." A glance up at him told her that the twinkle carried humor. "We *are* walking my way. I live on Broadway just across from Lincoln Center." When she showed surprise, he slowed his steps.

"Where do you live, Melissa?"

She laughed. "Four blocks from you, in Lincoln Towers."

They took the bus across Central Park, stopped at a coffee-house on Broadway, and idled away three-quarters of an hour.

"How long have you lived away from home?" he asked between sips of espresso.

"Since I left for college. A little over ten years."

"Do you miss it?"

She thought for minute. "No. I guess not. Our home life was less than ideal." Hot little needles shimmied through her veins when his hand reached across the tiny table and clasped hers, reassuring her. She knew right then that he'd protect her if she let him.

"I'm sorry." His words were soft. Soothing. She wouldn't have thought him capable of such gentleness. "That must have been difficult for you," he added.

"Oh, it wasn't all bad. From time to time, I got lovely surprises that brightened my life."

"Like what?"

"Let's see. The occasional rose that I'd find on my dresser. The little crystal bowl of lavender potpourri that would appear in my bathroom. Books of poetry under my pillow. I remember I was so happy to find 'The Song of Hiawatha' there that I read it and cried with joy half the night."

His strong fingers squeezed hers in a gentle caress. "Who was this silent angel?"

"My mother."

His perplexed expression didn't surprise her, but she was glad that he didn't question her further. He looked at her for a moment, then shook his head as though dismayed. "Ready to go?"

She nodded. As they left, he took her hand, intensifying her wariness of him and of what she sensed growing between them.

"Walk you home?" he asked her. She wanted to prolong the time with him but thought of the consequences and tried to extricate her fingers from his, but he held on and then squeezed affectionately. Warmth flowed through her, a warmth that strengthened her, invigorated her, and enhanced her sense of self. She noticed couples, young and old, among the late evening strollers, some of whom were obviously lovers, enraptured, in their own world. Some seemed to argue, to be ill at ease in their relationship. Others appeared to have been together so long that complacency best described them, but they all held hands. Like small children clutching their security blankets, she mused. When they reached the building in which she lived, Adam assumed a casual air and looked down at her, silently awaiting a signal for his next move. What a cautious man, she thought as she prepared to head off any gesture of intimacy on his part. Though wary of the guaranteed effect of his touch, she extended her hand.

"It's been nice, Adam. Since we've just had coffee, I won't invite you for more. Maybe we'll meet again."

His displeasure wasn't concealed by the dancing light in his eyes, she noted. "Are you always so cut and dried?" When I'm nervous, yes, she thought. Without waiting for her answer, he went on. "Your tendency to dismiss people could be taken as rudeness. Why are you so concerned with protecting yourself? Trust me, Melissa. I can read a woman the way fortune-tellers read tea leaves. You'd like this evening to continue, but you've convinced yourself that it wouldn't be in your best interest, and you have the fortitude necessary to terminate it right now. I like that."

He grinned. She hadn't seen him do that before, and she couldn't decide what to make of it. Why didn't he leave? She didn't want to stand there with heat sizzling between them. Tension gripped the back of her neck, and her hair seemed to crackle with electricity when he took a step closer. She moved, signaling her withdrawal from him, and he pinned her with the look of a man who knows every move and what it symbolizes. His brazen gaze told her that her reprieve was temporary, that he knew she was susceptible to him, and that he could easily get her cooperation in knowing him more intimately. Her blood raced when his right hand dusted her cheek just before he nodded and walked away.

Melissa closed her apartment door, leaned against it, and sighed with relief. Adam Roundtree was quintessential male. An alluring magnet. But she wasn't fool enough to ruin her life— at least she hoped not. But the uneasy feeling persisted that Adam Roundtree got whatever he wanted, and that her best chance of escaping him was if he didn't want her. Just the thought of belonging to a man like him was drugging, a narcotic to her libido. With his height, fat-scarce muscular build and handsome dark face, and those long-lashed bedroom eyes with their brown hazel-rimmed irises, he was a charismatic knock-out. Add to that his commanding presence and… A long breath escaped her. She recalled his squared, stubborn chin and the personality that it suggested and concluded that if he softened up and stayed that way, he would be a trial for any woman. She heard the telephone as she entered her apartment, and excitement boiled up in her at the thought that Adam could be calling her from the lobby.

Her hello brought both a surprise and a disappointment. "I thought we agreed that you wouldn't call me again, Gilbert."

"You suggested it," he said, "but I didn't agree." At one time she couldn't have imagined that this man's voice would fail to thrill her or that her blood wouldn't churn at the least evidence of his interest.

"You don't say." His weary sigh was audible. Women didn't dangle Gilbert Lewis, and she found his impatience with her disinterest amusing.

"Well, if you didn't agree, what's your explanation for this long hiatus? Do you think I've been twiddling my thumbs waiting to hear from you?" She didn't approve of toying with a person's feelings, but where Gilbert was concerned, she didn't have a sense of guilt—if he had feelings, he hadn't made that fact known to her. She grinned at his reply.

"Honey, you don't know how many times I've tried to reach you, but you're never home. Let's get together. I'm giving a black tie party next Saturday, and I want you to come. And bring Roundtree." The latter was posed as an afterthought, but she knew it was the reason for his call. Ever the opportunist, Gilbert Lewis had called because he wanted to meet Adam Roundtree. He had no more interest in her that she had in him.

"And if Adam has other plans, may I come alone or bring someone else?" She had evidently surprised him, and his sputters delighted her, because she'd never known him to be speechless.

"Well," he stammered. "I've always wanted to meet the guy. See if you can get him to come." She imagined that her laughter angered him, but he was too proud to show it. When she could stop laughing, she answered him.

"Gilbert, you couldn't have been this transparent four years ago. If you were, there must have been more Maryland hayseed in my hair than I thought. Be a good boy, and stick to your kind of woman. I'm not one of them." She hung up feeling cleansed. What a difference! Her thoughts went to Adam. That man would never expose himself to ridicule or scorn.

Minutes after he left her, Adam sat at a small table in the Lincoln Center plaza drinking Pernod, absently watching the lighted waters spray upward in the famous fountain. Across the way, the brilliant Chagall murals begged for his attention, offering an alternative to his musings about Melissa Grant, but he could think only of her. His strong physical reaction to her mystified him. He sipped the last of his drink, paid for it, and walked across the street to his high-rise building.

"This has to stop," he muttered to himself. He'd never mixed business with pleasure, but when they'd reached her apartment building, he had wanted more than the coffee she refused to offer or a simple kiss—he'd wanted her. She would never know how badly. Sound sleep eluded him that night. Another new experience. Like a flickering prism, Melissa danced in and out of his dreams. Awakening him. Deserting him. And waking him up again.

Adam walked into his adjoining conference room promptly at eight o'clock to find coffee and, as he expected, his senior staff waiting for him. Their normal business completed, he detained them

"Where might an abusive man look for a woman who'd defied him and escaped his brutality?" he asked the group. Anywhere but a small town was the consensus. He returned to his office and began redrafting plans for a women's center in Hagerstown, Maryland, an unlikely place for one. His secretary walked into his office.

"Are you planning to open another one?" He nodded, explaining that "this is more complicated and more ambitious than our place in Frederick."

Her gaze roamed over him, with motherly pride, it seemed. "If you need help with this, I'll work overtime at no cost to you. It's a wonderful thing you do for these poor women, supporting these projects from your private funds."

He leaned back in his big leather chair. "I can afford to pay you, Olivia, and I will. You do enough for charity."

"Pshaw," she demurred. "What I do is nothing compared to the help you give people. These homes for abused women, that hospital ward for seriously ill children, and the Lord knows what else. God is going to bless you—see if He doesn't."

He shook his head, rejecting the compliment. "I'm fortunate. It's better to be in a position to give than to be on the dole." Abruptly he changed the topic. "Olivia, what do you think of Melissa Grant? Think she'll find me a manager for Leather and Hides?"

"Yes. She seemed very businesslike. Real professional. Anyhow, I trust your judgment in hiring her. When it comes to people, you don't often make mistakes."

Adam slapped his closed left fist into the palm of his right hand. Not in the last fifteen years, he hadn't, but the thought pestered him that where Melissa was concerned he was ripe for a blunder of the first order.

Melissa. He had the sense that he'd been with her before. She reminded him of a woman he'd danced with in costume one New Year's Eve. He'd been dancing with the woman, but at exactly midnight she'd disappeared, leaving an indelible impression. As farfetched as it seemed, whenever Melissa spoke in very soft tones, he thought of that unknown woman. Perhaps he'd wanted the woman because she was mysterious. His blood still raced when he thought of her. Warm. Soft. He'd like to see her at least once more. Yet he wanted Melissa. He rubbed the back of his neck. His elusive woman was at least two, maybe three, inches shorter than Melissa, but he couldn't dismiss the similarity in allure.

He picked up the business section of *The Maryland Journal* and noted that the price of sweet crude oil had increased more rapidly than the cost of living index. His folks were no longer in the natural gas business and had sold their property in Kentucky, so fuel prices didn't concern him, but every day his family had to combat the scandal brought on by Moses Morris's unfair accusation of seventy years earlier. Anger toward the Grants and Morrises surged in him as he reflected on how their maltreatment had shortened his grandfather's life and embittered his mother. His passion for Melissa cooled, and he strengthened his resolve to stay away from her.

He dictated a letter pressuring Melissa to find the manager at once, though the contract specified one month. He rationalized that he wasn't being unfair, that he was in a bind and she should understand.

Several hours later Adam told himself that he would not behave dishonorably toward Melissa or anyone else, that he should have investigated MTG and identified its president. He tore up the letter and pressed the intercom.

"Olivia, get Jason for me, please." Melissa hadn't been in touch with Jason, and that riled him. He paced the floor of his office as he tried to think of a justifiable reason to telephone her. Finally, he gave up the idea, left his office and went to the gym, reasoning that exercise should clear his head. But after a half hour, having conceded defeat, he stopped as he passed a phone on his way out and dialed her number.

Adam held his breath while the phone rang. She's in my blood, he acknowledged and wondered what he'd do about it.

"Melissa Grant speaking."

"Have dinner with me tonight. I want to see you."

She had dressed when he arrived at her apartment. He liked that, but he noticed her wariness about his entering her home. He didn't put her at ease—if she didn't want to be involved with him, she had reason to be cautious, just as he had. It surprised him that she didn't question why he'd asked her to dinner, and he didn't tell her, reasoning that she was a smart woman and old enough to divine a man's motives. He'd selected a Cajun restaurant in Tribeca, and it pleased him that she liked his choice.

"I love Cajun food. Don't you think it's similar to soul food?"

He thought about that for a bit. "The ingredients, yes, but Cajun's a lot spicier. A steady diet of blackened fish, whether red or cat, would eat a hole in your stomach. Reminds me of my first trip to Mexico. I'd alternate a mouthful of food with half a glass of water. I don't want that experience again. Come to think of it, that's what prompted me to learn to cook."

"You cook?"

He knew she wouldn't have believed it of him, and neither would any of his staff or business associates. "Of course I cook, Melissa. Why should that surprise you? I eat, don't I?"

"Aren't you surprised that we get on as well as we do?" she asked him. "Considering our backgrounds, I'd have thought it impossible."

He let the remark pass rather than risk putting a damper on a pleasant evening. Later they walked up Seventh Avenue to the Village Vanguard, but neither liked the avant-garde jazz offering that night, and they walked on.

Adam took her arm. "Let's go over to Sixth Avenue and Eighteenth or so. The Greenwich Village Singers are performing at a church over there, and we may be able to catch the last half of the program. Want to try?" She agreed, and at the end of the concert, Handel's *Judas Maccabeus,* he walked with her to the front of the church to shake hands with two acquaintances who sang with the group. While he spoke with a man, his arm went around her shoulder, automatically, as if it belonged there, and she moved closer to him. He glanced down at her and nodded, letting her know that he'd noticed and that he acknowledged her move as natural, but he immediately reprimanded himself. He'd better watch that—he'd been telling the man with whom he spoke that Melissa wasn't available, and he had no right to do it.

"That was powerful singing," he remarked, holding her arm as they started toward the front door. She nodded in agreement.

"That mezzo had me spellbound." He tugged her closer.

"Would you have enjoyed it as much if you hadn't been with me?" She looked up at him just before a quip bounced off of her tongue. She'd never seen a more serious face, but she had to pretend that he was teasing her.

"I doubt it," she joked, "you're heady stuff."

"Be careful," he warned her, still serious. "I'm a man who demands evidence of *everything.* If I'm heady stuff, you're one hell of an actress." His remark stunned her, but she recovered quickly.

"Oh, I've been in a drama or two. Back in grade school, it's true, but I was good." Laughter rumbled in his throat, and he stroked her fingers and told her, "You're one classy lady."

Melissa looked around her as they continued walking down the aisle of the large church toward the massive baroque front door and marveled that every ethnic group and subgroup seemed to be represented there. She stopped walking to get Adam's full attention. "Why is it," she asked him, "that races and nationalities can sing together, play football, basketball, tennis and whatever together, go to school and church together, but as a group, they can't get along? And they make love together—what's more intimate than that? You'd think if they can do that, they can do anything together."

"But that's behind closed doors," he explained. "Two people can resolve most anything if there's nobody around but them, nobody to judge them or to influence them. Take us, for instance. Once our folks get wind of our spending time together, you'll see how easily a third person can put a monkey wrench in a relationship."

Melissa quickened her steps to match those of the man beside her. He must have noticed it, because he slowed his walk. Warmth and contentment suffused her, and when he folded her hand in his, she couldn't make herself remove it. Was the peace that seemed to envelop her the quiet before a storm? She couldn't remember ever having felt so carefree or so comfortable with anyone. Adam was honorable, she knew it deep down. But that didn't mean he wouldn't leave her to cope alone with the problems that they both knew loomed ahead if they continued to see each other.

As if he'd read her thoughts, he asked her, "Would your family be angry with you if they knew we spent time together?"

Looking into the distance, she nodded. "I'd say that's incontestable. Furor would be a better description of my father's reaction." She tried to lift her sagging spirits—only moments earlier they had soared with the pleasure of just being with him. He released her hand to hail a speeding taxi, and didn't take it again. She sat against the door on her side of the cab.

With a wry smile, Adam commented, "If you sat any farther away from me, you'd be outside this cab. Scared?"

She gave him what she intended to be a withering look. "Of whom?"

"Well, if you're so sure of yourself," he baited, "slide over here."

"I read the story of 'Little Red Riding Hood,'" she told him solemnly, careful to maintain a straight face.

"Are you calling me a wolf?"

She was, she realized—and though he probably didn't deserve it, she refused to recant. "You used that word; I didn't. But I bet you'd be right at home in a wilderness." Or most other places, she thought.

She controlled the urge to lean into him, when his long fingers stroked the back of her neck. "Don't you know that men tend to behave the way women expect them to? Huh? Be careful, Melissa. I can howl with the best of them." Tremors of excitement streaked through her. What would he be like if he dropped his starched facade?

"What does it take to get you started?" she asked idly, voicing a private thought.

"One spark of encouragement from you." He flicked his thumb and forefinger. "Just that much, honey." She couldn't muffle the gasp that betrayed her.

"Move over here," he taunted. "Come on. See for yourself." Tempting. Seductive. Enticing her. The words dripping off of his smooth tongue in an invitation to madness. She clutched the door handle and prayed that he wouldn't touch her.

"Melissa."

She clasped her forearms tightly. "I'm happy right where I am." Her heart skittered at his suggestive, rippling laughter.

"You'd be a lot happier," he mocked, "if you closed this space between us."

"Speak for yourself."

"Believe me, honey," he purred, "I'm doing exactly that." If she didn't control the impulse, her fingers would find his and cling.

He took her key to open her door for her and held it as though weighing the consequences of alternative courses of action. After a few minutes during which he said nothing and she was forced to look into his mesmeric eyes while she fought rising desire, she had the impulse to tell him to do whatever he wanted—just get on with it. But seemingly against his will, as if he pulled it out of himself, he spoke.

"I'd like to spend some time with you, Melissa. I don't have loose strings in my personal life nor in my business affairs. I need to see whether our friendship, or whatever it is that prevents our staying away from each other, will lead anywhere. I'm not asking for a commitment, and I'm not giving one. But there's something special going on between us, and you know it, too. What do you say?"

"We'll see." Even if she hadn't already learned a lesson, she had good cause to stay away from Adam. The most optimistic person wouldn't give a romance between them a chance of maturing, because no matter how they felt about each other, their families' reactions would count for more. So that settled it—she wouldn't see him except with regard to business. But how could she be content not knowing what he'd be like if she let herself go and succumbed to whatever it was that dragged her toward him? Oh, Lord! Was she losing sight of the storm that awaited her when Rafer Grant learned of her passion for Adam Roundtree?

Adam awakened early the next morning after a sound and refreshing sleep. He'd made up his mind about Melissa, and as usual he didn't fight a war with himself about his decision. That was behind him. He suspected that given the chance, she'd wrestle with it as any thinking person in her circumstances would, but he didn't plan to give her much of a chance.

He scrambled out of bed as the first streaks of red and blue signaled the breaking dawn, showered, poured coffee from his automatic coffee maker, got a banana, and settled down to work. He liked Saturday mornings, because he was free to work on his charities, the projects whose success gave him the most pleasure. The Refuge, as the Rachel Hood Hayes Center for Women that was situated in Frederick was commonly known, had become overcrowded. He had to find a way to enlarge it and expand its services. His dilemma was whether to continue financing it himself or seek collaborative funds. If it were located in New York City or even Baltimore rather than Frederick, raising the money would be fairly simple, but corporations wouldn't get substantial returns from humanitarian investments in Frederick, and he couldn't count on their support.

He looked out of the window across Broadway and toward the Hudson River, knowing that he wouldn't see Melissa's building. He had had years of impersonal relationships and loveless sex, and he had long since tired of it. After the humiliation of that one innocent adolescent attachment, he'd sworn never to be vulnerable to another woman. The lovers he'd had as a man had wanted to be linked with Adam Roundtree and regarded intimacy as a part of that. They hadn't attempted to know or understand him. Hadn't cared whether he could hurt or be disappointed. Hadn't dreamed that a hole within him cried out for a woman's love and caring. But Melissa was different. He sensed it. He knew it. He pondered what his mother would think of Melissa. She'd probably find reasons to shun her, he mused, and none of them would have anything to do with Melissa herself. Mary Hayes Roundtree was bitterly opposed to the Morris/Grant people for having vilified her family's name without cause. And he suspected that Melissa's fair complexion might bother her, too—his mother liked to trace her roots back to Africa, and she ignored all the evidence of miscegenation that he could see in the Hayes family. A muscle twitched in his jaw. He couldn't and wouldn't allow his mother's preferences and prejudices to influence his life.

He spent an hour on his personal accounts, then lifted the receiver and dialed her number.

"Hi. I mean, hello."

He could barely understand the mumbled words. "Hi. Sorry to wake you, but I've been up for hours. Want to go bike riding?"

"Biking?" The sound resembled a lusty purr, and he could almost see her stretching languorously, seductively. "Call me back in a couple of days."

"Come on, sleepyhead, get up. Life's passing you by."

"Hmmm. Who is this?" He had a sudden urge to be there, leaning over her, watching her relaxed and inviting, seeing her soft and yielding without her defenses. Her deep sigh warned him that she was about to drop the receiver.

"This is Adam." He heard her feet hit the floor as she jumped up.

"Who? Adam? Bicycle?" A long pause ensued. "Adam, who would have thought you were sadistic?"

"I didn't know I was. Want to ride with me? Come on. Meet me at the bike shop in an hour."

"Where is it?"

"Not far from you. Broadway at Sixty-fifth Street. Eat something."

"Okay."

They rode leisurely around Central Park, greeting the few bikers and joggers they encountered in the still cool morning. Melissa knew a rare release, an unfamiliar absence of concerns. It was as if she had shed an outer skin that she hadn't known to be confining but the loss of which had gained her a welcomed freedom. She looked over at the man who rode beside her, at his dark muscular legs and thighs glistening with faint perspiration from their hour's ride and at the powerful arms that guided the bike with such ease. From her limited experience, she had always believed that it was the man who wanted and who asked. She shook her head, wondering whether she was strange, decided that she wasn't, and let a grin crease her cheeks. Self-revelation could be pleasant.

"Let me in on it. What's funny?"

"Me." She replied and refused to elaborate, watching him from the corner of her right eye. He slowed their pace and headed them toward the lake. At the shed he locked and stored their bikes and rented a canoe for them. He rowed near the edge of the lake. The ducks made place for them amidst the water lilies, and some swam alongside the canoe, quacking, seemingly happy to provide entertainment. Melissa looked around them and saw that, except for the birds, they were alone. The cool, fresh morning breeze pressed her shirt to her skin, and she lowered her head in embarrassment when she realized he could see the pointed tips of her breasts. Her restless squirming seemed to intensify his fixation with her, and she had to employ enormous self-control to resist covering her breasts with her arm.

"Don't be shy," he soothed, "let me look at you. I've never before seen you so relaxed, so carefree."

"If you saw it all the time, you'd soon be fed up with it," she jested in embarrassment. "And maybe worse. One Latin poet, I believe his name was Plautus, said that anything in excess brings trouble."

His half smile quickened the twinkle of his eyes, and her hands clutched her chest as frissons of heat raced through her. "I prefer Mae West's philosophy," he taunted. "She said too much of a good thing is wonderful. You stick with Mister What's-his-name's view." Melissa stared at him. Did he know what he'd just done to her?

His eyes caressed her while she squirmed, rubbed her arms, and moistened her lips. As though enchanted, he dropped anchor and let the boat idle.

"You're too far away from me. If I wasn't sure this thing would capsize, I'd go down there and get you."

"And do what?" she challenged. Heat seemed to radiate from him, and she shivered in excited anticipation.

"When I finished, you'd never think of another man. You know you're playing with fire, don't you?" She wrinkled her nose in disdain.

"Keep it up," he growled, "and I'll go down there to you even if this thing sinks." The air crackled and sizzled around them, and she fought the feminine heat that stirred in her loins. Sweat poured down her face as his hot gaze singed her, but she struggled to summon a posture of indifference. Nose tilted upward and chin thrust forward, she teased him, her voice unsteady.

"Planning to rock the boat, are you? Well, if you let me drown, the Morrises and Grants will have your head."

She thrilled from head to toe as his laughter washed over her, exciting her. "I'm scared to death, Melissa. I'm shaking in my Reeboks." Her right hand dipped into the lake as a duck swam by, and she brought up enough water to wet the front of his shirt.

"Lady, what do you think you're doing?"

"Cooling you off." She hoped she'd made him give her some room. She hadn't. He looked at her steadily and spoke without a trace of humor.

"If you think I'm hot now, Melissa, you're in for a big surprise."

Adam watched as her eyes widened and knew she was at a loss as to how to handle him. He regretted that—he wanted her to handle him and to enjoy doing it. He pulled up the anchor and began rowing. The trees heavy with green leaves and the quiet water provided the perfect background against which he could appreciate her beguiling loveliness. His fingers itched to replace the breeze that gently lifted her hair from her shoulders and neck, and his lips burned with the impulse to taste her throat, to… They had the lake to themselves. If he dared… He raised his gaze from the water surrounding them and caught the naked passion unsheltered in her eyes. Watched, flabbergasted, as she licked her lips. Desire sliced through him, and he had to fight to rein in his rampant passion.

He rowed back to the shed, surrendered their boat, and retrieved their bikes. He was in control, he assured himself. He could stop the relationship, walk away from it anytime he chose. Or he could have until he'd seen the heat in her eyes and the quivering of her lips—for him.

He stood in front of the building in which she lived, looking down at her, trying to keep his hands to himself. She squinted at him and licked her lips. Did she want him to…? He ran his fingers over his short hair in frustration.

"Melissa, I… Look, I enjoyed this." He settled for banality, when what he needed to tell her was that he wanted her right then. She smiled in an absentminded way and responded to his meaningless remark: "Me, too."

Maybe he'd spend some time with Ariel on Sunday and get his desire for Melissa under control. Abstinence wasn't good for a man. He smiled grimly as he bade Melissa good-bye, admitting to himself that self-deception wasn't good for a man, either. The next morning, Sunday, it was Melissa whom he called.

# Chapter 3

A soft sigh escaped Melissa when she awakened and realized that Adam wasn't with her, that she'd been dreaming, and that the glistening bronze male who'd held her so tenderly was an illusion. Had she leashed her emotions so tightly these past four years that her defenses against masculine seduction were weak and undependable, that a man, who'd never even kissed her, could take possession of her senses? She didn't think so. What was it about Adam? She reached for her glasses, looked at the clock, decided she could sleep another hour, and turned over. Wishful thinking. She answered the ringing phone.

"Hello," she murmured, half conscious of the seductive message in her low, sleepy tones.

"So you're awake. Thinking about me?"

"No," she lied. "I was thinking about the weather."

"First female I ever met who gets turned on by thoughts of the weather."

She frowned. He was too sure of himself. Then she heard his amused chuckle and couldn't suppress a smile, then a giggle, and finally a joyous laugh.

"Want some company? I want to see you while you're so happy. You're uninhibited when you first wake up, aren't you?"

"Why did you call?" She twirled the phone cord around her index finger and waited while he took what seemed an inordinate amount of time answering.

"I didn't intend to—it just happened. How about going to the Museum of Modern Art with me this afternoon? There's a show of contemporary painters that I'd like to see, and browsing in a museum is my favorite Sunday afternoon pastime. What do you say?"

"Depends. I'm going to church, and then I'm going to shoot pool for an hour." After his long silence, she asked him, "Are you speechless? Don't tell me I shocked you. Women do shoot pool, you know."

"Surprised, maybe, but it takes more than that to shock me. Should I come by for you, or do you want to meet me?"

"I'll meet you at the front door of the museum. One thirty."

She hung up and immediately the telephone rang, sending her pulse into a trot in anticipation of what he'd say.

"Mama! Are you alright? Why aren't you going to church this morning?"

"Oh, I am, dear, and I'm just fine. I wanted to say hello before your father and I leave home. Schyler called. He just got a promotion to vice president and head of the company's operations in Africa. I knew you'd want to know." They talked for a few minutes, but Melissa's pleasure at receiving her mother's call had ebbed. Her parents took every opportunity to boast of her brother's accomplishments. She hoped she wasn't being unfair, but if they boasted about her, she hadn't heard about it.

Melissa's status within her family was far from her thoughts while she roamed the museum with Adam. She could have done without many of the paintings, she decided, but an hour among them was a small price to pay for a stroll with Adam in the sculpture garden. She had to struggle not to betray her response when he slung an arm around her shoulder as they stood and looked at a Henry Moore figure, splayed his long fingers at her back as they walked, and held her hand while he leaned casually against a post, gazing at her with piercing intensity—letting her see that his plans for them included far greater intimacy than hand-holding. She had to conclude that Adam Roundtree was a thorough man, that he left nothing to chance. He'd said he wanted to find out if there could be anything between them, and he clearly meant it. He was also stacking the odds. He might need proof, but she knew they had the basis for a fiery relation-ship, and he couldn't want that anymore than she did, but he was in a different position. He was head of his family, and his folks might not try to censor him as hers surely would, but she couldn't believe he'd be willing to drag up those ancient hatreds.

Adam let his gaze roam over Melissa. Her wide yellow skirt billowed in the breeze, and he could see the outline of her bra beneath her knitted blouse. Her softly feminine casual wear appealed to him, made her body more accessible to his touch, his hands. He grasped her arm lightly. "I've got a friend in West-chester I'd like you to meet. Come with me." He sensed her re-luctance before she spoke.

"I have to be home early—I've got a lot to do tomorrow."

"Come with me," he urged, his voice softer, lower. Persuasive. "Come with me." He watched her eyelids flutter before she squinted at him and insisted that she should go home. He knew she wanted to escape the intimacy between them, but he was de-termined to prolong it.

"I'll take you home early. Come with me."

She went.

They boarded the train minutes before its departure. Melissa didn't know what to make of Adam's mood, and his invitation to join him in a visit with a friend perplexed her. She was certain that he hadn't planned for them to go to Westchester when he'd called her that morning.

"Are we going to visit one of your relatives?"

Adam draped his right ankle across his left knee and leaned back in his seat. "If that were the case, Melissa, I'd warn you. I would never spring a member of my family on you unexpect-edly, and I think you know that. Winterflower is a very special friend. You'll like her. She has an aura of peace about her that's refreshing—the best preparation for the Monday morning rat race that anybody could want. I go up to see her as often as I can."

"How old is she?" She could see that the question amused him.

"Oh, around fifty or fifty-five, I'd say. But I could be way off—I don't make a habit of asking women their age."

"I got the impression from what you said a minute ago that she's different. Is she?"

"In a way. Yes. Winterflower doesn't fight the world, Melissa—she embraces it." He shrugged elaborately. "Flower defies description…you have to experience her." So he had a tonic for the New York rat race after all, she mused, pleased that the woman wasn't his lover.

A tall Native American woman of about fifty greeted them with a natural warmth. Adam introduced them, and Melissa liked her at once.

"What are you two doing together?" she asked Adam before telling him, "Never mind, it will work itself out. But you'll both hurt a lot before it does."

Melissa watched, perplexed, as Adam hugged the woman and then admonished her. "Now, Flower, I do not want to know about the rough roads and slippery pebbles ahead, as you like to put it. You told me about them three months ago."

The woman's benevolent smile was comforting, though her words were not. "You're just coming to them." Melissa had a strong sense of disquiet as Flower turned to her and extended her hand. "It's good that you are not as skeptical as Adam is. You complement him well."

Adam snorted. "Flower, for heaven's sake!"

Flower held her hands up, palms out, as though swearing innocence. "Alright. Alright. That's all—I'm not saying anything else."

They walked around the back of the house to the large garden and seated themselves in the white wooden chairs. Adam moved away from the two women and turned toward the sharp decline that marked the end of Winterflower's property, impatiently knocking his closed right fist against the palm of his left hand. He didn't need Winterflower or anyone else to tell him that Melissa was well suited to him, that she could be his match. She was unlike any woman he had ever known. Independent, self-possessed, and vulnerable. He didn't turn around—he was vulnerable himself right then, and he'd as soon she didn't know it.

Winterflower served a light supper. The late, low-lying sun filtered through the trees, tracing intricate patterns on them, patterns that moved with the soft breeze and seemed to cast a spell over the threesome, for they ate quietly.

Melissa spoke. "Are you clairvoyant, Flower?"

Winterflower nodded. "I see what chooses to appear. Nothing more." Melissa nodded. Not in understanding, but acceptance.

"Why were you surprised to see Adam and me together?" She thought her skin crawled while she waited for what was without doubt a reluctant reply.

"I've been associating the two of you with the end of the year." Winterflower nodded toward Adam, who frowned. He may not agree, Melissa decided, but he didn't suggest that the woman's words were foolish, either.

Winterflower's soft voice reached Adam as if coming from a long distance, intruding in his thoughts. "How is Bill Henry?"

Adam shifted in his chair, aware that her mind was again on the metaphysical. "He's well enough, I suppose. I haven't been home to Beaver Ridge recently, and I haven't spoken with him by phone since I last saw you."

"You will learn something from him," she told Adam. "He has taught himself patience, and he has stopped racing through life. Now he has time to reflect, and soon his heart will be overflowing with joy." She looked from one to the other, nodded, and relaxed as though affirming the inevitable. "And he is not the only one." Then she turned to Melissa. "Ask Adam to bring you back to see me."

Adam stood and hugged his friend. "See you again before too long." Melissa shook hands with Flower and thanked her.

"You're very quiet, Melissa," he said, as they trudged downhill toward the train station. "Was I mistaken in bringing you to visit Flower?"

"No. I'm glad you did." She appeared to pick her words carefully. "You seemed different with her."

He couldn't help laughing. "Melissa, I expect everybody's different around her. She's so totally noncombative, so peaceful. Life-giving. Sometimes I think of her as being like penicillin for a virus."

"But she's also unsettling."

He slid an arm across her shoulder and drew her closer. "That's because you were fighting her good vibes."

"Oh, come on!" she said, and he thwarted her attempt to move away by tugging her closer.

"Now, you're fighting *my* vibes."

"Adam," she chided, "you could use a little less self-confidence."

He squeezed her shoulder. "Be reasonable. Nothing would lead me to believe that you like wimps." She wiggled out of his arm. "Go ahead. Move if you want to. You still know I'm here." She reached up and pulled his ear, delighting him with the knowledge that she needed to touch him.

"Feel better?"

"About what?"

"About giving in to your desire to have your hands on me?" From the corner of his eye, he saw her frown dissolve into a smile, and he stopped, grasped both of her hands in his, and stared down at her.

"You're delightful, even when you're trying to be difficult." Her eyes narrowed in a squint, and she wet her lips with the tip of her tongue in a move that he now realized as unconscious. His breath quickened. "You make my blood boil." She parted her lips as though to speak but said nothing, and his passion escalated as she merely looked down the tree-lined street, escaping the honesty of his gaze. He held her hand as they walked to the train.

"Somehow I can't picture you with a close personal friend like Flower," she said as they seated themselves on the train. "You belong to the modern era; she doesn't."

"She does," he corrected. "Winterflower is her tribal name. She is Dr. Gale Falcon, a history professor, but she manages to stay close to her origins. My uncle, Bill Henry, introduced me to her. She and I can sit on her deck for hours at night without saying a word, yet we're together. I value her friendship."

"She's clairvoyant."

"Oh, yes," he confirmed, "but that stuff works only if you believe in it."

"And you don't?"

His cynical laugh challenged her to accept his premise. "It implies that life is guided by fate, that whatever happens to you is preordained. I can't accept that. Life is what you make it."

His hand covered hers to assist her as they left the train, and her inquiring look drew a grudging half smile and an unnecessary explanation. "I don't want you to get lost."

"If I get lost, it will be deliberate."

"I'll bet," he shot back. His arm around her shoulder held her close to him as they walked through Grand Central Station. The eyes of an old woman who pushed a shopping cart of useless artifacts beseeched him prayerfully. Melissa thought that he would give the woman a dollar and continue walking. Instead, he stopped to talk with her.

"What do you want with the money?" The woman seemed to panic at the question. "What are you going to do with it?"

"Well, I need some food for myself…." She paused, as though uncertain. "And for my cats, please."

"Where are you cats?"

"In my room on Eleventh Avenue." The woman looked into her hand and gasped at the bills he'd placed there. He bade the woman good-bye, and within a few paces a man asked him for money.

"Are you planning to buy a drink?" Adam asked him.

"No, sir," the man replied. "I'll take groceries. Anything, so long as I can feed my kids. You wouldn't have a job, would you?" Melissa's heart opened to Adam, and she didn't fight it, couldn't fight it, as she watched him write down the man's name and address before giving him money. It made an indelible impression on her that he didn't ignore the outstretched hand of a single beggar, and she couldn't dismiss the thought that he might not be as harsh and exacting as he often appeared. She was unable to avoid comparing Adam's response to people in need with her father's behavior when accosted by beggars, whom he despised.

"You're quite a woman, Melissa," Adam told her as they walked to her apartment door. Her eyebrows shot upward. "You're straightforward," he went on. "No roughness around the edges. A man knows where he stands with you. And you're not a flirt." A smile creased his handsome cheeks. "At least not with me. And I like that. I like it a lot." His gaze roamed over her upturned face, as if he searched for clues as to what she felt. He pushed a few strands of hair from her forehead and then squeezed both of her shoulders, letting her know that he wanted more than he was asking for.

"You're not entirely immune to me, though," he told her in a near whisper, "and I like that, too. Good night, Melissa."

Melissa upbraided herself for having spent the day with Adam. She couldn't fault his decorum, though: no cheap shots, no attempt at intimacy in spite of the almost unbearable sexual tension. He could brighten her life. Oh, he could, if he chose to do so. But he wasn't for her, and she intended to make sure that, in the future, Adam Roundtree would be just a business acquaintance. She sighed, remembering having made that resolution on two previous occasions.

After leaving Melissa, Adam strode quickly up Sixty-sixth Street to Broadway, crossed the street, and entered his building. Melissa was beginning to tax his self-restraint. He rubbed the back of his neck in frustration. Aching want settled in his loins when he thought of her high firm breasts, her rounded hips, and those long, tapered legs. He stopped undressing. It was one thing to desire an attractive woman, but it was quite another to be captivated by her because she was special, because she had an allure like none other. It bore watching, he decided, pulling off his shorts and getting into bed. Careful watching.

But she was there when he closed his eyes. Deeply troubled, he sat up in bed and turned on the bedside lamp, fighting a feeling he hadn't had for years. For all his wealth, his phenomenal success as a realtor, and his meteoric rise in the corporate world, his life lacked something. An emptiness lurked in him, a void that begged to be filled with the sweet nectar of a woman's love.

Three evenings later Melissa rushed to find her seat before the concert began. She hated being late and had been tempted not to renew her subscription to the museum's summer concert series, because it meant fighting the rush hour traffic in order to be on time. She shivered from the air conditioning and rubbed her bare arms as she realized belatedly that she'd left her sweater in her office. It would be a long, uncomfortable evening. As she weighed the idea of leaving, a garment fell over her shoulders, and large hands smoothed it around her arms. She looked down at the beige linen jacket that warmed her, felt the gentle squeeze of masculine hands on her shoulders, and fought not to turn around. But she couldn't resist leaning back, and when his hand rested softly on her shoulder, she tapped it lightly to thank him. So much for her resolve to avoid a personal relationship with him.

They left the concert together, stopped for coffee at a little café on Columbus Avenue, and though there was no discussion of it, she knew he'd walk her home. Maybe this time he wouldn't leave her without taking her in his arms. But when they entered the lobby of her building, she shuddered at the sight that greeted her. Wasn't it like her father to appear unexpectedly, giving himself every advantage? Rafer Grant rose from a leather lounge chair and walked toward them. He stopped, gazed at Adam, and fear ripped through her as his mouth twisted the minute he recognized the man whose family he detested.

"What is *he* doing here with you? Is this why you can't come home and look after your mother?" He didn't give her a chance to reply. "How could you consort with this...this man after what he and his kin did to our family? Aren't you ashamed of yourself?" Adam's arm steadied her.

Her voice held no emotion. "Hello, Father. I needn't say that I'm surprised to see you. There's no reason for you to be displeased. Adam—"

He interrupted. "Adam, is it? I'm shocked and disappointed at your bringing this man here to your home. It's disloyal, and I won't stand for it."

Adam pulled her closer to him, possessively and defiantly. "How are you planning to prevent it? This isn't the Middle Ages when you could have her shackled to the foot of her bed. She's an adult, and she can do as she pleases."

"It's alright, Adam." She was used to her father's harangues, having endured his reproofs and censure for as long as she could remember, but until now no one had called him to task for it— not her mother nor her brother. She needed her father's approval—it seemed that for most of her life she'd striven for it. Yet she couldn't remember a time when he'd praised her. She reached toward him involuntarily, but he waved her aside, glared at Adam, and marched huffily out of the building without having told her why he'd come.

She looked up at Adam, trying to read him. "I'm sorry you were exposed to this, Adam. My father never wanted a daughter, and sometimes I think he's not sure he has one. At least that's how he acts." She'd meant it in jest, but Adam's dour expression told her that he was not amused. Upon reflection, she wondered if her father might be more caring if she showed him that his opinion of her didn't matter. Should it matter so much, she pondered, as she and Adam walked without speaking to the elevator, her hand tightly enclosed in his.

At her apartment door he held his hand for her key, and she gave it to him and watched him open her door. Inside, Adam asked her, "Does your father always behave this way with you, or was he disrespectful because you were with me, a Roundtree?"

"Both. He's that way when I do something that displeases him," she explained, "which is fairly frequent."

"How does he act when you brother displeases him? Or does that ever happen?"

She hesitated; even though she was displeased with her father and ashamed of his behavior toward her, she couldn't criticize him. Especially not to a man whom he considered an enemy.

"Adam, my brother doesn't displease my parents." Then as the implications of her words hung between them, she joshed, "He's the good kid.

"Come on in the kitchen with me while I make some coffee." She had to change the subject—she didn't want Adam to see her as an ineffectual person. They were business associates, and she'd better remember that. She gave him a mug of coffee, and when he nodded in approval after having sniffed it, she was glad she'd made it strong.

"I like it straight," he told her, when she offered sugar and cream. "I also like your taste. I wouldn't have thought that beige and a dark gray would be so comfortable to look at, but this kitchen is attractive. Of course, the yellow accents don't hurt."

Her surprise at his interest in colors must have showed, because he shrugged and explained, "I dabble in watercolors." Then he asked her, "What's your hobby?"

She hesitated. "I go to a library in Harlem on Saturday mornings in the winter and conduct a children's story hour."

"That's not a hobby, Melissa. That's volunteer work. What's your hobby? I mean, what do you do for fun, just to please yourself?"

She didn't reveal that part of herself to acquaintances. Only her mother knew of her secret pleasure, though she hadn't let her mother read her verses. A desire to share herself with Adam welled up in her. She didn't look directly at him. "I like to write poetry. When I was at home, before I went to college, I used to sit in my room writing poems, and if I heard my father or brother roaming around or calling me, I'd hide what I was writing under my mattress."

His grim expression disconcerted her. "You don't think much of poetry writing?" He stood, his gaze boring into her. "I was thinking that I've known you less than a month and yet I know you better than your family does." Lowering her eyelids, she tried to veil her emotions from his probing stare. Her sudden self-consciousness must have been evident to him, for his casual posture suddenly changed. As though attempting to rein in an uncustomary wildness, he jammed both hands in his pants pockets and rocked back on his heels before turning swiftly and heading toward her hallway. Her ingrained courteousness overcame her diffidence, and she followed to see him out. At the door he turned to her.

"It's too bad that my presence caused you problems with your father. I expect you have enough trouble with him without having to explain why you were with me." She sensed that this impatient, demanding, and sometimes harsh man could be gentle, tender, and he would be that way with her. Her gaze drifted up to his face to the yearning, the fiery passion in his eyes and unconsciously she moved to him.

"Adam. Oh, Adam." Both of his hands reached out and wrapped her into his embrace. Her senses reeled at the feel of his big hand behind her head, positioning her for the force of his mouth. Heat shot through her when his marauding lips finally took possession of her, imprisoning her in a torrent of molten passion. He nipped her bottom lip and quickly, as if she'd waited a lifetime to do it, she opened for him and welcomed his hot tongue into every crevice of her hungry mouth. She reveled in the savage intensity with which he loved her, crushing her to him, then caressing her with a gentleness that belied the strength of his ardor. She opened her mouth wider, and as if he sensed a deeper need in her—one that he wanted to fulfill—his hand stroked her bottom then pulled her up until the seat of her passion pressed against the unmistakable evidence of his desire.

More. She needed more. To be a part of him, to crawl inside of him. One hand moved to his head to increase the pressure of his mouth on hers while the other caressed his face and neck. Frantically she undulated against him. His groan warned her to stop it, but she couldn't make herself move from him. The feel of his hard chest against her tender, sensitive breasts, his hands moving slowly over her back, and the intimacy of her position against him enticed her closer. She wanted… His hands gently separated them and held her from him. When she dared look at him, she saw his difficulty in maintaining control. Honest to a fault, as always, when she could restore her equilibrium, and without thought to sparing either of them, she told him, "If you hadn't waited so long to do that, it might have been easier."

He released a grudging laugh. "Easier? You're kidding. Woman, kissing you *is* easy—it's the consequences that'll sure as hell be rough." He continued to let his gaze roam indolently over her, and she knew his passion hadn't cooled.

She backed away from him. What had she been thinking about? If she had doubted that an involvement with Adam would rekindle the hatred between their families, her father's behavior when he saw them together was proof. Adam folded his arms and leaned against the wall, obviously judging her reaction to what had just happened.

"I see you intend to break off personal relations between us. I agree that we ought to at least decide if we want to go where we seem to be headed, but I hope you know that breaking it off and staying away from each other will be easier said than done." He brushed her cheek with his lips and winked at her. "I'll call you."

"At my office on business only," she quickly interjected. His raised eyebrow did not signify agreement.

She closed the door, drew a deep breath, and sat down to assimilate her feelings. One minute she had thought he'd walk away from her as usual, but in the next she was reeling from the jolt of his strength and passion. She knew that trouble lay ahead of her, so why was she already anxious for that telephone call? A famous actress once said that she'd have swum the Atlantic to be with her man—I still don't know exactly why, Melissa reasoned, but I sure am in a better position to guess.

Two days later, one day short of the month allowed in her contract, Melissa decided that she'd found a candidate with flawless credentials, one whom Adam couldn't reject. As was her custom, she escorted the candidate, Calvin Nelson, to his potential employer. Jason Court like the man and assured her that his boss would. Adam hired Nelson after an interview that confirmed Melissa's opinion that Adam was hard, but fair, and that he had a keen mind. And her relief was nearly palpable when

Adam made no allusion to the intimacy they had shared the previous Sunday evening.

"You're African American and so is Mr. Court," Calvin Nelson commented to Adam. "When I saw you, I was sure I wouldn't get the job, that you wouldn't hire a man who wasn't African American for such a high position in your company."

Furrows creased Adam's brow as he leaned back in his chair and weighed the words. The man was open, unafraid to speak his mind; he liked that. "I'm an equal opportunity employer, Calvin. What I want in an employee is competence, integrity, and honor. I don't give a hoot about a person's sex or ethnicity." He stood and shook Calvin Nelson's hand. "Welcome to Hayes/Roundtree Enterprises, Calvin. Oh, yes. We use first names here and in Maryland. Let me know what I can do to help you get settled in Frederick."

Jason shepherded Melissa to the reception room so that Adam could speak privately with his new employee. She blinked to make certain that her eyes weren't betraying her when Adam followed them and told Calvin to make an appointment to see him the following morning.

"Let's get some lunch," he called to them, pausing by his secretary's desk. "Olivia, call Thompson's and tell the maître d' I'm bringing three guests."

Melissa couldn't hide her surprise at Adam's odd behavior. "I thought he'd want to talk to Calvin alone, Jason. And another thing, I didn't say I was free for lunch." Her resentment flared at his cavalier disregard for her preferences, forcing her to squash what would have been a rare display of temper. One kiss didn't give him the right to take her for granted.

"He's marking his territory," she heard Jason say.

"What do you mean by that?" she asked him and warned herself to be calm—an agitated person didn't think clearly.

Jason nodded toward his boss. "He just told me to stay out of his territory, meaning you."

She reflected for a second. Jason had given her an appreciative glance. More than one, in fact, but she hadn't thought that Adam noticed.

"How can you say that? I haven't given him the right to do that."

Jason's shoulder flexed in a quick, careless shrug. "You don't have to give it to him. Adam doesn't wait for doors to open—he opens them himself. You believe what I'm saying. A man knows when another tells him to back off from a woman. Melissa, I have never lunched with Adam. Unless he has an important client, he doesn't go to lunch. He has a sandwich and coffee at his desk. You're the reason he's going to Thompson's."

She turned on her heel and headed for the elevator, but Jason must have guessed her intention, because he detained her. "Melissa, it isn't smart to belittle Adam. You wouldn't get away with it, and there's no point in making an enemy of him. Besides," he grinned lazily, "the food at Thompson's is first class. Worth a try." She looked up as Adam approached the elevator with Calvin Nelson. His disapproving scowl told her that he knew what she'd threatened and dared her to do it. Jason looked from one to the other. He didn't know that she and Adam were more than business associates, she remembered, forced a smile and got on the elevator.

Adam stopped abruptly as they walked out of the restaurant, and his companions stared while he greeted a woman with such warmth that neither of them doubted she was a close friend.

"Ariel! What a pleasant surprise!" A smile drifted over his face. He shook hands with his guests, excused himself, and left with the elegant woman. Jason's knowing look confirmed what Melissa knew: Adam had repaid her and had enjoyed doing it.

"He's not vindictive," Jason said, so that only Melissa heard, "but he believes in letting you know how he feels about a thing." They waved Calvin Nelson good-bye.

"What is this about?" she asked Jason.

"Melissa, surely you know that Adam has cut you away from the pack. He knew you intended to leave his office with me and without telling him good-bye, and he didn't like it. You didn't show much enthusiasm for his company and he's just let you know that he isn't pining for you."

"Who was she?" She hated herself for having asked him, but she had to know.

"I don't know," he replied, "but I don't think she's anyone special, because she made a pass at Nelson but, well...you never know."

Melissa swore to herself that she hated Adam, that he was just another of the four-martini corporate types she disliked. She wished that it was Jason Court who attracted her, but *Adam was the one.*

Adam settled down to work on that August morning, after telling himself that he'd done the smart thing in not calling Melissa over the weekend. They'd moved so fast in the short time they'd known each other that he figured he'd better step back and take stock of things, decide what he wanted. Maybe he'd been wrong last week in not asking her if she wanted to lunch with the group, but she'd been wrong in threatening to walk off in a huff, too. He flicked on the intercom.

"Yes, Olivia. Sure. Put him on." He lifted the receiver of his private phone. His eyes widened in astonishment at Wayne's incredulous request. Could he get away for a few weeks, go down to Beaver Ridge, and settle the strike at the hosiery mill? It was becoming increasingly clear that, except for Wayne's newspaper, the family businesses had been held together by the force of their father's personality, rather than by his managerial abilities.

"That's asking a lot, Wayne. I'll need an office manager for the time I'm gone, and it may be a few days before I can get one. I'll get back to you." He hung up and called Melissa, and the anticipation he felt as he awaited her voice surprised him.

"MTG." His customary aplomb seemed to have deserted him, and seconds passed before he could respond in his usual manner.

"Melissa, this is Adam. I need an office manager right away. Can you get one for me without Jason having to spend hours drafting a contract? I'm in a hurry for this." He walked around his desk cradling the phone against his left shoulder while he squeezed his relaxer—a plastic object that he kept in his top drawer—with both hands.

"Why do you need one? If your secretary can't manage your office, maybe you should be looking for one of those, not an OM."

He hoped that his deep sigh and long silence would warn her that he didn't have time for games.

"Well?" she prodded.

"Melissa, would you please stop while you're ahead? When I say I want an office manager, that's what I want. If you can't attend to that without lecturing me about how to run my business, I'll try another service."

"Yes, sir. Whatever you say, sir. Just fax me a job description," she needled, her tone cool and sarcastic.

Olivia's voice came over the intercom, and he realized he hadn't turned it off. "My Lord, Adam, what could she have said to make you mad enough to break the telephone? And I didn't know you knew those words." Her chuckle didn't relieve his boiling temper.

"I'm sorry, Olivia, but Melissa Grant strips my gears, and she gets a kick out of doing it."

He turned off the intercom, grabbed Betty—as he called his relaxer—leaned back in his chair, and squeezed the plastic object. What was it about her, he pondered. Why did that one woman get to him that way? She could make him madder than anybody else, and she could heat him up quicker and make him hotter than any woman. If he couldn't get her out of his mind, maybe the solution was to take her to bed and get her out of his system. He dropped the relaxer, pushed away from his desk, and put a hand on each knee as if to rise, but didn't. That could work either way, and if it brought them closer together, what would he do then?

Adam locked his hands behind his head. She questioned his motives and grilled him about his decision—*nobody* did that, not even his brother, his closest friend. He could get the response he wanted from most people with just a look, but not from Melissa. Was her attitude toward him part of the old Roundtree-

Grant antagonism, or was it just Adam and Melissa, a part of the storm that seemed to swirl around them and between them even when outward calm prevailed? His intelligence told him it wasn't their last names and that their family ties were irrelevant. He sat up straight, his nerves tingling with excitement. Melissa was worth the cost of getting her.

Melissa began the search for Adam's office manager, deliberately looking for a man, because she knew he would expect her to find a woman. He'd repaid her for threatening to defy him in the presence of Nelson and Court. Well, she'd give it back to him. Nobody put her down and got away with it, she vowed, still smarting from the warm greeting he'd given that woman at the restaurant.

Within an hour after speaking with Melissa, Adam received another call from Wayne.

"Adam, one of the older workers discovered what appears to have been foul play or, at best, an uncommon accident in the Leather and Hides plant. Nearly seven hundred pounds of cattle hides that we've earmarked for women's shoes and luggage have been given chrome tanning rather than vegetable tanning, and the lot is now too soft and too elastic for its intended use. These valuable hides will have to be made into cheaper and less profitable items, and we haven't been able to trace the error to any worker."

"Do what you can, Wayne. I'm working on getting that manager."

He hung up and phoned Melissa. "How's the search for my OM going?" She was peeved with him, and he knew why, so he kept his tone casual and friendly. He didn't want her to have an excuse to needle him.

"Don't worry. I've been working on it ever since you made the request an hour ago. When I find one, I'll notify Jason."

He couldn't resist correcting her, but he kept his tone gentle. "Melissa, Jason Court is not in charge of this—I am. Please remember that." He hung up and stared at the phone. Somebody ought to tell her that he never walked away from a challenge. And she was that…in more ways than one.

Melissa walked into Adam's office the following morning with his new office manager, a forty-six-year-old man who had impeccable references. She entered his suite with her head high and defiance blazing across her face.

"Good morning, Mr. Roundtree. I've got the perfect person for you. Adam Roundtree, this is Lester Harper." Adam narrowed his eyes and glared at her for what seemed an interminable minute. Abruptly he extended his hand in a welcome to Lester.

"Have a seat, and tell me about yourself."

"Well, Miss Grant said I'm just what you need, so I thought—"

Adam interrupted, pulling rank, Melissa thought.

"We'll see about that," Adam said, spreading his hands in exasperation. His lips tightened as he ground his teeth and looked Melissa in the eye. "If you'll excuse us, please."

Her triumph dissolved into remorse as she realized that he'd practically ordered her to leave them alone. Shivers sprinted along her nerves when his twinkling eyes delivered an icy rebuke. She was teasing a tiger, she realized belatedly, and his whole demeanor told her that he wouldn't be soothed until he got proper recompense. His gaze held her, refused to release her even when she struggled to look away. And she had no doubt of their message: *retribution is mine* was their promise.

The day passed too slowly. He had to let her know what he thought of her smart trick, bringing him a man when she knew he would have preferred a woman or anyone less officious than Lester Harper. The man was bound to try lording it over Olivia, and Jason had winced at the sight of him. Clever, was she? Well, he'd see about that! He sighed heavily. She infuriated him—but, heaven help him, he wanted her.

She answered her door uneasily around seven thirty that evening, knowing intuitively that her caller was Adam. What had possessed her to toy with him, she asked herself, as she slipped the lock.

"You aren't surprised to see me?"

"Not very." Why tell him she'd known he'd come after her? When he stepped inside the door without waiting for an invitation, she wouldn't let him see her eager anticipation of his next move, nor her erotic response to the danger and excitement that his determined look promised her. Goose bumps popped up on her arms, and she rubbed them frantically. He didn't give her time to regroup.

"Come here to me," he growled as if he'd waited long enough. She thought she didn't move, but she was in his arms, his fiery mouth moving over hers, possessively, unbelievably seductive. Her hands moved up to push at his chest, but instead they wound themselves around his strong, corded neck. She felt him growing against her just as he stepped back, though he didn't release her.

So he was holding back, was he? He'd fire her up, but he wouldn't let her know how she affected him. Darn him, he wouldn't play with her and do it with impunity. She pulled him to her and held him so tightly that he could release himself only if he hurt her. And she knew he wouldn't consider doing that. She felt him then, all of him, and she gloried in his male strength, his heat and energy until his fire threatened to overwhelm her. Now it was he who wouldn't let go, he who groaned while he spun her around in a vortex of passion, he who held the loving cup and tempted her to drink from it. And how she wanted that sip. But she couldn't take the chance—there was so much at stake. And he didn't intend to commit to her, he'd all but said it. It wasn't Gilbert Lewis whom she was facing; that relationship had been child's play. Adam's gaze warned her that he intended to go all the way, and even with her nearsightedness, she couldn't mistake the storm raging in his eyes.

"I think we're being reckless." She spoke softly as if she could barely release the words. "Adam, there would be the devil to pay back home if my family knew what we're doing." She hoped her words didn't make her appear as foolish to him as she did to herself.

"We're of age, Melissa." He didn't sound convincing, she noticed, sensing that his folks would also be furious. "And why do they have to know?" She moved back, farther away from him.

"I refuse to have a secret, back door affair with you or any other man, Adam, and I'm surprised you'd want something like that. I wouldn't have thought it your style."

His right index finger moved back and forth along his square jaw, a sure sign of frustration. "You're right. I don't want it. My one brief experience with a secret affair, if you could even call it an affair, was disastrous. But then I was only fifteen." Her eyebrows shot up. He'd started early. When she was fifteen, she hardly knew what boys were for.

They hadn't moved from her foyer. "Come on in." He followed as she glided into the living room.

"Melissa, I'm relocating for a couple of months. That may cool things down between us, and if it does, I expect it will be for the best." She couldn't argue with that, nor could she understand why it pleased her that his heated look belied his words.

"You're right again," she said. "It would be for the best. I think we ought to avoid each other so we don't reopen those old family wounds, because I don't want to stir up that mess."

"Neither do I." He walked a few paces, turned around, and let her see the desire in his eyes. "But I want you." A note of finality laced his tone.

His words sent tremors racing through her, but she maintained her composure. "And you always get what you want?" she goaded.

He shrugged. "Why should I want something and not get it if all that's required is effort on my part? I go after what I want, Melissa. I work hard—I leave nothing to chance, and I get what I go after."

"This time you may get what you don't want," she told him, seeing in her mind's eye the ugliness on their horizon.

Adam walked home oblivious to the light misty rain. The minute Melissa had opened her door, she had guessed his reason for being there, and her demeanor had become that of a defenseless person at the mercy of a Goliath. Not that he'd been taken in by that. She could defend herself with the best of them. But she'd parted her lips and squinted at him, and he'd lost it. Getting her to him had been the only thing he'd cared about. He weighed the chances of dashing safely across Broadway against the light, noted the speeding cabs, and decided to wait. Thinking about it now, he admitted that his reason for going to Melissa had nothing to do with the office manager. He'd needed to see her. His displeasure about Lester had been a weak excuse.

# Chapter 4

Adam closed and locked his office door, spoke at length with Olivia, took the elevator down to the garage, got into his newly leased Jaguar, and headed for Beaver Ridge. He hadn't told Melissa where he would spend the next two months or so, because he wanted to find out whether a complete break would have any effect on their feelings for each other. He couldn't imagine that they'd lose interest though, because a mutual attraction as strong as theirs had to run its course. He loved to drive and had missed having a car, which he considered more of a nuisance than a convenience in New York, but he'd forgotten the frustration of driving bumper to bumper. After more than four hours in heavy traffic, he turned at last into Frederick Douglas Drive, the long roadway that marked the beginning of his family's property.

Wayne met him at the door of the imposing white Georgian house that Jacob Hayes had built for himself and his heirs sixty-five years earlier. Remodeled and modernized inside, it was home to Adam as no other place ever would be. He could close his eyes and see every stone in the huge, marble-capped living room fireplace. As a youth he'd slipped numerous times out of the room's large back window that oversaw his mother's rose garden and, as many times, the thorns had ripped his pants. He had loved the solitude that its many rooms assured him, and cherished the stolen fun he'd had with his brother when they secluded themselves in upstairs closets or the attic away from parental eyes. Coming home was a feeling like no other.

\* \* \*

He and Wayne exchanged hugs in the foyer that separated the living and dining rooms and slapped each other affectionately on the back, appraising each other with approval, before Wayne took one of Adam's bags, and they climbed the wide staircase to Adam's room.

"What do you know about the new manager you hired for Leather and Hides? I'm sure you investigated his references. From what I've seen of him, he's competent…but, well, can we trust him?"

Adam rubbed the back of his neck. "He came with excellent references, but if you're suspicious…" He let the thought hang. Wayne's question raised a possibility that he hadn't considered. He went to find his mother, to let her know he'd come home.

With several hours remaining before dinner, Adam decided to visit Bill Henry, his mother's youngest brother. He figured he'd be seeing a lot of his uncle. If any man had come to terms with life, B-H was that man. And with a stressful two months ahead of him, he was going to need the relief that B-H's company always provided. He entered the modestly constructed, white clapboard house without knocking. When B-H was at home, the door was always unlocked, and in summer the house was open except for the screen doors. It amused him that his wealthy uncle chose to eschew the manifestations of wealth, while his neglected investments made him richer by the minute.

"Why're you home in midsummer, Adam? You usually manage to avoid this heat." Not only did Bill Henry take his time speaking, Adam noted—his uncle, though still a relatively young man, did everything at a slow pace.

"Wayne asked me to come home. I expect you've heard about the near fiasco at Leather and Hides. I hope it was a simple error, but I'm beginning to suspect that someone wants to sink Hayes/Roundtree Enterprises. We don't know who's master-minding it, or even if that's the case, but one of our employees had a hand in it. It couldn't have happened otherwise."

Bill Henry rocked himself in the contour rocker that he'd had designed to fit his six-foot four-inch frame. "What kind of mix-up was it?"

Adam related the details. "That's burned-up money, B-H." He wiped the perspiration from his brow. If Bill Henry chose to live close to nature, he could at least have something handy with which his guests could fan. The man must have sensed Adam's discomfort, for he passed an old almanac to his nephew, and Adam made good use of it.

"Any new men on the job?" When Adam shook his head and then looked hard at him, as though less certain than he had been, B-H probed.

"Anybody mad at you?"

Adam shrugged. "I've thought of both possibilities, and I've got some ideas. But I can't act until I'm positive. In the meantime I'll install a variety of security measures. If you have any thoughts on it, give me a call."

Adam took his time walking the half mile back home in the ninety-six-degree heat. A new man was on the job, but what did that prove? He had no reason to suspect Calvin Nelson. The man was too experienced to have permitted such a blunder, so he couldn't have known about it. If it was deliberate... But why would he want to do such a thing? Unless... Adam didn't want to believe that Melissa would engineer the destruction of his family's company, that she would participate in industrial sabotage, producing the perfect candidate for the job. One who could destroy his family's livelihood. No, he didn't believe it. But she was a Grant, and there had never been such a mishap at Leather and Hides in the plant's sixty-five years. Not until Calvin Nelson became its manager. It was a complication that he'd prefer not to have and an idea that he couldn't accept.

He didn't want to think about Melissa, but he couldn't get her out of his head, because something in him had latched on to her and refused to let go. He'd taken a chance in letting her think their relationship was over. If she knew him better, she'd know that he finished what he started, and that she was unfinished business. He meant to have her, and leaving her for two months only made it more difficult. Melissa was special, and she appealed to him on many levels. He liked her wit, the way her mind worked, her composure, the laid-back sexy way she glided about. And he liked her company. He was tired of games, sick of hollow seductions, disgusted with chasing women he'd already caught just because good taste demanded it. It was always the same. A woman allowed him to chase her until she decided enough time had elapsed or he'd spent enough money, and then she let herself be caught. He never promised anything, but she'd go to bed and then she chased him. He was sick of it. Done with it. Melissa didn't engage in such shenanigans, at least not with him, and that was part of her attraction. He wondered if she'd miss him.

A phone call from her father was reason for apprehension, though Melissa had learned not to display her real feelings when his treatment of her lacked the compassion that a daughter had a right to expect of her father. But when her father called her office and began his conversation with a reminder of her duties to her family, she knew he was about to make one of his unreasonable demands. She geared herself for the worst, and it was soon forthcoming.

"Melissa, you've been ignoring your mother," he began, omitting the greeting. "I'm taking her to the hospital so the doctors can run some more tests. They can't find anything wrong with her, but anybody can see she's not well. Your mother's getting weaker every day, and I want you to come home." She didn't want to argue with him. She had talked with her mother for a half hour the day before, and Emily Grant hadn't alluded to any illness, though she had said that she got tired of taking test after test just to please her husband. But Melissa knew that her father's views about his wife's health would be the basis on which he acted, not the opinions of a doctor.

A strange thought flitted through her mind. She had never

heard her father call her mother by her given name. Did he know it? It was my wife, your mother, she, her, and you. She didn't want to go back to that depressing environment. It wasn't a home, but a place where trapped people coexisted. Her brother had found relief from it by taking a job in Kenya.

"Father, I have responsibilities here." She'd told him that many times, but he denied it as many times as he heard it.

"And I've told you that if you come home, I'll support you." She didn't want that and wouldn't accept it, but if her mother needed her, she couldn't ignore that. Annoyance flared when he added, "And I need a hostess and someone to accompany me on special occasions. Your mother isn't up to it, or so she says. She isn't up to anything."

She terminated the conversation as quickly as she could. "I'll call you in a day or two, Father, and let you know what I can do." Why hadn't she told him no? That he could hire someone to help with her mother. Wasn't she ever going to stand up to her father, stop begging for his approval? She closed her office door, kicked off her shoes, and began analysis of her financial situation to determine the effect of a move to Frederick, Maryland. Her father was insensitive in some ways, but she'd never known him to lie. Maybe her mother didn't want to worry her by admitting that she was ill. She thought for a while. Yes, that would be consistent with her mother's personality. Three hours later she walked down the corridor and knocked on the door of two lawyers who'd just begun their practice. If they agreed to her proposal, she'd move her business to Frederick. Later that afternoon she telephoned Burke's Moving Managers and set a date.

Melissa entered her apartment that evening and looked around at the miscellaneous artifacts that had eased her life and given her pleasure for the five years she'd lived there. She loved her home, but she could make another one, she rationalized, fighting the tears. Ilona's phone call saved her a case of melancholy.

"Melissa, darling, come down for a coffee. I haven't seen you in ages."

"You saw me yesterday when I was hailing a taxi. Give me a minute to change."

Ilona hadn't indicated that she had a guest, and Melissa winced when she saw the debonair man. A boutonniere was all he needed to complete the picture of a Hungarian count. Melissa had dressed suitably for one packing to leave town with all of her belongings, but not for the company of an old-world gentleman. At times she could throttle Ilona.

"You and Tibor remember each other, don't you?" Ilona asked with an air of innocence that belied her matchmaking, as she placed three glasses of hot espresso and a silver dish of chocolates on the coffee table. They nodded. Melissa suppressed a laugh. She was glad he didn't click his heels, though he did bow and kiss the hand that she'd been tempted to hide behind her. After a half hour of such dullness that not even Ilona's considerable assets as a hostess could enliven, Tibor bowed, kissed Melissa's hand once more, and left. Ilona turned to Melissa.

"He is crushed, darling. He has been begging me to invite you down when he is here, so last night I promised him that if he came over this evening, I would ask you, too. I couldn't warn you to wear something feminine, because then you'd give me an excuse not to come down. But Melissa, darling, you could have showed him a little interest." At the quirk of Melissa's eyebrow, Ilona added, "Just for fun, darling. A real woman is never above a little harmless flirtation." The more Ilona talked, the stronger her accent became.

"Ilona, you spend too much time thinking about men. I've—"

Ilona interrupted her, clearly aghast at such blasphemy. "Melissa, darling, that's not possible. Ah...wait a minute. What happened with that man?"

"Nothing happened. He built a fire, and he's going away for a couple of months. Before you ask, the fire is still raging."

Melissa looked with amusement at Ilona's open-mouthed astonishment. "You mean he didn't take you to bed? What kind of man is this?" Both shoulders tightened in a shrug, and her palms spread outward as if acknowledging the incredulous.

"He's your kind of man, Ilona, believe me." She grinned as Ilona shrugged again, this time in disbelief. "Anyway, that's irrelevant now. I'm moving back to Frederick."

"You couldn't be serious, darling. The town doesn't even have a ballet company—you told me so yourself. Who could live in such a place?" Ilona would have been a wonderful actress, Melissa decided, grinning broadly, as she took in her friend's mercurial facial expressions and impassioned gesticulations. And all because a town of forty thousand inhabitants didn't have a resident ballet company.

"I've decided to try it for two years." She had to keep the uncertainty out of her voice. Ilona would pick it up in seconds and start punching holes in the idea. "My mother isn't well," she went on, "and… Look, I've made the arrangements, and if you hadn't called, I'd be packing right now." Melissa watched Ilona's eyes widen.

"Really? Well, darling, you know I don't do anything laborious, but I'll help you pack. This is terrible. I hate to see you go but…" She paused, and a brilliant smile lit her face. "Maybe you will find there the man for you."

Melissa couldn't restrain the laughter. Was there a scenario into which Ilona couldn't inject romance? "Thanks for the offer, but my biggest problem is finding a tenant. I'll pack my personal things, but the movers will pack everything else."

"You're not selling your apartment?"

Melissa wondered at her keen interest. "No. I'm going to rent it unfurnished for two years. If I find life in Frederick intolerable, I'll move back here."

Ilona beamed. "I have a friend who would take your apartment for two years. That would suit us both, darling. Your place would be in good hands, and I'd be assured of seeing him every night, even if New York got two feet of snow. Shall I tell him?"

Melissa couldn't contain the peals of laughter that erupted from her throat at the gleam in Ilona's green eyes. "Sure thing," she told Ilona when she recovered. "Tell him to call my office tomorrow morning."

\* \* \*

Two weeks later Melissa sat on a bench facing Courthouse Square in Frederick, exhausted. It hadn't occurred to her that finding an office in her hometown would be so difficult. In the short time since she'd made her decision, she'd arranged to share her secretary with the lawyers who had offices down the hall from her own in New York, made similar arrangements in Washington, D.C., and Baltimore, and shifted her business headquarters to Frederick. With fax, e-mail, telephones, and the use of electronic bulletin boards, she had expanded her business while cutting her expenses in half. But coming back home also had its darker side. She hated that the bed she slept in was the one she'd used as a child, and her father, satisfied that he had her once more under control, ignored her most of the time.

Melissa's mother had remembered her daughter's love of pink roses and had placed a vase of them in her room. A bowl of lavender potpourri perfumed Melissa's bathroom, and the scent teased her nostrils when she opened the doors of her closet. Emily Grant had greeted her daughter with a warm embrace.

"Welcome home, dear. I knew he'd keep after you till you gave in." Melissa returned the fierce hug, though she thought it out of character for her usually undemonstrative mother.

"I'm not sure you've done the right thing, coming back," Emily continued, "but I'm glad to see you. I've missed you."

"I missed you, too, Mother, and I hope we'll get to know each other again. It's been a long time since I lived at home."

"Over ten years. I know you'll be busy, but you come see me whenever you have time." Thereafter Melissa saw little of her mother, who, she recalled, preferred the solitude of her room and who, she'd decided, looked the picture of health.

She unfolded *The Maryland Journal,* checked the real estate ads, and walked four blocks to investigate the one office that might suit her needs. With its attractive lobby and wide hallway, the redbrick, five-story building enticed her as she entered it. The office suite that she liked had high ceilings, large windows, parquet floors, and a comfortable adjoining office for her secretary. Her excitement at finding exactly what she needed ebbed when she learned that the building was owned by the Hayes-Roundtree family. Unfortunately, if she wanted prime space, she'd have to take it.

She didn't mind renting from Adam's family, although she knew her father would explode. How could he harbor such intense hatred? It wasn't even his war. He hadn't known about the feud until he met her mother, but he'd since used it to justify every disappointment, every failure he'd had. She had to shake her guilt for having thought it, but she rented the office nevertheless. For the sake of peace, she had sacrificed her feeling for Adam and come home, but there were limits.

Raised eyebrows greeted her when she introduced herself to her office neighbors: a Grant renting from the Roundtrees. She'd almost forgotten about small town gossip. One friendly woman who introduced herself as Banks told her, "I see you've emancipated yourself. Good thing, too—when hell breaks loose, everybody will sympathize with the good guys." Melissa grimaced. She didn't need an explanation as to who the good guys were.

Melissa didn't have long to wait for an indication of the problems that her move into that building would cause. Her cousin Timothy stood at the corner light as she left the building, and she smiled as she walked toward him.

"Hi," he greeted her. "I heard you'd come back home, but what the hell were you doing in there? That's the Hayes Building." Cold tension gripped her as she noted his angry frown.

"Where else can you find decent office space in this town?" Her attempt to dismiss it as irrelevant didn't please him.

"You've been gone a while, but the rest of us have been right here watching them flaunt their money. Find some other place. Why do you need an office anyway? Uncle Rafer said you were coming home to be with Aunt Emily."

"Long story," she said, unwilling to explain what she considered wasn't his business and waved him good-bye.

He yelled back at her. "Get out of that place. You're just going to start trouble." *I seem already to have done that,* she thought, her steps slow and heavy.

Melissa worked late the next evening, arranging the furniture, books, and fixtures that had arrived that morning from New York. That done, she decided to acquaint herself with one of her new computer programs, but she had just begun when the screen went blank, the lights in her office flickered, and darkness engulfed her. She didn't have a flashlight and hadn't bothered to locate the stairs, and a glance at her fourth-floor window told her that the moon provided the only relief from darkness. She didn't get a tone when she lifted the telephone receiver, so she prepared herself mentally to spend the night there and tried to remember where she'd put her bag of Snickers.

"If you don't have a lantern or flashlight, go into the hallway and stand right in front of your door. I'll be along shortly with light."

She looked toward the loudspeaker as tremors shot through her, and she struggled to still the furious pounding of her heart at the sound of Adam's voice. She hadn't known that he had come home to Beaver Ridge, only that he'd left New York. It had to be Adam. She couldn't mistake anyone's voice for his—no other sounded like it. Did he know she was there? Would he be glad to see her? She opened the door and waited.

The air conditioning was off, but goose bumps covered her bare arms, and chills streaked through her as the lights approached. He stopped a few feet away.

"Melissa! What— What are you doing here?" Her eyes beheld his beloved face before taking in the length of him, as though assuring themselves that it was he. "Melissa— Am I hallucinating?" He took a step closer.

"Adam— Adam, I...I'm standing in front of my new office."

*"My God!"*

He didn't want her there. Why had she thought he cared for her even a little? She wanted to back up, but the eerie, unsettling atmosphere and the shock of seeing him kept her rooted there. Her gaze followed the two lanterns as they neared the floor, and then she looked up at him walking to her, a determined man whose motives she didn't need to guess.

"My administrative assistant didn't say she'd rented this suite. Tell me why you are here." He stood inches away, so close that she breathed his breath and smelled his heat.

"I—" He stepped closer, and her hand went to his chest. "I—Adam!" Quivers began deep inside of her when his hands grasped her shoulders, pulling her closer, and then wrapping her to him. She couldn't wait for his mouth, but stood on tiptoe and pulled his head down until his lips reached her moist kiss. She refused to let herself remember that he'd told her good-bye. She had him with her, and she had to have what he was offering her. Her parted lips took him in, and with unashamed ardor she sipped from his tongue's sweet nectar and fitted herself against his hard body. He thrust deeply into her mouth as though redis-covering her seductive honey, and she arched her hips into him. Her shameless demand must have threatened his control, for he eased the kiss and lightened his caress.

"I take it you're glad to see me," he said, a smile softening his face. He looked down, saw the two lanterns, and laughed as he reached for them. "Sweetheart, you're so disconcerting that I forgot about the blackout. There may be some more tenants waiting for me. Come on."

She couldn't believe he'd said it. "Adam, you just kissed me as though we'd never get another chance, and now you're acting as though you only patted your dog."

The man grinned. "I don't have a dog. Pets never appealed to me, and I don't think of Thunder as a pet. He's my friend."

She gaped. "Who the devil is Thunder?"

"My stallion. Try not to be outraged, Melissa. For a moment there, I gave myself the choice of moving away from you and cooling things down or seducing you into letting me put you on the floor. You do not belong on any man's floor, Melissa—so cut me a little slack, will you? Now tell me why you have an office in this building."

He showed surprise at her explanation.

"I'm glad I worked late tonight. You would have been here alone if I hadn't. We don't have night watchmen in our buildings here, and most people don't stay after hours, so if you plan to work after seven, notify my secretary."

"Your secretary? Is there where you'll be spending the next two months?" He nodded.

"Good Lord!" She didn't want to know that instead of avoiding each other, their respective moves guaranteed that they'd be together more frequently now than ever.

The first repercussion from her having moved into the Roundtrees' office building greeted her when she got home. News that a Grant had rented office space in the Jacob Hayes Building wouldn't need wire service. She'd bet everybody in Frederick knew about it before dark. Rafer seemed to have been waiting to pounce.

"Now you've done it. You've really done it. You've moved into that building, and you're paying them good Grant money. Haven't they done enough to us? Don't you have a bit of pride?" He paced the length of the foyer, turned and glared at her. "I assume you're paying rent. You ought to be ashamed of yourself."

"I'm paying rent, and it's my money, not Grant money." She had expected his anger, but not his constant harassment. Rafer put his thumbs in the watch pocket of his vest, paced as he did when he had a judge to admire him, and told her, "I want you out of the Hayes Building tomorrow and not a day later."

Melissa looked at him, snugly wrapped in the splendor of his self-righteousness, and knew two things: if she didn't have her own home within two weeks, she'd go crazy; and she was going to learn not to care what her father said or thought. Her cold smile conveyed the message that the Melissa who returned home was different from the one who'd left ten years earlier.

"You're a lawyer, Father," she reminded him, "so I'm sure you know the penalty for breaking a lease without provocation."

The following morning Rafer used different tactics. He

arrived at her office minutes after she did and, with her office door ajar, lectured her for not being attentive to her sick mother, who Melissa suspected wasn't sick, and demanded that she leave her office and go home.

She wouldn't dignify it with an answer, she decided, and was about to close the door when she heard her friend Banks's voice.

"Well, I'll say, Mr. Grant, you're a real sweetheart. I always ignored the things people said about you, since I figured nobody was all bad—but, honey, you make me rethink my philosophy."

Melissa recalled having witnessed her father's upbraiding once before. She heard Adam's voice again and knew that as long as she was in her office, she'd have peace. But she had no doubt that she'd pay when she got home. Her father would never let her forget that, because of her, Adam Roundtree had ordered him off Hayes-Roundtree property.

She'd known he'd come. He walked through her open door at six o'clock that evening, an hour after the normal end of the workday, as if he'd expected her to be there. He closed the door.

"You'll get more of that when you get home, won't you?" he said without preliminaries. "Does he get violent?"

Alone with him, worn out and vulnerable after her father's antics, she crossed her arms beneath her breast. "Yes, he'll have his say, but he's never been violent nor showed a tendency toward it." Her words must have reassured him, because he became less tense.

"I hadn't realized that your mother is sick. How is she?" A half laugh that was little more than a sigh slipped through her lips, and her shoulders flexed in a shrug as she pushed the frizzy hair away from her temple.

"I don't think my mother's sick. As far as I can see, she's the same as always. She stays in her room as much as possible and doesn't disagree with anything my father says or does. But I have noticed that when he's away she comes out of her room more often, even goes shopping."

"You came home because Rafer asked you to, or maybe he demanded it. But can you live in the house with him?"

She fidgeted with a rubber eraser and avoided his eyes. "I'm looking for a small house. I love the Federal town houses like the ones in North Court and Council, but I don't believe anybody would sell me one of them."

He inclined his head. "You're right, but it's a moot point, since they're never for sale. Whoever has one is keeping it. Some of those houses have been held by the same family since the Civil War. Have dinner with me this evening."

She sensed that he wanted to postpone the time when she'd have to deal with her father, and asked, "Why do you want us to have dinner together?"

His incredulous look brought bubbling laughter from her throat, and in her amusement she didn't noticed the change in him. The breath escaped her in a sharp gush as he drew her into his arms. "Wha—" Her hands clutched the lapel of his jacket and then tried to pull him closer to her. His answering sigh encouraged her exploration of him, and her fingers eased first into the tight curls at the back of his head and then found their way inside his jacket, roaming over his chest and shoulders.

He broke away from her, walked to the window and turned his back to it, facing her. "Melissa, I'd thought that if we didn't see or speak with each other for a couple of months, if we were out of touch, we'd either lose interest or discover that what we felt was more than the physical. But instead, here we are. How can you ask why I want to have dinner with you? I want you and I want to find out whether it's mutual."

How could he have a doubt? Surely, he knew…

"Do you want me?" he persisted. She knew that his relaxed, casual stance as he leaned against the wall was misleading, and she sensed his vulnerability, that by asking the question he had exposed himself to an extent unnatural to him. Her pride wouldn't let her lie, so she hesitated, searching for a way around it. He held her glance, waiting.

"Adam," she began in a hesitant voice, "what I want or don't want may prove irrelevant in this case." His eyes dared her to look away, and she couldn't doubt the importance that he attached to her answer.

"Irrelevant? That may be, but I don't think so. I'm not asking what you plan to do about it. I just want an answer—yes or no."

The fire in his eyes set her lips to trembling in anticipation as both fear and excitement clutched at her. If she said no, would he ignore it and attempt to seduce her? And if she said yes, when would he claim what she told him was his? She kicked at the half empty box of items that she planned to place on her desk and in its drawers.

"Well?"

"You…you know I do. Why are you forcing me to say the words? Will saying what you want to hear satisfy you?"

He walked toward her, shrouding her in his captivating aura, a male animal stalking his certain mate. "Say it, Melissa. Say the words. Tell me that you want me."

"Yes. Yes, I want you, and you've had plenty proof of it. But nothing can come of it. My father is out of joint because I rented an office in your building. What do you think his reaction would be if we…if I—"

"If we became lovers?" he interrupted. "Can't make yourself say it? Well, I don't share your fear. Rafer is concerned about himself, his family name, another loss to the Roundtrees. Not about your virtue, I'm afraid. A man who loves his children doesn't ridicule them in public. I'm sorry to say this, sorry if it hurts you, but it's true. If you go on trying to please him, you won't have a self to give. He doesn't deserve you. I'd hoped we could have dinner together, but if you don't want to—"

"Where would we eat?" The smile in his twinkling eyes stole her breath.

"I know just the place."

Adam stopped the car at Rafer Grant's front door, put the car in park, turned and looked at Melissa. She was preparing to get out quickly and leave him sitting there, as he'd known she would, and his right hand stilled her departure.

"Melissa, when have I ever left you to walk to your door unescorted? You underestimate me."

She opened the door. "Please, Adam, not tonight. I'm not ready to do battle with him. I enjoyed dinner. Good—"

In an abrupt move, he took her gently to him. "You may refuse me permission to see you to your door, but not this—I'm taking this." His kiss was hard and quick, but he knew he'd shaken her. He stayed there until the front door closed behind her and a figure, no doubt Rafer, approached her. He wanted to go into that house, to shield her from her father's unkind words, from the torrent of abuse that awaited her. For the first time in his adult life, he faced what he regarded as an insurmountable barrier, but he refused to consider the one certain way around it, and he wouldn't back away. She was in his blood.

Adam headed for Beaver Ridge, pensive and restless. He didn't fool himself. If he had to see her every day, his desire for her would grow, not diminish. He cursed—since when had he spent so much time thinking about one woman? Bitter laughter spilled from his lips when he reminded himself that no woman had stood against him as she had. With any other one, he would have long ago plucked the bud, sated himself, and gone his way. It was the reason that sophisticated women had suited him. This one was different, very different. She would want it all, and he wasn't ready to spring for that.

He realized that he hadn't driven home, that Bill Henry's house was at the next turn. He parked, remembered with considerable relief that it wasn't necessary to lock the car, and started up the modest walkway.

"Well, what brings you here tonight, Adam?" His uncle's voice came from a corner of the shadowy front porch, hidden from the light of the moon. "Come on up. Mosquitoes are hiding ever since I lit one of those lemony candles that Winterflower insists on sending me. 'Course, you didn't come here this time of night to discuss mosquitoes. I was in town this evening—heard an awful lot of whispering about you. What's her name?"

He regarded his uncle with affection. A tall, powerfully built and energetic man with smooth dark skin and a pencil thin mustache, he had been Adam's childhood idol. B-H had had time to listen to his dreams for the future while his father strove to preserve the family legacy. He'd never wanted to be like his uncle though, because Bill Henry didn't care about money or building empires; he was a seeker of contentment.

"What's her name?" B-H asked again, and Adam noted that as usual he didn't mince words, nor was he reluctant to get personal.

"Her name is Melissa Grant, and she's head of the search firm that located my newest Leather and Hides employee for me, the one I probably ought to suspect."

B-H nodded. "I see. And you think she might be in cahoots with this fellow—"

"The fellow we're speaking about is my manager of Leather and Hides," Adam cut in. His uncle released a long, sharp whistle.

"So you think she wants to sink the business? I know you'll handle that one way or another, so that's not all that's bothering you." When Adam didn't respond, B-H allowed a considerable amount of time to elapse, before he asked, "Are you talking about Emily Morris's daughter?"

Adam swung around. "Yeah. Why?"

B-H stood and walked toward the front door, signaling the end of their conversation. "Just watch your step. There hasn't been a real blitzkrieg around here in over thirty years, and it looks like we're in for one. Stop by again soon."

Meals in the Roundtree home had always been a time of family bonding, and Adam raced down the winding stairs knowing he'd find his mother and brother waiting at the breakfast table. It was one of the reasons why he didn't eat breakfast in New York. He couldn't get accustomed to being alone at a breakfast table. Mary Roundtree didn't spoil her sons, but she gave them as much mothering as they would tolerate. In Adam's case that wasn't much.

"It's so good to have you home, Adam. Sit down, and I'll get your breakfast." He was about to tell her that he'd get it, when he remembered the tradition that she dictated what the family ate for breakfast. She couldn't prevent their eating junk for lunch, she told them, but she could put a good, heaithful breakfast in them. Adam had noticed Wayne's unusual silence, but he waited until their mother left the room before inquiring about it.

"What's on your mind, Wayne?" The brothers occasionally went fishing or played tennis on Saturday mornings when both were at home, a carryover from their boyhood days. "It's too hot for tennis. How about spending some time with me at the office?"

"I'd rather we went over to Leather and Hides. Last night while you were out, Nelson called to report another vat of improperly tanned calf skins. He was so outraged that I've begun to wonder if he's involved in this."

They discovered nothing at the factory that Calvin hadn't reported. Adam was more certain than ever that he was dealing with sabotage, because someone had brought formaldehyde from a locked cabinet in the basement up to the third floor and added it to the chrome tanning when zirconium salts should have been applied.

"What's the damage?"

"We'll have to find a buyer for this glove leather," Adam told Wayne, "and we won't be able to fill our orders for first-quality shoe leather. Whoever's doing this is trying to destroy the family's reputation along with the business. Somebody on our payroll is at the bottom of this." As if he didn't have enough to think about: he had to know whether Melissa had a role in it, whether she'd selected someone whom she could depend on to wreck the business. He didn't want to believe her capable of it, but the possibility existed, and his desire for her wasn't going to overrule his common sense. "I'm going to the office to think about all this. I'll let you know what I decide."

Adam closed his office door, locked it, and stretched out on his luxurious leather sofa. He'd come to appreciate the solitude that living alone afforded, and he could only be assured of that total separation from others on Saturdays or Sundays in his office. Sunday was out—small town people went to church on Sundays, and if you had any standing in the African American communities of Frederick and Beaver Ridge, you'd better be there. To go to one's office was to risk being labeled an infidel, and the brothers and sisters did not associate with nonbelievers.

He turned over on his stomach and remembered that he hadn't eaten lunch, but food wasn't what he wanted. He wanted Melissa. He had to see her, but where could they be together without the wrath of their families or the speculations of gossip mongers? He couldn't go to her house, and she wouldn't be welcome in his, and if they went to a public place, the news would float back to their families within the hour. Did he dare even to telephone her? He sat up. For himself, he feared nothing, but he didn't want to trigger her father's mean behavior. He paced the floor, but with each step his desire to see her, to be with her, intensified. She'd said that her father was never violent. He dialed her number.

To his chagrin, Rafer answered. "This is Adam Roundtree. I'd like to speak with Melissa, please." He hadn't hesitated to identify himself, because surreptitious behavior wasn't his style.

"What do you want? Isn't it enough that your family stole her birthright? Now you're after *her!* I won't allow it."

He listened to the man's discourteous remarks with as much patience as he could muster. "If you won't allow me to speak with Melissa, please tell her that I—" He broke off when he heard Melissa's voice.

"Give me that phone. How could you speak that way to another person, Daddy, especially when that person is calling me at the place you said would be my home? If I came back, you promised this would be my home. You listen to me, Daddy—if I'm at home, I should be able to receive calls and entertain my friends without your interference. So it's clear that I'm not home now, but I soon will be." She disregarded her father's stunned expression, aware that she had never before defied him to his face, and turned her back.

"Adam. I apologize for my father. You wanted to speak

with me?" Her spirits rose as the deep timbre of his voice warmed her heart.

"I would have preferred not to call, but I had no choice. I want to see you. Where can we meet?"

Melissa looked at her father, saw the veins that protruded at his temple, the rapid breathing that always accompanied his moments of extreme displeasure. When she tried to please him or when, as now, she finally defied him, his reaction was the same.

"Pick me up in a half hour," she told Adam, hung up, and waited for the inevitable. She figured her father needed at least one minute's worth of verbal explosion, gave it to him, and went to her room.

Adam strode up the steps and rang the bell at Rafer Grant's front door. He was certain that Melissa had planned to wait for him on the front steps and had arrived ten minutes earlier than agreed in order to forestall her. He greeted Rafer with as much civility as he could, looked up and saw Melissa coming down the stairs, a vision in a wide-skirted dress of buttercup yellow and knew that, if he had to, he'd take far greater chances in order to be with her.

He took her hand, turned, and looked Rafer Grant in the eye. "Good night, Rafer." The man's whipped expression said that he'd gotten the message, clear and unmistakable: Adam Roundtree did not hide his actions from *anyone.*

Neither spoke, and both knew that their relationship had changed, because each of them had risked something in order to preserve it. Adam drove two blocks, aligned the Jaguar with the curb, parked, and turned to her. She had to know that he'd needed to see her or he wouldn't have called, that her defense of him to her father had heightened his desire to possess her, to be one with her. He reached for her and took her to him hungrily, shocked at first to realize how badly he'd needed to have her in his arms and then stunned by the ardor with which she returned his kiss, clung to his embrace. Again, a nagging memory pestered him: where and when had he known her before?

She nestled in his arms, and he held her there as he marveled that words seemed unnecessary, that they seemed to belong together. Yet he knew that it couldn't be. He wasn't ready for it, not with her, not with a woman who might be guilty of the epitome of treachery, not with the daughter of a man who hated him. Reluctantly he released her. He had to get his emotions into harmony with his brain. Her hand remained on his chest, warm and sweet, and he wanted to pull her back to him. To feel again her soft breast against his chest and her eager mouth welcoming his tongue. He ignored his craving for her and started the engine.

Her words reminded him of what she faced, of what they both faced because of their attraction. "I pray to God that I never have to stand between you and my father. Nothing would have convinced me that he was capable of such acrimony if he hadn't directed it to me, if I hadn't been the butt of it. I've seen a house that I want, and I'll be moving as soon the deal is closed. I shouldn't have let him persuade me to come back here, but fate seems to have had a hand in it, so I'm not knocking it."

"Fate is an excuse people use, Melissa. I don't believe in it," he said, working hard at combating his vulnerability to her.

"I know. You told me that."

He knew that their circumstances troubled her, as they did him. He could feel it, but he couldn't relent and comfort her. His desire for her already neared fever pitch, and he had to keep his counsel, had to resolve the problems at Leather and Hides. He couldn't—wouldn't—think beyond that.

He drove toward Baltimore and stopped at an elegant little mom-and-pop restaurant just on its outskirts, where they were unlikely to encounter anyone from Frederick or Beaver Ridge. But as they entered, Adam saw his brother, Wayne, at a center table with a woman whom he didn't know.

"Do you see someone you know?" Melissa asked.

"My brother and a companion." He sat back, looking in

Wayne's direction until his brother acknowledged his presence. That accomplished, he opened the menu and concentrated on what he'd eat.

"So much for privacy. I doubt we'll get any before you move into your house." He couldn't bring any humor to his chuckle. "And then we'll have more privacy than will be good for us." He could tell from her reply that she didn't have her sense of humor with her right then.

"Will your brother come over here? Do you think he'll join us?"

A smile touched the corner of his mouth. Her feelings about additional company couldn't have been clearer. She didn't want any, at least not his brother's.

"Wayne wouldn't engage me in a public confrontation, Melissa. My brother and I respect each other." They ordered cold minted pea soup, Maryland deviled crab cakes, salad, and peach cobbler a la mode for dessert. Adam contemplated the soup in which he normally delighted, but which he could not enjoy. He had looked forward to being with her as they'd been that Sunday with Winterflower, but he knew she wouldn't let down her guard, that Melissa Grant wouldn't drop her public persona so long as they were under his brother's watchful eye.

Heat pooled in his middle when she idly stroked his left hand.

"Will Wayne be angry with you?"

He realized then that she had a deep concern for his family's reaction to their being together. He told the truth.

"Wayne is angry, and he will continue to be for some time."

He watched, fascinated, as the gray of her eyes lessened and the brown grew more striking. Obviously appalled, she exclaimed, "Don't you care?"

"Every bit as much as you do, I assure you," he replied, "but I try not to allow the opinions of others to dictate my behavior."

"Doesn't *anything* get to you?"

"Sure. You get to me, Melissa. What do you suggest I do about it?"

She glanced anxiously toward Wayne.

"Don't be provocative. We're not alone." No, they weren't. But if there had been no one around them, it would have made no difference. The communion he needed with her couldn't be expressed in words. Frustrated and fearing that he'd spoiled the evening for her, he squeezed her hand and suggested that they leave.

"I'm not a masochist, but the longer I sit here with you, the more I'm beginning to feel like one." Tenderness for her surged within him, and he longed to cherish her for the world to see, to protect her from the berating he knew she'd get at home because of him. Their circumstances chafed him, its reality like bile in his mouth. He wanted to kick something.

When they got back to her parents' home, he parked and cut the motor. Her hand reached toward the door, and he told her in a voice soft but firm, "Don't even think it, Melissa. I went in and got you, and I'm taking you back in there." He took her key, opened the door, stepped inside, and took her into his arms. Her passionate trembling when his fingers streaked down her cheeks and her neck nearly cost him his self-control. He didn't consider whether he had an audience, didn't think of that, only that he needed her fire, her woman's heat, her total surrender.

Blood pounded in his brain as the heady scent of her desire tantalized her nostrils. The slight movements of her hips against him stunned him and then, as though giving in to her feelings and dismissing caution, her action became rhythmic undulations that sent blazing heat to his groin. At his swift, powerful erection, her arms tightened around him, and she sucked his tongue into her mouth and gave herself to him. He nearly buckled from the force of his desire. He demanded, and she gave. Gave until the blood coursed through him like a rising river rushing out of control; gave until he thought he'd lost possession of his big muscular body as it quivered with rampant passion; gave until the salt of her tears brought him back to reality, and he released her. He stood for long minutes looking into her eyes, looking for the woman that he wanted her to be. Looking for himself. At last he forced a smile, ran his hand over her frizzled curls in a gesture of affection, and left her.

The next morning, Sunday, he got out of bed at eight o'clock after having slept barely three hours. Frustrated because she was who she was and at himself because of the dilemma he'd gotten into, he had to settle at least one thing. What was her tie to Nelson? To his relief, it was she who answered his telephone call. He greeted her warmly before asking, "Melissa, did you know Calvin Nelson before you interviewed him for my company?"

He had to admit her genuine surprise at his question. "I met Nelson the day before I brought him to your office. Prior to that he was a name on my computer screen. Why?"

"I needed to know."

"If you doubt my integrity, say it right out."

"If I find fault with you, Melissa, I'll tell you to your face."

"Watch your step," she shot back, her voice cool and business-like. He hung up. He'd annoyed her, and he hadn't solved one thing.

Melissa dressed for church in a white seersucker dress and white low-heel sandals. Disconcerted by Adam's odd question, she told herself that it couldn't mean anything, that a man couldn't kiss a woman as he'd kissed her the night before unless he at least respected her. She stopped by the breakfast room for a cup of coffee and found her father seated at the table deep in thought, his place setting undisturbed.

"Good morning, Daddy."

"You're a traitor," he began with obviously controlled fury. "You know Jacob Hayes stole your birthright and that every one of his descendants has laughed in our faces, flaunting their millions at us. And you have the nerve to go consorting with Adam Roundtree, parading yourself with him right in front of me. You've got no shame and no family pride. I ask you to come home and look after your mother, and what do you do. You open an office in a Roundtree building and walk out of my house with Adam Roundtree holding your hand. You're—"

Melissa couldn't listen any longer. She left the room without having gotten the coffee and started up the stairs. For the first time, she wondered about her father's unnatural hatred for the Hayes people. He isn't a Morris, she reflected; he only married one. "I'm tired of this."

Banks knocked on Melissa's office door the next morning and walked in with two cups of coffee and a box of powdered sugar doughnuts. Except for her beloved Snickers, Melissa confined her junk food intake to late night snacks, but that morning she ate two of the doughnuts, arousing her friend's curiosity.

"Most mornings, I can't get you to eat half of one of these things. What's got into you?"

"How does tall, dark, and handsome sound?" Melissa asked, in an attempt at jocularity as she idly braided the curly hair that hung over her right ear.

Banks gulped her coffee. "You're sweet on Adam? Good Lord! Why don't you just drop the bomb and start World War Three?"

Melissa shook her head, conceding her dilemma. "My father is outraged because I went out with Adam Saturday night, says I've disgraced the family, and that Adam's motive in seeing me is suspect. I enjoy being with Adam, and I'm sick of this ridiculous feud, but I can't let my family down, Banks. I can't betray my folks."

Banks removed the cigarette from the corner of her mouth, and when she didn't see an ashtray, put it out against the sole of her shoe. That done, she settled into the room's most comfortable chair and looked at Melissa. "I don't know how meddlesome you allow your friends to be, but you might as well learn right now that I speak my mind. So if you don't want to hear it, push the rest of my doughnuts over here and tell me to leave."

Melissa returned her friend's steady gaze. "If you've got the guts to say it, I can take it."

"Well," Banks began after a long pause, "have you ever wondered whether Moses Morris, your grandfather, just stood silently and naively by while Jacob Hayes took him to the cleaners? Do you think a man smart enough to swing a loan for a high-risk venture with no capital behind him was stupid enough to let another man soak him? Think, Melissa. That was nearly three-quarters of a century ago, when most of the black people in this country didn't have a reason to go to a bank."

She lit another cigarette, puffed it, and sent a perfect smoke ring drifting its way to extinction. "And what about the court ruling, Melissa? Don't you think that has any validity? From what I read of it, the jury consisted of ordinary people living in the county here, and none of them stood to gain anything. You can read the trial record in the library on Market Street, or you can read the newspaper reports preserved in some of those glass cases in City Hall." She laughed, though it was more of a snort. "Or you can take the town tour that old lady Aldridge sells the tourist; she never fails to mention it. The Hayes-Morris feud is almost as famous around here as the one between the Hatfields and the McCoys." She glanced at Melissa to gauge her reaction. "I like it," she joked, not bothering to veil the mockery. "I like the fuss the townspeople make over it. It legitimates us black folk as social beings."

"Anybody would think you invented sarcasm," Melissa said, her tone conveying admiration.

Banks feigned modesty. "Aw, shucks, you know I didn't invent it, honey. I just know how to make good use of it."

She extinguished her half smoked cigarette in the manner previously adopted. "You know, Melissa," she continued when she saw that Melissa didn't object to her candid words, "all this sounds like jealousy to me, like your grandfather wanted to kick himself for his own rash behavior. Even *I* know you don't bring in gas or oil overnight. If he took his money out of that speculative venture before the find, he didn't have a claim. And, honey, if you let this ridiculous grudge keep you from a man that just about every woman within driving distance would like to have, you're doing yourself a disservice. And you're crazy. Plain looney." She crossed her leg and swung it. "Her highness, Mary Roundtree, is going to see red. Ha. Serve her right. She always was too highfalutin for me." She sighed and got up...a bit dramatically, Melissa decided. "I'm going back to work, Melissa. You can tell me what you think about this at lunch."

An afternoon several days later, Melissa put the keys to her new house in the pocket of her slacks and began the ten-block walk to her parents' home. She hoped the workers would complete the renovations within a couple of weeks, because she needed her own place, and soon. Her father had stopped speaking to her, and her mother stayed in her room reading the world's great books, the purpose of which Melissa sensed was to legitimate her refusals of Rafer's company, if indeed, it was she who did the refusing.

Her mother welcomed her visits, but rarely went to Melissa's room. Melissa had begun to suspect that Emily Grant would do most anything to avoid her husband's anger. Did that account for the times when she'd find chocolate under her pillow, a pink rose in her bathroom, or a book of verse on her night table? But never a word of it from her mother. Or when, as a child, she'd find a new doll or other toy in her drawer or closet. She had attributed that to her love of surprises and had thought that her mother knew that and catered to it.

She couldn't help pondering Banks's caution of her loyalty to her parents, especially her father, an allegiance that her friend believed to be misplaced. Why shouldn't she enjoy Adam's company? He hadn't hurt her in any way, and even with her limited knowledge of men, she knew he was honorable. Proud and at times arrogant, perhaps, but honest. Yet she hadn't been able to forget how he'd queried her about Calvin Nelson nor the questions he'd asked: how well and how long she'd known the man. She disliked the subtle implication that she might have recommended a personal friend after taking a retainer for an executive search. The more she thought of it, the closer she came to getting mad.

She walked into the house, went to the telephone, and called him. "Why did you ask me the other day how long I'd known Calvin Nelson before I brought him to you? I've been thinking about that, and I do not like the insinuation."

"I told you not to worry, that I was covering all bases."

"What kind of an answer is that?" The lilting cadence of his voice always thrilled her, but waves of joy washed over her at the sound of his deep, vibrant laugh, a wondrous sound that he so rarely let her hear. He must have heard the warmth in her voice, must have detected how well his brief answer had charmed her.

"I want to see you tonight."

She wouldn't let him bend her to his will. "I don't think so. What did Wayne have to say about our being together last weekend?"

"Don't let that concern you," he replied with evident lack of concern. "He means well. They all do—Rafer included—in their way. What time should I call for you?"

The man wasn't accustomed to hearing the word no, and as Jason Court had warned her, he didn't like it when he heard it. Well, he should know by now that she was as independent as he. "Not tonight, Adam," she insisted. "A war broke out in our house after you left here the other night."

"You mean I'm not worth your defense of me?"

She heard his laughter and figured it was time he got some of his own. "You've got the courage to come to my house and create a storm. Well, suppose I come by for you at, say, seven o'clock tonight. Be ready." She hung up. And you can be sure, she murmured to herself, that I'll ring your bell at a quarter to seven.

She grabbed the phone before its second ring. "What's the matter? Chicken?" she asked. But Adam was not the caller.

"Melissa, this is Timothy Coston, your cousin Timmy."

She sat down, glad that she hadn't said more and that she hadn't called Adam's name.

"How are you, Timmy? I'm surprised to hear from you."

"Yeah. I guess you are. I hear you have an employment agency. That's what your dad said, and I'm looking for a job." Some more of her father's shenanigans.

"I locate executives for corporations, Timmy. I don't run an employment exchange, but if I happen upon an opening, I'll keep you in mind. I'm in the Hayes Building. Send me your CV." She terminated the conversation as quickly as she could. She would not hire her cousin no matter what her father said or did. She'd lose control of her business, and her father would have been the instigator.

# Chapter 5

Melissa's breath stuck in her throat as she waited at the front door of the Roundtree house. She had never before stepped on the property, hadn't even had a clear view of the house, though, like most of the area's residents, she'd heard about its sumptuousness. She'd been taught from early childhood that the place was off limits. To her relief, no wild, vicious dogs barked furiously and snarled at her feet, which, as a child, she'd imagined was the reason for her father's stern edict that she, Schyler, and their cousin Timothy avoid the place. She listened for footsteps, heard none, and pressed the bell again. The doorknob turned, and she released her breath at last, only to suck it in sharply when the door opened and Mary Roundtree faced her. Lord, she hadn't counted on this.

"Good evening, Mrs. Roundtree. I'm Melissa Grant." The woman's manners matched her regal bearing. "Hello, Melissa." Though her voice was pleasant, it lacked warmth, Melissa noted.

"Won't you come in? I assume from what I've heard that you wish to see my son, Adam." What had she expected, Melissa asked herself—small towns and secrets were incompatible.

"Thank you. Would you please tell him I'm here?" She reflected on their behavior toward each other, so pleasant and so civilized. A stranger would have gained the impression that they had always been on friendly terms, but those were the first words they had ever exchanged. She stood straighter with her shoulders squared, faintly amused at the barely leashed anger she saw in Adam's mother's eyes. Parental possessiveness wasn't limited to her father. Mary Roundtree turned to leave, and Melissa heard

Adam's footsteps as he loped down the stairs. She looked up with a start. Would she ever get used to his arresting, masculine good looks? She stared into the depth of his gaze until the sound of his mother's throat clearing restored her presence of mind.

As she stood there admiring him, she wished she could enjoy their relationship without reservation. There was so much about him that she liked. Cherished. If he had spoken, if he had said one word, she would have quickly gotten herself in hand, but he didn't speak, merely ambled toward her without taking his gaze from hers. She backed up a step and tried to shake the tension, but it flooded the room like a powerful, invisible chemical and settled over her. Again Adam's mother cleared her throat, and he turned to her.

"Mother, this is Melissa Grant. Melissa, my mother." Mary Roundtree nodded, told Melissa good night, and left them. Melissa watched her walk away and couldn't help thinking that the woman could give her father lessons in manners.

She relaxed within the arm that he slid around her waist, nestling her to him as he opened the door for them to leave. She wanted to turn around, to know whether Adam's mother watched them, but he didn't give her the chance.

"How'd you get here?" he asked her, looking about for a car.

"Towne car service. I'd have been in a pickle if you had forgotten and gone off."

He walked around to the driver's side, got in, and turned to her. "So you got even. Why is it that I'm not surprised? Don't be too proud of yourself, though. The last time anybody in my house reprimanded me was the day I finished high school. And I only got it then, because I'd brought a girl home the evening before when my parents were out. That was the number one no no around here, but I never gave them the satisfaction of knowing that we only sat in the kitchen and drank root beer." He started the ignition. "Let's go."

She slid comfortably down in the bucket set. "I figured if you'd made my father mad with me, you wouldn't mind a little turbulence in your own household. You call that getting even? Tut-tut."

He looked down at her and grinned. She could give as good as she got. Soft, but strong. Clever. He liked that.

She stole a peek at the man as he glanced over his left shoulder, swung into Route 70, and revved the engine. Her heart lurched at the sight of him sitting behind the wheel of that powerful car, strength emanating from him. She looked away from him at the passing scene. With her glasses in place, her eyes skimmed the late summer cornfields as he sped past them, and she wondered whether a woman awaited the lone man who trudged through a field toward an old farmhouse. She longed for the day when she'd have a man of her own, one who loved her so much he couldn't stay away from her, one who would never be content with her sleeping in any room but his. One different from her father. A man who wouldn't be too proud to love a woman with every atom of his being.

"You're unusually quiet. Maybe you're not pleased with yourself, with your little devilment?"

She marveled that he wasn't annoyed by what she'd done. Or was he showing her that she couldn't dent his unflappable cool, that she wasn't of such importance that her little misdeed would make him mad?

"Do you think your mother's angry?" she asked.

"You betcha. Mad as hell." He took his attention from the highway long enough for a quick glance at her.

"And you don't mind that she's mad?"

"Of course I mind." She detected impatience and something like sympathetic understanding in his voice. "What do you take me to be? That woman is my mother, and I care about how she feels. But I'm a man, and that's my home, so I don't seek anybody's permission and don't expect anybody's condemnation about what I do there." He reached over and patted her hand.

"What would you do if I abducted you, took you to my lair and kept you there for a couple of weeks?"

She saw that he'd ended that topic. She turned toward him, and her eyes dared him to do it.

"Well?" he prodded.

"Grin and bear it," she joshed. His warm, throaty laugh that seemed to come from deep inside him sent frissons of heat racing through her. If he knew how much ground he could cover with just a laugh, she reckoned, the man would be unbearable.

Darkness encroached as he turned off the highway and into the only asphalt side road that she'd seen since leaving Beaver Ridge.

"We've passed plenty of them," he told her when she commented. "Don't tell me I've cast a spell on you, closing your mind to all but me." He laughed, and she imagined that her face mirrored her startled reaction. He did it often now, and she thought back to the day shortly after they met and the first time she'd heard his laughter. He'd been stunned at himself. Now he seemed to enjoy it, as though it released something that had been dammed up inside him. He stopped the car, got out, took her hand, and began walking up a gravel path. Melissa looked up at him, perplexed. Where were they going in the darkening woods? A strain of happiness wove through his laughter and swirled magically around her, exhilarating her like a warm twilight breeze frolicking in her soul. She gave herself over to the moment and let his joyous mood infect her.

They paused at an old mill lodged a few feet above the dawdling waters of a once busy brook, and his arm slipped around her shoulder while the moon let them see their reflection in the clear stream below. Melissa wanted to lean against him, but she didn't. If he had squeezed or patted her the tiniest bit, she would have moved toward him, but his large warm hand on her bare arm evidently didn't communicate to him the feeling it gave her. She moved away. Men were not meant to be understood.

"What's over there?" she asked, pointing to a footpath that led into dense woods.

"Not much of interest this late in the year, but in the spring you see a lot of trails littered with wildflowers and small streams alongside them. It's idyllic—a man's best ally if he's got a woman he wants to sweet-talk."

"I can't imagine you'd need help."

"Of course not." And you're proof of that, his eyes mocked. In spite of the lectures she gave herself, she knew she was becoming increasingly susceptible to Adam, but she told herself that she wasn't going to sell out her family by having an affair with him. And he was going to stop kissing her, too. Then his strong but gentle fingers reached for and squeezed hers, and she slipped a little farther into his universe, his world of riveting tension and longing.

Hours later, as he parked in front of her parents' home, she reflected on their evening together. Not once had he alluded to anything personal between them. Not one sexual innuendo. Not a single pass. And yet his twinkling eyes had held such fire and his smiles had triggered such excitement in her as to make her wonder whether he had special powers. He had made no effort to seduce her—but captivate her, he did. She told herself that she wouldn't kiss him good night, that he didn't deserve it. She had learned that he loved to read, liked football, tennis, horses, Mozart, Eric Clapton, and Duke Ellington, and disliked atonal music, baseball, washing dishes, and strong, gusty winds. Yet he hadn't even hinted at what he felt about her. Well, if he was satisfied with an evening of impersonal togetherness, so was she. And she'd show him.

"Adam, you haven't told me what you think of your new office manager. How's he doing?"

He took his hand off of the doorknob, turned, and looked at her in a way that suggested her question was not in order. "He's efficient and competent, but I think Jason's getting tired of him."

"Why?" So, she surmised, a problem did exist, but she wouldn't have known about it if she hadn't asked.

"The man doesn't accept supervision well, especially from someone he considers beneath him."

"He thinks Jason is beneath him?"

"Yeah. Lester's a snob, Melissa. To him, anybody who didn't go to Yale is illiterate. Jason was graduated from Morehouse and got his master's degree at Georgetown. I'm sure the reason they haven't clashed is because Jason is boss when I'm not in the office, and he just calls rank on the man. Anybody who pushes Jason too hard usually regrets it. I think Lester knows that, and he likes having a good income."

"He didn't behave that way with me, but then he was looking for a job. I'm surprised at his snobbishness, though, because several of the references I checked suggested that until Lester was in his late teens, a lot of that Mississippi mud found its way between his toes."

Adam cut short a laugh. "So you do check references?"

Melissa whirled on him. "What do you mean by that question? I run an honest, efficient operation. I've placed executives in some of the most successful businesses in this country, and I want to know how you get the temerity to suggest that I don't have integrity." She jumped out of the car, and he caught her just as she reached the front steps of the house.

"Don't get so riled." He paused as though weighing his next words. "Riled isn't the word—I've noticed that little if anything upsets you, or if it does, you don't show it. Where business is concerned, I don't insinuate anything, Melissa. If something needs saying, I say it. You can be sure that if I have a complaint against an executive hired through MTG, I'll tell you."

She handed him her key, and he opened her front door and walked in with her. Rafer stood in the middle of the foyer, facing them, his face mottled with rage.

"Now that you've discovered this house, you can't seem to stay out of it," he told Adam. His derisive tone and dismissive glance at Melissa was evidently calculated to annoy Adam. Melissa stepped toward him. "Daddy, if you want to bait Adam, please do it outside so he'll have as good a chance as you at winning a case of assault and battery." She heard them snort, but she wouldn't let that prevent her from having her say. It was overdue. "I am twenty-eight and self-employed, and I've established my business without help from anyone. I'm not used to your concern for my well-being after all these years of disregarding me, and I wish you'd stop it." She turned and kissed Adam, well aware that she surprised him when she pressed her lips to his in a lingering caress. "Good night, Adam. I had a lovely evening. Good night, Daddy."

Shivers streaked down her back as she walked up the stairs to her room, aware that they both stood as she'd left them, staring in her wake. Why had she kissed Adam when she had told herself that she wouldn't, not even if he tried to seduce her into it? She closed her bedroom door and turned the key. This was merely the beginning. Her father's pride was his most damning trait, and she had just embarrassed him, exposed him in front of Adam Roundtree. She'd pay. Oh, she'd pay plenty. She reflected on her brother's comment that their father wasn't a bad person, only a pathetically insecure man, and that he'd give anything to know what accounted for it.

Adam got into his car and drove off. He neared the house hoping his family had turned in for the night. He needed to be alone, to think over the evening's events, beginning with his turmoil before he'd brought Melissa home. He had promised himself that never again would he let a woman scramble his brain and hijack his hormones. But another woman had gotten inside of him, one who could be his family's enemy, who could have engineered the sabotage of his family's business, who could be the greatest actress since Waters or Barrymore. He'd strung her along all evening, touching but not caressing, drawing her to him while making sure that she didn't get close, and talking about any and every thing except the two of them. It had been hard work.

Adam shook off the autumn chill as he entered the wide foyer of his home and continued upstairs to his room for the privacy he needed. But as soon as he closed his door, his mother knocked and, like her elder son, she didn't skirt the issue.

"Adam, why are you pursuing a relationship with Melissa Grant? Is it because you like her, or because you're suspicious of her? Do you mind telling me?" He knew that she found prying into his personal life distasteful and was certain that that accounted for her uncharacteristic diffidence. She wanted his answer to be that he was suspicious, but he wouldn't lie.

"I see her because I like her, Mother." He noticed that she tensed.

"But what about the problem at Leather and Hides?"

"I don't have any proof that she's in on it, and I'd give her the benefit of the doubt until I was certain even if I had never met her." He locked his hazel-rimmed, brown-eyed gaze on his mother's identical one. "That's the way I was raised." Her affectionate smile assured him that she understood and accepted the reprimand. He told her briefly of their confrontations with Melissa's father.

Mary Roundtree grimaced. "Why did she come here tonight? Were you expecting her?"

He smiled. "I think to show me what she went through with her father because I insisted on ringing her bell and going inside her house for her, as I would any other woman with whom I had a date."

"Well, she paid you back, and I have to admire her strength. Looks as if she has grit."

"Oh, she has plenty of that." He sighed, deep in thought, private thought. "And she has something else, too. A quiet dignity that hides a deep-seated vulnerability, a softness…" He rubbed his brow with his long, tapered brown fingers. "A sweetness that I haven't—" Suddenly reminded of his mother's presence, he was himself again. Quiet. Uncommunicative.

"You think a lot of her." He'd opened the door, and now she'd have her say. Alright, he'd listen.

"Do I? I'm not so sure."

"Well, you *feel* a lot for her—that's clear. What I can't understand is how you let it happen, knowing what you know." Her tone held deep bitterness. Adam shuttered his eyes, shielding his emotions.

"I care about your feelings, Mother, and I know what you think of Melissa's family. But if I conducted my personal life according to your wishes, nobody would be more surprised or disappointed than you. And you know there isn't an iota of a chance that I'd do that, so please save us both some heartache;

don't get into this. I chart my own course." He walked over and kissed her cheek. "Good night, Mother. I'll see you in the morning." He mounted the stairs slowly. Where the Morris/Grant family was concerned, his mother was matched for intolerance and hatred only by Rafer Grant's attitude toward the Hayeses and Roundtrees. He wished he could see the end of it.

Adam stretched out in bed, wanting to clear his mind and go to sleep. The chirping crickets had as their backup a loud chorus of croaking frogs, familiar notes that had lulled him into many of his most precocious childhood dreams. As though back in time, he responded to the night music, and his mind drifted to Melissa, cataloging her lush feminine assets. What did she have that caused his pores to absorb her the way mushrooms drink water? Why did her woman's scent stay with him always? And why couldn't he stop feeling her lips? He wiped his mouth with his naked arm and turned over on his belly. In every way that counted, she was the kind of woman he liked, that was why.

His gut instinct told him she was honest, and he'd learned to go with his instincts. But he wouldn't swear that he hadn't let his emotions fog up his reasoning about Melissa. He had to have some proof. Sleep. He'd be willing to pay for it.

Melissa showered, got ready for bed, slipped on a robe, and knocked on her mother's door. What kind of marriage was it, she wondered, when the couple didn't share a room, not to speak of a bed?

Emily Grant opened the door, still dressed as though expecting guests for afternoon tea.

"I hate to disturb you, Mother, but I need to tell you what's going on with me these days." She looked around her mother's sanctuary. That's what it was, she saw, a hideaway, her mother's own place with her own decorative taste, own things, and, especially, her own books. Unlike the foyer, living, dining, and family rooms that had been decorated in dull, muted, and socially correct tones by the most expensive interior decorator Rafer could find, her mother's room shouted with joy in hues of green, yellow, and sand with an occasional red or orange accent. Melissa sat on a brilliantly patterned Moroccan leather footstool and watched in surprise as her mother kicked off her shoes, sat on her red chaise lounge, leaned back with both hands behind her head, and waited. Had she been missing something about her mother all these years?

"You know I came back home to be with you, to see you through this terrible illness that Daddy described to me, don't you?" Her mother sat up as if waiting for the ax to fall, but she remained silent.

"Mother, I can't stay in the same house as Daddy. I've bought a place on Teal Street, and I'm going to move as soon as possible." She watched Emily walk over to a small antique cabinet and return with two brandy snifters and a bottle of cognac. I don't know my mother, she mused, accepting the drink.

"I've done a lot of thinking since you've come back," her mother began, "and I'm ashamed. I made unforgivable mistakes with my children, and if I got what I deserved, you'd still be in New York. Rafer doted on Schyler, and I did whatever pleased Rafer, even when I knew it was wrong. I parroted him until I had no self left, until I couldn't stand him or myself.

"I wish I had challenged him, for you, if not for myself. Instead I tried to comfort you with little presents, when what you needed was the solid support of knowing that your mother loved you. You needed my absolute defiance. I should have battled him over his treatment of you. I admired you for your strength in getting out and making a life for yourself. I missed you, but I was glad you left, and I prayed you'd find the love you'd been robbed of at home."

Melissa leaned forward, hoping that her mother couldn't see how astonished she was. She didn't want to appear censorial, but she had to ask. "Why didn't you leave him, Mother?"

"No woman in my family had ever been divorced, and I didn't want to be the first."

"Was there a chance of that?"

Emily sipped the brandy. "Oh, yes. There was more than a chance. If I had chosen to behave differently, we would have separated. And I've often thought I should have let it happen. I should have forced it myself. We would all have been happier."

Melissa knew from her mother's strained expression that she found the conversation painful. She emptied her glass, indicated that she didn't want more and told herself to relax, to listen even if the words she heard hit her like sharp darts shot into her chest.

"Don't let him bully you."

Melissa gasped. She hadn't known that her mother knew how her father treated her since she'd come home.

"And don't let him interfere in your life. I spoiled your brother, because it was what his father wanted, and I didn't stand up for you against Rafer when I should have. I don't ask you to forgive me, because I can't forgive myself." She stood and turned her back. "Would you unzip me, please? I love this dress, but I hate back zippers—they're too much for my short arms. Be glad you're tall." Melissa did as she asked, then waited for her mother to face her.

"Why did Father have so little tolerance for me when I was a child? I used to think he couldn't stand me." She fought back the tears. "I tried so hard to make him love me, to make him think I was special...like Schyler was special."

Cold fear gripped her as she waited for Emily's answer, but her mother's deep sigh of resignation told her she'd have to wait.

"And you're still trying. But we've said enough for tonight. Someday, you'll know everything, Melissa. A lot of this furor about Adam and his family is my fault. I'll say this much: Mary Roundtree must be proud of Adam. I would be, if he were my son. It's time we got some sleep. Good night, dear."

Her mother's words had pained her, but they had also given her comfort. She wasn't sorry that she had made the move from New York. Her financial position had improved, and she had as many clients as she could serve. But most important, she had just shared genuine intimacies with her mother, a first. Her mother didn't disapprove of her relationship with Adam as her father did and as Schyler might, and that could set them against Emily. If she didn't stop seeing the man who was coming to mean more to her than any other had, she could destroy her family.

Timothy's presence in her secretary's office when she arrived at work the next morning astonished her. He hadn't sent his curriculum vitae as she'd directed, but he expected nevertheless that she'd find work for him.

"Complete this and send it to me, and I'll see what I can do." As he strolled out of her office, it occurred to her that she could be years finding her cousin a job.

Two weeks passed and Melissa's house wasn't ready, but after her meeting with the roofer that afternoon, she figured that she'd be able to move in within a few days. The cool October nights came early now as the days grew shorter. She didn't have much confidence driving the secondhand car she had just bought, so she worked swiftly to finish her chores and get to her parents' home before nightfall. She noted the low-lying, dark clouds as she left the house and had no sooner begun the short drive than a torrent of rain pummeled the car's roof.

She drove by a middle-aged man who struggled against the downpour, his shopping bags nearly useless, remembered small-town neighborliness, backed up, and offered him a ride. When he opened the door, she recognized Bill Henry Hayes, though they hadn't been formally introduced, and held her breath fearing that he'd rather drown than ride in a Grant's automobile. He got in, and she introduced herself.

"I know who you are, Melissa, and I'm sure glad you came along. I didn't like the idea of my groceries littering this street." She wondered at his remarkable resemblance to Adam, most evident in his smile.

"I'm glad I happened along." She'd never been good at making talk, and for once she wished she was more adept at it, because she didn't want to appear unfriendly to Adam's uncle.

He turned to her. "You and Adam have just about lit up this

town. Anytime you see two African Americans stop each other in the street and start a long conversation, you can bet they're back on the Hayes-Morris saga. If the Ringling Brothers came to town tomorrow, they'd probably just break even. Our own show is better."

A sense of dread overcame her, and she wondered if she'd been foolish in stopping for him. She let her silence tell him what she thought of the town gossips.

When he spoke again, his voice had lost its merriment and warmth. "Answer me this. Do you mean to do Adam harm?"

She couldn't control the sharp intake of breath that betrayed her astonishment at his question. "Of course not." If her tone sounded bitter, she didn't care. "Is that what he thinks?"

The conciliatory timbre of his voice did nothing to soothe her. "Nobody knows what Adam thinks but Adam." At least he shoots straight, she admitted to herself.

"Yes, I know," she answered.

Bill Henry's deep sigh warned her that she could expect more. "I could ask you what he means to you, but I don't expect you're foolish enough to tell me. I don't know a finer man. Never have. If you're after him, you'd better be one hundred percent straight. As far as I know, Adam's never learned how to forgive deceit nor forget a wrong deed. He's hard, but he's a solid rock of a man. And he's never been known to use his power against a helpless person. I watch him sometime. There's a fountain of goodness deep in that man."

She wondered if he realized how nervous she had become. "Why are you telling me this, Mr. Hayes? Adam hasn't indicated that I'm special to him in any way. Furthermore, we haven't made a commitment to each other, and there's little chance that we will." She glanced quickly at him as they neared his house.

"Well, he's indicated his interest to me and to the rest of the family."

He must have noticed her astonishment, because he patted her arm when she asked him what he meant.

"Adam wouldn't flaunt his defiance of Mary's wishes unless the situation was extremely important to him, and he did that when he walked out of her house with you on his arm."

She parked, rested her right hand on the back of her bucket seat, and turned to face him. "What will everybody think about my driving you home? How much fallout should I expect?"

"I couldn't say, Melissa. It's been decades since I gave a hoot about what anybody said. My guess is that Adam will appreciate it. Mary won't. Rafer will behave as only he can. And Emily, well…" His voice softened perceptibly. "How is Emily?"

Alerted by the strangely melancholy tenor that his voice took on, she told him in greater detail than she otherwise would have that her mother hadn't been well and that it was because of Emily's health that she'd returned to Frederick. His long silence caused her to wonder about his reason for asking. Then his words and tone mystified her.

"I'm sorry," he said with a slow shake of his head. "I'm so very, very sorry. Thank you for the ride and for the chance to meet you. And please call me B-H." She hadn't realized that the rain had stopped until he got out, retrieved his shopping bags, and started toward his front door, trudging very slowly, she thought, for a man as young as he. She backed up, turned the car around, and started home. Something in addition to the fight over entitlement to that gas field had mired their families in hatred. She was sure of it.

"Are you declaring yourself as my competition?" Adam enjoyed putting Bill Henry on the defensive. It wasn't often the man gave anyone the opportunity to do that. His uncle had wasted no time telling him that "the lovely Melissa" had been his savior during the late afternoon downpour. He had the impression that B-H wanted his relationship with Melissa to become permanent, but he didn't want that encouraged. He hung up the phone, stretched out on his bed, and answered his beeper. A foreman at Leather and Hides had discovered more skullduggery. In the pretanning process, someone had failed to add the correct amount of lime to the sodium sulfide solution that gave the company's shoe leathers their distinctive quality.

Frustrated and angry, he beeped Calvin Nelson. "Meet me at my office in an hour. I need to talk with you." He sprang up from the bed, tucking his T-shirt into his jeans as he did so. He listened.

"Don't interrupt your wife's plans. I can drive by your house. Yeah. Twenty minutes."

They sat in Adam's office sipping coffee from one of the building's automatic coffee machines. "Cal, this is the fourth such incident at the plant since you took over as manager, and nothing like this had happened before. Do you know of a worker who might dislike or resent you, or who has a gripe of any kind?"

"I've been on the lookout for that, but…no, I don't think so. I circulate as much as I can, but it's impossible for me to be everywhere in that plant at once."

"I know that." Adam resisted the urge to ask him whether he had a personal connection to Melissa. "I think it's deliberate, and if it continues, whoever's doing it will succeed in trashing the plant's reputation. I want it stopped."

"Have you considered hiring an undercover man who knows the business? We could make up a job that would justify his roaming all over."

"Good idea. Thanks." Adam brushed his index finger back and forth across his square chin. Would a guilty man made such a suggestion? He didn't think so.

He wasn't prepared for the coolness with which his brother greeted him at breakfast the next morning, and he guessed rightly that Melissa was the issue.

"Cut me some slack, Wayne," he said with dwindling patience. "I'm not impulsive—you know that. And you also ought to know that I keep my own counsel. If I want a woman and she wants me, it's between us and no one else. And if I decide that I want Melissa Grant, she's the only one whose feelings and opinions will matter to me."

"But what about Leather and Hides? What about her

family's seventy-year crusade to blacken our name? That means nothing to you?"

Adam disliked unpleasant arguments with his brother, but he refused to let Wayne censor him as Rafer had done Melissa. And he wouldn't tolerate a baseless indictment of her.

"If you've got any proof against Melissa, bring it to me, and I'll see her in jail." Good Lord, he hoped it wouldn't come to that. Less agitated now, he stopped pacing and sat on a stool at the breakfast bar. "Wayne, has she ever slandered a member of this family?"

His brother looked over his shoulder and returned Adam's probing stare. "Not that I know of."

Adam walked over to the window where Wayne stood, dropped a strong hand lightly on his shoulder, and spoke in a gentler voice. After all, they both were concerned about the family's welfare.

"You were always fair, Wayne. Why are you making her a scapegoat? What has she done? Get to know her. Then if you think she's poison, you'll be entitled to say so." He walked over to the refrigerator and took out a pitcher of orange juice. "Don't hope that I'll stop seeing her without good reason. The time I spend with her is the most relaxed, the ha—" He looked into Wayne's knowing eyes and bridled his tongue.

"Alright. Arrange a meeting with the three of us. Not dinner. That's too formal. Let's drive to Washington Sunday and catch the Redskins and Giants. I'll get the tickets. Does she like football?"

Adam shrugged. "I think so. I'll ask her."

"I'll be on my best behavior," Wayne assured him.

"You bet you will."

Forty minutes later Adam closed his office door, checked his messages, sat down at his desk, and picked up his private phone. "What happens between the time you lift the receiver and the time you say hello?" he asked Melissa. "I always get the feeling you're going to hang up without speaking. What are you doing for Halloween?"

"Hi, Adam. The answer to both parts of your question is 'nothing.' Before I met your uncle yesterday, I hadn't realized there were any poor Hayeses." His amusement must have been noticeable by phone, he figured, when she asked him, "What's funny?"

"Honey, B-H is rich." At her exclamation, he explained. "He's also a loner and a nature lover. His Vietnam experience changed his outlook on a lot of things. He came back, wounded, in 1963, and even though he'd nearly lost his life fighting at the behest of good old Uncle Sam, he had to risk it again in the civil rights movement before he could get a decent meal anyplace but somebody's house. He says he could handle that, but a year later something happened that alienated him from the family. Whatever it was left a big hole in him."

"Don't you know what it was?"

"I've asked, but the answer is always that some things are best left alone. Mother said he built that little house, and for years he isolated himself with his animals and his garden. He's back in the fold now, but he prefers his clapboard sanctuary. He doesn't have much use for money. Told me not long ago that what he wanted most in life wasn't for sale."

"You sure have raised my curiosity about him, and you make me feel kind of sorry for him, too."

"Save it—he doesn't accept pity. Want to watch the goblins with me tonight?"

"Where?"

"Melissa, you couldn't be as innocent as some of your comments suggest. We can watch from anyplace you want to, as private or as public as you like." He leaned back in the big, leather desk chair and twirled the telephone cord, hoping she'd throw him one of her little witticisms. A slender young boy— one of the many Adam had plucked from the jaws of the Goans and the Pirates street gangs—walked in and placed letters in Adam's incoming tray.

"Hold on a minute, Melissa." He addressed the boy. "Pete, I know you're memory challenged, but I gave you a tie, and you're going to wear it to work every day. I don't want to repeat this to you again. You're not a Pirate anymore. You're working on becoming a gentleman. Got it?"

"Yes, sir."

Adam waved the boy out of his office. "Now where were me, Melissa?"

"Adam, why did you call me?"

Adam laughed. He knew he'd done more of that since meeting Melissa than in his first thirty-four and a half years.

"Lady, you can ask some of the most astonishing questions. I like your company. Don't you need to know what's going on between us? I do. I want to see you, but when I leave you, I'm dissatisfied. I told you I don't walk away from problems—I solve them. And you, Miss Grant, are an enigma."

"I am not," she huffed. "What am I supposed to do when you come on with the hot stuff? If you'd keep your hands off of me, maybe we could get to know each other."

"What an ingenious piece of wisdom," he scoffed, rocking back and resting his crossed ankles on his massive oak desk. "Well, if you'd control your libidinous gazes, I might be more inclined to do that."

"Your ego's run amuck, mister. My libido doesn't know you're alive."

He rolled his eyes skyward. "Excuse me a minute, will you? I'll get back to you."

Melissa congratulated herself on having bested Adam. She closed the office door, and with the intention of hanging the remainder of the pictures that had arrived with her last shipment of belongings from New York, she started to climb back on the chair that she'd been using as a ladder when he called.

"Owee," she yelped, as strong hands circled her waist. He pulled her to him, and she raised her knee. But at the same moment that she would have attacked, she caught his scent. "Adam...Adam, have you lost your—"

The words died in his mouth, but the lust swished out of him when he stepped back and gazed into her trusting eyes. Tenderness for her suffused him, and his instinct was to protect and care for her. He relished her soft, womanly surrender, the nuzzling of her warm lips against his jaw, the points of her nipples teasing his hard chest. He covered her face with soft kisses. Then with exquisite tenderness, he set her away from him and kissed her, but didn't release her.

Her forehead grew hotter with the slight pressure of his lips there, as he breathed erratically, telling her of his struggle for self-containment.

"Adam… Oh, Adam…" The feel of his warm hand sliding up and down her back, easing her tension, protecting her, sent a different message to her senses than he intended. She didn't want to be protected from him.

"It's alright, baby. I'll get it together in a second. If I told you I didn't plan for that to happen, would you believe me?"

She looked at him, and her tongue darted out, moistening her lips, as she moved toward him. He wrapped her to him in a gentle hug, and she knew he was back in control.

"Would you believe me?" he persisted.

She let her head loll on his chest. "I don't think so. Maybe you didn't intend for it to go that far, but you sure left your office and came in here to give me my comeuppance."

"What about your libido? Think it knows I'm alive now?" Her hand accidentally grazed one of his pectorals, and his demeanor changed, the playful tone gone. "Don't ever do that, Melissa, unless you're planning to make love with me right then and there."

"You don't take rain checks?" she asked, feeling devilish.

His gaze stroked her sensually, though his words were contradictory. "I usually smile if I'm joking." He pinched her nose. "You take that piece of information and use it wisely." His behavior disconcerted her. She wasn't used to that side of him.

"What do you say I drop by for you here around five thirty and we go goblin hunting tonight. Hmmm? No telling what we'll catch."

# Chapter 6

"I'd forgotten that the lights in this town are always dimmed on Halloween. It's eerie walking behind a skeleton on these dark streets, Adam. Ghoulish things give me the creeps."

"Don't be such a namby-pamby." He draped an arm around her shoulder. "That's just a man wearing a costume, but if you're going to be chicken, we can turn around and follow that mummy we passed back there, see how many people he scares."

"Give me the mummy over this thing anytime. At least I can't see what's on the inside." They strolled along closely behind the shrouded figure for the next twenty minutes until the rising wind and the night's chill made their walk uncomfortable. Adam quickened their pace until he caught the mummy and tapped him on the shoulder. Melissa stepped back a few feet. Whatever was in those wrappings might be alive, but from its appearance, she wouldn't swear to it.

"You deserve the prize, Wayne, but I'll have to abstain from the vote."

"No problem. I still have six other chances." He nodded to Melissa. "You're not a judge, I take it?" he asked hopefully. Adam's incredulous look made an answer unnecessary, but he seemed compelled to make his point.

"Make sense, Wayne. This woman's scared of her shadow."

"Am not." She squinted at Adam, wanting to be certain that he was aware of her displeasure. He gazed down at her, his brilliant smile tender and possessive. Warmed, secure, she stepped toward him, and jolts of pleasure rioted through her when his strong arm welcomed her.

"Then you're scared of the dark," he teased. "When you saw that skeleton, you were ready to dive into my pocket." Wayne looked from one to the other and laughed.

"Don't let him get your number," Wayne advised Melissa. "He's been known to wear a joke thin."

"I've already got her number," Adam argued. "She's only tough before sundown."

"Am not."

"Are, too."

"It ought to be a while before you two get this settled. Adam, I've got to frighten some more kids and shore up my position, since your ethics won't let you vote for me. See you later. Hang in there, Melissa." He darted into a darkened side street.

"Wayne wasn't antagonistic toward our being together. In fact, he was friendly."

"Melissa, my brother is my best friend. I hope he'd be civil to any woman I had my arm around. Besides, he probably doesn't even know how a mummy acts when it's angry. Let's go over to Banks's Watering Hole and get a drink."

You never had to guess when he'd finished with a topic, Melissa mused. "I don't mind. At least the town gossips will be spreading the truth for a change." She had a sense of devil-may-care when he squeezed her shoulder and pulled her closer to him.

"Many a lie has begun with the truth, but if that bothers you, I'll take you home."

"You're not calling me chicken twice in one night."

They walked into the crowded, noisy bar, and in less than a minute not a sound could be heard. Melissa released a long breath when she saw her friend, Banks, rushing to meet them.

"I see you two decided to stonewall it and defy the gossip mongers. Come on back here to my table, give 'em something else to talk about. Bill Henry stopped by here a few minutes ago asking for lemonade, and I had to rescue him from that little number posing over there at the end of the bar. Everybody's going to swear that your folks have me in their pocket, Adam. Not that I'd mind hanging out in such nicely lined pockets." She paused at a table and crushed her cigarette. "Sit down, and I'll get your drinks. What do you want?" They each ordered a gin sling.

"I hadn't connected this place with Banks. I take it her family owns it, since she's working here."

Adam looked around, certain before he did it that most of the other patrons were gazing at him and Melissa. Rafer's law partner sat at a nearby table eyeing them intently, and Adam figured that guaranteed Melissa another scene with her father. He lifted her hand and stroked its back gently, idly.

"The place belongs to Banks's father," he said at last, "but she never works in here. She's waiting on us as a courtesy. I can't imagine Banks waiting tables in a bar. The place would be out of business in weeks."

"Why?"

Adam smiled at some tantalizing, imaginary scene. "The first unfortunate Joe who couldn't resist temptation would have to explain his adolescent behavior to a judge. After she dumped whatever she had in her hands right on top of him, of course." Banks joined them with the drinks and sat with them until they'd finished. Melissa's eyes widened when her friend walked them to the door and told them good night there.

"What was that about?" Melissa asked.

Adam's shoulders jerked upward. "Beats me." Minutes later they understood as Rafer's car moved out of the parking lot and into the street at a pace well above the speed limit.

At Melissa's questioning glance, Adam told her, "Your father probably walked out just before we got there. She knew he was out there and wanted to make certain he didn't lose his temper in the Watering Hole." He walked with her to her door.

"I don't want you to come in tonight, Adam. There's no reason for me to flaunt you before my father. It's enough that I defy him. I know he's wrong in this, but I don't want to humiliate him."

Scattered pellets of rain dampened her red designer jacket, a carryover from her New York dress-for-success wardrobe.

"I enjoyed checking out the goblins with you."

"Me, too," she replied, "and I'm not scared of my shadow."

"Are so," he teased, rubbing her nose with his thumb. He opened the door and kissed her quickly, so quickly that she didn't know whether her upturned face had invited the kiss or his finger under her chin had signaled his intent. She stared after him as he dashed through the raindrops to his car. Her father awaited her, but he only nodded when she greeted him, and she thought she detected sadness on his face.

Melissa got ready for bed, put on a robe, and knocked on her mother's bedroom door. She couldn't get used to her mother's open affection, and she cherished it in her heart. She must have been a difficult child for her mother, she mused, for she had been so concerned about getting her father's love and approval that she hadn't reached out to her mother, hadn't been responsive to her silent pleas for affection. She'd taken her mother's secret acts of love for granted, hardly ever acknowledging them.

"It's been years since I went frolicking on Halloween," Emily said. "From your father's temper when he came home, I assumed he saw you out with Adam."

Melissa nodded. "I guess he did, though we didn't see him."

"Do you love Adam, honey?"

"I don't know, Mama. But I feel so good when I'm with him. No matter what kind of shenanigan I pull off, what I say or do, Adam is equal to it or better." She couldn't help comparing Adam to other men she'd known. "When I was in undergraduate school," she recalled, "I went out with a guy a few times, but I couldn't get along with him, because every time I used a word with more than two syllables, he accused me of being uppity. After a while I did it just to annoy him. It didn't take me long to figure out that airheads weren't for me."

"Well, I presume Adam is well educated. Isn't he?"

"Oh, sure. He has an MBA from Columbia." Emily's happy smile jolted Melissa; her mother was a beautiful woman.

"I didn't realize you two had so much in common. The same degree should make you sympathetic with each other's work. It's a good basis for—"

Melissa interrupted her mother's wistful thought. "You shouldn't be counting on anything coming of this, Mama. We've got too many obstacles, and there's no commitment between us." She could see the disappointment mirrored on her mother's face.

"We haven't talked about things like this, and it's another way that I failed you. Did you ever love another man?"

Melissa thought back to the time when she would have given anything to be able to discuss Gilbert Lewis with her mother. The pain, the disappointment, had been severe, so much so that it had shoved her into womanhood. She had later marveled that the first man to whom she had been attracted should have displayed the kind of callousness toward her that her father did. She took her mother's delicate hand.

"I don't think I've ever been in love, although I once thought I was. I was naive until I discovered that he…well, he was sophisticated, successful, and not interested in any one woman. You know the type. After we'd gone out together for a while, he told me that if I wanted to continue seeing him, I had to go to bed with him. He gave me that ultimatum because he thought I was crazy about him. I told him to get lost."

Emily patted the edge of the bed, inviting Melissa to sit beside her. "You were hungry for love, the love you should have gotten right here at home or you wouldn't have reached out to a man who was obviously wrong for you. I hope you've gotten over it."

Melissa rested a hand on her mother's knee in assurance. "The only thing I'm carrying around from that experience is the lesson I learned, and the only thing I feel for Gilbert Lewis is contempt."

"And Adam?"

"Oh, Mama. They're nothing alike. Adam is honorable. I wanted to fall in love with Gilbert—or somebody, but I'm scared to death of loving Adam. I say I'm going to stay away from him, but if I know I'll see him, I can't think of anything else. He's so strong, so…. I can't explain it. When I'm with him, it's like lightning wouldn't dare strike." She heard her mother's deep ragged sigh and turned to face her. "What is it?"

"That last says it all, honey, because you've been afraid of lightning all your life. I just hope your feelings for Adam don't turn bitter in your mouth." That was the second time her mother had alluded to the misery a person could experience for having loved, Melissa recalled, and decided to risk the question that had nagged her for days.

"Mama, did you have an unrequited love?"

"No, dear. It was returned fourfold, but I was a victim of my own stupidity. He pleaded with me to marry him, but I did what my father wanted me to do. I married Rafer instead, and we've both suffered because of my cowardliness." Melissa's heart constricted as tears flowed untouched down her mother's cheek. Whatever she had expected, it wasn't this.

As if she had waited years to tell someone, had struggled in combat with her fate and then been whipped into submission before glimpsing freedom's light, the words rushed from Emily's mouth.

"Don't let the same thing happen to you. If you love Adam, take him. Don't let his family or yours get in your way, because if you do, you'll spend your life regretting it. I've been a good wife to your father, as good as he would let me be. I did what he wanted, loved what he loved, and went against everybody and everything that he didn't like. He favored Schyler, so I did, too, and I'm sorry. I did all that trying to prove to myself that I loved Rafer."

Breath whirled sharply through Melissa's lips, and she stared at her mother, stunned beyond words. How could she have known this woman for twenty-eight years and yet not known her at all? How could she not have seen the sadness, the suffering? She shifted at her mother's side, uncomfortable because in many ways she, too, had seen the world through Rafer Grant's eyes. Silence hung between them until, after a time, Melissa questioned her mother.

"Good Lord! I never dreamed— What happened?" Melissa

knew from her mother's sigh of relief that she had been awaiting what she feared would be a harsh verdict.

"Our parents threatened armed conflict to keep us apart, and they succeeded. I should have known that our fathers, pillars of the community, wouldn't engage in a public battle, but I believed them and broke my engagement to Bill Henry. God alone knows what that did to me."

Air swished from Melissa's lungs. Stunned, she repeated, "*Bill Henry?* You mean—?"

"Yes. Bill Henry Hayes. And Rafer never lets me forget that Bill Henry was my first choice, my first love." Melissa could not miss the silent confession, *and my only love.*

Melissa clasped her mother around her slim shoulders in belated comfort. Encouraged, Emily leaned against her daughter and expressed her concern for Melissa's fate with Adam. "If you tie up with your father about this, I doubt I'll have the strength to go against him. I never have, and it's probably too late for me to start—weakness is habit forming. But you fight for what you want, Melissa. Either you walk the whole mile for him and step over every obstacle or you'll end up like me. If I had the chance again, I'd face an army in order to be with Bill Henry."

Melissa hugged her mother and went back to her room. She stood by the window, pulled the curtains aside, and stared at the night. Small wonder that her father harbored such hatred for the Hayes-Roundtree family, that he opposed any contact between Adam and her with such vehemence. The alleged loss of a family fortune to Hayes and his descendants wasn't half the cause of Rafer's furor. A more personal, ego-shattering ordeal nurtured his rancor. His wife's heart belonged to Bill Henry Hayes. Always had and always would. Melissa could understand that with those two insults, her father couldn't help being irrational about the Hayeses and Roundtrees. She turned away from the window. What made him irrational about her?

The next day Melissa moved into her new home, a small, three-story house that wasn't the Federal she'd wanted, but a more modern facsimile. She raced from the basement to the top floor and stood at the edge of the stairs, panting for breath. The doorbell jarred her out of a self-congratulatory mood, and she loped with some anxiety down the two flights. Surely her father wouldn't leave his office just to bait her.

"Adam...what? How did you know I'd moved?" She stood back to let him enter.

"I called your office to ask if you'd like to see the 'Skins and Giants with Wayne and me this weekend, and your secretary told me where you were. I didn't know this place was for sale, but there's no reason why I should have. I left my real estate cap in New York." His glance swept around the foyer and living room, then across the hall to the small dining room.

"What's the kitchen like?" She walked with him to the little room at the end of the hallway and pointed with pride to the modern kitchen she'd had installed. "This is a nice house. What did Rafer say about your moving?" Neither his stance nor the heat in his eyes suggested an interest in Rafer Grant's views.

"He didn't know about it until I'd made a binding down payment, and my father doesn't believe in wasting money." Adam had stepped closer in order to hear her murmured words, his eyes blazing with passion. She moved backward a step.

"How come you're here in the middle of the day?" She looked away to avoid seeing the come-hither look in his twinkling eyes.

"You asked me a similar question at least once before, and I told you that I intend to find out what we've got going for us. Quit faking, Melissa. The football game, this house, and any other excuse we can find for being together be damned. I'm here because I want to be alone with you, and you invited me in because you want the same."

She looked at the hand he extended toward her in silent invitation and opened her arms. If she'd expected a searing kiss, a sample of his torrid passion, he surprised her. His arms enfolded her gently, carefully as if she would splinter like fine porcelain. Soft kisses on her cheek exacerbated her longing for the sweet pressure of his mouth, until she stopped fighting for passion and enjoyed his gentle loving. Her heart fluttered as she savored the thrill of his embrace, his tender stroking of her back and arms.

His strokes and caresses continued until she curled into him as her senses drank in his sweet onslaught of loving. She looked up at him, and a smile eclipsed her face when she glimpsed the soft adoration in his eyes. He had cherished her, had given her something of himself, perhaps for the first time, because he'd never before made her feel like that. As if he hadn't wanted to take, only to give. She closed her eyes and let her head loll against him, ashamed that she had tried to move him to a frenzied passion when he'd wanted only to share what he felt.

His twinkling eyes brightened when he smiled at her. "I'd better get back to work. It isn't even lunch hour." He glanced up at the sculptured molding on the high ceiling. "When you've finished decorating, this place will look great. I'm glad you moved. Every time I've brought you home, I've had to fight the urge to go in your house and protect you from harassment, because I know it's due to me that your home life's been unpleasant." She turned to face him fully and wrapped her arms around him, but he hugged her and quickly disengaged himself. She smiled, loving her ability to arouse him.

"You've changed, Melissa, but your father hasn't accepted it. You were in New York on your own and you succeeded where many have failed. That would give you or anybody confidence and a right to demand treatment as an adult. You won't tolerate from your folks what you once did, but Rafer apparently hasn't realized that. I can't figure out his behavior."

"Long story." She wasn't going into that. "When is that game you want me to see?" Adam's laugh held little humor, and Melissa sensed his displeasure at her having changed the subject. Didn't he realize how often he did the same?

"Sunday. Will you go? Wayne's coming along." Both of her eyebrows jerked upward.

"Oh, yes, you did say that. If you'd said B-H would be going with us, it would make more sense to me. Why Wayne?"

"He wants to get to know you, and I want him to. What's wrong with that?" he asked.

"Nothing. It should be fun."

* * *

Adam knew he'd better leave while he could. He wasn't surprised at what had taken place between them, but he hadn't planned it, and he certainly hadn't known he would behave with her as he had. That would bear examination when he had the time and privacy. He could have used the phone to invite her to the game, but he hadn't. He admitted to himself that even though they'd been together for three hours the evening before, he'd gone there because he had needed to see her. He knew he teetered dangerously toward caring deeply for her, but swore that it wasn't going to happen. Still he had to admit that if he found that she wasn't involved in the sabotage of his leather manufacturing company, he'd probably go after her. He didn't let himself dwell on their families' certain reaction. Whether to tell her about the problem at Leather and Hides and how much to disclose bore heavily on his mind. He needed to share it with her, but he also had to be cautious.

"I hate to put a damper on this peaceful moment, Melissa, but I have to tell you something. Someone has been damaging leathers at our factory, and one of the reasons I came back to Beaver Ridge was to find the culprit." Her eyes widened in surprise. "So far, we don't have a lead," he went on, "but we know the person either works there or has an accomplice who does." He didn't tell her when it began.

"Oh, Adam, I'm so sorry. This must be terribly expensive. I can't imagine who would do it. You don't have any serious competitors. You have to get at the bottom of this." She seemed genuine in her expressions of regret and concern, but he still scrutinized her for any clue that would point to her guilt and couldn't find a single one.

He noticed her untidy appearance and looked down at the beige and brown tiles she'd been setting. "If I wasn't dressed, I'd help you with that. Why don't I bring over a batch of Clara's crab cakes or whatever you'd like this evening and do that for you?"

Her mouth dropped open at his suggestion. "You'd do that? Thanks, but I wouldn't want to inconvenience you."

He laughed. "Don't give it a second thought, Melissa. I'm not in the habit of volunteering to inconvenience myself. Setting those tiles for you will give me pleasure." His steady gaze must have been warm and inviting as he'd meant it to be, because she folded her arms and rubbed them with her hands. Feeling wicked, he added, "And so will you."

"You'd think Nelson Mandela was coming here, the way I'm acting," Melissa muttered, trying to settle the butterflies in her stomach. Confound it, she couldn't even put on a decent dress. Nobody got dolled up to put in a floor and hang pictures. Disgruntled that he'd see her looking frumpy twice in a day, she compromised and topped a pair of army combat fatigues with a tight-fitting, scoop-necked lavender sweater and went to answer the doorbell.

She couldn't contain her amazement. Adam Roundtree in jeans and an open-necked jogging shirt. "I didn't know you could look like this. Scruffed up, you're...well—" she scratched her temple as she searched for the right word "—you know... human, more accessible. I don't know. You're different." His stare knocked her off balance. She would never have expected the message she read in his eyes. He quickly shuttered his gaze, but in that brief, open moment, she saw him as she never had, as he'd never permitted her to see him. Vulnerable. And hurt.

She needed to make amends for her seeming callousness, to heal him. But a vision of the trouble ahead, of her mother's life flashed through her mind, and she wanted to suppress and to deny the compassion, the tenderness, that he wrung out of her. She pushed the warning out of her conscious thoughts, and her right hand lifted seemingly of its own volition to caress his jaw. He stood, wordless, while she stroked his jaw, his gaze sweeping her face repeatedly as though seeking some truths, some answers that she alone possessed.

Shaken, she stepped closer to him with her eyes narrowed in a squint and her womanly need to banish his anguish unguarded. "What is it, Adam? What have I said?" But he stepped back, away from her, as though unwilling to forgive her and loath to accept her succor.

"Adam?" His pained stare drilled her as surely as any bullet ever pierced its target.

"I'm human, alright. As you once said, I bleed just like you do."

She saw the change in him—from anguish to need—and without thought as to the meaning of her feelings or the implications of what she did, she opened her arms to him. "Adam, tell me what's the matter, what I've done."

He didn't try to stifle the groan that could have been torn from his soul, so violent, so wrenching, as he rushed into her outstretched arms, aware that he was giving her more of himself than he had ever given to another human being. He let her hold him while he drank in her murmurings, her soothing words that declared her respect and her appreciation of him as a man. Abruptly he covered her mouth with his own, curtailing her outpourings in a powerful, ravishing kiss. His fever for her blazed, but he got a grip on his emotions and dragged himself out of the clutches of desire.

Her glance locked on his face, but even as she continued to hold him tight, he read in her eyes repudiation of what they'd just shared and saw her uncertainty and her fear that she'd gone too far. He wouldn't deny the pleasure of being in her arms, and he wouldn't belittle what he felt. He believed in facing the truth even if it hurt, because you couldn't solve a problem unless you knew precisely what it was, unless you understood its nature and what caused it. And he had a problem.

"Melissa, where are we headed? I can't guarantee that if I have another angry exchange with Rafer, I won't fight back. It's against my nature to let a man impose on me with impunity. But he's your father and you love him. I don't want you between us." He set her away from him, though he was loath to separate from her, and pointed to the bag of food that he'd placed on the table by the door.

"Want to eat now, or after we finish? Me, I'm hungry right now, and the scent of those crab cakes makes my mouth water.

How about—" He turned abruptly toward the door, alerted by the sound of footsteps and braced himself for another encounter with Rafer Grant.

Melissa opened the door to her father, who looked past her to her guest. Adam sensed Melissa's discomfort in what was becoming an all too frequent occurrence, but he didn't give quarter. He'd known instinctively that the caller would be Rafer. By some ruse the man seemed to know just when he needed to be reminded of what could happen if he let himself get too close to Melissa. He let her take the lead.

"Is anything wrong with Mama?" Adam didn't believe he'd previously witnessed such courteous and thinly veiled antagonism. She could hold her own, alright, he thought with pride.

"No more than usual. You know why I'm here, and you know I don't want him hanging around you. This is why you moved, isn't it?" Adam stepped closer to her.

"I moved so you and I could live in peace, Daddy, and we wouldn't be a constant source of annoyance to each other. I'm tired of so much unpleasantness, and I'd appreciate it if you'd leave now." Tension gripped Adam as Rafer's nostrils flared, and his eyes shone with hostility.

"He's turned you against your family. After all they've done to us, you're throwing yourself at him. You can flaunt him in our faces, but you won't give your own cousin Timmy a job. You will regret this. I promise you. You'll be sorry."

Adam stared at the closed door. He pitied the man. Loyalty and love couldn't be had on demand and especially not from your child. That had to be earned from the child's birth onward. He turned to Melissa, saw that she had hung her head, and knew that their evening was shot: no friendship could flourish in an environment of suspicion and hatred. Rafer would gladly see him dead, and he and Melissa had misgivings about each other. Why couldn't she have been someone else? He took the bag of food in one hand and grabbed her arm with his other one.

"Come on, let's eat and get this floor fixed."

\* \* \*

Melissa prowled around in her basement after Adam left. Her father had a knack for spoiling her pleasant moments with Adam, and she foolishly let him do it. But she couldn't turn her back on her father, and now that she knew that a deep, personal hurt fueled his anger, she judged him less harshly. She shouldn't attend that football game with Adam and Wayne. In her view she and Adam were behaving as fatalists do, as if they had no control over the course of their lives when neither of them believed that. But she'd promised, she rationalized, so she'd go.

Melissa supposed that where Wayne was concerned, she was on trial, but she wouldn't give him the satisfaction of behaving as if she knew it. She sat between them aware that her body language was that of a woman with two casual male friends. Indeed, until Adam looped his arm around her shoulder, an onlooker wouldn't have known which of the two she cared for. She moved closer to him.

"Mind your manners, Melissa. My women do not root for the New York Giants," Adam said.

"In other words your women just go along with whatever you do. Sweet little things. My men do as they please. If they were patsies, they'd bore me." She watched her warm breath furl upward until it dissipated in the cold November air.

"Your *men?*" His sharp whistle split the air. "Tell me more." She ignored his taunt.

"If the Giants lose, you owe me," he challenged, apparently warming up to the easy banter.

"How much? Or should I say, what?"

Adam's gentle laughter warmed her inside, and she noticed that it brought a quick glance from his brother. "Me thinks you don't trust me," he replied in a voice that suggested she might be foolish to do so.

"Sure I do, but you can be very imaginative sometimes, and I'd as soon not be the victim of your agile mind. So no blind bets. What's the wager?"

"You're smart to get it up front," intervened Wayne, who had been silent until then. "I recall that when we were hellions in our teens and about to scale a neighbor's barbed wire fence, Adam bet me that my pants would tear worse than his. I forgot that he was high jumping in gym class and took him on. It wasn't only my pants that got torn, but he breezed over that six-foot fence as though it wasn't there and had the gall to suggest that I should have been wearing my thinking cap when I bet him. It's best to stay on your toes when you're dealing with Adam."

Anticipating a Redskins' score, Wayne jumped up but quickly sat down, his jubilation short-lived, when the perfect pass slipped through the wide receiver's outstretched hands. Melissa patted his shoulder. "You poor baby. Well, at least you finally got a chance to stretch." When the next play resulted in a Giants' interception of the Redskins' pass, Melissa soothed, "I'm sorry. I wanted my boys to win, but I didn't want them to romp all over your guys."

Wayne grumbled, "Get her to cool it, man." But Melissa knew from Adam's warm laughter that their outing was going as he'd hoped, had perhaps even known it would. His response reassured her.

"I'm congratulating myself on not having insisted that she take that bet, because I'd planned to ask her to put up a few months of her time as collateral."

Melissa sat forward, alert, when Wayne asked Adam, "What were you planning to wager?"

Her breath stuck in her lungs while she waited for Adam's answer, staring as his shoulders bunched in a half hearted shrug.

"Myself." Air zinged through Wayne's teeth in a loud whistle.

At halftime Adam stood and wound his scarf more tightly around his neck. "I'm going for coffee. Would either of you like anything else? Peanuts, maybe?" Melissa nodded agreement, wondering why Adam would deliberately leave her alone with Wayne. Adam's brother seemed friendly enough, but how would he behave once they were alone? She was still a Grant. In the heavy silence a less self-possessed person might have resorted to small talk or rambling, but Melissa didn't say anything. She knew Wayne would take advantage of the opportunity, so she waited for him to speak.

"Do you love him?"

Taken aback, she turned toward him, thinking that bluntness must be one of their family traits. "Adam doesn't know the answer to that question, Wayne, and you shouldn't know before he does."

"Do you know the answer?"

She noticed that his voice wasn't hostile, and from his relaxed manner he didn't appear to want to aggravate her. So she answered him honestly.

"I try not to think about it. I haven't faced it. I don't know how your family has reacted to the friendship between Adam and me, but because of it my father barely speaks to me."

"Scared?"

"You could say that. Maybe."

"Adam is a different man when he's with you. If I didn't see him laughing and teasing with you with almost childlike enjoyment, nobody would make me believe it. Well, the jury's still out, but I have a feeling that if the two of you break up, it won't be due to any outside force or faction."

"What do you mean?"

"I know the hostility between our families worries you. It plagues all of us, but it won't be the cause of permanent cleavage between you and Adam. Only the two of you can ruin your friendship."

She stared at him. "How can you be so sure?"

"Melissa, I know Adam. And you're not a patsy, either." He paused. "Adam hasn't told me anything about you. Where'd you go to school?" She told him, adding that her degree was a master's in business administration. Several people sitting below them turned around when Wayne's whistle pierced the air.

"So you two have the same degree. This gets more interesting all the time. Hold on, I'll get that for you." He reached between their seats and retrieved her umbrella. "What's this thing for?"

"We're supposed to have rain or snow, and I hate getting wet when I'm not dressed for it."

He laughed. "Cover all bases, do you? I thought we weren't expecting a change in weather until after midnight. Are you another of these people who leaves nothing to chance? If you are, Adam's meticulousness probably doesn't bother you. It can wear on me."

She looked up as Adam placed a tray of coffee in her lap. Wayne took it from her, removed the lids, and gave her and Adam each a cup. They drank their coffee and nibbled the nuts in companionable silence, but Melissa had the impression that Wayne had warmed up to her. He held his empty cup for her peanut shells and took her own empty cup before Adam could reach for it.

Melissa pulled up the collar of her coat to ward off the late fall chill as they walked to the car. Adam's arm snuggled her close to him, and his gloved fingers toyed with her cold nose, and she had a delicious feeling that he cherished her and was protective of her. Excitement wafted through her, and she reveled in Adam's attentiveness, though he always showed concern for her. His openness with it in his brother's presence lit up her whole being.

When they reached the car, Adam slapped Wayne's shoulder. "You drive back."

"You're ordering me to chauffeur so you two can make out in the backseat."

Adam attempted to stare Wayne down, feigning distaste for the presumptuous remark, but Wayne protested. "I'm telling it like it is, brother."

Melissa couldn't help but marvel at their camaraderie. Maybe a brother and a sister couldn't be that close, she surmised. Or maybe the environment in which she and Schyler had grown up hadn't been conducive to that kind of love and affectionate exchanges.

When Wayne eased the Jaguar toward MacArthur Boulevard and Route 270 to Frederick, Adam leaned back in the seat, winked at Melissa, and announced that he was sleepy.

"Watch your step back there, Melissa," Wayne warned. "He's a fox that I wouldn't let anywhere near my chickens."

"You sound downright friendly," Adam said in a voice that Melissa thought strained and tension-filled. The silence weighed on her, for she knew that if Wayne bothered to reply, both she and Adam would know his reaction to their relationship.

Wayne turned off the radio. "I am. To both of you." She didn't know what response she'd expected from Adam, but he didn't say that he was glad nor did he thank his brother. But as she mused over their afternoon and evening, she concluded that Adam hadn't brought Wayne and her together in order to gain his brother's approval, but to give him a chance to make a more informed opinion of her. What a man.

"Let yourself out at Beaver Ridge, Wayne. I'll take Melissa home. If Rafer sees the two of us anywhere near that house on Teal Street, he'll lose control for sure."

Wayne reduced the Jaguar's speed as he entered the town limits, glanced into the rearview mirror and spoke as though surprised. "I thought you'd moved, Melissa."

"She moved," Adam said, "but Daddy's omnipresent gaze sweeps a very wide area." Annoyance at the sarcasm in his voice jerked her out of her reverie and out of his arms.

He made no effort to bring her back to him, and she slumped in the seat. Another lovely evening had been derailed by that ridiculous feud.

Adam secured the front door and walked down the lengthy and richly carpeted hallway toward the family room, where he knew Wayne waited for him. About halfway there he glanced toward a portrait of Jacob Hayes that had hung there ever since he'd known himself. The old man's intelligent eyes with their piercing and unsmiling twinkle always seemed to follow him when he passed. He stared at his grandfather's likeness until he heard Wayne call to him, shook his fist at the old man and walked on, less purposefully than usual.

"You've got your work cut out for you."

"Meaning?" Adam knew he'd have to talk with Wayne about Melissa, but he didn't intend to discuss her merits or lack of them. Not with Wayne or anyone else.

Wayne whistled. "Touchy, aren't we? What I mean is you haven't won her, but you can get her, though, because she is susceptible to you. Your problem is you've got her kin and our mother to deal with, and by the time they wear you out, you may say the hell with it."

Adam walked over to the bar, got some ice cubes, and poured two fingers of bourbon over them. He twirled the amber liquid around in the glass in what Wayne had to recognize as a means of gaining time while he thought out his next words. He didn't intend to seek his brother's opinion of Melissa, but he couldn't resist asking, "But not you? You're saying that I don't have to deal with you?" He smiled at Wayne's elaborate shrug, his brother's signature gesture.

"You two were made for each other."

Adam quirked an eyebrow in disbelief. "You're not even skeptical?"

"I liked what I saw of her, and I know you well."

"In many respects, yes, but not in this context."

Wayne paced the floor with uncharacteristic deliberateness, his hands in his pockets. "I may not know what you want in a woman, but I know what you ought to be looking for, and I've gained a good sense of Melissa's personality. She's the perfect foil for your tough cynicism. She's patient, determined, and independent, but she's soft, too. And she's smart. She respects you, but unlike a lot of people who know you, she's not afraid of you. And she wants you. She's the woman for you, alright."

Adam shuttered his eyes. "Damned if you haven't become clairvoyant. Good night." Halfway down the hall, he turned and walked back to the family room where he found Wayne drinking the untouched bourbon on ice. "I'm glad you like her. Shows you that the words Morris-Grant and Satan aren't necessarily interchangeable. A lot of times, maybe, but now you'll acknowledge at least one exception."

\* \* \*

Melissa mulled over the afternoon and evening events, unable to fall asleep. Adam Roundtree was not a wishy-washy man. He knew where he was going, but he hadn't revealed it to her. Whatever he'd planned to do about their relationship, he'd guarded as closely as a miser does his money. She knew he had to consider his family just as she worried about the reaction of her father and brother, but she didn't doubt he'd decide independently of anything his folks said or did. So what accounted for his halfhearted courtship, his reluctance to go after what she knew he wanted? She had a niggling feeling that Adam's caution about her went beyond concern for the ruptured relationship between their families.

She had always been able to arrive at a decision and stick to it, but this time her head and heart were at odds, and where Adam was concerned, both exerted a powerful pull. She didn't fool herself: she loved being with Adam. But he's a Roundtree, an enemy of your family, her mind cautioned. He's a strong man with the temerity to stand up to your father, whom you've never known to back down, her common sense replied. And he makes you feel what you've never felt before, makes you want what you've never wanted before and what you know you can hardly wait to have, her unreasonable heart argued. She turned over in bed, exhausted by her mental struggle.

She sat up in bed and pulled the pale yellow bedding up to her shoulders. If only she'd switched off the phone. Surely her father wouldn't interrupt her sleep to harass her about Adam. At the sound of her mother's soft voice, she knew intense relief.

"I'm sorry to disturb you, dear, but I figured you hadn't gone to sleep. Your father's nephew—you know, Timmy, called this afternoon. He said you asked him to fill in a questionnaire and send it to you, but he said the questionnaire doesn't have anything to do with him. Call him, dear. He's called a few times since you've been home, and he always asks about you. Do what you can for him, honey."

"I will, Mama, but not at the expense of my hard-earned reputation. I wish Daddy hadn't started this."

"Well, you know how he is," Emily soothed. "Do what you can." Melissa hung up, frustrated and angry at her father for having interfered in her business.

Melissa put the pillow behind her back, propped her elbows on her knees, and tried to think. She'd try to help him, but how could she if he didn't do what she told him to do? I don't think he wants a job, she told herself. He wants to hang out in my office and get paid. No way.

## Chapter 7

A call from her New York secretary several days later sent Melissa scurrying to New York City. Before she'd agree to find an executive position for an employee of Jenkins, Roundtree, and Tillman, she'd have to make certain that the man's efforts to relocate weren't calculated to hurt Adam. She wouldn't work for him without first interviewing him and finding out why he wanted to change jobs. The slow, bumper-to-bumper taxi ride from La Guardia Airport into Manhattan and the impatient horn-tooting of the drivers reminded her of the things she disliked about New York. Still, she had missed its museums and galleries, the little West Side bistros, its music—classical, jazz, and unclassifiable, the multitude of bookstores, and the ever-changing street scenes.

She registered at the Drake Hotel, settled in, called the secretary she shared with Crow and Ankers, and arranged for an appointment with a man she discovered was Jason Court's assistant. She plodded across the modest-sized but beautiful room and looked down on Park Avenue, killing precious time while she gazed unseeing at the speeding cars, the fur-coated women of leisure, and the corporate males who were too macho to put on an overcoat as they went out to lunch in the thirty-six-degree weather.

Ordinarily she'd be making notes for the next day's interview, researching the type of business or industry in which the man wanted to work, but she did none of this. She paced the floor. If she didn't take the job, the man would get assistance elsewhere. If she worked for him and succeeding in placing him, how would it affect Adam?

She had to pull herself out of that mood. Ilona answered at the phone's first ring. "Melissa, darling, you became sick of this place with no ballet and came back to civilization? Where are you?" At Melissa's reply, she complained, "Darling, you should have stayed with me. We need to have a good talk."

Melissa knew she wouldn't have contemplated such a thing. She had heard Ilona recount her escapades and seen her swoon over thoughts of her past lovers so many times that she could put on the show herself. She didn't relish being Ilona's captive audience in a bachelor apartment. They agreed to meet for dinner at a restaurant on Columbus Avenue, a choice Melissa regretted when she recalled light, happy times there with Adam early in their relationship.

Melissa dressed in a chic, brown ultrasuede business suit, complemented it with a cowl-necked orange cashmere sweater, brown suede shoes and brown leather briefcase, put on her Blass vicuna coat, and stepped out into the morning cold. It didn't even take a day for me to revert to form and turn back into a New Yorker, she admitted to herself as though it was an indictment. Where else do women dress with a briefcase instead of a pocketbook?

If the man had been tardy, if he had behaved condescendingly toward her, or if she had disliked him for any reason, she could in good conscience have refused to take the job. But as she had once told Adam, her criteria for accepting a client were whether she thought she could fulfill the terms of agreement and whether her integrity would be compromised in any way. She signed the contract and collected her mail, went back to the Drake, packed, and got a flight to Frederick via Baltimore.

Within a few days she'd located three firms that began aggressive bidding for the man when it was learned that he had worked for Adam Roundtree and that it was his decision to leave. Wary of corporate spying, she called Adam.

"So that's where you've been," Adam said. She had to know that her having left town without a word displeased him. They were not committed to each other, and she wasn't obligated to inform him of her whereabouts, but they were more than friends.

Or were they? He'd been vexed and a little hurt and had refused to ask her secretary where she was. Her reply told him she'd detected his annoyance.

"Adam, when I left here, I didn't know what the man wanted nor when he wanted to leave Jenkins, Roundtree, and Tillman. I'm telling you, now that I have the facts, because it's the decent thing to do. I haven't placed him, but I can offer him one of three firms, all of which are anxious to get him, and one of them is your competitor. I hesitate to introduce him to your enemy, and I want to know what you think."

A muscle tensed in his jaw. She hadn't understood his comment on her whereabouts. Well, so much the better. "Dan's my best middle-level salesman, but if he wants to leave my shop, he can go. If you don't place him, someone else will, and I'd as soon you got the profit."

"I was planning to place him, but I wanted you to know. My question was where to put him." Her long pause alerted Adam to the possibility that her next words might not please him, and they didn't.

"Adam, I think you should know that your biggest competitor is trying to raid your shop."

"Not to worry. Ken Bradley is less of a competitor than he thinks." Still, he didn't like the man enticing away one of his most valuable employees.

"You told me not to tell you how to run your office, but I think you ought to get back to New York for a spell." His antennae up, he tried to figure out what she'd left unsaid.

"Are you saying—"

"I turned down two offers of a contract to get Jason Court away from you. The fat cats in New York think that because you're not there, you're a sitting duck."

Adam bristled, angry at himself because he might have left his flank unprotected. "If they think I'm not in control of my office, they're a pile of bricks short of a full load. I'll get up there. Thanks. Oh, Melissa," he added in an afterthought, "I should be back in a few days. Stay out of mischief."

"Stay out of… Me? Do what?" she sputtered. "You're full of it, Adam. Just keep it up. One of these days you're going to get a hole in your sails." Her laughter floated through the wire to him.

"Don't sweat over the thought, baby. With any luck, you'll be in the boat with me when it happens. I can't wait to drown with you. In fact there are times when I can think of little else." He waited, hoping to get her sharpest dart.

"I hate to be the bearer of bad tidings, but you'd better look forward to a long life, sweetie—" she emphasized the *sweetie* "—because I'm a survivor." A riot of sensations darted through him at the sound of her husky giggle. She wasn't satisfied to challenge him, she had to entice him as well. But he'd have his day.

"Any man with an iota of sense knows when he gets an invitation to try harder, Melissa." Insinuation punctuated his words. "And ignoring opportunities, however thinly veiled, is not something I do. See you when I get back."

He buzzed his secretary. "I need to be in New York tomorrow morning at eight o'clock. Do what you can to get me a plane out of here tonight. If necessary, phone Wayne and ask him to call in some favors." He leaned back in his chair and stroked his chin. Would a person who would double-cross him have done as Melissa had, and would she risk his asking her not to place Dan? He had yet to find any solid evidence that Melissa lacked integrity. But how else could the sabotage at Leather and Hides be explained? What if her warning was a ruse to get him away from Frederick? He tossed his head to the side and grasped his chin with his tapered brown fingers, pensive. How had he allowed himself to crave a woman he wasn't sure he could trust?

He walked into his suite of New York offices the next morning to find things as he'd left them. Olivia hovered about, obviously happy to see him. "You look good, yourself," he said in response to her compliment. "I want to speak first with Jason and then with Lester." He assured Jason that his arrival unannounced did not indicate a lack of confidence.

"I've been told the raiders are busy. Any truth in it?" Before

Jason spoke, his slow nod and straight-in-the-eye stare gave Adam the assurance he needed.

"Plenty, but as far as I know, you don't have anything to worry about. Dan wants to leave, and that's for the best. He's in love with Virginia, and she's engaged to marry another guy. He figures he can get another good job easier than she can, and he doesn't want to be around her anymore."

Adam's whistle alerted any of the staff who didn't already know it that the boss was in his office. "He's in love with his secretary? How long's that been going on?"

Jason shrugged eloquently. "Since the minute he first saw her, though she didn't reciprocate the feeling, but he didn't give up until she got engaged."

"Well, hell! I'm sorry to see him leave, but you're right—no point in staying around her, unless he's a masochist. What about you? My source also tells me they're after you."

"I've had several feelers and a couple of offers. But if I wanted to move, man, you'd be the first to know it. I believe in hanging out with the champ, Adam, and from where I sit, you're it."

Adam had to hide his relief. "What about Lester?" Jason's jaw hardened, and Adam worked hard at squelching a laugh.

"He rings your bell, does he?"

Jason grimaced. "I'd bet my AT & T stock that Lester rings his mother's bell."

Adam laughed outright. "Not to worry, Jason. Nothing lasts forever." He made a mental note to give Jason a raise. Loyalty was very important to him and deserved reward. He spoke with Lester and decided that when he returned to the office full time, he wouldn't keep the man, held a staff meeting, and satisfied that his employees weren't contemplating leaving him, headed back to Frederick that afternoon.

Why such hurry to get to Beaver Ridge? he asked himself. He hadn't even bothered to go to Thompson's and get his favorite pastrami sandwich or to Sognelle's Cajun Kitchen for some hot ribs and boudin, and he wouldn't get any of either until he got back. He settled himself into his business-class TWA seat. "It's time I had a talk with myself," he acknowledged. "She's the reason I'm in a hurry. I misjudged her this time, and…" Disgusted with himself, he opened his briefcase and tried to work. "Hell, nobody's going to scramble my brain like this." He closed the file and looked at his watch. Another couple of hours; if he was lucky, she'd be home.

He phoned her from the airport. "Have dinner with me."

"And hello to you, too, Mr. Roundtree."

He shrugged off her gentle rebuke. "At least you recognized my voice. I hope you don't have other plans. Do you?" When she didn't respond immediately, he continued. "What time shall I come for you? I'd like an early dinner, if possible." She asked if he'd skipped lunch.

"You might say that." Let her think what she liked. He wanted to see her. He went home and telephoned Wayne. Now for another test.

"Anything untoward happen at Leather and Hides last night?"

"Nelson patrolled with the new guard last night, but they didn't see or hear anything suspicious. He thinks the culprit is trying to lull us into complacency. How'd it go in New York?"

He hadn't realized that he was holding his breath. "Clean as fresh snow, but it was a good idea to check the place out, and I intend to do it more often. I'll be in touch."

Melissa stared at the molding in her ceiling, while the dial tone menaced her ear. She had good reason to meet with Adam, she told herself, since she'd placed Lester in Adam's office, and the man might be the cause of his problems. The telephone operator's tinny voice got her attention, and she hung up. But she dallied beside the pantry door with her hand resting on the cradled wall phone. What was the use of lying to herself? She wanted to be with him. She hadn't seen Adam for a week, not since she'd gone to the football game with him and Wayne. And their tepid parting had frustrated her and thrust her into a whirlpool of confusion, leaving her more than ever at sea about their relationship. The fault had been hers. She couldn't overcome the

452      *Gwynne Forster*

deepening conflict between her feelings for Adam and loyalty to her family. And her inner struggle had intensified, she realized, because she'd become more sympathetic to her father since learning why he was so irrational about the Hayeses and Roundtrees.

They didn't know how to greet each other, so they stared in silence. Finally she smiled and his arms opened to her. But Adam held her to his side, unwilling to risk the escalation of desire. She leaned away and looked up at him, but he let her see a bland expression and joked, "You know the old adage, 'an ounce of prevention...' and so forth. We're supposed to be going to dinner, and I'm hungry, but if you want to hang around here, my two appetites are equally demanding right now." Desire pooled in his loins at the double meaning implied in her lusty laugh, and he set her away from him.

"I'll get my coat. Have a seat." He didn't move.

"You do that, Melissa." He watched the devil-may-care way she walked, turned his back, and tried to think about the problems at Leather and Hides, but those thoughts didn't lessen the heat in him. She returned quickly, too quickly. One look at her—scented as she was with a subtle but extravagant perfume and bundled up past the neck, waiflike to thwart the cold—and he struggled against man's most primitive impulse. I'm in danger here, he admitted to himself and sought to introduce some levity into the situation.

"I can hardly see you in all that stuff you've got on." His gaze stroked her face; not pretty but strangely beautiful.

Melissa's shoulders hunched in anticipation of the outside temperature. "I don't like to be cold."

"No reason why you should be. I'll keep you warm."

"Said the spider to the fly," she shot back, gazing up at him as though to confirm his meaning. He watched her teasing look dissolve into awareness and knew that he hadn't reduced the tension, but worsened it.

"Let's go while we can still walk."

"Where are we going?" He helped her into the passenger's seat, awed as she struggled to sit down with what could pass for decorum.

"Wherever you like."

He gazed down at her. "If you're so afraid of getting cold, why are you wearing your skirt a yard above your knee? And it's so tight, you could hardly sit down. Didn't you ever hear of comfort?" Her glare might have been meant to shame him, but he held his course.

"You've practically hidden your neck and face, and they're least likely to feel the cold, but your lower precious parts are left to freeze." He tapped his forehead with a long index finger. "Universities ought to give courses in deciphering the female enigma, and the male students should be forced to take them."

"If you're not happy with the way I look," she huffed, "I'll get out and go right back in the house, and I'll stay there." The breath from his laughter fogged the mirror.

"You look great to me, always do, and like I said, it'll give me great pleasure to warm you."

He drove to the mom-and-pop restaurant where they'd once encountered Wayne and found comfortable seats in the nearly empty but charming room. Melissa smoothed the red and white checkered tablecloth, wondering whether it was the time to open a discussion of what they seemed to have been avoiding.

"Aren't you going to tell me about your trip? How did you find things?"

He took his time answering. "Thanks for the tip. You were right about the raiders, but my people are loyal to me. Go ahead and do what you can for Dan—he's in a difficult situation." She wondered why they spent precious time talking about his staff, her staff, and a myriad of unimportant, impersonal things. He must have shared her exasperation at it, for he reached across the still empty table, grasped her fingers, and asked her, "Did you miss me, Melissa?" But before she could answer, what passed for a laugh escaped him.

"You didn't have enough time for that. I was only away overnight." Their locked fingers appeared strange to her, as if they didn't belong together. She wanted to tell him about her mother and Bill Henry, but couldn't force herself to do it, because she didn't want to hide behind that tortured relationship. When she looked at him, sensations swirled within her at the brilliant twinkle in his eyes. He tipped up her chin, and she brushed his hand aside.

"I missed you."

"But you didn't miss me when *you* were away for a week. How was that?"

Melissa squinted at him, frowned and bit her bottom lip. "Are you trying to pick a fight? Or what?" His wry smile brought a catch to her throat.

"Not me. I'm a peaceful man. I figure that at this stage there ought to be some honesty between us."

"Adam, the kind of honesty you want is not good for your ego. How about you being honest?"

That grin should have warned me, she thought, when he said, "No problem. I want to make love with you, and I don't feel a bit casual about it."

"Oh," she blustered. "Is that a direct pass?" Adam laughed.

The waiter's long awaited arrival interrupted them, but Adam returned to the subject. "I've said before that you can't be as naive as you sometimes seem. You shy away from intimacy until I drag you into it. Why is that?"

"Adam, you enjoy digging into my personality and my life, but if we sat here until doomsday, I wouldn't learn one thing about you that everybody else doesn't know." His look was one of funereal solemnity.

"That's because I ask; you don't."

She placed her fork on her plate, leaned back in the booth, and looked directly into his eyes. "Have you ever been in love?"

"No, but I've been close to it." Her eyes widened in surprise, and he wondered how deeply she felt, but he didn't ask her. She'd veiled her emotions. Even her eyes told him nothing. He switched topics, hoping to smooth over whatever damage his answer might have caused.

"You never told me what you thought of Wayne as a mummy hell bent on frightening every kid in Frederick." Relief and something akin to joy settled over him when her eyes lit and a smile broke out all over her face. But when she said, "Oh, Adam, you're wonderful," he had to caress her and maneuvered to her side of the booth, squeezed her quickly, and feathered her cheek with his lips. Frissons of heat exploded in him as her hot gaze drank in the warm affection that he knew was reflected in his eyes. Oh, the wonder of her! His heartbeat accelerated and his senses whirled when she lowered her gaze, obviously embarrassed at her inability to hide her response. They finished the meal in contented silence.

He wanted to share with her his deepening concern about the sabotage at Leather and Hides. He needed desperately to confirm her loyalty to him. But if she were guilty of betrayal, he would have tipped his hand. And even if she were innocent, if one of her relatives had a hand in it, to whom would she be loyal? He needed to know that she stood with him, and he needed her. Badly.

He parked, walked with her up the short cemented path to her house, and stood looking down at her, hands jammed in his coat pockets and his back braced against the outer wall of the house. His breath hung in his lungs as she reached into her bag for her keys, then hissed through his lips when she didn't hand them to him, but opened the door herself. He straightened up, and tugged at her ear with his gloved hand.

"It was a lovely evening, Melissa, and an informative one." He brushed her cheek. "Good night." He didn't feel much like whistling when he got into his car, but he thought he'd better, because it was the only way he had right then to blow off steam. He knew his whole body had telegraphed to her his desire to be with her, to make love with her, and it hadn't escaped her, either. She was obviously less sophisticated than he'd thought—hard working, intelligent, her own woman, but afraid to take a chance. Concern for the reaction of their families wasn't stopping her from seeing him, nor from responding to him whenever he put his hands on her. So what had kept her out of bed with him?

He parked, secured the house, went into his room and closed the door, knowing that he faced a long, restless night. If he did the smart thing, he'd drop it, but he hadn't gotten where he was by accepting defeat. He wanted her, and he had no intention of giving up.

Ten minutes after Adam left her, Melissa answered her doorbell thinking it might be him. Her father glared at her.

"At least you sent him home. If you can't leave those people alone, you can consider yourself no longer a member of my family. No kin of mine is going to consort with them."

Anger paralyzed her tongue, and she stammered in frustration. Finally her calm restored, words that had long wanted release spilled from her lips, and she faced him defiantly and more resolutely than ever before. "You never treated me as a member of your family, and if you read me out of it, I won't lose a thing. I might even gain something."

No blow struck him, she noticed and marveled that a father could be so cavalier about his daughter's feelings. His only reaction was the lifting of his forehead and the movement of his jaw. He wasn't used to the posture she'd assumed with him.

"They've already turned you against us," he said. "Even your cousin Timmy is more loyal to us than you are. But you mark my word, young lady, you're going to be sorry for this. You're just like your mother."

She spoke in a gentle tone. There was no point in beating a dead horse. "If I am, I don't consider it a disadvantage. Is that why you've never loved me, never wanted me?"

"Did she tell you I didn't want you?"

"No. I feel it. I've always felt it." He looked into the distance and pursed his lips as though reminded of an unpleasantness.

"It was what came before you that I didn't want. A man can stand just so much."

"What did it have to do with me? Any eyes can see that I'm your daughter."

He quirked an eyebrow and in icelike tones informed her, "I've had no reason to doubt your mother's virtue. But once she had you, she didn't care about anybody or anything else."

Melissa stared at him in disbelief. "How can you say that? Both of you ignored me." He didn't deny his share in it.

"After your brother, Schyler, was born, I had to make your mother concentrate on him. She was too wrapped up in you. A baby, especially a boy, needs all of its mother's time." She didn't comment on that. Clearly he either couldn't or wouldn't tell her why he had rejected her. Indeed, he didn't appear to realize that he'd done it. She reached for the doorknob simultaneously with him.

"Good night, Father." He appeared to hesitate, but he only said, "Good night."

Adam jumped out of bed at the sound of his beeper and switched on the light beside his bed. Damn. Two thirty in the morning.

"Roundtree." He sat on the edge of his bed, while Calvin Nelson recounted the havoc he'd just discovered at Leather and Hides. Zirconium salt had been applied with great care to the grain side or upper leather intended for the manufacture of fine shoes, so that the tanning process produced a white rather than bluish, more elastic, leather used for such shoes. Some of the hides could be retanned with chrome salts and used for lower-grade clothing, Calvin told him, but most of that expensive lot had been rendered useless.

He rested his elbow on his knee and dropped his forehead in his hand. "Any leads?"

"Sorry, Adam. Not a one, but I'll keep after it."

"I know you will." He got back in bed. He'd been two hundred and fifty miles away the night before, and nothing untoward had happened. But tonight while he was a couple of miles away... He sat up. Was somebody trying to frame Melissa? From the time she came back, the saboteur had usually struck when he was with her, and nobody who was as smart as she would incriminate themselves with such strong circumstantial evidence. The

possibility that he might have found a clue that didn't implicate her enabled him to get to sleep.

Adam ambled into the dining room the next morning to find
his mother, brother, and Bill Henry waiting for him. Mary
Roundtree had called a family conference, and Adam's surprise
at Bill Henry's presence was evidence that he hadn't been consulted. He took his place at the table, and they knew his restrained good morning was nothing less than censure.

"Don't tell me you've taken to eating soul food, B-H?" He
needled his uncle whom he regarded as a health nut. "What's the
matter, sick of alfalfa and bean sprouts?" It didn't surprise him
that his comment wasn't lost on his mother. She had always been
able to detect his anger no matter how subtly he expressed it.

"I called the meeting, Adam, because we have to put an end
to this destruction of Leather and Hides. I'm going to be honest
with you. I believe this problem started because of your flirtation with Melissa, and that it'll continue as long as you're seeing
her. The Morrises and Grants are out to destroy us."

He had to suppress his irritation. "What proof do you have,
Mother? And let's get it straight that I am not flirting with
Melissa Grant. I'm involved with her."

Her lips curled in anger. "You know I don't have any proof.
But I'm an intelligent person, and I know that the problem began
when you hired her to find the manager, and it intensified when
she just happened to move back home after a little absence of
nine or ten years."

Adam leaned forward, planted both elbows on the table—in
a gesture that he recognized as one of defiance since his mother
counseled that no part of the human body should touch the top
of the table during a meal—and supported his cheeks with his
fist. Then he sat up straight and articulated his words with
Churchillian accuracy.

"If anyone present wants my job as CEO of Hayes/Round-
tree Enterprises, Inc., that person is welcome to it, and I can get
back to New York and take care of my business." His glance

swept the table. "No takers? Well, that settles it." He rose without having eaten or drunk anything and addressed his mother.

"Mother, I consider myself responsible for our family and its affairs, and I'll sacrifice a lot for our family, but I won't walk away from Melissa Grant unless I have proof—" he folded his right fist and slapped it into the open palm of his left hand "—unless I have indisputable proof that she isn't worth my…my attention. If none of you has proof, I don't want to hear this kind of talk again. How would you feel, and what would you do if you were in my place?" He walked to the door, but paused there as Wayne began to speak.

"I spent some time with her and Adam a couple of weeks ago, and I thought she was nice. In fact I rather liked her. If the Grants are involved in this, she doesn't have to know about it. I know you can't look at a person and tell whether she's honest, but she impressed me as being straight. But like I said, it was a first impression."

Adam walked on as though impatient for fresh air and failed to remember his overcoat until he'd driven halfway to his office. Wayne's endorsement had been weak and grudging compared to what his brother had said to him about Melissa.

Bill Henry Hayes finished his high-cholesterol breakfast, his first such meal in over twenty years, and walked around to the sideboard for another cup of mint tea. He leaned against it and commanded his sister's attention. "Some things never change in this family. The people come and go, but the mentality manages to stay a little below moronic, especially about people's private lives. You two are acting as if Adam isn't Adam. He can take care of himself and his business, too. I met the young lady, and I like her. I like her a lot, in fact." His gaze drilled his sister.

"You're ready to do the same thing to Adam and Melissa that these feuding families did to me over thirty years ago. You can't control other people's lives. Mary, I'd like you to guess what you would have done if anybody had so much as hinted that you couldn't have John Roundtree. I doubt the United States Marines could have kept you from him. You watched what they did to me, and you're willing to see the same thing happen to your first-born child. I suggest both of you consider the hell Rafer is putting Melissa through because of Adam."

"What about her mother?" Wayne asked.

Bill Henry set his cold tea on the table. "She's one person who won't stand in their way."

Should she walk or drive the short distance to her office? Normally she walked, but dark clouds hovered ominously above and the weather forecast hadn't made clear the severity of the coming storm. Finally she decided to walk, but as a precaution she put a flashlight and a bag of Snickers in her briefcase. Banks joined her a half block from the office building.

"I see your folks had a miniconference at the Watering Hole last night. Seemed kinda strange that you and Miss Emily didn't join them."

Melissa waited until they were inside the warm lobby before commenting.

"Take your time," Banks offered in a tone that suggested she was handing Melissa a gift. "Your teeth make such original music, Melissa. If mine danced around like that every time they got cold, I'd invent some mouth muffs. How'd you happen to miss that confab last night?"

"Easily. I didn't know anything about it, and since I was probably the reason for it, I'm not surprised that I wasn't invited. As for Mother, none of them would expect her to go. Who was there?" Melissa marveled that her friend's brow furrowed as though she was in deep thought, trying to recall what Melissa knew she had carefully memorized.

"Let's see, now," Banks drawled. "Your mother's sister Mable, your father, his brother Faison and sister Louise, her husband and her son Timmy. Uh…oh, yes, and Louise's sister-in-law." As if she'd just had successful acupuncture for excruciating pain, Banks beamed at her and declared, "I think that's all."

Amusement buoyed Melissa as she entered the elevator. Too

bad her mother hadn't known about the clandestine little meeting. She might have gone just to spite them, and Banks could have enjoyed relating it even more.

Banks got off at the third floor. "Sure you don't want some of my hot doughnuts?" she called over her shoulder.

"I want some, but I'm not going to eat any," Melissa replied, her tone laced with regret as she continued to her office on the fourth floor. The elevator door closed, and her lips pursed in disapproval. Though she liked Banks, she disliked gossip. For the local African American citizenry, the Watering Hole and the church were the vats in which gossip fermented. You could hear all about the righteous folk in church circles, but at the Hole you could get the goods on everybody, the devout included. That was one of the things she'd been happy to miss in New York. Your neighbors couldn't discuss your affairs, because they didn't know anything about you, and few cared enough to speculate.

She checked her e-mail, called her part-time secretary in Baltimore, and got the same message from each source: a Texan named Cooper needed a ranch manager. For persistence, the man rivaled Adam, she thought, not a little irritated. If she didn't answer, he should know that she wasn't interested. All she knew about a ranch, she'd learned from Clint Eastwood movies and romance novels. She put a cassette in her tape recorder, but before she could begin dictating a letter refusing the job, her phone rang.

"MTG. Melissa Grant speaking."

"I'm surprised you're in this morning. It's been snowing for fifteen minutes, and the streets are already white. It might be a good idea to leave." Her gaze followed the twirling pencil in her left hand. He'd spin me around like that if I let him, she mused. She tossed the pencil across the desk.

"Adam, do you think James Earl Jones ever identifies himself when he makes a phone call?" His chuckle warned her that her barb had missed the mark.

"He shouldn't have to. I doubt there're many people who wouldn't recognize that voice, and you can bet his significant other wouldn't be among the few who didn't. If a man has an intimate relationship with a woman, she ought to recognize everything about him."

"Humph. If the male ego needed physical space, men would be scarce as dog feathers. What size hat do you wear, Adam?" She leaned forward, placed her elbows on her desk, her palms beneath her chin and waited.

"I've never worn a hat. And no matter what you say about my ego, you recognized my voice."

"Yeah, but that's a defense mechanism," she teased, eyeing the window and the swirling snow.

"Against what?" he demanded, his testiness sizzling through the wire.

"Against being mistaken for a significant other," she replied, getting up to lock her door because she knew what would happen if she didn't. But to her chagrin, the cord's length didn't allow that precaution.

"What man would be so pea-brained as to hang such a nondescript title on you? You come under the heading of woman, babe." When he got casual and flirtatious like ordinary mortal men, she told herself with some amusement, she'd better watch her nervous system.

"Still there?"

"Haven't moved a fraction of an inch."

"I suggest you go home before you have trouble maneuvering your car through that snow."

'I didn't drive this morning," she said and would have liked to bite her tongue.

"Then you ought to consider putting on your boots and hiking it home. This stuff's getting bad."

She straightened up and weighed the folly of staying there for the sake of annoying him against getting home in reasonable comfort. She hung up and looked around for her bag of Snickers. If she ignored his advice, she could wind up bedeviling herself rather than Adam. Her door swung ajar, and she gazed up into a pair of fierce brown eyes, not a bit surprised that he was making sure she left the building before the weather worsened.

"Just as I thought. Settling in for the day, were you? I'm asking everyone to leave within the next thirty minutes. The storm is getting heavier by the second, and I'm going to turn off the heat to make certain everybody gets out of here. You'd get yourself snowbound just to vex me."

"Tut-tut! Really, Adam. You could do something about your tendency to be overbearing. Just a wee bit of improvement there would do wonders for your personality."

He had to struggle not to laugh. He'd seen Melissa in many moods and with a number of facial expressions, but he couldn't recall her having previously shrouded herself in innocence. Her serene countenance and angelic eyes proclaimed her blameless, and she even lowered her gaze, he noted, and folded her hands in her lap to enhance the effect.

He grinned down at her. "You're a dirty fighter, but you're one hell of a woman. Come on, let's get out of here." He took her coat from the coat tree and walked over to her with it. She pushed her chair back from the desk and glared at him. Then she reached in her desk drawer, pulled out a brown paper wrapper, and handed it to him.

"Have a Snickers while you find your way down off of your high horse." Her smile dared him as she leaned back in her chair and crossed her knees, displaying her endless legs to the greatest advantage. He swallowed the saliva accumulating in his mouth, glanced back at the open door, and rubbed his dampening palms against his pant legs.

"One of these days you're going to find out who you're playing with."

"Anytime, Mr. Roundtree."

He couldn't believe the transformation in her. Her smile had become sultry and her teasing blatant. He had to control the inclination to whistle. He'd regarded her as laid-back and cool, touchable but unavailable. Maybe he'd been right, but he was certain now that her dress-for-success suits and Brooks Brothers ties disguised a wild siren. He threw the coat to her.

"Melissa, this storm is intensifying. You may be satisfied

with candy for supper, but I'm not, and I'm not going to leave you alone here in an unheated building. So come on." She looked toward the window, then back at him, and he could see her judging the weather and knew the minute she decided to cooperate. She stood, began to put on her coat, and he reached out to help her, but she brushed past him, pulling his nose as she did so.

One spark. Her touch was as tinder to dry grass. His left arm imprisoned her shoulder and his right encircled her waist as he brought her into the heat of his body. He stared into her eyes, eyes that asked him for all that he could give a woman, and every nerve screamed for the release of himself within her. He had to summon every vestige of willpower that he possessed to resist opening himself fully to her, revealing every nuance of himself, for he knew that if they started loving each other, neither one of them would call a halt to it until they had sated themselves. He tried without success to focus his attention on the rattling of a partially open window somewhere down the hall. Having given in to his feelings, he stood with his back to her desk holding her, soaking up her warmth. Warmth he hadn't realized he needed so badly. Finally the tapping of a woman's stiletto heels in the corridor brought him back to himself, and he released her.

"Melissa, we have to do something about this and soon. If we continue to see each other, I don't give us much chance of avoiding it. You know, we're mature adults, and we're supposed to know what we want and don't want. You're as familiar as I am with the circumstances past and present that are against any lasting relationship between us, but logic isn't what we're dealing with here. We want to make love with each other, *and we will.* We both know that."

She locked her office door and walked along with him. Uncommunicative. "Let me guess," he said, frowning. "You're wondering whether Loraine saw us when she passed the door." Her eyes widened and she sucked in her lip. "Yes, Loraine. Nobody else in Frederick wears four-inch heels. By tomorrow night, half of the town will have heard her own version of it and the other half will have gotten it secondhand. I hope you've got better things to worry about."

When they reached his car, he brushed the grainy snow from the door and scraped the windshield. She remarked that Frederick didn't have any underground garages and few indoor ones, and that not having them was an inconvenience in bad weather.

"It's just as well," he replied, laughter taking the punch out of his words. "I'd hate for our first time to be in the backseat of a car."

"You're awfully sure of yourself," she grumbled. "For the last twenty minutes, you've been acting as if you're the one who decides this. But let me tell you: contrary to what that song says, *everything depends on me.*"

Adam glanced at her as the Jaguar's skidding wheels fought his efforts to get them home. "You're grumbling, but I see you're not disagreeing with me." He got out, opened the trunk, took out the two army blankets that he kept for emergencies, and threw them under the spinning wheels.

"I've used sawdust and dry leaves, but I never heard of anybody using blankets. Where'd you get that idea?"

Adam breathed deeply and adjusted himself as the car crawled away from its temporary prison. He got out and put the wet blankets back in the trunk. It didn't surprise him that she'd chosen not to respond to his challenge, because he had learned that she wouldn't let him push her into a corner. He looked over his shoulder as the car chugged into the main street and the snow pelted its windshield. "You will learn, Melissa, that I'm innovative. If it doesn't work one way, I go at it another way, and I usually manage to do what I set out to do and finish what I start."

He noticed that she adjusted her skirt, folded and unfolded her hands, and shifted away from him toward the passenger's door. Let her squirm. The sooner she realized that they were destined to be together, even if temporarily, no matter what their families said or did and no matter what happened at Leather and Hides, the sooner he'd get on with his life. He stopped in front of her house.

"I'll come around and get you. There's no point in both of us getting our feet soaked."

"Would you like some coffee?" She didn't look at him as she spoke, and he wondered whether she was eager to be alone with him or afraid of it. Who knew what she was thinking and feeling when she squinted like that. He shook his head. She'd be surprised how often and how thoroughly she perplexed him.

"I'll wait here while you check the faucets, the lights, and your radiators. A couple of inches of snow can put this town out of commission, and we've got four or five inches." He slapped her playfully on the bottom. "Hurry up. I've got to get going."

She spun around, her eyes like daggers. "My reaction to that is about the same as yours to getting your nose pinched. So keep your hands to yourself!" He didn't care if his laughter irked her as she stood with her hands on her hips glaring at him.

"You're trying to pick a fight—but sweetheart, when we tangle, I'd prefer it to be under different circumstances. Believe me. Now go check your house, because if I do it, that Jaguar may be sitting right out there tomorrow morning." She went, and he figured she could hear his sigh of relief as she walked down the hall. He watched her and wondered what, other than a fire, could make her rush or lose her cool facade. A casual acquaintance might think her aloof and frigid, but he knew better. She was like a fine, rare diamond: cold on the outside and fire on the inside. And he wanted to explore every facet of her.

# Chapter 8

Melissa awoke early that morning feeling as a tigress must while prowling and pacing alongside a barbed-wire fence too high to scale. She wanted Adam, and what she felt for him went deep—deep enough to shatter her if he walked away. But he promised her nothing, and if she made love with him, he'd leave his mark on her forever. She didn't want to be like her mother, married to one man and loving another, losing her sense of self because of guilt. But she wanted a family of her own, though honesty forced her to admit that she wanted it with Adam Roundtree. He had all but promised her that they would make love. And soon. Face it, she told herself, you know you're not going to stop him, and he knows it, too. She stepped into the warm shower, but chills coursed through her at the thought of her father's certain reaction when he discovered how far she had gone with Adam.

The municipal workers cleared the snow from her street around noon, and Melissa dressed warmly, put on an old pair of boots, and set out for her parents' home. She leaned into the rising wind and tried to walk faster. Few people greeted her along the way. A five-inch snowfall was rare in Frederick, and everything was closed except the post office. It would be too much to hope that her father would be at his office and she'd find her mother alone, but she felt the need to see her even if it meant a confrontation with her father. Did young girls unburden themselves to their mothers? She didn't know, but she figured women her age didn't do it. It didn't matter. Her new relationship with her mother was precious to her, and she wanted to spend every moment with her that she could.

Emily opened the door and held out her arms. Melissa hadn't felt an urge to cry, but her tears came. She hadn't been cold, but when she stepped into the warmth of her mother's love, her sense of drifting in an unfriendly, frosty environment dissipated. Until she found herself dabbing at her tears with the back of her hand, she hadn't been aware that she shed them. She stepped back and looked into her mother's warm eyes, so like her own.

"I don't remember the last time I cried." Her mother's gentle hands stroked her back, and she soaked in the healing that they generated.

"That's what mothers are for. You can be yourself with me. This just makes me even more remorseful for not always having been here for you when you needed me."

Melissa shushed her. "I have you now, and that's what matters. Where's Daddy?" Her breath hung in her throat as she awaited the answer. She had no desire to grapple with her father's blind hatred of Adam and his family.

Her mother's words comforted her. "Rafer went to his office same as always. I'll make us some tea, and we can talk."

When Emily led them up to her room, carrying a tray of tea and sandwiches, Melissa realized that her mother had a sense of well-being only in her own room—that within her home, she could relax only in her bedroom.

"Now tell me about those tears," Emily soothed. "Have you fought with Adam?"

"No, but I'm not sure I can talk about him. I've got to work out my feelings about him and about us." The look of understanding that met her gaze caused her to wonder how her mother had come to terms with the destruction of her plans for a life with Bill Henry. But she didn't ask her. Instead, she told her of her meeting with the man.

"I gave Bill Henry a ride during that downpour we had early last week. He asked about you, and I thought he was pretty upset when I told him that you had been ill. Quick as a flash, he changed all over. I thought at first that he intended to pounce on me. Said he was very sorry to hear about it." She paused. "He sure was concerned, Mama." Her mother's teacup clattered in its saucer, staining the green broadloom carpet with amber liquid.

"Until I told you about us, I hadn't mentioned Bill Henry's name to anyone in thirty years, and I haven't seen him in nearly as long. How does he look?" She didn't wait for an answer. "Very distinguished, I imagine. When I saw Adam, I saw Bill Henry as he must have been at Adam's age. Does he still live at the old Hayes mansion?"

Melissa told her about Bill Henry's life-style and his little clapboard house. "I thought you knew."

Emily leaned forward in the brightly upholstered wing chair. "Who would tell me? Everybody in our families knows the story, and half the town, too." She sat up straight, looked Melissa in the eye, and spoke in a hoarse, teary voice. "I tell you again, honey. If you want Adam, don't let anybody stop you. Imagine what it's like to live twenty miles from the only man you ever loved, want him every day of your life, know that he wants you, and not be able to have him. Be strong, and don't let them ruin your life."

Melissa sipped her tea, buying time, trying to find a way to tell her mother what bothered her. She chose another, less personal, issue and silently scolded herself for doing it. "Mama, I don't want to be the one to tear this family apart." Her mother's hand rose and fell disparagingly, as though slapping at the air.

"You can't destroy what doesn't exist. After Schyler was born, your father moved out of this room, and I didn't blame him. The bathroom between us isn't for intimacy, but for show. He had his son, and he finished the marriage. I did everything I could to keep us together, but it was never enough. There hasn't been any intimacy between us for over twenty-five years. We coexist, nothing more."

Melissa knew that her face must have mirrored her sense of horror. "How could you live like that, without love or affection for so many years? How could Daddy do such a thing?"

Emily slipped off her shoes, and her right foot found its customary place beneath her left thigh. "At least he was honest. Don't judge him too severely, Melissa. He's always had to walk in the footsteps and the reflections of other men. His tragedy is that it's always been high noon for him, and he never created a shadow of his own. That can make a man lose perspective, make him desperate."

Trudging back home in the howling wind, Melissa reflected that she hadn't told her mother the real reason for her visit. She loved Adam and wanted to tell her mother. Wanted to tell her that she needed to be with him in the most intimate way. Wanted to tell her mother that she needed advice. She walked through her door as her answering machine was recording Adam's voice and ran to the phone, but was too late. She telephoned him and advised him of his bad timing.

"What did you want?"

"I wanted to know if you were alright."

"I had expected you to say you couldn't live another second without hearing my voice." The minute she'd said it, she wanted to retract the careless statement. But he laughed.

"A modified version of that would be accurate. I'm going to New York this evening, and I wanted you to know. I'll be back in a couple of days."

"Anything wrong?" She had to cover her disappointment that she wouldn't see him perhaps for several days.

"Just loose ends. Stay out of mischief." He hung up before she could retaliate, and she called him back.

"Yes, Melissa. I didn't move, because I knew you'd need the last word. What is it?"

"Some rise by sin, and some by virtue fall," she quipped, quoting Shakespeare. "Have a good trip, Adam." His deep laughter still warmed her long after she'd hung up.

Sunday afternoon, three days later, Adam pushed his right index finger through the handle of his garment bag, dragged it from the carousel, threw it over his right shoulder, and strode out of the airport. He had ordered a limousine before leaving New York, because three days of sparring with employees and competitors had drained him. He'd worked night and day with little sleep and knew better than to drive. He ignored the half dozen newspapers that had been placed there for him, opened the bar, poured himself two fingers of bourbon over ice, and sat back to review the past three days. Melissa had been right—the corporate raiders wanted his best employees, and he didn't doubt that as soon as they weakened his staff, they'd go for his jugular. He had gotten things under control, but the sooner he found the culprit at Leather and Hides and got back to his own business, the better.

He leaned forward to replace the glass in the bar, and an envelope slipped out of his coat pocket. He opened it and read what he'd written. A puny declaration compared to what he felt and what he needed from her. But he couldn't ask for what he needed, and if she offered it, he couldn't accept it. His family's views about him and Melissa didn't matter, but the insidious annihilation of Leather and Hides did matter—and until he solved that mystery, he couldn't allow himself to become too deeply involved with her. He leaned back in the downy softness of the exquisite leather seat, leather tanned as only Hayes/Roundtree Enterprises, Inc., could, and his thoughts drifted to his growing dissatisfaction with his life. He loved his family and his work, but he needed a woman whom he loved and who loved him, and he wanted children. In his mind's eye he saw Melissa in his home with his baby at her breast. "Damn! I must be losing it." He reached for the handle on the door of the bar, decided against a drink, and turned on the radio. But he didn't need to hear George Strait sing "You Can't Make a Heart Love Somebody," so he flipped it off and asked himself why he was so restless. He had the driver go into Frederick and wait while he pushed the envelope into Melissa's mailbox. His heart pounded as he held his hand suspended next to her doorbell, but he resisted, got back in the car, and went home to Beaver Ridge.

\* \* \*

"Anything happen here while I was gone?" he asked his mother when she greeted him at the door.

Mary Roundtree bussed her elder son on the cheek. "Not a thing. Looks to me like those dreadful crooks do their devilment at Leather and Hides either when you're out somewhere with Melissa Grant or when you're over at The Refuge. Never when you're home. I guess they didn't know you were out of town." He kissed her quickly, grabbed his garment bag, and headed for the stairs.

"Sooner or later they'll show their hands and trip themselves up," he threw over his shoulder. He would not be drawn into a discussion of Melissa, and if his mother insisted on it, she'd learn exactly what he felt. He hung up the garment bag, his overcoat and jacket, pulled a chair up to the desk that faced the window, and dialed her number. When she didn't answer and had forgotten to turn on her answering machine, he hung up and stared at the wintry scene through his window, stunned at the intensity of his disappointment. He was full of her, day and night, and he had to do something about it. He changed clothes, got his sports bag, took the Jaguar, and set out for the sports center in Frederick.

Melissa put on her swimsuit under her fatigues, added a winter coat, and went to the sports center. She checked her mailbox as she left the house and opened the unaddressed envelope that she found there. A red, silver-tipped feather fell to the floor. She picked it up, looked into the envelope, and found a card on which was printed, "When I saw this, I thought of you. It's unique, elegant, and it's soft—just as you are—A." Excitement enveloped her. Had he put it there before he left? Or had he stopped by after his return? She had to fight the temptation to telephone him, and she walked less briskly than normal, skipped occasionally, and spun around a time or two.

"Adam." She wanted to scream his name. "Oh, Adam."

Melissa patted the water from her glistening body, threw the beach towel across a lounge chair, and prepared to relax after her vigorous swim. But she sat up abruptly when her eyes caught sight of a flawless male figure, his slim brown hips accented by a yellow bikini, as he stepped up to the diving board and arched his body into a breathtaking dive. Who was he and how could she feel an attraction for a man when she'd seen only his near naked form? Her breath hissed from her lungs as she watched his rhythmic strokes take him to the opposite end of the pool. He reached it, flipped into a turn, and she stood up, feeling his raw masculinity from her brain to her toes. She continued to gape at him as he swam toward her with his head down, impatient to see his face. He surfaced right at her feet and climbed out.

"Adam!"

"Melissa! I didn't know I'd find you here." He must have seen the fire in her, must have sensed her need of him, because his gaze reciprocated what she felt. Want. Hunger. Reluctance. Pain. She saw it all reflected in his eyes, eyes that also bore a sadness she hadn't seen in him. She knew she'd give him whatever he wanted, but could she handle the certain repercussions? She panicked and dove into the water. Within seconds she heard his splash and felt his strong arms about her.

"Get dressed, get your things, and come with me. We've got to settle this." Her breasts tingled, and a shudder shot through her as his strong fingers grasped her bare flesh.

"Come with me," he said, in a voice that soothed and cajoled.

She couldn't calm her runaway heartbeat. "No," she told him, reaching for control though she knew he held the cards.

"Yes. Come with me now. We aren't children playing games, Melissa. It's time for us. It has been for weeks, and you know it."

Melissa summoned her customary cool demeanor and told him in a calm, steady voice, "If I go, it will be because I want to, not because you shoved or wheedled me into it."

Adam stroked her arms and back. "If I have to shove you into it, as you put it, I don't want you to go. It has to be mutual, Melissa. But we can't continue this way." As if he didn't care who came in and saw them, he fastened his mouth to hers without warning. Shivers betrayed her tingling body as his lips took her nectar, his strong fingers roamed over her naked flesh, and she opened her mouth for the sweet torture of his hot tongue. Her senses whirled, and her feminine center pulsated wildly when he slipped his hand into the scant bra of her bathing suit and brought her full breast naked against his hard chest. Her moans filled his mouth, and she felt herself sag against him.

"Come on, sweetheart, let's go."

"Where?"

"Your house. Baltimore. A hotel. I don't care, as long as you and I are the only ones there."

She sat motionless beside him as the Jaguar raced toward the setting sun. She wondered if its now cool rays, hovering as if in silence over a declining sphere of the horizon, foretold what she would experience with Adam. Would their passion for each other peter out coldly like the dying sun? She thought of Gilbert Lewis, of B-H and her mother and the toll that thirty years with a broken heart had taken on her mother. The doctors hadn't found anything wrong with her mother, because medical doctors didn't have the tools with which to detect a broken heart. She couldn't count on a life with Adam, but she would at least have this one night with him. She remembered the red feather and the note and forgot her fears, her anxiety. She realized that he had stopped the car and cut the motor.

"Aren't you going to ask me where I've taken you?"

"You wouldn't take me anywhere that I wouldn't want to be," she replied, and she meant it.

"You're sure?"

"It's one of the few things I *am* sure of right now." She paused, trying to decide whether to thank him for the feather and his note. Uncertain about it, she didn't mention his gift, but said, "And if I decide I want to leave here or anywhere else you take me, I only have to tell you."

Adam's right thumb and index finger stroked his chin in slow sweeps. "Why are you so certain?"

She stared into his eyes, masculine eyes that mesmerized, that twinkled for no reason, and that demanded confidence. In minutes she would give herself over to his keeping, so she spoke with honesty and candor.

"I'm not positive of much where men are concerned, Adam, but you're the rock of Gibraltar, and I'd go anywhere with you."

She knew from his demeanor that her words had affected him. He spoke in a slow, deliberate manner, as though to make certain of his ground. "You're not setting me up, are you?" He got out and started around the car to open the door for her, but she met him in front of the hood.

"Setting you up? Haven't I always said precisely what I mean?" Heat coiled in the seat of her passion as he growled deep in his throat and locked his arms around her.

"Tell me more of what you mean."

She couldn't believe that he needed the assurance, that he could be vulnerable. With her head against his shoulder in symbolic submission, she told him, "I mean the earth wouldn't dare quake when I'm with you."

He looked hard at her, picked her up, and carried her into his lodge on the bank of the Potomac River.

She glanced around at her surroundings when he set her down, but he didn't let her dwell on it. His fingers under her chin brought her lips within an inch of his, and she breathed in his words— "sweet, soft"—just before her body absorbed the shock of his tender kiss. On more than one occasion he had let her feel his power, his maleness, and he'd been tender with her, too, but he hadn't drugged her with this sweet supplication. Hadn't whispered loving words of encouragement, assuring her that her beauty beguiled him, that she was all a man could want in a woman.

"I've never known a woman like you," he whispered as she hid her face in his shoulder until he tipped up her chin and kissed her eyes.

"Trust me, sweetheart. I want your happiness more than my own." Her heart believed him, and she slumped against him in submission. "I need to love you," he murmured, trailing kisses over her neck and collarbone, easing off her coat, "but I need to know that I'm giving you what you want, what satisfies you." She held him closer, loving the feel of his lips skimming over her flesh, barely touching her, inflaming her. Unsure of herself and of her ability to please him, she fought her body's urge to twist itself around him, to issue its own sensuous invitation. Fought until her nipples beaded and her hips moved forward in an urgent plea.

"Ah, Melissa. My woman! *I need you.*" She could no longer resist her body's wild hunger and its searing demand that triggered her frantic undulations when she felt him hot and hard against her belly.

"Slow down, baby, and let me get a handle on this." Out of control now, her hands stroked him inside his shirt in her eagerness to explore him, to know him. And her fingers became bolder, toying with his nipple until his unbridled moan thrilled her with the knowledge that she could excite him so easily. She looped her arms around his neck and took from his mouth the kiss that she needed. Her heart skidded, and she buried her face against his throat as he cradled her to him and started up the stairs. At the top he stepped away from her, giving her a chance to change her mind, and between quick, short breaths, asked her: "Are you sure this is what you want?" Her smile must have reassured him, for he kissed her quickly and by the time they reached his bedroom, she wore only her bathing suit,

He threw back the bed covers with one hand without releasing her, and with exquisite care, placed her in his bed. He undressed himself quickly, removed her bathing suit with gentle hands, lay down beside her, and took her to him. Her body screamed in frustration as his talented, knowing assault on her senses began.

"Your breasts make my mouth water," he murmured, and she cried out as he circled a nipple with his tongue, pulled it into his mouth, and sucked it greedily. She swung her hips eagerly up to him. Seeking, begging. But he retained control of their loving, nourishing himself at her breast while his hand skimmed slowly down her body, tantalizingly, until he reached her woman's treasure.

"Adam, *please!*" she begged. "I think I'll die if you don't do something to me." He released her breast, bringing a groan from her, and with his tongue deep in her mouth, began to simulate the act of love. She couldn't restrain herself any longer, and her hips undulated wildly, as his knowing fingers began their witchery, working their magic.

"Adam," she pleaded, "I need you." He quickened his strokes, heightening her pleasure while he murmured sweet, tender words of encouragement. She shivered as her heart hammered out an erratic rhythm, and an unfamiliar need seared the center of her passion, dampening her for his entry. Her love nectar poured out of her, flowing over his fingers, and she felt the involuntary movement of his steel-like erection against her thigh. Excited beyond reason, impatient to know him, all of him, she reached for him to bring him into her, but he resisted.

"In a minute, baby. This is the most important thing that will ever happen to us," he whispered. With skill and more patience than he'd probably thought he would need, he joined them. Afterward she nestled close to him, shaken by the intensity of her feelings, by the sense that he had become a part of her. She had already forgotten the pain of his penetration, but the awesome control and tender guidance with which he had accomplished the ultimate surrender of herself to him would remain forever with her. Her whole body had quivered uncontrollably in its final submission to him. She wanted to stay with him always.

Adam lay on his back and held Melissa close to his side. His lips brushed her hair as she relaxed against him in trusting slumber. He closed his eyes and suppressed a sigh. How had she come to mean so much to him? He'd controlled his release, because he hadn't wanted her to know how deeply she moved him. Hadn't wanted her to witness the effect that the powerful climax she drove him to would have on him. He'd feared that even in her innocence she would have recognized her power over him. And he had sworn never to give another woman the power to ring his bell. But if he wasn't careful, Melissa could do that.

She threw her left leg over his groin, and he sucked in his breath, his appetite for her whetted but far from sated. He tried to come to terms with her having been a virgin. His first. He wouldn't have thought that would mean anything to him, but it did. When his first affair had crashed around him, he'd been young, still in his teens and, as youth are wont to do, he'd mended easily. This was different. He was no longer a boy, but a man who knew the value of the kind of loving he'd just had with Melissa and who had sense enough to realize that he'd probably never find it in another woman. She wasn't as sophisticated as he'd once thought, and lovely as she was, if she was a virgin at twenty-eight, she had to care a lot to allow him to be her first man.

If he told her about his first sexual encounter, would she forgive him? And what would she say about his misdeed at age sixteen when he got his revenge? He doubted that she would overlook either. Feeling the need to be closer to her, he pulled her over on top of him, and she buried her face in his shoulder and went back to sleep. His grip on her tightened; how could he let her go? But what if she were in cahoots with whoever was ruining his family's business? He wanted her but for how long? Vexed with himself, he laid her on her back and tried to focus on the problem he'd caused himself. Why hadn't he straightened it out, as he'd intended, before he made love with her. Lovemaking so explosive as they'd just experienced didn't end after one session, and a man didn't offer Melissa Grant a one-night stand.

He felt her shift beside him and sit up. "Adam," she whispered as she leaned over him, "we've done a dangerous thing. We could rekindle that awful feud between our families."

"Maybe, but I don't think it'll reach its past furor. It's worth watching, but there's no fertile ground for it."

She nuzzled his neck and ran her hands over his broad chest. "No? Speak to your uncle B-H, and ask him if I'm right."

His hand stroked her tangled curls, and his gaze roamed over her lovely, sepia face. He wanted to know what she felt for him, but if he asked and she told him, he'd have to reciprocate. So he didn't ask her. "If you know something about this feud that you think I don't, tell me."

"Speak to your uncle. I'd rather he told you. You know, Adam, my father rides me constantly about you. He's never had any genuinely fatherly feelings for me, but he hates you and your folks so much that he's suddenly become very protective of me."

Adam propped himself up on his left elbow. "What do you mean, Rafer has no feeling for you. I thought you said—"

She spoke quickly. "I couldn't tell you then, and I hated misleading you. I'm his property, a member of his family, that's all."

He crooked his arm around her shoulder and pulled her close. "It's his loss, Melissa. Any father should be proud to have you for a daughter." He dropped a kiss on her nose. "What about us, Melissa? What do you see ahead for us?" Regret laced her voice as she recited her misgivings, her belief that they'd had as much as they could ever have.

"Do you mean that?"

"I don't want it to be true, but it's what I believe. I don't expect more, because our families come first."

"You're not speaking for me. If you're not prepared to deal with your family, I guess this is it."

She got up. "You can't harness the Atlantic, Adam."

"No," he answered, pulling on his fatigues, "but you can ride the waves. Let's go, Melissa, before we manage to paint this black."

As though upon reflection and with apparent reluctance, he grasped the back of her neck with his large hand and guided her to face him. Standing mere inches from him, she made herself look into his penetrating gaze, and his naked passion. His unshielded want jolted her. Her arms encircled his neck, and her body found its haven in his tight embrace as she molded herself to him.

He held her until her rapid breathing subsided, and she felt his fingers tilt her chin upward until she looked into his twinkling eyes.

"This isn't over, baby. It may never be over. We didn't seek this, and I don't think we wanted it, but it found us and we have to deal with it. And we have to decide whether we're going to do that together or separately." She started to speak, but he shushed her. "We're too raw right now, and there are too many unanswered questions and unsolved problems—at least from where I stand, so let's think about this." He kissed her without passion.

"Adam, one day I tried to list the things that I dislike about you."

Both of his eyebrows arched. "And?"

"Well, while I admire your self-control, it irks the hell out of me that you can turn off your passion at will, as though it were a kitchen faucet."

His eyes lighted with mirth, and she thought his deep laugh held more than humor, that it signified release as well. He pinched her nose and hugged her. "If I wasn't able to turn it off, you probably wouldn't be speaking to me." Arm in arm, they walked to his car.

They spoke little on the drive back. Adam reflected on what had passed between them and on the unpleasant, empty sensation in his chest. He'd thought, hoped, that the fever raging in him whenever he saw her or spoke with her would subside if he made love with her. He'd depended on it. It struck him that if he were so far off in his business dealings, he'd soon face bankruptcy, because she'd gotten into his blood and made herself as much a part of him and the red and white corpuscles that coursed through his veins and sustained his life. But hell! People lived without sight, auditory faculties, limbs, and even a kidney. And if he had to, if she couldn't come to terms with it, he'd live without Melissa Grant.

But Melissa's thoughts didn't lean toward life without Adam. Monday morning found her slouched in her desk chair, daydreaming. Alarmed at her unusual behavior, she went to the ladies' room to refresh her face with cold water and try to change her mood. She had to get started on the mound of work in her incoming box. She walked into the room and Banks stopped fingering her curls, observed Melissa from the mirror, and smirked.

"What are you licking your chops about?"

Immediately defensive, Melissa asked her, "What do you mean?"

Never one for subtlety, Banks retorted, "You didn't even see me. Whose arms were you in last night? I've never seen a more sated female in my life."

Annoyed at her suddenly hot face, Melissa denied it. "You're imagining things."

"Nooooo kidding. Is he six-feet-four or so with long-lashed, bedroom eyes and a body to die for?"

"That could be anybody."

"You think I was born yesterday? Not in my estimation, it couldn't. That man doesn't even come in pairs. If I'd spent the night in his bed, I'd be walking around with a silly smile on my face, too. Go girl!" She ducked into a booth, and Melissa checked her face in the mirror, but detected nothing different. Still smiling, she sauntered back to her office.

She examined her e-mail and called her New York office for confirmation. She'd read correctly, but the secretary she shared had no explanation as to why she would be the subject of a private investigator's sleuthing. The woman called a few minutes later to know whether Melissa would participate in a roundtable discussion on women in business. She said she'd consider it. She checked her mail again. The Houston lawyer named Cooper hadn't despaired in his effort to hire MTG to find a manager for his two thousand-acre-ranch. She wasn't inclined to take the job, but the man was persistent, and the search would be a big enough challenge to keep her mind off of Adam.

"It ought to keep me so busy I won't have time to daydream," she said, and asked the man to offer a contract. But two hours passed and she'd done nothing but relive those moments in Adam's arms. She'd been afraid to let herself go, but he had soothed, coached, and loved her until she did. Shivers coursed through her as she remembered his sweet urging.

*"Give yourself to me, sweetheart. I'm your man, and you belong to me—you'll never belong to anybody else. Give it up, Melissa. I'll make you mine, if it takes me a week."* She'd looked

*up at his perspiring face and into his desire-laden eyes, and he'd*
*twisted his hips and whispered her name. "Melissa, my baby, I*
*need to feel you explode all around me." And she had exploded,*
*had lost her will as though he'd tossed her in a whirlwind of*
*ecstasy.* Frustrated, she stuffed some papers into her briefcase
and went home.

She answered the telephone after the first ring, hoping to hear
Adam's voice. "If you had been home last night, you'd know that
somebody shot your cousin Timmy. Louise said he came home
with his arm bleeding, and he's sure it was one of the Roundtrees or their men. I guess now you'll stay away from Adam
Roundtree. It was probably him anyway, because everything
was fine here until he came back."

She tuned him out and realized it was the first time she'd ever
done that while her father spoke. She didn't want to hear Adam
criticized, but if a Roundtree or one of their men had shot her
cousin, she had disgraced herself with Adam.

"What time did it happen, Daddy?"

"About ten o'clock. Why?"

Her adrenaline began a rapid flow, and joy suffused her. "I
can't imagine who did it, Daddy," she said, "but I'm certain of
one thing. It wasn't Adam."

"You dare defend him when he's wounded your blood relative?"

She could imagine that his eyes narrowed and the veins in his
forehead protruded as they always did when his temper flared.
It occurred to her that what she'd say next might be the last words
he ever heard, but she had to say them.

"Daddy, I was with Adam until midnight. It wasn't Adam."

"You— How could you?" he sputtered and hung up.

"Now I've really done it," she moaned. "There's no way I can
continue to see Adam. Daddy will find an excuse to hurt him,
maybe even prosecute him."

With reluctance, she answered her doorbell to find her mother,
the first time Emily had visited her. Their greeting reflected

their newfound warmth, and they walked into Melissa's living room arm in arm.

"This is a wonderful surprise, Mama. Tell me nothing's wrong."

Emily Grant walked around the room, touching little objects, admiring her daughter's taste. She lingered before a group of family snapshots that Melissa had set in little silver frames. "I never realized that you were so well organized, so neat, or that you preferred these muted colors that your father adores."

Melissa laughed. She knew when someone was buying time. "Mama, surely you don't consider green and antique gold muted. You've got these same colors in your bedroom, along with a little hot orange, I should add. Now tell me what's bothering you."

"You're father's up to something. He and Booker—you know the deputy sheriff, that crooked brother-in-law of his—well, they've had their heads together all morning, and for some reason, Rafer didn't take him to the office but brought him home, and they're closeted in his room."

"Just a minute. Let me get the door. You don't think Daddy followed you over here, do you?"

"Hardly. He was trying to convince Booker about something, but I couldn't hear them too clearly."

Melissa opened the door. Adam. Excitement boiled up in her, and her heart started a fast gallop as she looked at him.

"Hi." He didn't speak but bent to kiss her at about the same time as his gaze fell on Melissa's mother, who stood in the foyer a few feet away. Adam straightened up and looked into the eyes of Emily Grant, then he pulled Melissa into his arms and kissed her waiting lips.

Melissa knew Adam wondered why she'd let him give her a lingering kiss in her mother's presence and why she didn't move out of his arms. Still holding on to him, she turned to her mother.

"Mama, you must know this is Adam Roundtree. Adam, this is my mother, Emily Morris Grant." Adam released her, walked over to Melissa's mother and extended his hand. His surprise at

Emily's warm response was obvious, and when she continued to hold his hand, he remarked on his delight in meeting her.

"I don't want to interrupt your visit," he added, "I can talk with Melissa later."

"Please don't leave on my account, Adam. I'll just run along. You didn't come over here midday on Monday without a good reason. And when I called Melissa's office and found out that she'd gone home so early even though she wasn't sick, I tell you I was mystified. You two must have something to talk about, and I don't want to get in the way."

Melissa wanted her mother and Adam to be friends, though she doubted that her father would tolerate it, and she knew she'd better seize the moment. "Come on in here and have a seat. I'll get us something to drink," she offered, ushering them into the living room. She rushed to make tea and fresh coffee, fearing that tension might develop between her mother and Adam if she left them together for too long. She returned a few minutes later to find them comfortably engaged in conversation, and her mother's words rang in her ear.

"I don't have any ill will against anybody, Adam. Hatred ruined my life."

She watched Adam scrutinize her mother as if he could see inside of her, and it struck Melissa that Adam adopted that penetrating stare when sizing up his opponents.

Emily must have sensed it, too, because she told him, "I'm not your enemy, Adam. I know Rafer would like to see the last of you and all your kinfolk, but I don't know of anything that he and I think alike on."

Adam patted her hand, crossed his knee, threw his head back as if meditating and then abruptly sat forward. Melissa knew he had just made up his mind about something important.

"Rafer has accused me of shooting your cousin Timothy," he told them, his gaze fixed on Melissa. She knew why he hadn't told her over the phone, that he wanted to watch her reaction.

"I told Daddy that charge was ridiculous, that you were with me until midnight." She carefully avoided looking at her mother.

"Why did you decide to be with me last night? There've been many other times when the situation was just as compelling, just as urgent, and you sent me on my way. But yesterday afternoon you went with me without hesitation. Are you for me or against me?"

Melissa bristled. "How dare you suggest that I'd cheapen myself by taking subterfuge to the point where I'd—" She remembered that her mother sat three feet away and tried to cool off.

"Do you think I haven't wondered whether you were keeping me occupied while Wayne or one of your men went after Timmy? I haven't read any proclamation attesting to the spotless lives of the Hayes-Roundtree clan, so back off."

"Adam. Melissa," Emily began in a troubled voice. "Will you two stop it? Can't you see what you're doing to each other?"

Adam turned on her. "You're not against a relationship between Melissa and me. Why is that?" Melissa watched in horror as tears glistened in her mother's eyes and prayed that she'd be able to hold them back. She knew that the loss of dignity in Adam's presence would humiliate her mother.

Emily opened her handbag, pulled out a tissue, and blew her nose. "I've been a victim of this stupid feud for the last thirty-one years, and I pray to God I live to see the end of it."

"I've never raised a gun to anybody," Adam assured them, "and I don't know that I could. Life is precious." His gaze shifted to Melissa's face, and she read his silent message. *Precious, as you are precious.* From the corner of her eyes, she glimpsed the silver-tipped red feather that she'd placed in a tiny crystal vase and walked over to the mantelpiece where it stood. She handed it to her mother, and Emily remarked on its elegance and uniqueness.

"This is lovely. Unusual."

Melissa was still learning her mother's ways, and Emily startled her when she grinned devilishly, as if she knew Adam had given her daughter the little gift.

Melissa's voice tittered with emotion. "Yes," she answered as her gaze adored Adam. "Someone very special gave it to me." The twinkle in his eyes glowed until it enveloped his face, and his lips moved with unspoken words that she couldn't decipher.

She glanced over at her mother, then back at Adam, and fought her need to rush to him and feel his man's strength surround her. As though compelled to touch her, he slid a finger down her right cheek while the impassioned turbulence of his eyes caressed her face. Mesmerized, she leaned into him and gloried in the feel of his strong arms around her.

"I'd better be going," he told them, his tone indicating a reluctance to heed his words. Melissa nodded and opened the door. Adam turned to Emily.

"I'm glad you were here. It was a pleasure to meet you."

Melissa watched Adam brace himself against the wind and strike out for his office and knew she couldn't turn their relationship around nor change what she felt for him. She loved him more today than yesterday. More now than an hour ago. Anxious that she and Adam had disclosed to her mother how intimate they had become, she pivoted sharply, ready for a lecture.

"I know what you're thinking, Mama, and I'm sorry you witnessed that exchange, but I couldn't let Adam take the blame for something I knew he didn't do." Her mother's intense scrutiny irked her, but the words she heard told her that she needn't have been concerned.

"Why apologize?" Emily asked her. "You're twenty-eight years old. When a woman and a man love each other and they're not obligated to anybody else, how they express their passion and their love behind closed door is their business. The government can't legislate it, and the courts can't ban it. I only wish I'd been as sensible. Well, I'd better leave—your father will be up in the air as soon as he discovers he's in that house by himself."

Adam inclined his head in brief greetings to passersby as he walked swiftly to his office, his dilemma about Melissa's possible culpability mounting with the seconds. He *had* to solve it—far more than his family's reputation and livelihood hinged on it. He wasn't certain he could give her up even if she was guilty, and if she was and if he didn't give her up, he faced a complete break with his family. All except B-H. Somehow he didn't think his uncle would side with Wayne and his mother if—B-H…twice in connection with their relationship, Melissa had suggested he ask his uncle about the long arm of their families' feud. He made a mental note to speak with B-H.

As though by agreement, they avoided meeting each other at work or seeing each other outside the building, and they didn't telephone for several days. Adam had decided he needed to at least talk with her when he answered his phone.

"Roundtree."

"Hi, Roundtree. Grant here." He wasn't fooled by her light response, because he figured she'd missed him as much as he'd missed her.

He shrouded himself in his office demeanor. "What may I do for you?"

"I thought you'd like to know that I've found a position for Dan with another real estate firm, and he's willing to accept it."

"I told you I wouldn't object to his leaving my staff since he has good reasons, so why are you telling me this? Is there something else?" He heard the hesitancy in her voice and wondered if he'd been too brusque.

"Sorry, but I thought you'd like to know before I completed the transaction. He's joining one of your competitors, but he's assured me that he won't reveal anything about your business. I do need to talk to you about something else, though." He listened as she told him of her contract to locate a managing officer for a Pittsburgh real estate firm and knew at once that asking him for tips on what to look for in the applicants was an excuse to talk with him. She didn't need his advice, and she must be aware that he knew it and that he'd guess she only wanted contact with him.

"If you need the information urgently, perhaps we could get together for dinner. I'm…" He paused, uncertain. "I'm busy just now. Suppose I pick you up at seven?" He'd planned to go more slowly with her until he solved the problems at Leather and Hides, but he'd detected a need for him in her voice and responded to it.

He leaned back in his chair, placed his feet with ankles crossed on his desk and buzzed his secretary to come in. "No calls and no visitors until I tell you." He ignored her inquiring look and glanced at the Jaeger-Lecoutre on his wrist. Three o'clock. He'd see Melissa in four hours. He put his feet on the floor and got to work. An hour later he was squeezing his relaxer, annoyed with himself. He was damned if he'd be a slave to his penis just because he'd found a woman who was his soul mate in bed. He'd have dinner with Melissa, take her home, and leave her there. He whistled just to prove to himself that he'd gotten rid of a burden. After another two hours, he realized he'd looked at his watch a dozen times, willing the moments to pass more swiftly. It irritated him. He'd thought that if he made love with her, that would be the end of it. But he'd gotten an astonishing surprise, and he'd need the will of Moses to hold his passion for her in check. But he'd do it.

Bill Henry's telephone call as she began dressing for dinner with Adam disconcerted Melissa. To her knowledge, he hadn't previously contacted anyone in her family. Her mother hadn't heard from him since she'd broken their engagement. Fear streaked through her at the possibility that something might be wrong with Adam, but B-H's tone reassured her.

"How is Em— How is your mother?" Stunned, Melissa told him with all the casualness she could muster that Emily had recently visited her, apparently well. His deep sigh and audible release of breath communicated to her his profound relief, jolting her. Would it be her destiny to love so deeply and lose so painfully? She hoped not as she tried without success to calm her mounting excitement at the prospect of being with Adam.

She knew she shouldn't have agreed to go to dinner with him, but she couldn't contain her eagerness to be with him and resigned herself to take whatever came. She dressed in a soft, figure-flattering, berry red, wool knit dress, smoothed her long curls into a French twist and wrapped a strand of pearls around it. She slipped on a pair of black suede dress slippers, dabbed

Opium perfume in strategic places, and walked down the stairs just as her doorbell rang.

"Hi. You look...beautiful. Is this all for me?" Blood rushed to her face, and she ducked her head. He took her hand and entered without waiting for her invitation.

"You...you look good, too," she told him. He stared at her, shaking his head, obviously denying something. As if transfixed, she didn't move out of his way. Her gaze feasted on him. Chills twisted through her whole body as the gong of her grandmother's clock announced seven o'clock, and she couldn't shake the thought that it tolled for her and Adam. She knew he could tell that he'd disconcerted her and that he sensed her need for his reassurance, because she read his emotions in that fraction of a second before he blanketed his feelings. She looked up at him, waiting.

His sigh and mild oath fell on her ears like music, but he disappointed her when he didn't take her in his arms. His eyes mirrored his remorse, and she knew he intended to put their relationship on the shelf. She lowered her head to hide her reaction when his deep sigh of regret confirmed it. It wasn't easy to stand casually before him while his eyes adored her and his thumb tenderly stroked her chin, even as his posture sent a different message.

"It's okay, Melissa. We'll survive it." She knew he meant that going their separate ways would hurt, but that it wouldn't kill him. Her smile had never been so brilliant.

# Chapter 9

Melissa read Magnus Cooper's signed contract and decided she'd made a mistake. She had quoted the man a very high fee and had expected him to bargain or at least complain. But if her eyes served her properly, he would pay double that if she could find a manager who suited him within two weeks. She telephoned him to bargain for three weeks at one and a half times the fee she'd quoted.

"Are you telling me the president of MTG is a woman? Well, a man I trust told me this was one of the best executive search firms in the country. Who's your CEO?"

"Mr. Cooper, *I* am the president and owner of MTG." Melissa iced her voice to put the man in his place, but to her astonishment, he persisted.

"Well, I don't know, ma'am. I'm not used to doing business with a woman…but, well…they say you know your stuff. Still, I just don't know."

Annoyed, she told him, "Mr. Cooper, I'm looking at a contract that says you do business with me. I hope legal action won't be necessary."

"Of course not," he cajoled. And she envisioned honey dripping from his tongue as he drawled, "Let's have dinner and smooth over this little misunderstanding." Unimpressed with the offer, she declined—Houston, Texas, wasn't around the corner. Magnus Cooper gave her the three weeks and fee she demanded and told her he'd forward an amendment to the contract. Pleased, she thanked him and said a polite good bye. Later, dispirited over her unsatisfactory relationship with Adam, she accepted Banks's suggestion that they browse in a few antique shops after work.

They walked through Bessie's Yesteryear, looking at old coffee grinders, grandfather clocks, alabaster candlesticks, a Tiffany lamp, an early Shaker rocker. Melissa paused beside an ancient brass scale and lifted one of its weights, thinking that if she polished the scale it would add a nice touch to her kitchen's bay window. She felt Banks jab her in the back and glanced up and into the unfriendly eyes of Mary Roundtree. She couldn't treat Adam's mother discourteously, but the woman didn't invite warmth. Melissa didn't know what kind of response she'd get, but she squared her shoulders and spoke.

"Good afternoon, Mrs. Roundtree. How are you?" For that, she received a stingy "Fine, thank you" and a nod of the head. Perplexed that Adam's mother behaved more coldly toward her than when they'd first met, she nevertheless introduced Banks, who retaliated on Melissa's behalf by accepting the introduction with a frosty "Nice to meet you, Miss Mary." Melissa watched in horror as Adam's mother excused herself and turned away in such haste that she crashed into an 1890 gaslight post and knocked herself out. Alarmed, she knelt beside the woman to assist her while Banks telephoned Adam and called for an ambulance. She gave silent thanks that both were only a few blocks away.

Adam rushed into Bessie's Yesteryear and stopped short at the unbelievable scene. Melissa held his mother's head in her lap and placed a cold compress to her forehead. He knelt beside them and tried to gain his mother's attention, but she didn't respond. The wail of the ambulance seemed miles away and, anxious, he felt for his mother's pulse. Satisfied, he looked again at Melissa and marveled as she continued her careful ministrations. Shaking his head, he sat up on his haunches and fixed his gaze on her face. How could she treat his mother with such tenderness after she had accorded Melissa the barest civility and all but dismissed her when she'd visited her home? He studied the woman who, without realizing it, had made him rethink his priorities and knew an unaccustomed softness in himself. She combined gentleness and tenderness with strength, determination, and efficiency. He remembered Wayne's assessment of her and reached out to touch her face.

"The ambulance is here now. I won't forget your kindness, Melissa."

"Please don't thank me. I'd like to go to the hospital with you. Do you mind?"

His gaze roamed over her face before resting on her eyes. He wished he could read her reasons, because he knew she'd be affronted if he asked her why. He agreed, though he suspected that she detected his reluctance, and it bothered him that he didn't welcome her company.

They waited three hours before a doctor advised them that Mary may have suffered a severe concussion, but that she had regained a fair amount of lucidity. Adam expressed his relief and went to the cafeteria to get coffee for Melissa and himself.

Melissa stepped closer when she heard Mary's weak voice. "What happened? Why are you here?" It struck her that a lack of strength didn't camouflage the hostility in Mary Roundtree's voice. Melissa told her what had happened, her tone devoid of feeling. More alert now, the woman attempted without success to sit up, and Melissa pulled up a chair beside her bed.

"Where is Adam? Are you here because you're after him?"

Melissa couldn't believe the displeasure in the woman's eyes as she turned her face away. "I'm sure you know your son well enough to realize that if he didn't want me here, I wouldn't be here."

"If you care about him, you'll leave him alone," the woman told her with trembling lips.

Melissa tried to push back her annoyance. Being Adam's mother gave Mary Roundtree the upper hand. Melissa told her, "I can't be with him if he doesn't want to be with *me,* so use your influence with Adam. Your words are wasted on me."

Adam returned to find his mother dropping silent tears, her

lips pursed in disapproval. "What did you say to her?" he asked Melissa. She looked the man she loved fully in the face, stared him down for several seconds, and told him, "I just answered her questions. Seems I overstayed my welcome here. I'll be seeing you."

"Melissa!"

She kept walking. Her world seemed filled with men who, like Gilbert Lewis, exacted a pound of flesh for every smile they'd given you. She didn't want to believe Adam would think her capable of doing or saying anything to hurt his mother. Deep in thought, she nearly passed Bill Henry without speaking.

"What's wrong, Melissa? You look as though you've just witnessed an execution."

"Maybe I have. *Mine.*" That tired voice couldn't be hers.

"What happened?" He stepped closer and touched her arm. She told him, beginning with her encounter with Mary in the antique store. B-H nodded in apparent understanding.

"Didn't Adam tell you that Mary Roundtree is a consummate actress? For years my sister belonged to the Frederick Players— she can switch from saint to siren in seconds. I can't believe Adam would let her antics rattle him."

"No. He let her rattle me, and with impunity. I've had it with the Roundtrees."

Bill Henry shook his head. "For now, maybe. Well, it's a good thing I'm a Hayes." She felt his soothing pat on her forearm and sensed that he felt a special kinship with her. He walked on, turned, and called her. "Melissa, how is Em— How is Emily?" She walked back to him.

"She's fine, B-H. Lately something about her reminds me of early spring. I don't understand it, but I'm certainly happy about it."

He nodded, and she thought his face reflected a wistful longing. "Are the two of you close?"

"We never were until I came back home, but we are now."

"She needs someone. I'm glad she has you."

"Me, too," she said, as much to herself as to him. She walked back to the phone booth and called Towne car service for a taxi home. She'd gone shopping to escape her thoughts and look what she got as a result. More to think about. She went home and began undressing almost from the front door, not bothering to wonder why a bath seemed the answer to her problem. You can't wash it away, an inner voice nagged.

Adam walked out of his mother's hospital room, displeased with himself for having asked Melissa such a thoughtless question after her kindness to his mother. She hadn't deserved it. But his mother never cried, and he'd thought that... It didn't matter—he had mistreated Melissa. His uncle's voice interrupted his mental meanderings.

"What's going on around here? First Melissa walks past me without speaking, and now you nearly knock me down. How's Mary?"

Adam looked into the distance, preoccupied. "She's improving. She'll be home tomorrow."

"Be careful with Melissa, Adam. That girl's very tender."

It struck Adam that his uncle regarded Melissa with a deep affection for which he could see no apparent basis, and he meant to ask him about it. "I know what she's like, B-H, and it isn't my intention to hurt her."

"But you did."

"I know." Adam hastened on without saying good-bye. He had to get to her.

He parked in front of her home and sat in the car considering the charm of her little house nestled among the four swaying pines, cloaked in brilliant moonlight. How much like her it seemed: simple, elegant, uncluttered, and lovely. Frustrated when she didn't answer her bell after five minutes, he went back to the car and called her on his cellular phone.

"I don't want to see you, Adam."

He exhaled deeply. "My question wasn't called for, and you didn't deserve it. My only excuse is the anxiety I felt for my mother."

It would serve him right if I hung up, she told herself. Instead she said, showing more irritation than she felt, "I've had better apologies from strangers. My father is good for a better one than that." She braced herself against her bathroom wall and forced out the words. "It's best we go our separate ways, Adam."

Annoyed with himself for needing her, for caring, he snapped in anger, "You can't see the forest for the trees, Melissa. If that's what you want, I bow to your wish." He remained there, silent, collecting his wits, pensive. The shock of regret pierced his system when he heard the click as she replaced the receiver. He had to accept that she meant more to him than anyone else. More than Leather and Hides. More than finding out who wanted to destroy it. More than any woman he'd ever known. More than he would have believed possible. He laughed derisively—for the first time since his misadventure of over a decade and a half earlier, he couldn't call the shots. He didn't like it, but there it was.

Melissa heard Adam's car as he drove away and lectured herself: no tears, even as she brushed them from her cheeks. She loved Adam, but at the moment she could dislike him. Not for long, she admitted. She had wanted so badly to see him, to hear him say that he cared for her, that he hadn't meant those words, but his apology had been stingy, halfhearted. She called Banks for company, but had a sense of relief when she heard the answering machine. She searched for Ilona's phone number, thinking she'd call her in New York, but before she located it, the phone rang. She raced to it, hoping to hear Adam's voice.

"Sorry to disappoint you, dear," Bill Henry said. "I called to find out how you are, since Adam's at home. Don't think too harshly of Mary. She's troubled about the sabotage at Leather and Hides, and she isn't certain who's responsible." He told her as much as he could about the incidents at the plant, and she knew he detected her shock and her hurt that Adam hadn't told her how serious the problem had become.

"How do you know I can be trusted? Adam obviously doesn't think so, because he hasn't told me much about it."

He ignored the latter comment. "Because I know you love Adam."

"What? How?"

"Melissa, I saw you and spoke with you as you left the hospital. A man couldn't hurt a woman that deeply unless she loved him. Make her furious? Yes. But he wouldn't have the power to break her heart."

She wrapped herself in a bath towel and sat on the edge of the tub. "Oh, B-H, I've done a foolish thing, loving him, and I know I'll pay for it."

"Only if you refuse to accept the truth."

"B-H, I know Adam didn't shoot Timmy. He was with me."

"Would you have been so certain if you didn't have that proof? The hatred between our families runs deep, Melissa. Adam is tough, but he's fair, and he's honest. Money doesn't protect you from everything, and he's had some hard knocks. If you look carefully, you can see that. Don't think you can wait until this clears up and your family is absolved and then let him know where you stand. He'd lose all interest, no matter how much he loves you. My nephew demands loyalty from everybody, and he gives it unstintingly."

"I've told both my parents that he was with me," she replied with a sense of virtue. "I won't let him down."

His next remark gave her pause. "If you won't listen to what he has to say, you're letting me down."

She rose to her feet. Surely Adam didn't discuss his personal life with his uncle. "How do you know? Did he tell you that?"

"Adam isn't a man to unload on another one. I doubt he'd tell anyone what's in his heart except the person involved. I know you didn't listen to him, because he's in his home and you're in yours, and it isn't even nine o'clock. Nothing would convince me that he hasn't tried to apologize."

A heaviness centered in her chest, a sense of dread, as she made herself ask him a question, seeking from him reassurance she had long needed—evidence of a man's great love for a woman. "B-H, I have to know this. Did you love my mother?" His long pause unnerved her.

"How do you know about this?"

"Recently my mother told me that you are the only man she ever loved."

She didn't let him know she'd heard him sniffle, but waited during the ensuing silence while he struggled to collect his composure.

"Yes, I love her. I will always love her, and I thank you for telling me, Melissa. Knowing how she feels means everything to me. Make certain it doesn't happen to you. The feuding, lying, and meanness has to stop. We are all victims of it. Hatred ruins people...destroys them. And it will break you and Adam if you don't learn to trust each other. You have only to look at Emily and me to know the consequences." She thanked him, hung up and dialed Adam's number.

"Adam Roundtree."

"Do you still want to see me?" Her pulse raced when she heard his words.

"I'll be there in twenty minutes."

Melissa slipped into her red velour wrap robe, combed her hair, and dabbed a bit of Opium perfume where it counted. She put on her white fluffy bunny bedroom slippers, started downstairs, and stopped. Might as well go for broke she decided, turned, went into her bedroom and lit the four candles on her dresser, switched off the lamp, and got downstairs just as the doorbell rang. She opened the door, and he walked into her open arms, kicked the door closed and clutched her to him.

"Melissa, Melissa, I need you!" She parted her lips and let her senses succumb to his loving. Her heart raced as his tongue danced against hers and his large hand slipped beneath her robe and captured her naked breast. Her breathing accelerated, and her hips moved voluntarily against him. He put her away from him, his face harsh with desire, and a charge shot through her at his heated gaze and wordless question.

"Yes," she whispered. "Oh, yes. Yes." He didn't need any urging, just tucked her to his side and climbed the stairs to what he knew would be heaven in her arms. Her eyes adored him as he threw back the coverlet and laid her on the lavender satin sheets. With her gaze still locked to his, she slowly loosened the tie on her robe and threw it open. Quickly he took it from her, removed his clothes, and leaned over her as her outstretched arms welcomed him in a gesture as old as womanhood. He bent to her and caressed her lovingly, his hands claiming her body. Her moans of delight must have excited him more, for he rushed her preparation for his entry.

This time, her innocence behind her, she made demands of her own. Her senses sharpened, and his salty flesh and musky scent heightened her desire. She grasped him and stroked him, and his every move, every gesture, told her she'd found the right torch.

"Melissa, sweetheart."

"Yes," she answered, eager for what she knew awaited her. This time they flew swiftly and unerringly to the sun.

He wiped the perspiration from their faces with the corner of the sheet, and remained within her body, his gaze on her face.

"Melissa, please look at me." His throat tightened when she smiled, and the trust he saw in her eyes sent his heart into a gallop. He hated that he'd held back again, but he couldn't let her know how deeply she moved him. Not yet.

"You said 'please.' We're making progress." Her finger traced his bottom lip, and he felt as if she'd touched his soul. His arms drew her tightly to him, and his mouth sought her soft, pliable lips. He felt himself stirring within her and raised his head. With so many imponderables in their lives, he had to be careful what he said to her, but he couldn't let her think that he would use her.

"I have very deep feelings for you, Melissa, probably deeper that I realize."

"But?"

He knew that his smile must seem feeble to her, considering

the explosiveness of their lovemaking. "Not buts. There are things you don't know, and other things I have to straighten out—and until it's all clean and clear, I can't commit myself and you won't want to either. Let's try not to hurt each other while I work it out. Will you promise me that?"

"You don't think we're making a mistake? It looks to me like we're going the wrong direction on a one-way street."

He shook his head. "Life is what you make it, sweetheart. We can let the folly of our parents and grandparents ruin our lives, or we can put that feud behind us and make our own way, base our decisions and what we do on merit. I chart my own course. What about you?"

"I've learned the value of that since I've been back here, and I've stopped begging for my father's approval. I'm my own person, and my mother supports me in that."

"Alright, it's settled. We stand together until we have reasons not to, reasons that concern only us and have nothing to do with our families. Agreed?" She smiled and wiggled beneath him.

"Vixen. I'll teach you who to tease."

Melissa rolled over and hugged herself. Adam's good-bye kiss lingered on her lips, and she pulled his pillow over her head to blot out the fast-breaking daylight. If she didn't get up, she'd probably oversleep and get to work late. She heard him close the front door and snuggled deeper under the covers, her nostrils tingling with his heady masculine scent and the lingering aroma of their lovemaking. Thoughts of her mother alone in her room, her love denied her, brought Melissa upright. "Back to reality, kiddo," she advised herself, scrambling out of bed. She padded over to her window to look at the birds and glimpsed a bluebird among the swarm of blackbirds. But she lacked her usual enthusiasm for them and went about preparing herself for the day. Leaving home later that morning she had a consoling thought. Adam didn't accept defeat; if he wanted them to have a life together, he'd move mountains for it. She knew, too, that if he came to a different decision, what she wanted wouldn't matter. "So I can stop worrying about it," she muttered to herself.

Adam drove into his garage as the first streak of dawn shot across the horizon. Teased with the stirrings of desire one moment and in the next irritated by uncertainty, he knew he had to take action. If he couldn't solve the mystery at Leather and Hides soon, he'd get more professional help. It was hell making love to a woman whom you wanted all the way to the recesses of your soul and holding back because you were suspicious of her.

Adam selected a red and gray paisley tie to wear with his gray shirt and gray pin-striped suit that morning. He remembered that whenever Melissa saw that tie, she fingered it absentmindedly, though she never said she admired it. He hadn't been alone with her since he'd left her sleeping in bed four days ago. Lunch at a restaurant wouldn't afford them much privacy, but it allowed them to be together without the temptation of lovemaking.

He stopped by her office just before one o'clock.

"She has a client with her, Mr. Roundtree," her secretary told him.

"For the tenth time, Cynthia, my name is Adam."

"Yes, sir, Mr. Roundtree."

Adam sighed. He believe in hiring seniors, but getting them adjusted to the changing social norms could be difficult. He didn't sit but leaned against the doorjamb to wait for Melissa. Within minutes, handsome Magnus Cooper stepped out of Melissa's office wearing his ten-gallon Stetson and alligator boots, drawling his appreciation and his wish to see more of her. Adam had the satisfaction of hearing her say she didn't date her clients, but Cooper dismissed the comment with a laugh. Fury shot through him, constricting his throat and burning his chest. By what right did that cowboy hit on his woman?

Her smile when she saw him helped him to calm himself. He and the man had height in common, Adam observed, then noticed the Texan's two-inch boot heels with mean satisfaction. He nodded at Melissa's introduction, but didn't offer to shake hands. Then he pointedly asked her, "Can you take off the rest of the day? I thought we might run over to Baltimore. The Great Blacks In Wax Museum is having an open house." He hadn't planned to ask her right then, maybe Saturday, but it served a purpose. Magnus Cooper had been warned that Adam Round-tree didn't tolerate another man on his turf.

He glanced at Melissa, figured he'd irritated her and didn't much care. The more she understood him, the better. He knew he hadn't fooled her, and that her professionalism wouldn't let her take him to task in front of Cooper. He watched her get rid of the man, and it amused him that she drew out their good-byes, obviously to deny him assurance that she had no interest in the Texan. They spent the rest of the afternoon in Baltimore, first at the museum and then wandering around the Inner Harbor.

"Those Maryland crab cakes were worth battling this weather," she said, referring to the fierce wind blowing off the Atlantic over the Chesapeake Bay.

He rested an arm around her shoulder. "I'm glad you think so. The food was delicious, but I'd wondered whether this breeze might be too much for you." They approached a toy store inside the mall, and he ducked into it, pulling her with him, bought a tiger-striped kitten, wrote Adam on its tag, and gave it to her. Then he asked himself why he'd done that, but the joy he saw in her eyes placated his guilt for having encouraged her.

They walked on, browsing in little shops and gazing at spectacles that held no interest for them. He took her hand and urged her into a quaint coffee shop, where he got a table off in a corner. He needed to clear up a few things, and he couldn't do that amidst the distractions. He ordered the coffee and pastries that she selected, but he didn't want to eat. He wanted to know whether she remembered her promise to preserve their relationship until he'd solved some issues.

"Melissa, do you like that man I met in your office this morning?"

She must have misunderstood his question, he decided, when she replied.

"So far I do. Why?"

He knew she'd revolt if he showed anger and did his best to contain his temper and his impatience. "I'll put it differently. What I mean exactly is this: *do you want him?*" He tried to ignore the mirth reflected in her eyes.

"He's just a client, Adam."

"That's your view. His differs substantially." He swallowed his annoyance. Melissa could give the appearance of naivete whenever it suited her.

"You saw him for only a little while this morning. Why don't you like him?"

"What was there to like? He's rich—but honey, money doesn't part rivers, not from where I sit. I can usually judge a man by what he laughs at, and I didn't like his laugh nor what he found funny."

"You ought to know how much money impresses people," she scoffed, "considering how much of it you've got."

He didn't smile as he looked at her. He was serious, and he wanted her to know it. "Yeah. I'd probably make out better with you if I didn't have a cent. This guy I met this morning—is he the one you found a ranch manager for?"

"I'm finding one for him. Yes."

He put his elbows on the table, made a pyramid of his ten fingers, and searched her face. "I thought it was your policy to take the executive to the employer. What was Cooper doing up here in Maryland?" He knew that if he kept it up, she might lose her customary cool, but he didn't let the thought stop him.

"We talked a few times, and I guess he got curious about me."

Adam straightened up and glared at her. "Curious eh? Remind him for me that curiosity killed the cat." He watched her clutch the little tiger kitten as if it were a security token, though she stuck out her chin in defiance. But he refused to feel guilty for having goaded her. He didn't want Magnus Cooper within miles of her.

\* \* \*

They left the coffee shop, and he looped her arm through his. An old-fashioned gesture, he realized, but one that he liked. "Say, didn't Harriet Tubman once live around here somewhere?" he asked as they left the harbor area.

"I'm not sure," Melissa told him. "Imagine a woman born into slavery in the first quarter of the nineteenth century managing to get her freedom and organize an escape route for other slaves. She was something."

He squeezed her arm in a gesture of affection. "Sure was. In those days people depended upon their wits for survival. I'm curious," he said. "Are you a feminist because of the men in your life or in spite of them?"

"Both," she said, as they reached his car. He buckled his seat belt, turned to her, and with his arm around her shoulder asked her, "Why did you let me make love to you that first time? You were a virgin. Why did you give me that honor? The question plagues me, Melissa."

He could feel her withdrawing from him. "If you have to be told, Adam, the answer wouldn't help you."

He put the key in the ignition, but didn't turn it. "If you'd rather I reached my own conclusion, I can certainly do that."

She reached over and rubbed his nose with her index finger, surprising him, because she hadn't previously shown him such familiarity. "You will do that, no matter what I say." He noticed that her hand fell casually into her lap, that she sat in the bucket seat, quiet, serene. He thought of Keats's poem and the silence "upon a peak in Darien." Might as well accept it, he thought. I may not be able to let her go no matter what she's done and no matter how badly I want to forget her.

He felt her delicate fingers pinch his thigh and smiled. "Feeling your oats?"

"Just testing the water."

"What's it like?" he asked.

"Hot." He stared at her. Twice that afternoon she'd goaded him, and he liked her new familiarity with him, her shy possessiveness. Her fingers walked from his knee halfway up his thigh while she hummed "Frère Jacques" in accompaniment. They reached her house, and he tipped up her chin with his right index finger, excitement wafting its way through him as she continued her play, running her fingers up his left arm. His gaze steady and unfathomable, he stated, "I'll pick you up tomorrow morning at seven thirty."

She squinted, as though not believing what she'd heard. "What for?"

He didn't make her wait for his answer. "The weekend. If you want to test the water, I aim to accommodate you."

"You asking, or telling?"

He grinned sheepishly. "I suppose I can learn to crawl if you force me to it, though right now I'm having trouble envisaging such a scene."

Melissa laughed. "It's giving me trouble, too."

Adam took Route 340 toward Harpers Ferry to where the Appalachian Trail hit the Potomac River, bore left onto an unmarked gravel road, swung up a bumpy strip and stopped at his lodge, twenty-four miles from Beaver Ridge. The overcast skies and the air, warm and stifling for mid-November, warned them not to expect beautiful weather. Adam went about storing their supplies, but her quiet demeanor and obvious wariness began to disturb him, and he sat in a straight-back dining room chair and pulled her between his knees.

"What's the matter? If you want to go home, I'll be disappointed, but I'll take you." He breathed deeply in relief when her hands wound around his neck.

"I don't want to leave, but this feels strange."

He put her away gently and stood. "Maybe we should have done this a while back. I don't want you to be uncomfortable, so if you want to leave, just tell me." He meant it, but he didn't expect to have to keep that promise, because he knew how to get the response from her that he wanted, and he'd get it. They ate the breakfast he'd cooked and cleaned the kitchen together.

Domesticity wasn't so bad, Adam mused, turning on the dish-washer. He could even get to like it.

The sun peeked through the clouds, and they put on light sweaters and jackets and hiked along the Appalachian Trail. They strolled into the forest, amidst trees of golden and rust-colored leaves that waved among the green pines.

"I could get used to being in this place with you. I come here to find peace, to shut out my problems, to rejuvenate as it were. And I always come here alone. But having you here with me feels good. Feels right." He let his gaze roam up the trunk of a tall elm. "Are you glad you came?"

"Yes," she whispered. "Yes, I'm glad." His heartbeat raced wildly when she reached up and tucked his scarf closely around his neck but wouldn't look at his face.

"Come on—let's walk," she said, though she grasped his arm and faced him, making it impossible for him to take a step. His fingers guided her face upward until he could see the passion glittering like soft lights in her eyes.

"Oh, honey. Sweetheart, we're insane," he said softly. Imme-diately her arms reached up to caress his broad shoulders.

"I know. Oh, Adam, I know." He watched, captivated by her soft, yielding manner, as she raised parted lips for his kiss even as the words left her mouth. He covered her mouth with his and drank in her sweetness. He needed her closer, and he needed all of her. She moved against him, but he stilled her. He needed all of her, to know her fully, to communicate with her at the deepest level. But how could he, when the level of trust that he needed eluded them? He tucked her to his side and walked on. Unsatisfied.

"Time to go," he told her abruptly after seeing a brown bear dash into the thicket. They walked swiftly through the high pines, white ash, and oak trees that thrived there. Riffling ex-citement, akin to fear, alerted Adam to danger, causing him suddenly to sniff the wind and look up at the black sky. He released her hand.

"Let's get out of here. We'll have to make a run for it." Drenched and shivering, they reached the lodge.

"Too bad we didn't wait an hour to take that walk," he lamented, as the storm moved on, and the sun peeked through the clouds.

"You're t-t-telling m-m-me."

"You're shivering. I'll get something warm for you." He removed her jacket and shoes and wrapped her in a woolen blanket.

"T-th-thanks."

"I think I'd better call a doctor."

"No d-d-don't. I'm scared to death of electrical storms—it's just nerves," she told him, and he stared at her, incredulous. He took her in his arms and rocked her until the tremors stopped. She'd shown no sign of fear while she sprinted a half mile in that electrical storm.

He reflected on Melissa's behavior as he set about preparing lunch. He'd never seen her so vulnerable as when she'd trembled uncontrollably because of fear, not even when she had lain beneath him and splintered in his arms, and he realized he felt a new tie to her, a feeling that she needed him.

After lunch he made a fire in the fireplace to ward off the sudden chill that followed the thunderstorm. They sat before it, and he took her hand.

"What do you want from life, Melissa?" He could see that she'd rather he'd phrased the question differently.

"A girl and a boy in whatever order they decide to show up."

He took no offense at her attempt to downplay its importance to her, because he knew she had a tendency to squirm whenever their conversation became too personal. "And?"

"Well, I don't want to conceive them by artificial insemination, and I don't want to be an unmarried mother."

Adam couldn't help laughing. She refused to admit that she wanted a husband. "Anything else? What about a father for those kids?"

A brief wistfulness flashed in her limped eyes. "He can be part of the package." Her manner changed. "Are we talking serious, here?"

"Not as serious as we might, but I need to know something about you apart from your intelligence, efficiency, wit, sexy beauty, and earth-shattering lovemaking." Her raised eyebrows and skeptical look said that he might have overstated it. Heat flooded her face, and she shrugged, her diffidence adding to her allure.

"Seventy-five percent of the men in this country wouldn't need to know any more than that," she said, "and the other twenty-five percent wouldn't know what to do with that information if they had it."

He hadn't thought her shy or so tender. Getting her to reveal herself proved as simple as getting blood from a turnip. His eyes narrowed as he remembered his first encounter with her father. "What—besides your father—makes you cry?"

"Adam, that's behind me. If I hurt, it's for my mother."

He rolled over, clasped her in his arms, and she spoke more readily of her life. They talked, holding each other until sleep claimed them.

Hours later they awakened in a chilled room beside a cold fireplace. Melissa snuggled closer to Adam. The tender protectiveness he'd shown her bound him more closely to her, and she forgot the reasons why she should avoid him. She wanted to tell him she loved him, but even in his loving, protective mien, when he'd held her while she trembled uncontrollably in fright, he'd withheld something. She looked down at him, his arms behind his head and his eyes closed for emotional privacy, and thought of his masterfulness under pressure and his awesome passion for her. Yes, he charted his own course, and he hadn't committed himself to her because he hadn't accepted their relationship. Something or somebody stood between them, and she had an eerie feeling that the chasm they faced involved her family. A deep intimacy had developed between them as they'd sat before the fire talking and sipping coffee, but he had told her little of himself and nothing of what he envisaged for them. Yet he'd filled her heart with himself. She had to hold back—she didn't want to, but she had to.

# Chapter 10

Melissa unpacked her small weekend bag and dropped the soiled garments into the hamper. A glance at her watch confirmed that she didn't have time to get to Sunday morning church. Who would have thought their weekend would pass as it had—first a storm in which they'd nearly drowned and then an afternoon and night of the deepest intimacy she'd ever experienced. They'd shared affection and their minds, but not their bodies. If they had spoken words of love and given of their bodies, too, she doubted she could have left him for any reason. But he'd kept their temperatures low, though she knew that wasn't what he'd intended when he took her there. She understood that their feelings for each other had changed, that they'd come to a reckoning point and had opted for caution and restraint. She hadn't been hurt nor had she attempted to seduce him when he bluntly suggested they leave early, because he couldn't spend another celibate night there with her.

She answered the phone reluctantly, since Adam had no reason to contact her that she could imagine. Her father's voice roared through the receiver.

"Where were you yesterday and last night? Your mother stayed in her room all day. I told you she's not well, and I thought you came back here to look after her."

Why hadn't she realized that her father manipulated her, using her mother, her brother, and one phony situation after another to control her? "I spent the time with friends," she said, and let her voice proclaim her right to do as she pleased. She hadn't lied, she'd been with Adam and the little creatures she'd met near the brook. For the first time his taunts had no effect on her. Loving Adam had made her strong, and her newfound relationship with her mother made her less dependent on her father for parental affection. She didn't want to hurt her father, though, so she didn't share with him her suspicion that Emily remained in her room to avoid him. She changed the subject.

"What do the police have to say about Timmy getting shot?"

"Your uncle Booker is dealing with it, and he'll bring Adam Roundtree to justice. Mark my word. You'll rue the day you turned your back on your own people." When she didn't answer, he added, "So you're ready to agree that he did it."

Annoyed, she told him in icy tones. "You'd save a lot of breath and energy, Daddy, if you'd get to know your daughter. I hold integrity inviolate, and I won't lie for a Grant or a Round-tree or anyone else." He hung up, dissatisfied with her as usual, but she shrugged it off, put on a top coat, and went out to buy milk. On an impulse, she stopped at a public phone and called her mother. Her father had just gone out, she learned, and decided to pay her mother a short visit.

"You're just glowing, darling," her mother said. "Were you with Adam this weekend? Rafer swears you were."

Surprised at the question and uncertain how to answer, Melissa only nodded. But Emily assured her that she hoped Melissa had been with him.

"Mama, are you suggesting—"

"I'm saying what it sounds like. I was a prude, insisting to Bill Henry that we wait until after we married. That was the fashion in those days. But we didn't marry, and I never knew him. A thousand times I've bemoaned the day I exacted that promise from him. Melissa, I've had thirty-one years to wonder what it's like to make love with a man who loves and cherishes me. Rafer and I both got cheated."

She noticed the quivers in her mother's voice and asked if she felt ill. "I don't feel sick, just weak all the time. Not a bit of energy. If I complain, Rafer takes me back to the doctor for more tests. I've been scanned so much I feel transparent. That's all these doctor do: tests and more tests and feed whatever it is they find into the computer. How the devil will the computer know what's wrong with me? It hasn't been to medical school." A wide grin spread across Melissa's face, and soon, peals of laughter erupted from her throat. Her mother had a devilish sense of humor, and all these years she hadn't known it.

In recent weeks she'd noticed an absence of the invisible weight, the aura of defeatism that she had always observed about her mother. She looked at her mother's rich brown, wrinkle-free face, naturally black hair, and svelte figure. Who'd guess she had lived for fifty-two years? The doctors wouldn't find her mother's illness in her bloodstream nor her vital organs. The name of Emily Grant's disease was despair, lack of a reason for living.

Melissa walked over to her mother and began to massage the back of her neck and her shoulders, all the while thinking and putting her mother in perspective. It should have been obvious that Emily's listlessness and myriad of complaints stemmed from discontentment with her life, that her total submissiveness to her husband was unnatural and partly phony, that she just didn't care enough to fight hard for her rights, that her reclusive behavior had the earmarks of a power play, a defensive tactic. Her fingers stilled, and she pulled a small footstool to the front of her mother's chair and sat down.

"Mama, why don't you get out of the house, volunteer at one of the shelters, teach in the Head Start program, tutor, read to the blind, anything except stay in this room. You have a college degree, Mama. And you're too young to fold up like this." Her heart constricted at the expectancy, the eagerness, mirrored in her mother's face, and hope welled up in her as they walked toward the foyer.

"Honey, I've never gone anywhere much without your father, except shopping, and I certainly haven't done a thing unless he wanted me to. Your grandfather wouldn't rest until I married Rafer and gave him some grandchildren, so I bowed to his wishes. You know the rest."

"Well, it's time you did something for yourself, Mama."

"I hear what you're saying, and I may try it, but you and I both know that nothing will give me back Bill Henry. And that's my problem. You make sure you don't ever have one like it."

"If I have a choice, Mama, I won't take the one that will make me miserable. So please don't worry about me, and get out of here and do something about your life."

Adam walked through the recreation room of the Rachel Hood Hayes Center for Women, talking to the women who had taken refuge there. Small children clung to several of them, fright still mirrored in their young eyes. He took pride in The Refuge, as it was popularly known, and he hurt for the women whose hard lives and cruel mates had forced them to leave their homes for a communal shelter. He had intended that the one being built in Hagerstown would have only private rooms and small apartments, but the continuing fiasco at the leather factory threatened to get out of hand, and since he used his Leather and Hides shares to finance his charities, including The Refuge, he'd had to retrench.

The crooks had struck again on Saturday night while he'd been at the lodge with Melissa. He forced himself not to think of her in connection with it. His heart dictated forbearance, but his common sense counseled him to challenge her. Reorienting his thoughts, he shook hands with a woman who had arrived at The Refuge so badly battered that he'd had her hospitalized for more than a week, patted an older woman, there for the third time, and headed for his small basement office.

Adam didn't wait for an elevator. He opened the door to the stairwell and stopped just short of colliding with Emily Grant.

"What?" They spoke simultaneously. Adam stepped back and held the door for her.

"Mind if I ask why you're here." He didn't care if she detected suspicion in his tone.

"I'm a volunteer. Why? Is something wrong?"

Adam braced a hand on each hip, took a deep breath and pierced her with an accusative gaze. "Did Rafer send you here?

He isn't satisfied with the damage we're getting at Leather and Hides and wants to start on The Refuge, is that it?" She appeared at first to wilt under his stern rebuff, but he could see her back stiffening.

"I don't know any more about Leather and Hides than what you just said, and I have no idea what Rafer is doing." That comment made him realize that Emily didn't know his relationship to The Refuge. Nothing on the door identified the place by its correct name, the Rachel Hood Hayes Center for Women. He took her arm and walked with her to his small office.

"Emily, I don't suppose you knew that I'm the founder of this place and its sole support. It's a memorial to my maternal grandmother." She told him that she hadn't.

"Melissa suggested that I do some volunteer work, Adam, but she doesn't know I've actually started. I needed something for myself and when I saw these women, I knew I could help them. My body hasn't been battered, but my brain certainly has. I've been happier here these past four days than at any time since...well, it's meant everything to me. I feel like a different person. Please let me stay, Adam. I know that when Rafer finds out, he'll want your neck and mine, too, but I have to do this and I'm not turning back."

He opened two of the soft drinks that he kept in a tiny refrigerator beneath his desk and handed one to her. "I want you to stay here as long as you like." He rubbed his chin reflectively. "Do you mean to tell me your husband doesn't know you're doing this?"

"It's a long story, Adam."

He forced himself not to glance at the elegant watch strapped to his left wrist. "I've got plenty of time." She gave him what he figured was a well-censored account of a troubled marriage, careful to omit mention of the main reason for it, and they spoke at length. He thought over what she'd told him and released his signature whistle.

"There's going to be hell to pay," he warned. Emily sipped some ginger ale and leaned back in her chair with all the serenity of a reclining Buddha.

"So what? I've always had hell to pay." He tapped the rickety wooden desk with the rubber end of a pencil and laid his head to one side, watching her carefully. He ruled out the possibility of her presence there as an effort by Rafer to manipulate him.

"And you say Melissa doesn't know about this?"

Emily leaned forward, as though to beseech him. "She suggested I do something, but she didn't mention this, and I haven't told her about it."

He nodded. According to the facts he now had, the cleavage between the two families didn't appear as great as he and other people thought. Yet it went deep. Wayne might feel strongly about it, but he wouldn't be unfair. And B-H disassociated himself from the feud. Its main keepers appeared to be Rafer and his mother, but two more fierce or more committed fighters he didn't care to meet.

"I'm happy to have you with us," Adam said, and walked with her a few paces down the hall to the elevator.

"Are we going to be friends?" she asked him, when he held the door open. In that moment, it cheered him that he'd adopted the habit of smiling.

"I think we are," he said with a smile and meant it. He went back to his office, feeling as though he and Melissa had a chance at happiness. He pulled the sheet from his fax machine and read, "Somebody mixed the chrome and zirconium samples, and we've got some useless fluids and a hell of a stench here.—Cal." So much for that, he muttered. He figured he'd just spent twenty seconds in a fool's paradise. Too much dirty water flowed under the bridge—seventy years of hatred, the sabotage, and the things about him that Melissa didn't know and for which she might not forgive him. They didn't stand a joker's chance.

A few days later, the Saturday after Thanksgiving Day, Melissa sat in Banks's kitchen while her friend altered a dress she'd recently bought.

"This is a great color for you," Banks said. "Turn around. It doesn't fit because your waist is too little for the rest of you." Melissa waited for the words that would follow Banks's melodramatic sigh and groaned when she said, "But I guess Adam likes it."

"Throw out all the bait you like, kiddo," Melissa said, "but this fish isn't biting."

"Come on. If he was my guy, I'd hire a blimp and trail a mile-high streamer behind it proclaiming 'Adam Roundtree is my man,' and, by damn, I'd sign it."

Melissa laughed. "You're hopeless."

"The least you could do is let me enjoy him vicariously."

"I don't kiss and tell, Banks, and I don't ask you about Ray."

Melissa knew her friend shrugged mainly for effect—she enjoyed attention and got a laugh when she said, "What's to ask about Ray? He fills the bill for the moment."

With the dress finished and pressed, they got into Melissa's car and went to look for antiques. Melissa saw an old, sterling silver apple designed with a bite taken out, teeth prints evident, and a loop at the bottom for a key chain. She had it wrapped and sent to Adam, ignoring Banks's raised eyebrow but not her succinct words: "What's he supposed to do, conquer or surrender?" They bought apple cider at a farm and stopped for lunch at the adjoining restaurant.

Melissa nodded toward an adjoining booth and asked Banks, "Do you hear what I hear?" They listened as two men aired their views on women working. One didn't want his wife to work, but the second disagreed on principle. He wanted an independent, interesting woman with a career of her own, one who stayed with him because she wanted him and not because she'd rather not work. His voice grew more persuasive when he admonished his companion, "Keep your ego out of the way and get a woman who's your equal. Who the hell cares whether bag carrots taste as good as the ones on a bunch or the kid's Reeboks last a week longer than some other brand? You can't stay in bed all the time, man. Then what do you do?"

Melissa glanced toward the familiar voice as she and Banks left their booth. Wayne Roundtree. She hoped Adam was as far ahead of most Frederick men on the issue as his brother appeared to be.

"Isn't that Wayne Roundtree?" Banks asked. "If I were a little younger...well, I could go for a man who thinks like that."

"You're always seeing a man you could go for."

"I'm not promiscuous, honey, but I'm not dead either," Banks assured her. "Take a hint and give Adam something to mull over. A man shouldn't be too sure of a woman." Melissa's deliberate smile denoted the contentment of a cat licking her whiskers. Let Banks think whatever she liked.

Adam pushed a shopping cart full of used books into The Refuge's small library and began shelving them. Ordinarily he didn't go to the place on Mondays, but he knew the volunteers— mostly older women—needed his help following the weekend's Thanksgiving celebrations, and he'd do as much as he could during his lunch hour.

"Let me do that, you must have more important things to do."

He turned toward the familiar voice and greeted Emily. "Thanks, but this will only take a minute. Do you still enjoy it here?"

"Oh, yes. I'm happier than I thought I could be. These women and girls are so grateful for the little care we give them that I'm humbled."

"Hasn't Rafer discovered this, or have you told him?" His left hand remained suspended above the cart, holding an old cookbook, while he awaited her answer. In the past few days, the sabotage at Leather and Hides had stepped up, though the incidents weren't major disasters, but small yet destructive acts. He had begun to look everywhere for clues and to suspect a widening circle of people.

"If he knew, he'd have said something." Emily's voice halted his musing. "Rafer isn't one to keep his peace about a thing that displeases him." Adam released a deep breath. How could a man not know what his wife did for four hours every day of the working week?

As if she'd sensed his unspoken question, she said, "We live separate lives, Adam. At least *now* I'm living a life." He told her that her health seemed improved, and she replied, "It's my mind that's finally working. Never let anybody force you into leading a double life." At his raised eyebrow, she added with a laugh, "Just listen to me. Nobody *could* force you to do that or anything else. All these years I've accepted public adoration and private scorn from Rafer—but like that old song 'New Day In The Mornin,' that's all behind me. I'm not living like that anymore."

Adam's hand grazed her shoulder in a tentative gesture. "Be careful. Don't provoke him unnecessarily." He finished shelving the books and glanced at the wall clock. Twenty-five minutes before he had to be at his office in the Jacob Hayes Building. He phoned a take-out shop to have a hamburger and coffee delivered there, told Emily good-bye, and strode briskly down Court Street, deep in thought. Rafer had accused him of shooting his nephew but had taken no legal action. Authorities hadn't even questioned him about it. Emily had been a volunteer at his charity for over two weeks, and Rafer didn't know it or pretended that he didn't. Meanwhile someone had found a nearly indecipherable way to destroy the very foundation of Leather and Hides. And that someone knew his moves and had the run of the factory. Melissa knew his moves, and Calvin Nelson had the run of the factory, but somehow they didn't fit, and the possibility of their disloyalty grew increasingly more remote.

He fingered the symbol of man's surrender to woman that he kept in his pocket. Almost every time he touched it, he laughed. Only a very secure woman with a riotous sense of humor would send a man a silver apple out of which a generous bite had been taken. Lord! He hoped she was innocent. He'd hate to give her up—at least not before it suited him.

Adam sipped his coffee, gripped his private phone, and listened to his brother.

"You remember that I ran a piece in the paper about industrial sabotage in general and hinted at our problems at Leather and Hides. Yesterday I got a call. The guy said that if Leather and Hides went down the drain, the Roundtrees deserved it, and that it was too bad Jacob Hayes wasn't alive to see it. I'm having difficulty believing that Cal is involved in this."

"So am I. Anything else?"

"What about Melissa, Adam? Are you holding back because you're passing time with her?"

Adam swung out of his chair and paced as far as the telephone cord would let him. "Wayne, don't make me tell you this again. Melissa Grant isn't time I'm killing."

He heard his brother snort. "Well, at least you recognize it. I don't suppose you'd be willing to enlist her help with this?"

"Leave it to me, Wayne."

"Alright. Alright. I haven't mentioned to anyone that you hired a private investigator."

"And don't. I'll keep you posted." He hung up, called Melissa, and invited her to dinner.


Bill Henry's visit around six o'clock surprised him. His uncle used that time to prepare his healthful meals, which he ate without fail at six thirty. "Noticed Wayne's short piece in *The Maryland Journal.* I see you still got problems at the plant. What do you make of it?"

"Inside job, but I think it's someone in cahoots with the Grants. Problem is who and why."

"Did it start before or after your began this thing with Melissa?"

"You're saying I started something with Melissa?"

"Yeah. And you're knee deep in it. Son, I hope you're not following in my footsteps. But then I don't suppose you will. I doubt that even the Grants and your mother could bring you to your knees, and they're masters at it."

Adam rubbed the back of his neck, remembering that Melissa had twice suggested he speak to B-H about their families' feud. He stared at his uncle.

"You want to explain that?"

"I thought you knew." He related to Adam the tale of his ill-fated engagement to Melissa's mother.

Horrified, Adam braced his hands at his hips and whistled.

"That explains plenty." Emily's behavior toward him. Rafer's hatred of him and his family. B-H himself, his bachelorhood and reclusive behavior. He walked with his uncle to the family room, opened the bar and poured a ginger ale for B-H and a shot of bourbon for himself.

Adam looked at the man who had played such an important role in his youthful development and for whom he cared deeply though he hadn't wanted to imitate him. Less so now.

"Emily volunteers at The Refuge four hours a day, Monday through Friday, and when Rafer finds out—"

B-H interrupted him, his face hard with incredulity. "Don't tempt me, Adam. She's still wearing Rafer Grant's ring on the third finger of her left hand."

Adam set his drink aside, gazed at his uncle, and then shook his head. His words bore a soft, funereal quality. "After all these years? Three decades?"

He went back to his room to sort out his thoughts. He ought to call Melissa and cancel their date, but he couldn't disappoint her. And he admitted that he needed to see her. His mother's footsteps in the hallway forced him into action, and he quickly left his room, greeting her in passing before loping down the stairs. He knew she'd read Wayne's article and had primed herself to speak to him about Melissa and her family. He barely heard the rain pummeling the roof of his car as he steered it against the windy gusts. Bill Henry still loved Emily Morris after thirty years. Could what he felt for Melissa become so powerful? And would it do to him what loving a woman had done to his uncle? Would it drive him into himself?

Melissa finished dressing in a black velvet pants suit just as the doorbell announced Adam's arrival. Breathless with anticipation, she swung open the door, but her smile quickly disappeared and her face lost some of its glow.

"Hi."

She didn't know how to respond to this no-nonsense, harsh, and businesslike Adam, the one she hadn't seen since before they'd first made love. Scanning his face, she greeted him with a careful smile, the kind she'd give a client.

"Hello, Adam. Won't you come in."

Adam followed her into the living room, declined her offer of a seat, and ambled with deliberateness from one end of the room to the other, his overcoat open and his hands stuffed in his pants pocket. She sat in a comfortable chair, perplexed at his pacing, but certain that it allowed him either to rein in his temper or to deal with his feelings for her.

She opened her mouth, aghast, when he stopped before her and asked in a voice devoid of emotion, "Why did you make love with me that first time? A twenty-eight-year-old virgin doesn't do that without solid reason. Why?" Stunned at the bluntness with which he'd asked that intimate question, and for the second time, too, and annoyed with herself for having spent the afternoon longing and waiting to see him, she replied in like manner.

"You're Wall Street's boy wonder. If you can't figure it out yourself, my explanation wouldn't mean anything to you, either."

He pulled her up from the chair and into his arms. "You tell me. I want to hear it from your lips."

She couldn't bear having his arms around her in that impersonal way—she wanted more of his warmth, the gentle caring of which she knew him capable, but she was damned if she'd show it.

"Tell me," he urged, his tone dispassionate.

"If you just came here to get your ego stroked, I'm sorry to disappoint you. Mine's been out of sorts since the last time I saw you. So nothing doing."

"What do you mean?" She knew he'd remember that when they'd last been together, they'd spend the night at his lodge, she on the sofa and he on the floor nearby. He'd reached up and held her left hand in his right one until they'd fallen asleep. She'd wanted to sleep in his arms, but he'd said they needed to wait until he resolved some undisclosed problems before becoming more deeply involved, that they already risked more that he thought wise.

"I think you know the answer, and I also think we shouldn't

see each other anymore until all of the problems you mentioned are cleared up. If ever they are." She had to look away from the lights twinkling in his eyes, challenging her to give in to him, to tell him what he demanded to know. "I want you to leave, Adam."

"This is another first. You're the first—and only—woman to give me her feminine truth and the first woman or man with the nerve, or perhaps I should say the chutzpa, to invite me to leave anyplace whatever." She twisted out of his arms and turned toward the foyer as though expecting him to follow, but his hand heavy on her shoulder detained her.

"You don't think I'm leaving here before you answer my question, do you?"

Her nose lifted upward. "What was your question?"

He grasped her shoulders, drew her to him, and looked into her eyes. "If you won't say it, I'll tell you, and I dare you to deny it. You gave yourself to me because I'm the only man you've ever wanted. Ever loved. Deny it, and you lie. Unless of course you want me to believe you used yourself as a decoy while your re-latives trashed my leather factory."

She gasped, appalled. "How dare you accuse me of such a thing!"

"I didn't. I gave you the choice."

"I don't care what you believe," she bluffed.

He pulled her closer. "Oh, but you do. You care, alright." She thought his demeanor softened. He'd never before made a de-liberate effort to seduce her. When they'd made love, he had led her, but only where she indicated she wanted to go. She knew he meant to push her over the edge, but she didn't intend to ac-commodate him.

"Which is it?" he murmured. "Tell me."

Loving him as she did, she cared what he thought of her and how he felt about her, so she threw caution aside though she knew she'd regret it. "You know I didn't throw myself at you. How could you think I'd make love with you because of some feud?" His heated gaze toyed with her.

"Adam, what do you want? Please!"

"If what you say is true, you did it because you love me. Which is it? Tell me," he persisted, never taking his eyes from hers, his breath harsh and uneven.

"Yes. Yes, I love you. Yes. Yes." He wrapped her to him, kissed her tears and hugged her until she hurt. Her whimpers must have alerted him to his use of strength, because he loosened his hold and soothed her with gentle strokes over her back and down her arms.

He wanted to tell her that he felt as if her words would cause his heart to burst, but he couldn't bring himself to divulge the two episodes in his life that she might not forgive, and worse still, there remained the slim chance that he'd have to prosecute her.

"Alright." He walked them over the couch, sat down, and patted his lap, inviting her to sit there. "My questions may make you angry, but I have to ask them." He hugged her to him and blurted, "Tell me what you know about Timothy's gunshot wounds." He'd expected her to attempt to get up, and he restrained her, nibbling on her ear to soften the gesture.

"You're wasting your time and mine," she threw at him, bitterness lacing her voice. "I haven't seen Timmy since that happened. We're not friends, Adam. He thought I could find a cushy job for him, though I suspect that was Daddy's idea. I referred him to a bus company in Hagerstown, but he hasn't reported back to me on it. Anything else?"

"Bear with me in this, please."

"Why should I? You got the confession from me that you wanted, and of course it didn't occur to you that I also need reassurance about your feelings for me. I want you to leave." He put his arms around her and held her close, needing her with every atom of his being, needing to make love with her, to make certain that she belonged to him. But he'd lost the moment. Her pride wouldn't let her allow him that intimacy, and he didn't want to see her without her elegant sense of self.

"Are you going?" she asked, though her voice didn't convince him of her sincerity.

He caressed her arms, inhaled her woman's scent, and let his gaze roam over the warm, feminine body that reclined in his arms. Shudders plowed through him, and in a voice hoarse with desire, he said, "I care. Dammit, you know I care. Why do you think I don't stay away from you? It isn't because I'm a masochist, though I'm beginning to wonder about that." He felt her relax against him, and sensed a giving of her trust.

"Melissa, I asked you about Timmy, because you know your father accused me of wounding him. But did you know that I haven't been officially charged with it, and I can't find out whether anyone has been formally accused? Did it actually happen?"

She nodded. "Mama says it did." He had to ask her about Leather and Hides, but considering how she reacted to the question about Timothy, he didn't care to risk it.

"Adam, tell me what's going on at Leather and Hides." His astonishment must have been mirrored in his face, because she explained that B-H had mentioned it to her. "Hadn't you planned to tell me about it?"

He stood but resisted the urge to pace. "I tried several times, but I couldn't represent it to you as it really is, because I didn't want to hurt you." He saw her back stiffen, and it occurred to him that he ought to be grateful for Melissa's even temper.

"What's it got to do with hurting me? I don't have anything to do with it."

Adam considered his words carefully. "There are some who think your family may be involved, though I'm certain that the culprit has help from at least one of our employees."

She leaned forward, squinting, and he could almost see her mental wheels spring into action. "Do you believe I'd knowingly hurt you?"

"I don't want to believe it." He watched her rise from the sofa as a woodland sprite would drift up from a spring, though her vacant eyes belied serenity.

"But you do?"

He couldn't lie. He considered her guilt in the sabotage unlikely, but he hadn't exonerated her, either. "I'm a cautious man, Melissa, and I—"

She interrupted him, walking out of the living room as she did so. "I'm going to the kitchen, and I want you to be out of my house when I get back here."

Her words stabbed him. He'd hurt her, and for once he knew that special kind of pain, a deep agony that only one woman could relieve. He walked into the hallway and looked toward the kitchen. He couldn't see her, turned in that direction, and stopped. Until he cleared up the mess at that factory, what could he say to her? He had no choice but to do as she'd asked.

Melissa wouldn't have believed she'd allowed herself to be duped a second time. He'd numbed her senses, coaxed her into submission with tenderness and with his blazing heat, and she'd spilled her longing, told him her heart's secret. Lost herself in him. He'd said he cared, but he'd confessed it grudgingly, and minutes later he had implicated her family and all but accused her of aiding the ruination of his business. If any member of her family had a hand in it, she'd find out.

Adam sat at the desk in his bedroom, planning his strategy to trap the culprits, when he received a call from his private investigator.

"I'm certain it was Melissa Grant," the man insisted, when Adam suggested that he might be mistaken. "I saw her here at the factory about an hour ago, but she only looked around outside the gate and left. I waited for any follow-up before calling you."

"Thanks. Stay there, and if she comes back, call me." He didn't welcome that news. He had discarded the idea that she might be involved—now he had to rethink his strategy. Had she intended to meet someone? If not, what had she sought? He called his manager.

"I secured the gates myself, Adam, but someone gained entrance, and that person must have had a key. I can't even guess who it might have been. This time the damage involved finished shoe leathers. The criminal has realized that it is more damaging to attack after we've spent the money and time tanning the leathers. Damned if I know what to make of it." Adam thanked him and hung up. He wouldn't call local authorities. Why waste the energy? Rafer had the deputy chief of police or deputy sheriff, as he preferred to be called, in his pocket. He'd deal with it tomorrow.

He got to his office around nine o'clock the next morning and called the Physicians' Registry. A young doctor named Grant practiced in Hagerstown. On a hunch, he called the office, and without hesitating the unsuspecting young receptionist gave him the information he cleverly wrested from her. He taped their conversation.

Next he headed for The Refuge, where he knew he'd find Emily, engaged her in casual conversation, and satisfied himself that she had no part in the crimes at his factory.

He'd begun to like Emily Grant. "Are you sure you're up to this work? It's mentally as well as physical demanding."

Her smile reminded him of Melissa when she teased him. "I love it. And I'm not frail, Adam. That's what I've been led to believe for over thirty years. Not a bit of it's true. I'm strong."

He squeezed her shoulder in a gesture of affection. "I'm glad you've joined us. I like your spirit. Have you discussed this with Rafer yet?"

She hadn't, she told him without any apparent regret, and asked him to let it be.

"What about Melissa?"

She shook her head. "This is my own. I'll share it when the time comes. When I have to." He patted her shoulder and headed back to the Jacob Hayes Building. Emily Grant could grow on a person. He could appreciate his uncle's passion for her: a lovely, giving woman. She must have been captivating in her youth, for she remained a beauty, and she could charm a mouse away from its cheese.

Adam called his New York office. He'd have to get back there soon, but he couldn't leave Frederick so long as his relationship

with Melissa hung in limbo, and to straighten it out, he'd first
have to unravel the mystery at Leather and Hides. A short conversation with Jason Court assured him that, for the time being,
he needn't worry about his New York office. He had two detectives working in the plant and had hired a private investigator,
but the criminal who wrought destruction in the factory seemingly at will remained undetected.

Impatient with their lack of progress, Adam dressed in jeans,
a sweater, leather jacket, and sneakers after dinner that evening,
and to avoid the noise and headlights of his car, rode his bicycle
to the factory. The moon had shone brightly all week, and he
considered himself fortunate that it settled behind the clouds as
he left home, affording him the cover he needed. He secured the
bike and leaned well hidden against a large oak tree. A red
Corvette appeared, and its driver parked and waited. Very soon,
another car arrived. Apprehension gripped him as the door of the
familiar car opened, and stark, naked pain raced through him
when he saw Melissa get out of the car and walk around to the
driver's side of the Corvette. He watched, motionless, as she
stood there and talked with the driver for at least ten minutes,
before the Corvette drove off and left her standing there alone
in the darkness. Minutes later she, too, drove away.

As if he shouldered the weights of Atlas, Adam moved with
slow steps toward his bicycle, numbed with pain. He mounted
the bike just when a third car arrived. The intrigue heightened
as the driver cut the motor, turned off the lights, and waited for
thirty minutes before driving. Whoever it was didn't get out of
the car. Crossed wires, Adam decided. Melissa would answer to
him for her part in the scheme.

# Chapter 11

Melissa sat in her office the next morning, tortured by what she'd discovered and bleary-eyed from the sleepless night it had caused her. She hadn't answered her phone nor the loud knocks on her door the night before for fear of reprisal or that she might get into a hassle with her father. Her head lolled against the back of her chair, and she tried to concentrate in spite of the intruding noise. She hadn't realized that it was she who kept up the consistent, rhythmic rapping until she noticed the wooden letter opener waving up and down in her hand. She laid it aside and attempted to make notes for her regular morning calls to her satellite offices in Baltimore and New York. But no sooner had she begun to gather her thoughts than Adam burst unannounced through the door, and she'd never seen a colder, more furious and feral expression on a human face.

"What's the matter?" she asked before he could speak.

"You ask me what's the matter?" he growled. She couldn't imagine what her facial expression had imparted to him, because his anger evaporated, and a sad, bitter expression cloaked his handsome face.

"You want to know what the matter is? I'll tell you." He spoke slowly and with deadly softness as though killing his feelings, shredding his emotions. "Have you known all this time who was ruining my business, trashing my factory? Why didn't you tell me, Melissa? Don't you feel that you owe me *any* allegiance?"

"You're out of your mind," she protested, trying to figure out why he seemed so certain.

He leaned over her desk, his face inches from hers. "I was, but not anymore. Just two nights ago you swore innocence, and you curled up in my arms and told me you loved me. You defended me against the charge that I shot your cousin. Was that a screen?"

She pushed her chair back and braced her palms against her desk. Horror gripped her at the depth of disappointment in his eyes. "You're wrong, Adam," she said in a strong voice, but one that held such sadness that she barely recognized it as her own.

He didn't give quarter. "Oh, no, I'm not. I saw you there last night. The three of you got your wires crossed, didn't you? Your other partner, whoever he was, drove up right after you left and waited a full thirty minutes for you. Did they meet at your house later? Is that why you didn't answer your door and ignored your telephone?"

She wouldn't have believed that she could endure such pain. She took a deep breath and told the man she loved—the man who still leaned toward her, his anger less apparent now and his face warped with sadness—that she'd done nothing for which she felt ashamed and that if he believed her guilty of so heinous a crime, nothing she said in her defense would matter.

Melissa sat tongue-tied, stunned, while he walked out of her office without another word, leaving the door ajar. Her glance fell upon the framed portrait reproductions that hung on her office walls, and she winced as every eye seemed to accuse her. None of them would have tolerated such an unfounded accusation without a history-making defense. Frederick Douglass wouldn't have, nor would Sojourner Truth, Thurgood Marshall, Martin Luther King, Jr., or Eleanor Roosevelt.

She'd heard that a thin line often separated love and hatred and took some solace in knowing that Adam could not have expressed such bitterness, such disillusionment, had he not cared deeply. He would discover the truth, she hoped, but in her present mood, she didn't give a snap what he found out about that factory.

She reviewed events of the night before and wondered whether she should have told Adam. She buzzed her secretary with the intention of asking her to dial her New York office, but to her amazement her mother walked into the room. Emily had

visited her at home once, but had not come to the office. She was
about to tell her mother of Adam's accusations, but Emily Grant
had her own agenda.

"You don't know it," she began, "but for the past few weeks,
I've been volunteering four hours a day at The Refuge. That's
the shelter for abused women and children that Adam operates
over on Oak Street," she rushed on, as though oblivious to her
daughter's air of incredulity. Melissa ushered her to a chair.

"Sit down, and tell me what you're talking about." Still trying
to adjust to the effects of her earlier episode with Adam, she all
but reeled under the impact of her mother's words.

"I'm talking about your father found out that I've been volunteering at Adam's charity, and he packed his personal things
and moved out of the house."

"He what?" Melissa reached for the corner of her desk to
steady herself. She'd had about as much as she could handle for
one morning. First, Adam's rage, and now this. "Are you sure?"

"Of course I'm sure. He raved at me for two hours last night,
and when I got downstairs this morning, he'd already packed two
bags and put them in the foyer. He said he's moving into an
apartment."

"Oh, Mama, I'm so sorry." She watched in awe as her mother
tossed her handbag into a chair, jerked off her coat, braced her
hands on her hips, and stood akimbo.

"I don't want anybody's sympathy. I don't need it," Emily told
her. "I want a divorce, and I'm going to get it. I've spent over
half of my life letting people walk over me, behaving like a nin-
compoop." Her pacing increased in speed. "That's my house,
and I'm the one with the prestige and the clout in this town, and
it's time I acted like it."

Melissa advanced toward her mother as though reluctant to
disturb her. "Mama, why don't you sit down while I run to the
machine and get you some tea." She blanched from her mother's
withering look.

"I forgot to add, honey, that I'm not going to let anybody pa-
tronize me and that includes you, much as I love you. Your

father's done me a favor, and I'm getting out from under his heel. He walked out of the door grumbling that the whole thing was a Hayes-Roundtree conspiracy, that they inveigled me into working at The Refuge just to humiliate him. To hear him tell it, they're the reason his party didn't nominate him for mayor, then for congress, and finally passed over him for governor. Damned if I'd admit anybody was that powerful."

"Mama!"

"What's the matter?" Emily asked her. "Didn't you ever stop to wonder where you got your spunk? You didn't think you got it from your father, did you?"

"I can't believe Daddy left you. He's always so concerned about what people think."

Emily shrugged with apparent disdain. "It isn't the first time. He left me once before, and you were born while we were separated. I think it's the reason he always treated you as though you were his stepchild, rather than his own blood daughter. I thought that after you grew to look so much like him, he'd behave differently, but you can't teach an old dog new tricks." She reached for her coat. "Well, I thought you should know, and tonight I'll call Schyler and tell him. We'll talk this evening. I've got an appointment with my lawyer in twenty minutes."

Melissa watched her mother swish out of the door, plopped down in the nearest chair, and expelled a long breath. *What next?*

"I might as well get this over with," Melissa told herself, dialing her father's office number. She identified herself, and it annoyed her that his secretary nevertheless asked him whether he'd care to take the phone.

"I suppose you and your mother have been talking," he said by way of a greeting. "I can't stand any more of their humiliating tactics, Melissa, and I won't live with a woman who's in their pay." Melissa attempted to explain that her mother volunteered at The Refuge and received no pay.

"I don't expect you to understand," he said. "You're having an affair with him, and she's working for him. A man can take just so much. Both of you seem to have forgotten that those people stole your birthright. Old Jacob Hayes bilked your grand-father, and you're consorting with his rich descendants. I'm ashamed of both of you." He hung up.

Tired of the tale and the excuse it provided, she decided the time had come to face him down. She drove to his office building, went in, and started past his secretary.

"You can't walk in there," the woman hissed. "Visitors have to be announced."

"I don't need your permission to see my father," Melissa replied, still miffed at the way in which the secretary had treated an earlier phone call. She opened his door, and he glanced up, then continued writing. She hated that his refusal to acknowl-edge her presence drained her of her anger. She attempted to reason with him.

"Daddy, why do you hold on to that myth? You know it isn't true. You know my grandfather withdrew his money from that venture and nearly ruined Adam's grandfather. Anyway, it isn't your feud, it's Mama's, and she dropped it years ago."

"How dare you speak to me about that?" She didn't ask him what he meant, but assumed he referred to her mother's broken engagement and shifted the subject to a more pressing concern.

"You know how Timmy got shot and who did it, don't you Daddy? And you know the Roundtrees had nothing to do with it, don't you?" She ignored his sputter and said what she should have said days earlier. "I told you Adam was with me that night. Well, if you accuse me publicly, I'll tell the town of Frederick where we were."

She heard the sadness in her father's voice and saw the grimness that lined his face, but she couldn't let that sway her. He had no interest in upholding the truth, only in besting the Roundtrees and Hayeses.

"I never thought I'd live to see the day one of my children would take sides with those people against me," he told her in the weary voice of one facing defeat. "Why do you defend him? He's nothing to us."

"You're mistaken, Daddy," she told him, her voice strong and sure. "Adam Roundtree is my life, and if you force him to go to court, I'll stand with him." What had she said? She stood looking at the man for whose love and approval she had begged most of her life and felt as though she had suddenly flown free of him. He—a lawyer sworn to uphold the law—would ruin a man's reputation in order to shield his nephew from what she was certain involved some kind of crime. He didn't deserve her blind devotion. Perhaps no one deserved that.

Rafer Grant stared at his daughter. "Just like your mother. Hot after the Hayeses." He picked up his pen and returned to his writing. "Well, both of you can have them." She stood there long after he'd dismissed her, giving him a chance to soften his blow, but he continued to ignore her. She left, thinking him a lonely man.

Adam despaired of getting any work done, and for the remainder of the morning, roamed around in his office shuffling in his mind his unsatisfactory conversation with Melissa. She hadn't attempted to defend herself, and he had seen the honesty in her shock and outrage at his accusation. He couldn't imagine why she would drive out to the factory alone on successive nights if not to meet someone. And she had met someone. Yet when he'd confronted her with it, she'd withheld information that he needed. He slapped his right fist into the palm of his left hand. Alright, so he'd gone about it wrong; he'd accused her. He'd try another tactic.

When he walked into Melissa's office early that afternoon, Adam brushed past Magnus Cooper as he left. Angered beyond reason, he skipped the greeting and demanded, "What's he doing here?"

"We have a contract. Remember? I've just found a ranch manager for him." Relieved that she ignored both his temper and his audacity, he said in a more even tone, "I thought you made it a policy to take the employees to the new boss, but at least you avoided that long trip to Houston."

"Magnus thinks I ought to have an office in the capital of every state. He wants to invest in my business."

Adam tried to shake off his annoyance at her use of the man's first name. "And what do you think?"

"He's impressed with my work, and he made a good case for a bigger operation," she said, letting the words come out slowly as if to keep him dangling.

"And?" She squinted at him and, in spite of himself, he softened toward her.

She shrugged. "Then he or somebody else would own my business. I said no thanks. He was very disappointed."

Adam blew out a deep sigh. "I'll just bet he was—he won't have an excuse to come up here to see you." He ignored her silent censure. "He may fool you with his trumped-up reasons for hanging around you, but he isn't fooling himself and definitely not me." He noticed that her voice lacked its usual verve and color and told himself to lighten up.

"Am I interrupting something private?" Banks asked, surprising them since neither had heard her approach. "Your secretary must have stepped out," she explained to Melissa. "Bessie called me. She just got in a load of stuff at Yesteryear, and if we get down there this afternoon, we can have our pick before she does her Christmas ads." She must have noticed their preoccupation, Adam decided, when she exclaimed, "Oops! See you later," and ducked out of the door.

"Melissa, we have to talk, but not here. We need to speak openly and honestly with each other, and we need privacy for that. Can we get together this evening?" He suspected from her deep breath and the way in which her fingers had begun to drum her desk that she intended to refuse.

"I'm not about to let you harass me the way you did this morning, so whatever you have to say, you may say now."

"Fine. Lock your door." She stood and moved toward it but stopped when he said, "Not even your friend, Banks, would resist broadcasting the fact that you locked the door with only the two of us in here."

He had the advantage, but that didn't mean he'd keep it. "Well?" He persisted, standing to leave.

"Alright, Adam," she said, with obvious reluctance. "I'll be home around eight tonight." But at seven o'clock that evening she called him, canceled their date, and refused to give an excuse.

"I can't see you tonight."

"That's it? No reason?"

"That's it."

Melissa hung up, threw off her robe, and crawled into bed. She had no appetite and hadn't bothered to eat dinner. The day's happenings crowded her thoughts. Her mother had filed for a divorce, and her unrepentant father pouted somewhere, sad and alone. She'd telephoned her brother, thousands of miles away in Kenya, in an effort to understand how it could have happened. His summation had astonished her.

"I used to wish they'd split up, because I didn't know which one of them to sympathize with, and they both needed it. Maybe they'll salvage the rest of their lives. I hope so."

The day's events had undermined her sense of identity, and she lacked the strength to endure another of Adam's interrogations. Tangling with him that morning had left her raw, and after that, the dam had burst. If she could have expected him to greet her with love and understanding, she'd have run to him. But he wouldn't come prepared to meet her needs, only to wring from her what he required for his own peace of mind. No. She couldn't see him.

Adam rose from his bed and stared out at the still dark morning. He had to see Melissa, to arrive at an understanding with her and to find out what she knew about the incidents at Leather and Hides. Although he'd seen her there and witnessed what appeared to be her collusion with people intent on destroying his property, he didn't want to believe her capable of it. Yet what was he to think? Why hadn't she defended herself? He dressed in woolen pants, a long-sleeved knitted T-shirt, crewneck sweater, and leather jacket and drove into Frederick. He parked four blocks from Melissa's house in order to thwart the local gossipmongers and strode briskly through the darkness to her front door. She probably wouldn't appreciate a visit at seven o'clock in the morning, but if her night had been as rough as his, at least he wouldn't awaken her.

She answered after several rings, and he wondered why she seemed relieved to see him.

"You could have been someone intent on mischief," she explained in response to his question.

He didn't wait for her invitation to enter, and once inside surprised himself by asking, "What about Magnus Cooper?" He hadn't realized that her relationship with the man bothered him that much.

She tightened her robe, walked into the living room, and sat on the sofa. "Where is it written, Adam, that I have to explain my behavior to you?" He wished she wouldn't squint—every time he saw her do it, she all but unraveled him. He pulled off his jacket and tossed it near her on the sofa.

"It is written in the tomes of common decency, Melissa. You've been in my arms, and I've been inside of you. That gives me some rights."

She sucked her teeth and waved her hand as though to say, Don't fool yourself.

Adam took a chair opposite her. "Let's not bicker. The problem at the factory is getting out of hand, and if I don't find out who is responsible, we may lose it. Who did you follow there? And who shot Timothy, Melissa? Tell me what you know. It if weren't for you, I'd go to the FBI about this, but I'll level with you. My list of suspects includes three members of your family. Tell me you're not involved, and I'll believe you."

"If you need my verbal assurance, there's no point in my giving it."

He saw her lips quiver and her composure falter as she fought tears, and he told himself he wouldn't let her tears influence him, but he couldn't remain unmoved by the sight of water glistening in her eyes.

"What is it? Don't. I don't want to cause you pain." He'd never seen her cry, never seen her lacking the calm assurance that defined her character. Alarmed, he stepped to her and put his arms around her. "What is it?" he whispered, bending to hear her broken words.

"My family's falling apart. My father has left my mother, moved out of their house with all of his personal belongings, and Mama's actually happy that he's gone. She retaliated by filing for a divorce. Schyler stays as far away from our parents as he can get, because he can't stand to see them live out their farce, making the best of their painful marriage. And Daddy attributes every misfortune he's ever had to the Hayes and Roundtrees. No matter how remote the issue, if it didn't go his way, he holds your family responsible. He's a failed man, Adam. He wanted to play football but couldn't make the varsity. He wanted my mother, but although she married him, in her heart she belonged only to Bill Henry Hayes. And he wanted a career as a politician, but he lost the most celebrated legal case this region's ever witnessed, one that he should have won, but for his own inefficiency. After that, he could never win his party's support."

Adam eased her out of his arms. The time had come—he'd known it would. But he hadn't expected that he would have to confess responsibility for something that weighed so heavily on her and to do it at a time when she needed his strength. And at a time when he questioned her role in the attempted ruination of his family. With his hands lightly on her shoulders, he urged her to sit.

"I have to tell you something, Melissa—something I've postponed mentioning because I didn't know how to broach it to you." He stopped talking and thought for a minute, aware that she didn't press him to continue though she scrutinized his every gesture. "That isn't quite accurate," he amended. "The truth is, I knew I should have told you the first time I took you to my lodge, but I wasn't ready to take the risk that you wouldn't forgive me. I'm not ready for that now, either, but I don't have a choice. When I was sixteen, I found a lawyer's briefcase that contained court papers in the men's room at a local restaurant, but I noticed that it belonged to Rafer Grant, and in an act of vengeance I left them there without telling Rafer about them. I hadn't cared what the next finder did with them." He paused, his voice softening as though in regret. "I later learned that the brief pertained to the defense of a prominent person, and that because he didn't have the papers, Rafer's summary to the jury had been sloppy and ineffectual. He lost the case."

He shifted his stance, uncomfortable in the silence that hung between them. He got the impression that she wanted to recall something that eluded her, and he waited with as much patience as he could muster. At last she spoke.

"I've heard about that case Lord knows how many times. Daddy's excuse was that he'd misplaced his brief." Her cynical laugh jarred him. "And that's probably the only thing that happened to him after he married Mama that he didn't blame a member of your family for." She folded her arms, running her hands up the wide sleeves of her robe. "You couldn't have been more than fourteen or fifteen at the time. What could have upset you so badly that you'd do such a thing?"

"I can't tell you without reflecting upon someone else. Remember that I didn't hide it or take it—I just didn't tell him I'd seen it. But I didn't care if someone else took it. I hated the word Grant."

Her eyes widened. "But you were a child. Why?"

"I had a reason, a personal one, but looking back, I admit that I didn't behave honorably. It taught me a lesson, too: I never carry important papers in a briefcase unless I've stored a copy elsewhere." The slow shake of her head, her pensive expression, were not the reaction he'd anticipated. She didn't show anger.

"I don't know what to say to this. Whatever made us think we could have a normal relationship as other men and women do? There's too much bad blood between us."

He wondered if she felt as ill fated, as resigned, as her seemingly careless shrug suggested. No matter, he had no intention of landing on his face because Rafer Grant hadn't shown guts enough to fight adversity.

"A man doesn't allow a single incident to bring him down,

to circumscribe his whole life. Such a man will use any excuse, any crutch."

Melissa opened her mouth to defend her father, but remembered that she had stopped doing that. She spoke mostly to herself. "Do you know what it means to spend your life trying to please someone, only to have the scales fall from your eyes, only to realize that such blind devotion is undeserved?"

"Rafer?"

She nodded.

"Blind devotion is never deserved." He kicked at the carpet, looked down at her, shook his head, and walked toward the opposite end of the room.

"Adam, will you please stop pacing. It's unsettling." He did as she asked, but his close scrutiny told her that he wanted to gauge her mood, to figure out what had prompted her remark. She didn't enlighten him. Why should she tell him what she felt when she watched his muscles ripple, or that the sight of his tight buttocks and long masculine legs cased erotically in his pants challenged her sense of propriety?

He returned to his seat, leaned forward, and said, "You're your father's only daughter. How could he not love you? How could *anybody* not..." He didn't complete the sentence, and she refused to raise her hopes by doing it for him. He sat with his right sneaker resting on his left knee, and her gaze caught his long slim foot sockless and unshod and the circumstance in which she'd seen it. Her mouth watered. Her right hand went to her tingling breast, and she shifted her position on the sofa. Flustered, she locked her gaze on a group of snapshots that rested on her mantelpiece and swallowed the saliva that accumulated in her mouth.

"Melissa!" She resisted the pull of his voice and wouldn't look at him.

"Look at me," he purred with the soft growl of a great cat preparing to mount its mate. As if programmed to do so, her eyes found his beloved face, and she drew in her breath when her gaze locked into his seductive stare, his knowing look.

She glanced away. Good Lord! She nearly panicked at the realization that she still wore her robe and her bikini panties. Did he think she'd sat with him dressed in that way just to entice him? She stood, tightening the robe as she did so. She'd greeted him in that robe once before, she recalled, and he'd spent the night with her. Not this time. She started toward the door.

"Where are you going?"

"To get dressed."

"Why?" The sizzling hot, steely expression in his eyes told her that her robe was more than she needed. She tugged it closer to her body.

"Come here and sit on my lap, honey." With a hand in each of his pockets, he uncrossed his knee, spread his legs, and leaned back in the chair. "Come here, sweetheart." Liquid legs propelled her to him.

"I don't want this, Adam. We can't solve anything between the sheets." He reached up, gathered her in his arms, and lowered her to his left knee. Tremors of anticipation raced through her at his deep, masculine laugh.

"That's the only place we ever solve anything. We want each other, so don't bother to deny what you're feeling."

She shrugged to display an air of indifference. "I've decided to deny myself. Self-denial builds character."

"And guarantees sleepless nights. Come on, honey. Open your mouth for me."

Her stubbornness gave way to compliance when she felt him rise strong and rigid against her hip, and she eagerly sought his lips. She reeled under the impact of his loving kiss. As soon as she returned his fire, his kiss gentled, and he showered her with tenderness, feathering kisses over her lips and eyes. Cherishing her. She reveled in it. Oh, it felt so good to be in his arms.

She wanted to hold him forever, but his reason for being there flitted through her mind, and she couldn't help withdrawing and knew that he sensed it. He held her away from him, studying her countenance.

"I need to make love with you, but I need more. I can't give myself to you halfheartedly, and I don't want you to do that, either. You're important to me, Melissa. Do you know anything about the problems we're having at the factory?" He curled her to him as one would hold a baby. "Can't you understand that I have to solve that problem, and that as long as I don't know where you stand in this, my loyalties are split and I'm unable to do my job effectively?"

She took a deep breath, mused over his words, and sought middle ground. "I can tell you that I don't know who shot Timmy. The other thing I know is that Timmy's daddy is the deputy chief of police, and Mama says he's always taken care of Timmy's numerous brushes with the law. I know that much, Adam." She leaned back and looked him straight in the eye. "But I will not exonerate myself for you. Not now or ever."

She welcomed his audible sigh of relief. At least she could give him that much without compromising her integrity.

He released her, stood, and walked to the far end of the room. "Will you lose any sleep knowing that I intend to seek the help of the FBI?"

She couldn't hold back the smile that curved her lips. "Not one wink. Crafty rascal, aren't you?" He ran his right hand over his hair, not taking his eyes off of her.

"So I've been told. You won't yield on this, and neither will I, but you've given me something and for now I'm satisfied."

She yawned. "Would you like some coffee?"

He slid his hands into his pockets and propped his foot on the rung of an antique chair. Then he laid his head to one side and cocked an eyebrow. "*Coffee?* You're kidding. I want *you.*"

Adam lay on his back, his left arm securing her to his side. He'd made love to her twice, and the first time he'd been able to hold back as he had with every woman since, as a boy of fifteen, he'd gotten the strength to walk away from the one who taught him to crave her and then humiliated him for it. With her every move, Melissa had asked him for more than he gave her, but still he'd been able to withhold a vital part of himself. And with all her sweet giving, he'd been left unful-filled, knowing he'd brought that on himself. She seemed to have sensed that his war with himself didn't involve her, and she'd stroked and soothed him as he rested above her spent, but unsatisfied.

Minutes later, still sheathed within her warmth, he had reached full readiness again. He'd kissed her with all the tenderness he felt for her, and with his eyes had asked her permission to continue. Her sweet smile of acquiescence had sent his heart soaring, and he'd cherished her, because it was what he felt, and she'd suddenly gone wild beneath him. Her body demanded that he give her all of himself, and at her zenith she'd repeatedly whispered her love for him and stunned him by telling him she needed his love more than she needed air. He'd lost it then. A feeling he'd never known. And he'd given himself because he wanted to, needed to, and finally because he couldn't help himself. His control had shattered, and he would never forget that feeling of scaling the heights, of having the earth move beneath him and the stars shooting all around him. She had pulled down his walls, blasted his safe, and left him vulnerable to her. If he discovered that she had a hand in the mess at Leather and Hides, it probably wouldn't make a damned bit of difference.

He leaned over her, clasped her in his arms, and feathered kisses over her cheeks. He knew he had strength, that his tough-ness had made him a success. But he didn't fool himself. The woman he held in his arms had a strength equal to his own. She had considered one of his "secrets" of little consequence. But he knew she wouldn't treat the other one lightly, and that she had the guts to walk away no matter what she felt for him.

Adam showered in Melissa's lavender-scented bathroom. He had thirty-five minutes in which to go home, change into business clothes, and get to his office in time for his first appoint-ment. He hooked a towel at his waist, stepped out of the bathroom, and began to dress.

"Where did you park?" He glanced over at her lying on her

belly, her chin supported by the heels of both hands, and told himself to think about blackened redfish, the Indonesian rain forests, or poison ivy—anything except the sleepy woman between those sheets. He had to be in his office in minutes.

"I parked four blocks away. Don't worry, I wouldn't do anything to make you the main topic of discussion at Martha Brock's 'Monday evening tea to help the homeless.'" Happiness flooded his heart at the sound of her infectious and uninhibited laugh, the laughter of a well-loved, sated woman.

"Don't forget Miss Mary's Wednesday night prayer service," she added, mimicking the old woman. "They'll race right through it so they can get to the good part, the coffee and gossip part of the service."

He sat on the edge of the bed, pulled on his socks and sneakers, and felt her hand stroke the back of his head.

"Do whatever you have to do about Leather and Hides, Adam. You would regardless of what I said, but I want you to know that I'd never want you to compromise your integrity—and no matter what you discover, do what you have to do. If I were in your big sneakers and faced what you do, I'd go for the truth and let the chips fall—"

He turned to face her. "Thank you... I think. It's easier to say that than to live through it, Melissa. I don't want to make a move against you or anyone dear to you, and I hope it won't be necessary. But I can only be who I am and what I am. I'll do what I know is right, no matter how much or who it hurts, and this ridiculous feud won't weigh in my decisions. We may face some difficult days. If we mean anything to each other after I get this mess settled, call it a miracle." He hugged her quickly, shoving his desire for her under control.

"Aren't you going to work today?" Desire stirred in him as the backs of her fingers trailed down his cheek and stroked his neck.

"I don't think so. A dear friend will be staying with me for a few days, and I'm going into Baltimore shortly to get her."

He allowed a raised eyebrow, but inwardly he felt relief that she didn't expect Magnus Cooper. "Anyone I know?"

"I don't think you've met her, but she'd love to make your acquaintance."

"What does that mean?" He stood, looked around for his jacket, and remembered that he'd left it downstairs. She rolled over, dropped her feet off the bed, and tucked the sheet around her.

"It means she's normal."

"Are you getting testy?" He had a feeling the look she gave him had been used repeatedly and to maximum effect.

"Not yet, but give me time. I just remembered that Magnus Cooper is coming here today. Business, he said. He thinks this town is ripe with investment opportunities."

Adam's hand remained suspended above the doorknob. "Remind him for me that when the great warriors of history lost a battle, they were usually on foreign soil. I'll call you tonight." He didn't wait for her reaction.


Melissa dressed, put in a call to her secretary, and left for Baltimore. She'd had the car tuned up and cleaned inside and out. What she'd consider an ordinary mishap, Ilona would view as a major disaster. Her friend didn't pamper herself to the point of being a bore, but she expected life to flow smoothly. She parked along a narrow street that ran perpendicular to the west side of the Pennsylvania Railroad station and walked the short block. A neatly attired older woman fell in step beside her.

"You look so nice, dear. You remind me of myself when I was your age."

"Well, thank you," Melissa answered, trying not to break her stride.

"I love to see our young people looking so prosperous," the woman went on. "Where're you headed?" Melissa told her that she was meeting a friend.

"I sure hope he's nice, and I hope you appreciate him," the woman droned. "Don't do like I did. I was going to be an opera singer, come hell or high water. Well, it was high water, because it turned out I didn't have the talent for it. The man I gave up in order to chase that windmill married my sister, and every holiday

I have to watch him being happy with her and my three nieces and nephews. Now I'm fifty with a cracking voice, fading looks, and myself for company."

Melissa slowed her steps to a halt. "I don't know what to say. I…I'm sorry, ma'am."

"Don't be," her companion said. "I make a very good living with my tarot cards, and the older I get, the more people seem to trust me." She shook her head, as if in sadness. "If I could just stop dreaming about him and waking up thinking he's with me." The woman drifted into introspection, and Melissa touched her shoulder, waved, and strode to the information booth. Her encounter with the stranger had lowered her spirits. She feared that she would love Adam Roundtree forever, just as her mother still loved Bill Henry hopelessly after three decades, a marriage to another man, and two children. But the next move wasn't hers to make.

She bought a copy of *The Baltimore Sun* and found a seat in the waiting room. But the newsprint danced before her eyes until she saw only Adam's face above hers. Adam in ecstasy, shattered, vulnerable, and bare. She had finally touched him. For the first time he'd given all of himself, had belonged to her completely. She wondered about the other times they'd made love. Best not to speculate, because she would never know unless he told her. But she'd keep the memory of it close to her heart. For those few moments, if never again, Adam Roundtree had been hers. Perspiration dampened her forehead as she recalled the fire-hot tension he built up in her, refusing her the quick and easy release she begged him for until at last he hurtled her into a star-spangled otherworld. And then he'd joined her.

"Melissa, darling, you must be thinking about this man. I've been standing here a full minute. Darling, it must be awful to sit in these wooden seats. How long have you been waiting?" A wide grin spread across Melissa's face, and she quickly stood to hug her friend.

"I didn't wait long." She picked up Ilona's bag and started for the car. "I thought we'd have lunch in the Inner Harbor before going to Frederick."

"Whatever you say. I'm in your hands." Ilona pointed to her new low-heeled shoes. "I bought these just for the trip. I wouldn't be caught dead in these things on Fifth Avenue."

"Well, at least you'll have some respite from your sore feet while you're here," Melissa commented, unable to resist needling her friend.

After lunch Melissa gave Ilona a quick tour past the Johns Hopkins University and along Charles Street and walked with her through the famous Lexington Market.

"I haven't seen so much meat since the last time I shopped with my dear mother in the Great Market in Budapest almost forty years ago," Ilona exclaimed. "Don't they have strawberries down here?" she asked, when they wandered through the produce section.

"Ilona, this is December. If you want strawberries, I'll stop by a specialty shop." Ilona told her not to bother.

"But darling, you should have strawberries to feed your man—one at a time," she explained, pausing for effect. "But we could get some grapes. Grapes are good for that, too, except then you feed him the whole bunch. Just make sure he doesn't choke—some men don't know the purpose of that." Melissa resisted asking her to explain it.

"Are you expecting company, Ilona?"

"No darling, but you must be. I'm going to be here four days, and no real vooman would let so much time go by without seeing her man. So when do I meet him? Tonight?" she asked, hope caressing her accented tones.

Melissa glanced at her rearview mirror when she backed up to park in front of her house and saw the gray Towne car ease to the curb right behind her. She counted to three under her breath, and turned to Ilona.

"We're home." She opened the trunk to retrieve Ilona's bag and the few items she'd bought. She knew that the male hand on her arm didn't belong to Adam, and suppressing annoyance, looked up into the hazel brown, expectant eyes of Magnus Cooper.

"You broke our appointment," he reprimanded in a gentle voice.

"I've been waiting to meet you," she heard Ilona say, mistaking Magnus for Adam. "But somehow, you're not what I expected. You're more my style than Melissa's." She looked him up and down. "I've had less pleasant surprises." Melissa watched Ilona's fun and felt some of her antagonism toward Magnus ebbing. His car parked in front of her door would be a feast for her nosey neighbors and fuel for Adam's temper. He wouldn't believe that a man of Magnus Cooper's sophistication would visit a woman unless he knew she would welcome him.

"Ilona Harváth, this is Magnus Cooper. Mr. Cooper lives in Texas and is here on business. Magnus, Ilona is a dear friend visiting me from New York." He nodded.

"Mmmm. How do you do?" Ilona's raised eyebrow and suggestive shrug told them what she thought of Cooper's business in Frederick. Melissa asked him to excuse her and promised to see him at her office the next morning.

Inside, Ilona looked around, complimented Melissa on her home, and got down to business. "Melissa, darling, if this man you are so taken with doesn't look as good as the one who just left here, I will kill you." She shook her head and rolled her eyes skyward as though savoring the tenderest fresh truffle. "Darling, this Cooper is a real man. If I was ten years younger, I'd separate him from the pack in a minute."

"You could do it now." She took Ilona's bag and walked upstairs with her to the guest room.

"Darling, don't make jokes." That expression always amused Melissa, as did the withering look that accompanied it. She raced to answer the phone in her room.

"Did your friend arrive?" She flopped down on the side of her bed, kicked off her shoes and swung her legs up on the coverlet.

"Yes. She's here. You want to run by for a couple of minutes after you leave the office? I'd like you to meet her." And she longed to see him, to reassure herself that what she'd experienced with him that morning had been real, that she hadn't dreamed it. She couldn't understand the long silence nor his seeming lack of enthusiasm when he replied.

"Why not? See you in a half hour." She combed her hair, refreshed her makeup, and dabbed a little perfume behind her ears and at her temple. She arrived at the top of the stairs simultaneously with Ilona.

"Don't tell me," Ilona said, folding her arms about her chest in a gesture of satisfaction. "That was *him,* and he's coming over. Let me get my heels. I wouldn't be—"

"—caught dead around a man wearing those flats," Melissa finished for her.

Melissa tried not to rush to the door when he rang, and she had to muster an air of casualness when she opened the door.

"Hi." He didn't speak but stood looking down at her, his gaze roaming over her upturned face. And after what seemed to her endless minutes, he opened his arms and folded her to him. Unable to wait longer, she leaned back and fastened her gaze on his mouth in a silent request, and he gave her what she wanted, crushing her to him and shivering against her when she opened her mouth beneath his in sweet union.

He eased her from him, and tugging her to his side, turned toward the living room.

"Where's your friend?"

"Is somebody asking for me?" Ilona queried as she strolled down the stairs from her perch where she couldn't help but witness their kiss. Melissa couldn't suppress a hearty laugh. She should have known that Ilona couldn't wait to see Adam. She introduced them, and Adam went to greet her before she reached the bottom of the stairs.

Ilona accepted the introduction with the comment, "Melissa, darling, this is God's country. I'm living in the wrong state."

Melissa needled her. "But we don't have a ballet here, remember?"

"Who needs the ballet? From my experience since I've been here, I can't see how you'd have time for it." She shook Adam's hand. "I'm happy to meet you, Adam. You mustn't mind my continental manners."

Adam's grin seemed to please her. "I doubt the continent has much to do with your manners. I know a free spirit when I see one. Welcome to Frederick, Ilona."

Melissa sensed his forced manners. She'd felt a distance between them during their phone conversation and when she'd opened the door for him. And she sensed it now.

"Would you join us for a drink? Ilona drinks only espresso coffee, but I'd like some wine. What about you?"

He glanced at his watch. "Thanks, but I've asked Jason Court to come down here, and I want to meet him at the airport this evening." He bade Ilona good-bye, and they walked to the door.

"I sense a problem. What's wrong?"

"Did you enjoy your visit with Magnus Cooper?" The question surprised her, and she suspected from his closed expression that he hadn't planned to ask her that. She wondered how he'd known that Magnus came to her house, but she ignored his sarcasm and his audacity.

"We didn't visit. I made an appointment to see him at my office tomorrow morning. Anything else?" He ran his right hand over the back of his hair and looked at her intently for a few seconds without saying anything. She knew when he made up his mind to tell her about it.

"Sometime between six o'clock and eight this morning, someone sprayed red, oil-based paint on a batch of leathers that Cal had planned to ship today. He's threatened to resign if this sabotage continues. I'll be busy with this for the next few days, but I'll be in touch." He kissed her quickly and left. Melissa forced a bright expression on her face and went back to get Ilona's extended verdict.

"What's that matter, darling?"

Melissa countered with another question. "Why do you think something's wrong?"

Ilona shrugged first one shoulder and then the other. "Am I a lamb born today? This man is fighting a war with himself, and he's strong enough to win it. He wants you, but something's dragging him back. Pull out the stops, Melissa, and don't give him a chance to breathe without thinking of you first. What a man! Hmmm. If I had to choose between him and Cooper, I'd probably lose my mind." She lit a cigarette. "My one vice since I gave up rummy, darling. As far as Adam's concerned, you belong to him. Well, that's something. Cooper's only hoping."

"What are you talking about?" Melissa had headed for the kitchen to start supper and beckoned Ilona to follow her. Ilona tried without success to blow a smoke ring.

"Don't make me spell it out. I saw you with Adam, darling. You've made each other happy. Very happy. Keep it up." She sat down and crossed her knees. "I'm not going to offer to cook—it's not my style. But if you want to eat out, I'll pay. Cooking is for servants. I don't know why you do it." She sipped the hot espresso. "I see you remember I like it in a little glass. Listen darling, all fun aside. You love Adam, and he thinks an awful lot of you, but he's a man who can put you behind him. You know what he needs, so give him plenty of it. Don't let anything or anybody get between you, because you won't find another like him."

# Chapter 12

Adam drove home for lunch with Jason Court. He'd invited Jason to stay with him in Beaver Ridge, rather than at a hotel in Frederick, reasoning that if he was seen with a stranger of Jason's description—big, tough, jaded, and possibly a crime buster—the criminal or criminals might be alerted to the ring tightening around them. His intention had been to have his assistant bring him up to date on affairs at his New York office, but he remembered that Jason had been a police detective until he'd quit after having been wounded. He told Jason about the problems at the leather factory.

"I suppose you've planted one or two specialists there whom you can trust."

"Yeah. But they're poor detectives—these incidents take place all around them."

Jason interlocked his long brown fingers and leaned back in his straight chair. "Adam, this thing could involve people in more than one state. Maybe you should contact the FBI."

"I've thought of that, and I've postponed doing it, but if nothing else, the Feds could give me some advice." A smile creased Adam's face when his mother walked in the dining room with a huge chocolate bombe, his favorite dessert, and a pot of coffee.

"You're a lucky man, Adam, getting this kind of home cooking," Jason said. He smiled at Adam's mother. "I wonder how you knew I'm a chocaholic."

"Chocolate is usually the safest dessert to offer men, if you don't know what they like," she replied in a softer than usual voice. Adam glanced sharply at her. He'd lived for almost thirty-five years and hadn't guessed that his mother was what he thought of as a man's woman. His fifty-four-year-old mother bloomed in a soft, womanly response to Jason's compliment. He scrutinized the man who sat across from him, lustily enjoying the delicious dessert, a man who commanded respect as much for his masculinity as for his abilities. He recognized a similarity with his father and smiled to himself.

Melissa walked to her office door with Magnus Cooper, told him good-bye, and prayed that Adam wouldn't meet him in the hallway as he left. She liked and respected the genteel Texan and appreciated his business. He had divined her interest in another man and hadn't been surprised to learn the man's identity.

"From what I've seen and heard, you've chosen well," he'd said, removing himself from the picture with consummate grace.

She checked her calendar for the day, hoping to have the afternoon free so that she could show Ilona the town of Frederick and the little picturesque villages nearby. Friday had always been one of her busiest days, and this one was shaping up similarly. She punched the intercom and dictated a short letter to a woman in Atlanta who needed a florist to baby-sit her nursery while she took a long-anticipated tour around the world. Melissa declined the job on the grounds that she couldn't be responsible for damage or loss that the nursery might sustain in the owner's absence.

She'd asked her secretary not to disturb her, but she accepted Adam's call. "Hi."

"Hi." Pleasure enveloped her at the sound of his deep velvet voice. "Have I seen the last of Cooper?" Melissa couldn't resist a chuckle.

"Search me. Your sight seems to pierce walls and dart around corners. I wouldn't be surprised if you did see him. Making any progress?" She must have asked the wrong question, because his silence seemed almost palpable. "Are you there, Adam?"

"I'm here. I haven't made any moves. What is Ilona doing to entertain herself while you're at work?"

Adam didn't invite a person to butt out—he merely changed the subject. "You never see a need for subtlety, do you?" she asked, a tinge of testiness in her voice. But with his self-confidence, she thought, he didn't have to resort to that. He ignored her taunt, and she thought it just as well.

"Like any vacationing New Yorker worth the name, Ilona is probably sound asleep," she told him. "She asked me to set the coffeepot for eleven thirty, and I did." She waited, wanting him to tell her why he'd called, needing his admittance that he just wanted to talk to her.

"I was in a rush when I left you last night, but like I said, I had to get to the airport. I could have done a better job of telling you good night."

She settled into her chair and felt her lips curl into a slow smile. "It isn't too late. Want to make up for it right now?"

His laugh warmed her. "Seeing through walls is nothing compared to what you're asking me to do now."

"Do you know something I don't? Why should making up for last night be such a chore? Especially for you?"

"You pick the damnedest times to toy with me, always making sure you're out of sight. The manner in which I should have preferred to tell you good night cannot be executed through these telephone wires," he said in exaggerated Oxford English and with a hint of belligerence. She didn't try to suppress her delight nor the wickedness with which she communicated it to him.

"Oh, you're up to the task," she teased. "I can't imagine there's anything you'd want to do that you can't manage. Don't let a couple of telephone wires deter you. 'A man's reach should exceed his grasp. Or what's a heaven for?'" she quoted from Browning. She couldn't figure out whether her deviltry excited him or annoyed him. All she had to go on was his cryptic reply.

"If heaven is in a receptive mood, the telephone wires be damned. I can burn up the distance between us in no time. Say the word."

"Oh, dear, did I say something wrong?" She put her hand over the mouthpiece. If he heard her snicker, he'd be there in short order, and she wouldn't bet on what he'd do.

"Never pull a tiger by his tail, baby. I'll see you tonight."

"What? I have to entertain Ilona. I may not be home."

"Oh, yes, you will—and nothing would delight your friend more than to watch you take your medicine."

"Adam!"

"See you at seven, babe." He hung up.

She hugged herself and swirled her chair around in delight as her heart raced in anticipation of the evening. Whatever medicine he'd planned for her, she couldn't wait to taste it. Her euphoria evaporated when Emily appeared in the doorway, her face the picture of anger and determination.

"Your father backed a truck up to the house and took out everything he'd put there. He must have kept a list. You know, it struck me as strange that he'd do that when he didn't seem to want to leave. If Schyler was here, he could talk to him. Go see if he's alright. I have to make some plans, and I can't do that if he's having a breakdown."

"Okay. Do you think he's home?" Melissa's deep sigh bespoke her reluctance to speak with the man as daughter to father, but she promised her mother that she would. "Come on. I'll drop you off at home."

Rafer Grant did not welcome his daughter's interference. "You know why I moved out. Your mother has sold out and gone over to them. Both of you have, and I'm not going to hang around and watch you throw yourselves at my enemies."

"I just came to see if you're alright, Daddy."

"Of course I'm alright. Are you sure you didn't come here to protect Adam Roundtree?" He gritted his teeth apparently in disgust at having to mention the name.

A surge of anxiety washed through her. "What do you mean? Protect him from what?"

His smile was that of a man who held the trump cards. "He has alienated my wife, causing an irreparable breach between us and, even if you get on your knees and beg, I'm still going to sue him for that."

"Daddy, that's ridiculous. Mama told me that the two of you have lived separate lives for twenty-five years. Adam didn't alienate Mama, and he didn't shoot Timmy." She regretted the words when he stammered and sputtered, unable to articulate his rage. She'd only fueled his passion for revenge.

"I warn you," he finally managed to say. "If you betray your family, you'll regret it. You'll lose your clients, and Adam Roundtree won't be so anxious for you when he learns that you instigated the sabotage of his leather industry." She couldn't contain her loud gasp. How did he know about the problems at Leather and Hides?

She left her father and walked down the hall to his lawyer's office. "My cousin doesn't have a case against Adam," she told the man. "On the night of the shooting I was with Adam from around seven until midnight, and I'm prepared to give public testimony to that effect. And it was I and not Adam who urged Mama to begin volunteer work."

"Why did she choose The Refuge? Plenty of places around here need volunteers."

"Mama had never associated The Refuge with Adam or his family. I didn't even know Adam had any connection with it until after Mama went there."

"You'd go against your father?"

"I will if he goes ahead with this attempt to embarrass my mother."

"You're pretty resolute about this."

She hesitated to say more, but she didn't want the lawyer to doubt her. "Yes, I am, and I won't omit the damage he's done to her psyche. He has treated her as though she were incompetent, deprived her of self-confidence. She can't drive a car, has never been allowed to go anywhere without him except the hairdresser, and he has insisted on choosing her clothes. Yes, I'll tell it!"

"I find this hard to digest." The man walked over to the window and looked down toward the street.

"He robbed me, too. All these years I thought my mother pre-

554 *Gwynne Forster*

ferred my brother to me, that she didn't love me, but she was only trying to please my father. I was no better—I begged for his approval and didn't try to understand my mother. He manipulated both of us."

"I'm surprised."

She shrugged. "He probably isn't aware that he's done these things or, at least, of their effect."

"Rafer said you'd witness for him."

"Tell me—do I look as if I might do that?" Her face must have mirrored her sadness, because he shook his head in sympathy.

"I'd say, not."

She walked to the door and turned. "And you'd be right. Good-bye."

Melissa laid back her shoulders, plastered a smiled on her face, and unlocked her door. She found a well-rested Ilona fresh from her scented bath doing her nails to the tune of Jimmy Lunceford's "Uptown Blues."

"I love your records, darling. Who'd believe that blues could be so sexy? I always thought they were supposed to be depressing. You know, somebody crying about losing their lover. That's the only thing worse than death that I can think of."

Melissa laughed and hugged her friend. One couldn't remain dejected around Ilona—she didn't allow it. "Adam will be over at seven."

Ilona beamed. "Want me to take in a movie?"

Melissa cast a dark glance in Ilona's direction and started up the stairs. "Thanks, but no thanks. I'm wearing an avocado green silk sheath an inch above the knee. Can you handle that?"

"Of course, darling. Mine's red, four inches above, but don't worry—I don't have your height or your legs."

Adam arrived at Melissa's home promptly at seven. He'd brought Wayne along as company for Ilona, and they'd dressed in dark business suits.

"What's she like?" Wayne had asked about Ilona.

Adam had replied, "You can't describe Ilona—she has to be experienced. But not to worry, she'll be good company."

He rang the bell and waited, wondering what kind of curve he'd get from Melissa after his audacious taunt and thinly veiled promise of earlier in the day.

My God, he told himself when she opened the door, she can still take my breath away. The ball is in my court, she seemed to say when she stepped up to him, ran her arms up his chest, grasped the back of his head, and kissed him.

"Hi. You're right on time."

"Hi." He looked down at her feet, getting a grip on his senses after her surprise assault. "You're very tall tonight. How high are those heels?"

"Three inches. Gives me an advantage, doesn't it?"

"Depends. I thought Wayne would like to meet Ilona." Melissa looked over Adam's shoulder at his brother.

"Oops. I didn't see you. Come in."

Adam watched Wayne kiss Melissa on the cheek and suppressed a flicker of annoyance. He had no need for jealousy and wanted to kick himself for feeling it. They walked into the living room, and Ilona stood as they entered. Adam enjoyed the smile that lit her countenance: here was a female who took pride in her womanhood. He introduced her to his brother.

"Now I know I'm moving down here," she joshed.

Adam suggested a restaurant in Baltimore. "Want to drive, Wayne?"

Wayne laughed. "Do I have a choice?" He nudged Ilona. "They want to make out in the backseat. What do you think?"

She grasped his arm. "Wayne, darling, never get in the way of lovers. It's not sporting."

Adam positioned himself in the right corner of the backseat, knotted his fingers through Melissa's and urged her closer. "This car is bigger than the Jaguar," he said of Wayne's car. "You've put three feet of space between us. What's the matter? Scared you'll have to back up that greeting you gave me this evening?" He urged her all the way into his arms and held her close.

"I'm on to you, sweetheart. You're full of pranks when I'm not around and you can get away with them." He let a finger trail from her cheek down to the cleavage that her dress exposed.

"How sassy do you feel right now?" he teased. She didn't answer, but to his surprise urged his face down to hers with the tips of her fingers and parted her lips. Caught off guard, he had to do battle with the unsteadiness that he knew she sensed in him as his blood coursed wildly through his body. Her lips moved beneath his, seeking, demanding that he lose his self-control and, however fleetingly, belong to someone other than himself. With effort, he eased the kiss and moved her away from him.

"Are you staking a claim?" he whispered, trying to come to terms with the depths to which she had embedded herself in him.

Her calm response that she didn't know what he meant didn't fool him. She trembled against the arm that he slung around her shoulder, and he wondered for the nth time if his uncle's fate would be his own.

Melissa watched Ilona slip off her gold earrings, unfasten their matching bracelet, lay them in her jewelry box and lock it. She didn't take chances. Melissa wondered what role chance had played in her relationship with Adam. Had Ilona not chosen that weekend to visit, and if she hadn't admonished her to be more assertive with Adam, would she know that her kiss alone could make him tremble?

"You should have sent me to the movies," Ilona said as if aware that Melissa's thoughts rested on Adam.

"Didn't you have a good time?"

"What a question! Darling, if a vooman couldn't enjoy herself in the company of those two men, she should see a psychiatrist. You can get Adam, if you don't make any mistakes with him. But that's easier said than done. He's a tough one."

Melissa bade Ilona good night and went to her own room. She moved about absentmindedly, her thoughts on Adam's reaction each time she'd kissed him without warning. She undressed and slipped into bed. Ilona's words bruised her mind: "He's a tough one." Yes, Melissa mused, he is that. He had been hers when she'd kissed him unexpectedly, but only for moments before he reasserted his self-control. He'd kissed her good night at her door, looked at her solemnly, and had spoken in an unmistakably serious voice.

"I assume Cooper has already left for Texas. If he hasn't, give him a reason to do that." Then he'd walked off without waiting for her answer. "He doesn't like the word 'no,'" Jason Court had once said. Well, she thought, frustrated at his continued refusal to declare himself though he could tell her to cut ties with another man, he's going to hear it if he doesn't take the same chance on me that he's demanding I take with him.

Adam read his private investigator's report a second time. Nothing in Melissa's behavior the previous Friday night nor when they spoke during the weekend had prepared him for what his eyes saw. He rose from his chair, paused and sat down, not trusting himself to enter her office. He picked up his private phone and dialed her number.

"Melissa, what have you done?"

"I don't know what you mean."

"Yes, you do." His breathless tone betrayed his emotions, and he paused in an effort to control his voice. "You've risked everything in order to protect me from personal damage, threats, and accusations that I didn't even know about. Why did you do it, Melissa. I have to know." His breath trapped in his throat while he awaited her answer.

"How did you find out?"

"Nothing remains a secret for long in this town—you know that. Why did you do it?"

"I didn't have a choice, Adam. I acted in the interest of decency. There've been too many lies, too much misunderstanding and suffering because of this feud, and I won't contribute to it. I want it laid to rest." Her disappointing words hurt him.

"You're asking me to believe you risked relationships with your family, everything you've worked for, your business for such an impersonal reason? Tell me the truth, Melissa. You've lain in my arms and told me you love me. Can't you trust me enough to level with me now? The truth, Melissa. I need to hear it."

"And my needs, Adam. Does it matter what I need?" He pushed back his chair when he detected a hint of tears in her voice, hung up, and raced down the hall and up the stairs. He strode past her secretary, opened her door, and closed it behind him. She sat with elbows on her desk, holding her bowed face in her hands. Without breaking his stride, he knelt beside her chair and cradled her in his arms.

"I care for you. I feel for you what I've never felt for anyone else, but I can't name it."

Her arms tightened around him, and as though exhausted by a traumatic experience she rasped out the words: "I couldn't let him destroy you. I couldn't let anybody do that."

He hooked his foot under the platform of her chair, dragged it away from the desk, and sat with her in his lap. His heart swelled and his breath quickened. How had he ever doubted that he could trust her? She would give up everything for him.

"I care," he repeated, stroking her back, tangling his fingers in her dense curls, and spreading soft kisses over her face. "I care, sweetheart." Love and contentment flowed through him and with eyes closed, he rocked her, cherished her. For the first time in his adult life, he knew total vulnerability to a woman and, at the moment, he didn't care.

Later that evening Melissa sat in her living room addressing Christmas cards, a chore that she always tried to finish by the fifth of the month. Her house seemed empty without Ilona. She reflected on her friend's philosophy that a great love made the pangs of birth and death worth experiencing. Ilona had known such a love with her husband, but had lost him to Hungary's political madness of the time and had since refused to settle for less. She flipped through the stack of cards looking for one suitable for Bill Henry. She couldn't understand her affection for the man, having spoken with him only three times, but she suspected that his love for her mother and hers for Adam bound them. She found one, addressed it, and put away her writing.

She tried to control the happiness she felt, to subdue it so that if Adam walked out of her life, she wouldn't have a painful letdown. Adam hadn't committed himself, but she'd felt his love, sensed the change in him, and had known that he cherished her. She knew their differences wouldn't be resolved until Adam had satisfied himself that the person sabotaging his factory had been apprehended. But she had hope now that he'd give them a chance.

She crawled into bed, turned out the light, and the telephone rang.

"Hello."

"I called to tell you good night. Sleep well."

"Adam," she mumbled. "Good night, honey." He hung up, and she fell asleep and dreamed that he kissed her in a field of early spring lavender.

Around noon the next day Adam lifted the receiver, swung his alligator-shod size twelves up on his desk, crossed them at the ankle, and cleared his throat. "Are you sure?" he asked Wayne.

"The announcement didn't come by mail, but by Federal Express. Emily Grant wants the world to know that she and Rafer Grant now live under separate roofs and that she has filed for a divorce. What do you think we should do with this?"

He didn't hesitate. "Print it."

Adam welcomed Wayne's presence at dinner that evening, grateful that he'd driven in from Baltimore to ease the strain. Both expected their mother to explode with rage at Wayne's decision to print the announcement in the family paper.

"What else is going on behind my back," she asked them, then turned to Adam. "Doesn't this have something to do with you and Melissa Grant? The whole community talks of nothing but the two of you."

"Mother, I'm sure I don't have to remind you that the community's reaction to my friendship with Melissa doesn't concern me. Besides, this had nothing to do with her."

"Of course it does," she stormed.

"Hear me out, Mother. It seems that Timothy Coston was shot, and Rafer has decided that only a Hayes or a Roundtree would have done it. He gave me the credit. But I haven't seen a newspaper account of it. It hasn't been reported to the police, and I can't get any details. I didn't do it, but he intends to indict me. I expect he hopes such a suit will distract attention from his wife's divorce suit."

Mary Roundtree's lips quivered in anger. "If he dares to charge you, I'll keep him in court until he doesn't have a cent. I don't suppose I have to remind you of my advice that Melissa Grant is poison. Now that you've found out for yourself, I hope you'll leave her alone. When we finish with them, they'll know who we are."

Adam left the table and walked from one end of the dining room to the other in a move that Wayne and his mother recognized as one intended to cool his temper. Oblivious to their silence, he paced the floor, embattled with an inner turbulence not unlike the Atlantic in the clutch of an angry storm. He stopped at the head of the table, the place vacant since his father's death, and took a seat. He was head of the family, and it was time his mother accorded him that respect.

He looked into his mother's eyes. "Melissa Grant risked her relationship with her family, her clients, and her business to stand up for me and deny that I had any part in the deeds with which Rafer wants to charge me. If any of you thinks that I won't stand up for her, you don't know me."

"But what if she's engineered that situation at Leather and Hides and went to your defense as a ruse to cover it up," Mary asked.

He leaned forward. "Mother, that woman loves me as surely as any woman ever loved a man. I told you once that I didn't want to hear another word against her, and I don't. She's important to me. I will make my move after I find out who is trashing Leather and Hides."

"Emily is behind this," he heard his mother say. "She's still chasing B-H after all these years."

"Emily Grant is a respectable woman. She may have thought of B-H for the past thirty years, but she hasn't chased him."

"How do you know her well enough to defend her?" Wayne asked.

Adam sipped the last of his cold coffee and stood. "Mrs. Grant has volunteered four hours each day, five days a week, at The Refuge for the last month and a half. That's how I know her." He excused himself, put his leather jacket over his sweater, threw a long cashmere scarf around his neck, and set out for Bill Henry's house.

"What brings you here tonight, Adam?" B-H relaxed in his rocker and inhaled deeply. Adam had long enjoyed his uncle's habit of roasting sweet potatoes and peanuts in the hearth while he sat before the blazing flames.

"I take it you haven't spoken with Wayne today," he said, preparing him for the conversation's potentially explosive nature.

"Can't say that I have. What's up?"

Adam looked directly into Bill Henry's eyes. "Emily Grant and Rafer have separated, and she's officially announced that she has filed for divorce." Something akin to pain settled around Adam's heart when his uncle jerked forward as though blown to the position by a cannon.

"Don't lie to me, Adam."

"You still want her?" His uncle looked steadily at him, not blinking an eye until his expression assumed a far-off, lost look.

"Oh, yes. I want her. I doubt that even death could put an end to it. Just let me know when the decree is final. There isn't a Grant or a Roundtree alive whom I'll allow to get in my way this time, and that includes Emily." Adam sought to lower his uncle's expectations.

"You think she'd still—"

Bill Henry interrupted. "I don't think. I know. At times I've actually felt sorry for poor Rafer. A morsel of bread is worse than having none at all. Emily Morris loves me—she has never loved anyone else, and she never will."

Adam shook his head in wonder. "All these years. It must have been difficult for you."

Bill Henry picked up the poker, knocked a few peanuts away from the coals, and fanned them. "It hasn't been easy, Adam— but I had solace in the knowledge that she loved me, that no matter what appearances might suggest, it was me that she loved."

"You're sure of yourself." Adam stroked his chin with his right thumb and index finger.

"And if you want Melissa, you should be, too. You'd better bind her to you. She's a fine woman, and I'd hate to see you lose her." Adam didn't ask B-H why he was so certain he wanted Melissa, because he wouldn't discuss her with anyone, not even his beloved uncle.

He held out his hand for the peanuts he knew his uncle had pushed aside to cool for him and which he'd nibble on the way home.

"I'll let you know when the decree is final, B-H, and I hope things work out for you."

"Thanks."

Adam forgot the nuts as he walked home in the pitch darkness. His thoughts centered on his uncle and Emily Morris. A love that strong could bring a man to his knees, even flat on his face. Could he withstand what B-H had gone through if Melissa sided with her family, or worse, if she turned her back when he told her what he knew he had to reveal—a secret he'd kept from her far too long. His steps slowed, and unfamiliar tentacles of alarm made him shiver: suppose he couldn't get along without her. Then what?

At noon the next day Wayne walked into Adam's office and handed him a copy of *The Maryland Journal,* the family newspaper. The society columnist's phone had rung constantly that morning, he told Adam, and Rafer had called disclaiming the pending divorce and threatening suit. He sat down and faced Adam, his demeanor more solemn than was normally his bent.

"Adam, do you think it's possible that your affair with Melissa might have opened Pandora's box?"

Hot anger lit Adam's eyes, and his quelling look wasn't one that his brother had witnessed before. His lips thinned as he spoke with frosty softness. "I am not having an affair with Melissa, but if I were, it would be my business and hers and not a matter for discussion."

Wayne's careless shrug didn't mislead Adam. He sensed his brother's worry and annoyance at the turn of events, as he watched him hunch his shoulders and walk out of the office. Adam leaned heavily back in his chair, himself displeased. He had never spoken so sharply to his brother, and he feared it was only the beginning. What would his passion for Melissa cost him?

Adam remained in his office until six thirty that evening in order to have the privacy he needed. Never before had the folly of mixing business with pleasure been clearer. He had to choose between two things dear to him: his family's best interest and his relationship with Melissa. He thought of her warmth, the way she molded herself to him whenever he put his arms around her. Hell! He lifted the receiver and dialed her office number.

"Hello."

"What are you doing here so late?" he asked. And before she could answer, he whispered, "I'd like to see you, Melissa. Tonight. Now. Will you have dinner with me?"

Her immediate reply warmed his heart. "Could we go to that little place where we went that first time?"

"Yes. I'll pick you up in a couple of minutes." When he reached her office, he found her standing outside the locked door. For the last few hours he'd thought of nothing but the feel of her warm and soft in his arms, sweet and loving. Easing the torment he felt over that angry exchange with his brother, and calming his apprehension about their relationship. He'd needed to hold her.

"What's this?" he asked, his frustration barely suppressed.

"I was going to meet you." She stood on tiptoe for his kiss.

He kept it light—he had to, or they'd be a spectacle for whoever passed them.

He drove past the Taney house on South Benz Street, and Melissa seemed to spit in its direction, mystifying him.

"It's a small pleasure I allow myself whenever I pass here," she explained. "Now that we have school integration, I wonder whether our children still learn that, as chief justice of the Supreme Court, old Taney in the Dred Scott Case of 1857 upheld the tenet that slaves and their descendents were not citizens of this country and couldn't sue in Federal courts, and that congress couldn't forbid slavery in the United States or its territories. I refuse to forgive even his memory. Pursing my lips as if to spit at the place isn't very ladylike, but it's oh so satisfying."

A deep chuckle rose in Adam's throat. "The lady's a bag of surprises. I never know what to expect of you." He glanced over at her after pulling into the interstate. "You're like a brilliant comet shooting through a bunch of ordinary stars." He had the pleasure of seeing her settle down in the soft leather seat, fold her arms in contentment, and smile as though she possessed the secrets of the ages. Maybe she did, he mused, as she rested her head against his shoulder—she certainly had the key to his closet.

At the little restaurant they got seats at a small table in the rear, away from a group of happy revelers.

"What's so amusing?" he asked as the waiter approached.

"This red tablecloth clashes with my fuchsia suit, don't you think?"

"Do you really think I'm looking at this tablecloth?"

"Oh!" Crimson tainted her cheeks, and he observed her more closely when she ducked her head.

"You seem a bit down tonight. Anything wrong?" The shake of her head denied it, but he soon realized that she'd been waiting for the chance to share her concerns.

"We both knew way back when…when this started that if we got close there'd be turmoil in our families. I barely have one left. Earlier today my father begged me not to continue seeing you, to testify in support of my cousin, and to dissuade my mother from getting a divorce. Adam, I can't do any of those things. I can't give up my integrity, and I don't know how he can ask me to. All my life, he drummed into my head how important it is to be faithful to the truth and to myself, that I should never compromise on those things. Do you think he's sick?"

He stroked the back of the hand she rested on the table. "No. But I think Hayes-Roundtree may be his Achilles' heel."

"It isn't his feud, and I told him so."

"Maybe not, but it's the excuse he uses. The thought of Bill Henry makes him feel like a whipped dog, and he didn't do anything to deserve getting the short end." Adam didn't think it a matter for grinning, but when she squinted at him, he couldn't avoid it.

"He isn't guiltless, Adam. Daddy went into that marriage knowing that Mama didn't love him." Adam stared at her in surprise.

"Oh, I was blind about their relationship," she said, "but since I've been back home, I view a lot of things differently. I hate to see him so desperate, though. He told me I'd be sorry for standing against him, but if I regret anything, it will be my loss of faith in him."

Adam seized the opportunity to press his point. "If you're standing against him for me, you're pretty quiet about it, because you still haven't told me what you know."

"We've already had this discussion, Adam. I want you to succeed, and soon. But you have to find out on your own. When you do, I won't deny the truth."

She couldn't be different, and that suited him. He'd met too many women and men who didn't have a conscience and who had a price. She knew that he was scrutinizing her right then, but she sat unruffled, letting a smile play around her lips so he'd know she didn't mind that he looked at her. He wanted to take her to his lodge, away from everybody and every unsolved problem, to lose himself in her. He needed her to bind the wounds he'd inflicted on himself when he blew up at Wayne. But he'd never run from anything, and he'd never used another person. As long as his thoughts were only of himself, and he had no right to touch Melissa.

A full moon lit their way back to Frederick. Tall, leafless trees cast eerie shadows across the highway as they sped through the night. And Adam's thoughts drifted to the night he'd first kissed Melissa and how he'd spent the rest of it, sleepless, preaching to himself that nothing but disaster could come from a romantic involvement with her. But he'd paid no attention to his common sense, and the damage lay all around them. Quickly he threw out his right hand to protect Melissa as he slowed down abruptly and swerved to avoid a doe. He noticed how she tensed, and at the next rest stop he parked, walked around to her door, and gave her a hand getting out of the car. He held her loosely, stroking her back, but keeping her far enough away to make sure he didn't succumb to his feelings.

"I'm sorry I frightened you back there, but I didn't want to hit that deer."

"I'm alright. I realized you knew what you were doing."

He urged her closer. "I wish I did. Ah, Melissa, I wish I knew where we're headed." They got back in the car.

"Moral of the story is don't speed," she teased.

"Or leave woolgathering to sheep shearers," he added with a chuckle. "It's early yet. Let's stop by the Watering Hole for a few minutes." They remained there for about an hour, watching the strange night pairings, the loners, and those afraid to be alone.

"This scene is wearing on me. Are you ready to leave?"

She nodded and drained her wineglass. He held her hand as they walked out, leaving their audience gaping. He felt good, and her comment that they had just made Miss Mary's Wednesday night prayer meeting a success brought a chuckle from him. They walked arm in arm in the brilliant moonlight to his parked car. Adam stood at the passenger's door, looking at her, wanting and needing a resolution of their relationship. A pain of longing shot through him, and he bent down to kiss her. She welcomed him lovingly, her embrace strong and her lips open for the thrust of his tongue. He gave in to his feelings and admitted to himself the joy he felt when she molded herself to him and clasped him to her.

A niggling thought that he'd had early in their relationship began to plague him again, telling him to walk away while he could, to remember his vow never to let another woman control him, to let her go before she reined him in and had him at her mercy. The words "I can't" exploded from him, and Melissa stared at him.

"Can't what?"

"Shhhhh," he whispered. "Just let me hold you." He hadn't ever asked her for tenderness, though he'd been tender with her. He felt her discipline her own want and, instead, let him take what he needed from her as she reached up to receive the kiss that tenderly possessed them both. He raised his head to break it off and looked beyond Melissa and into the eyes of Louise Grant Coston, Rafer Grant's sister. He held Melissa away from him, and as though ice suddenly flowed through his veins, he stared at the woman he'd detested for more than half of his life.

# Chapter 13

The following Sunday morning, Emily fell into step beside Melissa as they left church service. They had both dressed warmly for protection against the biting winter wind, and Melissa smiled inwardly when her mother tugged the luxurious fur more tightly around herself. She was learning that her mother loved beautiful things.

"I've never enjoyed walking so much as now," her mother told her as she hunched her shoulders against the cold. "I can almost appreciate this coat. Rafer always insisted on driving, and you know how he hated for me to go anywhere by myself." Melissa looked at the woman beside her. Her face and figure seemed to have lost years in a few short weeks, and her whole being seemed to proclaim the sweetness of life. Her rich brown skin glowed, and her eyes sparkled.

"You are more beautiful every time I see you, Mama. It's the most amazing thing."

"Well, I don't know abut that, honey," Emily demurred, "but if it's true, it isn't that I'm happy—maybe it's because for the first time in years, I'm free to do as I please." She glanced down a narrow side street that jutted off Court. "I haven't tasted a cloud nine in over thirty years. They used to serve them in the Watering Hole. Let's stop there." She took Melissa's arm and steered her toward the popular bar. "When I was young, this is where we hung out. But the Banks family bought the place, changed the policy, and the older crowd took over. I don't know where the young people go these days."

"Mama, are you sure you want to go to the Watering Hole

right out of church? It'll be crowded. And what's a cloud nine, anyhow?" Her mother's laughter heightened Melissa's spirits.

"In my day, every young person knew what that was. A cheap champagne cocktail. A cube of ice, a jigger of cheap champagne, and ginger ale to the top." Melissa's grimace brought another laugh from Emily. "Honey, sophistication is a matter of definition. Sojourner Truth or Phillis Wheatley would probably have been shocked at such carrying-on, but what they did stuns me." They talked amicably until they reached the local gathering place. Melissa knew that her mother couldn't even contemplate the reaction that her presence in that place would generate. A hush and gaping stares greeted their entrance, but to Melissa's astonishment her mother ignored it and strolled confidently to a vacant table.

She watched her mother sip the harmless drink with relish but contented herself with coffee, though she hated the chicory with which southerners delighted in ruining its taste. She glanced around when her mother nudged her and asked, "Isn't that Timmy sitting over there staring at us?" Melissa suppressed a catch of breath, nearly choking herself—she'd never known anyone to look at her with such distaste.

"He looks as if he'd like to murder me," Melissa said. "But why? I haven't done anything to him."

"I know Timmy's a coward, and I know his mind has never been infected with common sense, but he isn't that crazy," Emily assured her. "I never could figure him out. I was mother to him for almost a year, and you watch. He won't even walk over here and ask me how I am." She drained her glass. "A long-stemmed glass should be handled with white gloves." Emily strolled over to Timothy.

"I haven't seen you in ages, Timmy, not since I heard you'd had an accident. Are you alright now?" Emily asked him. Melissa remembered that her mother had always been able to coax him into being gracious.

"I'm fine," he said grudgingly.

"Good," Emily said, patting him on the shoulder. "You come

see me sometime, now. You hear?" A scowl marred his face as he looked up at her.

"Aren't you lost, Aunt Emily?" Melissa marveled at the new Emily Grant, who favored Timothy with a dazzling smile, and informed him, "Not anymore, son. Not anymore!"

Melissa smiled at the devilish twinkle in her mother's eyes and turned to leave. "Mama," she said, pronouncing the word distinctly, "you're having fun at everybody's expense. Come on, let's go." Melissa paid, and they left with even more attention than they'd gotten when they walked in. They soon knew why. Rafer Grant had entered the bar in the meantime and seated himself near the door. He attempted to intercept his estranged wife.

"Don't make a spectacle of yourself, Rafer," Emily admonished with apparent disdain for his status as one of the town's leading attorneys. "If you want to talk, come on outside. We don't have to be the sole source of town news. You go on home, Melissa; I'll call you." Melissa nodded to her parents, feeling oddly alienated from them both, and walked on home.

"You either drop these ridiculous proceedings, or I'll make certain that Melissa and Adam Roundtree won't want any part of each other. The state of Maryland isn't as big as the space they'll want between them."

"You wouldn't do that to your own daughter," she gasped.

"You go ahead with that divorce, and you'll see. That man has been nothing but trouble to us."

"I love my daughter, Rafer, just as you should, but if the feeling she and Adam have for each other won't withstand whatever it is you plan to tell one of them, then I'm sorry. I only have one life, and I've wasted too much of it already. I'm going to try and live the rest of it on my own terms. Do what you like."

"You asked for it." He left her standing there, bemused, wondering what he knew. Rafer was too much the attorney to engage in idle threats.

* * *

Snow banked high around her house prevented Melissa from opening her kitchen door Monday morning, so she eased up the window and threw seed out to the birds. She tested the phone line, found it operating, and relaxed. She knew she couldn't get to her office through that heavy snow, but she didn't mind working at home so long as she had access to her on-line services. She dressed in jeans and a sweatshirt and sat down to her computer just as her phone rang. Her father didn't waste time on small talk, but went right to the reason for his call.

"I thought you ought to know that you aren't the first woman in this family to have an affair with Adam Roundtree."

Melissa sucked in her breath. If her father heard her, he ignored it. "Your aunt Louise tells me she had an affair with him years ago. I guess he just can't resist Grant women." When she didn't respond, he needled her. "What have you got to say to that, young lady?"

"I don't believe you."

"Really?" he snorted. "Then ask him."

Melissa wrapped her arms around herself and paced from one end of her den to the other. Twice she started toward the stairs leading down to the second floor and twice she remembered that she probably couldn't open her front door. She had to talk with Adam, to know if her father's story had any truth, but she wanted to be with him when she asked him about it. Right then, she needed the reassurance of his arms around her, holding her. She didn't know what she'd do if he admitted having had an affair with her aunt, a woman known among the local people for her beauty and her feminine figure. Beauty that she had envied as a young girl.

She whiled away most of the day, unable to focus on her work, almost uninterested in it. When she could stand it no longer, she telephoned Adam at home in Beaver Ridge only to have Mary Roundtree tell her that Adam went to his office on weekdays, snow or no snow.

"How did you get to the office?" Melissa asked Adam as though hers was a casual call. "I don't think I can open my front door."

"Hi," he chided for her failure to greet him. "If you can't get out of the house, I'll come over and dig you out. I hitched a snowplow to my dad's old Chevy truck and got in here with no difficulty. I'll be over there in about an hour."

Melissa changed into an off-white denim jump suit and prowled aimlessly about the house until she glimpsed Adam digging his way to her front door. Four or five inches of snow wasn't much in New York, but it stilled the town of Frederick. She watched him for a minute, dropped the curtain, and went to the kitchen to make coffee. She could at least be hospitable, she told herself, if he cleaned her walkway and steps. And any way, a man was innocent until proved guilty. Wasn't that the American way? She resisted the temptation to serve the coffee in porcelain cups, laid two paper napkins on the table, and set two mugs on them. She rubbed her hands together, caught herself doing it, and dropped them to her side. Then she rubbed her thighs. When he finally rang the doorbell, she walked to the door on wooden legs.

"Hi. What took you so long to get here?" He stepped in, pulled off his gloves, and took her into his arms for a kiss. He must have sensed her resistance, for he leaned back and looked into her face.

"What's this? You don't want me to kiss you? After digging out there in the cold for the last half hour, I deserve some warmth, don't I?" His arms tightened around her, but she turned her head.

She knew that she'd gone about it all wrong, but she couldn't help her feelings, and she wouldn't pretend. His reaction did not surprise her. She sensed at once the psychological distance he put between them, knew that if he proclaimed innocence she trod on dangerous ground. But she had to hear him say it.

"Would you like some coffee?"

He looked her straight in the eye, the twinkle that she loved devoid of warmth. "You don't feel like offering hospitality, and I don't want any. Why did you call me?"

She locked her hands behind her to still her fingers. "Let's go in the living room."

"I'm fine right here." He leaned against the front door and folded his arms. "Say whatever you've got to say, Melissa. I'm going back to work."

She took a deep breath and slowly expelled it. "My father is accusing you of having had an affair with my aunt Louise. I told him I didn't believe it." She glanced up hopefully, but received neither confirmation nor denial from his hard, unfathomable stare.

"What's the question? I see you've already made up your mind."

"I told you that I denied it to him."

"But not to yourself." He straightened up, walked a few paces away from her, and walked back. "I refuse to defend myself, Melissa. I realize that I should have told you about this months ago, before we got so deeply involved, but I anticipated that you'd react this way, and couldn't bring myself to mention it." He stopped pacing, shrugged with an air of indifference, and stared at her when she brought her hand to her chest as though to regulate her heart.

"If you're interested in the truth," he went on, "I was fifteen years old, and your thirty-year-old aunt seduced me deliberately and vengefully. And she made it very pleasant," he told her in a voice hard with bitterness. "I didn't know what had hit me. She built my ego to the heavens to make certain that I'd go back to her and I— a boy with no previous experience—went back for more. I can still hear her laughing at me. Is that what you wanted to know?"

She turned her back and knew, when he walked around to face her, that he intended to have his say. Only she didn't want to hear another word. *Adam had slept with her aunt.*

"How could you? How could you?"

"Weren't you listening? Don't you know that a fifteen-year-old boy who hasn't had any experience is no match for a thirty-year-old woman? Especially one like Louise Grant. She flaunted her sexuality, and she had plenty to show off. It wasn't until long afterward that I realized she'd done it for the pleasure of belit-tling me—a member of the Hayes-Roundtree family. I hated her, and I still despise her. I wanted vengeance against her and her whole family, and I got some a year later when I didn't tell Rafer that I'd seen his briefcase with his court papers in the men's room at the Harlem Restaurant."

Pain seemed to squeeze her heart, and she put both hands to her ears and shook her head, denying what she knew to be the truth. "And was that the end of it?"

He glared at her. "Weren't you listening, or aren't you interested in the truth?"

She turned her back. The old jealousy of her sensuously beautiful aunt—who had once suggested that she, Melissa, was the family's ugly duckling—returned nearly to suffocate her. Louise had had everything that she as a gangling teenager had lacked; she had even been Adam's first woman. She knew her reaction was unreasonable, but she couldn't help it.

"I want you to leave, Adam."

"Are you saying you hold me responsible for something that happened when I was fifteen years old? For your own aunt's criminal act of child molestation?" he asked, clearly incredulous. She looked up at him, tall and proud, lacking even a semblance of warmth toward her.

"Adam, please, just—"

"I'll leave when I've had my say. You know you're wrong, but you're looking for an excuse to get back into your father's good graces. If you don't care enough to see through his scheme, I'm glad he told you. You could overlook my deliberate act of vengeance a year after your aunt seduced me, when I was sixteen and more responsible. You could ignore an act that ruined your father's political career, but you haven't the heart to understand that a boy is most any woman's easy victim." The fierceness, the coolness of his gaze made her heartbeat accelerate, and she suddenly hurt so badly that she knew she wasn't ready for him to walk out of her life. But she refused to absolve him.

"You said you went back to her, that you wanted it to continue. You should have told me before…you should have let me choose whether to— You don't know what she was like when I was a 'plain jane' teenager. My own aunt. Beautiful. Voluptuous. All of my dates talked about her, boasted about her. And now you tell me this."

He reached for the doorknob. "This is all my mistake. I wish you well, Melissa."

She gazed up at him as he moved to open the door, apprehension thundering like wild horses in her head. She backed away from the door, disbelieving that he would leave without another word, that he'd walk out of there as though she no longer existed.

"Is that all you have to say?" she mumbled. He stepped toward her and tipped up her chin with the tip of his right index finger, as though to be certain that she understood.

"What else do you want me to say? You don't believe in me." He opened the door and left.

Adam drove the truck into the garage adjacent to his family's home, parked, and sat there. During the drive from Frederick, he hadn't let himself think over what had just happened. How long had Rafer known about him and Louise and why—Louise's glacierlike look a few nights earlier as he'd bent to kiss Melissa flashed through his mind's eye. So she was going for the kill. She'd tried repeatedly and without success since he'd been an adult to get at him, to coax him into an affair, and he'd tired of her shenanigans and told her that she didn't measure up to the women he'd known as a man. He knew she hated him, but he hadn't dreamed that she wanted revenge badly enough to reveal her own indiscretion.

He got out of the car and paced around it in an effort to walk off some of the anger building in him. He'd been willing to sacrifice more for their relationship than Melissa could imagine. Even face down his mother. But Melissa hadn't believed in him. He stopped himself just as his right fist drove toward the truck's windshield. Her rejection had hurt him. He got a shovel and walked around to clean the snow from the steps of the combination sundeck and greenhouse that his father had built on to the exterior of the dining room wall. But he felt no better after the vigorous exercise. Up in his room he locked the door, fell across his bed, and began planning for his move back to New York.

Melissa stopped by her mother's house the next morning on her way to work. She'd never done that before, and her mother would guess that something was troubling her, something unpleasant. Emily waved a hand when Melissa tried to talk in a voice muffled with tears.

"I know. I know. He told me Sunday morning that when he'd finished, the two of you wouldn't be speaking. I tried to warn you, but you didn't answer your phone. Your father won't stand by docilely and let Adam have you. He's wrong, but I know the pain and humiliation he feels where that family is concerned. The feud is a screen—that was never his battle. Knowing that his wife would always love another man ate him up inside. Melissa, his hatred of the Hayeses and Roundtrees has had thirty-one years to harden and fester. Tell me what he did."

Melissa recounted it, and encouraged by her mother's stunned expression, she went on.

"Adam was taken with her. He said so himself."

"When did it happen?"

"When he was in his early teens. Oh, it doesn't matter." The tears that pooled in her eyes failed to fall, so startled was she when her mother grabbed her shoulders and shook her.

"*My God.* It *does* matter. Louise is fifteen or sixteen years older than Adam. You mean to tell me you've fallen into the same kind of trap that I did? You've put family above your love. You made up your mind to believe Rafer and Louise before you heard what Adam had to say. Don't you know about Louise's reputation when she was younger? How could you be so foolish?"

Melissa opened her mouth, closed it, and repeated the action, amazed at her mother's harshness.

"Adam won't dance to your tune," Emily told her. "And he won't swear off of women the way Bill Henry did. He'll go on with his life, and you'll be an unpleasant memory. I never could understand why you allowed Rafer to worm himself and his influence into everything you did. I was glad when you left town, even if I didn't see my own role in it."

"I only wanted his approval. I wanted him to feel the same way about me that he did about Schyler."

Emily reached up and put an arm around her daughter. "And he knew that and used it as a weapon to bend you to his will. Now that it doesn't work, he first tried strong-arming you and then blackmailing me. We both defied him, so he took revenge. But he couldn't have done it without your help, Melissa. Oh, yes. You helped him. I thought you loved Adam. Didn't you learn anything from my life?"

"I don't know why I stopped by here this morning. I just couldn't seem to go anywhere else. I think I've upset you, and I'm sorry, Mama."

Emily Grant shook her head as though in wonder. "Honey, you came to me because I'm your mother. But you didn't learn anything from my stupidity. Well, maybe you'll learn something from this: if Bill Henry will have me, I'm his. As soon as my divorce is final, I'm going to him, get down on my knees, and beg his forgiveness. Beg him to let me live my last years with him, married or not. I don't care. And I couldn't care less about the gossipmongers of Frederick and Beaver Ridge. I need him. I just want to go to sleep and wake up in the same bed with him."

Melissa's eyebrows shot up, and she stared in mute astonishment at her mother. Appalled. Was this what she had done to herself in letting Adam go? Why hadn't she listened to her heart? She found words, but it wasn't easy.

"Mama, how can you feel this way about him after all this time? It's been thirty-one years." She watched the tears gather in her mother's eyes.

"Thirty-one? It seems to me like thirty-one hundred."

Melissa hadn't expected to accomplish much work that morning, and she didn't. The pain of knowing she'd lost Adam was almost more than she could tolerate. Why, she wondered, had Magnus Cooper chosen that morning to call? She hadn't been able to summon either her normal professional demeanor nor to act her naturally cool self. Just when she'd feared her ability to continue the conversation, he'd asked her about her relationship with Adam, and she hadn't been able to lie.

"Any chance you'll give him the boot if he shows up?" Magnus asked her with a nonchalance that she realized was clearly forced. She thought of her mother and B-H.

"Not as long as cats scratch."

"What?"

"There's not much likelihood of that," she amended.

"Then I hope you've got sense enough to go to him. It's been my experience that pride isn't good company, Melissa. And it sure won't keep you warm. Roundtree impressed me as being a fair man. If he's responsible for your misunderstanding, he'll come to you. But if you're the one who messed up, honey, he won't budge. Invite me to the big event, and I'll send your first kid a thoroughbred pony."

Melissa hadn't needed Magnus's lecture. She was in the wrong, and she knew that Adam wouldn't come to her. He'd said his last word on the subject. She wanted to go to him, wanted him back in her life and in her arms, but he'd never given her a reason to think he wanted her to be a permanent fixture in his life. Twice she'd told him she loved him, and he hadn't yet said he loved her. Only that he cared. She knew he cared, otherwise she'd have to conclude that he had a streak of promiscuity.

Melissa welcomed Banks when she sauntered in around a quarter of ten with two cups of coffee and her usual box of hot, powdered doughnuts.

"Here," Banks said, holding out the coffee. "This won't cure what ails you, but it'll at least warm your tongue."

"Why do you think something is the matter with me?" Melissa asked her, reaching for the paper cup and realizing simultaneously that she would have been smart not to ask.

"Is this the first time you've seen me today?" Banks asked.

"Yeah. Why?"

"You've just answered your own question. You met me once in the hallway, and you stood almost on top of me in the ladies' room. You took your comb out of your purse, looked at yourself in the mirror, put the comb back where you got it, and left the place."

A flash of annoyance gripped Melissa momentarily at having exposed her emotions without realizing it. "Why didn't you speak to _me?_" she asked Banks in what she meant as a reprimand.

"I did, but it didn't penetrate." Melissa set the cup on her desk and waited for what her friend would say next. Banks always had a punch line.

"At least you didn't bump into me without apologizing, the way Mr. Roundtree did. I'm thinking of writing a manual on common courtesy and distributing it to some of the people in this building."

"I'm sorry, Banks. I didn't intend to be rude."

Banks sent a perfect smoke ring toward the ceiling. "I know. But you'd better get it together with Adam. The word's out that he's making plans to move back to New York, and that's strange, because a couple of days ago, he was over at Jack Pettigrew's place ordering a new desk. They sell those in New York, don't they?" Banks didn't give Melissa time to answer. Just picked up the remainder of her doughnuts, sauntered to the door, waved, and left.

Adam threw his briefcase in the back of the Jaguar, decided the engine had been warmed up sufficiently, and pulled out of the garage. A good rain that night had melted the remainder of the snow, and he figured on getting to Baltimore in thirty minutes. How could so much have happened in less than an hour? For months he'd thought of himself in relation to Melissa, and now he had to change that. He hadn't wanted to involve the FBI in the sabotage of Leather and Hides, because he hadn't wanted to risk an escalation of the antagonism between the two families. He didn't want that now, but the break in his relationship with Melissa had added urgency to his getting away from Frederick and back to New York. He had to get her out of his thoughts, and he wouldn't do that easily if he had to see her unexpectedly a half dozen times a day. He had wrestled with his feelings for her the whole night—even when he finally slept, she'd been there to mock him in his dreams. He pulled into the right lane to let a nervous driver pass, slowed down, and decided to remain there.

He'd have sworn that she loved him. She probably did, but— He took a deep breath, turned on the radio, and whistled along with a singer whose name he didn't know. When had Melissa become so important to him that he needed her trust? He'd never given a damn whether people had confidence in him. He'd never needed to—he knew he was trustworthy. He pulled up to the Federal Building, put a couple of quarters in the parking meter, and went inside. When he left an hour later, the Feds knew everything about the sabotage of the Hayes/Roundtree leather factory, and Adam had the name of an FBI contact who would serve as undercover agent at Leather and Hides. Adam marveled at the thoroughness of the man who interviewed him; he held everyone suspect who had any connection to the factory. Adam drove next to the office of the secret agent.

"Shouldn't take long," the man told Adam. "Crooks tip their hand without knowing they're doing it."

"These are slick, and they're greedy," Adam replied. "They want to bring me down. How much time will you need?"

"From what you've told me, I'd say a week at most, but probably only three or four days. One thing. No one—not even your manager—is to know about me."

"Right."

"I'll check in tomorrow."

"Check in at my home." Adam handed the agent his card. "And make it after dark. I'll be expecting you." The man read the card, dropped it in an ashtray and struck a match to it.

"By the way, who lives there with you?"

Adam looked at the man in surprise. It hadn't occurred to him that a secret agent would suspect members of his family. "My mother and, on weekends, my brother. He's managing editor of *The Maryland Journal*." The man nodded.

Adam left feeling as though the man had violated his privacy. But that didn't compare with what he'd experienced when he walked out of Melissa's house four days earlier. He still carried the sense of abuse and abandonment that he'd felt when she withheld her trust. But he vowed he'd get over that. He'd liked her a hell of a lot, but that was all, he assured himself. He was going back to New York and put her in his past.

He telephoned Emily that night and made a luncheon date with her for the following day at noon. She declined a drink.

"My ladies at The Refuge need me to have a clear head, Adam."

She didn't seem surprised when he failed to mention Melissa, and he supposed she knew that he and her daughter had broken off their relationship.

"Emily, I'm going back to New York soon, and I want you to know how much I appreciate the work you're doing at the shelter. I hope being there hasn't caused you any pain or regrets." He lifted her hand, and her delicate fingers reminded him of the times he'd held Melissa's hand while they talked, or laughed. Or fired each other with desire.

"My only regret, Adam, is that I didn't do this years ago. And my pain hasn't ceased, but it got noticeably duller the day Rafer decided he'd be more comfortable living somewhere else." She looked at him steadily, and he saw the truth in her clear, honest eyes. "If I get another chance at a pain-free life, just one more chance at a little happiness, I'll grab it and hold on to it with all my might as long as I live."

Adam took Emily back to The Refuge, where she'd switched to volunteering full time. He hugged her and realized that he had developed a deep affection for Melissa's mother. He made his way to his cubbyhole in the basement, checked his incoming box, and hurried back to his office in the Jacob Hayes Building. He'd gotten the information he wanted. His uncle had been right; Emily Morris still loved him. He was glad for B-H, but the realization that two people could care so deeply after so long a time and under such circumstances didn't console him about his feelings for Melissa.

At dinner that Friday evening, Adam told Wayne and his mother that he planned to move back to New York.

"But you can't go before we solve the problem at the factory," Wayne complained.

"I didn't say that I would, but as soon as that's settled, I'm leaving." His mother asked whether he planned to leave before Christmas.

"I'll be here for Christmas, but I'll be leaving the following morning." He knew he sounded curt and detached. Well, so be it. He had already begun to distance himself from Frederick and from Melissa. What might have been didn't interest him. And he wasn't sorry that he'd kept a tight rein on his feelings for Melissa, that he had resisted the temptation to let go and let himself love her. He might be many things, but he knew he was a survivor. You got to be that way by protecting your flank, and in this case that meant removing himself from wherever Melissa happened to be.

"What about Melissa?" Wayne dared ask.

Adam threw the remainder of his cognac to the back of his throat and stood. "That's in the past." He ignored their stunned expressions, strode to the hall closet, got his leather jacket, and headed for the little clapboard house down the road.

Adam walked up the modest steps and caught himself wondering whether he could be content to live as B-H did—a semi-recluse who rationed his ventures out among people, avoided ties with all but his family, and did as he pleased. Why the hell should I? he asked aloud, annoyed at having let himself contemplate that easy solution to his life. He heard familiar pops from the big stone fireplace in his uncle's living room as he let himself in the house.

"You roasting peanuts?" he asked by way of a greeting.

"Naaah. These here are pecans. Nothing like a hot roasted pecan." Bill Henry raked a few nuts away from the coals and put them in a wooden bowl that he'd bought in Haiti years earlier. "Come on in. How's Mary? She didn't look so well when I saw her yesterday."

Adam sat down, stretched out his long legs, and crossed his ankles. "Mother's fine, B-H. When you saw her, she was probably practicing the technique she'd use to cut down Melissa without my riding herd on her. When she first learned about Melissa and me, she behaved as if I was a grown man, although I knew she hated the idea. But she's gotten desperate and careless of late, and it's just as well that I'll be leaving soon."

"You're leaving Melissa here to deal with Rafer and that bunch by herself?"

"Why not? They're all cut from the same cloth; birds of a feather. It's over between Melissa and me, B-H, and I expect that within a week we'll have whoever's committing those crimes at the factory behind bars. My place is in New York running my own business." He could appreciate his uncle's stare of disbelief, because he was still unable to reconcile himself to the reality of not having Melissa in his life.

"I don't believe what I'm hearing. What happened?"

Adam rubbed the back of his neck with his left hand and tried to figure out where to begin.

"It's a pretty long story, B-H, and I'm not sure I want to tell it."

"I want to hear it." Bill Henry didn't speak until Adam finished. His uncle listened attentively, nodding occasionally and sometimes frowning. Adam remembered that Bill Henry's careful attention to his childhood dreams, stories, and complaints and his way of withholding harsh judgment were the traits that had bound the two of them for as long as he could remember. In a rare outward gesture of affection, he reached over and patted his uncle's hand.

"Adam," B-H began, as though bearing a heavy weight, "didn't you and Melissa learn anything from history? Do you think life has been so beautiful for Emily Morris and me that you'd like to walk in our tracks?" Adam didn't want to talk about Melissa and himself, yet he knew that he'd gone there to give B-H a chance to say what he thought.

"Do you love Melissa? Don't answer, if you don't want to. I know you love her."

Adam reached down for a couple of roasted pecans, cracked them together, and shook them around in his closed fist. Distracted.

"What is love, B-H? If it's the willingness to let one's entire life slide by for want of another person, I'm not in love and never will be." He sat forward at the sound of Bill Henry's soft, almost pitying laugh.

"You're a strong man, Adam, but you're not Goliath enough to rid your soul of Melissa. You've got the will to do just about anything you set your mind to. You had that trait at the tender age of five, and I've always admired your tenacity. But, son, I'm sorry to tell you that you've met your match." His disbelieving stare must have amused his uncle, for Bill Henry's lips curved into a smile that flickered across his face.

"What do you mean?" Adam asked him, disliking the turn of conversation.

"I mean love isn't something you can order around, arrange to suit yourself or just banish. It will greet you at breakfast, glare at you when you're in a business meeting, and laugh at you in the dead of night. And I'll tell you something else. What you feel for Melissa will defy you to take another woman to bed no matter how much your head tells you that's what you want. Yes, sir. You've met your match."

B-H laughed aloud, and Adam knew he'd been caught with a rueful expression on his face. "You think so, do you?" he asked.

"I know so."

"I've got to be going." He bit into the pecan, savored it, and relaxed. "Cook a few more of these. They're good. By the way, I had lunch with Emily Grant today." Bill Henry jerked forward, as though his five senses had just come alive, turned and looked into his nephew's eyes. He said nothing, and no words were needed. Adam saw in his expression the hopes of a man about to glimpse the light after years in darkness. He dropped his gaze. No man should see another's naked soul.

"Emily will be a free woman in a matter of days, and she wants to see you. She didn't call your name, but she left no doubt that seeing you was foremost in her thoughts." The two of them stood, and Adam wrapped an arm around his uncle.

"I wish you luck, B-H. If you need me, you always know where I am."

"Thanks, Adam. I can't hope yet. I won't believe this is happening until I've got her in my arms again."

Adam struggled against the wind, stronger now than when he'd left home an hour earlier. He had an urge to get Thunder and ride hell for leather until he and the stallion exhausted themselves. But he didn't dodge his problems; he faced them. And he'd face this one. He hunched his shoulders when the wind increased in velocity, and dry leaves and small sticks swirled around his feet. The bright moonlight cast his long shadow ahead of him, and as he walked faster, he swore, disliking the implication. An intelligent man did not chase his shadow.

Clouds raced over the moon, but none obscured its light, and he thought of his uncle's warning that no matter what he did, where he went, or whom he met, Melissa would always live inside of him. How could a man love a woman so deeply as B-H loved Emily Grant? Grant. Bill Henry never acknowledged her married name, he recalled, but referred to her as Emily Morris, discounting Rafer's importance in her life. And she loved Bill Henry. Her simple declaration of it had moved him, and he wondered what he'd do if Melissa loved him like that.

Melissa sat in her dining room, checking her Christmas gift list. Several times that evening, she'd walked to a telephone, lifted the receiver, dropped it back into its cradle, and walked away. She sat dispirited among the glistening papers, ribbons, and gift tags.

"I don't care about any of this," she declared, wiping her eyes. "Why did I do it? Why did I let Daddy manipulate me like that? I don't care what Adam did. I want him." She wrapped her arms across her breasts and walked the floor. Finally she went over to the window and looked up at the thin clouds that whisked past the full moon. Where was he, she wondered, and what was he doing right then? She looked back at her boxes and wrappings, went over to the table, and sat down.

"I'm not going to let this or anything else throw me," she vowed, and lifted a pair of green and gold tassels and attached them to a box intended for B-H. Her mother had remarked during a rare moment of reminiscence that Bill Henry had a fondness for blue jays, so she'd bought him a book about them and a little house said to encourage them to nest. She'd bought something for everyone on her list except Ilona and Adam. She planned to give her friend a pair of tickets to an American Ballet Theater performance of *Swan Lake*. That left Adam. Maybe he didn't want anything from her.

She raced to the phone and picked up the receiver after the first ring, praying that she would hear Adam's deep voice.

"Hello." She knew that her voice betrayed her anxiety.

"Hi, sis. What's the matter?"

"Schyler! Where are you? Is anything wrong?" She clutched her stomach with her left hand, anticipating the worst.

"Nothing's wrong, at least not with me. I'm in Nairobi. Daddy just phoned me and told me to talk to you. He had a string of complaints a mile long. What's going on over there? Are you having an affair with Adam Roundtree?" Before she could answer, he continued with a litany of their father's grievances.

"Slow down, Schyler. Are you Daddy's advocate? If you are, I'm hanging up right now." A warm glow spread through her at the sound of her brother's deep, familiar laugh.

"Are you suggesting that I've slid back into ancient times? I understand Daddy better that you ever did, Melissa. Now tell me what this is all about. You and Adam. I'll be damned!"

She told him only that she loved Adam and that she'd let herself be victimized by their father's clever machinations.

"I don't understand. Tell me everything. It's my dime."

She told him everything, including Louise's abuse of Adam as a child, Adam's revenge, their mother's love for Bill Henry and his for her. Their parents' divorce. The problems at the leather factory. Her mistrust of Adam. Everything.

"Well, hell! I'd better go home. I'm starting to understand a few things that always bothered me. Let's deal with you first. I take it you've cleared the sawdust out of your eyes, and you can see that Daddy's a user. It must have knocked him for a loop when you stopped worshiping him. Melissa, I don't have anything against Adam Roundtree. He's doing his thing and I'm doing mine, and I never did give two hoots for that feud. But if that guy hurts you, look for a revival of it."

"He hasn't done anything to hurt me, Schyler. I did that to myself—and to him. I'm history with him."

He disagreed. "Not necessarily. Tuck in your pride and go to him, but don't wait until some other gal starts easing his pain. Now, what about Mama? You think she'll make it with Bill Henry Hayes?" Melissa caught the anxiety in his voice and wondered whether he disapproved.

"I don't know, Schyler. I hope so. At least she's going to try—I'd bet MTG on that." She heard the long breath that he expelled and waited.

"I'd better call her and tell her what I think. Thirty-one years! She deserves every bit of happiness she can get. You do, too, sis. Go talk to that guy. And don't worry about Daddy—he may come out of this a new man. Maybe even a happy man. I hadn't planned to go home for the holidays, but I think I will."

She hung up and went back to wrapping her gifts. Abruptly she shoved the boxes, paper, and ribbons haphazardly into a shopping bag and started upstairs, her taste for Christmas gone long before the season began. She didn't know how she'd stand it if she had to wait thirty years before she could feel Adam's arms around her again.

# Chapter 14

Adam jumped up at the buzzing sound of his beeper. A glance at the iridescent numbers of the clock on his night table informed him that it was nearly one o'clock in the morning.

"Roundtree."

"This is your agent. Two cars rendezvoused near that pine grove behind the factory for twelve minutes and left. That was three minutes ago. I'd planted a couple of mikes around, but not out there, so I couldn't monitor their conversation. We can probably expect somebody to make a move tomorrow night."

"I take it you didn't get a license plate number."

"No, but every time a criminal gets away with something, he gets more daring, a little more careless. I'll get him. Trust me."

Adam didn't try to disguise his furor nor his eagerness to get the crooks behind bars. His heart thudded rapidly at the thought that one of the cars might have belonged to Melissa, but if she were guilty, she would have to pay. He asked for a description of the cars and held his breath until the agent said that one was an old model, but that he couldn't see the other one clearly.

"Don't arrive at any conclusions yet though—this may have been a ruse to distract us while action was going on somewhere else. And I have to check out a couple of men here tomorrow. Stay close."

Adam hung up. An old-model car. Melissa's car was eight or nine years old. Hell. He got back in bed, but didn't sleep. He didn't want it to be hers. He sat up in bed and dropped his head in his hands. Anything but that. He could take anything but that. Before breakfast the next morning, he phoned his brother in Baltimore.

"Can you come home tonight? I may need you."

At eleven o'clock that morning, the agent had further news. "Your deputy manager just gave one of your men instructions that would have destroyed seven hundred and fifty pounds of hides if the man had done as he was told. Fortunately he just pretended that he'd done it. If the men know this is going on, why haven't they told you?"

"Probably because a man's word doesn't count for much sometimes, unless he has a witness. Find out whether Nelson knows about this."

"He doesn't. I've made sure of it."

"Alright. I'll be out there tonight. Let me know where you'll be."

Wayne joined Adam in the family room after dinner. "Who do you think we'll get?" Adam leaned against the mantelpiece and ran his hand over his hair.

"Beats me, Wayne. I can see that one of our men might do this out of anger if he had a grudge against us. And what better time to get away with it than when a new manager takes the job and I blame it all on his incompetence? But if a Grant's in it, that's more puzzling. I can't believe Rafer would encourage or shield a crime and lose his license to practice law. He wouldn't do it—he's too proud of his standing in the community."

"How can you be so sure?" Wayne asked. "He covered up Timothy's accident, and I've got a premonition that there's a connection with us. Otherwise, why did he accuse you of it?"

Adam shrugged first one shoulder and then the other one. "Rafer doesn't need an excuse to go after one of us. The man wallows in hatred. He's been consumed by it for so long that he's forgotten what it means to be charitable, and he's paying for it." Adam sensed his brother's discomfort. He had to repair the breach between them that he'd brought on with his harsh words in support of Melissa. He loved his brother and disliked seeing him feel his way through their conversation, making sure that he didn't say anything offensive.

"I said some harsh things to you the last time we discussed

Melissa, and you're still smarting over that. I can't say that I blame you, but neither can I swear I wouldn't do it again if the circumstances were the same. Don't let it come between us." He shrugged off the annoyance he felt when Wayne laughed.

"Let me in on the fun, will you?"

"As far as I know, that's the closest you've ever come to offering an apology. I'd as soon forget that argument, but thanks for mentioning it." Relief buoyed Adam, but only momentarily. Wayne hadn't wanted him to become involved with Melissa, and he'd been right.

"We'd better take our bikes out to the factory tonight. If we drive, we might as well send a fax saying we're coming."

"Fine with me," Wayne said, tapping one of the brass andirons with his booted foot. "I guess you'll be leaving in a few days." Adam nodded. Wayne looked him in the eye and asked, "What about Melissa, Adam? Are you really going to give her up?"

Adam squashed the irritation that he knew was unreasonable. His brother cared about him, and he had a right to ask. He straightened up, started toward the stairs, and stopped.

"Nothing new. That ought to please you." He heard Wayne's chuckle and cocked his ear for the wisdom that their father used to say always followed.

"Please me? Oh, I don't know. If I were in your place, I'd tell the family to butt out."

"Make sense, Wayne," Adam said more sharply than he intended. "The family was never in this. You know very well my personal life is my own business. This was between Melissa and me. Now it's over."

"If you say so, brother. Don't ever tell me I didn't warn you that you're making a mistake. I always envied your clear sight and your ability to make the right moves. But I never thought I'd see you make an error of such gargantuan proportions, and I do not envy you the consequences."

"Wayne—"

"Alright. Alright. Those are my last words on the subject."

Wayne scrutinized him as though puzzled. "At least for now, Adam. Well, let's get ready. You got an extra helmet?"

Adam pressed the switch on his beeper. "Roundtree. Yeah. The tanning room, you think? Alright, but station yourself somewhere nearby. I'm after an arrest. Tonight." He switched off and said to Wayne, "That was our agent. He's fingered two of them. We'd better hurry."

"Right on. Adam, does it ever occur to you to say which Roundtree is speaking? I don't mind getting credit for your brilliance, but—well, you get the idea."

Adam didn't pause. "It's an office habit, but not to worry. I don't criminally implicate you, because I usually stay out of trouble."

Wayne touched his brother's shoulder as he passed on the way to his own room. "But like you said, that's in the past. Man, you won't know what trouble is until you head out of here and leave Melissa behind."

"How would you know?"

"The voice of experience."

An hour later Adam worked the combination lock on the iron grill securing a window that overlooked a marshy pond and was sheltered by a clump of high pine groves. He and Wayne slipped into the factory through the window and made their way to the basement. Armed with a powerful walkie-talkie, Adam waited alone in the darkened "finishing" room where the tanned leather was polished, while Wayne leaned against the doorjamb of an adjoining packing room, closing a potential escape route. A surge of anger gripped Adam as the smell of chromium sulfate wafted closer and closer, alerting him to the criminals' steady approach. The men set the heavy drum on its bottom and started to attack each other.

"You're going too far, now, Mack. If nobody's mentioned any of these accidents to you, it's because you're a suspect. After all, you're the assistant manager and you're supposed to know what goes on here. Man, if you burn holes in these hides, the jig'll be up. I don't want to risk any further involvement in this thing."

Adam couldn't place the voice. He waited for the other man's words, knowing now who would utter them.

"You getting cold feet again? You're repeating yourself, buddy. I'm reminding you for the last time that this was your idea, and that makes you as guilty as the one who does the job. You sold me on it, and I paid you for it. Of course, like I said, you can bail out anytime you give me the twelve thousand dollars you owe me."

Adam struggled to control his anger. So Mack was the one. He'd passed over him in favor of Cal, because Mack never got to work on time. Why hadn't it occurred to him that this one man had a reason for wanting revenge? Mack had been in his family's employ for a quarter of a century. He'd been right in not promoting him to manager. They began stacking the hides.

"Instead of whining all the time," Mack went on, groaning as he heaved the drum to its side, "you ought to be thanking me. If I drop you, who'll save your neck from that gang in Baltimore?"

Adam shook off the tension clawing his insides as he folded and unfolded his fists and finally rested his elbows on his knees, ready to spring. Patience, he told himself. In a minute, you'll know it all.

"They could have killed you," Mack said. "That shot in your arm was just a warning. If you ask me, you ought to get into therapy. One of these days, your gambling habit is going to be the death of you."

Adam didn't need to hear more. He reached over and clicked the light switch, flooding the room and stunning the two men. Mack started to lunge toward Adam, but Timothy, the bigger man, restrained him.

"Do you want to make things worse, man? Adam Roundtree didn't come in here by himself. Unarmed."

"Smart thinking, Coston," Adam told Timothy as Wayne and the agent rushed into the room.

"If you book them here in Frederick, the sheriff will release them in minutes," Adam told the agent.

"Why?"

Adam could appreciate the agent's obvious annoyance as he rocked back on his heels, and a scowl transformed his face.

"This is a small town," Adam said. "The deputy sheriff is this man's father." He pointed to Timothy.

"Then Baltimore it is," the agent said, walking off with the two in handcuffs. "I'll call a cop from Hagerstown and take them in."

Adam stood by his bedroom window, his foot resting on the rung of a dining chair that had been in the first house Jacob Hayes built. He'd kept the chair in his room since boyhood, but he couldn't remember ever having sat in it. Yet it had a special place in his life. Would it be that way with Melissa? He knew he wouldn't forget her. How could he? Shudders ricocheted within him at the thought that he'd never know what she might have been to him. He looked at his left wrist and remembered that he'd pulled off the expensive watch before leaving home earlier that evening to go to the leather factory. Anyway, he knew it was too late to call her.

"You can talk to her now," an inner voice counseled. "You've got the perfect excuse." Tomorrow. He promised himself.

Just before noon the next day, Melissa glanced up from the mound of papers demanding her attention and saw Banks standing in the door. Nothing unusual about Banks standing in her office door, she thought, but it alarmed her to see Banks wearing a troubled expression on her face.

"Come in. What's the matter?" Melissa got up and closed the door. She couldn't imagine what had precipitated such an obvious difference in Banks. "What happened?" Melissa noticed that Banks didn't cross her knee, nor did she light a cigarette, but sat forward in the chair with her palms pressing her kneecaps.

"Janie just picked up Adam's plane ticket. He's dropping his car off at the rental agency in Baltimore, and taking the seven forty flight to New York Saturday night." Banks drew a deep breath and expelled it slowly, her expression pitying. "You didn't make it up with him, did you? You still have time, Melissa. If you let him go, you'll regret it forever."

"Thanks for being my friend, Banks, but it's already too late. If he can leave without telling me good-bye, I doubt I'd accomplish anything by going to him. It wasn't meant to be."

"Since when did you become a fatalist?" Banks snorted in disgust, more in keeping with her normal demeanor. "By the way, I was hoping you'd introduce me to Wayne. I get a funny sensation, like stars exploding all through me, every time I see that man."

Melissa's lower lip dropped. "Are you serious?"

"I wish I wasn't, 'cause I don't think he's noticed me. But, hey, we're talking about you. Get with it, girl."

She doesn't have her usual saunter nor her crusty self-possession, Melissa thought as she watched Banks leave her office. She shoved aside a feeling of depression, turned on her computer, and got to work. If she had to live without Adam, she might as well start.

Melissa clipped a metal bookmark on page 192 of Sandra Kitt's book *Sincerely* and turned out the light. Joanna Mitchell would get her man by the end of the book, but as much as she enjoyed the story, she couldn't bear the thought of anybody else's happy ending. She felt ashamed at the tears that cascaded down her cheeks, mortified that she'd let herself love a man who could walk out of her life without a word of good-bye. Yet she admitted that it was she who bore responsibility for their breakup. She'd known that Adam would not beg, that he'd state his case…maybe a second time, and you could take it or else. She'd turned him away, and he wouldn't give her a chance to do it again.

Excitement gripped her at the sound of the telephone. "H-Hello."

"Melissa, this is Adam. I'm calling to let you know that last night we caught Timothy Coston and Andrew MacKnight destroying cowhides in the leather factory. They're both in a Baltimore jail. That finishes my work here." Melissa later asked herself why she responded as she did when she hadn't cared about the answer.

"Who arrested them?" She wanted to bite her tongue, for she knew that with those words she'd completed what she started the afternoon that he cleared the snow from her walk and door-steps.

"An agent of the FBI. You don't think I'd hand them over to your uncle Booker, do you?"

"Adam, I—"

"I wish you the best, Melissa. I'm leaving in a few days for New York."

"Aren't you staying for the dedication of the Gardens for the Physically and Mentally Challenged?" Anything to keep him there, to postpone hearing the sound of that dial tone.

"That's set for noon on Friday, and I'm leaving Saturday night. Incidentally my mother has renamed the gardens for my father. She's calling them the John Roundtree Gardens. We already have over a hundred applicants, some from as far away as Baltimore and Washington."

"I see," she stammered, feeling powerless to curb what she saw as the inevitable. With each passing second, the gap between them broadened, and he didn't give her an opening. She couldn't have begged her case if she'd wanted to. And she didn't. She'd give up a lot for him, but not her pride.

"Well, I— Good-bye, Melissa."

Just before noon that Friday, Melissa joined other Frederick and Beaver Ridge notables in the heated, plastic-domed garden plot that covered three acres not far from the Monacacy River. The gardens were to serve as therapy for handicapped children, who would be encouraged to tend their own small plots. From her place in the front row, Melissa watched as Mary Roundtree rose from her seat between her two sons on the makeshift dais and told her audience how proud her husband would have been to see the project he loved so much completed. A rumble of noise overhead distracted her, and she didn't hear Adam's mother introduce him. Shivers crept up her arms when she heard a second, closer and much louder burst of noise above that she recognized as a clap of thunder. A glance at Adam told her that he'd fixed his gaze on her, and she braced herself. She wasn't going to let him see her fall to pieces.

The lights went out, and she knew from the noonday darkness and the unseasonably warm weather that a wild storm threatened them. She wrapped her arms around her middle as though to shield herself from it, but a brilliant streak of lightning and a sharp clap of thunder completely unnerved her as rain pelted the roof with the force of golf balls. Shaking, she stood up. She had to get out of there. Flashes of lightning illuminated the domed garden, and she covered her mouth with her hand.

"Melissa, what's the matter?" Banks asked her. Her breath lodged in her throat, and her lips formed a mute gasp. Another burst of thunder ripped the silence, and flashes of lightning seemed to burst into the dome. Her mouth opened in a sound-less scream just before she felt a pair of steel-like arms cuddle her to the haven of a man's chest.

The scent of his skin, the rough texture of his jaw against her temple, and familiar feel of his hands eased her terror. Adam held her. Then the sharpest flash of lightning and the loudest clap of thunder she thought she'd ever experienced filled the domed garden. Petrified, her arms tightened around his neck, and she couldn't hold back the wrenching scream.

"It's alright. I'm here and I've got you—I won't let anything happen to you. Just take a few slow breaths." He hurried to the entrance and put his coat around her. She didn't ask him what he intended to do. She didn't care—she was with Adam, and he would protect her. She didn't offer resistance nor question him when he picked her up, dashed through the pelting rain, and put her in his car.

"Give me your door keys." She fumbled in her pocketbook and placed them in his hand.

"Try to relax, I'll make some tea," he stated after removing their coats from around her. Melissa wanted to tell him that she didn't want tea, only his arms around her. She leaned into a corner of the sofa while he left her to go into the kitchen. Another clap of thunder shook the house, and she clasped her hands tightly over her mouth and put her face between her knees. He handed her a cup of tea and placed his own on the glass coffee table.

"How do you manage these storms when you're by yourself?" She felt his arms around her and, though she knew it was childish, she suddenly welcomed the storm.

"I'm sorry to drag you into this, Adam, b-b-but this is the worst one I've experienced in years. One of the reasons I liked New York is that there aren't many storms like this one." She snuggled closer, but his arms remained loosely about her. "I don't know how to thank you for getting me out of there. I was scared, and I didn't want people to know it." He stood, and she looked toward the window. His gaze followed hers.

"Appears to be over. You'll be alright now."

"You—you're not leaving."

"Yes, I am. Mother and Wayne need transportation home." Fear shot through her. He didn't intend to patch it up with her. He could walk away just like that. He had acted the part of a gentleman, helped someone in distress. She could have been anybody. She looked from his shuttered eyes and his impersonal manner to his wet clothing and led the way to her front door.

"Thanks for helping me." She tried to form the word "goodbye" but couldn't.

He nodded. "I couldn't have done otherwise." She opened her mouth to speak, but she couldn't make a sound, and her right hand didn't obey her command to reach out to him, but dangled at her side. She watched, helpless, as he saluted her in a gesture that struck her as sarcastic, stepped out of the door, and sprinted to his car. Gone.

Her heart pounded at the sound of the Jaguar's engine taking him away. She grabbed her chest as though to slow down her heartbeat and leaned against the front door. After a few minutes she could take deep breaths and managed to calm herself. She took his untouched cup of tea to the kitchen, emptied it into the sink, and washed it along with hers, wondering if she'd ever do anything else for him. After an hour during which she distracted herself with "Oprah," she got a pencil and sheet of paper and began to list the things she had to do before she could consider her slate with Adam clean. Their relationship had ended, but her responsibility to him had not. She finished writing, typed it on her word processor, printed it out, and climbed the stairs.

The next morning Rafer summoned Melissa to a family conference, and she alerted her mother, certain that Emily hadn't been included.

"I don't know who else will be there, but I want you to come along. There's no telling what he's up to." She told her about Timothy's arrest.

"I was afraid Timothy had gotten in with the wrong crowd. When he was a boy, he was always into something unwholesome."

Melissa found her aunt Louise, Louise's husband, Timothy, and her father speaking in hushed voices when she arrived. Seconds after her father began to speak, her mother walked in wearing a chic Armani pants suit and her fur coat draped on one shoulder. Emily Grant could have passed for a fashion model had she been a few inches taller. She marveled that her father could camouflage his surprise so well, and she suspected that she alone knew how angry he was. Her mother paid him no attention.

"Adam Roundtree has gone too far," Rafer exploded. "Blasting a hole in Timmy's arm wasn't enough for Mr. Round-tree. He's framed our Timmy and had him arrested. I bailed him out an hour or so ago." He nodded toward his nephew. "Well, we've indicted Adam for the shooting and for defamation of character. I won't have our family name smeared by Adam Roundtree." In answer to Emily's question, Timothy revealed that he had been charged only with trespassing, but that Mac-Knight had been booked on a far more serious charge. Melissa saw Adam's lenient hand in that.

"He could have thrown the book at you, Timmy," Emily told the man. "Don't you think you ought to tell us truthfully who shot you? We know Adam didn't do it."

Melissa regarded the players in their little family drama.

Her father glared at her mother though she thought she detected his admiration for her as well, and to the irritation of all present but herself, her mother sat relaxed with the serenity of a bejeweled regent surrounded by her loyal subjects. Melissa smothered a laugh. Adam's mother wasn't the only consummate actress of her generation in Frederick— Emily Grant could hold her own with any of them. Among those present, she didn't doubt that only she and her mother cared about the ruination of an innocent man. Adam. She stood to leave.

"I think I ought to tell you, Daddy, that I just mailed the district attorney my sworn affidavit that Adam was with me at his lodge on the Potomac when Timmy was shot, and I also sent Adam a notarized copy. I'm prepared to say the same thing in any court. Adam did not shoot Timmy, and I won't be party to a frame-up." Emily stood as though preparing to join Melissa, but instead she walked over to Timothy.

"How'd you get mixed up in this? Might as well tell the truth—it will come out anyway."

He shrugged before mumbling, "I've been gambling, and one thing led to another. When I tried to quit and didn't go to the gaming tables, one of the gang took a shot at me. Said it was a warning. Mack paid off a couple of my debts."

Rafer's voice rang out. "I don't believe you. Are you saying that because you're afraid of Melissa? Have you forgotten who I am? Your attorney, that's who."

Melissa looked her father in the eye. "And for a gambling debt, you're ready to sacrifice a man who's made a unique contribution to this town, a citizen in the fullest sense. Come on, Mama, I'll drop you off at The Refuge on my way to work." To her amazement, her father followed them out of his office and stopped them in the hallway.

"I thought you'd be through with this volunteer work by now, Emily. I thought you'd have gotten it out of your system. I want us back together, but not while you're playing up to those people."

Emily's face bore an expression of astonishment before

laughter spilled from her throat. "Be serious, Rafer. Only a chicken is stupid enough to rush back into a cage after having been free all day." She looked at her watch. "My divorce will be final in fourteen hours and one minute. Our farce is over." She reached out to touch his hand, but he quickly withdrew it.

"We made a mess of our lives, Rafer, and I'm sorry for my part in that. I intend to get mine straightened out, and I hope you do, too. Schyler has avoided the curse of this feud, because he got away from here and didn't let any of it touch him. And when Melissa hurts badly enough, she'll go to Adam and undo the mess she's made of their lives. But she'd better hurry."

Adam packed for his return to New York. He didn't want any of his mother's questions, but he knew she'd stay with him until he left, so he reconciled himself to the inevitable.

"What are you doing about Melissa?" He didn't answer at once, but picked up a brush and used it to clean a pair of soft leather moccasins while he thought.

"You asked me that two or three days ago, Mother. Nothing has changed." If he sounded a bit testy, she should expect that. He tucked the shoes into a sack, turned, and went into his private bathroom. He propped his left foot on the edge of the tub and rested his left elbow on his knee. He'd finished the job and caught the troublemakers, but the letdown he felt was a new thing, as though he lacked completeness. As if he'd lost something of himself, something on which he had unwittingly relied. He looked at his watch, went back in the room, and resumed his packing. As he expected, his mother remained where he'd left her, sitting on the side of his bed. If he had to talk about Melissa or listen to his mother talk about her, he knew he'd succumb to his urge to call her. He'd done that last night, and her first thought had been of her family. Had Booker Coston arrested his own son? She hadn't said the words, but that was what she'd implied. He walked back into the room and resisted kicking the side of the armoire.

He'd never express to anybody what he felt when he walked

out of her house that afternoon. He had wanted, needed her
words—that he'd done nothing wrong, that her aunt Louise bore
responsibility for what had happened between them. Melissa had
wanted affection, maybe lovemaking. He didn't know. Who the
hell could figure out her mind? But she hadn't taken that first
step, and he'd figured she wouldn't. So he'd left. He'd handed
himself something akin to a death sentence. But he'd left, and
he wasn't sorry.

"Just tell me this." His mother hadn't been in the habit of
nagging him, and she wouldn't do it now, he decided, if she
didn't need satisfaction about her son's well-being. She didn't
want a Grant in his life, but she didn't want him to be unhappy,
either. Could she be mellowing? He gave her his full attention.

"Were the Grants involved in the trouble at Leather and
Hides? You said Mack engineered it. Who helped him?"

"Timothy Coston was the lookout, but he's guilty only of
trespassing. Poor fellow—he let himself be blackmailed into it.
The Grants had nothing to do with it, Mother." He stopped
packing and sat beside her.

"I'd rather not talk about this, but you seem compelled to get
the details. Melissa had no part in MacKnight's havoc at Leather
and Hides." He tossed the affidavit to her. "She's gone to some
lengths to support me against Rafer's accusations."

"Then why are you leaving like this?"

He got up and locked his suitcase, uncomfortable with her
queries, but unwilling to hurt her by refusing to answer. In three
hours he'd be on the plane, and nobody he knew in New York
dared question him about his behavior.

"Let's just say I've paid for an innocent, youthful indiscretion.
Nobody can screw up your life for you, Mother. You have to do
that yourself."

She frowned. "Is yours screwed up?" He released a grudging
smile. His mother hated that word.

"Is it?" she persisted. Adam dropped a hand lightly on her
shoulder, at once consoling her and attempting to stop her. She

shook it off, and he knew that she'd have her say, but he didn't have to answer her.

"Why can't you wait until after Christmas?"

How could he tell her that he needed distance between Melissa and himself, that he had to push aside temptation? How could he tell her that Melissa had erased from his consciousness every other woman he'd ever known? That he'd come close to loving her?

"I'll fly down Christmas Eve and spend the night," he threw out as he set a case down in the hallway. Mary unfolded the paper that he had handed her and read its contents.

"Adam, do you love her?" Her voice sounded less firm than it had a little earlier, as though she fought tears. He was about to tell her he didn't think so, that he wasn't certain, when Wayne walked in and saved him the necessity of a reply.

"We'd better get moving, if you want to stop by B-H's place." Adam kissed his mother's cheek. "Don't worry about me, Mother, I can take care of myself." He noticed her somber expression and the absence of her usual confident air.

"You always could do that," Mary said, "but you haven't ever hurt like you're hurting now." He felt the heat of his blood burning his face.

"Let's go, Wayne." They didn't speak during Wayne's demonic drive the short distance to Bill Henry's house. Adam got out of Wayne's car, glad to be alive, and wishing he'd driven himself in the Jaguar as he'd originally planned.

"This thing won't fly no matter how much gas you give it, don't you know that?"

"Thought you could use a little diversion," Wayne answered, obviously unperturbed by the faint rebuke.

"Like having my heart plummet to my knees? You're so considerate."

They sat around the fire on either side of their uncle, prepared to tolerate one of the latest herbal teas Bill Henry had received from Winterflower. He did hand Wayne a warm glass fragrant with rosemary, but he opened a bottle of fine VSOP cognac, gave Adam a glass, and poured him a drink.

"I expect you'll be full of this stuff by the time you get to New York. If I were in your place, I know that's what I'd do. The day Emily married Rafer Grant, I stayed sober until after the wedding, making sure the deed was done, you might say. But an hour later I was three sheets to the wind and stayed that way for two weeks. Then I sobered up, and signed on for Vietnam. I must have been the only man in the service who didn't want to go back home." He changed the subject so quickly that Adam had to laugh. His uncle knew just how far to go with him.

"Run over to see Winterflower first chance you get and tell her what's happening with me. 'Course I expect she knows. Go anyway. Westchester's beautiful this time of year with its hills and snow and the Christmas lights decorating the houses and lawns. And I like the peace—it's so quiet there." He raised his head as if to bring himself back from a dream. "You go and see her. Maybe she'll put some sense into you."

Adam sipped the drink, savoring its flavor and aroma, but he remained silent. When Bill Henry wanted to say something, he said it. He was that much like his sister, Mary.

"I hate to see you walk away from something you want, Adam. There's no virtue in useless martyrdom. If life has taught me anything, it's that one lesson." Adam turned toward his uncle to announce that he was leaving, but the faraway look in the eyes of that strong man stopped him.

"I didn't pressure Emily enough to stand up to Mittie and Moses Morris, and I should have. I've paid for that every day since."

Adam downed the remainder of his drink, stood, and signaled Wayne to join him, but his brother remained seated. "I know what you're saying and what you're trying to protect me from, B-H," Adam said, "but don't let it bother you. I can handle it."

"Then you're a better man than I am, son."

Adam's eyes widened, their often luminous twinkle dulled by his vision of the future. For the second time since he'd left home for college, indeed in the last five days, his uncle had called him "son." Somewhere in that was a message. He slapped B-H on the shoulders in a gesture of affection.

"You're making too much of this. I feel like I've had more lectures today than in my first week as a college freshman. Hang in there, B-H, and if you want me for—well, for whatever, call me." He brought himself up short. B-H didn't want his hopes raised, and he had almost offered to be his uncle's best man.

Wayne drove through Frederick, past the Taney house, and Adam felt his heart constrict when he glanced out of the window and remembered Melissa's funny and foolish little habit of spitting in its direction. He spread his knees and slid down in the soft leather seat.

"Want me to drive by there? Just for a minute?" Adam didn't ask where, and the negative movement of his head sufficed for an answer.

Sitting at last in an aisle seat in front of the curtain that separated first class and cabin class of his Piedmont flight, Adam released a deep breath and surrendered to the fatigue that had dogged him for days. He'd been hoping that he wouldn't have a seatmate, but one arrived and immediately attempted to press him into service. Would he put her carry-on in the overhead bin? He would and did. Would he excuse her so she could go to the lavatory? He did. She returned, sat in her seat beside the window, and decided she needed a magazine. Would he—? Adam turned to face her.

"Madam, this is a fifty-minute flight. Please resist the temptation to spend the entire time getting in and out of your seat."

When her scowl failed to move him, she offered her feminine charm. Adam laughed.

"Lady, I've had it up to here with women." He sliced the air above his head. "You're wasting your time."

She crossed a pair of long brown legs, adjusted her suit jacket to avoid wrinkling the hem and leaned back in her seat. "That's no surprise. I'm out of practice." She opened her lizardskin handbag and took out a deck of cards. "How about some black-jack? I usually play against myself, but it's nice to have a real game for a change."

He didn't want a conversation with her, and he didn't want to play blackjack, but she had aroused his curiosity. A good-looking woman, around thirty-five, he supposed, who dressed with taste and money. And she'd just admitted to not having a man in her life for some time, at least not one susceptible to her brand of allure.

"Deal."

She dealt him two jacks, and he thought of the song about new fools. "I'm really not interested in a game," he told her, and turned away. She pushed a business card toward him.

"You wouldn't happen to need an office manager, would you? I just got fired from a big insurance company, and I have a child to support."

He tried not to listen, but compassion was as much a part of him as his skin. "What for? What were you accused of?"

"I refused to lie for my boss. I could fight it in court, but I need the money. Besides, I wouldn't win—it would be my word against his. I worked there for ten years, and I can't get a reference."

Adam sat up straight, adjusted his pants at the knees, and looked her over. He asked her the name of the company and what her duties had been. The flight attendant offered drinks, and he took a bourbon and soda, but she declined. One in her favor, he noted. He steered the conversation to other areas while he wondered how an office manager could afford such expensive clothes. She answered his unasked question when she told him. "Half of my salary went for clothes, because my boss demanded that the women working there dress like socialites."

Adam heard the change in the thrust of the engines and made up his mind. "Come to see me Monday morning." She looked at the card he handed her and drew back.

"You're—I didn't know who you were, honest. I mean, I wouldn't have—" Her hands dropped into her lap. "Mr. Roundtree, please don't build up my hopes for nothing." The pilot turned off the seat belt sign, and Adam stood and took her bag out of the overhead bin. "And to think, I asked you to...I don't know what to say."

"I know. I'll see you Monday morning at eleven." He looked back at her. "The women who work in my office wear whatever they like."

Adam walked rapidly through LaGuardia Airport. If the energy pulsing around him was an omen, he wouldn't have time to think of Melissa. And at least he wouldn't have to go back to her for another office manager.

Melissa opened her door reluctantly, hoping she wouldn't have to deal with her father. She stared, tongue-tied, at Bill Henry until he asked her if he could come in.

"Why, yes. Yes, sure," she stammered.

"I know you're surprised," he said, "but probably not much more than I am. I've been sitting home counting off the hours, and it just got to be too much. About the only other person whose company I could stand right now is Adam's, and he's not here." When Melissa's raised eyebrow allowed him to see her skepticism, he explained.

"I wouldn't want to be near your mother, either, until after midnight tonight, because I've never yet put my hands on another man's wife and the temptation to do that would be too great. Three more hours."

"But that's nothing compared to how long you've waited already." He took the chair she offered and stretched out his legs. So much like Adam, she thought.

"Melissa, don't you believe that. I could bear it before, because I didn't think of Emily in relation to the passing time. She was lost to me forever. I came to terms with it, but now I have hope. I trust I'm not intruding—I just wanted to while away the time with a friend."

"I won't ask if you'd like coffee, because Adam said you don't drink stimulants, just those teas that Winterflower concocts. How about some mint tea?" He accepted her offer, and she brought large mugs of the fragrant tea for them both. He took a few sips and set the cup aside.

"Melissa, have you decided to give Adam up? Is there a

chance that you two could learn what happened to your mother and me and let the same thing occur to you? Adam told me Emily bloomed into a different woman when Rafer moved out, and I know how much more like a live and breathing man I've felt since then. Looks like we both just shriveled up inside, and I hate to think that the same thing will happen to you and Adam. Did he call you before he left?"

"Yes, but only to tell me about the arrests." His look of disbelief disconcerted her.

"Come, now, Melissa. He wasn't obliged to do that. Sounds to me as if he used it as an excuse to call you. Didn't you talk?"

"Not really. I was so surprised and pleased to hear from him that I blurted out the wrong thing, and I knew it. He didn't call me again, just left town without another word."

"You're a businesswoman, and I hear you swing some heavy deals. So use your head. Adam is strong, and he's tough, but you can bend him with your little finger. Just apply what you already know." He stood to go, and she walked with him to the front door.

"B-H, I'm glad you stopped by. I'll pull out of this, but it may take me a while." He bent and kissed her cheek, and she stood with the door ajar until he reached the sidewalk. Ten o'clock. She hadn't known a night could be so long, and it had only begun. She went to the kitchen, put the mugs in the dishwasher, doused the downstairs lights, and started up to her bedroom. She got the phone on its fourth ring.

"Melissa, darling. Tell me you're watching this beautiful black dancer with the long neck right now on the public television station. She is exquisite. Such a ballerina!" Melissa told Ilona that she hadn't been watching.

"Then you are with Adam. Hmmm. What eyes this man has!" Melissa tried to pull herself together before Ilona sensed her mood, but she didn't succeed. "He isn't with you?"

"Ilona, Adam is in New York, maybe four blocks from you. We've split." Ilona's silence told her more than words would have.

Finally her friend asked her, "Is it over for good? It can't be."

"He didn't tell me good-bye."

"I'm sorry—" then after a minute "—but darling, turn on the ballet. You can be unhappy and still enjoy this wonderful ballerina. Call Adam and tell him you made a mess of things and you want to make it up."

"How do you know it's my fault?" Melissa huffed.

"Because I'm sensible. He didn't give you up voluntarily, darling. I saw him with you. Remember? You're the one who needs to have the head examined."

"Alright, I'll watch the ballet. And don't worry, I made my bed hard, and I won't complain about lying in it."

Ilona snorted. "Big words, darling. Just think how much more fun it would be if the bed was a little less hard and you weren't in it by yourself."

# Chapter 15

Melissa closed her desk drawer and opened the wrapper of her fifth Snickers since she'd returned from lunch an hour and a half earlier. She stared at her blank computer screen while she devoured the miniature candy bar. She had dialed her mother and hung up before the first ring. Her walk up to Banks's office had been without reward, and as she stood looking at Banks's empty desk chair, she remembered belatedly that her friend had gone shopping when they separated after lunch. At the other end of the long hallway, she found that all of the paper cups had been used, and she had to drink from her hand. Where was everybody on Monday afternoon, she wondered, though she ordinarily wouldn't have noticed the desolateness, because she, too, would have been busy. She trudged back to her office suite.

"Just a minute, Mr. Roundtree, she just walked in." Melissa's secretary punched the hold button, and she went into her office and closed the door. Her heart fluttered and excitement flared up in her as she anticipated the sound of his voice. Maybe this was it—maybe this time he'd tell her he cared, that he couldn't wait to be with her. She calmed herself.

"Hello, Adam. How are you?"

"Hello, Melissa. I'm just fine. I'm calling to tell you that I have decided not to extend Lester's contract. We all agree that he's competent and efficient, but we—my staff, from Jason to the new messenger—dislike him. You're entitled to know why I'm letting him go. It's his officiousness. Olivia threatened to quit, and that settled it. She's indispensable."

"Are you planning to hire another office manager?"

"I've already done that." He said it too quickly, she thought, as though being able to do so held a measure of triumph. "I didn't use a search firm this time. I met her on the plane coming up Saturday night, and I think she's exactly what we need." You mean what you need, Melissa surmised as she fought a feeling of melancholy, but she refused to allow him the pleasure of knowing it, and her response concealed her real feelings.

"I see. MTG is glad to have been of service, and I hope we may continue to count you among our clients." She found his silence aggravating, but it was his call, his next move, and she remained silent, refusing to ease the way for him.

"Have you ever done anything that you later regretted?"

"Hasn't everyone?" she asked, wondering about the question and stalling because she couldn't figure out what had prompted it.

"You're not everyone," he told her in a voice that was a little rough and lacked its usual authority. "I'm interested only in you. Have you?"

"Of course. Why?" She picked up a pencil and began tapping its eraser rhythmically against the phone.

"How did you manage to forgive yourself, Melissa? Or did you?" She stopped the tapping.

"How did I—?" He interrupted and spoke rapidly as if anxious to release something he'd held for a long time, to finish an unpleasant task.

"Something else I've wanted to ask you ever since we met."

"What?"

"What do you think of masquerade parties? Do you like them?"

At first she thought he might want to invite her to one. Then she wondered if he was accusing her of some pretense.

"Adam, this isn't the best day I've had recently, so would you just say whatever it is that's bothering you?"

"Sure. How about answering my question?"

"I can take masquerade parties and most other kinds or I can leave them. Some of the most unforgettable ones have been distasteful, but I remember others because they brought pleasure that I least expected and that had a lasting impact." She tried to fathom his sigh of obvious dissatisfaction at her remark.

"Tell me about it!" he said, affirming his frustration. His pause led her to expect more, something he'd forgotten, something more personal. But he only added, "Give my regards to your mother, Melissa. I'm glad I got to know her. Take care."

"Adam—"

"What is it?"

She thought she detected hope in his voice, but he'd been so distant in recent days that she couldn't risk more evidence of his disinterest.

"Adam, I— Take care." She hung up.

Melissa struggled with the turmoil into which her conversation with Adam had plunged her. She couldn't decide what his questions implied. The man with whom she'd just spoken had not displayed the tough candor that she thought of as such an essential part of Adam's makeup. Furthermore, he hadn't even mentioned the affidavit, and she knew that the document was of importance to him. The oversight bordered on rudeness, a trait that she couldn't associate with him. She wished he hadn't called her.

"I'm not sitting here moaning over that man or any other one," she lectured herself. She went to her lavatory, splashed cold water on her face, applied a touch of makeup, and went back upstairs to look for Banks.

"Let's go look for some antiques after work," she suggested to her friend. Banks lit a cigarette and took a few draws, looked Melissa up and down, and declared, "You sure won't find him wandering around in Bessie's Yesteryear, honey. Adam's in New York. For good, I heard."

"I know that, Banks. Do I ever."

"What are you planning to do about it? Just sit around here and dry up?"

"Right now, I just want to make it through today. I didn't send him packing—he left."

Not many people could match Banks's expressions of disgust, Melissa decided, watching her arched eyebrows and tired shrug.

"He's still breathing, isn't he?" It was more a statement than a question. "But if you like being miserable, you won't find a better opportunity. Let's call it a day." Everybody told her that she had to go after Adam, but she didn't know how she could. "Everybody" didn't know that Adam had never professed to love her, and without that armor she couldn't make herself approach him.

Why did he continue punishing himself, calling her under any reasonable pretext in the hope that she'd tell him what he wanted to hear? He'd spent one night in his apartment, and already he hated it. Not that he minded living alone; he didn't. But he'd gotten used to looking forward to seeing her every day, often many times. The last two weeks hadn't been easy ones. He needed her, and he sensed that she wanted them closer, but he couldn't compromise on the issues of trust and faith. He stood on his balcony looking toward the Hudson River and the building where she'd lived. Once, he hadn't doubted his ability to walk away from her and stay away. But he hadn't counted on the pain he felt when she showed him that she didn't have faith in him, didn't trust him.

A harsh wind swirled around him, bringing below freezing air that penetrated his heavy cashmere sweater, and he walked back into his living room. Why couldn't he get her out of his mind, out of his system, out of his— He sat down on the oversized leather sofa, spread his legs, and rested his elbows on his knees. Was she really in his heart? He cared. He cared a lot. But did it really go that deep? He walked into his den, picked up the phone, held it, and returned it to its cradle. He wasn't about to whip himself again, getting his hope raised and his libido unruly from the sound of her voice.

"Damn! I've got to get on top of this thing. I promised myself that I wouldn't give another woman the upper hand with me." He looked at his watch. "And that includes Ms. Grant."

He picked up the phone again—and dialed. "Hello, Ariel," he said when she answered on the first ring. He resented that habit of hers even before he greeted her. As he expected, she commented on his long absence and wanted to know when they might get together. But to his surprise, he demurred, telling her that he'd just gotten into town, that he was only touching base and would call her in a few days. His uncharacteristically inconsistent behavior disgusted him, and what he considered a softness in himself made him uneasy.

He tied a scarf around his neck, threw on his coat, and went out. Twenty minutes later he stood in front of Carnegie Hall. It hadn't been his intention to go there, but he figured the Preservation Hall Band might be just the thing. If he concentrated on Dixieland jazz, he couldn't stew over Melissa. He paid thirty dollars for the remaining forty minutes and went in. Twenty minutes later he left. The last time he'd heard live jazz, the fingers of Melissa's left hand had been entwined with his right one. He pulled up his coat collar and headed up Broadway. He loved New York. Hell, no, he didn't. He couldn't stand it.

Melissa steadied herself and took her mother's arm as they entered the district attorney's office where an attendant directed them to seats behind her father, Timothy, and his mother, Louise. The chairs had been arranged to make the office resemble a courtroom, with rows on either side of an aisle that led to the DA's desk. Before she succumbed to the urge to look for Adam, she put on the dark glasses that she'd bought for the purpose— to shield herself from his knowing looks and the seductive twinkle in his eyes. He sat with Wayne on the other side of the aisle, and she knew at once that with the seating arrangements putting her in her father's camp—against him—the gulf between them would widen the minute he realized it.

And as if by a magical ability to read her mind or to divine her concerns, he looked back and locked his gaze on her face, nodded briefly, and turned around. Less than a week had passed since he'd gone back to New York, but those few days had given her a glimpse of what forever without him would be. She recognized the gentle squeeze of her mother's hand as a gesture of support and wondered how she'd ever gotten along without the wonderful woman at her side.

The assistant district attorney breezed in with an air of importance greater than that to which her status entitled her. She stopped to shake hands with Adam and Wayne, nodded to Rafer, who sat away from the aisle, and began the proceedings.

"Mr. Grant, as Mr. Coston's attorney, would you repeat the charges, please."

Rafer made the accusation, but Melissa thought he lacked his usual verve, that his heart was no longer in it.

"Miss Grant, would you please read your sworn affidavit." The clerk brought the document to Melissa, and she stood and read from it. When she finished, she had to look at Adam, had to see his reaction to her public confession that she had spent half a night with him at his lodge. Their first time together. Her first time. She brushed away the tears that coursed down her cheeks. He had turned to look at her while she read it, and he didn't alter his gaze. But from where she stood, she couldn't see his expression, though she did know that the twinkle in his eyes seemed to remain still. Dull.

Suddenly Timothy stood, resisting Rafer's efforts to make him sit down and be quiet. "I don't want to go on with this," he said. "I never did want to accuse him." He nodded toward Adam. "He didn't have anything to do with it. I got into some trouble in Baltimore, and the guys warned me with that shot. That's all." The DA's office concluded the proceedings, and Melissa hurried out, pulling her mother with her. Adam and Wayne stopped them in the lobby.

"Thank you for the affidavit, Melissa. The DA has assured me that it exonerated me, so even without Timothy's confession, I wouldn't have been indicted." So cool and formal, like a dash of cold water, she thought.

"I only did the decent thing," she said, adopting what she took to be his demeanor. She watched Adam hug her mother in a warm, tender greeting and felt an unreasonable tinge of jealousy.

"I'm glad to see you, Adam," Emily said. "By the way, have you met my daughter?" Neither Wayne's laughter nor Adam's indulgent grin sat well with Melissa.

"My mother's a comedienne, now," she said to no one in particular. Adam introduced Emily to Wayne, and the two stood there making conversation, while Adam and Melissa gazed at each other. She wanted to reach out to him and couldn't understand why he didn't respond to the longing he must have seen in her eyes. She swallowed the bitterness she felt at his determination to withhold himself from her, to be oblivious to the needs he had cultivated in her. Needs that he alone had fulfilled. She waved at them and left.

Twenty minutes later she walked into her office, pulled off the dark glasses, and threw them across the desk.

"Oh, dear," she sighed, awareness dawning, "how could he know what I was thinking or feeling? He couldn't see my eyes." With a humorless chuckle she tipped her hat to herself—she had outfoxed Melissa Grant. Her purpose in wearing the glasses was to protect her emotions while she read that paper, and when she'd looked at him, he hadn't seen her, only her glasses.

She switched on her computer, lecturing to herself while it checked itself out. "I will not wonder when he arrived, whether he'll call before he goes back, or when he's leaving. I will not give a hoot." She looked at her e-mail and enjoyed a provocative message from Magnus Cooper.

"I suppose by now the men of Maryland are in mourning, having lost you to Roundtree," he wrote. "But if I'm wrong and you're slower than I think, drop me a note."

"You're wrong, and I'm slower than you and everybody else think," she answered, switching to her "talk" mode in the hope that he was at the computer and she'd get an immediate answer.

"Come down here for the holidays, and give him something to think about."

She laughed. He was there. "Sorry. That's family time. I'd have to bring my mother," she teased, enjoying the fun.

"Fine with me. If she's half your equal, don't hesitate to bring her."

"The question is whether I'm half her equal. Emily Grant is a beauty."

"This machine doesn't transmit whistles—I'll have to get another one. You coming down?"

"Maybe another time." She signed off.

By five o'clock she knew she wouldn't hear from Adam. She trudged home, went through the motions of eating and, completely out of sorts, crawled into bed and counted sheep, butterflies, horses, and cows until she fell asleep around two o'clock.

Melissa arrived at her office a half hour earlier than usual the next morning. If she couldn't be with Adam, she wanted to be alone, and she couldn't manage that unless she'd closed her office door before the tenants on her floor arrived for work. She missed Banks. Not that her friend wouldn't happily provide company, but Banks had fallen hard for Wayne Roundtree—and apart from work, didn't allow herself to think or speak of anything except her schemes to make Wayne reciprocate.

*I've got my own problem with a nonreciprocating Roundtree,* Melissa grumbled to herself. She got up and went over to straighten Eleanor Roosevelt's picture that hung on the wall facing her desk, and the door burst open bringing a whiff of fine French perfume. And Emily Grant.

She gaped as her mother strutted forward, waving her left hand before here. "Mama. What on earth—? Mama?" Emily swung round and round, her head thrown back and laughter spilling from her lips.

"Look. Look at it. Look!" She held her left hand within inches of her daughter's face. Melissa's shrieks of joy filled the room, and she gripped her mother in a loving embrace.

"Oh, Mama, I'm so happy for you. When? You didn't call or say a word, and yesterday morning you acted as if nothing had happened between you two. And I was scared to ask you. Tell me, when did—?"

"He gave it to me this morning, the same one I took off thirty-one years ago."

"But when? I mean, how did you get together?"

"My divorce became final midnight last Friday, and nine o'clock the next morning, I knocked on Bill Henry's door. I didn't have to get on my knees and beg; he was waiting for me. I didn't leave him until yesterday morning when I had to go to that hearing. And I left the courthouse, went home and put some clothes in a suitcase, and went right back to him. Are you really happy for me?"

"You know I am. I don't think anything could make me happier."

Melissa marveled at the swiftness with which her mother's sparkling face sobered with concern. "Nothing? *Nothing?* Oh, honey, go after Adam. Now I know what you're throwing away. At last I know what the fuss is about. Don't lose the chance to love him in the bloom of your youth. 'Of all sad words of tongue or pen—'"

"I know, Mama. 'The saddest are these: "It might have been!"'" When is the wedding?"

"New Year's Eve at five o'clock. I've already hired a caterer, and I'm going to get married in white satin. Don't look so shocked. I don't care about tradition. Bill Henry said he used to dream of seeing me coming up the aisle to him dressed in white satin and lace and carrying white calla lilies, and I'm going to make his dream come true."

Melissa quickly wiped the frown from her face, though she doubted that anything she did or said could diminish her mother's joy. Yet she couldn't resist adding, "Won't people think that you and B-H— I mean, so soon after the divorce?" Melissa stared, aghast, when her mother arched her eyebrows and shrugged with disdain.

"I know better. So do B-H, Rafer, and my children. I couldn't care less what the gossipmongers of Frederick and Beaver Ridge think. What people might think circumscribed my life for over a quarter of a century, thanks to Rafer." What's come over this woman, Melissa wondered, when Emily suddenly beamed and told her. "Sorry I can't have lunch with you—we're going to see an architect. B-H wants us to start fresh, and he's going to build us a home just off that grassy slope near his little house. Oh, honey, I'm so happy. Get a dusty rose gown made to match my wedding dress. You're going to be my maid of honor."

Melissa finished wrapping her Christmas gifts and held the one she'd bought for Adam, a silver business card case that bore his initials, and wondered what to do with it. At last, unable to decide, she placed it under her brightly decorated Christmas tree. She stared for a few minutes at the twinkling lights that reflected off red and gold bells, trying to summon a modicum of Christmas spirit. Finally she threw up her hands in frustration and ran up the stairs to shower and dress.

Around five o'clock, as dusk settled over the brightly lit town, she joined Banks and her sister, and the three went in search of carolers. With other singers, they stopped at homes decorated with a Christmas tree or wreath, sang a verse or two, and walked on. Melissa had thought that their tour of the hospital wards and at the seniors' center would depress her, and she couldn't understand how she could feel uplifted and unhappy at the same time. At home later she dressed and waited for her mother and B-H. She knew why she prowled from room to room, glanced frequently at the silent telephone, and in frustration shook her fist at the air. Her affidavit should have told him where her heart laid, but maybe he'd had enough of her. Enough of the Grants.

She opened the door to B-H and her mother, both radiant, and had to squash her jealousy of their happiness.

"You two could light up a dark night," she told them, ashamed that she'd envied her mother the joy that had been denied her for so long.

"If you and my nephew ever come to your senses, you'll outshine us, believe me," B-H said. Melissa waved a hand, gainsaying the thought.

"Don't worry, dear, they'll get together as soon as one of them hurts badly enough," Emily said, gazing at him in adoration.

"When did you get a car, B-H?" Melissa asked as they reached the Lincoln. "What about the air pollution?" she needled.

"It was a trade-off. I figured I'd looked after the environment for thirty years. Now I'm going to take care of Emily, and I need a car for that. I've got a list of places I want to take her right around here. Then we'll take one of those African-American heritage tours, go down to New Orleans for some real jazz, see the Metropolitan Opera, and the museums in New York City. Ah, Melissa, there's so much." He put an arm around Emily, love shining in his eyes. "I've got to make up for lost time. And after I've showed her the United States, I'm going to take her around the world." Melissa wiped her tears with the back of her index finger.

"Adam's in town," Bill Henry said as they neared the church.

"I figured he would be." But I won't let him get me down, she swore to herself. They entered the little church from a side door, and her heartbeat escalated as soon as she glimpsed Adam sitting with Wayne opposite the entrance. She had to pass close by him and wondered if Bill Henry knew he'd be in that pew and had taken that route to force them to notice each other. She managed a smile when he looked her way and nodded, but he didn't touch the hand she'd left dangling at her side, and she kept walking. Emily and Bill Henry could follow her or not—she was doggoned if she'd be manipulated into such a convenient arrangement. Her companions joined her, and she soon felt her mother's elbow.

"I think I'm disappointed in you."

"You'll get over it," Melissa told her and turned her attention to the program. Her mood soon changed into one of well-being. The little church glowed with hundreds of candles nestled among beautifully arranged red poinsettias, and carols sung by the local community choir filled the sanctuary. At the end of the service, she left the building by the front door and waited alone beside Bill Henry's car for him and her mother.

"I didn't see Mrs. Roundtree," she remarked to Bill Henry as he drove away from the church. "I would have thought she'd go to church with Adam and Wayne."

"Mary can't even tolerate the House of God if Emily and I are in it together. But that's her problem. I enjoyed the service, but she's so full of bitterness that she had to miss it."

\* \* \*

The next morning, Christmas, Melissa started out of her front door and rushed back to answer the phone, hoping to hear Adam's voice.

"Schyler! Where are you?"

"I'm home. I got in here late last night. Would you believe I found a note from Mama telling me she's in Beaver Ridge and I should go out there. Now I don't have a car, don't know the address, and there's no phone where she is. I take it Hayes is some kind of a recluse."

"You can borrow my car after I run by to see Daddy. I was on my way there."

"Drop by here, and I'll go with you."

Melissa couldn't help being nervous while they waited for her father to answer the door.

"I'm glad you're with me, Schyler. I was not looking forward to this meeting."

"His bark is louder than his bite."

Rafer Grant opened the door, dressed as though he was going to his office, and stared at his offspring. Melissa clutched her chest as she waited for his words. To her surprise, his smile didn't dim when his gaze moved from Schyler to her.

"Well, this is a nice Christmas present. Come on in."

Anything is possible, Melissa mused, when her father made coffee and served it along with Oreos. She'd forgotten his passion for those cookies. He questioned Schyler about his activities in Nairobi and his trip home, and she began to wonder when he'd get around to his favorite subject. Schyler hinted that they had to leave, and Melissa handed her father his gift—a pair of initialed cuff links. She knew he'd have to say something to her then and braced herself for the worst.

"I didn't expect to see you. I thought you'd be with your mother—" his head dropped "—and with Adam."

"Daddy, I told you almost three weeks ago that Adam and I aren't seeing each other anymore."

"Yes, you did, but I didn't believe it. What happened?"

She shrugged. "We had a misunderstanding. I don't know what it was exactly, but we can't breech it."

"That's strange," her father said, his expression one of amazement. "He doesn't strike me as foolish. After what you did for him, he must know how you feel about him. Well, I thank you for coming and for my present." He handed each of them an envelope and looked at Schyler. "I hope I'll see you again before you go back."

"Of course, Daddy. I'm staying until January third." Rafer walked with them to the door and opened it with apparent reluctance.

"Merry Christmas, and thanks for coming to see me."

Melissa clutched her brother's arm as they left. "Was I seeing a ghost in there, Schyler?"

"Don't ask me. I was wondering the same thing, but ghost or not, it sure was refreshing. I can enjoy being with him if he stays like that."

She nodded, rushing along to match his long strides. "Me, too."

Adam savored his lemon custard pie, the finale of a flawless Christmas dinner, and reflected on the emptiness he felt. For the first time in his memory, Bill Henry hadn't joined the family for the holiday meal, and throughout it his mother hadn't mentioned his uncle's name. Worse, he'd been within inches of Melissa last night, but she'd been miles away from him. He couldn't pretend to enjoy himself.

"Do you need your car for the next hour?" he asked Wayne.

"I'll be here for the next hour and a half." Wayne reached in his pocket for the keys and handed them to Adam.

"Dinner was delicious, Mother. I'm going to Frederick." He didn't pause at the clatter of her demitasse spoon against the saucer. He'd upset her, but he couldn't help that. He wouldn't allow her or anybody else to control his life. Twenty minutes later he knocked on Melissa's door.

"I couldn't leave without telling you Merry Christmas." His breath caught in his throat when she squinted at him, parted her lips, and then seemed at a loss for words. "Are you inviting me in? Or should I leave?" She opened the door wider.

"I'm kind of surprised. Merry Christmas." He stepped through the door, and she turned and walked into the living room.

"I took a chance coming here without calling. You might have had a date." She seemed disconcerted, and his gaze swiftly searched the room. "Are you alone, Melissa?" He nearly laughed. Her chin jutted out, and she surveyed him with the cool detachment that he had always admired and which he knew she'd forced. He handed her a small package, asked her to open it after he left, and accepted the lone one under the tree when she handed it to him.

"I'm glad I decided to come—at least I know you've been thinking of me." He watched her eyes widen in obvious amazement before she frowned and gave him a mild rebuke.

"My father said this morning that you'd never struck him as a foolish man. Wonder what he'd say to that remark." In what he'd come to recognize as an unconscious gesture, she moistened her lips and dropped her head slightly to one side. Stunned, he realized that he was learning her all over again. The peculiar little habits that he'd gotten used to seeing…hitting him now. Fresh. And the smell of her perfume that had been in his nostrils since the night before when she'd drifted by him, and that brought saliva to his mouth right then. And her eyes. Sparkling and sad at the same time. Why couldn't she tell him she believed in him?

He heard the guttural sigh that filled the soundless room and knew it came from his soul. He reached out and felt her warmth in his arms. He'd meant to vent his frustration and to torture her as she tormented him. But she parted her lips for his kiss, and current after current zinged through him. He lifted her until her mouth was an easier target, and his fire pressed against her fire. He tried to banish the loneliness he'd felt without her, to ease the pain of her rejection, and to cushion himself against her failure to understand what he needed from her. Her whimpers were the sounds she made when she needed him inside of her,

her love call, and he felt himself answering her. She moved against him, her demand becoming more insistent. Why am I holding out, he asked himself as he felt his ardor begin to cool. Memory flooded his thoughts. He had vowed that until she told him she'd been wrong, that she didn't believe he'd had an affair with her aunt, that she believed him and believed in him, there could be nothing between them. He needed her trust and her faith in him, and he couldn't accept less. She must have sensed his withdrawal, because she released him at once. But her eyes clouded with unhappiness. He couldn't leave her that way.

"I shouldn't have let things get out of hand, Melissa, but you know what happens when the two of us are together." He tried to manage a smile and knew he failed.

"Yes, I know," she said, and with her eyes she begged him for an answer to their predicament. If you'd only say it with words, he wanted to tell her, we could at least work toward a solution. But she said nothing. The next move was his, and he walked to the door and stood there for a minute. Then he clasped her within his arms—more roughly than he'd intended—and kissed her on the mouth.

"Merry Christmas." He heard her close the door, and he walked faster. He had to put some distance between them and to do it quickly. Even a shift in the wind could send him back to her.

Melissa walked up the stairs carrying the small rectangular red package, resplendent in its gold-speckled green silk bow, and laid it on the table beside her bed. He'd asked her to open it after he left, but she dreaded knowing its contents. She needed a token of his love, something more than the pulsing fire of his kiss, the kiss he later regretted. She supposed that he was in as much of a dilemma as she about their relationship, but he at least had control of his feelings. Not that that surprised her. From the beginning she had been impressed with his mastery of himself and his refusal to allow others that role. She sat on the side of her bed, her gaze fixed on his gift, and thought back to their happier times. Maybe she'd squandered a precious moment with him—she didn't know, but something had made him withhold his love.

When she'd seen him at her door, joy had suffused her only to be extinguished by his cool manner. They had been as strangers. Polite. Careful. And then he'd reached out for her, and she didn't remember how she had gotten into his arms. Only that she nestled where she knew she belonged. His harsh kiss had quickly turned worshipful, and she'd thought her prayers had been answered. Maybe he didn't love her, but he couldn't deny that he wanted her. She turned out the light and swung her feet beneath the cover, leaving the gift unopened. She could wait until morning for another letdown.

"Mrs. Roundtree's residence."

Melissa assumed it was the maid who spoke, gave her name, and asked for Adam.

"Sorry, ma'am," came the reply. "Mr. Adam already left for New York." Melissa fingered the little book of verses, a selection of poems that Adam had chosen and had bound in leather with gold tooling especially for her. Each one brought to mind something of their relationship, pleasant and painful. But not one contained the phrase "I love you," though she couldn't swear that each wasn't an ode to love. I'd better not assume too much, she admonished herself and decided to write him a thank you note.

Adam stood by his window, looking across at the snow-blanketed promenade of Lincoln Center, holding Melissa's note crushed into a ball. What had he expected? He moved away from the window and wandered aimlessly around his apartment. Discontented. Drifting for the first time in his adult life. "What the hell's gotten into me?" he asked the silence that surrounded him. None of the things he usually enjoyed doing on Sunday mornings in winter attracted him. He thumbed through the books on his shelf, books he longed to find the time to read, and walked away. Disinterested.

It's this apartment that's getting to me, he decided. An hour later he was on the train to Westchester. Winterflower opened the door before he rang. He accepted her generous hug and marveled at the sense of calm that he immediately experienced.

"You're troubled. What's brought you here?" she asked him.

"I needed a dose of your company." He followed her to the basement and leaned against the edge of a wooden sawhorse while she unveiled a clay mural.

"Perfect timing," she told him. "I want this to dry in the garage. It's less humid there." He stored it as she wished, walked out into the sunlight, and stood transfixed by the idyllic scene. The great trees stood burdened with icicles. Evergreen shrubs peeked through the snow, and birds darted in and out of the birdhouses that hung from branches and porch eaves. A blackbird tripped across his foot, unafraid. He couldn't hear a sound, and he knew he'd come for the peace and for Flower's calming presence. How different the setting from his last visit—a time when his body had just begun to churn with desire for Melissa. He looked in the direction of the rock on which she had sat with her hands in her lap. Relaxed. Serene. He turned quickly to open the porch door, but as he reached for it, it swung open and he looked into Winterflower's knowing eyes.

"Why can't you admit that being without her is tearing you apart? You've tallied some superficial reasons why you can't go to her and just give yourself to her. The problem begins with you, Adam. Not Melissa. She told you that she loves you." He cocked an eyebrow, remembering her ability to see beyond the ordinary.

"Yes," she continued. "And she risked her standing with her family and the community for you."

"There are things you don't understand, Flower."

"Like what?" she scoffed. "The fact that you're fooling yourself? You are a realist, a man who rejects sentimentality, who despises the shortcomings that afflict most of us mortals. A man who demands the truth of his associates. But not of yourself, Adam?"

He frowned. The assistant district attorney had been more understanding. "What are you getting at, Flower? I want it in English."

"Your complaints against each other are excuses, though hers make more sense." He tried to associate her words with what he felt. "You're both scared to go the other mile," she went on, leading him into the kitchen. "You'll give fifty percent, but not fifty-one. There's virtue in self-pride, Adam—but none whatsoever in self-centeredness. You can't expect Melissa to bare her soul to you when you've never told her that you love her."

"Why are you so certain that I love her, that I want a permanent relationship with her?" He watched, amazed, as Winterflower threw up her hands in exasperation, the closest to being disgusted that he'd seen her.

"When did a man, especially one such as you, tie himself into knots over a woman he didn't love?"

His gaze swept over her, but his thoughts were of how badly he'd wanted to include Elizabeth Barrett Browning's sonnet—*"How do I love thee? Let me count the ways."*—in the collection that he gave Melissa at Christmas and how dissatisfied he'd been when he'd forced himself not to do it. A rueful smile played around his lips.

"See what I mean?" Flower changed the subject. "B-H must be bursting with happiness along now."

"Yes," was his quiet answer as he recalled her special talent. "He's a lucky man. Emily is a wonderful woman."

"Not more so than her daughter."

Five o'clock in the afternoon, three days later at the Good Shepherd Presbyterian Church in Frederick, Melissa started up the aisle as the organ began to play, but her steps faltered when she saw that Adam stood beside Bill Henry as he waited for his bride. He turned slightly until he saw her and locked his gaze with hers. She hadn't thought to ask her mother who would be best man, but what would have changed if she'd known? No wonder her mother hadn't needed a rehearsal. She fought to hold her tears in check, but she couldn't banish the heartache that threatened to rob her of the self-possession she needed in order to make it through the rest of the day. Her hands trembled as she passed him, her eyes diverted, and took her place on the other side of the groom.

She saw Bill Henry throw custom aside and turn fully to the front to watch Emily Morris approach him, escorted by her son. Melissa didn't doubt his happiness, for her mother had given him his dream and dressed in a white beaded satin and lace gown with a headdress of beaded lace, and she carried his white calla lilies. She didn't think she'd ever heard a couple repeat their wedding vows so clearly and so loudly. Amused, she glanced over to find Adam watching her, the twinkle in his eyes aglow. After Bill Henry kissed his wife and walked up the aisle with her, Melissa saw Adam approach and offer her his arm. She had to fight a feeling of giddiness—what a time to experience a bout of hysteria!

Adam must have sensed her feelings for he tugged her a little closer and said, "That was almost enough to make a man cry. They're very happy." She looked up at him and knew that her face mirrored her surprise, but she only nodded, unable to speak.

"The bride is beautiful," he went on, "but not more so than the woman on my arm." Her shoe heel caught in the red carpet that Bill Henry had ordered laid down for his bride's satin-slippered feet, and Adam stopped, removed her other shoe and carried both of them in his hand. At the door he knelt and put them back on her feet.

They followed the bride and groom to the reception, and after the newlyweds drank a toast, cut the three-tiered cake, and began the dancing, Adam rose and extended his hand to Melissa. Custom demanded that she dance with him. She'd be lost, she told herself, hoping that she alone knew how her body quaked.

The band played a fox-trot, but he danced the one-step. She looked into the distance, past his shoulder, but he lifted her chin with his index finger and forced her gaze to his own. She missed a step, and he held her closer.

"Adam… Please…" She couldn't avoid his eyes, as fiery as she'd ever seen them.

"I love you, Melissa. You're my life. Everything." She missed several steps and had to cling to him for support.

"Do you still care for me? Or have I killed what you felt?" Her heart thundered in her chest and she couldn't help trembling in his arms. She fixed her gaze on his mouth and moistened her lips.

"Melissa, what do you feel for me?" He had stopped dancing.

"I love you." He bent closer to hear her words. "I love you, too, Adam."

"Come on. Let's go." His hoarse voice sent trills of excitement through her. He turned and started for the door just as the bride's beautiful calla lilies brushed Melissa's chest. Grateful for her good reflexes, she caught them, looked around the room for her mother, and when she found her, waved and grasped Adam's arm.

Wayne met them at the door. "Where to?"

"Thanks, buddy. Thirty-eight Teal."

"Right on."

Adam didn't speak again until his shoe heel kicked her front door shut.

"I'll put the flowers in some water. You wait here." She removed her coat, hung it in the closet, and stood with her gaze on the hallway, waiting for him. She made up her mind to accept the explanation he gave her, to take whatever he offered. He loved her—that was enough, all she would ever need. She raised her arms when he stopped in front of her. The twinkle in his eyes danced in a lover's smile as he looked into her eyes before he lifted her and sprinted up the stairs, his arms tight around her.

Her impatience for his possession mounted as he stood beside her at the foot of her bed. "I expected more from you than I was willing to give, Melissa. I know that now. Subconsciously I asked for proof that you loved me, while I withheld that from you." She placed a finger over his lips. She didn't need the words, but realized that he might and gladly gave them.

"Shhh. I didn't have any basis for believing that you had an affair with Aunt Louise, that you would lie to me. I was wrong in not listening to my heart, in not believing in you. When I…when I read those poems, I looked for one that said you loved me, but—"

He interrupted her. "How could you not know? Why do you think I carried you out of that garden in the presence of half the population of Frederick, defying my mother when I was there to support her? Why would I wrap my coat around you and allow myself to get drenched in that icy rain? Why do you think I sat on the edge of your sofa, chilled to my bones, and drank cold, sugarless tea—which I hated—while I waited for you to calm down?"

She sucked in her breath and shivers raced through her as she beheld the storm that suddenly swirled in his eyes. "Nothing and no one is as important to me as you are," he said. She heard the unsteadiness of his voice and saw desire blazing on his countenance. Her mouth opened beneath his, and she clung to him, nearly delirious with happiness and reveling in her womanhood, when the movement of his tongue in and out of her mouth reminded her of the way he could make her feel. With eyes that had become pools of warmth and blatant desire, he asked permission to love her.

"Yes. Oh, Adam. I've waited so long for you. So long." He reached behind her and released the zipper of her dress, while she held his face lovingly between her hands. The touch of his fingers trailing down her spine triggered her feminine heat, and her body arched to his in unmistakable demand. He turned back the coverlets, laid her in bed, and quickly joined her. Pleasure radiated through her when he covered her body with his own, and she felt his love flowing in her and through her until she lost herself in him.

Adam lay on his back, holding Melissa in his left arm. "Let's talk, sweetheart. I want to begin the year with nothing between us hidden or unsolved, with everything out front. I once asked you how you felt about masquerade parties, but I didn't get much of an answer. Tell me where you were five years ago tonight." She sat up in bed, and he had the impression that he'd triggered her memory.

"What was I doing? Let's see. I went to a party, a masquerade party. Why?"

"Where?" Her face clouded as though she had an unpleasant memory. I won't stop now, he told himself and waited.

"The Roosevelt Hotel in New York. It was an AKA sorority affair. Why?"

"Why did you run away from me?"

"That was *you?*"

"Yes. I want to know why you ran."

"A few minutes before I met you at that party, I broke off with a man whom I had believed loved me; he'd just proved that he didn't. I had walked away from him and stumbled right into you. I left you, because I didn't want another man's kiss."

"Did you get over it?"

"Long ago."

"I looked for you, and I never forgot you. Occasionally I'd think you were the same person, but she was much shorter."

"I wore flat shoes that night. Ballerina slippers." She grazed his shoulder tenderly with her fingertips. "I didn't see your mother tonight. Was she at the wedding?"

"I'm sorry to say that she wasn't, but her absence didn't mar my uncle's happiness, Melissa, and her attitude toward you won't influence my feelings." He pulled her down beside him and leaned over her.

"Will you marry me? I'll love you forever, Melissa. I swear it. And no matter what my mother and your father think, we can't permit them to wreck our lives. We may not be as fortunate thirty years later as Emily and Bill Henry. Will you take me for your husband and the father of your children?"

She squinted at him. "Shouldn't you be on your knees right now?" He reveled in the laughter that poured out of him, release that he'd learned through her and because of her.

"Don't keep me hanging here, lady."

"How about Valentine's Day? That should give me time to have a dress made. Oh, Adam. I'm so full of love for you."

# Epilogue

Adam leaned against the doorjamb of the room he shared with Melissa in the family home at Beaver Ridge and wondered when again his wife would have a chance to hold her son of ten days. They had come back to the family home after Melissa's delivery, so that their child could spent its earliest days among their families. Grant Roundtree had already found his niche as a force for peace. Mary Hayes Roundtree cooed at him from her chair on one side of the chaise lounge on which Melissa reclined, and Emily Morris Hayes made goo-goo eyes at him from the other side. Wayne, who was currently in possession of the little prize, insisted that he saw a clear likeness to himself. A five-foot teddy bear and a Lionel train bore testament to the love of Grandfather Rafer, who used his lunch hour to visit his daughter and grandson, and Schyler had come home from Nairobi for the event. Wayne had been so impressed by the changes he saw in Melissa on his visits to New York, and with his nephew, that he had stopped running from Banks and had begun to see her in a different light. Adam stood straighter when a hand rested on his shoulder, glanced around, and saw that his uncle B-H had joined them.

"Feels good, doesn't it, son?"

"Yeah. Unbelievable!"

# ECSTASY

# Prologue

Mason Fenwick paced the length of his brother Steve's living room, turned, and retraced his steps.

"I know you feel I've let you down, Steve, but that's the way it is. I'm quitting." He didn't have to glance at his older brother and surrogate parent to know that the beloved face held a mixture of sadness and incredulity.

"For good? You mean you're leaving medicine for good?"

"For good."

"Did you lose your nerve? If so, I can understand your doing this. The type of surgery you perform requires nerves of steel."

"No. I didn't, I've got the gall to do anything I ever did." He paused and walked once more toward the other end of the room. "What I lost, you might say, is myself. When I think of the chances I've taken with people's lives and gotten away with it, I get cold chills. I've healed a lot of people, but I could have killed every one of them." He stopped within inches of Steve and drew a deep breath.

"I relished the challenge that the disease's complications presented to me, as though it didn't affect a human being. As though the possibility of failure were implausible. I took the Hippocratic oath, and I've done my best to honor it but, for the last couple of years, I've only been serving myself. Risking human life for my own glory. Filling my calendar with names of rich, famous people who get a headache then schedule a five-hundred-dollar appointment with me. Living it up with people, who wouldn't know me from Adam if they saw me in jeans, a sweat shirt, and a baseball cap. Choosing my dates from the socialites who call and beg me to take them to Mrs. X's party. Women who'll do anything to be seen with me. I've backed myself into a corner, Steve. When I had this horrible accident, some papers made a big deal of it, but not one of those people who swore I was indispensable to them called me. I sweated out three lonely and anxious weeks beside Bianca Norris's bed, doing what I could to get her out of the coma. And that wasn't much. I promised God that if she regained consciousness and survived, I'd quit pretending to be him. I've got to straighten out my life."

"And you have to leave your practice in order to do it?"

"The kind of change I need to make has to be done decisively and completely, if I'm going to respect myself. I can serve mankind in some other capacity."

## Chapter 1

Alone in her little white frame house, located in a picturesque valley in Pilgrim, New York, Jeannetta Rollins sat at her desk holding the telephone. With her lips agape and her eyes rounded with disbelief, she stared at the grains of sand that filtered slowly downward through her late father's hourglass, signaling the passage of time. It couldn't be. The great oak that she loved to watch from her window, no matter the season, the snow-covered garden, and the brilliant blue sky blurred into nothing as she savored the incredible words. Her tests revealed the need for delicate brain surgery that most neurosurgeons hesitated to undertake. Without it, the prognosis for her sight was poor, and the longer she waited for treatment, the slimmer the likelihood that she'd be as good as new.

"I've checked with the surgeons to whom I normally refer patients, and none of them wants this job," Dr. Farmer said. "A Dr. Fenwick has had spectacular results with the surgery you need but, for personal reasons, he's terminated his practice and operates a travel business."

She hung up and looked around; within ten minutes, the world had become a different place. But she wouldn't give up. Surely that doctor would take her case if he knew about her. How could he not help her? She called her doctor back.

"Dr. Farmer, couldn't you talk with this Dr. Fenwick and ask him to take my case? Maybe if he knows that I'm young, that I'm a writer, and that my livelihood depends on my eyes, he'll relent and perform the operation."

"Alright, Jeannetta, I'll try my best, but it's been a couple of years since he operated, and I'm sure a lot of people have wanted him to treat them. So don't hold out too much hope." Within the hour, she answered her doctor's call.

"I'm sorry to disappoint you, my dear, but he flatly refused, saying that he's no longer a doctor. I begged him, but to no avail. I'm sorry, indeed."

Jeannetta looked at the pages of her novel and thought of the deadline for its submission five months hence. She'd have to slave over it night and day to complete it on time. She'd have to... She sent the hourglass crashing against the door. She'd done nothing to deserve what she knew awaited her. But she was more subdued after reflecting on the uselessness of anger and vowed to find that doctor and convince him to help her. Calmer now, she got up and went to the kitchen for a glass of cranberry juice and sipped a little. Maybe the radiologist had read the test improperly. She ought to get another specialist.

She went out in the back garden and gazed at the snow-covered mountains rising in the distance and the maze of green pines that stood in proud contrast to the glistening white snow, a scene of which she never tired. She put food in the birdhouses, talked to the blue jay that ate from her hand, threw peanuts to the lone squirrel who came to greet her, and breathed deeply of the crisp, late winter air. Smoke curled high several blocks down the street, and she knew that Laura prepared to roast a turkey or a fresh ham on the outdoor rotisserie for her dinner guest. She'd have to tell Laura.

Her sister operated Rollins Hideaway, a ski lodge that had twelve guest rooms and two apartments and which they had inherited from their deceased parents. Jessie and Matthew Rollins had left the South shortly after their marriage, unwilling to raise a family in a climate of segregation, and had invested their savings in the ski lodge. The profitable venture had enabled them to raise their children comfortably and to send Jeannetta to college. Laura hadn't wanted to study beyond high school, so they had given her three-quarters interest in the lodge.

The odor of roasting pork perfumed the air as Jeannetta neared the lodge. She loved the smell of food cooking on a chilly day; it was as though you'd been invited to feel at home. She walked around the back, where her older sister poked at the hot coals.

"I hadn't expected you so early," Laura told her, reaching up to dust a kiss on Jeannetta's cheek. At thirty-five, Laura was older than Jeannetta by six years, a difference that had cast her in a protective relationship with her younger sister, "Come on inside. I saved you some apple cobbler."

Jeannetta had to force a smile; if she didn't show enthusiasm for apple cobbler, Laura would immediately become suspicious. She sat in her usual place at the kitchen table and picked at the cobbler.

"What's the matter?" Laura asked her. There was no use trying to postpone the inevitable, so she summarized the doctor's report. Laura groped for the back of a chair, nearly falling to the floor as she did so. She sat down, stared blankly, as would a catatonic, and began to shake her head in mute denial. Jeannetta rounded the table and knelt to comfort her sister. She knew that, although their relationship had at times been troubled, they loved each other and could depend upon each other no matter what happened.

"What will you do?" Laura asked when she was able to control her near-hysteria.

"I'm going to find that doctor, get on my knees if necessary, and convince him to help me. Dr. Farmer wouldn't tell me where he is, because he doesn't want my hopes raised. He considers Fenwick's 'no' as final, but I don't."

"Suppose he won't help you?"

Jeannetta whirled around, unwilling to entertain that possibility.

"He will. I won't take no for an answer. I'll remind him that he took that Hippocratic oath and that he'll have to answer to God if he has the skill to cure me and refuses to do it. He'll do it, or I'll be on his conscience for the rest of his life; I'll make certain that he doesn't forget me." She rose and had to grope for a chair, exhausted. "If he wont' help me, I won't stop living; I'll learn how to live without that surgery. I won't be anybody or anything's victim."

Laura looked at her as though seeing her for the first time. "I always thought you were fragile, but you aren't, are you?"

"No, I'm not, but you wanted to take care of me, so I let you."

"You'll find him. Something tells me that nothing will stop you. How are you going to convince him?"

"I don't know, but I will. Could you give me a pen and some paper?" She ignored Laura's obvious confusion—opening first one drawer and then another, as if she were lost in her own kitchen.

"You're going to write him?" Laura asked, a look of incredulity masking her face.

"I don't know where he is, but I know what he's supposed to be doing; I just hope he isn't headed for skid row and that his hands are steady." The apple cobbler suddenly had appeal, and she bit into a forkful of it, savored the cinnamon-flavored tart, and ate some more. "I'm going down to New York City tomorrow," she went on, dismissing her sister's expression of amazement, "and while I'm there I'm going to the Metropolitan Museum of Art. I'm writing down a list of the paintings I want to see."

"Jeanny, for the Lord's sake, don't be morbid." Jeannetta shrugged her left shoulder.

"Morbid? Don't be dramatic, Laura, life's full of battles. You change what you can; the rest, you learn to live with. And I'm going to teach myself to come to terms with this, with or without Fenwick."

"I felt better when you swore you'd get him to help you. Now, you're..."

Jeannetta interrupted to put Laura's mind at ease. "Don't worry. I'll find him."

She promised herself that she wouldn't be disappointed if the first clues led nowhere. From the hospital at which he'd practiced, she learned that he'd given a post-office box as his forwarding address. After several days, she located a Fenwick Travel Agency in New York City and wrote for brochures.

"What are you planning to do with those?" Laura, a skeptic, queried.

"Learn all I can about him."

"Are you sure it's him?"

Jeannetta had had years in which to accustom herself to her sister's tendency to mistrust everything and everybody. "That's what I'm trying to find out." A smile moved over her smooth, ebony skin. The man guided a special round-the-world tour, a two-month venture with twenty personally selected individuals.

"You can't do that," Laura objected, when Jeannetta mentioned it. "That must cost a fortune."

Jeannetta pooh-poohed Laura's concern. "If I succeed, it will be more than worth the cost." She telephoned the agency.

"Is this the *Mason* Fenwick personally guided tour?"

"It is, indeed," a friendly voice replied. "Would you like to speak with Mr. Fenwick?" *Mr.* Fenwick indeed!

"Yes, please," she replied, quickly remembering her goal.

"Mason Fenwick speaking. How may I help you?" She'd made contact. She knew where he was. But her elation was temporary; tiny hot pinions fluttered through her, crowding her throat, churning in her belly. His low, dusty, and mellifluous voice disarmed her, robbed her of the aplomb so natural to her and left her speechless. "Fenwick speaking," he repeated patiently. Thinking fast, nervous and bewildered by her reaction to him, she asked for more details about the African portion of his tour.

"Any special reason why you're interested in that part of the tour?"

Though annoyed with herself, she couldn't still the dancing organ in her chest, nor the trembling of her fingers.

"I've never been there," she managed in a small girl's voice.

"Then you'll enjoy the countries we visit," he assured her and added, "I usually have a fascinating group, too. Most parts of the country, and different races and religions, are represented." His chuckle surprised her. "On every tour, at least one couple meets and later gets married." She tried without success to resist his seductive voice, and found herself imagining what he looked like.

"I hope you aren't too far from New York," she heard him say. "I insist on interviewing all prospective tour members in person. Two months is a long time to spend with nineteen incompatible people. Let my secretary know whether you're interested." He told her goodbye, and she heard the secretary's cheerful voice again. They agreed upon a date and time for the interview, and Jeannetta hung up, finally able to release a long sigh.

"How do you know you're doing the right thing?" Laura wanted to know. "That man could be a charlatan and, from the looks of you when you were talking to him, he probably is. Anybody would've thought that was the first man you ever said a word to." She sat down, reached over, and patted her sister's hand. "I'm not as smart as you, but I always had mother's wit. It doesn't make sense to take your savings and go chasing around the world with a bunch of strangers when you may need every penny."

"I know you love me, Laura, but I have to do this. I'll take every precaution I can, but I'm going to do it." Laura had never been easily placated when she set her mind on something, so Jeannetta let her have her say. Then she told her, "I'll hire a private investigator for a report on him. If it's negative, I'll ditch the idea. Okay?" Laura nodded.

Jeannetta contacted one the next morning and couldn't shake the feeling of guilt when the investigator assured her that he'd "get everything on him down to how many teeth he's had pulled."

Mason Fenwick dropped the receiver into its cradle, leaned back in his chair and closed his eyes. He sensed something strange about that telephone call. The woman had barely said a word and the few she'd uttered had been with what appeared to be an infantile, almost frightened voice. After musing over it for a few minutes, he dismissed his concern; as usual, he'd decide after the interview. The ringing phone annoyed him; he needed to get some work done.

"Miss Goins on three."

He wished Betty Goins wouldn't interrupt him during office hours. "Hello, Betty. I'm sorry. I meant it when I said we couldn't continue this…this farce. How can you be satisfied with this…vacuous relationship? I deserve better, and so do you, and I want to be free to look for what I need and to go after it when I find it. No, I won't change my mind. I can't. In spite of the intimacy, we've never been more than friends; let's remain friends. I won't call you again. Good-bye."

Thank God she'd had too much pride to plead. He wanted more for his life than he could ever have with her. His fingers brushed the keys that lived in his right pants pocket, the keys to his late father's house. The keys to the only place that had ever been home. When he put medicine behind him, Betty had lost interest in a future with him, told him that she wanted a professional man. Travel agents—black or white—were a dime a dozen, she had said. At the outset, she'd sworn what they had was enough, that she would teach him to care for her. But in his mind, she couldn't do that, because she hadn't loved him, hadn't cared, and he had suffered for the lack of it. She had wanted a doctor, a man who'd give her the social status she craved. But he needed a woman's love, a family of his own, and a door in which to put a lock that would yield to the key in his pocket. He signed three letters, took them to his secretary, walked back into his office, and closed the door. Freedom: how good it felt! He couldn't help jumping high, clicking his feet together in the manner of a dancer, and smiling broadly before sitting down to work.

A light snow blanketed the streets of New York the morning of Jeannetta's interview with Mason. She'd spent the previous night in the city to avoid being stranded in Pilgrim by the late March storm. She combed her thick, curly black hair with unsteady fingers. Then she donned a fashionable rust-colored woolen jacket and a matching knee-length skirt, pulled on a pair of brown leather boots, slipped her arms into a beige camel-hair coat, reached for a pair of brown leather gloves and her brown Coach hobo bag, and struck out for Mason's office. She couldn't suppress the sensation that she journeyed toward her destiny. Walking west on Fiftieth Street, she reached St. Patrick's Cathedral and, as she had done many times, she entered the Fiftieth Street door, paused for a minute to say a silent prayer, left by the front door, and continued down Fifth Avenue to East

Forty-sixth Street. Her steps slowed—but her heartbeat accelerated—when she reached the building. She should have consulted another specialist, she told herself. It didn't make sense to go to such lengths because of one man's word, but Dr. Farmer had consulted several specialists about her case, and each had referred him to Fenwick. She glanced up at the imposing structure, took a deep breath and opened the door. She looked neither left nor right, but counted the floors as the elevator sped to number twenty-six. Lead feet took her to suite twenty-six-hundred. She reached out to ring the bell and withdrew her hand. A long masculine arm reached across her shoulder, rang the bell, and pushed open the door.

"Who did you want to see?" That voice. A faint odor of sandalwood cologne reached her nostrils, but she knew at once that he wasn't wearing it. I've got to handle this like a pro, she told herself.

"I want to see Mr. Mason Fenwick," she answered, and made herself turn around and look at him. Her left hand flew to her chest as he stood smiling down at her. She couldn't shift her gaze from the blackish-green eyes that held her captive, entrapped. His smile evaporated and the deep, sensuous voice became crisp and businesslike.

"I'm Fenwick."

She had to be certain. "*Mason* Fenwick?"

His eyebrows arched sharply in a look of surprise. "Yes. I'm Mason Fenwick. And you are?"

"I thought I heard your voice," a woman who must have been his secretary said as she stepped into the little hallway. "Your coffee's ready." He told her he'd take it into his office, then gestured toward Jeannetta.

"She's here to see me; get her a cup, would you?" Jeannetta stepped into Mason's office, her poise intact. She removed the sunglasses she'd worn to deflect the glare from the snow, and took the chair that he offered her. It wasn't his physical appearance that unsettled her. He stood before her, tall—around six feet, four inches, she surmised—very dark, and, by any measure, handsome. No, it wasn't that. He had an aura, a mystique, an appeal that sucked her in as though he were quicksand. She got hold of herself.

"I'm Jeannetta Rollins."

He extended his hand, a bit reluctantly, she thought, though the possibility perplexed her, why wouldn't he want to shake her hand? Without her sunglasses, his strange eyes had an even more compelling effect, reaching inside of her, warming her, soothing her. She couldn't tear her gaze from them.

The buzzer on his desk went unanswered.

"Telephone, Mr. Fenwick."

If he heard, he gave no indication. Jeannetta watched, mesmerized, as his eyes darkened, losing their blackish cast, and seemed to radiate warmth in a change so drastic and so sudden that she hadn't time to hide her reaction. She gasped aloud, drawing him out of his trance.

"Who are you?"

In control once more, she repeated her name. He waved the words aside with a quick movement of his hand. "I mean, *who are you?*"

"A prospective tourist," she told him, though she cringed inwardly at the deceptive white lie. He picked up the black folder on his desk, read her name and opened it.

"You haven't filled in this form."

Noticing that it included, among other questions, two on the condition of her health, she told him she'd mail it.

"Better make it snappy; I have only four places left and fourteen applicants."

Unwilling to risk missing the tour, she took the form and completed it.

"You write sketches for stand-up comedians?" His voice held a note of awe.

"Among other things, yes. It's amazing what people will find comical."

He stared at her and shook his head as though disbelieving his ears. "Care to offer a sample?"

He didn't smile, so she couldn't know whether the request was a part of the interview or fodder for his curiosity. Well, she'd play it by ear.

"My samples are expensive," she told him, deciding that she wouldn't smile either.

"I'll settle for one of your cheaper ones." Not an expression on his face. Was he playing with her? She wondered what her demeanor conveyed to him when his peculiarly magnetic eyes became brownish and he leaned forward in an air of expectancy.

"Okay, here goes. Esther Ruth Hankin's good-for-nothing husband hadn't worked a full day in the twelve years since she'd married him, but Esther Ruth thought he was wonderful. Her hard-working, red-neck father disagreed and threatened to stop supporting them. 'It's time you left that bum,' he told her. 'The man's an absolute failure.' 'He ain't a failure, daddy,' she pleaded. 'He just started at the bottom and got comfortable down there.' The old man then turned to his other daughter, who crocheted happily nearby, and complained that her husband was too stupid to keep a job and that he was also going to stop taking care of them. Janie Dixon looked her father in the eye and asked him, 'Who's smarter, the man who can own a Cadillac without ever doing a lick of work, or the man who works his tail off to give it to him?'"

Mason Fenwick continued to stare at Jeannetta until she wanted the floor to open up and swallow her. Then his wonderful eyes gleamed with mirth; laughter rumbled in his chest and spilled out of him. He leaned back in his chair and gave his amusement full rein. Astonished at the change in him, intuition told her that this man could only be reached at a primal level with gut-rending overtures, that he could intellectualize as irrelevant any other kind of approach.

"That's pretty good." He scanned the form, his face again solemn and unreadable.

"It had to be better than pretty good," she told him, not bothering to hide her annoyance, "otherwise you wouldn't have laughed your head off." His long brown fingers strummed his desk, and he leaned back and watched her intently, like a cat eyeing a mouse.

"You're right," he said, after seeming to weigh the effect of yielding to her. He scanned the form that she'd completed. "This looks okay, but I'll have to check your references. You should hear from us within a week."

They both stood. He walked around the desk and extended his hand, and she felt her face throb with the rush of warm blood when she touched it. Did he grasp it longer than necessary? She didn't know, so caught up was she in his gaze, his whole aura. She never knew how she got out of his office.

He didn't move until the door closed behind her. He walked over to the window overlooking Forty-sixth Street and braced himself with both hands resting on the windowsill. What had happened in there? The churning in him couldn't have been more violent nor more enervating if he had just encountered a Martian. He couldn't help smiling inwardly; maybe he had. But he was master of his fate, and he'd proved it. Staring over at age thirty-four in what, for him, had been uncharted waters, hadn't been without pitfalls, but he'd done it and it had given him a sense of accomplishment and a measure of inner peace. Now, this stranger had bolted into his life and nailed him with a wallop such as he hadn't known he could experience. She'd looked up at him, her eyes sparkling with some kind of gut-searing, almost sad appeal, and he'd had a time steadying himself. If she had set out deliberately to pulverize his resistance to her, she had succeeded admirably.

"Well, what do you think, Mr. Mason?" He whirled around, strode quickly to his desk and punched the intercom.

"I haven't decided, Viv. What was your assessment?"

"I didn't see much of her, but I think she probably isn't demanding and won't be a trouble-maker, since she didn't ask me a lot of questions about the other tourists, sleeping accommodations, that sort of thing—and nothing at all about you. Most single women under forty-five ask if you're married. She'll be okay."

"Hmmm. Maybe." He hung up. Anybody as intelligent as that woman obviously was definitely should have asked some questions. He'd have to think about it. The buzzer rang again.

"She must be interesting, too, Mr. Mason. She's a writer, and she's got three books published. On top of that, she teaches writing at SUNY. Maybe she'll put the tour in one of her books, and you'll be famous again." He opened Jeannetta's file. Any writer had a perfect reason for taking a world tour, but she had stated "personal" in answer to the question. He recalled that he'd sensed an aura of mystery around her when they'd talked on the phone earlier; now he was sure of it. Well, he didn't have to take her. He had a peculiar feeling about her. Yet, she met his written criteria, and he prided himself in being fair. He'd sleep on it.

After that evening, Jeannetta sat on a hassock in Laura's tiny, cluttered office while her sister planned menus for the next week.

"Well, how'd it go with Fenwick?"

"You sure you want to know? That man's a keg of powder."

"Oh, Lord, don't tell me. I thought you were ready to move in with him just from talking with him on the phone. What happened?"

"What happened was I looked at him and felt as if he'd slugged me with a sledgehammer. Laura, I've never been a pushover for any man, but *that man!* Honey, he was all around me, everywhere. I could feel him, before he touched my hand. Just talking about him makes me want to… Gosh, I shouldn't be speaking to you like this."

"Shoot, honey," Laura said with her usual diffidence about such things, "at least let me live vicariously."

"He's a fantastic specimen, but it's more…I…I was practically traumatized, and he hadn't done anything but ask my name…and gaze at me. His eyes change from a blackish-green to brown when he smiles, and he…Laura, what if he's blunted my brain to the point where I can't persuade him to do what I want? Five minutes with him, and I was a bowl of mush."

"I don't believe that."

"Well, maybe I've overstated it a bit, but not by much. Trust me."

"What was his reaction?"

Jeannetta hadn't thought much about that but, upon recollection, decided that he'd at least noticed her. She described their encounter.

"Sounds to me like he wasn't exactly immune to you," Laura said. "You watch it."

"Don't worry. This has to be business; if sex gets into it, I'll lose everything."

"I'd like to have that problem with him," Laura said dryly. "You always did have what it takes with men, and you never used it. I'm thirty-five years old and still waiting for the first man to tell me he admires something about me other than my business smarts and my cherry pies. I'd give anything to be tall and slim with your long legs and hourglass figure. I'd even exchange my straight hair for your wooly stuff. A lot of men look right past short, plump women."

"You don't want to exchange places with me, Laura. Maybe this is fate's way of evening things out. I look like Dad and you look like Mother. When I was little, you got the roles in school plays, because you're fair. Nobody up here ever heard of a black fairy queen."

"And I never saw a fat drum majorette; you were the toast of the Pilgrim football team." She turned off the computer and rested her chin on the heel of her right hand. "Sex or not, what choice do you have? You need him, and if you two fall for each other, you'll just have to deal with that. Just you make sure he doesn't turn out to be another Jethro. That man chased you right to the day he married Alma."

"I know," Jeannetta replied, shaking her head in wonder, "and he's still at it. He must be a masochist. I detest him, and I let him know it. How could he possibly think I'd give him a second look after he slept with my best friend, when he was engaged to me. They both got what they deserve; she tricked him into marrying her, and he's still trailing after me."

Laura waved her hand in a gesture of dismissal. "Alma never was your friend. Biggest actress ever to walk these streets. Forget about them, and be sure that, if you fall for Mason Fenwick, he feels the same way about you."

Mason telephoned his older brother, Steve, the person who had been his spiritual, psychological, and economic anchor since they'd been orphaned at the ages of seven and twelve.

"I'll bring over some Chinese food, and we can have supper together, if you're not busy."

"I'm free this evening," Steve assured him. "Why don't I make a salad and chill a couple of beers?" Mason arrived at his brother's co-op apartment at about seven-thirty. The refined old building was situated on the south side of the dividing line between Harlem and the rest of mankind, as Steve liked to say, and was the only substantial gift he'd been willing to accept from his younger brother. Steve put the food in the microwave oven to be warmed later, divided a bottle of Heineken between two glasses, and took them into his living room.

"What's on your mind, Mason?"

He told his brother of his encounter with Jeannetta, by phone and in person. "I never felt so unsettled, as if I were in total disarray, unravelled, as I did when she left my office. I have a premonition that nothing good will come of it if I admit her to that tour."

Steve set his glass on the leather coaster and looked at Mason. "If she meets your criteria, and you said she does, you have no legal right or moral basis by which to exclude her. And since when did you base your actions on hunches and premonitions? It wasn't a premonition that led you to quit medicine, was it?"

Mason expelled a long, labored breath. He'd hoped that his leaving medicine wouldn't arise, but it nearly always crept into their conservations.

"Steve, I know you're disappointed in me, and that you'll probably always be, but I can't go back into that operating room. It warped me as a human being."

"You mean you let it warp you."

"Whatever. You worked most of your life to send me to

school, because I wanted to be a doctor, and you dedicated yourself to helping me realize my dream. I think of it all the time. You're forty-two, and you don't have a family, but you would have had if you hadn't cared so much for me." He covered Steve's hand with his own, in an attempt to convey the depth of his feelings.

"You weren't there, Steve. Everyone in that operating room saw it. For some reason, call it Divine Providence if you want to, I wasn't holding that scalpel right. If I had been, and my finger hadn't been as close as it was to the tip of that blade, Bianca Norris would be dead. She's in perfect health, and I don't plan to tempt fate ever again. I know it hurts you, and I lose more sleep over it than you can imagine, but that's the way it is."

"You'll go back. You'll have to. People need you. But you didn't come here to talk about that. You're here because of that woman."

Mason got up and walked the length of the long living room, stopped at a Shaker-style rocker, and propped his right foot on its bottom rung, rocking it.

"I don't want to take her along."

"Why? Seems to me you'd be glad to have someone your age on that two-month-long tour. When were you ever scared of a woman?"

"I'm not afraid of her, for Pete's sake." How would you feel about a strange woman strolling into your life and dulling your senses without uttering a word? he wanted to ask.

"Then take her." His wicked laugh seemed to carry immense satisfaction, Mason decided.

"Get down on your knees, brother," Steve continued jovially, "and see what it's like. We've all been there." Sobering, he asked, "What are you planning to do about Betty?"

Mason shrugged elaborately and ran his long fingers over his hair. "That's history."

"I'm glad to hear it," Steve said. "And at the risk of pontificating, I have to tell you it never should have started. She wasn't for you, but I suspect you know that. Any doctor taller than she is would have sufficed. When are you leaving?"

"May twenty-second. I have to ask you to go with Skip to his school program June first. He graduates from elementary school, and I can't leave him stranded. He needs support."

"Tell him to call me." He paused as though reluctant to raise an issue. "Mason, that boy's become so attached to you that, if you wanted to cut him loose, you couldn't."

Mason kicked at the carpet, as he frequently did when aggravated. "I have no idea why Skip began to tag along behind me. When my office was a couple of blocks from the upper East Side branch library, Skip used to sit on the steps, and, when I passed there every afternoon, he'd speak. I'd give him a thumbs-up sign and walk on. Seems he studied there to avoid the boys who were his neighbors in the projects. After a while he began waving at me when he spoke, and I couldn't help noticing him. Neat. Always alone and with an armful of books. Then, he began to walk along with me without saying anything, unless I asked him a question. One day, he rushed to greet me as though I were an old friend, even used my first name. I talked with him that day and, from then on, he waited for me. I didn't think to tell him I was moving my office down to East Forty-six Street but, after a couple of weeks, he found me and actually gave me a tongue lashing for not having told him I intended to move. I'd missed him, too, and told him so. He got to know my coming and going better than I did. He trailed along with me for months before he got around to asking me if we could be brothers, since his only family was a sick aunt who'd raised him almost from birth.

"He asked me to come to his school one night to root for his debating team. I went. As team captain, he introduced each team member and, to my astonishment, introduced me as his best friend. That gesture was out of place, and he knew it, but I never saw such a proud kid. By now, he means as much to me as I do to him, so don't think I'm going to want to cut him loose."

"What if you want to get married and your intended doesn't like Skip?"

"I won't want to marry a woman who doesn't like Skip." He ignored Steve's gestures of disbelief. "I'll tell him to call you."

They warmed the dinner and sat down to eat. Steve always honored their late father's custom of grace before meals, but Mason admitted that he rarely thought of it. They discussed the relative merits of General Colin Powell and Brigadier General Benjamin O. Davis, Jr., each conceding that Davis might have been great had he operated in a racially less difficult, less troubled era, and that Powell had made a more phenomenal imprint on the history of his time.

"You could have done the same in the field of medicine," Steve griped. "You developed a method of operating successfully where most doctors would rather not venture."

It always came back to that. Mason put the remainder of the food in the refrigerator, rinsed the dishes and placed them in the dishwasher, and prepared to leave.

"Is that the reason why you won't go into business with me? As partners, we could take turns touring, and one of us would always be in the office." When Steve failed to answer, Mason added, "I need you. If I ask often enough and long enough, maybe you'll give in." They embraced each other, as was their custom, and Mason left, knowing that Steve watched him from the doorway, as he had since their long-ago youth.

Mason took a taxi to the Amsterdam Houses on West Sixty-fifth Street, to the grim little apartment where Mabel Shaw lived with her nephew, Benjamin "Skip" Shaw. He surveyed the tidy but modest accommodation, wondering how Skip managed to study with the television, his aunt's only diversion from illness, blaring loudly, noise from outside and from surrounding apartments intruding, and the smell of decaying refuse drifting through the window with the dank air. At times, he was tempted to take the boy home with him, but Mabel was confined to the house, and she needed her nephew. He gave her some bills and inquired of Skip's whereabouts.

"Thank you, Mr. Fenwick. We couldn't live on what I get from the city, not even in this old dump. God bless you." Her weak hand dropped helplessly to her lap, and he knew a twinge of guilt. She needed better medical care and, under other circumstances, he could have gotten it for her.

"Where's Skip?" he asked again, and learned that the boy had gone to choral rehearsal. He told her he'd call Skip, and left. Two hours later, he walked into his apartment building to find the boy standing in the lobby wearing a hopeful look on his face. Although he'd eaten earlier with Steve, he sent out for pizza and nibbled some, while Skip devoured most of it.

"You don't need me to help you with your homework," Mason told the boy.

"Man, I have to know it's right. I have to stay at the head of my class.

Mason put the palm-sized calculator aside and looked Skip in the eye. "I do not like your calling me 'man'. How would you like me to call you boy? I have a name, so use it."

"Yeah, but…"

"I don't care for that expression, either, and I've told you so. The word is yes. Where's your math workbook?" Mason knew that what Skip wanted from him was attention. Though in Junior High School, the boy's knowledge of math was nearly equal to that of a high school senior.

Skip confirmed that, when he said, "Man, I'm way ahead of my class in math."

"Then we'll work on your English. You're not ahead of anybody on that. I want you to drop that street language."

The boy's eyes rounded and increased in size. "You want me to talk like you? I can't do that, man. The guys'll gang up on me if I start acting smart-assed."

"And clean up your mouth. You are not going to be like them, and you're not going to talk the way they do. You hear me?"

"Okay. Okay. I'm gonna be just like you. Right? I'm gonna get an education and learn everything. Me and my aunt are gonna move out of the projects soon as I get my first paycheck."

Mason resisted an urge to pat Skip's shoulder, to relieve him of his immense psychological burden. "My aunt and I. Read this page aloud." He listened, enraptured, as the boy read a long passage from Richard Wright's *Native Son,* interpreting it, giving life to the writer's words. Chills streaked through him as Bigger's furor, fears and then his dreams flowed from Skip's mouth. How could a twelve-year-old express another person's horror so eloquently? The boy had crossed Central Park and walked another twenty blocks to get to Mason's apartment near Eighty-seventh and Madison.

After Skip left, Mason sat alone, looking at the wood-panelled walls of his study, glancing occasionally at the expensive Tabriz Persian carpet beneath his feet. Without his brother's sacrifice, he'd have been like Skip—a good little ship with no rudder— or worse. Quitting medicine had been a tough decision, but living with it had been hell. He had gained a measure of peace, had learned to be comfortable and relaxed with himself, and with others since changing his profession. He got up and paced the floor, ill at ease now, stressed as he hadn't been since he'd pulled off those surgical greens for the last time, and he traced his discontent to Jeannetta Rollins. He didn't understand his reluctance where she was concerned, but he had to do what was right.

Mason didn't fool himself; his fitful sleep was due to his unsettled feelings about the woman who, in the space of seconds, had jarred him out of his sense of contentment, his hard-won equilibrium. He didn't doubt what would happen if he spent two months in her company. Hell: two days. At first light of morning, he called it a night, a sleepless one, dressed and walked over to Central Park. He had searched for an apartment on the East River so he could see the sunrise from a balcony or a window. But people who had the kind of place that he wanted and could afford seldom vacated. He leaned against a huge oak at the park's edge and enjoyed the chirping birds that darted freely about as though claiming nature's beauty and bounty for themselves before humans laid waste to them. He crossed Fifth Avenue on the way back home and greeted the newspaper lady who worked the corner of Madison and Eighty-seventh, collecting papers that she sold for recycling. She stored them in her shopping cart, and he saved his copies of The *New York Times* and The *Wall Street Journal* for her. She was a business-person, he remembered her having told him, and she didn't want handouts. At eight o'clock he telephoned Jeannetta.

"Hallo."

"Sorry to awaken you, but I thought writers started work early."

"They do if they get a good night's sleep. Who is…? *Mason?*"

"Right." So she recognized his voice and thought of him by his first name! He blew all the air out of his lungs. Maybe he ought to let nature take its course and stop worrying about what could happen. And he would, too, if he didn't have this strangely uneasy feeling about her.

"Do you still want to take the tour?"

"Yes. Does this call mean you're accepting me?"

"We fly out of Kennedy on the twenty-second of May. My secretary will send you a list of the countries for which you'll need visas, and information about the required shots. If you don't have a health card, your doctor will give you one. Any problems, call me. I know you're interested in Africa so, before you give me your word, I want you to understand that we'll be going to Northern and Western Africa, but not to any countries in the southern and eastern regions. That suit you?"

"Fine. I can go to east Africa some other…"

"Some other time?" He wondered why she hadn't finished the thought, and when she replied, "Well, maybe," he became curious.

"I know this trip is expensive; most people who take it have saved for a lifetime."

"It damages your savings, alright."

He recognized evasiveness when he heard it and decided not to push her. "Next time you're down here in the city, stop by the office and pick up your carry-on bag."

"I have to be there Tuesday morning. Is that too early?"

Excitement coursed through him, and he tried to suppress it. He wanted to see her. As soon as he'd heard her voice, his sexual energy had kicked into high gear and he'd felt the heat swirling in his belly. As though unaffected, he replied in a dispassionate voice, "That'll be fine. If you're free, say around one, we could have lunch, and I can outline our route for you."

"I…Thank you. I…I'd love that. See you around one on Tuesday."

He hung up, but didn't shift his gaze from the telephone. So she, too, was skeptical about a relationship between them. He fingered the keys in his pocket and told himself to stop thinking about Jeannetta Rollins. Not much chance of that…

Four days later, Jeannetta walked into Mason's suite of offices to find him standing by his secretary's desk with his right hand braced on his hip, examining his wrist watch. She'd tried to get there on time, she really had, but she hadn't been able to resist watching the harlequinlike couple in Grand Central Station who danced for their livelihood to the tune of Louis Armstrong's old recording of *Let's Do It*. The crowd had loved them, had showered them with money, and they had shown their appreciation with dazzling bluegrass clogging.

"Sorry I'm late."

"Something tells me you say that often." The thrill of his deep, comforting voice washed away her cares. She didn't care if he showed displeasure, as long as he kept their date. White shirt, red-and-navy-striped tie, and dark-gray suit. Did he dress that way every day? When she'd met him, he had looked good, Lord knows, but not that sharp. The thought that he might have dressed well for their luncheon sent her heart into a gallop.

"I can't resist enjoying things that are pleasing to look at," she said. "I hope you'll forgive me."

He asked if she liked Italian food and smiled his pleasure when her reply indicated they had that much in common. He took them to a restaurant on Sixth Avenue, not far from his office.

"Your usual, Mr. Mason?" the tiny dark-haired woman asked him. He nodded, and the woman led them to a small back room that had four well-separated and well-appointed tables. White linen cloths, vases of yellow, pink, and white snapdragons, long-stemmed crystal glasses, and porcelain dinnerware. Any ideas she had of insisting that they go Dutch went out the window.

"Do you eat here often?"

Amusement reflected itself in the gleam of his eyes, dazzling her. He held her chair, seated himself, and leaned toward her.

"When I can find the time. Yes. Now, let's get something straight before we proceed. *If you're not at the boarding gate for flight SK620 on May twenty-second when the flight is called, I'll let the plane leave without you, and I will not reimburse you. Got that?*" He didn't smile, wink, or do anything to soften the harshness of his remark. She avoided looking in his eyes and let her gaze find a spot over his shoulder, mulling over her reply before deciding to bait him.

"I won't be the first woman you left behind, but you'll be able to say you know at least one female who didn't chase after you."

"I'm serious, Jeannetta."

"Me, too, Mason." His handsome long brown fingers strummed the table lightly while his gaze fastened on her. "You aren't known for patience, are you?" she ventured.

"With people who don't deliberately provoke me into losing it. I've got plenty. Take you, for instance. You've got a built-in patience buster that stays on automatic pilot."

"How do you know all that?" she bristled. "We're strangers." She wished he wouldn't look at her so intently. Right then, his eyes changed color, jacking up her body's temperature and jellying her bones.

"Oh, I don't imagine that you do it deliberately. My guess is that you merely float around in your own world, laid back, unperturbed, wrecking other people's equilibrium without meaning to." She shifted in her chair. Laura must have accused her of something similar dozens of times over the years. Without thinking, she asked him, "Are you a psychiatrist?" She watched the light in his eyes dim and a defensive shield steal over his face.

"Anyone who cares about people can learn to interpret human behavior; one needn't be a psychiatrist."

She told herself that she'd gotten too close there, that she had better be more careful. In his mesmerizing features, she had glimpsed pain; just for a second, it had been there. Unmistakable. Perhaps he regretted leaving medicine. Or maybe someone for whom he had cared had betrayed him. This man carried scars, and trust probably didn't come easily with him. It wouldn't do for him to know too soon why she had chosen his tour. The waiter took their orders. Shrimp scampi with rice and a salad for him; spaghetti with pesto sauce and a salad for her.

He folded his arms, grasping his biceps, and leaned back in his chair. "Jeannetta, we might as well stop fencing with each other. It doesn't make sense and, besides, it's useless." Tiny pricks of warm sensation shot through her and anticipation simmered in her breast.

"I don't know what you mean." She hadn't been able to steady her voice, and his expression said that he knew it.

"Alright. Stick your head in the sand, if you think you'll be more comfortable that way." Before she could speak, he added. "And if you like mind-blowing surprises."

"I'm taking this tour because I want to see the world." Realizing that her voice had sounded plaintive, she smiled to soften the effect and, to her amazement, Mason abruptly leaned forward, his eyes simmering pools of brown heat.

"I'll show you the world." Tingling excitement shot down her spine at the sound of his passion-filled lover's voice. "The world through my eyes is a wondrous place, Jeannetta. Sunrises that explode from a kaleidoscope of colors, great trees with leaves that dance in a wind you can almost see, foamy ocean caps, long stretches of virgin sandy beaches, and moons that nourish your soul. I'll show you stars in your favorite colors, mountains topped with evergreen trees and pristine snow, green valleys with millions of wildflowers. If you travel with me, Jeannetta, you'll live in a new and different world. You'll bask in the realm of the ethereal."

She hid her trembling hands beneath the table cloth, pressed her arms to her side, and crossed her ankles. He wasn't speaking of the Fenwick Travel Agency tour, but of what she'd find in an intimate relationship with him. Strange that the picture he painted symbolized what she'd lose if he didn't help her. Somewhere from the archives of her mind came a reminder that if she fell for him all might be lost, and an admonishment that she ought to get away from him while she could. She knew she'd better get them back on an impersonal basis. But she sat there, imprisoned by his hypnotic stare, and said nothing.

"Well, what do you say?"

She called on her aplomb and managed to return his gaze. Sucking in her breath, she told him, "You paint a magnificent picture; I could see it all in my mind's eye, but…"

"But you're scared," he interrupted, his face bright and animated. Most of the time only his eyes expressed his feelings, and she had to force herself not to comment on the change. He regarded her carefully, and his demeanor told her that her words were important to him, but the effect of his rapt concentration was lessened by the gentle strumming of his dark fingers on the white linen cloth.

"Of all the things I may have been called in my life," she said, "I doubt that scared was one of them. But you'll have to admit that only a foolish woman would fail to question the words of a man whose tongue is as smooth as yours."

His eyebrows arched sharply, and he rested his fork.

"And the woman who does not recognize a man's truth when she hears it is to be pitied."

She didn't want him to know what his words had done to her, but the loud swish of air into her lips was all he needed. Her eyelids dropped, and she cringed at the prints that her nails had dug in the palms of her hands.

He must have seen her agitation, for he shook his head and told her, "A person's first duty to himself is to know who he is; I'm working hard at that, and you'd better start. Why can't you do what you'd like to do?"

"And what's that?" she asked, her tone less than friendly. He reached in his pocket for his credit card, placed it on the table and signaled for their waiter.

"Jeannetta, I promised myself three years ago that I would tell myself the truth no matter how much I hated to hear it. Although some inner sense—call it intuition—tells me I may regret it, you attract me as no other woman has, and I want to spend time with you. A lot of time. If you were as honest with both of us, you'd tell me that you feel the same way. Let's go. I've got a two-thirty appointment." Her penetrating, disbelieving stare must have gotten to him, because he explained his rapid change of mood. "I've grieved about two incidents in my life, and I doubt anything else could move me as deeply. I'll settle for peace and contentment. What about you?"

"Sounds good to me." She stood and hooked the strap of her hobo bag over her right shoulder. After their conversation, she had to start looking for a miracle. His fingers, splayed across her back as he guided her toward the door, gave her a sense of security that she hadn't often known. He was there—and he wouldn't allow anything to shatter her well-being—was the message that his warm fingers sent to her body. If only that were true. They stepped out into the early spring sunshine and she felt his hand through the fabric that covered her arm.

"Headed back to Pilgrim?"

She wished she could figure out what he was thinking. He managed not to communicate anything but the words he spoke.

"I'm going over to Columbus Avenue, find a sidewalk café, and do some people watching. It's my favorite hobby and provides me with a lot of material for my books. Have you ever done it?" She thought he stepped closer, or maybe it was a sensation. He seemed everywhere.

"A little. What I've done, I've liked." She could swear that his eyes changed to that brownish-green color with its hot, come-hither gleam. She couldn't help taking a step backward. "I like you, too, Jeannetta, and I wish I had time to join you. I'm sure I'd enjoy it."

"It would be nice to have company." What else could she say, she asked herself, needing an excuse for having encouraged him. She stepped away, preparing to leave him.

"May I call you?"

Flustered as well as delighted, she ignored the warning of her conscience. "Ye…yes. Well, I…Mason, it's…Well, alright."

"You've got misgivings?"

"Yes, I do, but…I'll be listening for your call." He appeared to mull that over. Then he squeezed her arm lightly and, for a minute, she thought he'd kiss her. Instead, he brushed her cheek with the back of his hand and winked. As she walked off, she knew that he scrutinized every movement of her body.

# Chapter 2

Jeannetta strolled into the Scandinavian Airlines lounge at John F. Kennedy Airport, dropped her bags, sat down, and pulled out her writing tablet. Airports afforded wonderful opportunities for people watching, and she had found several of her most intriguing fictional characters among the sometimes tired, sometimes excited, but always unsuspecting creatures who waited there. Her glance caught the tall, dark man who leaned with the support of his elbows against the airline crew's desk. Loose. Casual. Quickly, she tore her gaze away, but his had already captured her, and she knew he'd seen her admire him.

He straightened up and headed toward her.

"I could have sworn you'd be late."

She couldn't help laughing; she had expected him to say something like that.

"That's why I made it a point to arrive early; can't afford to let you think you can predict my behavior." His eyes darkened, and his glance swept over her. He nodded, as though putting his seal of approval on what he'd seen.

"A man who's foolish enough to think he can predict *any* woman's behavior shouldn't be allowed out of the house by himself. Woman has perplexed man since the beginning of time." Her delight in his company had to be obvious, so she didn't try to hide her pleasure in their bantering.

"Then 'man' ought to grow up." She laid the tablet aside, unconsciously inviting him to join her. He didn't accept the invitation.

"We've got nearly an hour before boarding time," he said, after glancing at his Timex watch. "Would you join me for a drink?"

The word yes sat on the tip of her tongue, but she remembered her doctor's advice and said, "I'd love to, but I'm not…I mean, I don't drink."

His face framed a set of flawless white teeth when his lips spread in a mesmerizing grin. She knew who'd win that one.

"Then we'll have coffee," he stated. She let him take her arm and usher her over to the bar. Their tour offered first-class accommodations, apart from the business-class seats. She put a few finger sandwiches on a salad plate, and he poured two cups of coffee.

"Let's sit over here where we can see the planes land," he suggested. When she declined cream and sugar, a curious expression that she couldn't fathom spread across his face. He reached for a sandwich.

"Caviar on cream cheese with black coffee, when the world's best champagne sits over there for the taking!" he exclaimed with a frown.

She remained silent while he stretched out his long legs on either side of the tiny table and pinned her with a penetrating stare. He always seems to want to dig inside of me, she thought, and put herself on guard.

"Why didn't you return my calls?" She had been expecting that question, but not the twang of bitterness that laced his voice. She'd thought he would shrug it off and forget about a personal relationship between them.

"That ought to be obvious." The blank expression that she now recognized as self-protection covered his face, and he pushed the coffee aside.

"Obvious to you, maybe. You told me I could call you. If you had changed your mind, one word would have been sufficient." She couldn't' tell him that the sound of his deep, melodious voice would have drained her of her resolve to avoid an entanglement. That admission would be as good as a confession.

"I should have returned your calls. I apologize."

"Tell me who you are."

Jolted by the low vibrancy of his voice, she repeated her name.

"I know that, and it tells me nothing. What makes you laugh? Cry?"

"Just about anything. It depends."

He nodded. "You're one vague woman. What do you want out of this tour?"

"I told you: I want to see the world."

"So you did." He stood. "Can I get you something?" She shook her head, and he strode to the bar and returned with a glass of club soda. She hoped her discomfort didn't show. She sat back in her chair and dropped her hands in her lap in pretended serenity, but her fingertips clutched the fabric of her green chambray slacks.

"Somehow that Timex doesn't fit the rest of you," she said, in an attempt to shift the conversation to him.

He looked at his wrist. "I've lost at least ten of these things. I always used to lay them aside when I walked into the op…"

Thank God he'd been looking at his watch and not at her, because recognition had to have been plain on her face. She waited for him to continue.

"Once you get in the habit of removing your watch when you're doing something delicate, you should buy the cheapest one you can find."

Nice cover, she thought, for the first time experiencing anger at his charade.

"What do you do that's delicate?"

"Wood carving. My favorite pastime."

"What do you carve?"

His deep breath and narrowed left eye told her to ease up, that he disliked personal questions. Tough, she decided; he didn't hesitate to dig into her life.

"Animals, people, whatever strikes my fancy. I like using my hands." He pushed his chair back from the table and looked at his watch. "Boarding in about fifteen minutes; I'd better round up my gang."

This man's got everything I want, she admitted to herself, and cautioned herself that if she didn't get her emotions under control, she'd damage her cause beyond salvaging, and she needn't even get on that plane.

He pinned her with a steady gaze. "You haven't told me what you're expecting from this tour."

She resorted to a half truth. "The experience of a lifetime. We're still strangers; perhaps if we get to know each other better, I…"

"We will," he interrupted, "put your life on it."

"How can you be so certain?"

He leaned forward. "We'll be spending eight weeks together. By the end of the tour, I'll know every one of my guests better." He leaned back in his chair, tilting it on its back legs, and let his gaze sear her with potent intimacy, its sensuality captivating her. Exquisite shivers pummeled her insides.

"You're so sure of yourself."

He raked his right hand over his hair, exposing his strong wrist and long-fingered lover's hands.

"No. I'm not, so you're wrong on that one. But life is short, Jeannetta, and I'm not going to spend it lying to myself or doing what makes me uncomfortable. I'm interested in more than pleasant chitchat with you." He paused as though seeking precise words, and let his chair rest on all four legs. "I don't like stewing over what might have been, so I try to avoid it. You interest me, and I'm probably going to pursue that interest." He stood. "See you in a few minutes."

Jeannetta avoided eye contact with Mason when he checked off her name as she passed him before boarding the plane. She stacked her carry-on luggage and found her seat, pleased that the entire business-class section had been sold to the tour. Minutes later, he touched her arm.

"Ignoring me won't make me go away," he told her. She looked up into his solemn face. "I'll try to make the trip as pleasant as I can but, if you still have doubts, I'll break my rule and refund your money. You have about three minutes to decide."

The investigator's report had described him as a man of honor, and she'd found no reason to disagree. "I'm taking the tour."

His smile, warm and genuine, flooded her heart with joy. His hand grazed her shoulder. "I'm glad."

Some mornings later, shortly after sunrise, Jeannetta strolled along the beach of the Tyrrhenian Sea, knowing a peculiar freedom as the warm May breeze whipped around her thin, wide skirt. Fresh, salty air invigorated her, and she released her cares and enjoyed her first view of the Lido di Ostia, southwest of Rome. Mason had scheduled one day there for the beach lovers. She had loved every minute of the week they'd stayed in Europe, but she'd gladly have spent most of the time in Italy. No other European country could match it for the sensual experiences it offered: great art; unforgettable food, music, and scenery; and, not to be overlooked, the adoration of the handsome Italian men.

She removed her sandals and strolled along the nearly empty shore, occasionally digging her toes in the warm sand, lifting them and watching the sand drift downward through them. The early-morning sun cast the shadow of her slim silhouette the length of a city block. She studied it as she did all things that she found pleasing to her eyes and, in her scrutiny of it, she nearly passed without seeing the figure stretched out before her.

She edged closer, glancing back occasionally to judge her chances of escape. A man lay sprawled supine in the warm sand, his bronze body glistening with beads of sweat as his pores soaked up the sun. She stared down at Mason Fenwick, his flawless physique bare to her eyes but for a tiny red string bikini swimsuit. His closed eyes and deep breathing suggested that he slept. She gaped at him in open admiration and whispered, "Thank God for my eyes." If she never saw anything else in her life, she had seen human perfection and reveled in it. Her tongue curled into the roof of her mouth, and she swallowed with difficulty. What would he say? What would he do if she fell upon him and took him right then and there? Shocked at her thoughts, she gasped aloud and ran.

\* \* \*

His years as a resident had trained him to sleep lightly, and Mason awoke at the sound of Jeannetta's gasp. He sat up quickly, and watched her run down the beach until she reached the bathhouse and disappeared from sight. Josh, the porter whom he'd hired to attend to the luggage, approached.

"That was Miss Rollins, wasn't it?" he said, making certain that it was she.

"Yes, sir," Josh confirmed. "She seemed kinda upset. You know, excited like, but she spoke to me like she always does." Mason got up and dusted the sand from his hips and legs.

"Sure hate to leave here," Josh told him.

"Yes, but you'll like Rome," Mason called back to him as he headed for the hotel.

Jeannetta stumbled into the bathhouse, breathless and confused about her reaction to Mason. She couldn't afford to fall for him. From the day she'd met him, she had questioned her ability to carry out her plan. Falling for a man made a woman vulnerable to him and put her at a disadvantage, no matter how you viewed it, and to lust for him as she had—only lust described what she'd felt—made her a pushover.

"Good morning, dear. You're looking fit, as usual," Geoffrey Ames confided to her in a near whisper. He had retired at age seventy-eight and had won the lottery the next day. By now, all of his touring companions knew how he regretted having no one with whom to share it. He'd treated himself to the tour, the first pleasure he'd known.

Jeannetta smiled, relieved that it was Geoffrey who had joined her.

"I didn't swim, but the weather is priceless."

The man appeared flustered, but she understood his embarrassment when he asked her in a tentative voice, "Would a lovely young lady such as yourself care to have dinner with me when we get back to Rome tonight?"

"Oh, Geoffrey, I'd love it. Rome at night. It will be wonderful."

"Then I'll find a place where we can eat under the stars. Would you like that?" She assured him that she would, collected the beach clothes that she had stored there, and trudged off to the hotel for breakfast.

Mason wrapped his beach robe tightly and slid into the booth beside her. Her refusal to look at him while she pretended to read a shaking menu and then attempted to drink the water before the glass reached her lips—with obvious results—told him what he wanted to know. She'd run away to avoid temptation. He hadn't tried to breach the wall she'd raised between them since their plane landed in Copenhagen, but he planned to put an end to the foolishness. Beautiful and statuesque, with an indefinable quality, she had a feminine something that he felt clear to the marrow of his bones every time she came near him. He had made it a point not to impose on his guests, and she'd indicated a desire to have space between them, but she would be his exception.

"Enjoy your morning walk?" He ignored her discomfort and considered himself entitled to do that. After all, she hadn't leveled with him; he was certain of it. Her eyelids closed for a second and furrows marked her brow, but he refused to let her discomfort sidetrack him. He repeated it. Her composure restored, she answered in a tone that belittled the importance of his question.

"Yes, but the sand wasn't as thick as I'd hoped it would be; I love to sink in it halfway to my knees."

"You've been avoiding me," he said, dispensing with preliminaries and small talk.

"Why would I do that? You've been the perfect host."

A muscle tensed his jaw, and he pushed back the irritation he felt. "You don't know what kind of host I've been, because you've managed to stay out of my path."

Her lips twitched, and he thought her breath quickened when he slid closer. "You're imagining that."

He caught the fingers of her delicate left hand in his right one, sensed a quick, involuntary movement of her body and watched her lower her eyes and moisten her glistening bare lips with the tip of her tongue. He squeezed her hand.

"Am I imagining this? Am I?" It didn't surprise him that she jerked her hand from his, but he wouldn't have expected the expression of pain mirrored on her lovely brown face.

She turned fully to face him. "Mason, be satisfied with things as they are. I can't give more." Her luminous eyes belied her words, and her obvious reluctance to say them fueled his hunger.

"You wrote on your application that you are not married. Are you engaged?" She shook her head.

"Alright. I want to know you better, and I think you want that, too, but I won't force myself on you or any other woman. Tell me you don't want anything to do with me, and I'll honor your decision." His fingers skimmed the back of her hand. "But could you walk away not knowing what might have been? Could you?" Encouraged by her silence, he let go of her hand, raised his own to her shoulders and tugged her closer to him. After a minute or two, she looked at him and released a quick breath, and he knew that she'd seen the tenderness he felt and the need simmering in his eyes. He lowered his head and kissed the corner of her mouth and, when her lids flew open to reveal a hot woman's desire, he swore inwardly for not having picked a more appropriate time and place to begin their intimacy.

Jeannetta looked at herself in the long mirror, shrugged, picked up her purse, and started toward the door of her hotel room. Satisfied with the way she looked, but not sure why she'd put on that sexy, lemon-yellow silk sheath for dinner with Geoffrey Ames, she considered changing into something less provocative. She hadn't bought it as a fashion statement, but because the color became her and the style suited her figure. Her hand rested on the doorknob. No point in lying to herself; she dressed with Mason Fenwick in mind. He socialized with tour members in the lounge at cocktail time, and she hoped he'd see her leave the hotel with Geoffrey. She leaned against the door, wondering when she had become a schemer. She could have been with Mason right then if she'd been honest and told him that she shared his feelings. She slapped her right cheek as though to knock sense into her head, opened the door, and headed for the lounge.

She looked from Geoffrey, bedecked in his dark-blue suit, white shirt, and blue tie, to Mason, who rested casually against the end of the bar wearing what even a child would identify as a mocking smirk. It was that obvious. Geoffrey greeted her in a manner that belied his modest education and humble background, and his pleasure at being with her shone on his countenance. They got into the waiting taxi for the trip across the Tiber River.

*"Buona sera, Signor, Signore,"* the driver sang in a proud operatic voice.

"Son, I'm lucky I can speak English," Geoffrey told the cabby. "These foreign words give me a headache. We want to go to Trastevere."

"Okay. *Dove in Trastevere?"* the driver asked. Geoffrey told him. The driver took them on a hair-raising ride down the Corso and stopped to give them a view of St. Peter's and the Vatican lit at night. Jeannetta thought his lecture in Italian unforgettable, as he used all but his feet to make them understand. She appreciated his effort, though neither she nor her companion could comprehend a word. Jeannetta couldn't suppress a gasp when they got out of the taxi at the restaurant, Alfredo's in Trastevere.

*"Alfresco?"* the waiter asked.

She nodded. That much Italian she knew, and the environment surrounding the famous restaurant invited them to take a table out of doors. They faced the Church Of Santa Maria in Trastevere that had dominated the small square and the Trastevere quarter since ancient times. The tiny white building, one of Rome's true treasures, boasted stained-glass windows and a colorfully tiled roof that gleamed in the clear moonlight. Its aura of unreal, unearthly elegance brought tears to her eyes. Nearby diners rattled their silverware and clinked glasses, but she stared, enraptured, her mind far from the gourmet food and its tantalizing odors of seafood, ripe cheeses, spices, and garlic. The setting lacked perfection only because Mason Fenwick didn't have his arms around her. Jeannetta reached over and patted Geoffrey's hand.

"I'll remember this for the rest of my life. If I've ever seen anything more beautiful, I don't recall it." She didn't imagine that the old man preened; her words must have touched him, for he seemed taller by inches.

"I didn't think I'd be so fortunate. I figured you'd be going out tonight with our guide. He's young and handsome and he's got all of his hair. He can't seem to keep his eyes off of you, either. I watched him."

"Don't read too much into that, Geoffrey. I can imagine that romances always bloom on these tours, and I expect they die when the plane gets back to JFK airport. Mason's nice to all of us."

Geoffrey shook his head. "You're wrong about this. I've been around a long time, and I know when a man's got the fever. He may be slow about it, but you've caught his eye real good, and he ain't planning to leave this earth without letting you know exactly what that means."

A part of her wanted that confirmation of Mason's interest, but an inner voice counseled her not to lull herself into forgetting why she knew Mason Fenwick. Her gaze held the lovely little church, and she savored the moment; she didn't need a better reminder.

"I think you're mistaken about Mason. He likes me, but not to that extent."

"Never mind. He'll let you know when he gets ready, and it'll do him good to see you with me. I've got a few years on me, but he'll be thinking about that lottery I hit. He knows money makes short men tall. Yep. It'll do him a lot of good."

To her astonishment, Geoffrey raised her hand to his lips and gave it a pretend kiss just as they stepped into the hotel lobby. She thought he'd overdone his appreciation of her company until she saw Mason sprawled in a leather lounge chair that directly faced the door. He stood at once, and she nearly laughed when Geoffrey patted her shoulder, grasped her hand, smiled and whispered, "It'll come sooner than you expect."

Mason walked to them, a scowl distorting his handsome features, and, ignoring Geoffrey, demanded to know where she'd been. She turned aside and told her escort that she'd enjoyed his company and that she would never forget their evening together.

"It was truly idyllic," she added, intentionally aggravating Mason.

"Miss Rollins, as you know, the first rule of this tour is that whenever members leave the group, I must be told where they're going. Lady, I sat here for three hours wondering whether I should call the police. You strutted out of here in that…that…walked out of here, got in a taxi and stayed for three solid hours. Three hours in a city you never saw before. You're…That's irresponsible."

"What are you so riled about? I was with Mr. Ames. You saw me leave here with him."

"You were with Ames?" He told himself to calm down, that she had returned apparently unharmed, and that he ought to forget about her. Then he ignored his advice. "I thought he only helped you get a taxi. You were with him all this time?"

"Sure was," she answered as though he'd find that scenario acceptable.

Well, he thought, she miscalculated. Ames might be seventy-eight, but he owned the standard male equipment, plus a pile of money.

"Ames told me where he was going, but he neglected to add that he intended to take you with him." He looked at her, standing there wearing that half-smile, the picture of innocence, and he wished he could do a few push-ups and cool down his anger. She had a right to do anything she pleased with whomever she liked. He stuck his hand in his right pants pocket and felt the odd-sized keys that were forever with him. Damned if he'd let her erase what he'd achieved in years of fighting to control his constant anxiety and trigger temper. He wanted to make her mad, but she just stood there smiling, refusing to budge.

"I hope you remember that we leave tomorrow morning for Paris and that you're to have your bags outside your door at six-thirty."

She took a step toward him. "I remembered. Why are you so angry?"

The balloon inside him burst, scattering his anger as chaff succumbs to the wind.

"I haven't been angry in years." Well, he hadn't until tonight. "I'm annoyed. Please try to be more considerate."

"I'll be ready in time, and so will my bags, so don't get your dander up. Losing your temper at me is bad for your health," she teased.

He stared at the mischievous grin that curled her lips, and he wanted to…

"Are you alright?" he asked, his demeanor having changed quickly to one of concern.

"Oh, I'm fine. Why?" Her smile didn't fool him. She'd experienced a vertigo-like sensation and grabbed the back of the chair. A second year medical student wouldn't have been fooled by that.

"I'll see you to your room." His hand at her elbow was all the support he knew she'd allow, but he wanted to take her into his arms, carry her to her room, and tuck her in bed.

"I can go alone. I'm fine; really I am."

"It will comfort me to know you're safely in your room. I'm going with you." In the elevator, where the lights shone brighter, a feeling of relief washed over him when he couldn't detect any pallor and she showed no further signs of dizziness.

"Too bad we aren't spending more time in Paris," she said. "I'll only have time to go to the Louvre and the *Jeu de Paume.* I would have loved to visit the Rodin museum and to find some of those new, off-the-beaten-path art galleries that feature folk art from central Africa. This may be my last… The other members of the tour will be shopping and sipping espresso at the Café de la Paix trying to feel what it's like to be French."

They got off the elevator and strolled to her room nearby.

"I doubt the French ever go to that café. If they want an espresso, they can get it cheaper and better some place where the waiters only speak French. Sure you don't want to shop?" She shook her head, and he found himself admiring her ability to get that thick, wooly hair into such an elegant twist at the back of her neck. A lot of things about her pleased him.

"Since we're both art lovers, why don't we check out those museums together, all three of them?"

Her quick smile told him that she welcomed his company. "I'd love that. Maybe we can find some of those galleries, too."

"Are you going to shop for African art?"

Why should the light in her eyes dim so quickly? Mason wondered.

"I don't want to buy anything."

He watched her closely. "Not even perfume?"

Her shrug must have been intended to suggest nonchalance, or maybe that perfume didn't interest her. She'd piqued his interest further.

"I don't need anything, and I don't like to own things just for the sake of having them. I only buy what I need. It would be fun, though, to sit on the Avenue de la Paix and watch the world pass." She took a step backward when he moved closer to her.

"You fascinate me. Why do you avoid me?"

She seemed flustered, but immediately covered it with a haughty tilt of her head.

"I haven't done that. Why should I? You seem harmless enough." That smile again. That curve of her lipstick-free mouth that made him want to devour her, to kiss her until she told him he could have whatever he wanted.

"You *are* harmless, aren't you?" she asked him. Well, hell. She was flirting with him.

"Depends on your definition of harmless. I'm your tour manager, and I'm responsible for you, but when the two of us are alone—like right now—my mating instincts are likely to surface. Like now."

Her eyes rounded into two beautiful brown O's.

"You're a very desirable woman, and I haven't forgotten that for one second since the first time I looked at you." The hot energy that shot to his belly must have been reflected in his eyes, because she broke eye contact with him. He wanted to take her and love her until he hadn't an ounce of energy left, but he understood women, and this wasn't the time to press it. Her inability to look at him and her insistent toying with her hands fuelled the heat in him. But he wasn't reckless. Not yet. If ever he'd been suspended over feminine quicksand, this was the time, and he admitted wanting the experience of being sucked into it. All the way. He brushed back the lapels of his jacket and eased his hands into his pants pockets while he stared at her lips. Desire choked him, and he coughed. If she didn't stop fidgeting…

"I'd better say goodnight. As you said, I have to rise early."

"Scared?"

"You could say that," she answered, though she didn't look it. He moved closer. "But you could also be wrong." She took the plastic card from her evening purse and would have opened her door had he not taken the card. He placed it in the lock, but didn't open the door. She shifted her glance; her lower lip quivered, and he had to admire her willpower. But when she swallowed hard, he nearly lost his own. A battle of wills, and she'd win if he didn't put some space between them.

"What do you want, Mr. Fenwick?"

"My name is Mason, and I think you know the answer to that. See you in the morning." He sucked in his breath. "Goodnight."

Mason reflected on their exchange as he rounded the corner to his room. She's delicate, he mused, but she's also strong; warm, but wary. And she intended to keep him at a distance. It had stunned him to realize how badly he wanted to kiss her, to feel her, soft and submissive, in his arms. He thought of that morning on the beach, still unable to decide why she'd run away. An aura of mystery clung to her, and he sensed an air of transience about her, as though she were only flitting through his life. He'd better watch his step with Jeannetta Rollins, because he'd had his last temporary liaison. Now he wanted a home and a family.

Jeannetta got into her room and locked the door. That had been close. Her thoughts had been filled with the memory of him lying nearly naked in the warm sand, beads of perspiration glistening on his washboard-flat belly. All but inches of him had been a feast for her eyes. The urge she'd had to fall upon him and ravish his body had come back to her. Six more weeks, and it didn't look promising. He hadn't allowed her to create an environment in which he could be approached as a surgeon, and she had avoided him when he socialized with the guests. She couldn't let him believe that she was courting his attention, but, no matter what she did, he steered their relationship toward intimacy. She had to keep it impersonal; if she didn't, she would pay dearly.

After the uneventful flight from Rome to Paris and a routine trip to a hotel near the Champs Elysée, Jeannetta stood on the balcony of her hotel room in the shadow of the Arc de Triomphe, savoring the sights that greeted her eyes. Preparing for the possibility that her ears would someday become her eyes, she relayed descriptions of the French and their antics into her cassette recorder. An old man riding what seemed an even older bicycle fell from his bike in his attempt to prevent his long skinny loaf of bread from falling to the ground. Unharmed, he threaded the baguette through a hole in the basket, looked up and shook his fist at the sky. A woman wearing a yellow, red, and purple beret dashed across the wide avenue after her monkey, stopping traffic as she went and leaving her organ grinder to the mercy of two youths, who stood playing with it when she returned with her pet. She promptly left the machine and the monkey and took off after the two pranksters.

Jeannetta rushed inside to answer the telephone and was rewarded with the sound of Mason's deep baritone.

"It's eleven o'clock. We ought to get started if we're going to three museums today. How much time do you need?"

She told him she'd meet him in the lobby in ten minutes.

"I thought I'd stop by for you."

And from the way he'd looked at her after placing her bags on the luggage rack in her room that morning, they'd never reach *one* museum. "Downstairs. Ten minutes."

His chuckle warmed her heart. "Okay, scaredy-cat."

She leaned against the doorjamb, studying a sculpture in the Musée de Rodin. She had to memorize as much as possible so that she could make an accurate recording of it that evening.

"Are you tired?" Mason asked her.

"No. Thank you. I can't rush through this. I want to see these sculptures with every one of my senses, not just my eyes. I want to be able to recall in my mind's eye every line, every bump; feel the cold texture of the bronze. Everything." From his strange, inquiring expression, she wondered what he saw.

"Do I seem odd to you?" she asked, and immediately wished that she hadn't, when he seemed taken aback.

"Why, no. I've just realized that you're a deeply sensual person." Her glance fell on *The Kiss*, Rodin's great masterpiece, and she wished that Mason hadn't witnessed her reaction to it, as he must have, when she sucked in her breath and her lips parted in awe.

"Exquisite, isn't it? A man's homage to his love." Stunned at his unexpected sentimentality, her eyes caressed him as she welcomed this new facet of the man who, with each passing moment, wedged himself more deeply into her being. His diffident smile betrayed his reaction to having exposed himself and, with a shrug, he grasped her hand.

"Come on. We've got a lot more to see." She might have removed her hand if an inner voice hadn't whispered that it belonged in his. The strong, smooth fingers communicated an eagerness to protect, and a need for her woman's tenderness and succor. She tried to ignore the swirling sensation that caught her up as would a dream and incited in her an eagerness for everything he could give a woman. And she couldn't help relishing the comfort of his stroking finger, as a strange, reassuring vibration flowed through her.

He squeezed gently, as though wanting to achieve greater intimacy, and she withdrew her hand.

"Did I hurt you?" The low timbre of his voice communicated a gentleness that she had begun to realize bespoke the true nature of the man. She shook her head, not wanting him to know that his touch had ignited a wild churning in her. She had never felt so close to him. Could now be the time to tell him? She didn't want to make a mistake, because she probably wouldn't get more than one chance.

*"On ferme dans les trente minutes."* Closing in thirty minutes, the loud nasal tones proclaimed, intruding on their intimacy, destroying the opportunity.

"Your fingers are calloused," she said, "and I didn't expect that. I thought they'd be softer, like… Not the hands of a blue-collar man." Her voice quavered and a harsh shudder shook her. She had almost revealed that she knew he'd been a surgeon.

"That's because I carve wooden figures," he said. She could breathe easily; he hadn't caught what could have been a crucial, fatal blunder.

"It's a hobby," he went on. "If I'd known your partiality to soft hands, I might have used some lotion." Laughter lightened his features. "And then again, I might not have." She joined his laughter, remembering her similar remark to him their last night in Rome. He looked down at her for a long time, his gaze, bland and unrevealing, roaming over her features yet obviously seeking some important answer. Abruptly, he smiled, shrugged, and took her hand firmly into his. She let him keep it.

Mason paused by one of Rodin's free-forms and ran his hand over it, fondling its lines, stroking it. He didn't hear Jeannetta's footsteps; only the stillness around him interfered with his absorption in the art beneath his hand. He looked up to find her watching him. Engrossed. His heart quickened at the sight of her parted lips, wide eyes, and the absence of the serene expression that ordinarily adorned her face. He noticed that she breathed erratically and that her gaze remained glued to the rhythmic movement of his hand. He stopped its stroking, testing her reaction, and she glanced up at him. His breath gurgled in his throat. Stripped bare, exposed, her eyes were windows of her aching, her longing. He didn't have to be told that she imagined his hands on her, stroking and caressing her, that desire had sucked up the coolness she always presented to him and left her emotionally naked.

"Jeannetta!"

She ducked her head and walked swiftly away from him.

"Don't run from me, Jeannetta; don't run from this. There's no point. It will catch up with you, with us."

"I don't know what you're talking about."

He watched her standing with her back against the wall. If she wasn't trembling, his name wasn't Mason Fenwick. He wanted to comfort her, to reassure her that nothing wrong, nothing painful could come of a relationship with him, that he'd as soon hurt himself as damage so vulnerable a woman.

"Denying it won't make it untrue," he told her, as gently as he could. "This is something you and I are going to have to deal with. And soon. We're like moth and flame, and, if we put an ocean between us, we'd only postpone the inevitable. Because, honey, we'd find each other."

"Think about something else, Mason. We don't have to get entangled."

He raised both eyebrows. "And we don't have to give this up, either. We're free, over twenty-one and…"

"You know what would be fun?" she interrupted, and he could see lights dancing in her warm brown eyes. alright, he'd give in this time; he had learned the value of patience.

"What would be fun?" he asked.

"Let's take the Métro to the Opera house, walk over to the Café de la Paix, get a sidewalk table, and watch the people."

He stroked his chin, the notion that Jeannetta liked to live outside of herself occurring to him for the first time. He mused over it, certain that he'd discovered something important about her.

"You like that sort of thing, don't you? I seem to recall your having suggested that I sit at a sidewalk café on Columbus

Avenue and freeze with you while you gazed at the passersby. What is it about watching strangers that gives you so much satisfaction?"

"I don't know." She waved a hand airily. "People-watching is an art. If I watch a person walking toward me and then away from me, I can tell you a lot of things about him."

The swirling skirts and dancing boots of a group of Gypsies caught his gaze, and he nudged Jeannetta. Immediately, she joined them. The dancers welcomed her, and Mason watched in awe as her feet seemed to take wings. Her head back and arms spread wide in abandon, her whirling skirt became a maze of brown, orange and yellow billowing in the breeze as she gave herself to the music. A glow of ecstasy glistened on her face, and he had the feeling that she tossed off burden after burden as she danced. But for her darker skin and thick, wooly hair, he couldn't have distinguished her from the Gypsies. When at last the music stopped, her new friends applauded her. She waved goodbye to them and, with his finger at her elbow, they continued down the crowded street. She seemed suffused with joy, but the incident depressed him, because he recognized an unwholesome desperation in it, a false *joie de vivre*.

"Gee, what pretty child. Look, Mason."

He noticed the little dark-haired and rosy cheeked girl who stared inquiringly at Jeannetta. She dropped his hand, walked over, and hunkered down to the little girl's level. His heart skittered in his chest as the child, wreathed in smiles and delighted with the attention, touched Jeannetta's cheek. The child's mother stood there and watched the exchange, her prideful delight in the beautiful little girl obvious. He had to turn away when a look of longing darkened Jeannetta's face. She's young and so beautiful, he thought. Why did she have that look of longing in her eyes? He stepped to her side, took her hand, and helped her to her feet. It occurred to him for the nth time that she needed his protection. But when he offered it, however camouflaged, she made certain he knew that she didn't need it.

\* \* \*

At the Café de la Paix, they found a tiny round table at the edge of the café, beside the sidewalk, a prize any time of the year in spite of its cracked marble top, myriad coffee stains, and rickety legs, and settled back to observe the changing scene on one of the world's busiest streets. Jeannetta could hardly contain herself.

Mason ordered two cups of espresso. "I was eighteen the last time I sat at this very table," he said, pointing to the initials he'd carved in the marble. "I had the world at my feet: a scholarship to Stanford and this trip to Europe that I'd been awarded for graduating at the top of my high-school class. My horizons had no bounds." He leaned back in his chair and spoke quietly, as though to himself. "Youth is a wondrous thing."

Alert to any clue that might tell her that she could safely broach the subject of her health and whether he'd return to the practice of medicine in order to help her, she cocked an ear. "Do I hear disillusionment behind those words?" she questioned, in an attempt to lead him into a discussion of his past.

"You're hearing the voice of reality. Man proposes and God disposes." He looked away, strummed his fingers on the tiny table, and she could see him detach himself. Well, another time.

"See that couple over there?" she asked him. "The man's wearing a black jogging top."

"Yeah. What about him?"

She cupped her chin with her palms and braced her elbows on her crossed knee. "She wants more from him than he's giving or wants to give." She paused, watching them closely as they passed. "See? She can hardly keep up with him. He's not a bit concerned about her." She pushed her sunglasses higher on the bridge of her nose and waited for his reaction.

"All that with just a glance? All I saw was two people walking past."

"You were looking. I was observing," she said. "That man has a serious problem. Hands in his pockets, gaze on the pavement, hunched over. I'd bet on it." She had his full attention and, deciding that she didn't want to relinquish it, she tossed her head back and looked at him from lowered eyelids. "You're a clever man. You can do as well as I can." Alright, so she was getting fresh with him; he wasn't above a little flirtation himself. His slow smile confirmed it.

"Your passion for people watching could be a very consuming pastime." He said it so softly that she had to lean toward him, showing more cleavage than she thought prudent. His smile told her he'd done that intentionally. "These characters who flow through your life, do you keep them in mind, forget about them, or what?"

"The ones that I can't forget..." she let her long pause include him in that group "...find their way into my novels."

"You're a writer? A novelist? I thought you wrote jokes and made dolls." His frown reminded her that she hadn't put "novelist" as her occupation on her application to Fenwick Travel Agency. He let it slide.

"Jeannetta, I'm enjoying this, but I have to get back to the hotel and make some overseas calls. Have dinner with me."

He'd take her to a swank restaurant with an idyllic setting; fine wine and elegant food. He was that type. And when he took her back to the hotel, she'd be a pushover. For the snap of his finger, she'd crawl all over him right then; a luscious evening with him would...

"I...I think I'd better turn in early tonight... You...you're marvelous company, but...maybe not." From the lights dancing in his eyes, and the amusement she detected around his twitching lips, she knew he had her number. Those wonderful eyes challenged, teased and coaxed. Oh, how she adored his eyes.

"I haven't bitten any pretty women recently," he bantered. "Besides, I'm responsible for you, so you can trust me. Or does Ames have first dibs on your evenings?"

"Oh, Mason, he's hungry for company," she said with pretended seriousness. "Can he come along with us? You won't mind, will you?"

Streaks of pleasure danced along her limbs when he gave in

to his amusement and let his face dissolve into an infectious, devastating grin.

"If Ames is hungry for company, I'll introduce him to Lucy Abernathy; she's practically starving for it. She took this tour last year and the year before, so I'd say she could use some good company."

She thought of dowdy Miss Abernathy and said, "What about Maybeth?"

His smile faded. "Don't tell me you've got a sadistic streak. Maybeth Baxter is a man-eater. In six months, Ames wouldn't have a dime of his lottery millions. Besides, he's too smart to go any place with that woman." He stood and waved for the waiter. *"Garçon. L'addition, s'il vous plâit."* The bill, please. He extended his hand to her.

"This is our only night in Paris. I don't want to eat; I want to dine, and I don't want to look across the table at Geoffrey Ames while I do it." His voice, low, soothing, teased her senses. "I want to look at you while I enjoy my meal." The huskiness of his tone and the soothing strokes of his fingers rattled her will to resist him. Face it, she told herself, you want to go with him; what's the use of being coy about it?

"Dinner would be nice. I'd like to get back early, though, since we're leaving in the morning." She didn't fool herself; he'd already shown her that she needed all of her wits when, as now, he challenged her, dared her, without so much as one word, with only the mischievous merriment or the smoldering suggestiveness in the extraordinary eyes that gleamed at her from his impassive face.

The man bowed from the waist and taunted, "At your service, ma'am."

She had to stifle a laugh. She wouldn't be outdone; her sense of humor was as good as the next one's.

"Mason, it's easy to forget, sometimes, that you're a mere mortal—but if the rest of us make that mistake, you be sure and keep your head screwed on right. Psychiatrists probably make even more money than surgeons."

She wanted to swallow her tongue. His eyes rounded and, beneath his sharply arched eyebrows, she could see every bit of the white in them. She couldn't let the unfriendliness in his penetrating stare disconcert her. Too much hung on this moment. She put an inquiring look on her face that questioned his change of mood, and prayed that her bluff would cover her slip. After a minute, he relaxed, but he didn't pursue the topic.

"Let's find a cab," he said, as they walked out in the warm sun. If he noticed her stumble, he didn't mention it.

"Seven o'clock," he admonished, as a reminder of her tardiness, and she left him and went to her room. She took off her sandals, got her recorder, and began to describe all that she'd seen and done since arriving in Paris that morning. But the practice that she had enjoyed in the early days of the tour weighed on her now as an unwanted chore. She put the instrument aside, flipped on the television news program and, minutes later, sat gaping at herself in a frenzied dance, whirling and cavorting on the rue du Chandon with the colorful Gypsies. She remembered the wildness of it, the wonderful feeling of abandon, the... She zapped the channel and soon turned off the television.

Paris was so close to Germany, less than one jet hour away. Maybe she ought to quit the tour, go to Frankfurt and see a specialist. Germans had always been leaders in medicine. She only had the word of two doctors, both of whom could be wrong. For all she knew, they had consulted with one another. Maybe she didn't have a tumor. She hadn't had any dizziness since the first days of the tour, and then only twice, and she hadn't had a headache in several days. Anybody could have a headache. Deciding that she'd think about it later, she undressed and got in bed for a pre-dinner nap.

An hour later, she awakened in the midst of damp, rumpled sheets, her gown clinging to her perspiring body. She hadn't had a nightmare since learning the nature of her illness. But this time, it had ended differently. In Mason's arms, his velvet tongue spreading sweet nectar in her mouth as he lay buried deep within her, powerful waves of sensation had banished the darkness. His hugs and kisses, tender murmuring and total giving of himself, had dissipated her fears, made her a whole, vibrant person again. She struggled out of bed, showered, donned a lavender-pink silk peignoir, and walked out on her balcony, hoping to see the sun set. She looked toward the Arc de Triomphe and gasped. Rays of the red setting sun filtered through the leaves of the flowering horse chestnut trees that lined the famous avenue, a humbling vision against the background of dark gray sky. Men and women rushed home, by bicycle, automobile, and foot— much as Americans did, though you wouldn't see any Americans carrying a long loaf of unwrapped bread.

Six o'clock. That made it noontime in the northeastern United States, she calculated, going to the telephone. Within minutes, she heard Laura's voice.

"Made any headway with him yet?" Laura's question took the place of a greeting, reminded Jeannetta that she had better treat the matter with the urgency it deserved. She couldn't tell Laura that she'd made headway, but not the kind she needed.

"I'm working on it. What's new?"

"Same old mountains, hon. You soak up all that Paris atmosphere, but you come back with a commitment out of that man, you hear?" Laura's ability to focus the way a racehorse does, with the help of blinders, had always amused Jeannetta, though many found it reason for faulting her intelligence. If she knew your problem, she didn't let you forget it until you solved it.

"Don't you get caught up in that man and forget why you're spending all of that money," Laura went on. "The Lord helps those who help themselves, and if you don't do your part, he'll think you don't care what happens." Jeannetta knew she'd better not tell her sister that Mason had come close to kissing her more than once.

"He hasn't given me the opportunity to bring up the subject, though I've made several openings. From what I've come to know of him, I don't think I'll accomplish anything by jumping in cold and asking him."

"You mean you've been with him for almost three weeks and you haven't even mentioned it? Since when did you get so shy? Something's wrong; you're leaving something out." She could see Laura rest the back of her hand on her hip, and a look of incredulity spread over her face.

"Don't worry, Laura. I'll work hard at it. I don't intend to fail." I'd better not, she admonished herself, as Laura blew kisses in the phone, reminded her that she'd have a big bill, and hung up.

Jeannetta meandered slowly back to the balcony, pensive, her thoughts weighted with misgivings, thanks to Laura's pessimism. She walked to the edge of the balcony, where she glimpsed a tall man of African descent strolling along the Avenue. He stopped, leaned against a big chestnut tree and looked toward the Arc, seemingly enraptured by the sunset. She had heard it said that one could connect with another person through the mind. Could she compel him to look her way? The force of her concentration produced the first headache she'd had in days. He's strong-willed, she decided, but she wouldn't give up.

"Look at me. Show me your face," she commanded repeatedly. As though in defiance, he straightened up, strolled to the corner, paused, then continued and, finally, as though against his will, Mason Fenwick looked directly into her eyes. She would have liked to evaporate. He stared at her for a long time, didn't smile, and turned the corner toward the hotel's entrance.

Cold shivers coursed through her, and she rubbed her arms furiously as she stumbled back into her room. She'd tried that trick dozens of times without having succeeded but, when she would have given anything to fail, she'd finally done it. Maybe the cards were not in her favor; she hadn't done anything right where Mason was concerned. Perhaps she shouldn't have plotted to win his concern, but should have gone to his office, told him her story and accepted the consequences. How could she face him? She laid back her shoulders, went to the closet and took out a scooped neck, sleeveless sheath, a luscious green that shimmered with green crystal beads and stopped four inches above her knee. She covered her long legs with sheer black stocking and slipped her feet into a pair of spike-heeled black silk evening shoes. A small black beaded bag completed what she referred to as her masquerade. She'd scrubbed her face with cold water, buffed it with a terry towel, and twisted her hair on top of her head.

"What you see is what you get," she said, reflecting on her refusal to wear make-up of any kind or earrings. She dabbed a bit of *Trésor* behind her ears and between her breasts, glanced at the mirror and left the room.

Mason pushed back the sleeve of his white evening jacket, checked his Timex, headed for the elevator, and leaned against the wall facing the door. She'd given him plenty to think about that day, half a dozen women in the same body. He'd never known such a changeable woman. He suspected that part of it was due to the anonymity one gets in a strange place. Her odd behavior on the balcony of her room. That wild dance, for instance; she would never have done that in Pilgrim, nor New York City for that matter. But the longing he'd seen in her when she talked with that child had been real. And she took that people-watching thing almost to an extreme. The writer in her. Maybe. Hard to say. He had no doubt as to the genuineness of her sensuous nature: art, music, and that intuitiveness about lovers. Maybe it was all real. One thing he didn't question was the fascination she held for him.

The elevator door opened. He supposed he'd have to get used to the tingling delight that shot through him when she stepped into the lounge. He could only stare, as a crazy, schoolboy kind of joy zinged through him when she saw him and it transformed her beautiful brown face into a glowing appreciation of his manliness. He knew that women thought him handsome, that they especially raved about his eyes, but he'd long since learned to ignore their shallow adulation.

"Your loveliness, so natural and so beguiling, takes my breath away. I'll be the envy of every man who sees us tonight."

She tossed her head to the side, in what he'd noticed signaled a flirtatious mood.

"French women aren't slow when it comes to appreciating men, either. From what I've heard, they may get fresh with you while I'm holding your hand." Her exaggerated deep breath made him wonder what else to expect. She didn't keep him waiting.

"I've never been in a cat fight, and I'd just as soon my first one happened some place where nobody knows me. Why not Paris? Ready to go?"

He didn't recall her previously having wrinkled her nose at him in playful flirtation as she did then. What a female, he thought, as he offered her his arm. With this woman, he'd have to keep his motor oiled and running. "Slow down, buddy," he cautioned himself.

He'd reserved a table at an elegant restaurant that seated twelve couples or parties of four. Potted palms between the tables guaranteed privacy, and the multicolored lights, reflected off the waterfall in the room's center and in the overhead chandeliers, gave the room a soft allure, a testimonial to the French preoccupation with *l'amour*.

"You like it?" he asked as the waiter seated them.

"Oh, Mason. It's the loveliest restaurant I've ever seen. Thank you for choosing it; I'll add it to the treasure of memories I've stashed away in the archives of my mind."

He couldn't tell whether she noticed his reaction to that revelation. Something wasn't right.

"Oh, you'll see lovelier ones than this," he said.

"Maybe."

It had been on the tip of his tongue to tell her that he'd show her the world, but she lacked the zest of moments earlier, and he thought light banter might unsettle her. He had to get used to her mood changes.

"You're still young." He covered her hand with his own. "You'll visit a few of them with me on this tour. We can have a wonderful time together, Jeannetta." He paused. "If you want it."

"Perhaps." He caressed her hand, and a sensation of sharp, hot darts pounded at his belly when she turned her hand so that her palm embraced his own. He'd better get them interested in another subject, anything to enable him to make it through dinner without an embarrassing show of male want.

"When will you finish your novel?" Oh, oh. Wrong topic, he realized when she placed her fork on her plate, sat back, and took a deep breath.

"That depends on a lot of things, some of which are beyond my control." Suddenly, she brightened. "I'd been writing about a woman but, when we were in Rome, I realized that was all wrong. My protagonist is a man and should have been all along."

"Anything to do with anybody you met on the tour?"

Her enigmatic smile curled her lip upward and settled at the corner of her mouth.

He hoped she couldn't hear the wild thumping of his heart. "Well?" he insisted.

"Everything and nothing."

"What kind of an answer is that?"

Her laughter wrapped around him; he could have listened to it forever.

"You inspired the change, but it isn't about you."

"I see. Gonna let me read it?"

"If I finish it, you'll be the first to see it. I promise." He resisted asking why she'd implied that she might not finish it, but they'd gotten out of one dump, and he wanted to see her happy, spirited, her normal self, not melancholy and withdrawn. Her hand moved against his, a little caress.

"If I wasn't certain I'd drive these French waiters up the wall, I'd move my chair around this table and sit where I could put my arm around you."

She hid her eyes behind lowered lashes, but trembling fingers nevertheless betrayed her, and he thought his heart had galloped out of control. When she threaded her fingers through his, still avoiding his gaze, he thanked God for the long white tablecloth that covered his lap.

"Some people are big on words," he heard her murmur beneath her breath.

"*What?* We're still in France, lady, so don't tempt me unless you'd like me to show you some wantonness of my own. I probably wouldn't dance in the street with a group of Gypsies, but, take my word for it, I know how to let it all hang out. You want to eat those words?"

She shook her head and corrected her posture, but didn't remove her hand from his. He reached across the table and tickled her chin with the forefinger of his free hand.

"Don't go getting prim on me, sweetheart, too late for that. Look at me."

Her long lashes lifted with snaillike speed. Lord, did this woman know how to flirt!

*"Pour dessert, Monsieur?"* The waiter must have understood his murderous glare, because the man glanced away, then back, as if to say: *Sorry, bad timing.* Neither of them wanted dessert, so he ordered two cups of espresso coffee.

He wouldn't press her. Time enough for that when he got her to himself. Her quietness didn't disturb him, because he knew she was feeling something new, just as he was, and that she was trying to deal with it. They left the restaurant holding hands.

"It's only nine o'clock; would you like to stop by *Bongo Ade's* for half an hour or so? It's walking distance. It caters to Francophone Africans, but you don't have to talk to them. How about it?"

"I'd love it. Unless their French is full of local accents, I'll probably be able to understand it."

Rays of yellow, orange, white, and blue lights, reminiscent of a Harlem disco, flashed like convoluted rainbows across the dance floor of Ade's home away from home. A low hum of voices melded with the steady rhythm of the drums to which patrons swayed even as they sat at tables or stood talking in groups. With its warm, homey atmosphere, *Bongo Ade's* needed no welcome sign. Mason found a table, ordered lemonade, which the waitress recommended, and settled in the comfortable rattan chair. He noticed immediately that the West Africans seemed to prefer lemonade and soft drinks, while the Frenchmen and other non-Africans drank wine or spirits. People-watching had a lot to recommend it.

"Excuse me, please."

He looked up as she started to rise, went around to her chair, and assisted her. "I'll be right back." He watched her glide away. He had wanted her because…well, a man wanted a woman like her, but he had begun to develop a reason for wanting her that had nothing to do with what he saw when he looked at her. He needed to have a good talk with himself.

Jeannetta closed the door of the ladies' room and leaned against it. She couldn't imagine why she'd teased Mason at the restaurant when she knew he'd exact payment first chance he got. She'd never been so irresolute as now, telling him that he could expect nothing intimate between them and then leading him to believe he had a chance. A woman who did that risked being known as a tease, and the description didn't fit her. At least it hadn't. Mason wasn't a man a woman could ignore, especially if he showed an interest. She had to admit that, with each come-to-me signal he sent her, with each tender gesture, her will to walk away from him weakened more. She rinsed her mouth and glanced up to see two West-African women enter the room.

"Where you from, love?" one of them asked in a most non-African fashion. She told them. The woman switched from French to English. She had spent seven years at the United Nations in New York before transferring to the UNESCO in Paris.

"You and your husband look good together," the woman said.

Surprised at the assumption, Jeannetta replied, "He isn't my husband."

"You'd better fix that," the other woman advised. "If you don't, some other woman will do that for you. He's nice. Real nice."

"He sure is that," the first woman added. "I never could understand how you American women don't see to your men." They talked for a few minutes, and Jeannetta remarked that they seemed less African than she would have expected. They told her, proudly, that they had lived, and worked in New York, married Frenchmen, and traveled extensively, and that they were as uncomfortable in their ancestral villages as she would be. She said goodbye, started back to her table, and stopped. Two women in West-African dress had joined Mason, and his flirtatious smile told her that he enjoyed their company.

She steamed, in what she recognized as a fit of jealousy, strode purposefully to the table, and stopped. Seeing her, the smile spread wider over Mason's face and he stood. He introduced Jeannetta and asked them to excuse him.

"I've enjoyed meeting you ladies," he added as they lingered.

Jeannetta could barely control an impulse to flinch when one of the women looked her over, showed a lack of concern for as competition and drawled, "When you leave your man alone in *Ade's*, you're asking one of us to take him." Jeannetta glanced at Mason from the corner of her eye and wanted to erase that smirk from his grinning lips.

"He isn't that easy to get," she said, running her left hand along his arm possessively and smiling into Mason's eyes. A broad grin animated his elegant features, and she could almost hear her heart sing with delight.

"I am *so* easy to get," he said, grinning as his gaze seared her. "All you have to do is wink."

"I wouldn't have thought you'd be a pushover," she said, her gaze fastened on his tantalizing lips as he bent over to seat her. She could almost touch them with her own.

"Maybe not for some people," he teased. "Go ahead. Push a little bit. See what happens."

The rhythm of the bongos increased, soft and sensual, and the heat in his eyes toyed with her. Desire tugged at her, but she fought it, finally crossing her legs in frustration. She knew the gesture hadn't escaped him but, gentleman that he was, he let it slide.

"Chicken. Don't you want to test your feminine power?"

"Get thee behind me, Satan." He threw his head back and released an attention-getting, happy laugh. A warm glow flowed through her, and his blatant joy drew her into a cocoon of euphoria. His cocoon. What was the point in fighting him?

# Chapter 3

He hadn't taken her hand when they left *Ade's*, because he couldn't hold any part of her and fight his battle with himself. Her quiet serenity during the ride back had suited him, given him time for reflection. They reached her door, and he held out his hand for her key. Wildfire shot through his veins when she opened her bag, took out the strip of plastic, and handed it to him without shifting her gaze from his. Be careful, man; you don't want any more fly-by-night affairs. No more convenient sex. No more…

"Here." Her whisper barely reached his ear. He held out his hand for the card and felt it scrape his fingers as her hand shook.

"Jeannetta." He heard the soft rasp of his voice, but did she? Only the rapid quiver of her bottom lip told him that she'd responded to his entreaty. He tugged at the card, but didn't take it. Waited. She glanced up at him with "I need you" blazing in her eyes, and he didn't care about the lecture he'd just given himself, didn't worry about her past insistence that there could be nothing between them. He shoved logic aside.

"I'm waiting for you to wink."

"I never learned how." He took a step closer, testing the water.

"If you can't close one eye at a time, close both of them." His breathing accelerated, and he finally had to shove his hands into his pockets while he wondered if the bottom would drop out of him. Like a slow-moving drawbridge, her eyelids covered her luminous eyes, and her hands crept up his lapel.

"Jeannetta. Jeannetta."

* * *

Her nerves skittered wildly when the voice that had shaken her before she met its owner produced that urgent, husky sound of need. She knew that her bottom lip quivered, because it always betrayed her nervousness. His large but gentle hands covered her slim shoulders, steadying her. Why didn't he kiss her, take her, love her out of her senses?

"Don't be afraid: I don't wound if I can help it; I'm a healer." She opened her eyes but couldn't move, didn't want to move, as his eyes turned a smoldering dark greenish-brown, and she could feel him inside her as he'd been that afternoon in her dream.

"Oh, Mason. Mason, I..." Goose pimples spread over her flesh and the air swished out of her. His lips touched hers, tentatively, as though he thought she might reject him. Clamoring for him, she parted her lips, slipped her right hand behind his head, and pressed his mouth to hers. His tongue swept and swirled in her mouth, and she savored the taste of him, sucked it, nibbled it, until he used it to show her how much more they could have together. Wave after wave of vibration pounded her center, and she undulated against him. Hot flames of desire engulfed her and, when she shivered, he tightened his hold on her, slipped his hand between them, and swallowed her keening cry. She twisted against his body until he held her away from him.

"We have to think about this, baby. I want to take this key, open that door, and lose myself in you but, tomorrow morning, you'd be sorry. You've told me enough times that you don't want an involved relationship with me." Still holding her gently, he sought confirmation that she had changed her thinking about them. "I want you to stand three feet from me and tell me you changed your mind." But she burrowed her face in his shoulder, and he opened her room door, took her in, kissed her cheek, and turned to leave.

"Mason." He turned around. "You're...You're...wonderful."

"I'll see you in the morning. Try to be on time."

* * *

He had planned to go straight to his room and hit the bed. Instead, when he passed the elevator, he punched the button and headed for the bar.

"Surprised to see you down here tonight," Geoffrey told him as he picked up his bourbon and soda and walked over to join Mason. "If I'm not welcome, just nod your head, and I'll go on back to my table."

"Why are you surprised to see me?" Mason asked him, hoping that it wouldn't be necessary to tell the man to mind his business.

"Well, you'll be rising with the chickens in the morning, and I figured you'd be turning in."

Mason smiled inwardly. Geoffrey Ames could take a dozen trips around the world, but he'd carry that Georgia country style of speaking wherever he went.

"I'll be turning in shortly. Enjoying the tour so far?"

"Well…yes and no. Accommodations are fine, but I've kind of set my sights on Miss Lucy, and I'm out of practice. I was married for well-nigh fifty years, and I guess I just lost track of how you go about getting a lady's attention."

"You didn't need any help last night in Rome," Mason retorted, referring to Geoffrey's date with Jeannetta.

"It's easy to ask for something if it don't matter whether or not you get it. I just wanted company, and she's a nice, gracious lady. Now, with Miss Lucy, I've got more than company on my mind." He sipped first the bourbon and then the soda. "I was so sure Miss Jeannetta would be going out with you that I just about fell over when she accepted." He took another round of sips, raising Mason's curiosity.

"Is that the way Georgians drink bourbon and soda?"

Ames rubbed his chin. "Can't say as they do. It's the way *I* drink it."

Mason held his gaze for a few minutes. "If you're interested in Lucy Abernathy, I suggest you walk up to her table, sit down, and start talking. She'll be delighted. Trust me." He downed his cognac. "See you in the morning."

He hadn't wanted company. He had a decision to make. He'd sworn off relationships that he knew would be temporary. So what was he going to do about Jeannetta? He had kissed more females than he remembered, but none had responded to him as she had, and none had fired him up as she did. She alone had made him feel as though he had the key to her heaven, that only he made the music to which she'd been born to dance. He knew that, after one night alone with her, he'd never be the same. If only he could understand his reservations about her. He walked into his room and swore. He tasted her; he'd gone to the bar to get her taste out of him, but not even the cognac had killed it. She hadn't been in his room, but he smelled her, not her teasing perfume, but her aroused woman's scent. He kicked off his shoes, stripped, dumped his clothes in a suitcase, and headed to the bathroom for a cold shower.

Jeannetta checked her room to make certain that she hadn't overlooked anything, closed her suitcase, and laid the key on top. She glanced at the uninviting bed, and walked past it to the lone window of her Paris hotel room. The Arc de Triomphe glowed with its brilliant lights, romanticizing the night. She would never forget it, nor Paris, nor that room beside the door of which she had known for the first time the mind blowing force of desire. She clutched her chest to steady her dancing heart as spasms of excitement rippled through her at the memory of his sweet tongue in her mouth and his aroused sex against her belly. Who could blame her for wanting him? She closed the curtain, turned back the covers, and got in bed. She hadn't had much experience with men, but enough to know that her dance with Mason Fenwick hadn't ended. If she let it go any further, her cause would be lost. Tomorrow, she'd ask him.

Resplendent in white pants, long-sleeved yellow silk shirt, and green aviator's glasses, Mason stood outside car number seven of the Paris-to-Istanbul express, checking off tour passengers as they entered.

"Glad to see you're early, Geoffrey. I've seated you at the table with Lucy Abernathy for meals. You take it from there, man." He grinned at Geoffrey's wink. Winning that lottery must have rejuvenated the old man. Well, bully for him. He looked at his watch: seventeen minutes before departure. Where *was* she?

"Give the baggage one last check," he told Josh, looking over his shoulder in the hope of seeing Jeannetta. A stab of anxiety pummeled his belly when the conductor issued the first call, *"all aboard."* He couldn't abandon his tour, and he couldn't leave not knowing whether she needed him.

"All aboard for Istanbul." Breath hissed out of him when the conductor climbed the steps. In another two minutes, he'd see that door close. An increase in the wind's velocity and the smell of rain alerted him to the possibility of a troubled journey, but he had to shake off that concern; Jeannetta was his only… The wind shifted, and he turned quickly as the scent of her perfume reached him. He rushed to meet her, grabbed her carry-on bag, lifted her onto the coach, and sagged against the door.

"I'm so glad you decided to join us." He heard the bite in his voice, but after the scare she'd given him, she deserved it.

"And hello to you, too. What's the problem? You knew I'd be here." He figured that the train's forlorn bellow and the chug of its wheels less than a minute after they'd boarded should set her straight.

She hadn't expected his annoyance, but his glare was nothing short of a reprimand.

"You knew I wouldn't leave here without you," he told her, "and you knew my responsibility to these people. Didn't you consider the dilemma you caused me?" He straightened up and stepped closer to her. "Do you always play it so close to the edge?"

"I'm sorry. I got here as fast as I could; the driver made himself a few extra francs at my expense." Her gaze locked with his, and she had to suppress the urge to reach out to him as the flash of heat in his eyes told her he remembered the night before. That he hadn't forgotten his pleasure in holding her body close to his. But, as quickly as it came, the moment of recognition was gone.

"This tour occupies car seven," he explained, his voice impersonal. "The dining car is at one end and the lavatories are on the other." He reeled off a list of do's and don'ts. She wouldn't allow him to put distance between them, not after the note he'd left her that morning: "My dear Jeannetta, neither of us wanted to become involved, but Providence decreed otherwise. I'm strongly attracted to you, but I'll do my best not to impose it on you nor on our tour members. The next move is yours. Mason."

"Thank you for the note I found under my door this morning. We'll work it out; I know we will. And I wouldn't have upset you this morning if I could have avoided it." His strong fingers gently stroking her cheek encouraged her to smile, stirring anticipation and want in her that must have been mirrored in her eyes, for he leaned forward and brushed her lips with his own.

"Come on. I'll show you to your compartment," he said, taking her bag with one hand and resting his other arm protectively around her shoulder. "You're in L-11."

"Where's yours?" She wanted to know. He placed her bag on the sofa-bed, raised an eyebrow, and frowned.

"Four doors down. Why? Do you sleepwalk?" Embarrassment flooded her until his frown dissolved into a wicked grin.

"Oh, you!" This man had a streak of devilment in him, but she knew she could hold her own in that department. "I don't think I've done it in the past, but I'm sure I could learn," she teased. "At what point do you think I'd wake up?" His rapt stare both censored her and heated her up and, when his eyes became that greenish-brown that she knew indicated desire, she had the feeling that she'd better not play with him. From his harsh intakes of breath and unsmiling face, she knew he didn't want any more jokes about their relationship.

"Find yourself down there, day or night, sweetheart, and I'll answer any question you can ask, close any door you open, and finish anything you start. Come around anytime the spirit moves you. Lunch at noon, today. If you need a snack before that, walk down to the dining room. If you need me, dial eight or push the blue button on your intercom. Remember that anything you say on the intercom can be heard by anybody who wants to listen. Have a good rest, and don't come to lunch late. See you."

She figured that by the time she got her mouth closed, he'd be in possession of his equilibrium.

Mason sat at the maître d's desk at the entrance of the dining room. Geoffrey and Lucy lingered over coffee, engrossed in conversation, but most other members of the tour had finished their lunch and either returned to their compartments or gone to the observation lounge. It seemed as though he had looked at his watch more frequently since meeting Jeannetta Rollins than in all his previous thirty-seven years. Didn't she ever go *anywhere* on time? He got up, went to the buffet table, and began filling a plate for her. That finished, he laid a few pieces of smoked salmon on black pumpernickel bread and wrapped it in cellophane paper in case she didn't like the cold plate. The woman needed a keeper. He grimaced at the niggling voice of his conscience that proclaimed: "You don't seem averse to looking after her." He refused to glance up when the door opened; he knew who it was.

"Do you always bring up the rear?" he asked, declining to glance her way. "Lunch hour will be over in seven minutes, and the dining room has to be readied for the one o'clock seating. I asked you to be on time." Her soft hand rested on the middle of his back, and he told himself to stay firm, but he couldn't help swinging around after the first soothing stroke.

"I don't mean to upset your schedules, but I've stopped rushing through life. There's so much to see, and so li...so few opportunities. I never used to stop and smell the flowers, as it were, or even to look at them. Nowadays, I savor every precious thing. Back in Pilgrim, the mountains have always been part of my life, and I've taken them for granted. But a couple of days before I left home to join the tour, I stood at my kitchen window late one evening and looked out. That time of year, the mountains are always snow-capped, but that evening, bright red streaked the peaks, and I thought for a moment that there'd been a terrible catastrophe. But I'd only seen the lustrous glow of a setting sun. I couldn't imagine how I had missed that awe-inspiring, majestic sight for so many years."

He knew something about achieving balance in your life, turning corners and taking control of your future, and he knew the feeling of satisfaction it gave. He'd done it. "Haven't you noticed that I don't rush?" he asked her. "I'm never late, either, and that's because I budget my time properly. Try it." He motioned toward the buffet table. "I fixed something for you. The dining room will close to our group in about two minutes, so I suggest you take this to your compartment." He watched the smile spread over her face and an uncensored gleam of admiration—or something more...dangerous—shine from her dark eyes. He turned away. *Before I do something foolish,* he cautioned himself.

"Here." He handed her the plate and sandwiches. "Why don't you go in your compartment and eat? I...I've got a few things to do."

"You're not angry because I came in here late, are you?" She put so much weight in that question, he thought, as though his opinion, how he felt about her, mattered more than anything else.

"Naaaah," he said, as casually as he could. "Now go eat your lunch." Why didn't she move? Why did she stand there sending him vibration after vibration of pure sweet hell, her eyes warm and inviting, smiling at him as if he were a king?

"Thanks for making sure I got something to eat," she said, and blinked both eyes in what he realized was an attempt to wink.

"Get out of here, Jeannetta. Right now." Her eyes widened, and he swore lustily and headed for the adjoining caboose.

He was sitting in the dining car, reading Colin Powell's autobiography, when she walked in around three-thirty for a can of lemonade.

"Thanks for sending me the *International Herald Tribune.* How'd you know I'd gotten hungry for some news of what's going on in the world?"

He glanced up from his book, vowing not to let her shackle his insides for the second time that day. "My pleasure. It's a courtesy to my guests."

Her mouth drooped in disappointment. "Sure, and I suppose you sent all nineteen of us a red rose to go with it."

He put the book aside and stood.

"You're welcome." Alright. Let her frown, he told himself without a trace of guilt. She'd knocked the wind out of him, and he hadn't decided he liked it. Trouble was, she could match him, mood for mood and stance for stance. An inner amusement lightened his thoughts. He never could understand why women felt so much more powerful when they stood akimbo, with their feet wider apart than normal. He grinned down at her. Like a little bantam-weight fighter squaring off against Mohammed Ali. He would have laughed if he hadn't been sure she'd feel hurt.

"Still vexed because I was late for lunch, are we?" she asked in a low don't-battle-with-me voice. "Well, I wandered into car number six and met some Swiss children. A whole car full of them." A glow spread over her face, lifting his spirits, drawing him into the pleasure she recalled. "We had a wonderful time, and I just couldn't leave them. A whole car full of five- and six-year-olds. It was wonderful." He couldn't help staring at her. This mercurial woman, who fascinated him and made him think of a warm fireplace on cold nights. He fingered the keys in his pockets, shook his head, and wondered about his sanity. Had he gone so far with her that he couldn't back up? It wasn't possible.

"What's the matter?" she asked, misunderstanding his reaction. "Don't you like children?"

He shook his head in awe.

"You'd be a full-time job for any man," he muttered under his breath.

"What?"

"I hope they'd all had lunch before you descended on them. They won't get another chance to eat until around five-thirty."

She cocked an eyebrow and gnawed her bottom lip.

"You're not overdoing this protective thing, are you?"

He grinned. "Sure I am."

"Well, I appreciate your concern, but don't ladle it out too thickly. Okay?" She turned to go, stopped, and reversed herself. "Thanks for the pretty rose. When I get back to Pilgrim, I'm going to press it and keep in the family Bible."

He gaped. "You're serious?"

She nodded.

"Why?"

"It's the first thing you gave me, and it may be the only thing. I want to keep it." Long after she left, he stared at the spot where she'd stood.

After dinner, Jeannetta sat in the lounge, sipping ginger ale and doodling on a paper napkin as she surreptitiously observed her companions. Leonard Deek, a university professor on a year's sabbatical, seemed to shrink in Maybeth's voluptuous presence. When she stood, her bosom dwarfed the little man. Chuckling to herself, Jeannetta quickly scribbled three one line jokes about the decline in breastfeeding and the refusal of increasing numbers of men to grow up. Her smile of delight greeted Geoffrey's arrival.

"If you're not expecting anybody, I'd love to join you."

She motioned toward the empty chair.

"I'd love your company, Geoffrey. Where's Lucy?"

"Couldn't say for sure, but I expect she's somewhere primping. Never seen a woman pat and primp like she does. I told her if she was any more perfect she'd have silvery wings, but she just laughed and patted her hair. I hope I'm on her mind when she's doing it."

Jeannetta had to fight a wave of melancholia. Was the need for love so powerful that it ruled one's life regardless of age? And could she live without it? She told herself not to think that way.

"I wouldn't worry, Geoffrey; Miss Abernathy cut you from the pack before our plane left JFK airport." She thought his shoulders straightened and his chin lifted. She liked his earthy chuckle.

"I must be slower than I thought."

Jeannetta nodded toward the door, warning him to change the subject, as Mason entered with Lucy Abernathy. That woman is really burning up his ears, she thought, observing the rapid movements of Lucy's lips. Geoffrey stood and waved them over.

"Sure we're not interrupting anything?" Mason asked.

She'd nearly asked what there was to interrupt, when Geoffrey's cool reply gave her a lesson in the management of men.

"Not a bit sure; we were sitting here in conversation, weren't we? Ya'll sit down while I get us all something to drink." He left the table without waiting for a reply.

Jeannetta nearly giggled as she watched Mason stare at Geoffrey's back. She wondered what Geoffrey had been telling Lucy; her serenity would have been worthy of a queen. It amused Jeannetta that Mason directed his conversation to Lucy, ignoring her. She didn't believe his ego needed bolstering, because no man with his looks, physique, and manners could have lacked the adulation of women. Wherever she saw him, he stood out, a belly-twisting example of virile manhood. Geoffrey returned with a loaded tray, and she helped herself to a glass of ginger ale.

With his gaze searing her, Mason raised his glass of cognac, sending dazzling sensations zinging through her body. Applying as much calm as she could muster, she lifted her glass to him and then brought it forward for a sip but, to her amazement the ginger ale poured into her lap. She couldn't control the trembling of her fingers, but she tried nevertheless to smooth over the incident, smiling as though it didn't matter. When she finally glanced up, his dark eyes were fixed on her, but they lacked warmth or sensuality; he had the look of a man deeply concerned. Quickly, she glanced away.

Mason flinched as the liquid streamed into her lap. He'd realized that the glass hadn't touched her lips and, if she'd been drinking wine or any other alcoholic drink, he'd have ascribed it to the liquor, but she didn't drink alcoholic beverages. He's seen that in his medical practice: the failure to judge distance correctly in relation to one's self. Sometimes that meant missing a step, sitting on the floor rather than in a chair, grasping air when reaching for something. But she didn't have any of the symptoms that accompanied the ailments that came to mind. Still, her fingers had trembled and what seemed like fear had settled in her eyes. He took a slug of cognac. He'd forced himself to quit that kind of fanciful thinking, and not even his concern for her was going to trick him back into it.

"If you'll excuse me, I think I'll turn in." She saw Mason glance at his watch, but where was it written that she couldn't go to bed at eight-thirty if she wanted to?

"I'll see you to your compartment," she heard him say, in a tone that discouraged rejection. At the door, he extended his hand for her key, his gaze sweeping over her. He opened the door and stood there. Waiting. She didn't dare look at him, because she knew he could turn her on with a smile, a wink, and all she could think of was that night in Paris, outside her room door.

"Aren't you going to invite me in?" He said it with reluctance, as though he wished she'd say no, but his posture suggested otherwise. Less than twelve inches separated them; bridge it, and she'd know again the sweet nectar, the pulsing ferment, of his loving. His unsmiling face and purposeful manner jarred her. Had he noticed? Maybe this would be a good time to talk with him and ask him if he'd help her.

"Mason, I…yes…if…"

He interrupted. "Ask me in. You ought to know by now that I don't bite." His unexpected smile sent a flush of heat through her, but she refused to let him see her lose composure.

"What excuse would I give myself?" she asked him, not caring how he took her flirtatiousness. "I can't invite you for coffee and I left my etchings in Pilgrim."

"Then ask me in because you want my company."

She backed in the door, and he followed, closing it with his elbow. He'd expected more feminine surroundings but, except for a jacket thrown across the sofa and the red rose he'd sent her, the compartment bore no testament to femininity. Bare.

He couldn't help showing his surprise. "Didn't you unpack?

When you walk out of here, this place might as well have been unoccupied."

"I told you I don't collect things. I'm satisfied with admiring lovely things; I don't have to own them. In fact, I don't like to accumulate stuff. With millions of people hoarding things, more and more must be made, and since everything we have comes from the earth and sea, think what that does to the environment." He leaned against the closet door and observed her beneath half-lowered lids.

"You're a nature lover?" The way she tossed her head back, and that half-smile that curved around her sweet mouth, Lord! He looked toward the writing table, any place but at that voluptuous invitation to forever that glowed before him.

"I love everything that's graceful and beautiful. Everything."

"You love children." He didn't ask himself why his heart pounded while he waited for her answer. She nodded, though he thought her smile forced.

"Don't you?" She asked him in turn. Her delicate hands slid up and down the sides of her hips, rubbing them. *A camouflage for her trembling fingers,* he noticed. He didn't want to torment her; she meant something to him. He didn't know what, but *something.* Yet, the scientist in him had to solve the riddle she represented. Something stood amiss. He'd bet his life on it.

"What are you seeking on this trip?" He swung away from the closet door and closed the space between them. "You want something. What is it?"

"I want to see the world."

He shook his head.

"But you've got plenty of time for that. This is my third year with this tour, and you're the first applicant I've had who was under forty. Young people usually don't have the money and two free months to spend on a tour." He paced a few steps while he waited for her to interrupt him. Nothing. He turned back to her. "My clients are retirees and newly divorced and widowed people who are trying to put order into their lives, to start over. What's your reason?" He hated that he had begun to sound accusing, but he teetered at the edge of caring for her, and he had to have some answers. He needed to know that the wild pounding of his heart that began whenever he saw her wouldn't some day suffocate him.

"Are you running from a broken love affair? Hit the lottery as Ames did? I'm curious."

"I told you; I want to see the world."

He shrugged.

"Sure you do. But why do you feel you have to satisfy this curiosity now? There's a reason, and you aren't giving it."

He'd have been a successful attorney, Jeannetta thought. She knew from his turn of mind that the opportunity to bring up the subject of her health had slipped past, if, indeed, it had been there at all.

"Why do you think my wanting to see the world is so unreasonable?" she asked, hoping that he would soon tire of the subject.

"It isn't unreasonable, but if you're twenty-nine years old and have a master's degree, you can't have worked more than five years and, unless college teachers make more than I thought, you've spent a chunk—maybe all—of your savings on this trip. A trip that began two weeks before the end of your school's regular term."

"Some deduction! If your tour had started two weeks later, I wouldn't have had to skip the last two weeks of school." She wanted to tell him that it was none of his business, but it *was* his business. *He* was her reason. When she could force herself to look him in the eye, she saw his skepticism mirrored there. Maybe she could find a way to tell him. She began slowly, fearfully.

"I've never found it easy to talk about myself, especially not with strangers—I mean, not with people I don't know very well. You're asking for personal information, and I'm not…"

He'd moved to within inches of her, and tugged at her hand.

"*Strangers?* Do you kiss strangers?"

"Of course n… Oh, Mason. I'm not sure you've ever been a stranger."

"How about that night in Paris?" His hoarse voice had lost its smoothness, and a rasp of desire greeted her ears. Perspiration beaded on his forehead, and she wondered why he didn't move. Where did he get that awesome control? She stood mesmerized as his eyes lost their blackness and took on the greenish-brown cast that signaled his arousal. Even as her breath shortened almost to a pant, his sexual heat bruised her nostrils. If she didn't get him inside of her, she'd…

"Come here to me, honey."

Somehow, her feet left the floor, and the steel-like grip of his powerful arms crushed her to him. His tongue invaded her mouth, and she sucked it feverishly. Hungrily. When he cupped her bottom, she let her long legs grip his hips, and a spiral of hot darts shot to her feminine center when his bulging arousal pressed between her thighs. He rubbed her erect nipple and, at the sound of her frustrated moan, he set her feet on the floor, reached into her blouse, released her breast and bent his mouth to it. With one hand, she pressed the back of his head, while the other one squeezed his buttocks. His mouth and tongue sucked and tugged at her nipple, sending pulsations to her core. Nearly out of her mind now, she cried out, asking for more. He picked her up and sat on the sofa with her on his lap.

His voice, still minus its natural tone and cadence, washed over her. "I don't want to leave, but I can't remain in here. I've already stayed longer than I should, and I can't break my own rule."

"You mean you've got a rule that says people can't make love on this tour?"

His weak, forced smile tempered her annoyance.

"That isn't the rule, but it amounts to that. Our time will come, Jeannetta. A time when we needn't worry about rules, beepers, intercoms, and lack of privacy, and I'd as soon that time came when this tour is behind us and our desire for each other isn't whetted by convenience and close proximity." He shifted her from his lap and stood.

"You're important to me. Don't forget that in the days to come." He leaned over her, and she tried not to respond when he brushed her forehead.

"I'll let myself out. Lock your door." With that, he left her.

She'd known before he touched her that he didn't want to start a raging fire, but she'd ignored the signals, had let her unappeased desire for him rule her. And she had nearly destroyed any chance she might have of getting his help. And even if he agreed, out of guilt, to operate, she'd lose him. What man would forgive a woman for allowing him to care for her, for making love with him, and then exacting a price? Not this one. She paced the narrow room, fell on the sofa, sat up, and slammed her newspaper across the room, knocking over the bud vase. Her anger subsided, and she told herself she'd take whatever came, but she went to bed knowing that she'd toss all night, uncertain of the future.

Mason jumped out of bed at the first sound of his beeper, glancing at his watch as he did so. Twenty minutes past three. The train had stopped. What the...

"This is Fenwick. What's the problem?" He didn't like the quiver in the conductor's voice. He grabbed his Bermuda shorts and jumped into them before the man could get his voice under control.

"Some soldiers, about eight of them, just boarded the front of the train. They blocked the track, so the engineer had to stop. We're only a mile from the Bulgaria border with the former Yugoslavia, so we don't know what's going on. They're not customs officers. I'm alerting the tour guides and the unescorted passengers."

"Are they showing their rifles?"

"Combat ready, sir."

Mason swore. "Thanks. Keep a cool front, pal. Never let a man know he's got you down." He flipped off the phone, hooked it to his belt along with a can of mace, grabbed his keys, and raced down the corridor to Jeannetta's compartment.

"Open up, Jeannetta." He hoped she didn't sleep soundly.

"Who is it?"

"Mason. Soldiers on the train. Put on a dress and open this

door. *Now!*" While she dressed, he alerted people in other compartments, getting a few surprises, as he did so. In different circumstances, he might have found the evidence of bed-switching amusing. Two men and one of the women were sleeping in a bed to which they hadn't been assigned. He dashed back to Jeannetta's door.

"Let's go, Jeannetta. Hide your valuables and money, but bring your passport. Come on, babe."

She opened the door, her eyes wide and unblinking. He didn't have time to allay her fear; later, if there was a later. He pulled her through the door, slammed it, and raced with her to his room.

"Wha...what's going on, Mason?"

"We don't know, but we're near the border and, European history being what it is, we may be in disputed territory. If they stop here, don't volunteer information, and don't discuss anybody but yourself; if those soldiers were friends, they wouldn't have their fingers on the trigger."

"We always stop at the borders. What's so different this time?" He wanted to hug her to him, but he needed his wits. He had to keep her safe, and nothing was more dangerous for a beautiful woman than sex-starved soldiers.

"Customs officers don't board these trains with rifles drawn." His glance swept her unsteady form. He shook his head. She'd brought her most valuable possession with her—a little doll. He'd ask her about that later.

"Button up your dress, honey. All the way to the neck. And pull your hair up on your head."

"Why?" He glared at her, partly in frustration and partly in anger at the situation into which he'd unwittingly put her.

"Because those soldiers will see exactly what I see, and they may not be averse to taking it."

Her shaking fingers couldn't manage the buttons, and he fastened her dress, his large fingers innocently brushing her soft mounds and threatening to disconcert him. If he got her safely to Istanbul, he was going to kiss God's good earth. He twisted her hair on top of her head and knotted it. The knock on the door of his compartment was loud and brutish. His lips brushed hers quickly.

"Don't be afraid, honey. If they touch you, they'll have to kill me." With his best nonchalant air, he opened the door, raised an eyebrow and asked," May I help you?" Only two of them. He hoped the rest weren't busy intimidating the other passengers. They swaggered in without waiting to be asked.

"What country you from?" He told them. The leader of the two examined their passports, and Mason couldn't help expelling a long breath when the man returned them to him. The other man had his gaze fixed on Jeannetta.

"Your husband?" Jeannetta nodded, the leader reminded her that her passport gave her status as single.

"It's over a year old," she told him, referring to her passport. Mason shifted his stance, and icy tingles hurtled along his spine as both men's gazes fastened on Jeannetta, their eyes ablaze with lust. His focus shifted from the can on his belt, and his mind adopted the attitude of the karate master that he was. He hadn't applied those principles since college, but he knew he could depend on them.

The soldiers must have noticed his change of demeanor, because the leader half-smiled and told him, "If she was my woman, I'd leave her at home. She is black American?"

Mason nodded. He couldn't let himself be lulled into thinking they were safe, only to have the trial of his life.

"You're the tour leader?"

Mason inclined his head.

"Everybody in this car is American?" the leader asked him.

Mason nodded.

The man appeared to have satisfied himself that whatever he sought wouldn't be found in that compartment, but the other continued to drool over Jeannetta. The leader nodded toward the door and spoke in a language that Mason didn't understand, but he didn't doubt the essence of the message: "Leave it. We don't have time for that."

The leader touched the door handle, looked back and asked Mason, "You see any soldiers with this on their sleeve?"

He pulled a small emblem that Mason recognized as the colors of a flag out of his pocket. He hadn't seen any soldiers except them, he said. The door closed behind them.

"Oh, Mason. Do you think they've gone? I'm so scared." He pulled her trembling body to him.

"We'll have to wait until the conductor signals. As sure as they see me alone in that corridor, one or both of them will make a beeline straight to you." She moved closer to him, but he stepped farther back; until he knew the danger had passed, he couldn't allow her nearness and patent vulnerability to scramble his wits. He pushed the buttons on his beeper and held his breath until the conductor answered.

"Motorman, here. All clear."

"Any problems?" Still holding, Jeannetta, Mason leaned against the wall. That had been close. The last time he'd been that strung out… He fought back the memory of his scalpel suspended over the lesion in Bianca Norris's exposed brain.

"Just a hundred-thirty-three scared passengers. Excluding yourself, of course, sir. They're after terrorists. We'll be on our way shortly."

Mason thanked him and looked down at Jeannetta.

"I'm sorry they frightened you." He sat on the sofa with her cuddled in his lap.

"I wasn't afraid for myself, as much as for you," she whispered. "If anything had happened to you because of me…Oh, Mason, you don't know how scared I got." He set her on her feet.

"I can imagine. I'll walk you to your compartment. You'd better try and get some sleep, because we reach Istanbul later this morning, and you won't be near a bed again until we get to Singapore."

Her hot, welcoming kiss wasn't something a man could easily shrug off. He had to marshal self-control to walk away from the invitation mirrored in her eyes. He wasn't Superman, but if he could turn his back on his profession, work he'd dreamed of enjoying for as long as he'd known himself—if he could make himself do that, he could do anything. He headed back to his compartment, certain that he'd walked away from the loving of a lifetime.

Later that morning, Jeannetta sat in the observation lounge, trying to glimpse the sunrise. A fierce headache, much as her doctor had told her to expect, had kept her awake for the remainder of the night. Geoffrey ambled in, carrying a cup of coffee, and she welcomed his company.

"You're not you usual bright self this morning, Jeannetta." He peered at her as though to verify his words.

"Geoffrey, what holds a man back when he's interested?" She had to wait while he blew the hot coffee until he could bear to sip it.

"Married, engaged, misgivings. Why?"

"Do you think Mason's married?" His face creased into a half-smile.

"Nope. I sure don't."

She liked Geoffrey, but his laconic responses sometimes got on her nerves.

"Engaged?" She pressed.

"No. Mason's no cheat."

She took a deep breath and asked the obvious. "Misgivings, huh?"

He let her wait while he finished his coffee.

"I'd say so. A lot of 'em. 'Course it's up to you to rid him of those. I'd best be getting on; Lucy gets spiteful when she sees us talking. Don't you set her at ease, though. Women never act right when they get too sure of a man."

Jeannetta had to laugh. "That's practically the advice you gave me about Mason."

Geoffrey Ames winked at her with his newfound sophistication. "It ain't done you no harm, neither. Has it?"

In a few hours, the train would pull into Istanbul and, seven hours later, he and the tour would be on a plane for Singapore.

Mason had dreaded this day as the most precarious of the entire trip; one hitch, and he stood to lose a bundle. He headed down to the observation car, hoping to begin the day in the way he most enjoyed—watching the sun break through the clouds, spreading its kaleidoscope of colors across the horizon. He walked into the observation lounge, stuck his hands in his back pockets and gazed at the glorious pinks, purples, reds, and the blues that shot across the sky. A cup of coffee and ten minutes of this would get his day off and running just right. He whirled around at the sound of a steady, low drone. Jeannetta. She didn't know he'd entered the car. But what...? She sat alone, dictating into an audio cassette a description of the sunrise and what she saw as the train whizzed past villages, farms, and endless hills. He started to speak, thought better of it, and stood quietly as she related the tiniest of details. Tremors in her voice lent an intimate quality to her dictation. Yes, and an eeriness, too. No one should eavesdrop on another's soul; he left. So much for his visit with the sunrise.

Alone in the dining room, he sipped black coffee and mulled over what he'd witnessed. Why didn't she photograph the scenes? What was the advantage in describing them? Upon reflection, he realized that he hadn't seen her with a camera. Among his tour guests, he'd seen all except her take pictures. He shook his head, and his fingers brushed the keys in his right pants pocket. He'd let her have her privacy, but he would rather have begun his day buoyed by that exhilarating sunrise.

A few minutes later Mason stood at the bar, checking the train's Istanbul arrival time with Josh, his porter; Jeannetta strolled by without seeing them, humming a tune that he didn't recognize.

"Miss Rollins is in that lounge every morning at sunup telling that little machine of hers what she did the day before," Josh said. "I've been trying to figure out why she does it if it makes her feel bad. Yesterday morning, she was making her recording and, man, you should have seen the tears. But she kept right on talking, like her eyes were dry. She's strange, that one. Couple of minutes after I sneaked out of there, she came out and greeted me with the biggest smile you ever saw."

"Yeah," Mason replied. "We've got forty-seven pieces of luggage and two crates of supplies to unload here and transfer to Singapore Airlines. I want this stuff at the airport by noon. No later. Got that?" He left the bar without waiting for Josh's reply. He didn't want men discussing Jeannetta. That was one of the problems with romances in groups like this one; you had to listen to things you'd rather not hear.

"Hi. Remember me?"

He whirled around. Lord, would he never get used to her eyes? Eyes that proclaimed the woman as a warm nesting place. He grinned down at her.

"If we'd ever met, honey," he drawled, "I'd remember it. My five senses are in flawless condition, and I'm a man in the prime of life. You know me from somewhere?"

Her laughter wrapped around him, warming him and unsettling him. Her presence gave him a feeling of contentment, and his fingers automatically went to the keys in his pocket.

"Need something?" he asked her, in his best low, suggestive tone. He could see the laughter starting to boil up in her. Laughter that said his question didn't deserve an answer. As quickly as it started, it stopped.

"Do I need something? How about tall, dark, handsome, and male, with a habit of strumming his fingers on any solid surface near him?" she asked with feigned seriousness. Unable to resist touching her, he tweaked her nose.

"All in good time, sweet thing." Her smile—natural and sincere, but so powerfully seductive—reminded him of the lecture Steve had given him when he left for college. If he made low grades, his brother had said, he'd lose his scholarship, be forced to work his way through, and probably wouldn't get his medical degree until he reached thirty; but a pretty woman's smile could get him kicked out of college, and he'd never get that degree.

She is as uncertain about us as I am, he told himself, watching her enter the dining room. Neither of them behaved consistently.

Small children played the game, go-away-come-here; it had no place in his life. He followed Jeannetta to the dining room.

"Remember that the plane leaves at six-forty and, please, for Heaven's sake, be there an hour and a half before flight time."

"I'll do my best, but I'd love to see a little of Istanbul. I might not get another…well, I might not come this way again." The childlike lights of eagerness that sparkled in her eyes endeared her to him; at that moment he could have denied her nothing.

"Would you like to see Istanbul with me, Jeannetta?"

"Oh, yes. I would."

He didn't want her to see how much she affected him, so he walked out of the dining room. And nearly knocked Geoffrey to the floor.

"Angry, or in a hurry?" Geoffrey asked him, adjusting his jacket.

"Neither. Where's Lucy? I want everybody in the dining room for briefing." Sometimes he wondered if Geoffrey's professed interest in Lucy might be a screen. The man spent a hell of a lot of time in Jeannetta's company. *Oh, heck, I must be getting paranoid.*

Mason had leased a bus to drive the group around Istanbul before taking them to a hotel. He and Jeannetta struck out on their own.

"I didn't know anybody still mixed cement that way," Jeannetta said as they passed a construction site. "Imagine, mixing that with a hoe. What if it gets hard before it's used?"

"This is a moderately developed country, but it isn't rich, it's… Say, this is the first time you've been outside the Western developed region, isn't it? This one's modern, compared to what you'll find in Africa and most of Asia." He realized that she no longer listened, but stood staring at… What *was* she looking at? A child dived into a large mound of sand, and another made a game of sifting sand through her fingers. In his book, that didn't classify as spellbinding. Yet, she stared, immobile, her face drawn.

"What's wrong, Jeannetta?" He watched, aghast, as her glance shifted in a way that suggested she searched for a way to escape something. He rushed to her.

"What's wrong, honey?" His fingers on her arms absorbed her trembling, and he didn't doubt that something had frightened her. He put an arm around her, drew her to his side, and waited for her answer. None came.

Minutes later, she exclaimed, "Oh, Mason, there's a big mosque. Can we go in?"

Relieved that the somber moment had passed, but worried that she hadn't confided in him, he forced a smile. "I don't see why not." They walked toward the mosque, but two young boys stopped them.

"You speak English, mister?" the more forward of the two asked Mason

"Yeah. Why?" Eager smiles spread over the two young faces.

"We practice our English. What you like? We show you." Mason turned to ask Jeannetta if she would like the boys to give them a walking tour. She'd disappeared. His heart surged powerfully in his chest. Where had she gone? He raced into the mosque, smaller than it appeared from the outside, and searched behind every one of the large marble columns, but he neither saw nor heard anyone. Perhaps she had gone outside...but she would have passed him. Had those boys acted as decoys, distracting his attention while someone spirited her away? He dashed outside, where the two boys waited, spoiling his theory that they had helped someone kidnap Jeannetta. If he ever got her to Pilgrim, he'd take that soldier's advice.

If she went to the police, the plane would have left for Singapore long before the officers finished questioning him and filling out forms. He could go to the American Embassy, he reminded himself, but to what end?

"You wait 'til the lady comes back, and then we take you tour? Okay?" one boy asked.

He had to get a plan, and quick. "What's your name?" he asked the talkative one.

"At'ut. We do business? Yes? Very cheap. Three American dollars." Mason sized up both boys as intelligent and resourceful. What choice did he have?

"At'ut, did you see the woman who was with me when I met you?"

"Sure." The boy gave Mason as accurate a description of Jeannetta as any warm-blooded adult male might have done.

"I can't find her. I think she went in there," he said, pointing to the mosque, "but she walked away and I've lost her. I'll stand here until noon. Find her and bring her back here, and I'll give each of you twenty-five American dollars." Both boys leaned toward him, as though making sure of what they'd heard, their eyes as round as saucers.

"You wait here," At'ut said. "We bring her back; you don't lose the American dollars. Wait here." They left at breakneck speed and, after loosening the collar of his damp shirt and wiping his neck with a handkerchief, Mason took a position against a post in the shadow of the mosque. Not an iota of breeze relieved the sweltering heat.

He could stand the heat; he could take anything, except losing her. He had to look for her—but if he left there, what if she came back and panicked when she didn't see him? He paced the cracked sidewalk, stumping his toe on the loose rumble. He couldn't leave her fate in the hands of two Turkish urchins whom he might never see again, though there was some comfort in the fact that twenty-five dollars would buy nearly one hundred and seventy Turkish lira.

He hated the feeling of helplessness that had begun to pervade him, a feeling he hadn't had since his first year of internship, when his team had lost a patient whom he favored. What if he couldn't find her? A burning sensation on his arms, neck, and face sent him back to the shaded post beside the mosque. Suppose someone had abducted her. He had no intention of leaving Istanbul without her but, if he deserted the tour, he'd get sued for every cent he had, and he could kiss Fenwick Travel Agency goodbye. He squinted at the blazing sun, bowed his head, and closed his eyes. He hadn't prayed for such a long time that he doubted he'd get a hearing.

# Chapter 4

"You are looking for the door?" The little man bowed from the waist, the picture of courtesy. Jeannetta glanced around, hoping to see another human being. The man's saintly persona could be a ruse, a trick, but she had despaired of finding her way out. Thick Turkish carpets in a multitude of bright designs covered the floor, the space relieved only by the dozens of silent marble columns scattered about. Each may have had significance for the worshippers, but they only gave her a feeling that she walked in circles. She sighted a paneled-off area, and wondered whether it hid a door. The quick glimpse she'd intended to take while Mason talked with the boys had turned into half an hour.

"If you wish to go out, I will show you," the man repeated, though with less patience than previously.

She didn't know the customs, so she bowed her assent. Her rescuer led her to a door so heavy that she could never have opened it. Tentacles of fear streaked through her at the thought that she might facing a fate worse than the loss of sight. The little man pulled at the door, and bright sunshine enveloped her. She smiled at him and stepped outside.

She stared at her surroundings, looked back at the door through which she had just walked, at the shops across the narrow street. *Where was she?* She took a deep breath and decided to walk to her left. A dump heap. She retraced her steps and walked several blocks, but she saw neither a mosque, a broad avenue, nor, worst of all, any sight of Mason. Her short-sleeved cotton shirt clung to her body; she searched her bag for a tissue, but couldn't find one, and had to use the tail of her long skirt to wipe away the perspiration that bathed her face. Hunger pangs irritated her stomach, but she didn't dare stop for food. She had to find Mason.

Hearing a buzz of traffic, she walked toward it, hoping to find the avenue where she'd left Mason at the entrance to the mosque. Every building that she passed seemed to house an open-front coffee house in which scores of men sat drinking coffee and watching her. Surely she didn't defy custom by walking the street at noon, but she remembered that she hadn't seen a woman. She would never forget the seas of dark eyes—some of them beautiful, but all of them disconcerting—that followed her the way the eyes in Van Gogh's self-portrait follow the viewer. In spite of the blazing heat, she hugged her middle as she walked, as though to protect herself from the unknown, the unseen.

The odor of raw lamb, pungent garlic, and a strong, strange pine-like odor bruised her nostrils. She longed to escape it, to breathe a different air. Dank, decaying scents greeted her from an alley as she passed it, and she welcomed the all-pervading aroma of cinnamon, cloves, and rose water that soon flowed from several bakeries. Gnawing hunger over her reticence, and she turned into the next bakery. She had discovered that bowing and smiling invited friendship if you didn't have language to do the work for you. The old man looked up from his mound of dough, pointed to a high stool and disappeared into the rear of the store. She didn't care where he'd gone or why; she welcomed the respite from the scorching sun and relief for her tired feet. He soon returned with a young boy, about eight or nine, she guessed.

"How can we help you, lady?" the boy asked her with a broad smile. After hearing that she was hungry and lost, he went in the back and a woman shrouded in black returned with him. Jeannetta quickly explained that she want to *buy* something to eat and drink and to get instructions back to the mosque. A rapid translation sent the woman scurrying away, only to return with three soft drinks and assorted breads, cakes, and baklava. The mosque, the boy happily informed her, was right around the corner. Replenished, rested, and relieved, she struck out for the mosque, carrying a sack of pastries that the woman had handed her. Around the corner stood the great Hagia Sophia, a fifth-century architectural miracle that she recognized from travel posters. She brushed away the tears, raised her head, and walked on. She tried to remain calm, to think, but the strange noises and peculiar and often unpleasant smells disconcerted her. She had to take comfort in knowing that he wouldn't leave her alone in Istanbul, that he'd find her, that he cared enough to search the city for her. Lord, let her see him before dark.

Mason looked at his watch for the nth time. Four o'clock, and not a word from the two boys. His feet had covered every inch of the pavement within a block of the mosque, because he hadn't been able to stand still. The pangs of hunger had long since become a painful ache, but he refused to leave the place long enough to eat. In another thirty minutes, he'd have to go to the United States Embassy and report her missing; he'd also have to phone Josh and tell him to take the tour on without him.

"Hey, mister! Hey, mister!" Mason whirled around and ran to meet the exuberant youth.

"You come. We find her." He grabbed the boy by the collar of his jacket and tugged him upward, nearly to eye level.

"Where is she? Where is your friend? You tell me something right here." He had to calm himself; the boy bore no responsibility for his state of near madness.

"She with my friend in Ataturk Square. I ask her to come with me, but she refuse. So my friend stay and I come. You still have American dollars?"

Mason nodded. "Let's go. If you're not telling me the truth, I'll take you to the police." The boy grinned, unconcerned about the threat.

"Police my uncle. You come now." Mason had to restrain the anxious youth, who couldn't wait for his prized American dollars; he had barely enough energy to walk, to say nothing of running. He wondered that he hadn't suffered sunstroke;

poor hydration had stopped his profuse perspiring, and his stomach cramped. Renewed strength flowed through him, however, at the thought that he'd soon see her, verify with his eyes that nothing untoward had happened to her. They reached the edge of the square and stopped for the traffic. He had to swallow hard to stave off the sorrows that welled up in him. Where was she?

"Come. Over there," At'ut urged. Mason searched the distance until his gaze fell on the blob of yellow at the edge of the monument. His heart surged in his chest, and he had to run.

"No. Wait. Come back, mister. The traffic, she kill you." Buses loaded with passengers lumbered by; automobiles raced past him; he dodged motorcycles, bicycles, vans, and a hearse. But none of them slowed his pace. He had to get to her, touch her, feel her, know for himself that nothing hade harmed her. Horns blared, words that must have been curses fell against his deaf ears; a stunned traffic officer whirled around as Mason whizzed past.

He saw the smile break out on her face as she glimpsed him, jumped up, and started toward him, and he silently thanked the boy for yanking her back, away from the rushing traffic. He jumped the curb and swept her trembling body into his arms. The hell with custom. He didn't give a damn if the Turks didn't embrace publicly. Her lips parted in a joyous greeting, and he filled her with himself, emptying his relief, longing, need, hunger for her and, yes, fear, into his powerful and explosive kiss. He ignored the tugging at his shirt.

"I've never been so scared in my life, not even when...I was on my way out of my mind when At'ut came back for me. Don't you ever do this to me again." His lips dried the tears that streamed down her cheeks.

"Say, mister, what about the American dollars?" He reached into his pocket and paid them each the twenty-five dollars he'd promised them.

"Thanks. You two were great." Joyous laughter erupted from them as they counted the money.

"When you lose her again," At'ut the entrepreneur of the two, assured him, "you come to mosque. We find her again, quick like today." He thanked the boys and told them goodbye.

"Where were you?"

She recounted her adventures, adding, "About an hour ago, I decided to get a taxi to the airport, thinking maybe you'd gone there, but the cabs didn't stop. There must be a thousand mosques in this city, and I'm sure I've seen most of them today. Oh, Mason: if you think you were scared—I've been terrified that I'd miss the plane, never get back home, never see you again." Her slender body moved closer, and a sense of well-being pervaded him.

"I would have let the tour go on without me, Jeannetta. There's no way I'd have left you here." He kissed each of her eyelids.

"Good Lord, Mason, we're the local attraction."

He looked over his shoulder and saw that the traffic had stopped and that the passengers leaned from automobiles to watch them. He remembered that kiss and grinned; it had been one hot one, and he hoped they had all enjoyed it half as much as he did.

"If it wasn't so late and I wasn't starved, I'd suggest you show me where you were today. I still haven't had a chance to visit old Istanbul. There's where you find the centuries-old mosques, quaint customs, ancient bazaars, narrow streets, and crumbling old buildings, the flavor of Turkey that tourists hope to see. I'm told that many of the inhabitants still cling to the old way of doing things. Too bad you were so concerned about finding your way that you couldn't enjoy the experience." Saliva accumulated in his mouth as he looked down at the pastry she took from a brown paper sack. "I'm so hungry, I think I've forgotten how to eat," he told her when she handed it to him, "I don't know where you got this, but let me tell you, I'm glad to see it." She gave him the bag.

Mason noticed a taxi driver among their audience and negotiated a ride to the airport.

"How do you feel?" he asked Jeannetta when she sagged against him in the cab.

"Stupid. It has just dawned on me that the nice little man who showed me how to get out of the mosque knew I'd get lost, but he didn't care. I had no business in that male sanctuary, or at least not in the place where he found me. What a day!"

"Women use a separate entrance, and you went in the main door." He settled back in the hot, bedraggled car, slid his right arm around her shoulder and his left hand into the bag of pastries. "In other words, if you want to live with Vikings, learn how the Vikings live."

She looked down at his long legs, close to but not touching her, as they sat in the Singapore Airlines business-class lounge. His head lay against the back of the seat, his eyelids covered his eyes, and his arms lay folded against his broad chest. She knew he needed those moments alone, to regroup after what must have been an emotionally gruelling day, so she used the time to record her experiences in Istanbul on her cassette.

"I was scared," she said, unable to control the tremors that laced her speech and the unsteadiness of the hand in which she held the recorder. "More scared than I've ever been in my life. It was worse than when they told me..." Startled at what she'd almost said, she glanced over to see his gaze on her, switched off the machine, and forced her attention to several of her fellow passengers. She could feel him scrutinize her, but she refused to acknowledge his pulsing hot vibes that stimulated every centimeter of her body, and she shifted her gaze everywhere but to his face. He had questions that she didn't dare answer. After a time, she closed her eyes and was soon deep in thought. Because his refusal to Dr. Farmer had been emphatic, she had procrastinated about asking his help, hadn't gotten the courage to open the subject for fear of hearing that "no" herself, that sentence to darkness. She opened her eyes and smiled at him, hoping to distract him from whatever thoughts he might have about what he'd heard her dictate into the recorder.

His attention was focused on her.

"Didn't you know I'd find you?" he asked, "that I wouldn't

leave you behind? Haven't you accepted that I'm going to take care of you, even if you test me to my limits? Even if you insist on being late, getting lost, attracting dangerous men, and I don't know what else?"

She wished she knew whether he'd just said he cared for her, or that he always took care of his tour guests. His dispassionate face told her nothing.

A sigh escaped her. "Thanks. I knew you'd try to find me, but I didn't know how you'd succeed without a clue. Of course, I hadn't reckoned on your psychic powers."

He shrugged. "'Psychic powers'? I can't remember the last time I prayed, before today." He flexed his left leg, stood, and held out his hand to her.

"I've got to check in my gang, the flight's boarding. Come with me?" he asked, smiling that warm, intimate smile that she loved.

"Oh, I don't want to get in the way, I'll get in line."

At his incredulous stare, she rose without hesitation.

"If you think I'm letting you out of my sight before you get on that plane, lady, you'd better think again. Not after what I went through today, I'm not."

He grinned—to soften his words, she thought. She tried not to stare at him, to ignore the way in which his mesmeric eyes gleamed whenever he smiled.

"Besides," he went on, "is being with me so unpleasant?"

She wrinkled her nose at him, aware that the day's adventure had augmented their bonds, but she couldn't resist a chiding remark.

"If you thought so, you wouldn't ask the question." But as she stood with him beside the desk while he checked in the tour passengers, she wondered. Tall. Handsome. Powerfully built. Charismatic. Capable. Intelligent. Could such a man feel the need for praise? She shook her head. Maybe her view of him differed from his own.

Mason led her to her seat and stored her carry-on luggage in the baggage compartment. After all his guests had found their seats, he took the aisle seat beside her. Jeannetta couldn't decide whether his having changed her seat should annoy her. She had originally been assigned 6D, but he'd changed it to 11-F.

"I didn't realize we'd be sitting together. To where do you think I'll disappear while this plane is in the air?" She appreciated his interest, but she had never tolerated well anyone's attempt to control her. "It's either the lavatory, the cockpit, or out the window. Which do you think I'll choose?" She bit her lip, surprised at her waspishness. Mason stood, rested his hand on the back of his seat and looked at her, his face impassive.

"You don't want me to sit with you?"

"Did I say that?"

"Well, let's get it straight this minute. Do you or don't you?"

She'd boxed herself in, and she didn't doubt that he'd let her take her medicine.

"A gentleman doesn't press his advantage. Besides, I'm not so cruel that I'd want you to stand all the way to Singapore."

"Who says I would?"

"Mason, would you please not make an international crisis out of this, and sit back down?" In his unwavering gaze, she glimpsed a semblance of pain, fleeting though it was. She held out her hand to him.

"If you're sure," he said, seating himself.

"I'm sure."

His mouth softened to reveal glistening white teeth. "I may hold your hand."

With a flash of insight, she knew that his glibness covered the pain she'd seen in him, and she prepared herself to indulge him.

"Okay, if you want to hold my hand."

"I may put my head on your shoulder and go to sleep."

"I guess I can handle that."

"I've been known to snore."

"Not too loudly, I hope."

"Like a buzz saw."

She produced the grimace she knew he hoped to see. "I've heard worse."

"I'll definitely kiss you."

She yanked on the hand he'd rested on the back of his seat.

"Will you please stop trying to bug me?" She found that she loved teasing him. She knew he could take it, that his self-discipline was well known among his medical peers. A dark shudder passed through her. What if he learned that she'd had him investigated before she took the tour? He'd have two counts on which to cross her off as a scheming woman, and her plans would go for naught, elusive like her dreams.

They dined in companionable silence, causing Mason to marvel at their ability to commune without speaking. Jeannetta didn't babble as many people did when conversation lulled, and it was one of her many admirable traits. Silence didn't make her nervous. He savored the fine cognac, inhaling deeply before rolling a sip on his tongue.

"When we get to Singapore," he advised, "don't go anywhere alone. We'll only be there six hours before we'll have to board the ship. I've arranged for a bus to take us on a two-hour sightseeing tour, with brief stops in Chinatown, the Botanical Gardens, Colonial Singapore, and Jurong Bird Park where handlers train birds to sing. If there's time, we'll drive past the Raffles hotel complex. Please stay with the group." He watched her from the corner of his left eye. If his guess was right, the lady would get her dander up. He couldn't help smiling when she turned fully to him and took a deep breath.

"Yes, *sir!* Anything else, *sir?*"

"You're not taking me seriously," he said in an offhand manner, smiling inwardly and pretending not to know he'd riled her.

"And a good thing, too. I don't speak that way to my students but, of course, they're all over eighteen."

He laughed. Nothing pleased him more than the company of a lovely, laid-back, witty woman. He put a couple of pillows on his shoulder. "Lean over here," he whispered.

She hesitated, as though questioning the pleasure she'd get from it.

"Come on," he urged, his voice warm and sugary, as he slid

an arm around her shoulder and waited for her to resist. When she didn't, he flipped back the armrest that had separated them. Pulled her close, and rested his head on her shoulder. No reaction. He let his fingers dance beneath her chin until she could no longer resist and began to laugh uncontrollably. Then he reached down for their blankets, covered them both, and felt her curl into him. He hadn't thought she'd get so cozy in the presence of their companions, but he hadn't noticed the lowered lights, either.

In those circumstances, a man's options were severely limited. She huddled closer, and he had to struggle to suppress the fire that raged in his blood. His pulse pitched into a gallop when her breathing accelerated. The scent of warm woman began to tantalize his nostrils, and he'd have given a day's income to jog five miles in thirty-two degree weather. He couldn't tell whether she knew her effect on him right then, and he wasn't about to ask her. She'd caught him on the blind side sometime during the last few days, and he'd as soon she didn't know how vulnerable he'd gotten. When had he begun to need her? He didn't know anything about her, but he wanted her, and didn't want another man near her. She sighed deeply and buried her face in the curve of his neck. If only he could get out of there. He rested his head on the back of the seat and counted sheep, but his passion didn't cool. He imagined himself eating sauerkraut, which he hated, but that didn't lessen the discomfort in his groin, or the pounding of his pulse. A waste of time, he decided, and wrapped his arms around her. What the hell! It wasn't the first time he'd done without, but he couldn't remember having previously enjoyed it.

Let him think her asleep, that she didn't realize the intimacy she'd created between them. She tried to ignore her nagging conscience and its caution that she'd pay dearly for every kiss, each caress, for every minute in his arms. But, even as a young girl, she had dreamed of a man's holding her as though she were precious, his morning sun and evening breeze; she couldn't help savoring this dream come true with a man who in so short a time had wedged himself deep into her heart. She knew she'd eventually have to face the inevitable, that moment when he knew everything and walked away from her. And there was no denying that, if he accused her of dishonesty, she would deserve it; she hadn't led him on, but her attempts to discourage him had been so haphazard that he'd probably seen no reason to take them seriously.

His right arm tightened around her and, in spite of what her head told her, she slid an arm across his chest and accepted his affection. She wanted to raise her head, touch his lips with her own, and taste the sweet agony that gripped her from head to toe every time she drank the burning passion of his kisses.

"Jeannetta, do you know you're caressing me? Do you?"

She'd been so absorbed in the feel of him that his low guttural voice reached her ears as if from a great distance.

"Do you?" He stilled her attempt to remove her fingers from the thatch of hair on his chest. "Answer me," he urged, his voice low and thick.

"I… Oh, Mason, I don't know what I'm doing. We're getting so close, and I know that nothing can come of it. I try to keep that in mind, but you're so tempting."

He held her closer when she made a weak and irresolute attempt to move back to her own seat, and she realized that the man in him paid greater attention to her actions than to her words. Who could blame him?

"You don't have anything to fear from me. I'm free, solvent, and thirty-seven, and I'm neither married nor engaged. So why can't I hold you in my arms? You're comfortable, aren't you?"

If only it were that simple.

"This is moving too fast, Mason."

"Too fast?" he scoffed. "We've seen more of each other on this tour than we would have managed in six months if we'd been in New York and Pilgrim, unless…" He sat up and gazed down at her, his eyes sparkling with devilment in that way she loved. "Of course, we would have seen a lot, I mean *a lot* more of each other if you'd taken me for a roommate. You still can; I always pick up my socks and, as far as I know, I don't snore."

She sat up abruptly, hitting her head on his chin, which he rubbed reflexively.

"We're getting kind of fanciful, aren't we?"

His hand stroked her back until she succumbed to temptation and moved back into his arms.

"Not in my book. Tell me, are you an only child?"

He hadn't previously asked her personal questions and hadn't given her a chance to ask him any. Maybe this was her chance.

"I have an older sister who lives at our family home in Pilgrim." He'd opened the gate. Maybe this was the time. "What about you? Sometimes I get the feeling that you're a loner."

The muscles tensed in the arm that held her, and she sensed his caution, his withdrawal. "I have an older brother who's like a father to me. He's…well, he's…a great guy."

She already knew that from the investigation, but maybe if she probed…

"How did you decide to start a travel agency? And this tour…it must have been a huge financial risk."

His right hand stilled on her back and the other one covered her own, and she knew he intended to take her hand away from his chest where, without thinking how it would appear to him, she'd teased his chest hair as though to coax him into answering her questions. She sat up.

"You like me, as long as I don't invade your privacy, and you'll kiss me with all the urgency and deliberateness of a patriot missile going after a scud…until I get out of my place." She knew that such tactics wouldn't get her what she ultimately wanted, but she couldn't help feeling hostile toward him. He had the power to heal, to sustain life, yet he chose to traipse around the world catering to people who had the means to indulge their selfish whims. Her back stiffened. "What made you choose this line of work?" She almost hoped he'd tell her that it wasn't her business.

He leaned back, ran his hand over his tight curls, and breathed deeply.

"I'm not used to answering direct questions about myself, and I've never liked asking them. You took this tour because you wanted to see the world. If I hadn't had something similar in mind, I'd probably have chosen another line of work. Let's get some sleep."

She closed her eyes to hide the pain she knew he'd see there. Bitterness churned inside of her, and she had to muster all her strength to hold back the tears. She'd thought she could face the future, no matter what happened, that she'd learn to accept her fate, but he was handing her a double dose of poison. She thought she could handle life without trees, snow-capped mountains, and brilliant sunsets, but a future in which he had no part? Anger surged in her, and she glanced up at him, expecting to see annoyance. But his face held no expression. In a flash of intuition, she saw that he cloaked his emotions behind his poker face, that his bland expression served as his shield, his defensive armor. Knowledge, someone had said, was power. She refused to allow him to dismiss her.

She leaned toward him, her voice calm. "You've practically told me to shut up; are you planning to kiss me anymore?"

He laughed, but she didn't place much store by that; she'd learned that this was a man who never surprised himself, and she could only admire his self-discipline.

"Well?" she insisted, but he was saved an answer when a flight attendant rushed to him.

"Mr. Fenwick, Lydia Steward says she's having chest pains, but we're not quite halfway. Should we turn around or keep going?"

He was on his feet in a flash, and Jeannetta knew that the physician had emerged, that it was Dr. Fenwick, and not the tour manager, who moved with such alacrity. She wanted to follow him, to see what he'd do, how he'd handle it. She longed to know how much of his secret he'd expose in such an emergency, but she dared not follow. She'd never forgive herself if she hampered his efforts to help the woman. After some time, he returned, outwardly calm.

"Will she be alright?"

"More than likely, provided she takes her medicine and

follows her doctor's advice, but if she has another incident like that one, I'm sending her back to Spokane."

"What happened?" she asked, hoping that he'd respond with a physician's language and manners.

He paused for a while as though gathering his thoughts. "She had a bad case of indigestion, or something similar. I could use a few hours sleep. How about you?"

She settled in her seat, disappointed.

"Sure. Every living thing has to sleep." If she sounded bitter, she didn't care. She wished she had never heard of him, that she hadn't taken his tour and that she didn't love him to the depths of her soul.

The big business-class seat had wide armrests and a slanted prop on which to rest her feet, but she didn't think she'd ever been more uncomfortable. She tossed about, shifted from one position to another, and prayed for the sleep that would take her out of her thoughts. After nearly an hour of it, she felt his strong arm gather her close and fold her to him. He rested her head on his shoulder and drew the blanket across her.

"Now, perhaps we can both get some rest."

She slid her right arm across his chest and cherished the moment.

Mason awoke to the smell of strong coffee, and Jeannetta's soft breathing. He glanced down at the delicate brown fingers that clutched the breast pocket of his shirt and covered them with his hand. He had a sense of well-being, of having the world by the tail, and he knew it came from the feel of her stirring in his arms as he awoke.

"Coffee? Orange juice?" the flight attendant asked him. He ordered coffee, remembered Lydia Steward and wanted to check on her, but controlled his urge. He had thought he'd laid to rest the physician in him, but now he wasn't so sure. He'd brought along a medical bag, complete with a stethoscope, that he was glad he hadn't had to use. Finally, unable to resist any longer, he swallowed the last of his coffee, woke Jeannetta, got his toiletries, and started back toward the lavatories. Lydia's smiling face reminded him of the feeling of accomplishment he'd always gotten when a grateful patient thanked him, a feeling he realized he'd missed. He paused beside Lydia, and her smiles and words of profuse thanks humbled him, making him want to get away from her, from all of them. Away from the charade he'd carried on for the last three years. He glanced up the aisle toward his seat, where Jeannetta stood, looking directly at him. Perhaps she's getting a much-needed stretch, he mused but, somehow, he didn't believe that.

He returned to his seat, shaved and refreshed, to find Jeannetta dictating into her recorder a description of the plane, the appearance of the flight attendants, the clouds, even the wagons from which the attendants served food and drinks. He couldn't figure out why a writer didn't take photographs of her surroundings, and that bothered him. He cleared his throat and, as he'd expected, she put away the recorder.

"You said you write fiction. Is this a story about travel?"

She hesitated before answering. "No. I'd thought I'd work on it during this tour, but the mood hasn't been right. I can't get into the man's character."

"What kind of man is he? You hinted that I'm not your model and, since I'm not a writer, you don't lose anything by telling me."

Their breakfast arrived, and he thought she'd take advantage of it to change the subject, but she didn't.

"He isn't the main protagonist, though he's central to the theme, and this isn't the story I had in mind when I left home. This is a troubled man who can't come to terms with his feelings, who believes that his strength lies in his ability to stand alone, to need no one, but whose true problem is his inability to give of himself. My problem is that I can't get a handle on his character, how he deals with people, with his surroundings, his adversities."

She talked on, but his ears roared with the hollow echo of his insides. He opened his eyes to shut out the portrait of himself in his white coat, his stethoscope dangling from his pocket as he walked off of that hospital ward for the last time. Cool dampness matted the hairs at his wrist, and he thought he'd strangle from the saliva in his mouth as he opened it to speak.

"How does it end?"

"I don't know. I've just begun to lay it out in my mind, to see how he looks and to understand him."

He forced himself not to cover his ears. Maybe she wasn't talking about him, but her words rattled around in his mind all the same.

"No, I don't know the end," she went on, "but I expect he'll have his moment of truth."

He sat forward and turned so that he could see her face.

"I've never met anyone who seemed more composed, more at peace, than you, but some kind of aura around you denies it. In these four weeks, you've come to mean something to me and, from what I've learned about you, I welcome that, but you're mysterious. You've got a...a...a quality that's unsettling. I can't help wondering why you're on this tour. Oh, I know you want to see the world. But why *now?*"

She lifted her glass to take a sip of orange juice and tilted it before it reached her mouth. He stared at her and at the juice on her egg and in her lap. She'd done the same thing on the train, only then it had been water.

"Good Heavens! I've gotten to be such an oink-oink. You'd think I could enjoy breakfast with a charming man without getting nervous and spilling everything."

He reached overhead and rang for the flight attendant.

"It's alright, Jeannetta. That can happen to anybody." He didn't believe it. She had tried to distract him, but he hadn't been taken in by her patter. Jeannetta didn't babble; she talked when she had something to say.

Their flight attendant cleaned her dress with club soda and, to his amazement, Jeannetta joked: "Mr. Fenwick didn't enforce his rule against babies on the tour."

He didn't join her laughter, because he could think of half a dozen ailments to which such symptoms could be ascribed—none of them good news.

* * *

Jeannetta excused herself to freshen up before the plane landed. She had experienced some of the symptoms her doctor had mentioned, and she couldn't help wondering whether her time might be running out. She hadn't had her period in months, and the headaches occurred with increasing frequency and severity. The thought of flying home from Singapore occurred to her, but she had never been a quitter, and she had invested too much in this scheme to throw in the towel without a try. She washed her face, brushed her teeth, and combed her hair, looked at herself in the mirror, and thanked God for wrinkle-free fabric.

He stood by their seats when she returned, a deep frown and a quizzical expression on his face. Strange, she thought, since he usually camouflages his feelings with a poker face. If he'd been as good a doctor as everyone claimed, he might have noticed something about her. Could she pretend she hadn't known what ailed her? She couldn't do it, and the thought nagged her as she left the plane.

Mason checked the passengers through customs and onto the sightseeing bus. He had had their luggage sent directly to the Southern Queen, the boat that would take them on a four-day journey from Singapore to Bangkok, Thailand. He stood by the bus, mopping his forehead, and was about to board when Lucy Abernathy grabbed his arm. She panted excitedly, as though she'd run a mile, and her words tumbled over one another, finally making him understand that Geoffrey Ames hadn't arrived.

"I don't know where he is," she yelled. He did his best to ease her fears, but she wouldn't be comforted.

"He said he'd meet me at the bus, and he's not here," she screamed, flexing her knees as though she were jumping.

"I'll find him," he told her, and moved away from the bus but, to his chagrin, she rushed along beside him. When they reached the terminal, she stopped, and a glance at her distorted face told him to expect trouble. He followed her gaze and saw Geoffrey Ames, surrounded by half a dozen Singapore beauties and autographing everything from a magazine to the front of one girl's blouse. And with her tube of lipstick.

Mason threw out his arm to block the irate woman's way, but she brushed past him, and he prayed she wouldn't commit one of the numerous crimes for which hanging was the penalty in the Singapore legal code.

"Don't ever come near me again," she told Geoffrey in a trembling voice, her hands planted firmly on her ample hips.

"Now, Lucy...Lucy, you don't mean that."

"Who doesn't mean it?" she fumed.

"He's so cute," one of the girls exclaimed, amidst a chorus of giggles.

"What?" Lucy glared at the happy old man, who seemed oblivious to her displeasure. "*Cute?* I've got your cute, Mr. Ames."

Mason stared in awe as she pranced off, stepping high as though leading a marching band. He couldn't help laughing at the unrepentant man, whose smile reached from ear to ear.

"We could have left you, Ames."

"I knew Lucy wouldn't let you," he said, still unperturbed. And still smiling. Mason wondered if the man's steps had a more youthful bounce than when he'd gotten off the plane.

"I see you and Miss Jeannetta been getting pretty close," Geoffrey confided.

"I was thinking the same about you and Miss Lucy," Mason rejoined.

"You planning wedding bells on board ship?" Geoffrey wanted to know.

Mason gawked. Had the man lost his mind?

"I just met her in March."

"Time's got nothing to do with it," a confident Geoffrey Ames replied. "When this tour's over, you'll go wherever she goes. Mark my word. Yes, sir. When a woman gets in your blood, she stays there. And there ain't nothing so miserable as having part of you one place and the other part somewhere else. Yep. You've been had."

He warmed up to his lecture, slowing his pace, though Mason had no doubt that the man knew they had a tight schedule.

"Yes, sir," Geoffrey went on. "In my day, romance was the step to marriage. You young people don't seem to understand your feelings, can't make a commitment. That's what a good marriage is—total commitment. The fires burn lower with time, and the hot coals die down. What's left is deep, abiding love. You don't think of yourself without her. She's you. You're happy when she's happy and miserable when she's sad. And if she leaves this world before you do, the best part of you goes with her. In my forty-six years of marriage, I never spent a night away from my Nettie. God rest her soul, and no more of the day than I had to in order to make a living for us—such as it was. And she was always there for me. I lot my job once. It wasn't much to start with—four hours every night cleaning rest rooms and floors in a bank building—but it kept us off of welfare. I got home and told her about it and said I didn't have a cent. She smiled and said, "It's a good thing I made pig's feet and hot potato salad for your supper. You always like that so much.' I never loved her as much as I did that minute. Miss Jeannetta is a simple person. Oh, she's smart and all that, but she don't have any of those airs that those sophisticated women have, otherwise she wouldn't a dressed up to eat dinner with an old man like me. She likes you a whole lot, son. I'd pay good attention to her if I was you."

They climbed on the bus, and Mason couldn't help laughing to himself; Lucy had seated herself with another passenger to foil Geoffrey's certain attempts at making amends.

"She's going to make you sweat," Mason told him.

"I can handle her," Geoffrey replied. "You're the one with the problem." He took the seat behind the driver and motioned Mason to join him.

Mason looked down the aisle. Maybeth had taken the seat beside Jeannetta, so he sat with Geoffrey.

"How're you going to manage? Miss Abernathy is furious with you."

Geoffrey gathered his pants legs up around the knee and made himself comfortable.

"Oh, she'd stay mad if I'd brought one of those beauties on

this bus, but I'm not crazy and she knows that. Take my advice and work on things with Miss Jeannetta. She's a diamond waiting to be polished.

"Don't lose any sleep over it," he advised the older man. "I'm dealing with it." He ignored Geoffrey's grunt of disbelief. His fingers wrapped around the keys that were his constant companions, and he leaned back in the seat and closed his eyes. He'd give anything to have a Nettie of his own. A woman who would smile at him when he told her he didn't know how or where he'd get her next meal. He turned to his seat companion.

"How long did you know your wife before you married her?"

Ames fingered his beard and a melancholy smile stole over his face. "Well, I asked her to marry me the first time I took her out. We went to see *Casablanca*. I'd already seen it, but she hadn't. Anyhow, she said yes, but it took two weeks to make the wedding dress. I declare I thought she'd never finish it. Every time I saw her, she needed another little piece of lace, more beads or something." Mason smiled as images of Jeannetta sewing beads on a lace wedding dress flitted through his mind. He'd bet that, like other modern women, she'd head for a good designer. Of course, professional women rarely had time to sew.

"You're quite a man," he told Geoffrey. "I'm glad I met you." It wouldn't hurt Ames to get a little of his own medicine, he decided and asked him, "What are you planning to do about Miss Abernathy? You going to cross this off as a vacation romance?"

"'Course, not," the man replied, a scowl marring his usually serene face. "I'm going to marry her as soon as I get back to Augusta. That's in Georgia, you know." Mason shut off what would have been a sharp whistle.

"But she's not from Georgia."

Geoffrey Ames's smug smile wasn't lost on Mason, and the man's self-confidence was even more evident when he replied, "No, but she soon will be."

Mason clicked on the mike. "First stop, Jurong Bird Park. Anyone who isn't back on this bus twenty minutes from now, get a taxi to the harbor; we'll be leaving on the Southern Queen at two o'clock." He moved so that Geoffrey could pass. With the tour members gone and the bus empty, he pulled the baseball cap he'd bought at the Istanbul airport over his eyes and slumped down in his seat, hoping for a twenty minute nap.

"Want some company?" He removed the cap and sat up.

"Everyone else went to the Park. Why didn't you go?" he asked Jeannetta. "I thought you'd be happy to see so many colorful birds. First time I went to Jurong, I could hardly believe my eyes." He slid into Geoffrey's seat so that she could sit beside him. He gaped when her hand went to her forehead as though to steady herself, but she smiled and sat down. He might have imagined it, he told himself. Hopefully.

"I would have, but I decided I'd rather use the opportunity to get rid of Maybeth. She'd a card. Of course, the possibility of having you all to myself wasn't easily ignored."

He raised both eyebrows. "Are you flirting with me?"

He thought her sudden interest in the floor, the top of her shoes, and her lap unusual, and a smile curled around his lips at the ingenuity she displayed in the art of finger twiddling. Might as well have a little fun. He tipped up her chin and held it until she looked at him. He winked.

"You were, weren't you?"

Hot shivers plowed through his chest when she bathed her bottom lip with her tongue and slanted him a sly grin.

"Why not? You're free, thirty-seven, and solvent, I believe is the way you put it. So I can have my way with you without getting into trouble with the law. Come here."

He sat forward. "Whoa, there," he cautioned. "Back on that plane, you implied that I ought to leave you alone, that nothing could come of this."

She slid toward him, positioned her head on the back of his seat, gazed up at him and let him see the warm welcome in her almond-shaped eyes.

"That was before I saw you wearing this silly cap."

He tried to ignore the dark, lusty hue of her voice. If he could hold out for another twelve minutes, the tour members would return and they'd have company, but he couldn't help responding to her. He'd sized her up as a woman who could and would hold her own, but he hadn't though her aggressive. Her jaw muscles twitched, his belly flexed, and he knew what would come next; the painful stirring in his groin jolted him, and he stared down at her. Her eyelids fluttered as if weakened by a powerful light, and she licked her lips.

"Come here, Mason." Longing replaced the welcome in her dark eyes.

"Baby, don't play with me."

"I've never played with you. I may change my tune, but I can't change what I feel."

Air swished out of him. She had never asked him for himself. He wrapped her in his arms, and her soft fingers at the back of his head guided his mouth to hers with a force that he wouldn't have dared apply. Her parted lips sucked his tongue into her mouth, and her arched back pressed her breasts to his chest. God, he couldn't stand it. Wave after wave of hot currents tore through him when she released his tongue and plastered kisses over his face, neck, and ears, murmuring things that he couldn't understand. She attempted to straddle his lap, but he used what sense she'd left him with, cradled her in his arms, and rested her on his knee. She leaned forward, getting closer to him, and her thigh grazed his engorged center. He would have shifted her position, but she caressed his jaw and whispered in his ear: "Maybe I shouldn't have done this, but all of a sudden I needed to know you. Don't move. Please. At least, I can have this much of you."

If only the runaway train in his chest would stop its mad tumble. He took slower, deeper breaths. "What do you mean by that? Are you trying to tell me something?" The clamor of voices reached his ears, and he quickly shifted her to the seat beside him, stepped out of the bus and counted the tour members as they boarded. He didn't feel lighthearted, but he couldn't resist a laugh when Geoffrey arrived holding Lucy's hand.

\* \* \*

Jeannetta took a seat midway in the bus. She wanted to sit with Mason, to be close to him, but she didn't dare. *Are you trying to tell me something?* Subconsciously, she had been but, because of the poor timing, she'd been grateful when their companions returned. She couldn't figure out what had prompted her to abandon her self-control as she had done with Mason, but had never done with any other man. Oh, she loved him, but did loving him mean she'd change her personality?

She adored birds and had looked forward to visiting Jurong Bird Park, but when she'd stood to leave the bus, everything in it seemed to swirl around her. She'd managed to steady herself and to walk as far as Mason's seat at the front of the bus, but the sensation hit her again, and she'd sat down beside him, because she had no choice. She supposed the experience had made her reckless with him, because she'd thought at first that her time had about run out. His eyes had changed to that greenish-brown she'd come to recognize as his red flag, his signal to stop or be prepared to go all the way, but she hadn't broken it off. One more bill she knew she'd have to pay. He hadn't accused her of being a tease, but he'd warned her not to play with him. She closed her eyes to discourage Leonard Deek's conversation. Had she been right in thinking she should leave the tour and give up? She turned her head toward the window, seeking as much privacy as she could get, wondering whether she loved Mason so much that she'd voluntarily condemn herself to half a life rather than have him know that shed' deceived him. She took a tissue from her purse and blotted away the lone tear on her cheek. If only she hadn't fallen in love with him. *If.* What a useless thought. She sat up, looked at Leonard, and smiled.

"Did you enjoy the birds? I wish I'd gone, too," she said to the quiet Latin teacher.

"At least you were spared that hundred-degree heat; if you've seen one of these preserves, you've seen 'em all." He took out his pad and began making notes.

"I haven't seen one." He went back over his sentences, dotting the i's with little round circles, a practice she disliked.

"Really?" he asked, without looking up. "Well, you can always come back to see them next year."

She turned toward the window.

Mason checked the tour through immigration and onto the Southern Queen for the voyage to Bangkok, Thailand. He looked at his faithful Timex. Seven o'clock Saturday morning in New York. He found a telephone station and placed a call.

"Hello, Skip, this is Mason. I'm about to leave Singapore."

"Wait. Let me get up and get my map you gave me. Where's Singapore?" Mason couldn't help smiling. He found immense satisfaction in the boy's eagerness to learn, to succeed, and he'd vowed that he'd befriend him as long as he showed promise. He'd awakened the boy on a morning when he didn't have to get up early, and he hadn't objected.

"It's in Asia, Skip, and I don't have time for a geography lesson. How's your aunt Mabel doing?"

"What part of Asia?"

Mason laughed. Tenacity was as much a part of Skip as his dark skin and wooly hair.

"Southeast Asia. I said, how is Mabel?" He held his breath. Skip disliked talking about anything unpleasant. "Well?"

"She's in the hospital right now, but..."

"In the...*what?* Who's looking after you?"

"I've been with Steve, but she's coming home this afternoon, so I stayed overnight to clean up the place. Steve was here 'til ten last night. You having a good time?"

"I'm working, Skip, although it's pleasant work. I have to hang up, because I want to talk with Steve. Be sure and do as he tells you, and give my regards to Mabel." He hung up. What a thing to happen with twenty-five-hundred miles separating them. Even so exceptional a boy as Skip shouldn't have such responsibility at age twelve. He'd been lucky to have his brother Steve. He's resisted becoming involved with Skip, but the boy had adopted him and followed him around until he became a leech on his conscience. He didn't regret his decision to look after Skip and his struggling great-aunt, and he'd developed a deep fondness for the boy. He wrote Steven's number on a pad and handed it the operator.

"Sorry to get you up so early on Saturday, Steve, but I'm just shoving off to Thailand. What's wrong with Mabel?" He listened, a plan forming in his mind. "That's serious. Do you have time to look for a bachelor apartment in one of those nursing-care complexes? Ask my receptionist to help you."

"Mason, I know their apartment wouldn't win a prize, but it's theirs and, if she leaves that, they'll have nothing."

"From what you told me, I know she won't recover and, unless I do something, Skip will spend the next couple of years taking care of her. I don't want to see his potential wasted."

"What'll you do with him?"

Mason didn't hesitate, because he knew it was right. "He can live with me. That's what he wants to do, anyway. Check the hospital. Get an ambulance to take Mabel home, and give her enough money to last them until I get back. Thanks for looking after Skip.

"He's taken to calling me Uncle Steve. You wouldn't expect me to neglect my nephew, would you?" Steve had said it jokingly, but the thought stayed with Mason.

He looked over the list of boarded passengers once more to make certain none of his tour members had stayed behind. Maybeth had been the first on board, followed by Deek. The woman toyed with the little man, but he tailed her wherever she went. He'd said he was on sabbatical, a year's leave for research, but what kind of research would a professor of Latin do on this tour? He wondered how many of them had lied about their reasons for taking the trip. He walked up the gangplank and looked back at the soaring buildings in Asia's most modern city. He'd left something of himself in that city, on that bus, something he knew he'd never regain. His ability to walk away from her had died there.

# Chapter 5

Jeannetta looked around her comfortable stateroom, pleased with the soft, feminine decor and glad the decorator hadn't liked wild colors. She had decided not to splurge on first class and was glad; her cabin-class quarters offered as much elegance as she needed. Light filtered through the windows, and she moved a chair in order to look out of one. Passengers strolled the deck, and large gray birds dived off the thick wooden planks at the edge of the water, caught unlucky fish, and flew away. Was everything on earth a predator, including herself? She unpacked, found an iron and ironing board in a closet, and pressed a few items of clothing. Restlessness hung on her like a heavy weight, and she knew its source. Pretending an airiness she didn't feel, she donned a pair of white slacks, a yellow T-shirt, and socks and white canvas shoes, but got only as far as the door before turning around. She had to do something about Mason, had to find a way to talk with him about herself; four weeks, and she hadn't found an appropriate occasion. Pricked by her conscience, she admitted that he'd given her a good chance on the bus, and that she'd used a handy excuse to forfeit the opportunity. Though she knew she was responsible for her predicament with Mason, anger seethed within her, and she couldn't help feeling hostile toward him for withholding his precious skills from desperate people.

Determined to find a way, she left the room and strolled down the deck. The fresh, salty air enlivened her as she walked along, greeting tour members and other passengers. She stretched out in a deck chair and watched the Singapore skyline, waiting for the ship to pull anchor and head out to sea. A tall man of indeterminate age and race walked over to her.

"I'm Rolfe Merchinson." He extended his hand and waited for an invitation to sit with her. "Would you join me for a drink?"

She shook hands; not to have done so would have been out of character for her, but she refused his offer.

"Thank you, but I rarely drink."

"Why not make this one of your exceptions?" he asked with the practiced smoothness of a worldly sophisticate. She picked up the magazine that she'd brought along for the purpose of discouraging unwanted acquaintances, glanced at it, and replied.

"I'm alone here, but I'm not by myself on this ship."

"You're with someone?"

She nodded.

Rolfe Merchinson straightened up, bowed briefly, and told her, "That is a pity. The gentleman is a lucky man, indeed."

She glanced up as Mason approached, slowed his steps, nodded, and kept walking.

"Excuse me."

She reached the bottom of the wide curving staircase just as Mason stopped and looked back as though to confirm what he'd seen. Not a smart move, she told herself. But she hadn't wanted Mason to think that, forty minutes after boarding ship, she'd struck up an acquaintance with a strange man. Rolfe Whatever-His-Name might have been nice enough, but she didn't play games with men, and she didn't want Mason to think her easy pickings. She slowed her steps in the hope that she wouldn't catch him, but he waited.

"Settled in okay?"

She nodded. "My stateroom's super; couldn't ask for better."

A smile enveloped his whole face, and the warmth in his eyes seemed to caress her. Even his stern top lip had relaxed. She detected a difference in him, a softness, a strange tenderness. Maybe now was a good time to lead him to thoughts of medicine.

"How's your patient?"

"She's..." His eyes widened, his lower lip dropped for a

second and, as though he'd programmed himself to do it, he looked over his shoulder. Something akin to anger flashed in his eyes. She'd have to brazen it out.

"Is she alright? I wondered why you had to stay with her so long last night if she only had indigestion."

"Jeannetta, Lydia isn't my patient. I don't have patients. She's a senior citizen, and I was concerned about her health. Still am, for that matter." His gaze bore into her. Searching, Judging.

"What on earth did I say to bring on this furor?" she asked as she struggled to present him with a bland, innocent face.

"Nothing. But try to remember that travel managers don't have patients, we have customers. I've got a few things to attend to. Please excuse me."

She watched his long, broad back as he strode toward his stateroom.

"That sure didn't work," she told herself. "You're in trouble, kiddo; the longer you wait, the worse it'll be." He stopped before turning the corner and looked back at her, and she remembered that late, sun-shrouded afternoon in Paris when he'd wanted to turn the corner and, by the sheer power of her mind, she hadn't allowed it. His gaze sliced through her until she did the only thing that she could; she smiled and held out her hand to him. She half expected him to walk on, but he stood there. She took several steps toward him, his own pain searing her, for she at last knew that he lived with discomfort and unhappiness for having disclaimed his true self.

"Just like I'm pretending to be an ordinary tourist." She moved another three or four steps in his direction. She wasn't guiltless; *who was she to judge him?*

She took another step toward him, and his gaze didn't waver. For the first time, she could see vulnerability in him. She walked closer, and he took a short step toward her. Encouraged, she took another. His smile was a brilliant lamp, a symbolic beacon in the darkness, and she opened her arms wide and sped to him. Mason met her three-quarters of the way, swept her into his strong arms and twirled around with her before setting her on her feet.

"It wasn't my intention to be short with you; I don't know what got into me," he said.

She had to steady herself when his eyes, a black sea of adoration, caressed her, and his gentle fingers grasped hers in a wordless entreaty that she follow him. He led them to his stateroom nearby, entered, and, before his portfolio hit the floor, he had her in his arms. She raised her lips but, even in her frantic eagerness to drown in him, she had the sense that he deliberately prolonged the tension, as though starving himself before a feast. His voice, strangely dark, dusty, and littered with the cobwebs of his unhappiness, penetrated her understanding, and tendrils of fear shot through her as she realized the responsibility of sharing his vulnerability. Open honesty had replaced his poker face.

"Look at me, Jeannetta. We're alone now. We're not in a public place, a bus. Put your arms around me and kiss me."

Her wide-eyed gaze searched his face for an answer to the change in him.

He stroked her cheek. "Kiss me. I...I need you."

A bolt of heady sensation shot through her, and she curled into him, wanting, needing to heal him. Desperate to belong to him. Her right hand grasped the back of his head, and she raised parted lips to his. It seemed light years before his mouth sent flames of passion roaring through her body. She felt the tremors that shook his big frame when she pulled his tongue into her mouth and sucked it. Emboldened, she slid her leg between his, and shuddered at the force of his arousal against her thigh. His hoarse groan stripped her of what reticence she had left, and her hand went to his buttocks and pulled his arousal tighter against her thigh. Frustrated with longing to hold him inside of her, she tugged at his belt buckle, but he pulled his mouth from hers and whispered, his voice harsh.

"Honey, do you know what you're doing?"

She couldn't hear his words for the thundering desire that roared in her head, numbing her to everything but her ravenous craving for him. Her hips rolled wildly, out of control, and his fingers grasped them and held her still.

"I need you worse that I need to breathe, but I have to know where this is go…"

The sharp buzz of his beeper brought them both to the reality of what they were about to do. He released her body and answered, though he continued to possess her with his fiery gaze.

"Fenwick speaking." He listened for a second and flipped off the beeper. "That was the first mate," he explained. "The ship's about to leave harbor, and cocktails will be served immediately."

The ship's bellow confirmed their departure. Mason moved back a step, though he held her hand firmly in his own. He hadn't known himself capable of such burning passion, such a powerful, humbling need. He had to go somewhere and deal with his feelings. Was this the woman with whom he'd share his life? How could he know? She hadn't levelled with him. *"Nor you with her,"* his conscience needled.

"I guess we can be glad you're wearing that beeper."

"Speak for yourself, honey. As far as I'm concerned, that was the same as being awakened from a deep sleep and routed out of your house in the dead of winter because the place is on fire." She leaned her head against his chest, and he locked her in his arms.

"I want you to sit quietly and decide what you want from me. Whatever it is, be honest with yourself. I've had my last take-care-of-your-needs kind of relationship. I deserve more, and I'm prepared to wait until I find it. I don't doubt that, if we hadn't been interrupted, we'd be lovers right now, and I'm also sure that both of us would have had second thoughts afterwards." He glanced at his watch. "I have to check on Lydia. I didn't like the look of her when she boarded. When we get to Bangkok, I may send her home. It would be a pity, though, because she wanted so badly to make this trip."

"Has she told you the truth about her health?"

He looked closely at her, certain that her voice had wavered.

"I doubt it; truth isn't too popular these days." The tightening of her fingers in his hand told him more than she knew. "But we'll settle it in Bangkok, if not before." His words held an ominous ring for him; a dark prophesy reverberating in his head. He gazed down at her in wonder that she could induce such a mood in him.

"I hope you don't have to send her home."

He shook his head. He'd told her to face what was happening between them, and she'd managed to skirt the issue. Did she think he didn't know that? She had discouraged him, but she'd also set him on fire and, on at least two occasions, she'd been deliberate about it. He grinned down at her, though he took pains to shut off his emotions.

"When we were on the plane to Singapore, you asked me if I planned to kiss you anymore. You may or may not have been serious, but, I assure you, if you get your ducks in a straight row, I'll kiss you every time I get the chance."

Her eyelids fluttered downward, and he tipped up her chin with his left index finger.

"What's the matter, you don't like the idea?"

She gave him a quick peck on the cheek and started for the door. "Don't we have to dress for dinner?"

He nodded, and she blew him a kiss and walked out. He smiled, a satisfied male reflex at the shakiness of her steps after their passionate exchange, until the doctor in him doubted kisses could make a person stagger.

He showered quickly, and changed into white shirt, white linen jacket, and navy slacks. Black shoes, red tie, and handkerchief completed his outfit. He left his room thinking how much simpler a surgeon's green cotton garb was than the stylish clothes he had to wear as a travel manager. He strolled along the deck, letting the fresh salty wind invigorate him, but an unsettled feeling stirred in him. He paused and propped his foot against the rail, stared out at the dark sky above him, and the South China Sea all around him, black but for the whitecaps of the rough water. So much like his life. He'd opened his soul to her, shamelessly let her see into him, into his heart. She had responded with a passion that he hadn't previously known, but she hadn't offered her trust, her truth, the person inside of her. Could he turn back? He didn't think so, but she didn't have to know that.

He shook off the mood, walked into the cocktail lounge, ordered a vodka and tonic, and leaned against the grand piano, his gaze glued to the door. She stopped in the doorway of the lounge and looked around, a vision in a red sleeveless sheath that defined a perfect feminine silhouette. Breath hissed out of his lungs when she saw him and a smile claimed her face. His passion steamed as though hot coals simmered in his blood, and the innocent undulations of her rhythmic movements triggered his desire as she glided to him. Damn. He tossed his drink to the back of his throat, and his fingers squeezed his parents' door keys that were always in his pants pocket. He didn't go to meet her. He waited.

"Hi. I hope you haven't waited long."

He shrugged. "Hi. I've accepted that you have a problem with time."

"I know. I'm sorry."

He couldn't help smiling. She didn't ask to be forgiven, because she knew she'd do it again. He let his gaze roam over her lovely form.

"My pleasure. You were well worth the wait. What would you like?" He touched her elbow and headed them toward the bar.

"Some of those stone-crab claws," she said, pointing to one of the many small tables laden with finger food.

"I meant, to drink."

"Mason, I don't drink anymore." Immediately she wished she hadn't said those telltale words, for both of his eyebrows shot upward.

"Anymore? Why did you stop?" Here was her chance, the perfect opportunity, and she couldn't summon the courage to tell him.

"Prudence."

He lifted another glass of vodka and tonic from the tray of a passing waiter and raised it to her in a salute.

"Prudence, eh?" A cynical smile flashed over his handsome face. "Well, here's to Prudence, whoever the hell she is."

Stunned, she gaped when he tossed the drink to the back of his throat. He grasped her hand, and her heart thudded beneath her breast as he stared down at her with mocking eyes.

"Beautiful. Innocent. Vulnerable. When such a woman lies, it's as though she's smeared grease paint on pristine snow. My table is number twenty. Care to join me?"

She wanted to be with him, but his mood gave her a sense of imminent trouble. She tried unsuccessfully to push back the dark feeling, to banish the intuitive notion that the piper wanted his due. She walked beside him to his table.

"I don't think I like you when you're drinking," she told him.

"Oh, you probably like me as much then as I like you when you lie." She stopped walking, laid back her shoulders and glared at him.

"If you'd rather have someone else' company…"

He guided her along, an enigmatic smile playing around his lips.

"On the contrary, my darling, you've pinpointed my problem. I've discovered that I don't want anyone's company but yours, and that's bad news."

"For whom?"

She couldn't say he'd been rude, but he'd certainly set aside his usual politeness. He looked deeply into her eyes until she shifted her gaze.

"Since you won't level with me, it's bad news for me, wouldn't you say?'

Mason stared, horrified, as she took a glass of tonic from a waiter's tray, only to have it slip through her fingers, as though she lacked the ability to grasp it. After the waiter cleaned the liquid from her shoes and off the floor, Mason led her to his table, held her chair, and seated himself beside her. He'd lost his taste for food, but he knew that, if he didn't eat, she'd know that her accident worried him. He smiled at their dinner companions, reached in her lap and gathered her right hand in his left one, but he couldn't banish the ache in the pit of his stomach. Gloom hovered around him when he let himself think of the horror that her syndrome of ailments suggested. It couldn't be true.

"How's your stateroom?" he asked Lucy Abernathy. Geoffrey had had it changed from tourist class to first class. She smiled up at him and told Mason it was the most beautiful room she'd ever seen.

"You come have breakfast with me tomorrow morning, you hear?"

At Mason's raised eyebrow, she informed her companions that her suite had a dinette as well as a living room.

"She's scared of the water." Geoffrey explained, "and I wanted her to enjoy this trip."

"I'm afraid of the water, too," Maybeth chimed in, "and I'm sure I saw a shark swim past my porthole." She and Lucy were the two tour members who had paid tourist class rates for the sea portion of the tour.

"Keep the window closed," Leonard Deek advised her, to everyone's amazement.

Maybeth gave him a withering look. "Do you think the people who made this ship were crazy? There's no window down there. I'd have to break open that porthole, and this ship might sink. Tourist class is below water level."

The laugher that followed lightened Mason's mood a little, and he glanced at Jeannetta.

"What about you? You scared of water, too?"

Several in the group twittered softly. He leaned over and whispered in Jeannetta's ear.

"What?" she asked.

"I said Leonard Deek must sit on his brains. Of course, he isn't the first bottom-heavy professor I've met. My freshman English prof fit that description, but her ancestors were probably Hottentots." Her hearty giggle was what he'd hoped his exaggeration would accomplish, and he managed to eat the remainder of what would ordinarily have been a wonderful meal, though his anxiety about Jeannetta had ruined any chance of his enjoying it. He looked around the table.

"I apologize for whispering, but I couldn't resist needling Jeannetta."

Geoffrey eyed him carefully, and he'd have given a few Thailand bahts to read the man's mind. For an uneducated person, he possessed a store of knowledge and wisdom. He hoped they would remain friends. He leaned toward Jeannetta.

"Walk with me a little?"

She smiled, but it bore no relation to the hearty laughter and happy grins that he'd grown to love. He held her hand as they left the dining room and, when they passed a florist, he tugged at her hand.

"I want to go in here."

She looked at him inquiringly, but didn't ask his motive. He hoped the starch hadn't gone out of her. If it had, he reflected, though he'd rather the thought hadn't arisen, it would mean that she'd know all along that she had a problem and what it was. If so, her condition could be more serious than he thought. He bought a red-tipped yellow rose and handed it to her, testing her. She reached for it, but failed to touch it. He pretended not to notice, but he no longer doubted that she had a problem with her peripheral vision.

"Would you like to see the floor show?" he asked her.

"Should be fun. Why not? I don't care to go to the casino, and I'm not a good bridge player."

He splayed his fingers at her waist and guided her back to their table. The floor show held little interest for him, but it would give him an opportunity to observe her closely without her knowing it. He helped himself to a snifter of fine VSOP cognac when the waiter offered it, and watched anxiously as she eyed it longingly, shook her head, and settled for a cranberry rickey.

Jeannetta tried to concentrate on the show and to ignore Mason's intense scrutiny. Her furtive glances didn't tell her whether his gazes were of admiration or curiosity. Maybe she'd fooled him but, if she had, he couldn't be much of a specialist; she'd shown every symptom in his presence except fainting, and she'd nearly done that twice. She wanted to direct some inquiries toward his profession, to prompt the right questions from him so she could give him the answer that she must. She'd had the chance twice, but the timing had been wrong. If she asked him about himself, he'd take that opportunity to begin delving into her life, and he'd tell her nothing about Mason Fenwick.

Billowing smoke and the reverberation of ancient brass striking brass gongs got her attention, and she watched a young belly dancer swish onto the stage and begin her monotonous, twirling undulations. Most of the crowd, particularly the men, found it entertaining for the first five minutes, but when minutes became half an hour, she noted with satisfaction that the Western men became bored. The Asian men sat in rapt attention.

"Are you enjoying this?" Mason asked her.

"Not as much as the different reactions, especially those of the men." She nodded toward an Asian at the next table. "He's really having a bang out of this. I don't get it."

Mason's smile, tender and intimate, warmed her heart. "He's not going home to a woman like you. If he were, he'd be as bored as I am."

The words had barely left his tongue when the belly dancer plopped into his lap. His gawk brought a laugh from Jeannetta, and she marveled that he sat without touching the woman, without showing a smile or a grimace, or indicating in any other way his reaction to her impertinence. The dancer managed to move, after her cool reception but, Jeannetta noticed her smile became real when she saw the tip her gave her.

An orchestra reminiscent of 1940s bands began to play, and couples flocked to the dance floor. She felt cherished when he held her hand and adored her with his mesmerizing black eyes, and she didn't know whether to feel hurt when he didn't ask her to dance.

"Mason, I hope you don't mind if I take this lady for a spin around the floor," Geoffrey said, though he didn't wait for a reply before extending his hand to Jeannetta.

Mason grinned, shrugged elaborately, and replied, "A man doesn't have the right to give another permission to put his arms around a woman and dance with her, not even if that woman is his wife."

Geoffrey, who by then held her hand, retorted, "Sorry, I must've thought I was talking to a man of my own age. I forgot chivalry's expiring with my generation."

Mason glared at him, but whatever he'd planned to say would probably have been an anticlimax, Jeannetta decided, when Lucy Abernathy walked over to her and bowed.

"Jeannetta," the woman said in a soft voice, "do you mind if I have this dance with Mr. Fenwick?"

She'd never danced with Mason, but that didn't matter. Lucy had provided the brightest spot of the evening, and she intended to enjoy it.

"Of course I don't mind, Miss Abernathy, but I wouldn't get into those fast dances with him if I were you; you'd have to watch your toes, and he wears a size eleven." The sounds of Mason clearing his throat and of Geoffrey's down-home laugh emboldened her, and she risked a glance at Mason. He'd taken Lucy's hand, but she could all but feel the hot sparks that blazed in his eyes. She nudged Geoffrey onto the dance floor; she hadn't seen Mason lose his temper, but she suspected he soon would.

"Now, Miss Jeannetta, something tells me you went a mite too far with your teasing. 'Course I aim to speak to Lucy about her manners, too."

"You dance a mean fox-trot," she complimented, and added, "Miss Abernathy showed the two of you the ridiculousness of the whole business. She carved a permanent place in my heart when she did that."

"It's no use trying to understand women," he huffed. "They want you to love 'em and cherish 'em, but if you try to protect 'em, they throw a fit. Don't y'all know it's one and the same to a man?" The fox-trot ended, but the band started a rhumba, and Geoffrey hardly missed a beat before he swung into it.

"You're a wonderful dancer," she told him.

"Thanks. My Nettie loved to dance, and she taught me. That's what we did on Saturday nights. This is the first chance I've had to dance since she left me. Now, she was some dancer, but you're a fine dance partner yourself." They walked back to the table, and Mason stood as they approached. He nodded to Geoffrey, and Jeannetta felt herself flush warmly at his intimate look.

"I expected to get drenched from these sprinklers," he told her, gesturing to the red cylinders lodged high above in the ceiling. "You and Geoffrey put on quite a show out there with that rhumba. I'll have to stop by some of those nightclubs next time I'm in Augusta." He glanced upward again.

"Out where I lived, we didn't go to clubs," Geoffrey corrected. "We went to dance halls."

"And I don't remember having set a boat or any other place afire," Jeannetta told them, "although I may have steamed up a few rooms." They sat down, and she shifted her gaze from Mason's rapt stare to his long, thin fingers, dark brown against the starched white linen cloth on which he strummed rhythmically. He leaned back in his chair and looked at Lucy Abernathy.

"I thought we were talking about dancing, didn't you?" Mason asked Lucy.

Jeannetta couldn't help marveling at the changes in the woman in one month. Maybe love wrought miracles.

"They're both of them showing off," she heard Lucy say, and it occurred to Jeannetta that she wouldn't have had the courage to utter such a remark as recently as a month earlier.

"Not me; I don't show off. I do what comes naturally," Jeannetta said, as she dared him with her eyes to take it any further.

"We're still talking about dancing, I presume," Mason said, mainly to Jeannetta. A slow smile played around his lips. "What comes naturally is what I do best," he parroted her.

"Stick to claims that can be verified," she challenged, and her pulse accelerated as she watched his eye color change in seconds from black to that brownish-green that made saliva pool in her mouth. He stuck his hands in his pants pockets, rocked back in his chair, and fixed her with his hot gaze, desire vibrating from him like atomic waves. She glanced nervously toward their two companions, a part of her wanting to be rescued, and the other part wanting to test him. Lucy and Geoffrey had left. Embarrassment suffused her when she thought of what they might have witnessed. She made herself look at Mason, and saw that the heat hadn't diminished—that, if anything, it had intensified.

"Do you want to eat those words now? Or later?" he asked, accepting the dare. With so many people around, what did she have to fear? She leaned back, as he did, and refused to hide the effect that his drugging masculinity had on her. If he could singe her with part of a table between them and a room full of people all around them, how soon would he have her rocketing to Heaven once he got her clothes off? What a man! He brought his chair upright and leaned forward, his chiseled brown face harsh and unsmiling.

"Well?"

She decided to bluff. "Can't say offhand. I'll have to think about it. I don't remember having tasted my words."

"Jeannetta. You're playing with fire. You're... What the devil?"

The slight sensation passed, and she managed a smile. "I got a headache all of a sudden. I'm not trying to get out of anything; I really did." She tried to avoid pressing her hand to her forehead. Immediately, he came to her.

"Come on. I'll walk with you to your room." He draped an arm around her, and his fingers lovingly cradled her to his side.

"Where're we going?" she asked, when he walked them past the staircase.

"We'll take the elevator." She had intended to discourage intimacy when they reached her room, but he didn't offer it. Instead, he opened her door, brushed her forehead with his lips and admonished her, "Call me, if you need me. Don't hesitate. You understand?" She wondered at the expression of deep concern that marred his handsome face.

"I will. I promise." She let her hand dust his cheek, forced a smile, and closed the door.

She tossed her evening bag on the bed, kicked off the red satin shoes, and sat down. Geoffrey had nearly worn her out with his fast, sexy rhumba; she'd have to avoid spinning around like that, but it had been such fun. Thoughts of the heat in Mason's eyes when she'd returned to their table sent her blood racing, and she hugged herself. After taking a couple of aspirin, she unzipped her dress and stepped out of it.

*His fingers feathered down her arms, eased over her back, unsnapped her bra and freed her round, tight breasts for his pleasure. She threw back her head as his lips possessed first one and then the other until her knees buckled, and she cried out. "Oh, Mason. I need you so. If only you knew!"*

She looked around, almost expecting to see him there beside her. The experience, the pleasure had seemed so real. She sat on the edge of the bed and let the steady sloshing of the waves calm her. Her headache eased, and she walked to her window and looked down at the deck. The moon had drifted from behind the clouds, and she could see a woman, her chiffon dress billowing in the southern wind, reach up to the man beside her as he gathered her in his arms and kissed her.

A dull ache of longing coiled in her breast when the man lifted the woman and carried her until she could see them no longer. She walked back to the bed and looked at her tape recorder. Suddenly, she kicked her shoes across the room and slammed her fist against the mattress. Why her? Why, now that she knew at last what it was to love a man, to want him and to yearn for his children beneath her breast…why this? Why couldn't she be open with him, share her dreams and fears with him? Why couldn't she reveal herself and level with this strong, caring man? The telephone interrupted her reverie.

"Hello?"

"Hi. You alright now?" His low, husky voice wrapped around her, settling her.

"I'm fine. I looked out a minute ago. It's so beautiful out there; nothing but moonlight, sky and waves as far as I could see, and not a man-made thing in sight. It's unbelievable."

His silence unnerved her.

"I take it your headache's gone."

"No, but it eased. Where are you?" Did he want to come to

her? Still raw and vulnerable after that spooky experience a few minutes earlier with what she'd only imagined, she didn't know how she'd feel about that.

"In my room. I wanted to know how you were before I turned in. Would you care to join me tomorrow morning around six-thirty to see the sunrise? A view from this boat in this part of the world can't be matched. How about it?"

"Six-thirty?" She knew he could hear her groan.

"Okay."

His laugh, warm, deep, and rich, floated to her through the wires, thrilling her. "Who'd have thought you were mush-brained in the mornings? Six o'clock air is good for you. I'll call you at five-fifteen and knock on your door at five minutes to six."

"You're a cruel, heartless man. You'll do that, and I'll have no way to get even."

"Sure you have. Tomorrow evening, you'll tell me goodnight and close your door."

"What?"

"That's exactly what you'll do," he said dryly, "instead of kissing me goodnight, reaching over and turning out the light. Hmmm?"

"I was way ahead of you, if you remember an evening some-where between Vienna and Istanbul, Mr. Fenwick. Don't tell me you've changed your tour rules," she baited.

"You and I are the only tour members on this corridor."

"What does that have to do with your rules? I accommodated myself to them, because I figured a man of lofty principles such as you wouldn't demand more of his charges than of himself. And I'm right, aren't I?" She didn't want to vex him, but she didn't want him in her room. If he crossed that threshold tonight, she wouldn't let him out of her sight until she'd drained him of every bit of energy. And she'd have the rest of her life to pay for it.

"I see. So what kind of relationship do you think we should have? Before you answer, keep in mind everything that's happened between us since we met, and include what you wanted to happen that didn't."

Keep it light, she told herself, wishing she could see the wick-edness in his wonderful obsidian eyes.

"Let's see," she stalled. "How about a nice warm friendship?"

"That's it?"

"Yes. Good friends. That's what I want for us."

"Hmm. I'll bet. See you in the morning. Sleep well."

She remembered that she hadn't spoken with her sister in several days, and telephoned her. It amazed her that, in seconds, she could speak with someone half a world away and hear that person as clearly as though she were in the next room.

"Rollins Hideaway. Laura speaking."

"Hi, sis. How's everything there?"

"Jeanny. Bless you, honey. I've been worried about you, since you didn't call. Where are you now?" Jeannetta brought her up to date.

"What about him? Have you mentioned it to him yet? What did he say?"

She expected the questions, and she had no choice but to tell Laura the truth.

"I'm having a hard time with this, Laura, because I've fallen in love with him, and I don't know how to bring it up without his thinking I've been leading him on just to obligate him." She was glad of the distance between them. When Laura got comfortable on her soap box, she could preach for hours, non-stop.

"You're not serious. Do you know what you're risking? You give me his name and phone number; I can ask him. You watch what you do off there in the middle of nowhere, and for heaven's sake keep that man out of your room. You girls nowadays don't have a crumb of sense. If it was me, I'd have asked him before that plane left JFK."

"If you're worried about my getting pregnant, forget it," Jeannetta told her. "One of my symptoms is amenorrhea—"

"What's that?"

"No monthly period."

"Well, there're other reasons for you to stay away from him. I sometimes wonder if there's a thirty-year-old single woman in this country who's still a virgin."

Jeannetta laughed. "I sure hope not."

"Jeannetta Rollins, shame on you. It's a pity what this world's come to."

"I'll call you in a couple of days. Go out and have some fun."

"You grab that man and tell him your problem, you hear. Take care of yourself, now."

Jeannetta mused over their conversation. In some respects, her sister took conservatism to the extreme. How could a normal woman be content to live a whole life and die without having loved a man? It occurred to her that her sister might be smarter than she. Laura wouldn't have gotten into the mess she'd made with Mason.

The sloshing of the waves had a bluesy rhythm, and she hummed along. Her good mood partly restored, she took out her recorder and began describing the evening's events. Recalling Mason's phone call and their conversation made her choke up, but she pushed back the tears. She tossed the recorder into a chair, slapped her fist into her right palm and got up. Just standing felt good. She'd do something; she *had* to. She'd never been one passively to accept whatever came her way, and she wouldn't do it now. She grimaced as she passed the mirror. With her life depending on Mason's help, why had she chosen this occasion to behave as though she was merely doing research for one of her novels?" "This is your life, girl," she repeated to herself, "and you'd better shape up." She'd tell him, and she'd do it before the ship docked in Thailand.

She stopped pacing the floor, crawled into bed, and turned out the light. Darkness flooded the room, and the vision of him all over her, around her, caressing her, making passionate love to her assaulted her senses. She sat up. When she told him everything, he wouldn't believe that she loved him, and even if she got her life back, she'd lose her heart's desire.

For the nth time, Mason looked at his watch and wrestled with sleep, longing for daylight. Disgusted, he stripped the sheet from his body, walked over to the window, and gazed out at the clouds that raced over the full moon. He found no comfort in it.

If he had the answer to one question, he'd know the nature of Jeannetta's problem. But if he asked her anything so intimate, he'd have to give a reason and, unless he told her that his concern was professional, she'd have every right to consider him auda-cious. But if he told her that, he'd have to tell her everything, and he wasn't prepared to do it. That life was behind him, and he intended to leave it there.

He showered, dressed in white slacks and a white T-shirt, slipped on white sneakers and went down to the ship's galley, where he got two large containers of coffee and some doughnuts. Then he bought a red rose from the florist and returned to his room. He stashed the coffee in a thermal bag and phoned Jeannetta.

"Who's this?"

"Mason. We've got a date in half an hour, remember?"

"You're making this up. What time is it?"

"Five-sixteen."

"In the afternoon?"

He laughed. One of these days he was going to roll her over on her back and love her until she was full awake.

"You promised to see the sunrise with me, so get up, unless you want everybody on this ship to hear me banging on your door."

"You wouldn't."

"You don't have any proof of that, so you'd better play it safe and get up. Want me to get a passkey and join you?"

"Alright. Alright. I'm getting up. You're a hard man, Fenwick."

He wondered at her wistful manner when she opened the door, until she asked him, "Would the captain really have given you the key to my room ?"

"Not in a million years, but I figured you were too sleepy to question it. Come one, let's get a good spot on deck." He let his gaze roam quickly over her and breathed deeply when he didn't detect outward signs of illness. She had her normal color, clear eyes, and steady gait.

"How're you feeling?"

"I'm fine. A couple of aspirin took care of my headache."

He relaxed. Maybe he'd been concerned without cause. "In

that case, I could have kissed you good morning." He shoved two chairs close together, and they sat facing the sea. He removed the lids from the containers of coffee and gave her one, and she closed her eyes, sniffed the familiar aroma, and smiled her delight. He didn't remember deriving so much joy from giving a woman a simple pleasure. He reached into the thermal bag, took out the rose and handed it to her. She'd never know how he prayed that she wouldn't drop it.

"Lean over here," she commanded. "This level of sweetness deserves a hug."

He accepted her quick caress, and held his tongue when he wanted to tell her that he'd like to have more, that he needed a steady diet of her. Instead, he said, "I was hoping for something more substantial." But he didn't look at her, because he knew she'd see in his eyes what his lips had wanted to say. He passed her one of the doughnuts.

"Here. Try this." For two cents, he'd take her in his arms and...

"Oh, Mason, look!" He let his gaze follow her line of vision. Red, gray, pink, and purple images greeted him from above, like multi-hued mountains resting amid the clouds. Red and blue shadows hovered over the sea, painting the shallow waves, and the sun began its slow, upward climb.

"It's breathtaking," she exclaimed. He stopped looking at the awesome display and turned to watch her, stunned by the longing that he'd heard in her voice. Something wasn't right. Half an hour later, with the spectacle over and nature busy clouding up the sky, he walked her back to her room.

"I wouldn't have missed that sight for anything, but if you hadn't dragged me out, I'd never have seen it. I can't thank you enough."

"The pleasure was mine. Coming down for breakfast?"

She shook her head. "I'd better work on my book."

He nodded.

"Lunch, then. I have to check on Lydia, and keep the rest of the gang happy. If you need me, here's my beeper number." He wrote it on the back of his business card, brushed her cheek with his lips and left her at her door, certain that she'd get her recorder the minute she walked in that room.

Seven-thirty. That made it about eight o'clock in the evening back home. He dialed Skip's number.

"I'm glad to see you're home," he said, when he heard the boy's voice. The possibility of losing the child to the streets was never far from his thoughts, because the boy's surroundings offered every conceivable opportunity for criminal behavior.

"Hi, Mason. 'Course I'm here. I do like you said. Besides, Uncle Steve's already ringing me when I get in from school. Man, he don't give me breathing room."

Mason didn't bother to hide his amusement.

"*Uncle* Steve?"

"Yeah. He said he's old enough to be my father, and he wants some respect. It was that, or call him mister." Mason laughed.

"What's wrong with calling him mister?"

"No, man. It's real second-grade stuff. I'm almost thirteen. You know that."

"Hmmm." He fingered the keys in his right pants pocket. He'd have to put some bricks under Skip while he could still make a difference. "How's Mabel?"

"Doing pretty good. She's sitting up watching television, and she can get to the bathroom. I don't know what I'd do, Mason, if she couldn't bathe herself. Uncle Steve brought me a big pan of his lasagna, a gang of baked sweet potatoes, half of a ham and a pot of collards for the next three or four days. I didn't tell you he put a freezer chest in here, did I? He's real cool. Wait a minute, and I'll let you speak to Aunt Mabel."

"How are you, Mabel?" He'd barely heard her weak hello.

"I'm better, and I feel pretty good. I don't know how to thank you and..." He cut her off.

"Don't thank us, Mabel. Skip adopted us, and we look after our family. Simple as that. If you have any problems before I get back, tell Skip to call Steve. How's the boy doing?"

"Wonderful. I couldn't ask for more of him, and I have you to thank for that, too."

"Put him on. How many classes are you taking this summer, Skip?"

"Three. Geography, something called Chaucer, and English. You know anything about a guy named Booker. T. Washington? I have read his biography."

"Of course I know about him." He thought for a minute. "Skip, why are you in summer school? Your grades are outstanding."

"I didn't want to hang out, so I figured if I was in school, the guys around here wouldn't expect me to."

"Good thinking. When I get back, we'll see some Broadway shows, maybe even go up to Stratford to the Shakespeare Theater."

"Wow! Broadway? Cool! But Shakespeare, man. I think I'd rather take cod liver oil."

Mason laughed. "Cod liver oil's good for you. I'll call you in a few days."

"Say, don't hang up. You didn't tell me where you are right now."

"I'm on a boat in the South China Sea headed for Thailand. That's in Southeast Asia. Okay?"

"Yeah. Gee whiz. I think I'll be a travel manager."

Jeannetta skipped breakfast and, on an impulse, ordered lunch in her room. The handsome Thai waiter, who seemed little more than a boy, served her lemon grass soup, shrimp salad, and assorted tropical fruits, bowed, and asked, "Madam, why you not on deck? All Americans want suntan; everybody out but you, I bring ship doctor if you sick."

She smiled her thanks and showed him the door. No use explaining if his eyes didn't tell him that she didn't need a suntan. She answered the phone. At least she wouldn't have to explain to any of her tour-mates why she hadn't oiled her body and stretched out practically nude to get a suntan. Most of them wouldn't be as dark as she if they sunbathed for a month.

"You okay?" She wondered if he could hear his voice. Low, husky, and sexy. Her temperature climbed up several degrees every time she heard it.

"I'm fine. Please go back to your sunbath."

"My what? Sunbath? You sure you're alright? I'm a moon person. I got enough sun one day recently in Istanbul to last a lifetime, while I waited for a missing female. What gave you that idea?"

She told him.

"Ignorance has its advantages," he said, when he could stop laughing. Her insides turned somersaults at the sound of his melodious merriment. Thank God, he didn't know how he got to her.

"Sure does," she managed to say. "Isn't it great that people in these countries look at you and don't think only of race?"

"Yeah. That's why I've been toying with the notion of bringing a young friend along next year. He'll be thirteen, a good age at which to learn this. Join me for happy hour?"

"Thanks, but I…I'd rather not. May run into you later."

"I don't like what I'm hearing. You began this tour spirited, eager to do and see everything, but, during the last couple of days, you've begun to fold up. I'm telling you again, that if you need me, I'm here for you. Meet me down in the green lounge or, if you don't feel up to dressing, throw on something and I'll go there. You're not alone. If you want to go home, my associate can fly to Bangkok and complete the tour, and I'll personally take you back to Pilgrim. Jeannetta, let me help you."

"You don't know what you're saying. If I thought you meant it… If I dared believe you…"

"Why shouldn't you believe me? And why can't you trust me?"

"Because I know you don't know what you're promising."

"Why do you insist in being mysterious? I've thought since we met that you're misrepresenting yourself." His voice had lost its gentleness. He spoke more rapidly, and his tone carried a harsh edge. She didn't feel the empathy he'd sent to her through the wires. She wanted him to hang up.

"Mason, I've been writing almost nonstop since you left me this morning, and I'm tired. For your information, I ordered lunch here in my stateroom. I have your beeper number and your room number. I'll be in touch."

But he persisted. "Why are you taking this tour? If you refuse to tell me, I may ask you to leave it."

"I've been as honest with you as you've been with me, so get off your high horse. Seconds earlier, you assured me that you're here for me, that I should trust you. Now, you're threatening to dump me in a strange country that doesn't even use the Roman alphabet, where I won't be able to read a word."

"My God, Jeannetta, you know I wouldn't. I only wanted to build a fire under you. I...I care about you, and I don't know who you are."

She suspected that he heard her deep sigh, for he added, "Alright, I'll stop pressuring you. I'll be in my room around six, if you'd like to have a drink then. Get some rest." He hung up, and she stretched out on the bed.

He didn't know who she was, but *she knew who he was,* and therein lay their problem. His threat had clarified for her both his dilemma and the measure of his frustration. She could see that he didn't tolerate well any disturbance of his scheme of things, of the way in which he'd ordered his life. She'd wanted to blurt it all out, but she wouldn't. She didn't doubt his strength; only a man capable of toughening himself to the dark potential of the unknown could walk away from success, wealth, and glamour as he had. But if she leaned on him, that brand-new castle he'd built could collapse all around him. If you loved a man, would you wreck his life? She didn't phone him.

A grand ball had been scheduled for their last evening on-board ship. Jeannetta dressed in a peach-colored chiffon evening dress, swept her hair up and secured it with an ivory comb, slipped into black satin slippers, picked up her black beaded bag, and paused before the mirror. A lot of décolletage, she thought, but since she wore no makeup, the effect ought to be prim enough. She grinned. Nothing prim about half of a size thirty-six C in full view. She found Lucy and Geoffrey leaning against the rail of the ship's leeward moonlit deck.

"Mr. Fenwick's in the lounge," the radiant woman informed Jeannetta.

"I expect they'll find each other when they get ready," Geoffrey said. "Trouble is they can't seem to focus on what counts."

Jeannetta laid her head to one side and looked at Geoffrey Ames. The casual observer would see a simple man and, in a sense, that's what he was. But he had depth and character and, at times, he could be intriguing. Like now.

"What do you mean, Geoffrey?" Jeannetta asked him. He rubbed his chin and looked skyward.

"It ain't something you can teach people. You and Mason got everything you need to be happy together, except what'll keep you that way. Even if I tell you, you won't understand; you'll have to experience it. If it comes, it comes; if it don't, it don't."

Jeannetta glanced toward the entrance to the lounge. Mason stood in the doorway, his gaze fixed on her. Light smoldered in his greenish brown eyes, betraying his desire, and the hungered look of a starving man replaced his poker face. Even the tilt of his shoulders emphasized his vulnerability to her. Her left hand sprung toward him involuntarily, and she had to force herself to stand there and not run to him. He must have realized from her reaction that he had exposed more than he'd have wanted, because he hooded his eyes, straightened up, and strolled toward them almost nonchalantly.

When he reached them, he smiled and nodded to her companions and stood silent, staring down at her. Uncertain or displeased: she couldn't figure out which. She hadn't called him as he'd asked, and she'd avoided the Green Lounge where he'd suggested they meet. She didn't want to encourage him more, because if he touched her they'd be lovers, and she had no idea what course she would eventually take. Ask him to repair her life and wreck his own? Risk his finding her deceitful and leaving her with a broken heart? Maybe… Could she have him for a little while? She lowered her gaze.

"You're a knock-out."

She jerked her head up.

"You are. So lovely. Beautiful. And it's all you." His gaze roamed over her, as though cataloguing her virtues, until she shivered in awareness. "I waited for you."

"I know. But we're getting too involved."

"You say that from time to time, Jeannetta, and then you forget about it. I thought the same, but now, I'm not so sure. Have dinner with me."

She turned. "Geoffrey, do you and... Where'd they go?"

"At least I had your attention. They walked off as soon as I greeted them." He looked out toward the sea. "Geoffrey's so certain that he and Lucy are right for each other. Wish I knew his formula for that."

She smiled. "Don't waste your time asking him. He'll tell you either you have it or you don't." The flashing lights announced the dinner hour, and he took her hand.

"Nothing's going to happen unless we both want it, Jeannetta, so let's relax and enjoy each other. You look wonderful, but how do you feel? Headache?"

"It didn't come back."

They sat at the captain's table along with Geoffrey, Lucy, and several people whom they didn't know. Mason passed the lobster Marnier through his teeth, tasted the real turtle bisque, the duck l'orange, saddle of veal, buttered parsley potatoes, steamed mélange of baby vegetables, and barely took his glance from her. He couldn't have remembered the selection of French cheeses, or the mixed green salad that followed, if he'd stood to lose a million. And he couldn't pretend an interest in the crème Courvoisier that the chef personally brought to the table. He finally had to admit to himself that the vision in peach who daintily tasted everything put before her was the woman he needed in his life. He had tired of worrying about the mystery that he sensed around her; he loved her, and he'd deal with whatever he faced because of it.

Soft. Elegant. Unassuming. How could she grow more beautiful right before his eyes? He hooded them and let himself enjoy watching her. Still so many unanswered questions, he thought, strumming his fingers on his knee. The dinner ended, and the orchestra members took their seats on the bandstand. He could barely contain himself when he heard the exchange between Lucy and Geoffrey.

"This was truly wonderful," the woman said to Geoffrey, who had donned his Sunday best for the occasion.

"Well, you could say that, and I'm glad you enjoyed it," Geoffrey replied. "'Course, now, if I'm gonna take in this much cholesterol, I'd as soon have it in southern fried chicken, candied yams, and some good old coconut cake."

A deep, throaty chuckle floated up from Mason's throat. He winked at his new friend, got up, and held out his hand to Jeannetta.

"Dance with me?" A saxophone wailed a love song from the 1930s, and he whispered the words, synchronizing them with the tune: "If I didn't care...more than words can say..." She missed a step, and he pulled her closer.

"Loosen up," he taunted, "and let it hang out the way you did in Paris with the Gypsies. There's no use pretending anything anymore. It's you and me, baby. Forget about the past, all your reasons for not getting involved, our doubts; they don't matter. It's where we go from here that counts."

"Mason, let's...let's sit down. You...don't know what you're saying."

"I hope I've heard that line for the last time."

The orchestra leader announced a request, and a seductive saxophone swung into *Body and Soul*.

"That's how I need you," he whispered, "just like that song says." He didn't intend to give her breathing space until she let him know what she felt for him—words or actions, he didn't care which—but he had to know something. A guitar whipped into a duet with the sax, and he wrapped her to him and brought her head to the curve of his shoulder.

"You'll regret this; we both will," she told him with such certainty that, for a second, he sensed defeat. Only briefly, however, because her supple body snaked around him, molded itself to him. Her knee moved with his knee, her hips swung when his did, and her pelvis tilted forward when his dipped to receive her. They danced as one person, and his blood ran hot and fast.

Her breathing accelerated and, with a deep sigh, she gave in to him and did as he'd asked. Her arms tightened around his neck, her breasts warmed his chest, and she seemed to let her body have its way. He tried to ignore the sweat that beaded on his forehead, the thundering of his heart, and the sensuous movement of her hips as she followed his steps. He swung her out in a two-step, intent upon getting some space between them, but the sultry expression in her eyes and the movement of her belly as she glided back to him accelerated his pulse, and awareness slammed into him. He thought he'd explode.

She slid her fingers around his neck and whispered, "You're warm and...and everything. Everything." He stopped dancing. Did she want him to make love with her? Hang his rules. Did she? She had closed her eyes and her lips brushed his jaw. He wanted to pick her up, run with her to his room, and lose himself in her.

"Let's go, sweetheart. Let's get out of here."

She nodded, although her luminous smile seemed shaky. He splayed his fingers across the small of her back and led her back to their table. She grasped his hand, smiled, then slumped against him in a dead faint.

# Chapter 6

Mason paced the narrow corridor outside the ship's infirmary. A nurse smiled at him, pausing briefly for what he didn't doubt was more feminine than medical concern. On a different occasion, she might have inspired a second glance, but his thoughts were on the woman in that room. He hadn't been allowed inside, because his answer, when the doctor had asked his relationship to Jeannetta, had been "friend." The doctor had shrugged and said, "Wait out there." He'd wanted to say, *but I'm a doctor, and I have as much right as you to be in there.* He'd said nothing and had watched the door close in his face. He'd given that up voluntarily almost three years ago, and he hadn't regretted it. Oh, there had been little twinges once and a while, when he read of a new medicine, ground-breaking test, or special equipment. He'd think how wonderful, how exciting or safer his work would be because of it, only to remember that he headed Fenwick Travel Agency and had no connection with medicine. Then he'd take consolation in getting a full night's undisturbed sleep on a regular basis, not having to deal with anxiety and stress about his patients every waking minute, and in not being the target of every long-lashed socialite whom he encountered. At one point he had fantasized about buying all present and future rights to the manufacture of false eyelashes and sending them to the moon with the next team of astronauts headed that way.

The nurse emerged, still smiling. "Can you tell me what the situation is with Miss Rollins?" he asked her.

"Nothing serious. The doctor will be out in a few minutes."

At that, Mason stuck his hands in his pants pockets, propped himself against the wall, and tried to relax. If he'd been away from medicine thirty years instead of two years and nine months, he wouldn't believe that—unless Jeannetta was a closet drinker, and he didn't believe that, either. He fingered the old keys and, in his frustration, knew an unfamiliar urge to slam them against the wall. So many years of longing. An hour ago, what he'd wanted for so long had seemed within his reach.

"Well, I see we're still here."

Mason bristled at the doctor's patronizing manner. "She'll be fine," the doctor said. "This rough sea doesn't agree with a lot of people, and she's just seasick. I've given her some Drama-mine. That ought to take care of it."

Mason stared at the man, wondering what Jeannetta could have said or done to mislead him.

"Thanks, Doctor." He had to work hard at containing himself, because he wouldn't gain a thing by questioning the man.

"You're still here? I thought you'd gone."

He offered the best smile he could muster.

"You gotta be kidding," he said. "I aim to see you safely in…well, I don't suppose I dare to tuck you in, although that's what I had in mind an hour ago, but I want to walk you to your room." He took her cool fingers in his hand and clutched them to his chest. "I told you that I'm here for you, and I want you to believe it." He refused to comment on her skeptical look. He had to decide whether to send her back to New York and, if so, what kind of advice he ought to give her.

Jeannetta awakened early after sleeping fitfully. She couldn't help regretting that the last night on board ship hadn't been what it could have, and certainly would have, if she'd been more for-tunate. She pushed the thought of the consequences out of her mind, though she conceded that Providence had no doubt rescued her from herself. More than once during the night, she had wondered whether it was Mason or her ailment that had made her knees buckle and caused her to faint. She swung her feet to the floor, showered and dressed hurriedly. She knew where to find him; he wouldn't miss the last opportunity to see that spectacular sunrise.

As she'd expected, he was leaning against the rail watching the awesome sight of the sun climbing out of the sea, its halo of colors straddling the sky.

"I knew I'd find you here." She joined him at the rail to watch the sight.

"And I hoped you'd come. This is so extraordinary; I wanted to share it with you." He took her hand in his, and she shifted her gaze from the spectacle before them to glance at the strong man at her side. He stared deeply into her eyes and gently squeezed her fingers, and she gloried in the shared moment. Still holding her hand, he let his gaze drift back to the brilliant hues surrounding the rising sun.

She continued to look at him. "Not even the sunrise can compare to you," she whispered beneath her breath.

"Let's walk," he urged, when the sun had fully emerged.

She didn't miss the envious glances that women sent her way, nor the covetous manner in which they eyed Mason. And she couldn't help thinking that her time with him would soon be over and that, if she didn't watch out, she'd blow this one opportunity to gain his help. She noticed the tall, beautiful, and expensively dressed blonde long before the woman reached them. To her surprise, the woman stopped before them and her heavily lashed eyes widened in astonishment.

"Why, Dr. Fenwick," she gushed. "I'm so delighted to see you. I had no idea you were on board." Before Mason could respond, she turned to her companion. "Brad, darling, this is *the* Dr. Mason Fenwick that I've told you so much about. I owe my life to this brilliant man. But for him, I'd be blind, maybe even dead. He's a marvelous surgeon. Believe me, I always want to know where this man is. You're still on East Seventy-second Street?"

Jeannetta stared at him when he smiled diffidently, and she couldn't help gritting her teeth.

"No. That's all behind me now. I'm happy to see that you're well, with no aftereffects."

Bile formed on Jeannetta's tongue, and she snatched her hand from his as fury roared through her.

"Jeannetta!"

She glared at him, her eyes brimming with tears. *All behind him.* Never mind who needed him; he could stand there and calmly imply that it didn't matter. She bolted for the stairs and ran to her stateroom.

If he didn't catch her before she got in that room and locked that door, he wouldn't have a chance. He didn't expect her to understand; his own brother didn't comprehend or accept his decision to leave his profession behind, though Steve had walked the floor with him while he'd agonized over it. She spun around and raced up the steep, winding stairs and down the heavily carpeted corridor. His hand shot out above her head as she pulled the key from the door and pushed at it. She leaned into the door, but he didn't allow it to budge.

"May I come in? I have to talk with you."

"There's nothing for you to say at this point. *It's all behind you,* you said. The devil with the people who need you. You could stand there and calmly consign human beings to a life of hell and not give a fig. Talent, education, and opportunity, and all of it wasted." She wasn't without guilt, but she didn't let her mind dwell on that; black terror had swept through her when she heard from his own lips that he'd finished with medicine. If he thought she trembled from anger, she didn't care, but she'd never been so scared in her life. He pushed the door open, walked in with her and closed it.

"You've condemned me, and you'd hang me without a hearing. All that's gone between us means nothing to you? Do you know what it's like to play God day after day and know you're doing it, to risk lives for your own glory, to do routinely what other surgeons regard as perilous? Do you? And then one day your arrogance almost kills a woman. You make a mistake that puts her in a coma, and if you had moved that knife one iota of a centimeter further, she'd be dead. You don't know what terror is until you have a narrow escape like that. When that doctor told Steve and me that he couldn't save our parents after their accident, I vowed to be a surgeon and to be the best. I gave up my childhood, went without friends, and sacrificed my dreams for a family of my own, because I wanted to be a doctor more than anything. And I walked away from nothing." She'd turned her back, and as he walked around to look at her, he recalled something that had hung on the edge of his mind.

"You didn't seem surprised to learn that I'm a doctor. Have you known all along?" He wondered whether her lips trembled from anger or from a pain around her heart that equaled what he felt. He had to lean forward to hear her whispered words.

"How could you stand there while that doctor misdiagnosed my ailment? I heard what he told you."

His face must have reflected the icy chill that plowed through him when he recoiled from her words, because her eyes widened. He stepped back from her.

"So you know what's wrong, and you've known from the start. That's why you're here, isn't it?" His voice had dropped several decibels, and he knew his temper would rise. "You went to all this trouble to get me back into harness, back into that operating room. What about your torrid responses to me every time I put my hands on you? And your kisses that promised me the heavens? What else had you planned to offer as part of your little scheme?" he ignored her loud gasp. "Well, I got a taste for you, Jeannetta, and I want you, but your price is too high."

"Would you please leave? Now. I... You've said enough."

Enough? He'd said too much, but the last time he'd hurt like this, he'd been seven years old. He gazed down at her and at his dream of a woman to cherish, one who'd give him the family he'd wanted for so long. His anger dissipated, and his hand went toward his right pants pocket, but he forced himself not to reach for those keys. Home. He could forget about that. He opened the door, walked out, and didn't look back.

She wanted to hate him, but how could she when she loved him so? She could hardly blame him for reacting as he had. He was right that she'd schemed to get him to help her, but her reaction to him hadn't been part of it. She tried to see it all from his vantage point. She hadn't been in his shoes in that operating room, and maybe she would have reacted to his trauma just as he did. But she couldn't help resenting him and her circumstances. He had with three words sentenced her to a life without everything that she loved most, including herself. She closed her eyes and started to the vanity for a facial tissue. When she stumbled over the edge of the bed, she straightened up and walked on. But neither the chair nor the magazine rack were where they'd been when she closed her eyes, and she bumped into them also. She picked herself up, opened her eyes and looked around. Clenching her teeth, she grabbed the magazine rack, tossed it against the door with all her strength and plopped herself into the chair.

Jeannetta wished for her old guitar; from childhood, she had found peace of mind by strumming or picking her favorite tunes. She hummed softly for a few minutes until she could restore her serenity. "I'm the one who's wrong," she admitted to herself. "I burst into his life and expected him to change it for me. I should have told him at the outset, just as Laura said." She sucked her teeth and leaned back in the deep cushions. "But I dreaded hearing him say no." She sighed and started to the bathroom to wash her face. "And I didn't count on our being attracted to each other nor on my falling in love with him." She looked skyward. "What will I do?"

The Southern Queen docked an hour before sunset. Mason stood at the edge of the gangplank checking off the passengers, but Jeannetta avoided looking at him when she passed. The few branches in view stood still. Within seconds, it seemed, her cotton T-shirt clung to her body, and she thought the heavy, wet air would burst her lungs. She wiped away the moisture that dripped down her face and beaded on her lashes, and would have run to the waiting bus if she'd had enough energy. She caught a strong whiff of the shellfish that fishermen heaped into huge vats, and needed a nose guard when she passed the pile of un-familiar, decaying tropical fruits that a laborer appeared to haul away. Lucy wouldn't like it, but she sat beside Geoffrey on the bus anyway in order to avoid Mason.

"You two spatting again? I noticed he spent his whole lunch-time watching the dining room door. And what were you doing? In your room trying to punish him?"

She had to laugh at the man's blunt words.

"Oh, Geoffrey. You know true love never runs smooth," she said, attempting to make a joke of it.

"Garbage. Who told you that?" She ran her hands over her hair and verified what she figured the sweltering humidity had done to it.

"It's over between us, Geoffrey."

The old man rolled his eyes and pursed his lips in disdain.

"There's just about as much chance of that as there is of me walking from Bangkok back to Augusta. Fenwick will be on your tombstone sure as Ames will be on Lucy's."

She looked at the passing scene, but didn't see it, as she pulled at her thumb, pensive. After a few minutes of silence and self-searching, she turned to him.

"Geoffrey, I didn't level with Mason about something impor-tant, and I don't think he'll forgive me." Geoffrey patted the back of her hand but, from his expression, he could have been miles away. She wondered if his long silence meant that he agreed with her.

"I don't suppose he's leveled with you, either, otherwise you wouldn't be sitting back here with me, snubbing him. The two of you have wasted near 'bout a whole day of your lives being foolish. If I upset Lucy, I tell her I'm sorry, that I'll try not to do it anymore and ask her forgiveness. Why can't you do that?"

\* \* \*

Along with the others, Jeannetta checked into the luxurious Oriental Hotel, said by some to be the world's finest, recorded the day's events, had her dinner in her room, and repacked her bags. Then she called Kenyan Airlines and booked a flight to Nairobi, Kenya, for the next afternoon. She chose East Africa because the tour would visit West African countries, and she wanted to avoid him.

"You wouldn't be checking out, would you?" Geoffrey asked when he met her as she walked out of the Oriental early the next morning.

"Yes, I'm leaving the tour." She reached into her handbag and gave him her card.

"I take it Mason doesn't know you're skipping out, does he?" She thought she saw sadness reflected in his eyes. "I guess he doesn't," Geoffrey continued, answering his own question. "You can't love him much, Jeannetta, if you're treating him like this. Even a condemned man gets to speak his piece before they hang him. No use saying I hope you won't regret this, 'cause you will sure as night follows day."

"That's the problem, Geoffrey; I love him so much that I can't risk destroying him." She rubbed her cheek where he'd kissed it before he walked off. She looked at the letter in her hand a long time before she dropped it in the hotel's mailbox. Within an hour, she had a visitor's visa and a ticket to Kenya.

She'd never been in an airport designed for passenger comfort, and this one was no exception so, after lying awkwardly across two chairs for several hours, she sat up. "I'd better finish this doll," she reminded herself, and took her crocheting from her carry-on bag. She couldn't work up an enthusiasm for it, so she put it away and made notes for her novel. Just before five o'clock that afternoon, she boarded a plane that, minutes later, took off for Nairobi.

Well past midnight, Mason sat at the hotel's bar, out-of-doors along the Klong, the major waterway that teemed with commerce and houseboats day and night. He could have done without the strange, sour odor of the thick, brown waterway, but he didn't want to go to his room, though he'd had to discourage dozens of the elegantly dressed Thai girls who worked the hotels. He didn't doubt the he could cure Jeannetta because, even without assurance that she didn't have her periods, he knew she had a brain lesion and suspected the implications. But he didn't want to believe that she had deliberately set out to seduce him, making him fall for her, and insure her chances of getting him back into the operating room. He'd spent almost six weeks with her, and he'd seen nothing about her that was less than admirable, so how could she… He let the thought die, pulled the damp T-shirt away from his skin, slapped at a mosquito that dive-bombed toward him and decided to call it a night. He thought of his brother Steve and the terrible sacrifices he'd made so that Mason could be a doctor. And he thought of Jeannetta and what her life would be like a couple of months or less from then. Tomorrow, he'd get with her and try to salvage their relationship. He'd do what he had to do; he always had.

"I'm Clayton Miles. How do you do?"

Jeannetta let her gaze move casually over her business-class seatmate, allowed him a half smile and replied, "I'm Jeannetta Rollins." That accomplished, she returned to crocheting a doll that she'd give to the Edwin Gould Foundation for distribution to homeless and other needy children. She hoped to have completed about twenty of them by Christmas.

"Is this your first visit to Kenya?"

It wouldn't hurt to talk with him, and it wouldn't interfere with her crocheting. She might even manage to stop thinking of Mason, at least for a while.

"Yes. I've never been to Africa, and I'm looking forward to being there. I've always wondered what it's like to be in a country where I'd be one of the majority and where black people governed."

He accepted a drink from the stewardess, and she got a good look at his hands. Neat. The hands of a cultured man.

"Depends on the country. It can be pleasant, and it can be downright awful. Over here, people care about their family and their tribe, and if you're not a member of either, don't look for compassion."

Curious about the handsome black man, who had the bearing of a university professor, she asked if he was on a business trip.

"I'm afraid those days of dashing around the world on business are over. I marketed a wrinkle-reducing product for a chemist who claimed to have tested it, but, after women used it for a while, their skin tended to get leathery. The lawsuits ruined my company. Up to that time, I had a real good business producing and marketing all kinds of chemicals. Fortunately, I managed my affairs so that I'm personally alright, but my reputation as a businessman is shot. The company went bankrupt, and it depressed me for months. Then I said, the hell with it—and decided to see the world while I figure out what to do with my life. I'm fifty-two and I've no intention of taking a powder. But that's enough about me; what about you?"

To her astonishment, she heard herself telling him about her health, Mason, the scheme she'd concocted to gain his help, and the way her hopes had shattered.

He downed his drink and ate a few Brazil nuts, all the while seeming to dissect what she'd told him.

"Sure you didn't overreact? If I were facing what's before you, I expect I'd have gotten on my knees and begged him." She wrapped the crochet thread around the doll and put it in the little bag beside her.

"Maybe that's because you're not in love with him." Heads turned when he whistled.

"That's a mean complication; if he cares about you, he's dealing with a shrunken ego."

That's nothing compared to what I'm trying to handle, she thought. With dinner over and the lights lowered, she tried to sleep, but whenever she closed her eyes, she saw the sadness that marred Mason's face when he walked out of her room. She feared she'd carry it with her always.

\* \* \*

"She skipped lunch and dinner yesterday, and she hasn't come down for breakfast this morning, and doesn't answer her phone," Mason told Geoffrey. "I think I'll scout the shopping mall next door." He said it casually so that Geoffrey wouldn't know how deeply concerned he was about her. He walked outside and, within minutes, his clothes began to cling to his body. Unmuffled sam lams—three-wheeled motorized taxis—roared through the streets, as did old trucks, poorly maintained cars, and more brand-new Mercedes-Benz cars than he'd ever seen. He clasped his hands over his ears when a big jet thundered low overhead and irate drivers honked their horns at the red light. The din nearly deafened him. He searched the mall without luck, figured she might have gone to one of the temples, looked at his map, and struck out for the nearest one. Babies cried, women cooked on the streets over primitive utensils; the smell of assorted strange foods tormented his nostrils, and he looked around for an escape. More of the same. Every place. He crossed the wide street, thinking that he risked his life, dodging among mad motorists hellbent on winning some imaginary race, walked into the Temple of the Emerald Buddha, a cool, quiet oasis, empty but for himself, and sat on the marble floor. He couldn't help reminiscing about his life, one that seemed so much longer than it had been. He wasn't afraid or nervous, but how would he feel when he went back there? He got up and walked toward the exit, the echo of his clicking heels shouting at him from every pillar and nook.

"May I help you?" a monk in saffron-colored robes asked in a soft voice. Mason thanked him and walked on.

"I think you are worried," the man said, quickening his steps in order to keep up with Mason, who stopped and looked at the short priest.

"Yeah. You might say that," he replied. They stood at the door of the temple, and Mason dabbed at the perspiration running down his face. How could the man not sweat in that heat? The priest bowed.

"Do what you have to do. Everything you possess is on loan

to you, even your intelligence. Whether your life has any value depends on what you do with it." He bowed and went away.

Deeply moved by the man's concern and his words, Mason failed to pay attention to his surroundings. During his lapse, he felt a hand in his pocket, turned, and saw the thief making off with his wallet. With legs nearly three times as long as the thief's, catching him proved easy. He retrieved his wallet and headed back to the Oriental.

"Miss Rollins checked out at eight o'clock this morning."

The telephone operator's words battered his eardrums like the toll of a funeral bell. He phoned Geoffrey.

"Jeannetta has left the tour. Do you know where she went?"

"Can't say as I do. She left around eight this morning, and the reason I didn't tell you before is 'cause I just couldn't bring myself to give you that news. I know what she means to you."

Mason didn't want any philosophy and definitely not any sympathy. "I'm going back to New York as soon as Lincoln, my assistant, can fly out here." Lincoln wouldn't want to leave his new bride, but Mason didn't plan to give him a choice. He hadn't remembered that option until he said the words. He felt almost dizzy as plans and possibilities took shape in his mind. He had to hurry. She hadn't seen the last of him.

After lunch, Geoffrey and Lucy joined him in the lounge. Lucy's sudden motherly behavior with him brightened his mood, and he considered the likelihood that approaching marriage automatically made women think of motherhood. But Lucy Abernathy? The woman had long since kissed sixty good-bye.

"I'll leave for New York as soon as I can get a flight. Josh can handle things until my assistant gets here day after tomorrow. So don't worry."

"I won't," Geoffrey assured him, then he cocked his head to one side and studied Mason. "How're you going to find her? She won't be leaving you any clues."

"You think I'll be looking?"

A deep frown creased the old man's face, and then a smile slowly erased it. Geoffrey laughed aloud.

"Why should you?" Geoffrey asked. "This ain't the end of the world."

Mason didn't hide his irritation at his friend's sarcasm. "Don't tell me it isn't; speak for yourself," Mason muttered.

Geoffrey laughed louder. "My question was as good as your answer. I've been watching people a lot of years, and I know when a man cares for a woman. You go ahead; everybody'll understand."

Mason packed, called Skip and his brother, got a seat on Scandinavian Airlines, and left Bangkok that night.

Jeannetta watched the sunrise from the plane's window and had to fight a wave of melancholy, until she closed the shade and vowed not to get upset every time something reminded her of Mason. She rode into town with Clayton Miles, and discovered that they'd chosen the same hotel.

"It isn't such a coincidence," he said when she commented on it. "There were only two choices. I'm going to sleep for a few hours. How about meeting me in the dining room about one?" She nodded agreement. He'd be in Nairobi for a week, and he'd never know how grateful she was for his company.

Mason walked into his apartment building after a twenty-two-hour flight, and found Skip waiting in the lobby. The boy rushed forward and threw his arms around him. He marveled at his feelings of contentment as he held the child. When had he developed this deep, paternal feeling for the boy, this sense that he'd come home to Skip? Inside his apartment, the boy didn't waste time reporting his news.

"I'm going to be a doctor, Mason. I made up my mind, because Aunt Mabel is so sick and the stupid doctors can't cure her. I'm gonna cure all of my patients."

Mason sat in the nearest chair. "What did you say?"

Skip repeated it, bubbling with excitement and oblivious to Mason's incredulity.

"I saved up three hundred and twenty-nine dollars toward it, and I want you to help me open a bank account. I have to put

away a lot of money, and I wouldn't trust anybody but you."
Mason listened as the boy poured out his dreams at a rapid rate,
unaware of the pain he caused. How could he encourage Skip,
when the boy would someday learn that he'd realized his own
dream—and walked away from it?

"You've thought this over and you're sure? You're not going
to change your mind?"

"I'm sure. It's all I can think about. I'm gonna work hard,
Mason. I just want you to open my account for me." He recognized the gleam in the boy's eyes as the child's vision of his
future, and remembered his own dreams. He shook off the inner
voice warning him that destiny stalked his heels. To go back...

"Alright, son. Be over here at eight-thirty tomorrow morning.
While bank do you want to use?"

Skip's face glowed, his lips curved upward to expose even
white teeth and, Mason realized for the first time, a dazzling personality. He stroked the boy's shoulder.

"Can't I use yours?"

Mason nodded. "Now, get going; I've got a million things to do."

"Why'd you come back so early?"

"I have an emergency, and I'll be leaving as soon as I get it
straightened out. A couple of days, I'd say. Run along, and tell
Mabel I'll get to see her before I leave."

"Steve, how are you?" He listened for a minute. "In my apartment. I got back this morning, but I'm leaving as soon as I
straighten out a few things. How about lunch?"

"Fine, we can lunch here in my apartment. alright?"

Mason agreed, hung up, and called the chief of ophthal-
mology at New York Hospital. Sweat poured off of him and he
paced the floor, to the extent the phone cord would allow, as he
listened to the familiar voice. He loosened his tie, ran his fin-
gernails over the back of his neck, and tried to control his breathing. The thudding of his heart reminded him of the surge of
adrenaline he used to get when he'd donned his greens and
walked into an operating room.

Gwynne Forster

"Alright. Eleven o'clock tomorrow morning." He hung up. He'd done it, and there was no going back.

"What brought you back here in the middle of a tour, Mason? It isn't like you."

"I'm going back to medicine. It was inevitable, I guess."

Steve's fork fell to his plate, his lower lip drooped, and he reached for his glass and gulped down some water.

"You're going back to... Are you serious?"

Mason nodded, and continued chewing his hamburger.

"Something must have happened on this trip?"

Mason pushed his plate aside and looked at his benefactor, the man who had sacrificed his own future to help him become a doctor, and who hadn't shown bitterness when he'd walked away from it.

"Yeah. Plenty." He told Steve about Jeannetta.

"A lot of people must have needed you these past couple of years or so. You love her, I take it. Suppose you can't find her?"

"I'll find her, but I don't have much time. When that tumor gets a grip, it can be horrendous. I've got a date tomorrow morning with the chief. Wish me luck."

Steve cleared away their plates and returned with two slices of chocolate icebox pie. "I can't tell you how happy this makes me, Mason. But I'm sorry you're starting again in these circumstances, because loving her will make it doubly stressful."

Mason put a forkful of the pie in his mouth and wrinkled his nose.

"Man, how can you eat this stuff?" He made himself swallow it. "It was always stressful, but I was so cocky, I didn't let it bother me."

He could sense from Steve's manner that his brother meant to air what had long been a contention between them.

"Mason." He cleared his throat a couple of times. "Mason, Bianca Norris is in good health, and she was out of danger when you called it quits. I've tried all this time to understand how you got so upset that you'd give up your lifelong dream just because you made one mistake? Did you think you were infallible?"

Mason shrugged and strummed his fingers on the table. "You

have to understand that people, even my peers and my chief, treated me as if I could do no wrong. If a case was difficult or out of the ordinary, they'd send for Fenwick. And Fenwick always did it, never questioning his ability or the danger involved. But that morning, right in front of everybody… Well, you know the rest. I realized, right along with them, that I was just a man, one who could make mistakes like the rest of them. I couldn't sleep that night and, when I woke up the next morning, the thought of going in there made me sweat. I didn't trust myself. In operations that delicate, self confidence is just as important as knowledge and skill. And those weeks of waiting— the lessons I learned. I had to turn myself around."

"And now?"

"If I don't try, I can't live with myself."

"I remember thinking, back when you were a small boy, that nothing would stop you; you showed guts and brilliance before you went to the first grade. You'll do fine in there, like you'd never left."

Mason spent the next two days at the hospital witnessing surgeries, operating on dummies, and reacquainting himself with his true profession. His fourth day back in New York, he stopped at his travel agency to check on the tour.

"A letter from Bangkok arrived for you this morning," his secretary told him.

He looked at the return address. Oriental Hotel. His pulse raced, his heart galloped, and his fingers trembled as he tore open the envelope on his way to his private office. He stood with his back to the door and read:

"My dearest Mason, I'm leaving the tour, and don't worry; I'll be alright. I know that I hurt you, and I'm sorry. I knew who you were, and I tried many times to tell you my problem and to ask your help, but I always got cold feet because, if you said no, it would be so final. When our attraction for each other grew strong, I feared that if I asked you, you'd think I had manipulated you. In the end, that's precisely what you thought. I have unshakeable faith in you, but I know that if you took my case and weren't successful, you'd persecute yourself forever. I care too deeply for you to wreck your life. Love, Jeannetta."

He walked to his desk, sat down, and reread the letter. He had to… Where was his mind? He punched the intercom.

"Viv, get me Jeannetta Rollin's file." He noted her address, phone number, and next of kin. When her phone went unanswered, he got Laura's number from information.

"Rollins Hideaway. Laura speaking."

Mason breathed a sigh of relief.

"Miss Rollins, this is Mason Fenwick, head of…"

"I know who you are. And if my sister can't ask you to look after her case, I sure can."

"Slow down, will you? She left the tour. Do you know where she is? She shouldn't be alone in a strange place, for one thing, and for another, she needs treatment. I have to find her."

"She called from Nairobi day before yesterday, but she didn't say where she was staying. You can't find her in a place that big."

"I can if you don't tell her I'm looking for her." He had been in enough developing countries to be able to trace an upper-middle-class American; in most, only a handful of hotels would appeal to them.

"Viv, get me a flight to Nairobi, Kenya, and call Sidu Adede and tell him I need a visa right now." He made a mental list of what he needed to take with him, called Mabel and Steve, and locked his desk. Twenty-six hours later, he stepped off the plane in Nairobi, went to a telephone, and began checking off hotels.

"Suppose this thing runs out of gas?" a young boy sitting behind Jeannetta in the six-seat Landrover asked his father, as their guide drove them through the game preserve not far from Nairobi. "How would we get past all these lions to get out of here?"

Clayton Miles turned to Jeannetta. "If I were as pessimistic as that boy, I'd probably end up selling used cars. I lost millions because I trusted a man, but I aim to make a few more millions before I check out of here. Never take adversity lying down, Jeannetta. Get hold of that doctor, and give yourself a chance at a normal life. My guess is he'll be waiting for you."

"I don't see how I can do that, Clayton. I can't ask him to mortgage his life for mine. I intend to put him out of my mind and enjoy this vacation." Her gaze swept the vast plain, and she looked with awe at the endless varieties of birds perched on the tall grasses that waved in the breeze. Her senses were heightened by the sight of the birds enjoying a free ride, while nature protected them from the small animals hidden among the grasses, waiting to prey upon them.

"When do you leave Kenya, where will you go?"

She heard his unasked question: how long would she run?

"Further south. Home. I don't know."

He didn't speak for a long time, and when she looked at him, she wondered why he'd closed his eyes when they were supposed to be sightseeing. When he spoke at last, she thought she detected a tremor in his voice.

"Come to Egypt with me? You'll love the pyramids, the Sphinx, Luxor, the desert. They're something marvelous to behold. Come with me?" Though the loneliness in his voice gave her a deepening sense of kinship with him, she declined.

"Thank you, but I want to see more of this part of Africa, to know more about life here. I want to meet some people and talk with them." Her eyes widened at the sight before her. Giraffes that had to be a couple of stories tall drank from a spring, all the while keeping watch for lions. Their guide drove up a narrow lane and stopped in the middle of the wildlife preserve. Nearby, a herd of elephants drank from a muddy stream, while some of them rolled in it.

"No danger," the guide assured them, "elephants downwind, we upwind." Jeannetta breathed deeply in relief, reached for her cassette, and recorded the sight.

"Clayton, isn't it strange that the elephants don't mind all those birds on their backs?"

"Not really," he replied. "According to my guide book, those birds pick off the insects that infest the elephants' hides. The poor beasts probably love those birds."

She closed her eyes and pasted in her memory all that she'd seen that day. As she opened them, a thousand gazelles swarmed by.

"You can bet there's a hungry lion right behind them," their guide explained.

"If you're determined to put Mason Fenwick in your past and to brave what you know is going to be a hard life, why don't you cast your lot with me? Marry me, Jeannetta, and I'll take care of you. I guarantee you'll never want for anything."

Her eyes widened, losing their almond shape, and she worked at the lump in her throat. Had she heard him correctly? He gazed steadily at her, and she frowned deeply, squinting in an effort to understand.

"You couldn't be serious. You've only known me for five days. If I accepted your offer, you'd probably spend the rest of your life berating yourself and hating me."

She felt his fingers lightly on her arm and looked at him. His solemn gaze pierced her.

"Why do you think I'm a frivolous man? Let me tell you that I am not. I think before I speak or act, and I've given this some thought. I enjoy your company, and I've been more at ease when I'm with you than at any time since I locked Miles Chemicals and walked away from it for the last time. When my business went belly up, my so-called friends had more important things to do when I called. Until we met, I'd been alone, in the truest sense, for the past eighteen months. You've changed that. And I'll be honest. Because of me, a lot of women lost their beauty and aged prematurely. Their class-action suit drained my business, but no amount of money can compensate for what happened to them. If I make your life a little easier, a little brighter, maybe I can ease my conscience. Now, what do you say?"

"But you did nothing wrong, and you have no reason to feel guilty."

He shrugged, looked out of the window, and spoke as though to himself.

"I should have carried out my own investigation before I packaged that cream under my logo and put it on the market. But that's beside the point; we get on well, and we could have a good life together if you'd marry me. Your presence, your carriage, and the way you're dealing with your problem uplift me."

She had vowed that she wouldn't cry about her condition anymore, so she sniffled and calmed herself. "You're a terrific guy, Clayton, and I've enjoyed these past few days with you, but I have to find my own way." She tried to hide her astonishment at his somber, almost sad expression. Even if he had meant that noble gesture, she wouldn't accept it. If she couldn't lose herself in Mason Fenwick, if she couldn't have the essence of him, she wouldn't share herself with any man.

She barely heard the guide's warning of the dangers of being in the preserve after dark, for she had been enjoying the prospects of soon having a few moments alone in which to contemplate all that had transpired that day and to think about her life. Clayton grasped her hand, detaining her as they left the land-rover, and she couldn't help being conscious of the difference between the feel of his hands and what she felt when Mason's fingers so much as brushed her flesh. Darts of electricity shot through her at the thought of how he made her feel.

"Look Jeannetta. Don't you feel as though our seeing this beauty together foretells something wonderful for us?"

She gazed up at the purple, red, and orange hues that blazed across the darkening sky as the sun neared its goal. Her free hand went involuntarily to Clayton's arm, and he looked at her inquiringly.

"At times such as these," she whispered, "I thank God for my eyes."

She felt his arm encircle her waist in a gesture of comfort, and his warm smile made her wonder how many women would reject the proposal of such a man. Distinguished, well-mannered, a wonderful conversationalist, wealthy, and handsome.

"Until you tell me you'll never marry me," she heard him say, "I'm not available to anyone else."

"Clayton, I'm sorry, but I…"

"Hush. You haven't thought it over. Give me your address in Pilgrim, so I won't lose touch with you."

She did as he asked. "Better give me your sister's name and address, too."

She did, though she knew Laura would be scandalized at the thought that she had spent so much time in the company of a strange man of whom she knew nothing.

"Meet me for dinner," he coaxed.

"I'll call you," she hedged. She liked Clayton Miles, but she hadn't forgotten that a lapse in judgment had complicated her relationship with Mason—though she doubted she could have staved off the fire that had roared inside her from the moment she met Mason.

Mason found the foreign-exchange booth at the airport, changed dollars for Kenyan shillings, and phoned the Nairobi Hilton. Jeannetta Rollins was not a guest there. That left the Intercontinental. If she hadn't registered, he had some work to do. He phoned the hotel and, half an hour later, he'd registered there.

"Miss Rollins went on a tour of the wildlife preserve," a bellboy told him, obviously fishing for a tip. A check with the tour agency enabled him to plan his day, and, after sleeping for the next eight hours, he showered, dressed, went down to the lobby, and sat facing the door.

Mason rose slowly, his heart slamming against the walls of his chest, when she walked through the door. He let his gaze sweep over her, searching every visible inch of her for evidence that she was no worse than when he'd last seen her. Her hair seemed longer, blown forward to frame her ebony cheeks. Nothing more. He relaxed for a minute, and then tensed. She had a man with her, but he'd deal with that later. Right then, his only concern was her health. He ignored the man and walked directly to her.

"Jeannetta, why did you leave? Didn't you remember my telling you that I'd always be here for you? Didn't you?"

Her obvious astonishment at seeing him—her audible gasp, dropped lower lip and widened eyes—held little surprise; she should have known he'd find her.

"Did you get my letter?"

He took it from the vest pocket of his linen jacket and showed it to her.

"You shouldn't have come."

Her hand went to her throat, and he stepped closer, ready to support her if necessary. Mason glanced at the man who remained beside her, and who cleared his throat—a bit insistently, Mason thought. He put a hand on each of Jeannetta's shoulders and looked the man in the eye.

Clayton Miles smiled wanly and introduced himself. But the man's smile lacked warmth. "I assume you're Dr. Mason Fenwick."

Mason nodded, but he didn't move his hands from Jeannetta's body.

"Am I to assume you're not free for dinner?" Clayton asked Jeannetta.

Mason looked from one to the other. They hadn't had time to develop close ties...or had she known him before she left the tour? When Jeannetta half turned to face Clayton, Mason released her shoulder and stepped back.

"I enjoyed sightseeing with you, Clayton. Perhaps we'll meet tomorrow."

He nodded. "Don't forget what I said. Good night, Dr. Fenwick. Good night Jeannetta."

Mason stared at the man's departing back, trying to recall why he seemed familiar.

"Will you have dinner with me?" he asked Jeannetta, when he could no longer see Clayton. She agreed.

"I'll be here in the lobby. Perhaps we can go to one of the French or Italian restaurants a few blocks away." He tried to shove his emotions aside, but couldn't. Butterflies darted around in his stomach, and need twisted through him as she stood there gazing at him with warmth and want blazing in her eyes.

"Can you imagine how I felt when I realized you'd gone? You could have left the note for me with the hotel's concierge, but you mailed it to New York, expecting that I wouldn't get there for another three weeks. It might have been too late then. Oh, Jeannetta, why couldn't you trust me? Don't you know that I couldn't live with myself if I didn't help you?"

Her bottom lip worked; she pulled at her hair and swallowed.

"You're returning to medicine?"

He nodded. "I'm back at my old job, and I'm ready whenever you are. But you'd better hurry." Her hand went to her collarbone, and her eyes widened before she lowered her lids, and a soft, dreamlike expression drifted over her beautiful face. He couldn't deal with what he felt for her right then; first thing first. And his priority was restoring her health. A man shouldn't operate on a woman with whom he was deeply involved. Nobody could argue with the reason but, in this case, neither of them had other options.

"I'll wait here," he said, and turned her to face the elevator. If she didn't leave there, he couldn't guarantee that he wouldn't follow her straight to her bed.

Jeannetta showered and changed into a pink strapless dress and jacket, slipped into white sandals, picked up her straw bag, and raced down the stairs, too excited to wait for the elevator. She'd thought she'd faced a mirage when she saw him standing in the lobby. I'm going to enjoy this evening with him, she told herself, and I won't worry about a thing. The bellboy grinned and bowed when she passed him on the stairs. She took her key to the desk, and the receptionist grinned knowingly. What is it with these people, she wondered. Since when did staff take such delight in getting into the guest's private business. When they left the hotel, she wanted to scream to the doorman that she wasn't spending the night in Mason's room. The man had actually winked at Mason. They walked to the restaurant, and she mentioned her mild annoyance.

"Jeannetta," he said, his voice filled with amusement, "they think you were playing around with that guy and that I came unexpectedly and caught you two together. These are boring jobs, and the guests are the only diversion."

She couldn't help laughing with him. "That explanation suggests that you've got a pretty healthy imagination, yourself."

They chose the Italian restaurant, because Jeannetta found its soft lights and elegant decor enchanting. He seated her, motioned to the waiter, and sat facing her.

"Why did you leave without telling me?" he asked for the second time. He took her letter from his pocket and pointed to it. "You said here that you don't want to wreck my life. Do you believe I could go on with my life as it was knowing what you faced? Didn't you have any faith in what has happened between us? Surely, you don't think a man can hold you as I have done and not care about you."

"I left because I didn't want to risk your having a failure with me, a tragedy that would haunt you forever. If a near-miss was enough to make you walk away, failure would destroy you. I believe in you, but I'm not sure that you do; after all, you said that medicine was behind you, a thing of the past. I don't plan to waste time feeling sorry for myself, I'll do and see all that I can, while I can."

"You didn't reply to the most important part of my question, but I don't suppose dinner is the place to discuss something this serious." His fingers strummed the table a couple of times. "Who is Clayton Miles?"

"I don't know." At his raised eyebrow, she explained, "I mean, I met him on the plane. He's interesting, has good manners, and he's a very pleasant company." She watched Mason carefully to gauge his mood, to determine whether he might be jealous. If so, she decided, he knew how to hide it.

"His name's familiar. What does he do?"

"He's a chemist." She knew from the set of his jaw and the way he ground his teeth that she wouldn't like his next remark.

"Why is he staying here?"

She glared at him. "This is where he had reservations."

She realized that her glare didn't carry much weight when he said, "Is that why you're staying here?"

"My last name is Rollins and yours is Fenwick," she told him, "and that should tell you what I think of your impertinent question."

He didn't give in. "I didn't suggest anything. I asked you a question."

"It will be a great loss if you hold your breath until you get an answer."

They finished the succulent shrimp brought up from Mombasa, Kenya's second city, and the waiter served their main course, which consisted of fried *talapia*—a fish common to East Africa—overcooked zucchini, and broiled locally grown mushrooms. Jeannetta couldn't figure out how the fish and mushrooms could be so tasteful and the zucchini, the only Italian dish on the menu, so awful. She said as much to Mason.

"Anybody can open a restaurant, decorate it in red, white, and green, and call it Italian. I wouldn't be surprised from the taste of this fish if the chef hadn't been working on a hundred and twenty Fifth Street in Harlem. This stuff is good."

She nodded. "Kenya is famous for its fruits; I'm going to have an assortment. Some of every kind on the menu."

He finished chewing his mouthful of fish, put his fork down, and assumed the posture of a man preparing to run. "Where are you planning to put it? You couldn't possibly have any more space in there." He pointed to her stomach.

"Alright. So I love to eat. Be a gentleman, and don't rib me about it."

He laughed, reached over, and tweaked her nose. "I like women who have a lusty appetite and aren't ashamed of it. What I can't stand is the woman who orders food, pushes it around on her plate and leaves it—as though that's supposed to be feminine—then goes home and wolfs down a couple of peanut-butter sandwiches."

"Not me. What you see is what you get."

He leaned back in his chair, and she could only guess at the reason for his sudden seriousness.

"Yes. I've known that from our first meeting. And I like that about you; I like it a lot."

Excitement ploughed through her as his voice dropped a few decibels, and grew dark and suggestive.

"I like everything about you. Everything. Right now I want to…"

She felt her eyes widen and her lip drop, and he must have noticed her impatience to hear what he wanted, for he suddenly clammed up, stood, and held his hand out to her. He walked with her halfway to the door, turned, and laid a bill on the table. When he rejoined her, he joked, "You've got me so damned befuddled that I forgot I'm supposed to ask for the check. Wait here while I go over to the cash register."

They walked down Mundi Mbingu Street, crossed Kenyatta Avenue, turned into City Hall Way, and walked on to the corner of Uhuru Highway without speaking.

"Tomorrow, we ought to check out the Conference Center and some of the government buildings," Mason suggested. "The first time I came here, it surprised me that Nairobi is such a modern city, at its center especially. What do you say we meet for breakfast around nine and walk through the city, huh?"

"It wasn't what I expected, either," she said. "It's well laid out, with broad, paved streets and avenues, traffic lights, and modern stores. Our guide said that you have to go to the city market to find traditional wares."

He squeezed her hand and urged her closer to him as they walked along. The clear bright moon cast their shadows before them as they turned off Uhuru and walked across the park toward the hotel. Jeannetta looked up at the sky that was bright as early morning, at the white swirls that played hide and seek with the moon, and she missed a step.

Mason dropped her hand and wrapped his arm around her. "It will be yours again, everything. All of it. I promise you. So don't let this depress you."

She looked up at him and smiled, the only response she could give him. Their brisk strides slackened into a stroll, and she knew that, like herself, he was reluctant to let go of these precious moments.

Kenyans went to bed early and got up early, so the streets were deserted except for the few tourists who walked back to their hotels after dinner, a movie, or local entertainment. She felt his fingers tighten on hers as two strangers staggered toward them. He switched sides, putting himself between her and the men, who appeared to be foreigners, and they staggered on their way.

"How about an aperitif? It's early yet," he said, heading them to the bar. "Jeannetta, I want you to go back to New York with me as soon as we can get a flight out. I don't want to waste any more time."

She rested her glass of tonic on the counter and made herself say those fatal words. "I'm not going with you, Mason. I've decided to take whatever comes. I don't want to be on your conscience, and I won't let you ruin your life for me. I have faith in you, but I don't believe you're sure. And even if you are, it's as risky as it ever was, and if your reasons for walking away were valid once, they're valid today. I won't let you do it."

He jumped up, knocking over his glass of cognac, and rubbed the back of his neck with his left hand, wet and smelling of the high-priced brandy. He shook his head as though to clear it, and she'd have sworn that he had difficulty focussing on her. He walked away from the bar, then went back and stood over her.

"Run that past me again. Slow and clear so I can understand it." He spoke in a low, strained voice that shook from frustration or anger, she didn't know which. When she reached out to touch his arm, he moved beyond her reach.

"Well?"

"I'm not going back with you." She took a bill from her purse and would have laid it on the counter, had he not stopped her.

"You're my guest. I invited you to have a drink with me. Remember?"

Breath hissed from her lungs when she saw the sadness, the distress, mirrored in his obsidian eyes. "Mason... Oh, Mason..."

"Come on," he interrupted in barely audible tones, "I'll walk you to your room."

They neared her door, and he stopped. "How can you deliberately do such a thing? You think you're brave, but not even Hercules would have volunteered for what you're choosing. Why, when it's unnecessary?"

How many times did she have to tell him that, with a fifty percent chance of failure, she wouldn't let him ruin his life on account of her?

"What changed your mind, Mason? Pity? You told that woman who'd been your patient that you were no longer a doctor, that you'd put it all behind you. And you knew right then what was wrong with me. I'm not the only person who's needed your services these past two or three years. What about them?"

"That's unfair. I went through hell after that last operation, reliving those times that I had heedlessly tweaked the devil's nose, and acknowledging for the first time how lucky I'd been. What scared me was the thought that I'd been playing God. My chief told me last Monday that he never enters that operating room without praying first. That never even occurred to me."

"But you did it successfully so many times. Did you lose your nerve?"

He shrugged his left shoulder and tilted his head to one side.

"I don't know. I don't think so, but I know I can help you, and I want to. I have to. Let me help you."

"I'm out of sorts. Seeing you here unexpectedly, and realizing what you've done… Let's talk at breakfast."

He walked her to her door and stood looking down at her. His wistful expression tugged at her heart, and she reached out to him.

"Jeannetta. Honey, come here to me."

She had told herself that she wouldn't let him wrap himself around her heart with his loving. But I need him, she thought, as she went mindlessly into the powerful arms that enfolded her in his adoring embrace. Her right hand caressed the side of his face, and he pulled back enough to gauge her feelings. He must have seen her hunger, for he pulled her to him with trembling, unsteady hands, covered her open mouth with his own, and let her feel the force of his longing. His tongue, bold and hot, swept every crevice of her welcoming mouth as if to learn it all over again. Her moans seemed to elevate the heat in him, because his left hand went to her hip, and he molded her to him, letting her feel his virile strength. She raised her arms to him, wanting to give him full access to her person, to let him have his way. Her hands slid to the back of his head, holding his mouth to hers while she sucked his tongue; she felt the shudders that raced through him when he grabbed her buttocks and rose heavy and strong against her. Blood pounded in her brain, and hot currents of desire stormed through her trembling body.

Should she drag him into her room or…? She loved him all the way to her soul. How could she make love with him and then carry out the plan that she knew would hurt him? She pulled his tongue into her mouth, held him as tight as she could, and loved him with every ounce of her strength. He stepped back, held her off, and gazed into her eyes.

"What is it? There's no reason to feel desperate, honey," he soothed. "We're in this together, all we'll come through it alright. Together." She relaxed in his arms, exhausted by her emotions.

"I think I'd better tell you good night," he said with obvious reluctance. "I'd rather not, and you know it, but I… You said you're exhausted, and I won't want to risk a mishap." He brushed his lips over her cheek. "Nine o'clock in the dining room."

Jeannetta sat on the side of the bed, her head in her hands. She'd made the right decision; any other would cripple Mason for life, and she refused to do that. She packed, phoned the airport, and went to bed. The next morning, she phoned Clayton Miles, thanked him for his kindness, and hung up before he could answer her. She left her note to Mason with the desk clerk. At a quarter past nine, she was on her way to Harare, the capital of Zimbabwe.

# Chapter 7

He had spent the night scrambling the sheets, tossing and dreaming. At dawn, he dragged himself out of bed, more tired than he could remember, dressed, and decided to watch the sun rise in Kenya before meeting Jeannetta for breakfast. He strolled along Uhuru Highway for a couple of blocks until the changing sky announced the coming sun, and leaned against the trunk of an old coconut tree to witness its rise. How could he make her understand the horrifying experience of having the certainty that a person's life can be snatched away by your error? She didn't want to accept that, prior to that near-fatal incident, he'd never thought of it in that way, because he'd never considered his fallibility where his work was concerned. He'd been cocky. All-powerful. But he'd gotten a dose of the humility that every surgeon must eventually drink. The sun was up in full, and he'd hardly noticed it. He walked back to City Hall Way, past the elegant government buildings, hardly aware of his surroundings.

"Got a couple of shillings, rich mister?" a boy of no more than seven asked him. Mason fished around in his pockets, careful not to expose any bills in the event the boy had accomplices, and gave the child some coins. To his amazement, the boy handed him a used toothbrush and, when he questioned him, explained that it was fair exchange; he didn't beg.

"I can show you around the town for some more shillings," the boy told him. Mason thought about it for a minute.

"What are you doing out here in the street so early?"

"Best time to find tourist. Make money. First bird gets biggest worms. I show you around." They walked along City Hall Way, and Mason had to admit that the boy knew the town and its buildings and monuments.

"How old are you, and what's your name?"

"Jomo. Almost eight."

Mason couldn't associate an American boy of that age with such sophistication.

"Do you go to school?" He was curious about the boy, but he had a hunch that if he got too close, he'd lose his shirt.

"Second grade. We go to marketplace now." Here was the Kenya of the common man. Hundreds of traders prepared their wares for the day's sales. Women hung colorful baskets, woven mats, wood carvings of animals, eating and cooking utensils, ornaments, hides, and an assortment of other goods. Jomo stopped at a stall and grinned.

"This is my grandmother, rich mister. You buy something from her?" Mason bowed to the woman and bought several wooden bracelets on which were carved heads of giraffes, lions, and other animals.

"I can take you to see the Masai for a hundred shillings," the boy urged. "For some more, my cousin will take you to see Kilimanjaro."

"What do you do with your money?" Mason had no intention of going miles away from Nairobi into Masailand with the boy, but he didn't doubt that Jomo could get him there and back.

"I save to buy a wife; I need many shillings." After questioning Jomo, Mason learned that the boy was a member of the Kikuyu tribe. He flinched as his gaze locked with Jomo's grandmother's piercing, unnerving eyes.

"Go back to your hotel," she said. A tremor of apprehension skipped down his spine, and he couldn't doubt that behind her gaze lay special knowledge.

"Why?"

"Go back." He forced a smile, thanked her, and asked Jomo to walk with him to the Intercontinental. He gave the boy the equivalent of ten dollars and watched the happy youngster accost another tourist. Skip saved to become a doctor, and Jomo saved to buy a wife. He could imagine the life that the enterprising little boy would have if he'd been born in the United States. He decided to leave his purchases in his room and to freshen up before meeting Jeannetta for breakfast. When he stopped at the desk for his key, the receptionist handed him an envelope. His heart plummeted when he saw her handwriting, and he didn't open it until he'd closed the door of his room. *Déjà vu!*

"Dear Mason, because I love you with every fiber of my being, I won't let you do it. Nothing that you have revealed to me will make me believe that you're willingly going back to medicine. I'm not happy with my decision, because I know I'm letting myself in for a bad time. But as I see it, I've got a fifty-fifty chance of losing my life either totally or partially and, if either happens, you'll lose yours altogether. I'm not convinced that you're ready for it; I know I'm not. Thanks for wanting to help. This is final. Jeannetta."

He crushed the note into a ball and slammed it across his bed. *Now what?* He sat down and reached for the phone, and his gaze fell upon the crushed note. He picked it up, pocketed it, took it out and reread it. She loved him. He had thought she did, but she had at last told him. He needed that love, needed it desperately. But if he didn't find her and get her back to New York in a hurry, she'd never be his, her pride wouldn't let her go to him unless she was a whole person. He packed, ordered a car, and went to the dining room. To his surprise, Clayton Miles joined him.

"I tried to find you," Clayton said. "I wanted to tell you that she was about to leave."

"Thanks. Any idea where she went?"

"Your guess is as good as mine, but it shouldn't be too difficult to check out. Around here, money buys more than goods and services."

"Tell me about it." He extended his hand. "I hope to meet you again." He stopped the chambermaid in the hallway.

"I'm trying to find out where Miss Rollins went," he said, holding a ten-dollar bill in his hand. "Did she leave anything behind? Any papers? Maps?" The maid opened the door.

"I haven't cleaned in there yet. You look around."

He found travel folders in the waste basket, and the phone numbers of the Zimbabwe Embassy, Kenya Airways, and the Princess and Sheraton hotels in Harare. She'd bought a ticket to Harare, Zimbabwe. At six-thirty that afternoon, he boarded a flight to Harare and, this time, he vowed, she wouldn't get away from him.

He called the Sheraton first and hung up before the operator connected him to her room. No point in tipping her off. He got to the hotel after midnight, slept fitfully, and rose early the next morning. He wanted to call New York, check on his business, Mabel, and Skip, but he had to give priority to Jeannetta. Steve would take care of Skip and, if necessary, Viv could handle the business while Lincoln guided the tour. He headed for the dining room and stopped. She stood in the lobby at the tour desk with her back to him, inquiring about a trip to Victoria Falls on the Zambezi River.

He walked rapidly to where she stood. "Jeannetta!"

She whirled around. Her bottom lip dropped and her hand went to her chest.

"Mason! How did…?" He took her in his arms and swallowed her words as his mouth covered her trembling lips. He didn't care if they had an audience, or whether the culture frowned on public expressions of affection. When she attempted to resist him, he deepened the kiss, holding her closer. Her groan of capitulation sent rivulets of heat cascading throughout his tall frame, and he had to struggle for control of himself. He eased their passion with light kisses on her eyes, cheeks, and forehead. And with his arm around her, he walked her to a cove near the elevators, away from the gaping onlookers.

"You ran away from me again. Didn't you know I'd find you? I'll always find you, Jeannetta. You can't tell a man you love him so deeply and kiss him off in the next sentence. At least, not this man. Come back with me and let me help you. We're losing precious time." His gaze swept her features, caressing, adoring.

"If you're going to talk about that, please go back where you came from. I want to enjoy my vacation, and I don't want to spend it worrying about the future."

"There's no use denying the truth. When the curtain falls, and—believe me—that could happen any day, it may be too late, and I may not be able to help you."

She attempted to move, but he'd placed her between himself and the wall. He felt her soft, sweet hands on his chest and had to stifle the urge to crush her to him.

"You didn't follow me this far to depress me, did you?" So she was in the denial phase, a problem he'd had with many of his patients. He'd use another tactic.

"Then let's spend the day together, enjoying being with each other. What tour are you taking?"

She told him.

"Sounds interesting. Mind if I join you?"

Jeannetta longed to get out of the minivan and touch the giant rock formations. Reddish, sandlike rocks of various shapes and sizes clung together, as though created by a master mason; to form massive, eerie shapes—some as high as thirty feet. The rocks sat in a wide area of reddish-colored sand. She dug the toe of her shoe into it, scooped up a handful, and watched it sift slowly through her fingers. Mason fingered the keys in his pockets. She'd done the same thing when they passed a building site in Istanbul, and he wondered at its fascination for her.

"These rocks are thousands of years old," the guide explained, but their rough appearance denied it. Jeannetta pulled Mason's sleeve.

"Look." They gazed at a male monkey meticulously grooming his mate, and Jeannetta turned away when the female expressed her loving gratitude. But the experience made her feel as if she'd been cheated, and she welcomed Mason's arm tight around her, stopped and turned to him. She sucked in her breath at the message of deep caring in his eyes and let him take her weight for a minute. He held her steadily, and she knew she could trust him; she had never doubted that, but she didn't want to expose what she feared might have become his Achilles' heel. And she didn't want him to tempt fate again because, this time, he might not win. They walked on behind others on the tour, arm in arm.

"I didn't bring a camera," Mason said when a flock of black birds with red beaks and red and yellow combs flew overhead. She wished for her recorder but had to settle for what she would remember. His arm slid around her waist and, as she nestled against him, it occurred to her that he might have begun to read her thoughts.

"Close your eyes, imprint them on your brain, and tell yourself to remember them," she said and she could have bitten her tongue when she saw his startled look; she was glad that he didn't comment on it. Instead, he squeezed her shoulder and advised her to think pleasant thoughts.

She grinned, glad for his light mood. "Now we're cooking together for a change. Look over there." She pointed to several cheetahs prowling behind a high fence. "They'd be handsome if they didn't have such small heads," she said.

"Yes," he agreed, "but with a large head, they probably wouldn't be the world's fastest animal."

The guide announced lunch, and shepherded them to a nearby restaurant with outdoor seating, that featured grilled meats, fresh fruits, and iced coconut milk.

"We'll have an hour at Victoria Falls before sundown, when it's most spectacular," the guide promised. "It's only a half hour flight, so we have plenty of time."

Jeannetta stood with her back to Mason, enjoying the feel of his arms around her and experiencing the mile-wide Victoria Falls as they exploded into the Zambezi River. Hundreds of rainbows in every conceivable combination of colors straddled the river, a halo for the falls. She turned her face to his chest and wept.

"You alright?" he asked as the little plane headed back to Harare.

She nodded. "I hope I didn't upset you back there, but it was so beautiful, so breathtaking, that I couldn't stand it."

"I've never seen a more riveting sight, either. The urge to sink to my knees and pay homage to it was almost irrepressible."

Mason disliked lying, but he figured that, in this case, the truth would do more damage. When she had wet the front of his shirt with her tears, the bottom had dropped out of him. He looked down at her, asleep with her head resting on his shoulder, and placed a protective arm about her. If only he could make her understand what she'd pay for her stubbornness. She stirred against him, and he leaned over and traced her forehead with his lips. He admitted to himself that she'd found a niche deep inside of him, and he wished he knew how their story would end. The plane circled the airfield to land, and he checked her seat belt, accidentally rousing her.

"You make a great pillow." She tried unsuccessfully to stifle a yawn, and sputtered out her next words. "That's the best sleep I've had in ages."

He looked at her and, since he didn't much feel like joking, he let his eyes answer her. She looked away.

"I can guarantee you an even better sleep, one you're not likely to forget soon," he boasted.

"But first…"

He didn't object to her needling him. She had backed away from their passionate exchanges as often as he.

"Yes. But first…If you're guilty, don't accuse," he admonished her.

"Humph. The only thing I'm guilty of is being sensible."

He released a mirthless laugh and followed her down the short aisle and off the plane. The hotel van awaited them and, as they drove past one of the famous jacaranda trees blooming with purple flowers, Mason asked the driver to stop.

"It was planted ninety-nine years ago," he said. "Would you believe it? And still blooming." She slid her arm through his, and he gazed down at her. "It's nearly as beautiful as you are."

"Meet you in the dining room in forty-five minutes," he told her as they collected their keys from the hotel reception.

"Okay."

"Can I take you at your word?" He asked her, and smiled, as though to soften it. "Don't tell me you have the nerve to be affronted by my remark. Sweetheart, we're down here almost to the end of Africa because you've skipped out on me twice. But not anymore, so don't even try it."

"I said I'd meet you for dinner," she huffed, "and I will."

Jeannetta took a leisurely bubble bath, dried off and applied *Trésor* body lotion to her skin. She sat on the edge of the bed, filing her toenails, and decided to call Laura.

"What're you doing way down there, girl?" Laura asked in a pleading tone when Jeannetta told her where she was.

"Laura, try to understand. I have to do this. If you knew what I've seen today, you wouldn't scold me."

"I don't care what you saw. You're out there denying what's happening, and I want you to come on home. You get the next plane back. You hear?"

"I can't promise you I'll do that." Jeannetta didn't want to upset her sister, but Laura could be difficult when she didn't get her way.

"What about Fenwick? Have you gotten in touch with him? Have you? I gotta see that man so I can figure out what he's got that made you lose your head. If you're not gonna speak with him, you'd better come on back here so I can look after you. You hear?" Jeannetta hung up. She had long thought that Laura would smash her ego if she let her.

She got out a pair of sheer stockings, a rose-colored garter belt, and matching bra and panties. "What am I doing?" she asked aloud. She sat down and thought over their relationship, all that they had experienced together. "I love him as I love my life, and this is my last chance to show him what he means to me. Maybe when he wakes up tomorrow, he'll understand what I've been trying to tell him." She slipped into a dusty-rose sleeveless sheath that ended two inches above her knee, and looked at herself in the mirror. She put on a pair of three-inch sandals, let her hair hang around her shoulders, and left the room, taking only her plastic door key.

\* \* \*

Mason paced in the lobby near the front door, his hands locked behind him so that he wouldn't look at his watch every two minutes. He had every other exit covered with the help of twenty-dollar bills so, unless she had climbed out of her sixth-floor window, she was in her room. He'd learned that she had a weak regard for time, but this bordered on...

"Guess who." She had approached him from behind and covered his eyes with her hands.

"The most beautiful woman in the world," he answered, his good humor restored.

"Methinks you exaggerate, sir."

He looked down at her, drinking in her loveliness, that ephemeral something about her that drew him as ants to sugar, nails to a magnet.

"Arguing with you usually gets me nowhere," he said, unable to hold back the grin that he knew had spread over his face. "What do you say to your being the second most beautiful?"

He couldn't help laughing aloud when she tilted her head to one side and looked at him inquiringly before asking, "Who's number one? You never told me whether you have a girl back in New York. Do you?"

He looked toward the heavens in a gesture of feigned exasperation.

"If you had been satisfied with being the most beautiful, that question wouldn't arise. Let's go out. I want to show you off."

Jeannetta tried without success to gauge Mason's mood. He vacillated between playful and serious, but his facial expression didn't alter.

"I hope you're enjoying this," he said at one point, "French food is all sauce and no substance, and that endless talk about '*l'amour*' is so much babble. Outward manifestations of it end with marriage."

"You know this first hand?" she asked, needling him. He sipped the wine.

"About the food, yes. But where that love business is concerned, I only know what I've observed in my French friends. Those guys can woo an alligator out of its hide, but as soon as they say those vows, they forget how to do it."

She couldn't imagine that he would. "I'll bet nobody would ever be able to say that about you."

"Not in this life."

Shivers skittered from her breast to her belly when he lowered his voice and promised her everything with just a look. She wet her lips and swallowed, and she had to clutch her middle as sparks shot from his hot gaze.

"You sound as though you've got a notarized certification of it," she dared to say.

His look turned somber. "You like to play with fire, it seems."

She gazed steadily at him. "When I'm cold, Mason, really cold, I get as close to it as I can."

He stopped eating. "What would you say the temperature is in here right now?"

She knew what he was asking, and she wasn't backing down. She rubbed her bare arms. "Feels like the left side of thirty-two degrees Fahrenheit."

He reached in his pocket for his wallet and glanced at their waiter, who held two dessert menus.

"What would you like for dessert?" he asked her.

"Nothing, thank you."

"Coffee?"

She shook her head. He held his hand out to the waiter for the bill, never moving his gaze from her eyes. She wouldn't have believed herself capable of such a fit of nerves, though she knew that her demeanor belied what she felt. He stood and held out his hand, and she looked at him for a long minute before placing her right hand in his. They walked the two short blocks back to their hotel. He didn't speak, and she was glad for that, because she didn't trust herself to say anything. He walked straight to the elevator, punched his floor, and looked at her. She said nothing, and he pushed the button that closed the door and then released her hand. The elevator stopped, the doors opened, and butter-flies flitted around in her stomach while he stood there looking down at her.

"Come with me?"

She gave him her right hand, and he held it until they reached his room; he paused and he let her read the question in his eyes. She squeezed his hand, and he opened the door.

"What happened to your misgivings, Jeannetta?" He tried to control his anxiety, his fear that she'd overcome her need as she had so many time times in the past.

She looked him in the eye and didn't evade his question.

"I still have them, but I..." She shook her head slowly and diverted her gaze.

He tipped up her chin with his left forefinger.

"You said you love me." Fine tremors wafted through him at the new lights in her eyes and the smile that curved her sweet lips.

"Yes. Oh, yes, I love you. But what about your misgivings?"

"I still have them, too, but they're no longer strong enough to keep me out of your arms. I've never held a woman who con-fessed to love me and made me believe her, and I've longed for that. When I met you, I knew I wanted you, but I resisted because I'm tired of casual relationships. I'm convinced now that what's between us isn't casual, Jeannetta, and that it won't ever be." He stepped toward her. "I've never needed anyone or anything the way I need you. Let me love you." He didn't want to pressure her, but he was desperate to bind them so tightly that she'd stop pushing him away. If she let him love her, the way he knew he could, she'd go back with him.

He hadn't known her to be so quiet, softer than flower petals, yet the answer in her eyes didn't include submissiveness. A bolt of sensation shot through him, hardening him, when she wet her lips, rimmed them with the tip of her tongue, and gazed up at him. He watched her swallow the damp heat of desire and run her hands from her hip bone down her thighs. Her lower lip dropped, and he had her in his arms. He covered her mouth with his and showed her with his marauding tongue what he intended to do to her. Her hips moved against him, and he stilled her with his hand firmly on her buttocks. Her groan of frustration heated him to the boiling point, and he rose firm and powerful against her belly. His senses whirled dizzily when she took over the kiss, sucking on his tongue, caressing his hips, holding his head while she took her pleasure.

"Slow down, sweetheart. I don't want this to get away from us." He could have been speaking to the moon. She sucked on his bottom lip and rubbed her body against his leg. He had to set her away from him; another minute of that, and he'd be over the hill. He slipped her shoulder straps down her arms, watched her dress pool around her feet, picked her up, and carried her to his bed. She clung to him while he turned back the covers and lay her on the white sheets.

"Trust me?"

She nodded, and he leaned over and dropped a quick kiss on her lips. He stood close to the bed and stripped off his shirt, never taking his gaze from her desire-filled eyes and welcoming smile. He took in her scantily clad body, peeled off her garter belt, the sheer hose, and reached for her skimpy panties. When he glanced at her for permission, she lifted her hips and, a second later, his mouth watered, and he stiffened as he stared at her beautiful, thickly tufted love nest. Her hand went to his belt buckle, freed him of the pressure around his waist, and he gazed down at her and waited. When she unzipped him, he sprang free and ready into her hand, as his shorts and trousers dropped to the floor.

He leaned over, gathered her in his arms, unhooked her bra, and buried his face between her full breasts. She shifted to give him access to her nipple, and he pulled it into his hungry mouth, and nourished himself.

The full power of his virility loomed before her, and she wet her lips in anticipation. Hot darts danced inside her and then zoomed straight to her petals of love, and she couldn't help spreading her legs and raising her arms to him. He seemed to hesitate, and she thought she'd die right that minute if he didn't get inside of her.

"Mason. Please, I need you. I need you."

He positioned his knee on the bed, and his gaze swept her nude body. Her hips moved upward to him of their own volition, and she felt a gush of love liquid when he groaned and tumbled into her waiting arms.

"Not so fast, honey," she thought she heard him say, when she fastened her lips on one of his flat pectorals. His hips moved and she caressed the little nub with her tongue while she rubbed the other one with her fingers.

"Slow down, baby," he crooned. "Ah, Jeannetta. *Jeannetta!*"

She reached down, found him thick and ready, and stroked him lovingly. She sighed impatiently, adoring the feel of his mouth on her neck, ears, and shoulders. His lips found her nipple again. She jerked upward, because nothing had prepared her for the feel of his strong, talented fingers as he separated her secret folds and stroked her. Tremors shook her, and her heart slammed in her chest.

"Mason, darling. I can't stand any more." She threw her leg across his hip, and he leaned over her.

"This is important to me; you're important to me. Forget everything, and let's love each other. Look at me now. I want to see your face when I lock us together." His rough, smoky voice sent shivers of desire through her.

"Yes. Yes. Please." She pulled him over her, and looked into his desire-filled, greenish-brown eyes.

"Now!" She lifted her body to meet him and, when she felt him at her portal, she cried out.

"Mason, please." Oh, the wonder of it, as he slid into her depths. He was iron-hard, hot, velvety smooth, and big. He let her adjust to him and then began to move. Immediately, she felt the tension build within her as he whispered encouragement, told her that she was wonderful, all he could ever need or want. She caught his rhythm, but lost it when her body disobeyed her and went wild. Spirals of unbearable tension coiled upward from her feet to the nest of love that he masterfully stroked, and she felt herself begin to grip him rhythmically, until her spasms clutched him. He increased his pace then, and she tumbled out of control, screaming his name.

*"Mason! Oh, I love you. I love you so."* She wrapped her legs around his hips as that heaven-and-hell pleasure took control of her, and then relaxed, replete and exhausted. Restored, she gripped his thigh and held him to her as she drove for his pleasure and, in seconds, his arms tightened around her and, with a shout of joy, he splintered in her arms.

He let his elbow take his weight as he rested in the circle of her arms. "I ought to move over. I'm too heavy for you." The feel of her hands on his shoulder muscles, gently stroking, gave him a sense of belonging that he couldn't remember having had before.

"You aren't too heavy," she corrected. "You aren't too anything for me. You're perfect for me."

"I hope you mean you're happy right now."

"It was wonderful. I didn't know I could feel as I did with you."

He raised up and looked into her face. Sated. No other word would describe her. Well, if he wanted to go for absolute truth, he could say she looked like the gal who'd just been elected campus queen. Or the cat who'd just finished off the canary. Pleased with herself. He dropped a kiss on her flaccid nipple and watched it harden. He attempted to move away from her but, even as he shifted, he reached full readiness.

"Don't move," she protested. "You belong right where you are."

He gathered her closer. "Don't you know what's happening? I want you."

Her eyes widened, and he kissed the tip of her nose.

"You started this. I was resting, teasing a little bit maybe, and this nipple of yours acted up and, well…what's a man supposed to do?" She wrapped her legs around him and shifted her hips, sending waves of current all through his body.

"A man's supposed to do what a man's supposed to do," she answered and parted her lips for his kiss.

The ride was short and sweet. They knew each other now. She opened herself to him, holding back nothing, and she gave. And gave. Whatever he asked, she gave fourfold, and then she took, drawing his inhibitions out of him until he could withhold nothing of himself. Shaken, trembling, he knew himself for the first time in his life and, in triumphant submission to her, he filled her with his essence. He collapsed upon her, strung out, glad she hadn't asked him for his soul, because she'd taken the rest of him. He separated them, fell over on his back, and pulled her close. In seconds, she slept. He looked at her, as beautiful in the grip of orgasm as she was in a long flowing gown, and his pulse quickened. It was best that she slept; her tender loving had loosened his tongue. He flipped off the light. An unaccountable eeriness crept over him as he dozed drowsily, and the blackness of the darkened room seemed to thicken. "I don't want to live without her, and I couldn't bear to see her suffer. I…"

He slept.

Jeannetta stretched languorously and curled into the warm man who cuddled her to him. His soft murmurings lulled her, and she nuzzled his shoulder and dozed off. Awakened by his restlessness and the low drone of his words, she sat up and gazed down at him. She felt the moisture on her right side, noticed the dampness of his body and the sheet that half-covered them, and leaned over him to hear his words more clearly. His hand went out, brushing her shoulder.

*"I can't fail. I…can't both this. I won't. I can't make a mistake with her. I can't…I…mustn't let my finger slip. My finger is slipping…I'll fix it. I have to. She needs me…I can't fail."* She patted his hand, awakening him as gently as she could. Drawing in quick, heavy breaths, he turned on his right side and slept.

What had she been thinking? She'd made up her mind to go wherever he took her. Anywhere. The sweet, tender way in which he'd loved her, giving her what she had reached for and longed for, but never achieved—a thorough and powerful completeness—had given her a lapse in judgment, she decided. She had gone to sleep looking forward to his reaction when she told him she'd go back with him and do as he suggested. But not after what she'd just witnessed. She stole out of bed, dressed, and slipped down the hall. She wouldn't be on his conscience; you couldn't love man as she loved Mason Fenwick and knowingly ruin his life. This time, she wouldn't leave a note.

The Oxford Hotel sat on West Queen Street about eight blocks from the Sheraton, and one-third its size.

"If a man asks where you took me, tell him the airport."

The taxi driver looked at the twenty-dollar bill and smiled.

"Yes, mum. He won't get it from me.

She checked in, amused when asked to pay for the previous night because it was seven o'clock, five hours before check-in time. The small hotel had its advantages, she decided, when she walked out on the balcony and saw that it overlooked a well-tended garden and a small waterfall that served as a bath for the birds. She called her sister.

"I wanted you to know where I am."

"Why don't you come home?"

It was no use trying to explain. "There's one more place I want to go, and then I'll call it quits. If I had the opportunity, I'd go to South America and take a ride down the Amazon, but I don't suppose I'll get to that."

"Jeannetta Rollins, don't you dare do anything like that. Have you lost your mind?"

"Stop worrying, Laura. You'll send your blood pressure sky high."

"A Mr. Miles has called here a few times asking about you. Seems like a real nice gentleman. Who is he?"

"A friend. Someone I met in my travels. If he calls again, tell him I'm fine." It occurred to her after she hung up that Laura hadn't asked about Mason, and that didn't ring right.

Jeannetta smiled when she saw that the hotel served breakfast on a terrace facing the garden. She relished the cool crisp air, the smell of perfume from the rose garden, and the flitting and chirping of birds, and she wished she'd brought her cassette recorder. A matronly woman approached.

"Mind if I join you? I used to live here years ago, but I live in London now. I'm on vacation."

Jeannetta put the local morning paper aside and gestured to the chair facing her.

"Please. I'd love some company," she told the woman, wondering where she and her family had stood politically when the former Rhodesian government ceded power to the African majority.

"How does it feel being back?" she asked the English woman.

"It's easier than I thought it would be. I do miss the old days here with my family and all that." She spread her arms in an all-encompassing gesture. "But time marches on, and it's good to see that the blacks have done a good job of preserving the country. Salisbury—I mean Harare; it's hard to keep up with these name changes—is still clean and beautiful, and so many new buildings, new schools and such. That's progress, I suppose."

"That's because you people gave it up graciously and didn't tear it up fighting to stay in power."

"Yes. I've thought about that a lot, but look at what's happening in Liberia. You can't blame that on colonialism. And look at some of these other countries that are torn apart by tribal conflict." Jeannetta took a deep breath. She had heard this argument before. Which was best? Colonial control or tribal conflict and devastation?

"Don't forget that the colonial powers cut across tribal lands and boundaries when they carved out these countries, establishing nations without regard to tribal affinity. Arch-enemies under one flag? In this region, one's tribe is more important than country will ever be. You know that. What can you expect?" The woman heaved a deep sigh of resignation and sipped her morning tea.

"What we're getting, I suppose. But it's such a waste of human life and resources. Kids ought to be able to play without dodging gunshots. Thank God, the children here can grow up normal."

Jeannetta wondered about the woman's sad expression until she heard her say, "The whole world needs to clean up its act."

She told her breakfast companion good-bye and went to her room, but she couldn't fit her key in the lock, and had to try repeatedly before her shaking fingers found the keyhole. She went in and laid down with her eyes closed. A few minutes later, she opened them and said a prayer of thanks. She walked out to the balcony, and her eyes widened as she exclaimed with pleasure, "Let me get my recorder."

Dozens of colorful birds perched on the banister of her balcony, and she spread cookie crumbs to keep them there while she described each one. She went back inside and attempted to write in her novel, but didn't like the story line and couldn't think of a way to change it. Mason crowded her mind, but she pushed thoughts of him aside. She'd sell her house in Pilgrim and buy a small bachelor apartment in New York City, one in which she could easily maneuver.

"No, I won't," she swore, as the bile of it seeped into her mouth. Why should she give up everything she loved? Her little house? Her work? Her mountains? *And Mason!* She answered the phone.

"Grace Tilden here. We took our morning tea together."

Did we? Jeannetta, who wouldn't taste tea before noon, smiled inwardly at the British manners.

"I have a friend who would take us for a spin around the city, out to the zoo and back to her house for dinner, if you'd like."

Jeannetta thanked her, but declined. "I've got to get back home, and put my life in order." No more running from the inevitable. She threw her suitcases on the bed and started repacking.

## Chapter 8

Mason woke up with a start and patted the rumpled sheet beside him. He hadn't been dreaming; the musky scent of their love-making confirmed what his body remembered. Their night of loving had lifted him to heights he'd never known. And still she'd left his side. He had sensed her desperation that second time but, after what they'd shared, he wouldn't have thought she'd leave him. He phoned the desk.

"Miss Rollins checked out, sir, and I don't think she used a hotel taxi, because none of the hotel drivers logged in a trip for her."

He thanked the clerk, and called Laura.

"She checked out," he said, "and I don't know where she is. Think she'll go back home?"

"I don't know, Dr. Fenwick, but, when we talked, I got the feeling she was getting tired of running from place to place. What will you do now?"

"Find her." Telephone calls to the local hotels yielded no clues. He headed for the airport and bought a ticket to New York. When he found her, he wouldn't let her out of his sight until he had her under anesthesia. But that had better be soon.

Two days later, wearing a thick beard, his body weary from the loss of sleep during forty-eight hours of flights and layovers, he got off the train in Pilgrim, New York. At the local post office, he telephoned Steve.

"What in Job's name are you doing in Pilgrim? Viv hasn't heard from you in days, and she wants your okay on over a dozen appointments. Some of the cases are urgent." Mason put his right hand in his pocket and fingered the keys. Wasn't this what he'd left? This stress, race after race against time? A lot of people wanting immediate and undivided attention? Steve would have to understand.

"Tell Viv not to make any firm appointments. Man, I haven't even announced that I'm reopening my office, and I'm not available to anybody until I take care of one thing. Someone needs me, and she comes first. After that, we'll see. How's Skip doing?"

"I suppose you'll get around to telling me who *she* is. Skip's fine. He got a scholarship from his choral group, and he's anxious about when you're coming back. He's real proud of that scholarship."

"Me, too. I'll call him tonight." Mason went to the postal clerk's window.

"Can you tell me where I'll find the Rollins family?"

"Sure can," the pretty woman replied. Part Native American and part Caucasian, he judged. He wrote the directions to Rollins Hideaway, put the note in his pocket, and turned to leave. He had to call Skip.

"Mason!" The boy shrieked. "Where are you? Can I come over right now?"

"Calm down, son. I'm upstate, and I may be here for a few days, but I wanted you to know that I'm back in the States, and I'll see you soon. Congratulations on that scholarship. I'm proud of you."

"You are? Gee. Thanks."

"How's Mabel?" He sensed from Skip's diminished buoyancy that his aunt might have deteriorated.

"Not so hot; she wants see you."

He had to look into that situation as soon as he got Jeannetta to see reason and treated her.

"I'll call her tonight. And don't worry, I'll take care of things there."

He hung up, got into a taxi and headed for Rollins Hideaway. The woman who greeted him bore no resemblance to Jeannetta, so he assumed she wasn't Laura.

"Don't ever come up here in winter without a reservation,"

the woman said. "You want something on the first floor or the second? Second's quieter."

"I'll take one on the second. Is Miss Rollins here?" He hoped she'd say no, because he wanted Jeannetta's sister to be friendlier and more…

"She's at the market. I'll tell her you want to see her." He got a shower and lay down for a few minutes, only to be awakened by the ringing phone seven hours later at six o'clock in the evening.

"Dr. Fenwick, this is Laura. Nice to have you with us. We start supper at six-thirty, but if you don't want to come down, you may eat in your room."

"Thanks, but I'll be down in a couple of minutes." He pulled on jeans, a T-shirt and sneakers, and walked down to the lobby. Laura met him, but he noticed she didn't offer to shake until he extended his hand. After an exchange of greetings, he watched her size him up. And frank about it, too, he mused.

"She's not as foolish as I was beginning to think," Laura said, dryly, as she motioned him to sit down.

"Any idea where she is?" he asked.

"She's been wrong all through this," Laura said, "but she didn't plan for it to happen like it did. I hope you can talk sense into her."

But what about answering my question, he wanted to ask her. Instead, he told himself to have patience.

"Tell me where you stand in this; I have to know precisely what I'm dealing with."

"Do whatever you can for her. She thinks she's strong, that she can face anything, but she hasn't dealt with blindness. Except for music, everything she loves comes to her through her eyes."

He nodded. "I've noticed that." He stretched his legs out in front of him and strummed his fingers on the arm of the chair. "I have to find her, because she doesn't have that much time left, and I don't want to be faced with the impossible. Where do you think she'll go?" Laura looked intently at him, and he didn't doubt that she judged him.

"You want to put another trophy on your mantelpiece, or do you care about her? Which is it?"

He tilted his head and weighed his answer. Her audacity didn't bother him, but what he felt for Jeannetta was private.

"Because of her, I'm returning to a profession that I gave up when it began to bring me more pain than pleasure. Going back will not be easy, but I'd walk off a cliff blindfolded before I'd refuse to help her. I *have* to do this, as much for myself as for her, and I hope I have your blessing."

"And my prayers. Her train pulls in tomorrow afternoon, but I wouldn't meet it, if I were you. You'll be more successful if you wait until around six-thirty, when she's home." She looked squarely into his eyes. "Do you love my sister?"

"She's everything to me."

Her deep sigh told him that his answer wasn't what she wanted, but that she accepted it.

"Alright. I'll let you know when she gets home."

The following evening when the sun hovered low, near the time of day that Jeannetta loved most, he covered the few blocks from the Hideaway to her house, with his heart hammering at his chest. He couldn't force Jeannetta to do what was best for her, and if she refused help, he didn't know what he'd do. He took the neat brick walkway to her door in three long strides, his eagerness to see her overcoming his anxiety. The door cracked open, but the chain separated them.

"Who is it?"

His stomach muscles tightened, moisture beaded his forehead and he could hear the thudding of his heart. She stared directly at him and asked who he was.

"Open the door, Jeannetta." A painful knot clutched his insides when she squinted in an effort to bring him into focus.

Her whole body came alive when she heard his beloved voice, but immediately she tensed. He had outmaneuvered her and, now, she wasn't able to get away from him. She'd talk with him, but she wouldn't budge from her position.

"Why did you come? Haven't I made it clear that I don't want your help?"

"Open the door, sweetheart, or I'll break it down, chain and all."

A warm glow enlivened her, raising her spirits. Did he care that much?

"Why?" She kept her voice cool, a part of the armor she'd have to wear in order to stand her ground. She heard the tired exasperation in his voice and felt herself softening.

"You ought to know by now that I will not give up. You don't know what you're facing, but I do."

"Please go away." She would have closed the door, but he prevented that with his foot.

"I need you, Jeannetta. You let me make love to you, and you held me in your body and loved me until I lost touch with myself. And now you tell me to please get lost. Just go to hell and leave you alone. Haven't you thought about what I felt with you that night and what I went through the next morning, when I reached for you and you weren't there?"

"Don't make this more difficult that it already is. Please, I…"

He interrupted her, and she wished she could see his eyes more clearly; she'd always depended on his eyes rather than his words to tell her what he felt.

"How did you think I'd react to your leaving like that after you pulled out the stops and showed me what loving you could be? Did you lie when you told me you'd love me as long as you had breath in your body, or were you just caught up in the moment, in getting what you wanted?"

Her hand reached out involuntarily, but she let it drop to her side. She couldn't let him think she'd used him to satisfy her physical needs, but she couldn't let him risk performing that operation.

"Please, Mason. You don't believe any of that; you couldn't. So, let it rest. I'm glad you've gone back to your profession, because I know that's where your heart is, but you can't jeopardize your chances of succeeding by making me your first case. I won't let you." She wished he'd leave, because she wouldn't hurt him by closing the door and, if he stayed there—his

824

presence more palpable than when she'd been able to read his mesmeric eyes, and her need to feel his arms around her overwhelming her—she knew she'd give in. He shifted his stance then, and the low hum of excitement that had teased her since she'd cracked open the door and heard his voice suddenly galloped through her nervous system. His male aura curled around her, and she sucked in her breath.

"I nearly went out of my mind when I realized you'd disappeared again, and you didn't leave me a clue as to where you'd gone. Don't you care that I need you? Don't you? Open this door, baby, and let me get you in my arms."

She lifted the chain.

A groan tore from him as his hands encircled her body, and he crushed her to his big frame. She had no shame about the desperation and passion that he must have heard in her answering cry. Her pulse leapt, and her heart nearly burst when at last she could clasp his head with her hands and feel his mouth possess hers in a plundering kiss. She savored his tongue swirling in her mouth as though he had to relearn every crevice, and an unearthly sensation heated her blood as his arms tightened around her, fitting her to his body. She moved against him. It wasn't enough. She needed more. All of him. Everything. But he broke the kiss and held her away.

His fingers traced her eyes, opening the lids as his fingers moved from side to side, and she realized that he examined them.

"Thank God," she heard him whisper, and he seemed to release a gush of air.

"What? What is it?" she asked, as he pulled her back to him and rested his head in the curve of her shoulder.

"I don't think I'm too late. I read your tests last week, thanks to Dr. Farmer's help. You've lost your peripheral vision, and there's more, but I can handle it. Oh, honey, why don't you trust me?"

"I do. Oh, Mason, I do. But you're human, and I don't want to be on your conscience."

He didn't move, but she could detect the restlessness in him from the muscle that twitched in his jaw where her fingers rested.

"You're worried about me?"

She shook her head, unwilling to burden him or to give him ammunition with which to persuade her to do as he asked.

"Then, you do love me. That's what this is all about, isn't it? You were willing to let me take the chance; in fact, you wanted me to take the chance until you loved me. Isn't that right: *Tell me!*"

She couldn't lie to him; the words wouldn't come. She nodded.

"Jeannetta. Sweetheart." His arms went around her and brought her into the protection of his warmth and caring.

"Mason. Oh, Mason," she sobbed. So near to her, and yet so far. It was more than she could bear. She leaned away from him, and her hands traced his face until his skin warmed her palms. Her fingers caressed his closed eyes, roamed over his lips, nose and ears, and her palms grazed lightly over his cheeks and forehead until tremors shook her body. She hadn't wanted him to know that she only saw his shadow, but she couldn't help herself; she had to see him, really *see* him. He must have realized why she'd done that, because he beseeched her.

"Sweetheart, don't. It will be alright, if you just trust me." His arms brought her closer, and she relaxed in their loving circle.

"I do. I trust you implicitly. I have from the moment we met." She sensed the quickening of his breath and the easing away of his tension, and she raised her lips to his. The deep and rapid thrusts of his tongue sent the fire of desire shooting through her. She needed to feel him against her, inside of her, and her right leg raised to grip his hip as her groan of passion echoed through the foyer. Her need became a flame burning out of control. He rose against her, pressing into her belly, and her fingers caressed him, encouraging, urging until his cries pierced the silence, and the powerful man shuddered against her. She undulated wildly, all control dissipated.

"Jeannetta. Stop it, baby. Give us a chance to make this memorable. Let me love you the way I want to. The way I need to." He carried her up the stairs, strode unerringly to her bedroom and set her on her feet.

\* \* \*

Mason knew he couldn't communicate with her with his eyes, so he asked her, "Do you want this, Jeannetta?"

"Yes. Yes. Oh, yes." All woman and all his. His blood quickened when his hands met the thin sheen of moisture on her arms, and he knew he'd find more where it counted most. She grasped him eagerly, and he drew the snug fitting T-shirt over her head, gripped her shorts and heard the button hit the bedpost. Her fingers fumbled with his tie and the buttons of his shirt, and it saddened him that he had to still her hands and do it himself. His blood began to simmer when her fingers grazed his pectorals, and he grabbed her bra, pulled it up over her head and bent to her swollen nipples. With unsteady hands, she unbuckled his belt, eased her fingers past his navel, groped for him and found him. Her busy hands made him want to relax and take it, but his heart wouldn't let him do it. He thought he'd blow up before he could finish undressing them both and lay her in bed. He looked down at her, arms raised to him in a gesture as old as woman, and sprang to full readiness. Her nostrils flared and perspiration beaded on her forehead as he knelt to her embrace.

His senses whirled dizzily as she guided him to her lover's portal, and he sank into her sweet heaven. He felt her relax, stop driving for what she needed, and give way to his lead, and he had to push back the tears. Home. She tightened her grip on him, and he thrust gently, careful not to let her push him too far too soon. Even so, when she caught his rhythm and joined his dance in perfect harmony, giving him everything as she'd done in Zimbabwe, he had to think of something other than the passionately hot lover beneath him. Her long legs wound around him, and the sound of his name on her lips nearly sent him over the edge. He murmured to her.

"You're mine, and I'm yours. You do whatever you want with me. Let it go. Give in to me, baby." He put his hand between them, caressed her as he accelerated his movements, and she rewarded him with a keening cry and the beginning ripples of completion that clutched at him until he shouted his release and she yelled his name in ecstasy.

"Oh, Mason. My love. I love you so."

He wanted to tell her what he felt, to open his heart to her, but the words didn't come. He kissed her eyes and her lips and laid his head on her shoulder.

"You...I've never known anyone like you. You're the only woman who's given me this feeling of completeness. Wholeness." His lips brushed her shoulder, and he looked down at her breasts, their smooth olive skin and dark aureoles, hard with desire. She moved beneath him, exciting him, making him proud that she wanted him when he knew he'd satisfied her thoroughly only minutes earlier. This time, she exhibited no submissiveness, but demanded what she knew he could give her, and he gloried in her womanliness.

She's what I need, he thought, as her hands grasped his buttocks and she lifted herself to his loving, drawing him deeper until she pitched over the edge, draining his essence and tearing at the shield in which he'd shrouded himself for thirty-seven years.

He lay awake in the darkened room, glad that he'd slept during the day, because he didn't intend to go to sleep nor to leave her side until she gave him her word. She stirred beside him, and he drew her closer.

"Are you awake?" For an answer, she kissed his shoulder.

"Be prepared, Jeannetta. I am not going back to New York City until I can take you with me. I intend to stay with you until you give me your word." He felt her tense, but he plowed on." Nothing and no one will make me leave here until you come with me."

"What about your business?"

He turned on his side, propped himself up with his elbow and gazed down at her.

"My next tour is ten months from now and, in the meantime, my secretary and my assistant can run the business. If they need my advice or opinion, you've got a telephone."

She looked away from him. "Are you accepting any patients, yet? What about them?"

"Not to worry. You've my only patient right now." He couldn't understand her stubbornness nor what she thought she'd gain with it, so he punctuated his words. "You. *Only you.* And it'll be that way until you give up this notion of being a martyr." He could see that she bristled at the remark.

"What are you saying? If I don't let you operate, what will you do—go back to surgery or keep your travel agency?"

"Honey, I own Fenwick Travel Agency. I've been hoping that my brother would operate it but, if he won't, my assistant can do it. I'm a surgeon. I know that now, and that's what I'll be no matter what. A dozen people have asked their doctors to try and persuade me to help them, and the guilt of ignoring that far outweighs any concerns I have about performing that surgery." He fell over on his back and encouraged her to relax on top of him. She slid into his open arms.

"I suppose this crisis in my life has forced me to develop some humility," he went on. "I hadn't had much of that since I completed my internship. To tell the truth, I doubt I was ever humble, but it's been brought home to me with hurricane force that I'm not all-powerful, and I needed to learn that." *I won't push her right now,* he told himself, reasoning that their lovemaking had probably exhausted her.

"Can you sleep in that position?" he asked, hoping she wouldn't move and he'd have the upper hand if she attempted to leave him. He breathed more deeply when she nodded, wrapped her arms around his shoulders, and closed her eyes.

She rolled off of him and burrowed into her pillow.

"You've been awake for at least half an hour, and I'll bet you've been lying there plotting. Your mental wheels are already preparing you for flight," he said, his tone light as though her behavior didn't concern him.

"G…go back to s…sleep," she slurred.

"Not this time. I'm a morning man, remember? If you'd planned to move on, you've missed your chance. You're my woman, Jeannetta, and I'm sticking with you; no man could do what you're asking of me. If you don't give me your word that you'll go to New York city with me as soon as I can make arrangements—Tuesday at the latest—then I'll just stay here."

"You make the alternative sound like a threat. Believe me, I never heard of such delicious punishment." She yawned, raised her arms above her head, stretched and purred. "It's like giving a kid an allowance for misbehaving. Will you stay forever?"

"Stop playing with me, woman." He looked down at her, watching her breasts jut forward when she twisted and stretched, and his voice lacked sincerity. She couldn't see them well, but she knew from his hoarseness that his eyes had become greenish-brown. And it didn't surprise her when his fingers skimmed her thigh and his hot breath teased her skin seconds before she felt him suck her nipple into his mouth. She squirmed, and he couldn't doubt that she liked it, but he raised his head.

"You want me to make breakfast, or…"

"Ooh," she gasped, as his lips encircled the little brown aureole, pulling and sucking, while his fingers danced wickedly and wantonly inches away from where she wanted them to be.

"What do you want for breakfast?" he teased, his voice dark and lusty. She swallowed hard; damned if she'd beg him. His fingers inched closer to their prize.

"What do you want?"

She buttoned her lip and swallowed more. If he wanted to play games, she'd do her best to accommodate him.

"Won't talk, eh? Okay by me." He bent to her breast. Exasperated at his teasing, she reached for him and lovingly encircled his velvet steel. A groan erupted from his throat, but he wouldn't give in to her. Suddenly she remembered what she'd wanted to do to him when she found him lying on the Lido beach, and she led him to his back, straddled him and took him mercilessly, wantonly, withholding nothing, until he surrendered. Until they both surrendered. Spent. She gazed down at him, but when she couldn't make out his expression, she let her fingers graze lightly over his face. Yes, he smiled. She thought her heart would burst.

Mason held her against him while the fingers of his left hand played in her wooly curls. Contentment permeated his whole being. Her lovemaking hadn't been desperate; he was sure of that, but he'd give a lot to know why she'd gotten aggressive with him. He couldn't think of anything more alien to her character. Or was it, he asked himself, remembering their tryst in the tour bus? Her arms encircled his neck, and she stretched out on top of him. Then it came to him: *Jeannetta hadn't been able to see him clearly, and she hadn't been able to judge from his eyes his reactions to what she did, so she had let her inhibitions fly.* Great for their lovemaking, but that was as far as it went.

He got up, walked downstairs, got the reports on her clinical tests that Dr. Farmer had sent him, and reviewed them briefly. Then he went back to bed and pulled Jeannetta close. "Trust me?" She nodded. "You know I do." He reached for the phone on the night table beside the bed, placed it on her back, picked up the receiver and dialed.

"This is Dr. Fenwick. Schedule surgery for tomorrow morning. The patient's name is Jeannetta Rollins, and I'm checking her in this afternoon. Thanks." He hung up and held his breath while he waited for her to protest or to accuse him of seducing her in order to get his way. But she said nothing, and the muscles of his belly tightened while he awaited her next move.

Wet drops splashed on his chest. He raised her from where she lay prone on top of him, and the sight of tears bathing her face tore at his insides.

"What is it, baby? Have I gone too far? I only want to help you before it's too late. You have to know that I'd rather hurt myself than you. Talk to me, honey." He listened to words that came haltingly, but firmly.

"No. You haven't hurt me, and I know you won't if you can prevent it. You've made me feel special. Please promise me that if it doesn't work out the way you want it to, you'll be satisfied that you gave it your best shot, and you'll understand that I'm content no matter the outcome. Promise me that, and I'll go with you this afternoon." He stared at her, his emotions so near the surface that, for seconds, he couldn't trust himself to utter a word. Had his month of gruelling torture and guilt ended at last, and could he find the words to let her know what her trust meant to him? He held her face and he kissed her, because no words could tell her what he felt.

"I promise. And all I ask of you is that you trust me. My chief told me last week that we doctors don't perform miracles, but that miracles are often performed *through* us. If I remembered that, he added, everything would fall in place."

She'd been quiet while he spoke.

"You alright?"

Her answer was a kiss on his neck.

"Can you be ready to go to New York with me this afternoon?" He held his breath for fear she'd procrastinate.

"I'll go with you." Air gushed out of him, and he gave silent thanks.

"I don't have much time to get things together here," Jeannetta told Mason, who watched her fumble her way around the house.

"Just pack a gown, robe, slippers, and your toothbrush, honey. We're not going on vacation."

She wrinkled her nose at him, and his hand went to his chest as if he could steady the fluttering of his heart from the simple gesture. He could see the pieces of his life marching toward each other and fitting themselves together in a perfect whole. Only six weeks earlier, he wouldn't dared have imagined it. "Aren't you going to tell Laura?"

Jeannetta turned toward the direction of his voice. She didn't mind the haze in which she had awakened the previous morning, because he was with her, thought she knew now that she would have hated experiencing it alone. She groped for the phone, but failed to touch it.

"Where's the phone?" She didn't even care if he knew how bad things had gotten. He handed it to her.

"Laura, I'm going to New York with Mason this afternoon. The surgery is tomorrow morning."

"Thank God. I didn't want to see you ruin your life for some supposed altruistic reason. I've never been in love, but if it makes you do unreasonable things, I don't want any part of it. Mason looked capable to me." Jeannetta sat down, because, once Laura got going, she preached a sermon.

"You always did attract men, and some were good ones, too. I used to envy you, because you had the beauty, smarts, height, and all that. And I never could see why you couldn't accept one of those nice men and settle down. Maybe now, you will. Honey, I sure hope so. I can't close the Hideaway and go with you to New York, but, I'll be praying for you."

"Thanks, Laura, and don't worry. I'm in good hands." Laura envious of her? She couldn't believe it.

"By the way," Laura added, "that Mr. Miles called here this morning, and I told him you're back. He is one persistent man, and you know I don't lie." She paused for a second, and Jeannetta knew she was about to get some unsolicited advice. "Don't you think you should rent out your house and stay here at the Hideaway 'til you get healed up?"

"Thanks for the offer, but it'll be time enough to think about that when I start recovery. I have to get over this next step before I worry about the future. Mason will let you know how I am. And Laura, for once, I appreciate your meddling and telling him where to find me."

Mason waited with Jeannetta in the admitting office and, later, accompanied her to her room. She placed her recorder on the little night table, sat on the edge of the bed, and Mason took a chair beside her and held both of her hands.

"Have you so little faith in me that you brought the recorder with you?"

She removed her hand and tugged at his arm. "I believe in you with all my heart, but this gives me something to do. I can't sustain an interest in my novel, and that hasn't happened to me before, so I think I'm going to scratch it. A different story plays around in my mind, and I'm going to have to write that one as soon as I recover. That's why I need the recorder, so I can put down these ideas."

The phone rang, and Mason handed it to her.

"This is Clayton."

"Oh, Clayton. I'm so glad to hear your voice. I've decided to do it, and now that I've made up my mind, I can't wait to put it behind me."

"You have company?" He must have deduced that from the stiltedness of her conversation. She told him that she did.

"Fenwick, no doubt."

It embarrassed her to admit that Mason hadn't left the room when she got a personal call.

"Yes.

It probably didn't make sense, but she could suddenly sympathize with the filling in a sandwich, and she didn't like the feeling. "Mason is my surgeon, Clayton, though he's with me right now as a friend."

"Alright. Good luck. I'll see you in a day or so. And don't forget that I asked you to marry me, and that you haven't answered yes or no. So you're half engaged."

"We'll discuss that some other time." She hadn't thought she would ever be glad that she couldn't see Mason's eyes, but she was.

Mason reminded himself that he'd long ago mastered his temper. "A friend, huh? I can't wait to know how you'll act with me when you decide I'm your lover." He took the old keys out and looked at them; the night before, with her in his arms, he'd thought she might be his home. He tossed them about a foot high, caught them, and put them back in his pocket. Miles was after her, but what was *he* after, his conscience prodded. He had no answer; one step at a time, he told himself.

"There's nothing between Clayton and me. Surely, you don't think I could…"

He cut her off. "Of course I don't think you'd make love with me if you had an intimate relationship with another man. But Clayton Miles wants you."

"Okay, I'll print a sign telling men it's illegal to want me and stick it in my hair where everybody can see it." The laughter that rang in her words warmed his heart and eased his concern that she might get a pre-op case of nerves.

He moved closer and took her hand. "You'll have to add in big letters: 'except for Mason Fenwick'; otherwise I might find myself behind a grilled fence dressed in regulation drab blue."

She pooh-poohed the remark. "Not even a barbed-wire fence could hold you."

He draped his arm lightly around her and asked her, "Do you remember that morning on the Lido beach?" She nodded.

"Why did you run away? I know you did, because I saw that wide gauzy shirt you wore trailing behind you as you ran. I was half asleep, but I knew someone stood there watching me. The first thing a doctor learns when he begins residency is not to sleep soundly. What happened?"

Her left hand grazed his chest, and he held her closer.

"You'd be shocked. You should have seen yourself lying there at my mercy, almost completely nude with sweat beaded on your body."

He heard her swallow and told his libido to get lost.

"I almost gave in to an impulse to strip that little G-string off of you and make love to you then and there. My hand had actually reached toward you when I came to myself. If you'd felt what I did, you'd have run, too. The violation of your person would have been against the law."

He couldn't suppress the mirth that boiled up in his throat and came forth in peals of laughter.

"Baby, believe me, you wouldn't have done anything illegal, because you would have had my complete and eager cooperation. I can't think of anything that could have excited me more."

She gasped in astonishment. "On a public beach?"

He grinned as the picture of it flashed through his mind. "Well, hell, honey. You were barely speaking to me in those days, so I'd have taken what I could get when I could get it."

"I can just see the salacious newspaper headlines for which the Italian *paparazzi* are famous: African-American man and woman heat up the Lido. Or maybe: American blacks show how it's done."

"Alright. Let's not get carried away. Anyhow, I think you ought to get some rest, because you and I have an early appointment in the morning. I'll stay with you until you're asleep."

"They gave me sleeping pills, but I don't want them."

He tried to concentrate on *Essence* magazine while she prepared for bed.

"I'd sleep here in the room with you, but hospital regulations don't permit it." He kissed her with a gentle brush of his lips over hers, and his anxiety for her dissipated when she kissed him without a hint of desperation. He lowered the light and sat opposite her in a chair. Twenty minutes later, he gazed down at her, brushed her forehead with his lips, and left.

Jeannetta fought the clutches of sleep; she'd wanted to tell him something. Oh, yes. That business about having a private investigator dig into is life and give her a report on him. She shouldn't have done it, and she had to tell him so she'd have a clean slate with him. The sound of his light footsteps receded… She had to tell him…

At six o'clock the next morning, scrubbed and ready, Mason looked down at his gloved hands and remembered his chief's admonishment that miracles were performed not by doctors, but through them. He had decided not to see Jeannetta before she'd been anesthetized, because he wasn't sure how he'd react if she seemed afraid. He didn't deserve to be heard, but he said a prayer nonetheless. Then he put the past and the future out of his mind and concentrated on the now. He knew that the group assembled in the operating theater was unusually large, that the interns, residents, nurses, and surgeons not in attendance had come to watch him make it or lose it. He smiled inwardly. They were entitled to their skepticism but, by damn, he'd show them. He looked down at her sleeping peacefully, her trust evident even in unconsciousness. He extended his right hand to the head nurse, looked at the instrument she handed him, winked at her as he'd always done in earlier times, and went to work.

Four hours later, he found a telephone and called Laura.

"It went well," he told her. "She's resting in the intensive-care room. It was a neat job, my best, Laura, but I won't know for weeks, maybe longer, whether I've been completely successful."

"Well, if you did your best, I couldn't expect more. Thank you isn't much at times like this," she said, her voice breaking, "and I know all this has been hard on you. But I do thank you, Dr. Fenwick, and I have to tell you that I admire you. You get some rest and come on back soon as you can. You hear?"

"Thanks. And Laura, call me Mason." He stopped by ICU to check on Jeannetta and, as he stood there, his fingers automatically went to the pocket in which he kept his keys but, instead of them, he grasped the note that an attendant had handed him after he completed the surgery.

"My love," he read. "You've done your best, and I'm happy. I shall always be happy, and I shall always love you. This is your true calling, so, no matter what happens, stay with it. Love, Jeannetta." His lips brushed her cool forehead, and he turned quickly away, blowing his nose to camouflage his emotions as he strode swiftly down the hallway.

He got coffee at a take-out shop on the way home, savored it, took a quick shower, and fell into bed. "I'm not tired," he marveled, sitting up. He flipped on the radio and turned it off as soon as he heard the country music. No use going to the other stations, because he couldn't stand rock or rap, either, and he didn't feel like concentrating on classical music. He needed to see Steve and Skip. He'd turned a corner, found his stride, and he had to share it with them. A call to the hospital satisfied his concern about Jeannetta, and he struck out for Steve's apartment.

His brother opened the door, and contentment washed over him as Steve welcomed him with open arms. He couldn't remember the last time they had embraced so heartily.

"Well, how did it go?"

Mason shrugged his right shoulder and brushed his fingers over his tight curls. "So far, so good."

Steve walked off a few paces, turned around, and looked at him. "That's all? What did you feel going back in there?"

Mason hadn't let himself think much about that. "I can't say, truthfully, because I tried not to think about anything except the job."

"How bad was it?" They walked to Steve's study, two men of commanding height and presence. Regarding Steve from the corner of his right eye, Mason had to wonder what his brother might have become had he been selfish and ignored his younger brother's needs.

"Another month or so and it might have been too late," he said, adding that, "it's difficult to reverse the disease after the patient loses sight. I won't know for a while whether we have a complete cure." When Steve raised an eyebrow, he amended it. "I mean I can't be certain yet that I've corrected the problem and that she's good as new. I don't expect she'll get any worse." But the operation had been a success, he reminded himself, and released a long breath.

"Want a drink?"

A half-smile played around Mason's lips. His conservative brother considered daytime drinking to be a form of debauchery.

"Not until I've done an examination. She has to have an MRI, a skull x-ray, a thorough ophthalmoscopic exam. Everything. I need my wits. Jeannetta's my priority."

"You can't focus entirely on her," Steve said, clearly aghast. "You'll be a nervous wreck. Take on some other patients; they're waiting in line."

Mason watched as his brother's eyes narrowed, warning him to expect a drilling.

"You planning to quit if you don't cure her?"

Mason leaned against the edge of their father's old roll-top desk and folded his arms across his chest.

"I know you're not proud of some of my decisions, but every one of them expressed the truth as I saw it. My integrity is intact, and I take pride in that."

"Yeah. Me, too. I didn't mean to lecture, but you're getting on with your life, so it's time you forgot about that one almost-error." He grinned, and Mason thought of their father; Steve's likeness to him had made it easy for both of them to remember the man whom they had loved so much.

"Now that they all know you're human, how did they act this morning?"

"Funny," Mason said, a laugh lacing his words. "This morning, I had a room full of 'em, and they all looked as though they expected me to tear it. Man, that was a good feeling—no place to go but up. None of that idolatry I thought I loved."

"Maybe it's a good thing you slid on your rear. I can't remember the last time you came over here after surgery. I've missed these times we had when you couldn't contain your excitement after you'd taken a difficult case and succeeded. Sometimes, I wondered if I'd have to tie a lodestone on you to get you back to earth. Then, women discovered you. A physician shouldn't allow himself to become a socialite." He walked over, patted Mason on the shoulder, and must have seen the emotion mirrored in his brother's eyes, for he turned quickly away.

"I'm glad you made it back. Come on; how about some hamburgers and a beer?"

"Hamburgers sound good to me, but save the beer." In the kitchen, Mason pulled a straight back chair from the table, straddled it, and rested his chin on his forearms.

"How about taking over my travel business? You can do it. I'd be a silent partner, and knowing you were in charge would free me to concentrate on my patients."

Steve looked him in the eye. "I've told you a hundred times that you don't owe me anything; you're my brother. Whatever I did, I'd gladly do all over again." And he would, too, Mason realized.

"There's a woman who takes that tour every year. A high school teacher. She once asked me if I had a brother and, when I told her about you, she said the two of you were cut from the same cloth. At least, take the tour. You'll like her." Interesting. Steve's hamburgers needed a lot of attention all of a sudden.

"Why do I have to wait until next May to meet her?"

Mason tried not to show his astonishment. "Good point," was all he said, but he made a mental note to get in touch with Darlene Jones when the tour returned.

"What are you planning to do about Skip? He wants to be a doctor?" Mason meant to bite his hamburger and nicked his tongue.

"This is good stuff, and it would be even better if you'd left some of this onion in that bin. Skip's a great example of what some care and a little help can do. If he makes good grades, I'll send him to school."

Steve pushed his plate aside and leaned back in his chair. Now what? "Skip wants you to adopt him, and he says his aunt wouldn't mind."

Mason coughed up the crumbs that stuck in his windpipe and reached for water. "This is a day for surprises. What else did he say?"

Steve reached for a pickle, pointed it toward Mason and grinned. "Well, if you want to know, he said he tricked you when he asked you to be his big brother because, from the outset, what he wanted was to be your son. You might say he wormed his way in."

Mason couldn't suppress an outright laugh. "Slick little devil." He glanced at Steve, who watched him closely.

"He's very special to me, Steve, and he needs me. He needs you, too. I'm going to listen to what he has to say." He washed his hands, stretched out on the sofa, and went to sleep.

Several hours later, he jumped up, startled. He'd have to get used to that beeper again; it was one of the things he hadn't missed during his hiatus from medicine.

"Dr. Fenwick." That sounded strange, too, as he'd gotten accustomed to referring to himself as "Fenwick."

"An ICU nurse at the hospital called to say that Miss Rollins is awake and asking for you," Viv said. His stomach unknotted, and he breathed deeply. Mention of a nurse had sent his heart racing and twisted his belly.

"Should I start looking for another job, Mr. Fen...I mean, Dr. Fenwick?"

"Viv, for pete's sake. I'm not closing the travel agency; in fact, you'll probably get a raise, because you're going to have more work. Anything I need to do there?" Assured that there wasn't, he headed for the hospital. He'd done it. He hailed a taxi that seemed to stand still even as it moved and, as he walked through the hospital door, he strove for professional decorum, but when he got off the elevator, he chucked it and ran.

# Chapter 9

Jeannetta shifted in bed, reaching for the elusive sun rays as she tripped through the beautiful forest. Great elms, oaks, and pines, heavy with branches, bowed as she drifted among them; hyacinths and roses showered her with perfume; and the squirrels, raccoons, foxes, and bears smiled at her with greenish-brown eyes as she passed. She wandered out of the forest and down to the beach and dug up a handful of sand but, when she tried to sift it through her fingers, it wouldn't leave her palm. Four little black dolls that she had crocheted for the Edwin Gould Foundation to distribute to poor children at Christmas danced around her. And from somewhere far away, Mason called her. But his voice was such a lovely masculine velvet that she didn't want to answer for fear he'd stop. She smiled in joyful appreciation. The animals ran away, the dolls disappeared, and the forest, beach, and ocean dissolved into a lovely white cloud.

"Darling, talk to me. Let me hear your voice. Answer me, sweetheart. How do you feel?" The blur slowly disappeared, and he was there, close. His own masculine scent, his special aura, enveloped her, and she knew that the hand holding hers belonged to him. His lips brushed her forehead, and she had to struggle not to slide back into the Heaven from which she'd just come.

"Come on, baby, say something to me. Anything." She squeezed his hand, and her face dissolved into that luminous smile that always thrilled him to his soul. Thank God, they'd passed the first and worst hurdle.

"Hi." He needed to hear a few more words so that he could judge her speech, but that one was worth a gold mine.

"Hi," he said, as casually as he could. "How do you feel?"

"It is over? What time is it?"

"About seven-thirty." He did a few simple tests and, satisfied with the results, sat beside her bed.

"Did you leave me with any hair?" she asked, as though reluctant to know the answer. The strength of her voice pleased him. "Plenty. When the bandage comes off, you'll be able to comb your hair so that it hides that bare spot. In a few months, you won't know it was shaved." She patted his hand, and her smile tugged at his heart.

"Where were you just now, honey?" He listened to her tale and almost wished he'd been there with her.

"I'm glad you had such a pleasant adventure; it means things are going well."

She reached toward him.

"Could I give you a kiss?" she asked him, her voice low and sultry. The woman had a penchant for testing his self-control at the most inconvenient times. He grimaced at the thought of what a hot kiss would do to him right then and stood, removing himself from temptation.

"Don't you think we'd better wait a while for that? Wouldn't want to raise your blood pressure," he joked, though there was little likelihood of it. She mumbled a few incoherent words, which he recognized as evidence of grogginess.

"You always jack up my blood pressure," she said, her words distinct and husky. "I only have to think about you, and it shoots up."

"Really?" He sat down beside her bed again. "I'd like to hear some more of this."

She smiled, shakily, he thought.

"That's because you know you're sexy and…hmmm. Men like you should be banned; we females don't stand a chance around you." She nodded sleepily, and he settled back, enjoying himself.

"I thought you'd gotten your revenge for yourself and half the other women in this country, considering what you've laid on me." He didn't want to overtax her, so he brushed her cheek lightly with his finger and rose to leave. This little touch wasn't the kind of contact he needed with her, but she smiled in return, and his heart fluttered in gratitude. He glanced at the IV that sent life-sustaining fluid into her body, checked her vital signs, and started toward the door.

"Mason…" He'd never get enough of the sweet sound of her voice, trusting, soft, and seductive. He turned to face her.

"There's something about your hands. Long tapered fingers. Smooth and perfect as though you'd never worked. Beautiful hands. First time I…saw…looked at them, I imagined…wondered how they'd feel on my naked body. Hmmm."

He walked back and leaned over her. "And how do they feel?" he asked, keeping his voice low.

"Hmmm. Hot. They make me want to scream for you to get all…all…" Her voice trailed off.

He should be ashamed of himself for taking advantage of her, but he wasn't. He'd been through hell in the last fifteen hours, and he deserved a boost. He watched her as she slept, kissed her cheek again and left, fingering the keys in his pocket. In about two months, he'd have some decisions to make.

Jeannetta gazed out of the same window that had framed her dreams as a child. Yellow leaves peppered the green mountainside, signaling the approach of autumn, though the heat of mid-August still nourished the garden and the little animals that munched on its produce. She wondered about Laura's strange behavior. Her sister couldn't have cared for her more faithfully since they'd decided she would recuperate at the Hideaway, but Jeannetta knew she hadn't mistaken her sister's coolness. She busied herself by dictating notes for her novel, since Mason had urged her not to strain her eyes with reading or writing, limiting her options for whiling away the time. She had begun a new novel, fully cognizant of Mason's role in her decision to drop the other one; he'd shown her how special a man could be, that he could care deeply for you and still not let you inside of him. She picked up her old standby, the guitar that her father had given her on her seventeenth birthday, and began to strum and sing, but a headache and the needlelike sensations around her wound reduced the pleasure that the music usually gave her.

She wondered how much hair she had; a thick bandage covered most of her head, and she had to sleep on her left side. She didn't care how it looked, though, because what it symbolized meant more to her than her thick crop of wooly hair. Mason had promised her that the wound would heal in a few weeks and that, if she wanted to, she could wear a wig. She didn't think she would.

She wrapped a yellow scarf around her head and ambled into the breakfast room with the intention of serving herself from the luncheon buffet table, and what she saw made her think her heart had tumbled to the pit of her stomach. She muffled a gasp and blinked her eyes, wondering whether she had lost her sanity. Surely she wasn't looking at Clayton Miles perched on a stool at the breakfast counter and staring, as though lost, into the eyes of her enraptured sister. She opened her mouth to announce her presence and stopped herself as Clayton spoke.

"I'm not free to say what I feel, Laura, because I'm committed. I don't have to tell you that I'm sorry. You have to know it. Never in my fifty-two years have I felt anything so strongly. Forgive me." She watched Laura, a woman without guile or feminine ego, and understood for the first time the true meaning of loneliness.

"Nothing to forgive," she heard Laura say. "I've been a wallflower all of my life, and I don't expect that to change. I'm average, maybe even less, and that's the way people have always treated me. So don't worry; I'm used to it." Jeannetta flinched at Laura's self-derision.

"If I had the right, I'd make you see that you're talking nonsense, that you're precious. You're the most..." Jeannetta spun around and left; she didn't want to hear it, and she didn't want them to see her. Clayton married? Then how had he planned to marry her? Had he deliberately set out to mislead her sister? And why? She walked back to her room, taking care not to hurry and make herself dizzy. But she did that automatically, because she didn't think of herself, but of Clayton. She'd considered him a man of principle; now she wasn't so sure. She turned the curve at the top of the stairs and bumped into Connie, the chambermaid.

"Connie, is Mr. Miles a guest here?"

"Yes, ma'am. Since yesterday. He must have come yesterday afternoon, I think, 'cause he had dinner here last night and I sure made his bed up this morning."

Jeannetta wished she could check his arrival and departure dates on the office computer, but Mason had forbade her to use one until he gave her the okay. She walked on toward her room and, on a hunch, turned and called Connie. Better not to ask the woman if Clayton had been there before, because Connie had perfected gossip to a fine art. She chose her words carefully.

"When was the last time Mr. Miles was a guest?"

"A little over a week ago, but he only stayed a couple of days."

Jeannetta nodded. Maybe he'd visited her in the hospital while she slept, or when she'd still been under anesthesia. How peculiar. When had Clayton gotten to know Laura well enough to speak to her as he had? She couldn't figure it out. With his money, a twelve-room, low-profit ski lodge couldn't be the reason. She sat down at the little desk in her room, picked up the phone, and ordered her lunch.

Jeannetta had never known Laura to be the object of a man's affection; maybe it was better for her to have the experience, even with a man committed to someone else than to spend her life without it. She didn't know, and didn't think she had the right to judge. She and Laura had always been so close, but lately...Maybe she'd better not mention it. The phone rang.

"How's my favorite patient?"

She grasped her chest to stop her runaway heart. "Feeling fine. She'd like to see her favorite doctor."

"Really? I promised Skip I'd help him apply to the YWHA for

a music tutor. It'll be late before I can get up to Pilgrim, but if you want to see me, count on it. Any vacant rooms in the Hideaway?"

"I don't know, but you may sleep on the sofa in my sitting room if you don't want to sleep with me."

You could almost see him bristle. "What kind of remark is that? You think I'm a piece of deadwood? Woman, don't you remember what happened the last time I was in your bed?" Fear rioted through her body. Had she been in bed with him? She had or he wouldn't have asked her that question. Dear Lord, what else had she forgotten? She'd be cool about it, as though it didn't matter. "Uh…"

"Don't you?" he interrupted. "Well, sweetheart, that doesn't compare to what I need with you now. Not by a mile."

Jeannetta had to force back a swell of apprehension and tell herself to stay calm. Maybe he hadn't meant that they'd actually made love with each other. After all, they had shared some sizzling kisses, and some of their petting had taken them right to the brink. She'd play it safe.

"You've pulled out the stops more than once, so I'm not sure which one of those heady sessions you're talking about. You want to be more specific and refresh my memory a little bit?"

"Don't tease me, Jeannetta."

Tension gripped her as the seriousness of his voice warned her that she had a problem. Her fingers clutched the bed sheet. "We made love in my room in a Zimbabwe hotel," he went on in a dry, hollow voice, "and in your bed in your house up there in Pilgrim. Do you remember, or don't you? This is your doctor speaking now. Do you?"

Dumfounded, she struggled to remember, and her delay in answering must have increased his suspicion, because his tone lost its lover's groove and assumed the determined professionalism of the doctor.

"What plane did you take from Zimbabwe to New York?"

"Mason, I'm…I…"

"What happened after you left Nairobi?" She knew from the huskiness in his voice that he was anxious about her condition, that the man warred with the doctor for expression of feelings. She fudged the truth.

"That escapes me right now, 'cause you're pressuring me. Anyway, I was teasing…or I think I was. I remember us talking about your hands and me in a forest. Look…I think I'm mixing things up. I don't remember Zimbabwe, or you in my house down the street. I…Oh, Mason, is that bad?" She paused. "Mason, did Clayton Miles come to see me while I was in the hospital?"

Mason had begun to think that she wouldn't have a problem with short-term memory.

"Miles? Yeah, he did. On consecutive days. Are you asking me about that because you don't remember?"

Her answer was too long coming, and he knew she was denying the truth.

"Uh…Oh, Mason, I don't remember. Will it ever come back?"

"Usually. And soon. Don't try to remember things, and don't upset yourself about it."

"Are you coming up here tonight?"

"I'll be there, but don't wait up. If you're asleep, and if it isn't too late, I'll wake you." She could bet he'd be up there, because he didn't like what he'd heard. To think that she didn't remember the powerful, gut-searing way in which she'd pitched her inhibitions and loved him until she'd taken everything from him but his soul. And he'd bound her to him as securely as flesh could cement itself to flesh. But she didn't remember, and that made her vulnerable to the ubiquitous Clayton Miles.

"Okay."

She sounded reluctant. He'd learned that he wasted time when he tried to anticipate Jeannetta's thoughts. So he waited.

"I'll connect you to the desk," she continued, as though her mind were elsewhere. "As for a double room and, if they have one, bring Skip. I'd love to meet him, and he'd enjoy this environment."

He hadn't expected that one. "Skip's looking for a job for the next month. He had one delivering homemade bread, but his employer took a month's vacation, and he needs work." He didn't want Skip sidetracked from his goal of saving a hundred dollars each summer month toward his education, but a short stay out of the city wouldn't hurt him.

"Bring him, Mason. You can never tell what might happen."

Mason smiled inwardly. "You've got that right. Once Skip enters your life, I can promise you it's never the same. See you later."

Laura brought up her lunch. Jeannetta had thought she'd have sent it up by one of the help.

"Thanks, hon," Jeannetta said. "I didn't expect you to bring it, because I know how busy you are. You work from the time you get up until you hit the sheets at night, and I'm just adding to your work load."

"Nonsense. Gives me a chance to see how you are." Her words lacked conviction, and Jeannetta could see that she'd forced the smile.

"Laura, what's the matter?"

"Nothing. Maybe I'm just tired." It wasn't like Laura to avoid looking at the person to whom she spoke, but she did just that. Jeannetta stared at her sister, who turned to leave without a semblance of a conversation. Laura, who never missed an opportunity to delve into your private affairs, hadn't mentioned Mason's name.

"Sit down a minute, Laura." Jeannetta didn't believe in procrastinating, especially when it came to Laura, who could hold a grudge or nourish a misunderstanding until clearing up the matter became impossible.

"Something's happened to us, Laura, and it's not good. What is it and what brought it on?"

"Has anything changed?" Laura asked with an unlikely look of innocence.

"You're not talking to me, Laura. You're fencing. Have I done something?" She watched, disbelieving, as her sister sighed deeply and curled up her thin lips at the edges in an expression that Jeannetta hadn't previously observed.

"No. You haven't done anything, Jeanny, except be yourself. You never had to do anything; you only had to *be*."

Stunned, Jeannetta asked her, "Whatever are you talking about?"

"Haven't you ever noticed how different we are? No, I guess

you haven't, because you've had it all. You're beautiful, with your flawless, ebony complexion, perfect face and figure, lovely hands, and soft voice. And you didn't do one thing to deserve it; just an accident of birth. But it's brought you so much. Everything. My hair is straight, but it's thin and stringy, while yours is long and thick, and you can do whatever you want with it. I'm forgettable, short and dumpy, but you've got a model's height and a siren's figure. I've worked so hard to make this Hideaway a four-star lodge that my hands look as if they belong to an old woman. Mom and Dad left me the controlling interest in it, because you were too precious for this kind of work. I love you, but I resent you; I always have."

Her cup clattered in its saucer, spilling tea in her lap, as Jeannetta tried to steady her hand and place the saucer on her lunch tray. With trembling fingers she clutched at her throat. Dr. Farmer's revelation that she had a brain lesion hadn't given her a bigger or more alarming jolt than Laura's words.

"Laura! You don't mean…" The thought trailed off when she looked into her older sister's implacable gaze. "I'm sorry. I never guessed. I always looked up to you, loved and admired you as my older sister, never dreaming how you felt. Does this have anything to do with your not telling me that Clayton is here?"

Her sister was the old Laura again, and she didn't allow an expression to cross her face.

"Did he come here to see you, or me?" Jeannetta persisted.

"Both of us. You might as well know that if it weren't for you, I'd have a man of my own at last. After all these years of watching you and all the other women I know with their men, I'd have my own."

Jeannetta stared at her in astonishment, unable to suppress an audible release of breath.

"Why don't you tell him about Mason?" Laura went on. "That the two of you are lovers. Why do you keep him dangling like you do Jethro? No wonder Alma's upset."

Jeannetta jumped up from the bed, stood over Laura, and shook her finger.

"Don't be cruel, Laura. You know I don't dangle Jethro, that I avoid him. And you also know Alma's paranoid about that man. She's welcome to him. Where did you get the idea that Mason and I are lovers and that I'm dangling Clayton?" She bit her tongue when she remembered Mason's words earlier that day. "From what I heard him say to you this morning, you'd better be careful. He's a married man."

It was Laura's turn to bristle. "Who told you that? It's not true. He said he's committed to someone, and when I asked him a few minutes ago who it was, he said he asked you to marry him so he could take care of you. He's trying to make up for his past mistakes. Either marry him or tell him you can't because you love Mason. You're playing your cards pretty close to your chest, anyhow. When the illustrious Dr. Fenwick finds out that you had him investigated and that you plotted to meet him so you could get him to operate on you, he may decide you had an ulterior motive for going to bed with him."

"*Laura!* For God's sake, what's gotten into you? Yes, I schemed to get to meet him, but all that happened before I ever saw him." She stopped speaking, and her gaze bore into Laura's steady stare.

"What gives you the right to say I've been intimate with Mason? I haven't but, if I had, it wouldn't be anybody's business but ours. We're both free, and I love him."

"Maybe you do, but if he finds out all of this, you'll be in the same boat as I'm in." Her face must have reflected the alarm she felt, because Laura's belligerence suddenly faded. "Don't worry, he won't know it from me, but you remember that old saying, 'Birds don't go north in winter.'"

"No, they don't," Jeannetta, replied after musing over her sister's words. "I gave Clayton my card so he'd know where to find me, but it looks like he found you." Laura's breath quickened and a deep crimson brought a youthful glow to her round face. Jeannetta reached out to her. She didn't want to hurt her sister, and especially not about herself and Clayton Miles.

"You're telling me that you and Clayton care for each other?"

The older woman fidgeted nervously, but she looked Jeannetta in the eye and nodded.

"Then I misunderstood what I heard. He's free, Laura. I never intended to marry him, and I told him his offer was too generous. I've never hidden from him my feelings for Mason. I'll straighten it out." Laura's face brightened so quickly and so luminously that Jeannetta's lower lip dropped.

"Clayton is a wonderful man," Laura said, barely above a whisper. "If he'd wanted you, I would have understood. He hasn't told me exactly what he feels, but he's made me know he cares."

"When did he get here?"

"Last night. You had gone to bed. He... Oh, Jenny, when I knew he'd be here, I almost went out of my mind, waiting. The feeling... It's like something's consuming me. Like something burst wide open in me and is just waiting for him to close it." Jeannetta pulled Laura into her arms and hugged her for a long time, stroking her back, healing their wound.

With wisdom she hadn't applied to herself, she held Laura at arm's length. "You're in the wrong place, hon. When Mason gets here tonight, I won't leave him alone while I chat with you."

Laura stood there, letting her know that their chasm hadn't been breached, that their slate wasn't yet clean. "Are you going to...to talk with Clayton?" So that was it. Laura wanted Clayton freed of his presumed obligations.

"Ask him to come up here in about half an hour. I'll talk with him. And you get out of that apron and those green slacks and put on something pretty. Make it bright-colored and, preferably, knit fabric. Something feminine and clinging. Put on some perfume and go up to his room and wait for him."

"I couldn't do *that!*"

Jeannetta laughed aloud as Laura gaped at her. "It's time you got over being so straight-laced and gave in to your feelings. I remember a time when I probably wouldn't have said that, but I wasn't in love then. Now, go on. You're in for something special."

Laura whirled around with more speed than Jeannetta associated with her sister. "You're not saying that I...I mean that we…I…" She let the thought die, but Jeannetta was now the wiser, the more experienced.

"I'm suggesting that you loosen up and enjoy him, that you do whatever feels right. Now, go on."

Jeannetta remade her bed, slipped into a simple green coat-dress, and went into her sitting room. If Clayton Miles was misleading her sister, he'd pay for it.

Mason looked over his new medical office, checking it against his specifications. He'd gotten what he wanted, a large suite at Ninety-sixth Street and Fifth Avenue—the dividing line of wealth and poverty, because he intended to serve both. He'd have office hours from twelve noon to six-thirty weekdays, leaving mornings free for surgery. He'd see the wealthy on Tuesdays and Thursdays, those less able to pay on Mondays and Wednesdays, and those who couldn't afford to pay on Fridays. Some rich people were uncomfortable around people who weren't like themselves, and he needed their patronage in order to serve those who couldn't afford to pay. But when patients had an emergency, he'd scotch that schedule.

He liked the restful colors, sand and a soft, yellowish green. He'd hung two landscapes, silkscreen prints by the painter, Louis Mailou Jones, in his waiting room, and a nearly life-size photo of the dancer Judith Jamison dressed as Josephine Baker hung in his private office. He could still remember how she'd held him spellbound on the Broadway stage in *Sophisticated Ladies*. Limited-edition prints by Selma Glass decorated each of his examining rooms. He loved the great painters, from Michelangelo and Rembrandt to Miró and Catlett, but he'd hung some originals by less expensive contemporary African-Americans in his office. He meant to put captions under each, so that his patients would know about the painters' lives.

Mason looked at his watch as Skip bounded into the waiting room. "Skip. I've told you a dozen times that a man is worth no more than his word. If you say you'll be here at two o'clock, I don't expect you to walk in here at twenty minutes past. And I don't ever want to have to repeat this. Got it?"

"Yeah. Sorry, but I…"

"Skip. Yes, sir. I'm old enough to be your father." The boy's sheepish expression belied his character. Now what?

"Yes sir. That's what I've been getting at. Sort of. Why can't you adopt me and be my real…?"

"What the…? Say, man what is this?" The boy's eyes rounded, then he narrowed his eyes and took in his surroundings. Mason observed him closely; Skip never bothered to pretend what he didn't feel, and hostility flared from his piercing eyes.

"Ain't this a doctor's office?"

Mason stared right back at him. If he didn't deal with it openly and honestly, he'd lose the trust he'd so carefully built.

"*Isn't* this a doctor's office? Yes, it is." Skip moved around jerkily. Prowl was more like it, Mason decided.

"But I thought you said meet you at your office. You ain't no doctor. What *is* this, man?" He ran his hand over his hair and pierced Mason with a hostile stare. "You been acting strange lately." He paused, less certain, and asked. "Are you a doctor?"

"Don't say 'ain't,' and yes, I'm a neuro-ophthamologist. I…"

"Can the lessons, man. What about your travel agency?" Mason explained as succinctly as he could, and ended with, "and you are not to address me as 'man' anymore." Mason could see the boy's gathering rage, as his jaw worked involuntarily and he began to clench and unclench his fists. He sought quickly to dispel it.

"You don't have to like everything I do, but if you're going to hang out with me, you'd better learn to respect my decisions, and fast."

Confusion replaced the boy's rage.

"How come you didn't say nothin' about it when I told you I wanted to be a doctor?"

"I didn't see it as relevant."

"You didn't see …" The boy resumed his catlike prowling around the room, slapping his fist against his palm. "Let me get this straight. If it hadn't been for this…this bird of yours, you'd still be a travel manager?"

At that, Mason conceded himself the right to a show of temper.

"You've got a problem with that?"

Skip didn't yield.

"I don't know, man. I mean, Mason. Like I'm dying to be just like you, but if I get to be a doctor, I sure as h... —I sure ain't gonna check out and go around the world. I don't think I like this."

In for a penny; in for a pound.

"Sit down, Skip." He related his story in detail, beginning with his near-accident while operating, sparing nothing. "Being a doctor is more than glamour, more than ego and self-importance. It's healing sick people, but when you take chances with their lives and do it for self-aggrandizement, there comes a time when you have to stop and take stock of what you're doing and why. I reached that point the morning my hand slipped and my patient almost paid for it with her life. I realized at that moment that some force beyond me, greater than I, had saved the woman's life, that I wasn't infallible and that I was capable of irreversible damage to my patients. I didn't quit because I got scared, but because I had dared to play God and I found out that I'm not all-powerful."

He didn't have to be told that he had deeply impressed Skip. The boy sat watching him as though mesmerized.

"I wasn't accusing you. I just couldn't understand how you could give up what I want so badly. You were A-one, right?"

Mason nodded. "Yes, but I got cocky, and that's dangerous."

"So what about Jeanny? Is she your patient or your bird?"

"Jeanny?"

"Jeannetta's too long a word."

Mason laughed. His hours with Skip gave him so much pleasure that he sometimes wondered if he could ever repay the boy.

"She's my girl and my patient, but that's an accident, and it's not a good thing."

"Is she okay? Nothing went wrong?"

Chills danced down his spine as the possible scenarios flashed through his mind.

"She's okay and nothing went wrong. I expect she'll be good as new in a couple of months." He watched Skip rub his chin, run his hand over his tight curls, and shake his head.

"Gee, man weren't you scared walking in there after three years and picking something outta somebody's head? Especially when she was your bird?"

Mason smiled to himself at Skip's choice of words.

"I didn't let myself think of anything but what I had to do. I wasn't scared, but I had a good talk with God when I'd finished. We'd better get moving."

"Like wow, man… I mean, Mason. How big is this place we're going?" Mason laughed at the boy's enthusiasm and patted him on the head.

"Bigger than you are. Did you bring your biology books?"

"I brought all of my books," Skip said, and patted the school bag that had been a present from Mason.

"Okay, let's get started." He glanced around, admiring what he saw, glad to be back where he knew he belonged.

"Who's this trip for, Mason? Me or you?" Mason raised an eyebrow at the boy's astute question.

"Both of us. This is your big chance to get some polish." And mine to find out where I'm going, he added to himself.

"Come in." Jeannetta looked at her watch. Nearly four hours had elapsed since Laura had left her room. Had a dread of seeing her detained him? "Hello, Clayton."

"Hello." He rushed to kiss her cheek, but she sensed a new reserve in him, and emotional distance where previously none had existed.

"How are you, my dear?" Banalities. Forced conversation. He meant to stick to his promise to marry her until she voluntarily released him, though he had to know that that kind of gallantry had made a lot of people miserable.

"I'm glad to see you, Clayton. How long have you been here?" Maybe she shouldn't put him on the spot, but she meant to find out as best she could and as quickly as possible whether he intended to hurt Laura. He looked her straight in the eye and she had the uneasy feeling that he'd judged her. Then he raised his head and looked toward the ceiling.

"I asked you to marry me, Jeannetta. More than once I've told you that I'd be honored to have you as my wife. I'll be happy knowing that you're well-cared for. What is your answer?"

"I'm honored, Clayton." He paled visibly—dark though he was; his eyes widened and his breath quickened. She couldn't help marveling when his left hand jerked voluntarily toward his chest, only to have him force it into his pants pocket. She put him at ease.

"I appreciate your gesture more than you can know, but I'm sure you'll understand that I can't marry you when I love another man."

Air flowed out of him with such force that he released it through his lips, and his entire upper body sagged as the tension eased out of him .

"Are you going to marry Fenwick?"

She shook her head. "That's irrelevant. The point is that he's the one, and I can't marry anybody else. So don't worry; I'm going to be fine."

"Has he told you that the operation succeeded?" he asked doggedly, causing her to wonder whether she'd been unfair to him .

"He won't know for a few weeks or maybe months. Are you in love with my sister?"

Both of his eyebrows arched sharply. "She told you?"

Annoyance pricked at her. How else would she know? "She told me that you wanted to declare yourself but couldn't, because you're committed." Jeannetta couldn't help remembering how she had allowed Alma to think that she encouraged Jethro's advances in revenge for Alma's having seduced Jethro and tricked him into marriage, although Jethro had been engaged to Jeannetta. She had tried several times to set it right, but Alma's vicious gossip and supercilious behavior had discouraged decency on Jeannetta's part. So she had let the woman worry. But that lesson was all the motivation she needed to avoid future tangled relationships. She stared hard at Clayton, scrutinizing him in a way that must have surprised him.

"You and I are friends, or so you said. But you'd been here twenty-four hours and hadn't greeted me. Surely you wouldn't marry a woman if you felt that way about her."

He's a fighter, she realized, when he straightened his shoulders, tilted his head and wordlessly dared her to question his integrity.

"I didn't want to hurt Laura by going to you, and, though I would have honored my proposal, I dreaded knowing I'd have to—feeling as I do about your sister."

"Laura looks and acts tough," she told him, "but she isn't. People think I'm fragile, but they're invariably surprised to learn otherwise. If anybody hurts my sister, they'll hear from me. You get the message?"

His wan smile and cold eyes told her that he wouldn't take much more, but his mild words denied it.

"Too bad you think you have to warn me, though that was more of a threat. You'll learn that I'm honorable."

"I'll be watching for it, too," she replied, refusing to weaken her stance. He grasped her hand before she could move away.

"This isn't the way friends should talk to each other. I'd prefer to have your blessing."

She tried to release her hand, but he held it firmly.


"What are you doing up here? I want you to move around." At the sound of Mason's voice, her glance shot toward the door. "You're not to stay in…wh…what's going on here? What the hell *is* this?"

"Mason!" She smiled, her heart bursting with joy at the sight of him, as Clayton released her hand, but her smile evaporated when she noticed the scalding fury reflected in Mason's dark eyes.

"What is it? Oh," she exclaimed, when she followed his gaze to Clayton. "You remember Clayton Miles, don't you?"

"Bad pennies don't *let* you forget them. So give it to me straight, Jeannetta. What is this man to you?"

You'd think a man of his brilliance wouldn't need her public declaration.

"He's a man who wants my sister, Laura," she said, mainly for Clayton's benefit.

"If he can't see how you feel about him, you ought to let him sweat!" Clayton said, as he left the room but, if Mason heard that, his next words didn't indicate it.

"If he's nothing to you, why were you holding his hand?"

Her joy at seeing him didn't mean he couldn't make her mad, and she bristled.

"How did you get the temerity to walk into my rooms without knocking or having yourself announced?" He folded his arms across his chest, accentuating his maleness and teasing her with his provocative posture.

"'Scuse me, baby. I wanted to surprise you." The natural seductiveness of his low, husky voice addled her, and she rubbed her arms and swallowed while his gaze pierced her. She watched, mesmerized, while his eyes changed to greenish-brown, and she got a whiff of his man's scent and felt moisture on her skin. Like a hawk, he watched her, and she took a few steps backward, knowing that he'd come after her. She sprang to him when he held out his arms and lost herself in his drugging kiss. His lips, his skin, his smell besotted her, and she had to hide her face in the curve of his neck while she fought for composure.

"I didn't mean what I said," she murmured. If he'd thought she did, he wouldn't be holding her. He had wanted to see her face light up when he walked into her room, but conceded that he shouldn't have done it. He held her away and gave her what he hoped was a stern look.

"We have to avoid these hot scenes, honey, because I don't want you to get overly upset; anger is just as detrimental as passion. Try not to get excited." He had to laugh at her raised eyebrow and rueful expression.

"Where's Skip?" Jeannetta asked.

"Downstairs in the office at the computer. He was as happy sitting there as a worm in a barrel of apples."

"I want to meet him." He walked them to a floor lamp and removed the shade.

"Time enough. I want to examine your eyes." He dressed the wound.

The cool early morning breeze of late August drifted into the room, and Mason grabbed a fistful of it and stretched his long body, his arms extended toward the ceiling. He glanced toward the other bed and had to laugh, though he was barely awake. Skip sat up in bed waiting for Mason to open his eyes. "I'll go back to New York the day before school starts," the boy said at the end of a long and rapid discourse. "Since you're going to get a place for my aunt Mabel, and I won't have to worry about her, I can stay up here. Can't I?"

He heard the worry and anxiety in the boy's voice.

"You really want to stay up here for the next six weeks? This room's expensive."

"Laura said I can have the maid's room, since she lives at home with her folks. And she said I can mow the grass, wash all the windows, polish all the floors, dry clean the carpets, wax her car, and a couple of other things she named. I'll get the place ready for winter, and she'll pay me eight bucks an hour, room and board. Man...I mean Mason, that's money." Mason wanted Skip to stay at the Hideaway, but he didn't like the idea of his doing such heavy work.

"Skip, that's hard work for a twelve-year old. Whose idea was it?"

The boy grinned cockily. "Mine. If there's any work around, I find it. Okay?" That's what he'd thought.

"We'll see."

"*Merde,* man. I work that hard at my aunt's place and don't get a cent. Just think; I can put fifty dollars a day in the bank. "That's twenty one hundred bucks." Skip jumped off the bed. "You're not going to make me give that up, are you?"

Mason yawned. He'd gotten accustomed to Skip's bursts of energy, and he'd handle this one with some words to Laura.

"I'll think about it, and watch your language. You aren't the only one who's studied French."

"Okay. So how come you didn't stay with your bird last night?"

Mason had to stifle a laugh; the boy was incorrigible.

"Skip, do not refer to Jeannetta as my bird, and try being your age. This is not a subject for children, of which, believe it or not, you are one." He grinned broadly at Skip's expression of amazement. "And, son, men mind their business when it comes to such things. You shower first, and make it snappy; I'm ready for breakfast."

He watched the boy dash into the bathroom, and the memory of Steve's sacrifices for his own well-being settled in his mind. Was he about to take on an even greater responsibility? And what if Jeannetta didn't want to mother someone else's twelve-year-old?

# Chapter 10

Jeannetta had never thought she'd have occasion to envy Laura her relationship with a man, but when she walked into the kitchen and saw the glow on her sister's face she could only stare at the transformation and know that Clayton had brought it about. Feminine softness radiated from Laura, her movements and gestures had taken on a new daintiness, and her fair complexion reddened whenever she risked a glance at Clayton, who seemed unable to look at anything or anyone but Laura. If she'd made love with Mason, wouldn't she know it, and wouldn't she react to him as Laura did to Clayton? She knew she loved Mason, but she sensed a peculiar gap in their relationship. She turned and went to find him.

The handsome young boy was talking animatedly to Mason, as though pleading his case for something important, and she saw that he had the man's rapt attention.

"You must be Skip," Jeannetta said as she walked toward him with her right hand extended.

The boy started to meet her, turned back, and asked Mason, "This is your...I mean, is this Jeanny?"

"Yes. I'm Jeannetta."

"Wow, man." A grin spread across his face, and his whole visage brightened as though a floodlight had been turned on him, and Jeannetta knew she would like him. Still, her raised eyebrow bespoke her astonishment when he declared, with a hefty shot of confidence, "It's time I met you, 'cause me and you are gonna be seeing a lot of each other."

She glanced at Mason for an explanation, but he limited his visible reaction to a dry smile.

"Skip has problems trying to be a child and keeping his imagination in check." The boy whirled around.

"But me and her are gonna be tight. Right?" Jeannetta saw the boy's desperate need for love and, when Mason walked to him and slung an arm loosely around his shoulders, she understood that the man she loved knew how to give it.

"Stop lapsing into that street language, and speak the way I've taught you. If you behave yourself, I'm sure she'll want you to be her friend," Mason told him, adding, "now stop worrying and go talk with Laura. You may work five hours a day, but not a minute more, and you're not to get on a ladder that's over six feet high. Got it?"

"Yes, sir. But...Mason..."

*"Skip!"*

"Okay, Okay."

Jeannetta couldn't miss the parental pride with which Mason watched Skip as the boy sped from the lounge. "He's very attached to you."

"Yes. He is. He'll keep you busier than an ant, but he's a great kid. If you still want to go fishing, we'd better do if before the sun gets too high."

"Can Skip go along?" Her heart fluttered at the suggestion in his obsidian eyes when they swept slowly over her with half-raised lids.

"What's the matter? I'm boring, or you don't trust your virtue with me out there in the woods?" A flirtatious grin added fuel to his seductive glance and wicked tone.

She laid her head to one side, and rested her right knuckle on her right hip bone. "Are you playing with me? I don't seem to remember your getting this familiar with me. Not that I don't like it; I'm just burning my brain up trying to figure you out. I understand you when you're being the doctor, but when you're somewhere between suitor and lover, I'm lost."

"The doctor told you not to tax yourself trying to remember, but the lover is going mad wanting to hold you to your words and behavior when you spun out of this world in his arms."

She touched the bandage on her head, winced, and smiled with what he knew involved a good deal of effort to ignore the discomfort.

"When I say out of this world, I mean heaven on earth," he emphasized. He watched her swallow hard just before her lips parted and her eyelids dropped, the way they did when desire claimed her, and he told himself that they would recapture what they'd lost, even if her memory of their loving didn't return.

"I can think of at least one way for you to restore my memory of that in a hurry."

"Honey, if you're thinking that, don't mention it to me, because I remember, and I don't need that provocation. When your doctor says you're well, you won't have to ask. Trust me." He tried to soften the words with a smile, but he didn't feel like smiling. He picked up their fishing gear and a folding chair.

"What's that for?" She pointed to the chair.

"Jeannetta, I know you don't like having me coddle you, but cut me some slack here. You are recovering from serious major surgery, and I have to see that you act like it. I can't stop being your doctor just because I've got something going for you. Come on." He settled Jeannetta on the short pier at the edge of the lake, baited her hook, slipped off his fatigues and dived into the water.

Jeannetta forgot about the fish. Mason's long lean physique with the rippling muscles, slim hips, and broad chest presented a feast to her eyes. Clothed in the tiniest of swim suits, the vision brought back the memory of him lying in the sand on the Lido beach wearing only his red bikini. Picture of sea and endless sand forced their way to the fore of her mind and, with it, another experience begged to be recalled. She could feel it thumping against her cerebral walls. Strange; she had forgotten everything of that part of the tour except Mason on that beach. The red, white and yellow ball on her line bobbed in the water, but she ignored it. Powerful strokes brought him past the pier, and she would have loved to strip off her clothes and join him.

"This isn't like me," she told herself, trying to bring to her conscious mind the strange something in her that *knew* him. He'd suggested that they had become more intimate than she'd remembered . If they had, she'd give anything to know how he'd made her feel.

"You've got one terrific kick," she called to him, when he pulled up to the pier.

"I'd better have, big as I am. What did you catch?" She laughed, recalling that she'd ignored the "bite" for the pleasure of swooning over his near-nude body as he flashed through the water.

He had eyed her surreptitiously and watched her hand go repeatedly to her forehead.

"Do you have a headache?"

She nodded, but he saw that she did it reluctantly.

"Are they frequent?"

She smiled that wonderful way in which her face seemed to welcome the opportunity to show pleasure. He hopped up on the pier and observed her closely.

"It's getting too warm. Come on, let's go back to the lodge." Mason grimaced at the scowl on her face; she wasn't thinking what he was thinking. No doubt about it. As they walked back to the lodge, he prayed that she'd remember the powerful and explosive, brain-branding loving they'd had together—not once, but twice. He didn't want to entertain the thought that she'd never remember. He saw her staring down at the ground.

"What do you see there, Jeannetta?" He stroked her shoulder in gentle encouragement. "Tell me."

She let a handful of sand stream through her widespread fingers.

"I remember trying to do that, and the sand stuck in my hand and wouldn't fall out. But when?"

"You were coming out of anesthesia after the operation, and that was a kind of delirium. What else do you remember?"

She shook her head.

"Nothing? Not even the night before I took you to the hospital?" He had to hide his sadness and consternation, so he turned his face away from her.

"Let's take the shortcut through the forest," he suggested, "I don't want you to get too tired." Minutes later, he wished the thought had never occurred to him.

Thought the wind was nonexistent, a dank, dusty odor assaulted his nostrils. He stopped. The cracking of dry sticks and leaves hadn't come from their footsteps, so he waited. Almost at once, a brown bear ambled across their path, glimpsed them and stopped.

"Don't move, and don't say a word, honey." He surveyed their surroundings as best he could from the corners of his eyes, to find out if the bear had cubs, and whether he and Jeannetta stood between them and the big animal. At least that posed no problem. He hoped the bear was nearsighted, but he wasn't about to test it. His belly knotted to a figure eight when the animal took a single step toward them and stopped. His fingers gripped Jeannetta's waist. This was one time when his black belt in karate would be of little help, but it would take more than that bear to get her away from him. The animal suddenly turned and bounded into the thicket, and he breathed again.

"That was close, and we'd better get out of here. Next time, we'll use the main road." He could be thankful that Skip hadn't wanted to come with them, because the inquisitive boy would have wandered around and might have bumped into the beast. He didn't want to rush her, but he wouldn't be at ease until they crossed the highway.

"I sure wouldn't want to be within kissing distance of one of those boys."

Mason squeezed her to him. For the second time, he'd been willing to give his life for her. "Being that close doesn't mean you'd get kissed. I'm pretty close to you," he needled, "but, if kissing me crossed your mind, you did a great job of keeping it to yourself."

She covered his hand with her own and squeezed his fingers. "Ask, and it shall be given," she said.

Without thinking, he playfully patted her bottom, bringing a gasp of surprise from her, and he had again the painful reminder that she didn't yet recall their intimacy as lovers.

"I have to ask?"

She raised an eyebrow and glanced at him through half-lowered lids. "Do you?"

They'd reached the highway, and waited for the traffic to ease. He cupped her chin, raised her face to his, and covered her mouth with his own in what he'd meant as a quick exchange. But when she parted her lips and stepped closer to him, he dropped the chair and fishing gear and brought her into the strength of his body. Her mobile lips asked for his tongue, and he couldn't, wouldn't, deny her. But he wouldn't let her drag him into hot, seething passion as she'd done so many times. He cooled the kiss, gently put her away from him, and grinned.

"Just checking." He held her hand as they walked on to the lodge. Maybe he ought to turn her over to another doctor. But who? He knew many competent physicians, but he didn't think he'd be able to entrust Jeannetta's well-being to anyone. Perhaps he should ask her whether she'd accept a change. But what if she agreed?

"Do you have a friend named Geoffrey Ames?" Laura asked Jeannetta when she and Mason entered the lodge.

"Yes. What about him?"

Mason's broad smile told her of his delight that she remembered Geoffrey.

"He wants to come here with his new bride for a couple of weeks. Said you'd vouch for him."

Jeannetta turned to Mason, her heart singing with delight as she recalled her fondness for Geoffrey, and their shared good times. "Oh, Mason. Isn't this fantastic? They really did get married." He stared deeply into her eyes, and she didn't doubt that he hoped being with Geoffrey and Lucy would trigger in her mind what he wanted her to remember.

"I never doubted Geoffrey's intentions," he told her. "Nor Lucy's. Wish I could be here with them."

"They'll get here tomorrow," Laura told him. Jeannetta asked if he could stay for the weekend.

He needed to stay, to be with her as much as possible, because he had to do whatever he could to make her know what he'd done with her and to her on those nights when she'd screamed his name in ecstasy and told him she'd love him forever. And he wanted to examine her incision and change the dressing. After thinking about it for a minute, he decided he could do it at Pilgrim's small General Hospital. He'd stay.

"I'll call my offices and see what's going on. Laura, where's Skip?"

"In the back with Clayton learning to clean things with natural ingredients. You know, without chemicals." She looked up from her bread making. "Is he any relation to you?"

"No, but he may be one of these days. He wants me to adopt him, and I just might do that." He pinned his gaze on Jeannetta as he said the words, and when her eyes widened, he could see that she was taken aback.

"Don't you want children of your own?" she asked.

He looked directly at her, but she had found something interesting across the room. He didn't let her off.

"You're not against adoption, are you?"

"No."

That simple answer left him unsatisfied. He called his medical office, learned that he didn't have any urgent business, and decided to take Jeannetta to the local hospital that afternoon. He phoned and made the appointment.

"Laura, you got any snacks? I eat a lot," Skip exclaimed, barrelling into the kitchen with the speed of one fleeing vipers. He glanced around and saw Mason and Jeannetta.

"Oh, hi. Mason, you ought to get into this environment thing. It's a gas, man...I mean, Mason. I already learned that you can do almost as much with vinegar and baking soda as you can with those detergents. I'm gonna learn a lot up here." He glanced over at Jeannetta, and hardly broke his stride. "While you're getting well, Jeanny, you and me can be buddies. I'll take you down to the lake, and we can pick berries. You ought to see the raspberries around here." His grin blessed them all. "Stuff like that. And you can teach me stuff. Mason said you teach college. Wow!" He paused finally to breathe and Jeannetta was able to comment.

"I see you like to learn."

"Yeah. I want to learn everything, and that'll take a lot of time." Apparently unimpressed by the laughter that followed his words, he plowed on.

"Mason's going to adopt me, but maybe he has to get married first. I dunno." The boy looked hopefully at Jeannetta, and Mason knew that she had locked her gaze on him, but he looked into the distance.

Mason pushed his hands into his pockets. Hauling her into his arms wouldn't solve one thing. The tension bounced off of Skip, who seemed suddenly ill at ease.

"Any fish in that lake, Laura? Jeanny didn't catch any," the boy said, as though deliberately breaking the silence.

"Plenty," Laura assured him. "Water's full of 'em. Clayton caught the ones we had for supper last night."

Skip looked hopefully at Jeannetta.

"You know much about fishing, Jeanny? Boy, I sure could use a lesson, and I don't have anything to do right now."

"I want her to rest," Mason intervened. "You two can fish some other time. You're making great progress, Jeannetta, so don't push too hard and ruin it."

"Is she really sick," Skip asked him, "or are you just manning your turf?" Mason couldn't help laughing at Skip's choice of words, thought the first thing he'd do if Skip came to live with him would be to clean up the boy's language.

"Skip, I thought we agreed that you don't get into my personal affairs. Right?"

"Kids ask their parents anything they want, don't they? Right, Mason? And I'll be your kid as soon as you sign some papers. Right? That way, when you get old, you'll have me to take care of you." The boy's hopeful expression tore at his heart, and he knew a peculiar and strange new feeling of pride and contentment. It wasn't the satisfaction he'd known after successfully completing a difficult operation, but was more similar to the pleasure he knew as a young boy tending his vegetable garden, nurturing his seedlings and watching them grow. That garden had been his greatest joy, but he hadn't thought of it in years. Until now.

"I'll keep that in mind," he said, and he'd come to a decision. He saw the fires of love dancing in Jeannetta's eyes, walked over to her, and let her read his own.

Jeannetta held his gaze. Warm coils of comfort flowed in wave after wave from him, directly to her heart. The protective heat from his big body enveloped her and strengthened her. Why couldn't he tell her how he felt about her? His eyes said "I adore you," but it wasn't enough. She nodded to him in a mute excuse for herself and walked upstairs to her quarters. Clayton met her on the stairs, turned and walked up with her.

"We haven't had much of a chance to talk. I want you to know that Laura has given me a sense of stability. I can imagine that you've been worried about my rootlessness; I've always known where I was going, but losing my life's work knocked the starch out of me. I have reason now to pull my life together and get moving."

"I'm happy for both of you, Clayton. You must be good for Laura, because anyone can see she's glowing with happiness." Jeannetta kept her other thoughts to herself, though she couldn't suppress a smile when the man reacted with an expression that bordered on cockiness.

"Just wanted you to know that a lot has changed since we first talked on that plane." He turned around and went downstairs.

Jeannetta closed her door and lay down. Laura had to live her own life and, if Clayton made her happy for only a short while, it would be more than her sister had ever known. She removed her jeans and shirt, closed the blinds, and tried to sleep. An hour later, she awoke with a headache, and with images of green malachite columns, waterfalls, and gray sandstone carvings flashing through her mind. She took a tablet that Mason had prescribed for her, dressed, and went to find him.

Mason watched Jeannetta walk away from him on her way to her room. As a travel manager, his life had been relatively uncomplicated. Cut and dried. Now, Skip wanted to drag him into unchartered waters of parenthood; his dual role of doctor and lover complicated his feelings about Jeannetta; and, in a couple of weeks, he had learned that maintaining businesses as disparate as medicine and travel reduced his fitness for either. He couldn't allow Jeannetta to complicate her recovery by becoming over-confident, but discouraging her and forcing her to slow down brought a stabbing pain to his heart. And his affections for Skip went deep, but…parenting was another matter. He walked out of the kitchen, leaving Skip to trail after Laura, and headed for the back porch where he could get a good stretch. He found Clayton there, cleaning tools.

"Skip's quite a boy, Mason. He says you're going to adopt him."

Mason shrugged. "He seems to want that, and he operates on the principle that wanting it makes it so."

Clayton smiled, as though to indulge the younger man. "Why not? Faith has worked many a miracle. Jeannetta had faith that you'd help her, and she believed that your best would be good enough, but she was also willing to sacrifice her sight and her future so that you wouldn't have it on your conscience if you failed. And you didn't fail."

Mason walked to the end of the porch and looked toward the setting sun.

"Not in the way that I could have, but she isn't out of difficulty yet." Why was he discussing Jeannetta with a man whom he barely liked, he wondered.

"She seems to have confided a lot in you," Mason told Clayton, in a tone devoid of friendliness. "I hadn't realized the two of you had grown so close."

"Slow down, man," Clayton chided. "We were soothing our individual wounds, not each other's. We were strangers, and I suppose you know that sharing your concerns with a stranger whom you never expect to see again can be a powerful healer, because you're totally honest. You ever try it?"

Mason's attitude toward Clayton probably needed some repair work, but he didn't much care. "What do you mean?" He glowered.

"You and I have more in common than you know."

Clayton had done nothing to invite his disrespect, but his behavior hadn't been entirely above question, either.

"Let's hear it," he said, his tone harsh and sarcastic.

But Clayton chose not to respond in kind. "That's right. She told me about you. Well, I started Miles Chemicals with a seven-dollar-and-ninety-five-cent beaker and built it into a multi-million-dollar company. Then I made the mistake of trusting another person's research reports on a cream that removed wrinkles, when I should have checked. Money poured in, and then the bottom fell out. After several months' use, the product toughened the skin; the women didn't have wrinkles, they had leather. I lost a class action suit...and my business."

Mason stared in disbelief. "You're *that* Miles?"

Clayton nodded. "I made financial restitution, but that hasn't restored my reputation nor erased my guilt feelings."

Mason's head snapped up. "Jeannetta isn't part of your absolution. Don't even think it."

"No. But Laura is."

They were talking, so now was as good a time as any to air his reservations, so he looked directly at Clayton. "Few men would have the nerve to go after sisters, especially in such quick succession."

He'd touched a nerve, alright. Clayton stiffened and assumed the posture of an adversary.

"I never went after Jeannetta, as you put it. I offered her an honorable way to a comfortable life, because I didn't believe you'd do that operation. I knew all about your celebrated case, more than she could tell me, and I didn't expect you ever to operate again."

Mason nodded absentmindedly, his thoughts partly in the past. "Neither did I."

"I fell for Laura minutes after I first saw her."

*I'll bet,* Mason said to himself, and then remembered how he'd wondered what hit him when Jeannetta walked into his travel office. He had to admit the possibility. A thought occurred to him, and he found himself advising Clayton to prove that the maker of the wrinkle cream had lied about the tests and to clear his name. Within minutes, they had begun plotting Clayton's course of action.

His conversation with Clayton had disturbed him; Jeannetta knew her diagnosis before she took the tour, but how much did she know of his background as a surgeon? He walked out of the lodge and headed toward the lake, because he needed to be alone, to think. But Skip caught up with him.

"You can go on back to New York City, Mason, and I'll take care of Jeanny for you. I won't let her out of my sight. I swear it. That's another reason, why you ought to adopt me. I can keep your bird in line."

Mason laughed aloud and put an arm around the boy's shoulder.

"Stop calling her my bird. And another thing. You don't keep women in line; they're capable of doing that themselves." He stopped at the edge of the lake, and Skip moved closer to him and assumed an identical posture.

"I'll be real good, Mason, and I won't give you any trouble. Ask Aunt Mabel. She never has to worry about me. The problem is she's going to wind up in a nursing home."

He hurt for Skip. The child hadn't been able to ask what would happen to him when his aunt could no longer live at home. She hunkered down to Skip's level, and looked him in the eye.

"Stop worrying. I won't let anything happen to you." Skip kicked the dirt and looked afar.

"That's not good enough for me. I want you to be my dad. Most of the guys in my school have a dad, but I never had one. I'm gonna be tall, and I could even look like you if I get rid of this Chelsea hair cut. Couldn't I?"

"Maybe, but that's not important." The child's burden weighed heavily on him. How did a father act when his son hurt so badly?

"You scared Jeanny won't like me?"

"Forget that. I'll have a talk with Mabel when I get back to New York, and we'll take it from there. Right now, I want you to stop worrying. Where I go, you go." He stood and put his hands in his pockets to prevent his arms from going around the child in a fierce hug.

"If I go everywhere with you, Mason, what're you gonna introduce me as? Just Skip?"

At that, he hunkered down before the boy again, gave in to the powerful urge, and clasped Skip to him. Skip wrapped his arms around the strong man's neck, and clung in an unspoken plea so violent that emotion surged in Mason. He summoned what composure he could manage, pried Skip's fingers loose, took his hand, and started back to the lodge.

Jeannetta saw at once that marriage hadn't changed Geoffrey Ames's demeanor, though Lucy had obviously guided him to a good tailor.

"This here's my bride," he exclaimed to Laura and all within earshot as he registered at the desk. Jeannetta noticed that Lucy had also adopted a classier style of dress. She dispensed with the banalities of formal greeting and clasped them each in a big hug.

"You're looking good, Jeannetta," Geoffrey announced, "but you're lacking some of that spice you used to have. You ain't been sick or nothin', have you? How's Mason?"

She'd forgotten the man's directness.

"Well, actually, I'm recovering from surgery right now. That's why I'm wearing this African-looking head dress; it covers my bandages. I had a brain tumor, but Mason says I should be good as new within the next couple of months."

"Mason said...? I don't get it." She told him that Mason had performed the surgery, and watched the old man gape in amazement.

Geoffrey rubbed his chin and shook his head. "You mean he's a doctor, too? Well, I always figured him as a smart one. Doctor, huh? Imagine that, Lucy?"

She took his hand and smiled up at him, but didn't say

anything. Jeannetta couldn't help wondering what had happened to still the woman's once-verbose tongue.

"Everybody's surprised," Skip ventured. "I'm Skip, and Mason's going to adopt me."

Mason walked in and seized Geoffrey's hand in a warm handshake. "Congratulations. How'd the rest of the tour go?"

"Great," Lucy said, "but I was sure glad when we got out of Bangkok. Those girls don't care whose man they chase." She poked her husband in his ribs. "And *my husband*"—she emphasized the words, savored them and continued—"Geoffrey here, was a kid in a toy store; he just ate up the way they fussed over him. By the time we got to Nigeria, I was ready to come home. Two months is a long time, and I wanted to get married before it got cold so I couldn't wear my mother's wedding dress." Moisture formed at the corner of her eyes.

"It's seventy years old, and I thought I'd never get a chance to wear it."

Jeannetta shifted her glance to Mason, and tremors raced through her at the sight of so much feeling mirrored in his dark eyes.

"This calls for a celebration," Mason stated. "Drinks are on me."

They seated themselves in the lounge, and Skip helped Mason serve the soft drinks to all but Geoffrey, Clayton, and himself, for whom he set out champagne. Lucy and Laura didn't want any, and alcohol was contraindicated for Jeannetta, whose medicines included an antibiotic. She noticed, with amusement, that Skip took a seat between Mason and herself.

"Don't I get any of that like the rest of the men?" he asked Mason, pointing to the champagne and placing his other hand possessively on Mason's thigh.

"As soon as you're twenty-one, son."

Jeannetta watched from the corner of her eye as Skip moved closer to Mason, settled back in his chair, and sipped his ginger ale.

The newlyweds went upstairs to settle in and Skip went with Laura for a promised lesson in the art of making fudge brownies. Mason sipped the last of his champagne, saluted Clayton, who returned the gesture and left them alone, and cradled Jeannetta in his arms.

"What will you do about Skip?"

"I'll probably adopt him if I find there's no reason why I shouldn't. He wants my word on it, but I can't promise him until I investigate the obstacles. I don't want to disappoint him."

"He's become possessive of you, and he copies your every gesture."

Mason said he hadn't noticed, but his obvious pride in the boy warmed her heart.

When Laura served them a family-style dinner that night in her personal quarters, Geoffrey's keen old eyes took in the state of affairs, and he remarked, "Looks to me like cupid's been pretty busy," as he glanced from one couple to the other. "'Course, I was expecting to see something on your third finger, left hand," he said pointedly to Jeannetta. "If y'all knew what you were missing, you'd tie the knot."

Jeannetta wished he'd change the topic, but he wouldn't, she knew, until he'd made his point.

"This here sure is one fine piece of roast pork, Laura. Nothing like good home cooking to keep a man satisfied and his feet in front of the fire."

"We bought you a bolt of ecru lace for your dolls," Lucy interjected, as though allying herself with Jeannetta's discomfort.

"That'd make nice trimming for a wedding dress, too," Geoffrey put in. "'Course, like I said, it ain't none of my business if y'all want to waste precious days making up your minds."

"Here, Geoffrey, have some more biscuits and some of the greengrocer's fresh-churned butter," Laura said. "No use making Jeannetta miserable. A snake couldn't move her 'til she's ready. Y'all don't let that potato soufflé go to waste, now. You hear?"

If you wanted a fire extinguished, send for Laura, Jeannetta mused.

Clayton assisted Laura in serving the dessert, and Skip bounded into the kitchen to help them. Mason noticed later that, as the boy savored his raspberry cream pie, his gaze swept repeatedly over his surroundings.

"Do you always have flowers, candles, and stuff like this on the table when you eat?" he asked Laura.

She explained that the table settings depended on the occasion.

"Gee, this is great. I'm really gonna learn a lot up here. Say, Laura, are you Clayton's girl?"

Laura frowned, before her face creased into a warm smile. "I sure am, honey. I sure am."

Mason got his linen jacket from the closet, walked over to Jeannetta, and rested his hands lightly on her slim shoulders.

"Let's go catch some air."

He walked them along the highway, and when she rubbed her arms to warm them against the night's coolness, he took off his jacket and draped it around her shoulders. Their long shadows preceded them, and a ghostly silence hovered around them in the eerily beautiful and stark moonlight. Mason wondered how he withstood the city's noise and distractions, how he lived without the peace that pervaded him at that moment. The rustling breeze swayed the compliant trees, and somewhere a dog barked. The wind shifted, the smell of pine drifted to his nostrils, and visions of a blazing fireplace, his children, and Jeannetta flashed through his thoughts. And not for the first time. He reached for her hand, stopped, and turned her to face him.

Her gaze seemed to beseech him, to implore him. But for what? She unmasked her vulnerability and, in the midst of the strange, shifting shapes of the trees swaying against the moonlight that filtered through their leaves, he witnessed her naked need of him. Joy suffused him but, in the next minute, his heart pounded with his uncertainty. He put his hands in his pockets and looked steadily into her eyes. If only she remembered what they'd been to each other.

"Marry me, Jeannetta." He hadn't kissed her or even touched her, and he could see that his words had stunned her. They surprised him, too, but he knew at once their rightness.

"Wh...what?"

It hadn't occurred to him that his proposal would take her aback to such an extent.

"I want to marry you." Now that he'd said it, he wanted it badly, more than he had ever wanted anything in his life. He sucked in his breath and waited. Surely...

"You don't mean it. You...you couldn't."

"I've never meant anything more, or been more serious, in my life." A man wanted to see thousands of glittering lights dancing in his woman's eyes after he told her he wanted her for all time, but when she looked up at him, hers held only a strange sadness.

"I...I don't know. Let me think about it."

Ice-cold metal balls vied for space in his belly, and he was glad of his ability to conceal his feelings. He spoke carefully, so that the tremors so near the surface wouldn't control his voice.

"You don't know? I'd have thought you'd already made up your mind about that."

Why wouldn't she look at him?

"In a way, I had. I don't take your proposal lightly, but I can't give you an answer right now."

He opened his mouth to ask her what she had to consider other than that she loved him, but his vocal cords failed to respond. They walked back quietly. He wanted to take her hand, to feel her close to him but, after that rejection, he couldn't make himself do it. He told her goodnight in the lounge and went to the room he shared with Skip.

After a restless night, Mason walked slowly down the stairs and into the breakfast room, hoping to see Jeannetta there and, at the same time, fearful that he might. Her place setting was untouched, so he surmised that she hadn't eaten. He was about to look for her in the garden when Clayton walked into the room.

"I'm going to stay around for a while and handle my appeal from here. You gave me sound advice, and I think Laura would be more accepting of me if I straightened out my life. She's very conservative."

Mason refilled his coffee cup and motioned Clayton to sit down.

"If Laura's concerned about that, it's not for herself, but for you. She'd marry you today, if you asked, and I'd bet my last dollar on it. If I can do anything to help you with your appeal, give me a ring. Laura knows how to reach me."

Clayton stood.

"Thanks. I won't forget this."

Mason resisted looking for Jeannetta. She knew he would be leaving early and, if she'd wanted to see him, she would have been in the breakfast room. He wanted to see her, to hold her, to… He looked to the ceiling. He'd had some difficult times in his life, but not one had pulled him under. This wouldn't, either. He raced upstairs, awakened Skip, and told him good-bye.

"I'll take good care of your girl," rang in his ears as he headed for the door and New York.

Jeannetta sat in the broad stretch of sand that separated the lake from the glassy slopes that bordered it. She dug her bare feet into the cool yellow grains, raised them and watched the sand drift down between her toes. She picked up a handful of it and sent it into the morning breeze. How slowly time passed when you waited for a man to open his heart to you, to let you inside of him. Let you *know* him. For all his competence, strength, kindness, compassion, and gentleness, Mason didn't know how to love. He couldn't reveal himself to her. She had no idea what hurt him, what angered him, or even at what point you transgressed in an area of importance to him. She couldn't read his facial expressions, because he fixed them at will. Yet she loved him beyond all reason.

His reaction to Geoffrey's remark had showed that he wanted a home and a family. She tossed some crumbs to a starling at the edge of the grass and pondered what she knew of him. Skip needed him, and she surmised that he needed Skip. She got up and started back to the lodge walking slowly as Mason had urged her to do. Why had he asked her to marry him, and why would a man want to marry a woman without ever having told her that he loved or cared for her? Without ever having revealed himself? Protectiveness? Guilt? Those had been Clayton's reasons.

"Mason's gone?" Laura asked when Jeannetta walked into the kitchen. She nodded.

"I have to tell you," Laura began, "I know he did the surgery and all that, and you could say he's a terrific specimen of a man, 'cause he is. But I'm not sold on him yet; it took him too long to get down to business."

Jeannetta pushed back her annoyance. "Don't criticize him for that. He did the surgery as soon as he could get me in the hospital."

"Well, I guess you did give him a hard time. No matter. He did it, and you got a new lease on life." She poured the last of the coffee into her cup. "You told him about that investigation yet?"

"I remember telling him I wanted a clean slate, so I must have. Still, I'm not sure. But not to worry. No PI discusses his client's business, so it may be best to let sleeping dogs sleep."

Laura took a long sip of coffee. "If you say, hon, but I wouldn't trust it. When you get caught doing something wrong, Providence is usually sound asleep, and you can't get any help there."

Jeannetta marveled that her sister slipped back into her pre-Clayton personality whenever her man wasn't near her. Habit could be a curse.

"About time something happened between you and Mason, isn't it?" Laura said. "He doesn't seem to me like the type to let things drag on and on. Don't you think it's out of character?"

"What? Oh. Yes, I suppose so. The PI's report described him as a man of action. Decisive. A take-command person." She felt her face sag. "He was also reported to be very popular with glamorous women. Nobody would call me glamorous."

"You don't show a lot of cleavage, and you don't wear your skirts slit up to your waistline, and you don't layer a lot of junk on your face, but you're as good-looking as any woman I know. You want me to ask him what his intentions are?"

Jeannetta had to laugh. "Hon, that's out of fashion."

"Humph. Fashion never did make sense to me," she snorted. "A bunch of men telling women what to wear? Things are good between you?" she asked, her voice filled with hope.

A deep sigh escaped Jeannetta. "Sometimes, the physical attraction between us has the force, the power, of a hurricane; it almost consumes us."

Laura's eyebrows shot up. "Then how come you haven't made love?"

"Mason says that we have, but…" She tried to still her trembling lips and to stop the flow of moisture from her eyes. "But I can't remember it."

Laura's whistle split the air, and Jeannetta glanced around to identify the other person in the room. Seeing no one, she looked back into her sister's empathetic face.

"If you can't recall it," Laura advised with her newly acquired wisdom, "let him show you what it was like. That's probably what's wrong with the two of you; you're in different stages of your relationship."

Jeannetta stared at her. "You think it happened?"

Laura shrugged. "What would he gain by misleading you? Nothing. Besides, he can prove it. Ask him if you've got any little moles, what they look like, and where they are. He'll tell you."

"I will," Jeannetta said in a subdued voice. "I would already have done that, but he's my doctor, and whenever doctor and man do battle, the doctor wins."

Laura chuckled, shaking her head as though perplexed. "Honey, you always were one to do things in a big way," she reminded Jeannetta. "From the time you were little, if you laid an egg, not even a magician could sweep it under a rug. If it was me, he'd do what I want him to do."

Jeannetta gasped at her. "You're a quick study."

"Clayton's a great teacher," she retorted, as she turned her back and walked out of the kitchen.

Minutes later Skip charged in. "How you doin', Jeanny?"

She glanced up from her writing and smiled at the rambunctious child.

"I'm doing fine, Skip. Want some ginger ale?" he removed his baseball cap and regarded her with a sheepish look.

"You already on to my habits. Thanks. Er…Jeanny. Look, if

you wanna go downtown before it gets too late, I'll take you. I promised Mason I'd look after you while he's gone. He'll be my dad soon, and I'll be responsible for everything when he's not around. Mason is a class cat. He got my aunt into a nice place where she can get good care—she's very sick, you know—and he's seeing about getting to be my dad right now. He said so yesterday." He gulped down the ginger ale and wiped his mouth with the back of his hand. "If you get to be my mother, I won't care if you pop my bottom when I do something wrong…you know…like other kids' moms." The pain of his loneliness tore at her. He wanted a response, she knew, and when no words would pass her lips, she stood, opened her arms, and wrapped him in the love that flowed out of her.

"Let's go," she said.

Skip's eyes rounded. "Is it okay?"

She assured him that a walk toward town wouldn't hurt her. They reached a small square still some distance from Pilgrim's center, and Skip suggested they sit on the bench, since he hadn't seen any Pilgrim, but she knew he feared having tired her. Jeannetta sat there enjoying her favorite pastime. A few paces away, she noticed that two women restrained their dogs on leashes while they talked. Only Alma, in all of Pilgrim, owned a French poodle. The little dog turned up his nose and pranced off when the big mutt attempted to establish a friendship. Jeannetta couldn't help laughing.

Later, she told Laura, "You should have seen that little poodle looking down his nose at the low-class mutt. Well, I've heard of dogs taking on the personality of their masters and mistresses, but that's the first time I've seen it. That dog did precisely what Alma would have done."

"I don't suppose you know Jethro called here several times while you were in the hospital."

"What'd you tell him?"

"I told him if he had rocks in his bed, he's the one that put 'em there, and he oughta leave you alone. When he had you, he was sniffin' around Alma, and ever since he married her he's been after you. He gives men a bad name, and I told the scoundrel as much."

Jeannetta curled up on the sofa in Laura's living room, and glanced at Clayton, who sat nearby making a list of the records he needed from his safe-deposit box in a New York City bank. Her straight-laced sister Laura was actually living with a man to whom she wasn't married. She couldn't believe it.

"Maybe I should tell Alma she's mistaken about Jethro and me; I haven't said a word to that man since he admitted to me that he'd gotten her pregnant."

"Forget it," Laura snorted. "If your best friend sleeps with your fiancé, she deserves what she gets. I never could see what either of you wanted with him. 'Course, this is a small town, and you didn't have a lot to choose from."

"My excuse is that I was twenty-three."

Clayton answered the phone. "She's right here, Mason. Right. I'm getting it together now. And thanks, man." He passed the phone to Jeannetta.

"Hi. Could you call me on my phone in about two minutes?"

"Ten minutes. There's no need for you to rush. Later."

She answered on the first ring. "Hi. I wasn't sure you'd call."

"Why's that? You're still my patient...aren't you?"

Oh, Lord, was it like that now? Well, she was fighting for her happiness, and she wouldn't sell short. "Yes, I'm your patient, Mason." Uncertain of his mood or his reason for calling, she decided to let him lead the conversation.

"Skip called me a few minutes ago." She should have known he would, after his self-proclaimed role of caring for her in Mason's absence.

"He did? I thought he was in the office exploring the Internet."

"He wanted me to know that he'd taken you into town. How do you feel after that walk?"

She winced at his impersonal tone. "I got tired, but I enjoyed it. Mason, I'm not sure I can handle this detached, doctor persona. How can you treat me as though I'm precious, coddling and loving me and then talk to me as though I'm only a case in your files?"

"How can you give me so much of yourself, responding to me with every nerve in your body—and I'm not talking about making love, which you can't recall—leading me to think I'm the most important person on earth to you, and then calmly tell me I'm not husband material? I'm thirty-seven years old, and it's never occurred to me to ask any other woman to marry me."

"I didn't say you're not husband material; I promised to think about it." She looked down at the telephone wire that had somehow gotten twisted around her arm. Just like my life, she thought.

"Well, hell! You think it's flattering to have been as close to a woman as I've been to you, and have her admit she doesn't know whether she'd marry you? Woman, you've practically taken my clothes off of me, and I'm not including the times we made love. We've faced danger together; we've stood waist deep in nature, stripped of all sophistication, and we've laughed together." She heard his harsh release of breath. "Jeannetta, don't you remember sitting with me on the deck of the *Southern Queen* and watching God's paintbrush lift the sun out of the South China Sea? I thought we were as close, that moment, as two people could be."

She groped for a chair and sat down. He'd told her more about himself in that minute than in all the weeks she'd known him. And yet, he's said nothing personal about himself. How could she explain it without sounding foolish?

"I don't know how much has transpired that I can't recall, Mason, but I do know that I love you, and have for some time. Something's missing between us, something that I need, and it's holding me back."

"What are you saying? What do you need? If I don't know what it is, I can't give it."

She leaned forward in the chair, placed her elbows on her knees, and propped up her chin with her left palm. He wouldn't like it, but he deserved her honesty.

"I don't know what's inside of you. I know what I see, but not

Forster

who you are. Maybe I didn't make myself clear, but I don't know any other way to say it."

"And yet you love me."

"Yes."

"Where does that leave us?"

She knew that her answer would end the conversation, but she could only speak the truth. "I don't know."

"Well, if and when you do know, share it with me. Will you?"

Was it defeat, or frustration, that she detected in that remark? She couldn't be sure, because it sounded so alien to him. Yet he'd said it.

"Nothing's going to change what's in my heart."

She remembered to tell him about the strange images that had played in her mind. "Mason, do green malachite columns in a huge lobby-like enclosure, a lot of rainbows and waterfalls, say anything to you."

"Did you dream this, or did you envision it while you were awake?"

From the urgency of his voice, she knew he thought it important.

"I was trying to go to sleep, but these images stayed in my mind until I got an awful headache. Why?"

"The lobby of the hotel at which we stayed in Zimbabwe had about six of those big round columns, and on our sight-seeing tour outside Harare, we went to Victoria Falls. It had I don't know how many rainbows forming arcs above it. You're beginning to remember, but your head ached because you pressed too hard. It'll come."

"I hope so. I want to remember…everything."

"Not any more than I want you to recall it."

# Chapter 11

Mason left his lawyer's Wall Street office, took the Lexington train to Ninety-sixth Street, and walked the block to Steve's apartment. At the corner, he stopped at a bank to arrange an income for Mabel, and the aroma of hot coffee greeted him as he entered.

"What's this?" he asked the bank officer with whom he was discussing opening an account for Mabel. His gaze locked on a man, obviously homeless, who filled a bag with muffins and brioches, poured himself a cup of steaming coffee, and left without saying a word or even resting his glance anywhere but the food-laden counter.

"That must be his seventh or eight trip in here today. We asked him what he was doing with it, and he said he had some friends who couldn't get around as well as he, and he wanted to help them."

"How old would you say he is?" Mason asked the woman.

"He looks forty-five or more, but from his sprightliness, I'd say he's probably in his late thirties. The coffee and breads are for the customers, but the manager told us that he needs it more, and we should let him help himself until it's all gone."

Mason finished his business and followed the man out. When asked where he lived, the man replied, "Under the elevated up by a hundred and eight street."

"I got what was coming to me," the man said in response to the empathy he must have seen in Mason's expression. "I'm supposed to be an engineer, but I wanted to make a fast buck, and I let myself get lured into the brokerage business. The firm engineered some unsavory deals and got kicked off the stock exchange, I was out of a job, lost my apartment, and my wife took a walk. If you can't get cleaned up decently, you can't look for a job. You know the rest."

"I wish I knew of a way out of this for you," Mason said, thinking that he'd been lucky that he hadn't floundered as a travel manager, and that he could still practice his craft.

"Don't sweat it," the man replied. "There's a way up, but I have to decide to take it, and I haven't done that yet. You stay cool, man." Mason walked on, realizing for the first time what a gamble he'd taken with his life, and the measure of his good fortune in not having to pay for what he now saw as a gargantuan error.

When Steve opened the door, Mason regarded his brother carefully. He hadn't gone beyond high school, but he'd made a decent living, enough to support them and to send his younger brother through school.

"Steve, you're forty-two years old, and you could have a much easier and more fulfilling life if you'd come into partnership with me. Managing your emergency office-machine repair service wears you out, because half the time your workers don't show up, or one of them ruins something and you have to do the job, sometimes three jobs in one night. The travel agency is a money-making concern, because I've been there to manage it, and I can't do that when I restart my practice. I won't have time." He explained his plan to open his office two days for the rich, two for those of modest means, and one day for people unable to pay.

Steve nodded. "Pop would be proud of you for that. When are you going to start?"

"I told you that, until I can discharge Jeannetta, I won't take on another patient."

"When do you think that'll be?"

Mason shrugged both shoulders and fingered the keys in his right pants pocket.

"Soon, I hope. She has flashes of recall, and that means she's on the way." He leaned back in the chair and locked his hands behind his head, but his words were barely audible. "I asked her to marry me, and she turned me down."

Steve gawked. "You asked her to...Good Lord. And she..." He released a piercing whistle. "You love her, or you want to protect her?"

"Both." He understood Steve's look of perplexity, because he couldn't figure it out either.

"Did you ask her why?"

"Yeah," he said, shifting his long body into a slouch, "but her reason didn't make sense to me. Look, man, it won't kill me; if I could go back into that operating theater and perform that surgery with that bunch eyeing every move I made and waiting for me to make a mistake, I can take *anything*."

Steve leaned against the roll-top desk, put his hands in his pockets, crossed his ankles, and looked at his brother.

"I hope you don't think there's any similarity between that and not having the woman you love. Before this gets cleared up, you'll find that you're the problem. You probably know a lot more about women than I do, Mason, but the ones who trailed around after you when you got to be a famous surgeon were pretty shallow. They wanted to be seen with you, to have you escort them to the Jack and Jill gala, the Urban League banquet, or some Delta or AKA shindig. For that, they'd accept whatever you offered and give you anything you asked for. Jeannetta Rollins is different; she's demanding more. I don't know what it is, but I'll bet it's something you never had to give up. Bring her down here sometime; I want to meet her."

Mason spread his palms on his knee caps and grinned at the picture he'd conjured up. Imagine *bringing* Jeannetta Rollins anywhere.

"I'll ask her nicely."

Steve laughed. "Bully for her. You're not giving up on her, are you?"

Mason pushed himself up to a standing position, stretched luxuriously, and shook his head. "Man, you know me better than that. Problem is, I don't have a clue as to what she wants that I don't give her." He reached down for his brief case, but straightened up without lifting it. "When she has her full memory, I'll know better where things stand with us." And I'll know whether she loved me or merely used me, he said to himself. Steve detained him when he would have left.

"I didn't get to see Mabel over the weekend; how is she?"

"She won't make it," Mason said with a sad shake of his head. "She's used up that extra something that makes people live when medical science says they shouldn't. I'm going to start adoption proceedings. Skip wants it badly, and I'm not turning him over to Family Services and heaven knows what kind of foster home. I want him with me."

"You'd better hurry up and do it while Mabel can help you. Skip's a great kid; if you wouldn't adopt him, I would. Get a lawyer."

"I did that this morning. He's drawing up an affidavit for Mabel's signature, and he'll take it from there. But I won't feel easy 'til I have those adoption papers in my safe-deposit box."

"Skip will be one happy boy; when he's with me, he can't seem to talk about anything but wanting you to be his dad."

Mason had to laugh. "He says I'll have him to take care of me when I'm old."

"And you will, too, so don't sell him short."

Mason frowned and looked toward the ceiling. "Well, I've cast the die; I'm going to be a father." He took in his brother's broad grin. "What's so amusing?"

Steve laughed. "Don't worry about your approaching fatherhood; Skip will give you all the advice you need."

Approaching fatherhood wasn't his worry; his main problem was the widening chasm between himself and the woman he'd come to love with every fiber of his being. The woman who seemed comfortable knowing that they had slipped away from each other.

\* \* \*

Jeannetta wanted to telephone Mason, but what could she say to him? That she'd changed her mind about being his wife? The phone rang. She turned over in bed, struggled to release herself from the tangled sheet and the twisted gown that clutched her tired body. She pulled the coverlet from the floor where she'd kicked it as she wrestled with sleeplessness, knocked the pillow off her head, and tried to sit up. She peeped at the clock as she lifted the receiver.

"Hello."

"Hi. I awakened you, and I'm sorry. I wouldn't have thought you'd turn in so early. Any problems?"

"No, but you said I'm not to read or to write much, though I did write for a few minutes yesterday afternoon, and I'm not to watch TV, so what's left? The bed."

"Don't trash it. The bed's probably been the scene of more awesome, mind-altering experiences that any other place on this planet. If the company's right…there's no limit. Trust me."

"Hmmm."

"What does that mean? Oh, yes, I said the wrong word."

Jeannetta stood up. "In a game of words, you'd probably win, but I'm after something more meaningful."

"I'd ask what, if I wasn't sure you'd dress it up so much that I wouldn't know what you're talking about."

"Did you call me to pick a fight?" She poked her tongue at the mouth piece. "Because if you did, I'm hanging up and going back to bed."

"That wasn't my intention, but I won't back away from one. In fact, honey, a good fight with you would do me a world of good right now."

"Too bad; I'm not going to accommodate you." She had a sense that he was warming up to a good verbal sparring, but she ached all over from bouncing around in the bed trying to sleep, and she wasn't in the mood for it.

"Don't want to fight, huh? How about making love? Would you do that if I were there right now?"

"And disobey my doctor, who thinks that a little thing, so mild by comparison, as a tongue darting in and out of my mouth, would raise my blood pressure to crisis level?"

"Don't get out of line there," he growled. "I can stay at fever pitch for longer than it takes me to get from here to Pilgrim, and then let's see how brave you'll be."

"You don't scare me. If I stood within thirty yards of a horde of wild elephants and didn't trem...Mason. Mason, when was I that close to elephants? I've got to get dressed and find Clayton. Maybe he was with me."

"I was with you, Jeannetta. We were on a preserve in Zimbabwe outside Harare. You and I." Excitement streaked through at the urgency in his voice. "What else did you see, baby?"

"I don't know...there are some monkeys, a male and a female, and they seem to be intimate...I...do you think it's all coming back?"

"Yeah. You're on your way. I read your last tests, the ones taken in Pilgrim and transferred here electronically. They're very encouraging. Read or write about an hour at a time, no more than four hours per day altogether, and wait a while for TV. Don't walk alone too much, and try to avoid the midday sun."

He could switch from hot to cold faster than a hailstorm. She'd love to cuff him. "Thanks, doctor." If he heard the sarcasm, so much the better.

"Wait a minute there." She knew she'd annoyed him, because he spoke rapidly with no inflection. "Are you saying I'm just your doctor? Nothing more than that?"

"Oh, Mason, how can you ask such a question?" If she hadn't already known that academic degrees didn't give men an understanding of women, he'd have convinced her.

"Why shouldn't I ask? You turned me down."

She took a deep breath and weighed her words carefully. After all, she didn't want to drive him from her, only to help him understand.

"I don't know you, Mason, and I can't marry a man whom I don't truly know. I don't understand what goes on inside of you.

I know that you want to protect me, to take care of me, and I appreciate that, but it isn't what I need. I don't need you to be my fail-safe in case I stumble." His silence cut like hot acid, but she had to tell him. "I can take care of myself. I appreciate all that you've done more than I can express it but, unless and until you offer me what I need, my answer is no."

"No? That's it? *No?*"

"I love you but, as things stand, marriage isn't for us."

"I see. Well, thanks for setting me straight."

She wouldn't react to the harshness of his voice, she told herself. "I don't think you see at all. *And how I wish you did.*"

"You're still my patient, I take it."

"Of course."

"Alright, I… Look, Jeannetta, we…we'll be in touch."

Mason replaced the receiver carefully, deep in thought. Needles and pins produced a tingling in his fingers and toes, and lightness claimed his head as though all the fluid had been wrung from his body. He told himself to get a grip on it, but he needed time to digest what had just happened to him. For the first time in his life he had let himself love a woman, a woman who believed that he didn't meet her needs. He swallowed a curse; anger wouldn't solve anything. Maybe he should have given her the details about the two occasions on which she had thrashed beneath him, calling his name as he kept her hanging at a precipice, begging him for ecstasy while he branded her with one powerful thrust after another. Maybe he should have told her all the things he knew about her that would leave no doubt in her mind that she'd made love with him. Like the little red mole beneath one of the chocolate brown nipples that he'd held between his lips, teasing her, while she begged him to suck them. He could have told her that they tasted like Tia Maria. Just as good and just as heady. Or should he have merely reminded her that a man had to have known a woman intimately to know how many moles she had at the edge of her pubic hair.

Mason paced the floor of his bedroom. What he wanted was

to get her back in his bed, and then he'd show her, love her until it all came back to her. He knew that she would eventually remember everything, but would that time come too late? He stopped short. He didn't want to believe it, but maybe she had never loved him—had enticed him, used him to get what she wanted. Pain flowed through him, enervating him. It couldn't be, he told himself. Not even Ethel Waters was reputed to have been that great an actress. Maybe he ought to get back up to Pilgrim and have it out with her.

After Mason's call, Jeannetta gave up the idea of sleep, dressed and went down the lounge, where Geoffrey held Lucy's hand and lectured Clayton about the importance of clearing his name. Jeannetta couldn't help being amused; all was right in Geoffrey's world, and he wanted smooth going for all of his friends. She had turned to leave when he asked why she wasn't in New York with Mason.

"I just spoke with him, Geoffrey. Quit meddling."

Geoffrey cocked his head to one side and peered at her. "He wasn't too happy when I saw him, and you ain't exactly bouncing. So, seems to me that you two need to spend more time together. I don't expect to let Lucy here out of my sight for more than a couple of hours at a time. We don't have misunderstandings when we're together, only when we're separated and start thinking about things that ain't got nothing to do with what glues a marriage. You don't see Clayton here leaving Laura with all these fellows that come up here to fish, do you?"

Jeannetta looked from Geoffrey to Lucy. She doubted that she had ever seen a happier woman, and she smiled in delight as Lucy inched closer to her husband. Geoffrey leaned back, propped his left foot on his right knee and looked at Jeannetta.

"I knew all the time that you two hadn't leveled with each other." Geoffrey looked up toward the ceiling. "That kind of thing does a lot of damage, and takes a lot of healing." He patted Lucy's hand and stood. "Where's Skip?"

"In the Internet," Clayton responded. "I'll bet my last dollar that this visit of Skip's is going to cost Mason a state-of-the-art computer." He glanced at Laura and smiled the secret smile of a lover. Everybody seems to have that something special except Mason and me, Jeannetta thought. Maybe Geoffrey was right; their relationship had been flawed from the outset. She walked over to her sister.

"Laura, I need to write, and I'll have to get away from here to do it. Pleasant company represents too much of a distraction, and Mason said he wants me to be active but quiet. My house is leased for three more months; I don't start school until January—if Mason will let me, I need to begin relying on myself. I have to look for a place where I can work."

Never at a loss for advice, Laura told her, "You shouldn't be in New York City and you shouldn't be too far away from Mason. You're not out of the woods yet."

"You're right; Kay and David Feinberg will be in Europe until mid-October, and I think, maybe I'll ask them to let me baby-sit their house and their dog while they're gone. I think I'll do it. You remember Kay; we shared a room at NYU." She watched Laura put on her worried look.

"Child, that's way past Fire Island. I don't know...doesn't seem right." She looked to Clayton as though seeking support for her argument. "West Tiana is a little inlet, and it's probably safe from storms but, honey, it's so far. What if she needs Mason?" She directed her question to Clayton.

"You're worrying unnecessarily, sweetheart," Clayton replied. "If Jeannetta needs Mason, she can probably signal him by mental telepathy. If I guess right, the man's antenna is pointed straight at her. I'd better see why Skip is so quiet." He headed for the office.

"And other thing," Jeannetta said, hoping to circumvent Laura's open disapproval of her plans. "Mason said the environment out on Long island will be good for me—clean air and a lot of natural scenery." She watched Laura purse her thin lips and knew she wouldn't like the words that were about to pass through them.

"Honey, you sure you don't want Clayton? Is that why you're content to let things slide with you and Mason? I don't want to see happen to us what happened to you and Alma when she slept with..."

Jeannetta interrupted, her tone harsh. "Laura, I don't want to have to tell you this again. I wouldn't see Clayton if he strolled past me butt naked. Okay?" She watched Laura's lower lip drop and her eyebrows arch sharply.

"Your eyesight couldn't possibly be that bad."

"It isn't. We're not talking eyesight here, Laura; this is a matter of chemistry. You should have had a look at Mason lying on the beach wearing nothing but red G-string bathing trunks. If you'd seen that sight, honey, you'd be fired up for life."

"If you say so. But I didn't see it, and I *am* fired up." She had paused for effect, Jeannetta realized, when she added: "For life. Mason isn't the only hot stuff on this planet; my Clayton can start fires with the best of them."

Who *was* this woman? Jeannetta squelched a laugh as she eyed her newly liberated sister.

"From the looks of you these days, honey, I don't doubt it."

Laura's quick change of manner startled Jeannetta. Now what?

"Now that all of Pilgrim knows a celebrated doctor comes here regularly to see you, Alma's out for revenge. I've been meaning to tell you," Laura said, her mood pensive. "The jealous woman's threatening to take that lie about you and Jethro to the dean of your department at SUNY. She tells everybody that you never denied having an affair with Jethro."

"No, I didn't deny it; the idea was too ludicrous. Besides, that was the only way I could punish her for what she did. My closest friend sleeps with my fiancé and tells him she's pregnant, when she isn't. That hurt. I'm sorry they aren't getting along, but whether I tell her the truth won't matter. She'll believe what she wants to believe. If she used her brain, she'd know that, as far as I am concerned, Jethro Williams ceased to exist when she told me they'd gotten a marriage license."

"What about the dean?"

"Alma was once on the dean's staff. Enough said."

"Don't be so smug about it. She tricked him into marrying her, because she was jealous of you; now she knows you got the better part of the deal and she'll do anything to upset you. 'Course, if you ask me," Laura went on, warming up to the subject, "Alma's got a big blob where her head's supposed to be, and sometimes I think she manages to sit on *that*. You be careful."

"Okay. Okay."

"And don't go too far from Mason," Laura nagged, following Jeannetta up the stairs. "I know you're going to do whatever you want to, but I don't like this. Anything could happen."

"But nothing will. How about driving me to Payne's Drug Store first thing tomorrow morning; I don't know what I'll find out there in West Tiana."

Laura nodded in agreement.


The two sisters were standing at the cashier's station in Payne's, joshing with the proprietor's daughter, when Laura nudged Jeannetta.

"Look over there. Darned if it isn't her royal highness."

Jeannetta followed her sister's gaze, knowing that she'd see Alma Williams; she had already started toward them.

"I heard you'd had a brain operation," she said to Jeannetta. "I suppose that means you have to give up teaching."

"Hello, Alma." Jeannetta had to force a smile, because she refused Alma the knowledge that she'd been disturbed by the woman's gossip-mongering. "Actually, I signed a new contract a couple of days ago." She scrutinized the woman carefully for her real reaction; anybody who lied with as much finesse as Alma had to be a consummate actress.

"Well," Alma said, "contracts have been broken. By the way, did you know that that doctor of yours practically killed a woman?"

"You ever been sued for slander, Alma?" Laura asked. "Well, prepare yourself, because you're about to get it, you hear?"

Jeannetta almost admired Alma's arrogant toss of the head as the woman prepared for her parting shot.

"You don't say. The dean said she'd be getting in touch with you, Jeannetta."

\* \* \*

They returned to the lodge to find Geoffrey, Lucy, and Skip still at the breakfast table. Jeannetta asked Geoffrey whether he and Lucy would like to spend a few days at West Tiana with her.

"No thanks. We left the Georgia heat and came up here for some cool air. You go ahead. Lucy's fallen in love with Skip and that great big oak out back, and Skip wants to learn everything Lucy knows. They'll have a good time. You're not going to drive, are you?"

"Hadn't planned to."

Skip left his place at the table and rushed to Jeannetta. "You going away some place?" She told him her plans.

"What about me? Weren't you gonna tell me?"

Her heart skipped several beats as she observed the boy's crushed demeanor; she hadn't considered that he cared for her.

"Yes, of course," she assured him, "and I'd let you go with me if you hadn't agreed to work, and if Mason didn't mind."

Lights danced in Skip's eyes, and a smile beautified his young face. "You going off somewhere with Mason, huh?"

She hated to disappoint him, but she couldn't mislead him. "Don't hope for that, Skip." She watched his enthusiasm fade along with the gleam in his eyes, as he hung his head. His painful need to belong somewhere stabbed at her and she folded him in her arms.

"You'll be special to me, no matter what happens between Mason and me," she tried to assure him but, unappeased, he stared into the distance.

Geoffrey tried. "She'll be back, and while she's gone, you and my Lucy can bake cookies." Skip looked at Geoffrey, and she didn't remember having seen so vacant an expression on a child's face.

"I promised Mason I'd look after Jeanny, but I can't if she's checking out. He'll think I lied."

Jeannetta decided to telephone Mason and let him ease Skip's worries.

"I've decided to stay out at the Hamptons for a few weeks," she told him, "but I'm afraid I've upset Skip, because he's staying here and won't be able to look after me." She bit her lip as she forced herself to sound serious for Skip's sake.

A comforting feeling of security settled within her as she listened to his dark, husky voice, reassuring her, telling her that he'd be there for her when she needed him.

"You need a good rest, though I'd prefer that you were some place nearby." He listed a number of signs that she should regard as foretelling an emergency. "If you experience any of them, call or beep me. But don't waste time about it. Promise?"

She promised and gave him the address and phone number.

"Let me speak with Skip." His abruptness stunned her, but she later realized he'd had a good reason. She handed the phone to the eager boy. Seconds later, Skip tossed the phone in the air and let out a whoop. Jumping and slapping his fist into his palm, a gesture he'd taken from Mason, he yelled, "Mason is adopting me." Immediately, he became subdued.

"But my aunt's pretty sick and wants to see me, so I have to go to New York." He looked at Laura as she entered the dining room with fresh muffins.

"Can I still have my job when I come back?"

Laura nodded. "Of course you can. You come right on back to the Hideaway, you hear?"

Making a quick decision, Jeannetta told Skip that he could go with her to New York.

Mason looked at his watch for the nth time since he'd spoken with Skip. Two-thirty. The boy should have been there. His office door opened, and Betty Goins sauntered in, unannounced, as usual.

"Heard you'd come to your senses," she said in greeting, leaned forward, and pressed a kiss on his mouth.

"Yeah, and I bet you heard it less than an hour ago." He needed a lot of self-control to refrain from wiping his mouth with the back of his hand.

"Don't be mean, Mason," she pouted.

He couldn't help laughing and wondering what he'd ever seen in her. "Alright, but don't you be so obvious." He lightened his tone, but he stared directly into her eyes; he wanted her to believe him when he said, *nothing doing.*

"We can still see each other, can't we?" She moved closer to him.

"Sure," he replied, backing his chair away from the desk and her, "but with my present preoccupation, that's all we'll do. I'm involved with someone." He pointed to his temple. "And she's right here thirty-six hours a day. You wouldn't get a rise out of me no matter what you did. Trust me."

She sauntered a step closer. "You're sure of that?"

Mason threw his head back and laughed. "Does water flow downstream? Let's leave it where it is, Betty. We've been friends, and I'd like to remember us that way."

"Oh, Mason, darling don't be like this." He watched her lower her lashes, drop her head to one side and rim her lips with the tip of her tongue, and he started to lose patience with her.

"If you want it crude, just say so."

Her head snapped up. "Alright. You can't hold it against me for trying. How's your precious patient?"

"Doing great." He paused, remembering Betty's wide contacts. "You remember that class action suit against Miles Chemicals?" Betty took a seat beside his desk, swung one of her long legs over the other one, and let her red silk skirt rise high above her crossed knees.

He grinned at her. "No dice, Betty. What about Miles Chemicals?"

"Sure, I remember that. One of my friends joined the suit, but her skin is already back to normal. I used it, and nothing happened to me."

Mason leaned forward. "How long did you use it?"

"As long as it was on the market. A year and a half, or two, I'd say. Why?"

Mason strummed his long fingers on his desk and thought for a minute. "The owner of that factory went belly-up because of that suit. He's a good guy, and he doesn't think he deserved what he got. He doesn't want the money returned; he wants to clear his reputation. He'd been assured that that formula had been properly tested."

Betty swung her knee and eyed Mason for effect. Seeing none, she got down to business. "I'd go back to court, if I were in that man's place. The instructions said that, if your skin felt dry, smooth it liberally with olive oil. That's what I did. He ought to make those women get their skin examined. I'll bet there're isn't a one whose skin isn't back to normal."

"Thanks. I'll pass that along."

"Well, if we can't get together, I guess I'd better take off."

He dialed the Hideaway with the intention of speaking to Clayton, but Betty opened the door to leave, and his heart pounded as though it were a runaway train. She stood facing Jeannetta and Skip. He dropped the receiver in its cradle. She glanced back at him, but his gaze seared the woman who occupied a permanent place in his heart.

Skip raced to him, his arms wide. "Dad! Dad! When will we get the papers? I started to think they wouldn't let you do it." He turned to Jeannetta. "Can you believe it, Jeanny? He's my Dad now." Mason didn't bother to correct him, because the only thing lacking was the judge's seal, which would be affixed within a week. He saw the tears of happiness in Jeannetta's smiling face and the lack of understanding in Betty's. Thank God, he'd avoided that pitfall. He let his arms tighten around Skip, stunned at the swell of love that flooded his senses. He reached one arm out to Jeannetta.

"Sweetheart, come here, please." He held them both until the three of them broke apart at the soft sound of Betty closing the door.

"You think Jeanny should be going out to Long Island by herself, Dad? She said it's almost three hours on the train."

Mason looked at her and hoped that his eyes mirrored what he felt, that she knew they reflected the heart of the man, not the doctor. "We can't run another person's life, son. We can only say what we believe to be the truth, wish them well, and let them go." He tried to ignore Skip's startled look. The boy had learned some archaic assumptions about women and their capabilities, and he intended to set him straight. He looked at Jeannetta, and hated the feeling of helplessness that stole over him when tears swam unshed in her beloved eyes. Why did she keep them apart with the cryptic explanation that he didn't meet her needs? He didn't believe a word of it, but she left him with no choice, and he had to accept it. He looked down at her small suitcase.

"You shouldn't be carrying luggage."

"I can carry it, Dad," Skip exclaimed. "I can go to the station with her." Mason smiled at the boy, whose voice caressed the word "dad" as though it had magic properties.

"No, son. You have to come with me to see Mabel. We'll get a taxi for her."

"Can the taxi take her all the way to the Hamptons? Huh?"

Mason rolled his tongue around the left side of his jaw. "It's a thought. A good one."

"No way," Jeannetta interjected. "I know you fellows mean well, but I'm taking the train."

"Call us when you get there. We'll be home," Skip advised.

"Where's home?" Jeannetta wanted to know.

"With my Dad," the boy answered proudly.

Jeannetta sat on the terrace facing Shinnecock Bay and the distant Atlantic Ocean, anxiously awaiting her first glimpse of the sunset. Robins, a finch and a few blackbirds serenaded her, and the cool ocean breeze sent her inside for a sweater. She couldn't see the sun, but the sky had become a rainbow of colors, settling slowly into a dark bluish gray with flashes of red and pink, the only sounds the rustling of the birds. Her longing for Mason intensified as darkness closed in, but she worked hard at shoving the yearning aside and concentrating on her work. She couldn't help being amazed at the way in which her fingers had flown across the keyboard of her laptop. She hoped Mason would lengthen her work time. She hadn't written about him; she couldn't bear to commit her thoughts of him to paper. But the hero of her story had closed his heart to everyone, even to himself. Neither the woman he loved and needed nor his precious golden retriever was allowed to sense his sadness and the way in which his soul ached. She saw her task as that of imbuing the hero with such self-knowledge as would bring him to share his inner self and, in so doing, accept himself and let the love of his woman heal him. Close to home, she reasoned, but once begun, she hadn't been able to steer the story in any other direction.

She nibbled absentmindedly on a cold chicken sandwich as darkness settled around her, fireflies rose from the grass, and crickets began their evening song. She sucked in her bottom lip and told herself that she had gambled for high stakes, wanting all of Mason and not that small portion of himself he'd so readily given. The sound of the telephone crashed into her reverie.

"Yes?"

"How're you getting on out there, Jeannetta?"

"F...f...fine." She hadn't expected his call, and she hoped the man and not the doctor was on the other end of the wire. "It's wonderful out here, Mason. Quiet, cool, and a sunset you wouldn't believe."

"Ah, yes. I remember that you have a passion for sunsets. I love the sunrise."

"I know."

"You know?" She wondered at his surprise. "You remember?" he asked.

"I don't know why I know it, but I do." Tendrils of fear sneaked over her nerves at the thought that she might have a permanent disability. "Why are you asking me that? Am I having chronic memory problems?"

"A few problems, but you're getting over them. We've discussed this at least once since your operation. Do you remember that?"

"Well, yes, you said we've made love, and I'd give anything to remember it. You wouldn't fool me, would you?"

"Fool you?" She thought she detected testiness in his voice. "I'll be delighted to prove it, and maybe I'll shake up your memory in the process."

"You sound pretty confident," she replied lamely. She'd been so certain that he'd been having fun at her expense, but if he could prove it...Laura's words came back to her.

"How can you prove it?"

"Jeannetta, if you're interested in the proof, just say it. Do you want to know?" That impersonal tone, again.

"With whom am I speaking now? The doctor, or the man who kissed me on a road in Pilgrim as though he could eat me alive? Which one?"

"Both." He shot back. "And if you think you can stand another round of that, I'll be in my car in five minutes."

"What'll you do with Skip?" she asked, not sure that she'd done the right thing in challenging him, and certain that he wouldn't come prepared to divest himself of his emotional armor.

"Skip's back at the Hideaway; I can't pry him loose from the place. Well?"

"I...uh..."

"You want to see me or not?" he broke in.

"I want to see you."

"It's six-forty; I'll see you in two and a half hours."

She begged him to drive carefully, and gave him the directions.

"Who else lives at the end of that road?"

"Just me."

"That wasn't what I wanted to hear. I'll be there soon."

Had she lost her mind? Unless he offered more than when he had proposed, what did she stand to gain from an evening with him? She took the menorah that David had inherited from his grandfather off of the mantelpiece to ensure its safety, and lit the fireplace. The evening had cooled and, face it, she thought, dancing flames would drive a man's heartbeat into a trot quicker than warm radiators. She put on a long red cotton shift and shod her feet in gold thongs. As usual, she didn't wear make-up or jewelry; she didn't want props. She wanted him to know exactly what he got—*if* and when she gave herself to him .

Mason called the Hideaway, and Skip answered. "Hiya, Dad?" He had to get used to his new title, but he didn't think he'd find that difficult. As any father would, he had called to tell Skip where he would be if needed.

"You gonna stay with Jeanny for a while?" the boy asked hopefully.

"Skip, you're still twelve, and you don't get into my personal business. Right?"

"No, sir. But you're going to see her?" The boy was incorrigible.

"Yes. Get Mrs. Ames to go over your chemistry and geography with you."

"I don't need that, but I don't guess it could hurt. Say, Dad…" here it comes.

"What is it, son? I've got to be moving."

"That's just my point, Dad. Hurry up and get going and…and…"

"And what?"

"Stay as long as you want to. That's not meddling, is it?"

"Not really." He had to laugh. Skip was determined to have Jeannetta for his mother and had begun to nag his soon-to-be father about it. The night before, Skip had practically lectured to him on Jeannetta's virtues, though he couldn't imagine how the boy had been able to chronicle them so accurately. He supposed that Skip's difficult life had equipped him to evaluate people; it certainly hadn't left him shy about going after what he wanted. And what he seemed to want and need most was to be a part of a normal family with his own mother and father, something he'd never known.

Mason bought a large vase of red roses, stargazer lilies, and calla lilies, and two bags of fresh-roasted unshelled peanuts. He slid into his Cougar, strapped his seat belt, turned the radio to WKCR jazz and headed for Long Island. With rush hour over and the traffic sparse, he'd see her in less than three hours. And when he left her, she'd be a different woman. He caught himself. If she had used him, he'd know it, and if she had leveled with him, he'd know that, too. He settled back, flipped on the cruise control, and quit thinking; he intended to greet her with an open mind.

He followed her perfect instructions, arrived at the end of

Burkes Road, and killed the motor. A dead end. As he sat there getting his bearings, a bloodcurdling sensation plowed through him. She walked toward the car shrouded in bright moonlight with a big German Shepherd leashed close to her side. He released a long harsh breath and gripped the steering wheel. She could never know what that image had engraved in his mind, kicking his heart into runaway palpitations. If he hadn't done the job and done it well, that would have been her life. She tapped on the window as he sat rooted to the driver's seat, appalled by that sickening symbol of what might have been.

"Hi." He relaxed as her brilliant and intimate smile began to warm his soul. Could she smile at him that way if she didn't care deep down? He started to unlock his door, but she motioned him to remain inside.

"Hi. Roll down the glass and stick your hand out. I have to introduce you to Casper." He tensed as the big dog smelled his fingers, looked up toward their owner, and sniffed again before wagging his tail.

"Now, pat him gently on the head a couple of times." Mason complied, and waited for the next ritual. Finally, Casper sat down and thumped his tail, and Jeannetta told Mason that he could safely open the door, but that it would be wise to get out slowly. Out of the car at last, Mason thought he'd better pat the dog again for insurance' sake, did as much, and was rewarded with a wagging tongue and a thumping tail. He opened the trunk, removed the flowers, nuts, and his medical case.

"I take it he's a guard dog." He watched the animal from the corner of his eye as he stepped closer to Jeannetta. Her smile broadened, and her lips met his in a kiss that was warm and brief, too brief. They walked around the back of the house, and he stopped them at the patio lamp.

"Let me look at you." Stepping back, he let his gaze roam over her face, her slim rounded figure, and he sucked in his breath. He wanted to hold her, love her, and keep her close to him for the rest of his life. Couldn't she see how much he loved her and needed her? She grasped his hand, and he hoped that meant she felt what he felt.

"I have to take Casper to his house, because he won't go in otherwise. He's trained to do as he's told." She patted Casper's head, and the dog went inside his elegant dog house. Mason didn't attempt to guess the implications when she glanced up at him, took his hand and said, "Let's go in."

Inside, she took the flowers, and he watched her hips assert themselves beneath the simple red dress. On some women, it would have been an ungainly sack, but she wore it with sexy, feminine grace. He had expected a beach house but, looking around the living room, he saw a well-appointed place for year-round living. His gaze landed on the menorah.

"Your friends are Jewish, I take it."

"Yes. Kay and I roomed together in undergraduate school, and I was one of her bridesmaids. We've had a lot of fun together."

He nodded. "I had some good times in my college days, too." He tried to figure out her mood. She seemed accepting, but was she?

"It's strange, your being here, but I'm glad you came."

"Me, too." He hoped she hadn't forgotten that he'd come in response to what amounted to a challenge from her. He opened his medical bag. "Let's get this over with, so we can send the doctor packing." He couldn't help grinning at her skeptical look and raised eyebrow, which he took as a warning that she wouldn't bend easily. How could he have fallen so deeply in love with her without knowing important things about her, essential aspects of her character? This woman had a backbone of steel. He examined her and, satisfied, closed the bag.

"Where do I put this?"

Her answer should have told him what to expect, but she didn't tip her hand when she suggested the foyer. Not in her bedroom or the guest room. He stuck his hands in his pants pockets, wiped his face of all expression, and gazed at her.

"We're acting like strangers, Jeannetta."

"Our last conversation left me feeling like one," she said. Funny; she had a habit of remembering things one way when he saw them from a different perspective.

"The last time we were together, I hugged you, woman."

"A hug and a conversation are different forms of communication."

He frowned, although he took courage from the fluttering of her long, thick, black lashes, but a smile fought for and won possession of his face. He caught her looking at his mouth and sucking the inside of her lip, and his smile became a broad grin.

"What kind of communication is kissing?" That was what he wanted right then, some mind-boggling loving, not the flirtatious bantering at which she was such a genius. But when she tossed her head back and propped her left fist on her left hipbone, he knew that sexual fencing was what he'd get.

"You should know; you're a master at it." He tried not to show too much pleasure at her remark, but he must not have succeeded, because she frowned and asked him, "What are you up to, Fenwick?"

He spread his hands in a gesture of defenselessness. "Who, me? I'm just trying to make some headway here. And if you'd just take your hand off your hip, I'd feel a lot more comfortable. I had an aunt who used to stand like that, only she usually waved a heavy skillet with her other hand. No offense meant, of course." He ran his hand over his tight curls. So far he hadn't made any progress with her. He looked around for some help, saw the screened-in side porch and took her hand. "Let's sit out here."

She went with him, but protested that the night air chilled her.

"That's why I'm here," he said with a wink. "to warm you up."

He reclined in the chaise lounge with his arms around her. "Can't you imagine us growing old together like this, after our kids are grown and married and we have a gang of grandchildren?" His hand smoothed her thick hair away from her face as he talked, and it excited him when she snuggled closer and wrapped her arms around his waist.

"What do you say? Wouldn't we make terrific grandparents?" She giggled almost to the point of strangulation.

"Mason do you realize how far out of character you're being?"

"Sure I do, but being myself got me nowhere, so I'm trying to imagine how all those married fellows did it."

"This business is woman-specific, honey," she purred, "and each one of us has…uh…different requirements."

"I'd hoped that when you finally got around to addressing me with an endearment, it would at least have the ring of intimacy."

The clock chimed, and she leaned away from him. Regarding him intently, she spoke softly, almost as though to herself. "Romance is like everything else, you gain by giving."

"Now, we're getting somewhere." He gripped each of her shoulders and stared into her eyes. "What do you want? Name your terms." Her narrowed eyes and the sound of her throat clearing weren't reassuring, but he refused to back down.

"Well?" he urged. "You can be pretty frisky when we're talking on the phone and, come to think of it, you know how to be aggressive when it suits you." He paused and decided to let if fly. "I hope you haven't forgotten the way you nearly seduced me on that tour bus when we were in Singapore, and in broad daylight, too. I knew what you wanted then, because you telegraphed it to my brain, my nervous system, my libido, my whole body. Use a little of that ingenuity right now, and tell me what you want." Her eyes seemed to search for something deep inside of him, and he found himself automatically closing an emotional gate. Her eyes dimmed, and he knew she had discerned it. He'd deal with that later, but right then he had to know what she required of him.

"You told me you love me," he went on, "and I can't find a reason to disbelieve you. Yet, you won't agree to marry me. What do you want that I'm not giving you? You've got a price. Name it."

"You," she answered, boldly meeting his gaze. His eyes widened in astonishment. Hadn't he offered to give himself when he proposed? Perplexed, he shook his head.

*"Me?"*

"You. Your whole self." Her hand caressed his jaw and, with a tenderness that amazed him, he trapped her wrist, but her lips parted in surprise, and he released her.

"Shut-eye time," she announced, standing and suppressing a yawn. He took his time getting to his feet. She walked ahead of him, turned, locked the door after he'd entered the dinette, and faced him, questions mirrored in her face.

Did she know that her body had relaxed, her pelvis tilted toward him, and her nipples were little hard pebbles peeking at him through that dress? He sucked in his breath and gave himself a silent lecture. This night could be the most important one of his life. His gaze settled on her mouth as she absentmindedly licked her lips, and he rubbed his damp palms against the sides of his pants, swallowed, and reached out to her, unable to withstand their fencing, incapable of denying himself any longer.

Jeannetta hurled herself into his waiting arms. Shivers of anticipation crept over her limbs as she waited for the touch of his mouth. Of their own volition, her lips parted for him in her longing for greater intimacy with him, and her body pressed itself to his. He tried to slow it down, to pull away, but she clung to him until he relented, thrust his tongue between her lips and let her feel his virile power. Her body rocked with the awareness that slammed into her, and her control shattered when he trembled against her. She had forced him to that point, but she didn't care; she needed it, needed some evidence that he belonged to her, that she could somehow pierce his emotional shell and know the man whom she loved. With obvious strain, he moved away from her, though his fingers rested lightly on her arms.

"Sweetheart, I wanted a kiss, but you know we can't take this any further until your doctor releases you."

"You don't think my doctor is being overly cautious?"

He pulled her back into his arms, and she welcomed it, loved the feel of his hands stroking her back.

"No, I don't. Hell, he wouldn't approve of the heat you turned on there, either." His grin sent her heart into a dizzy trot. "Woman, you pick the damndest times to put me on a rack."

"Are you going to spend the night?"

His rueful smile touched her heart.

"That's right; turn the knife." His demeanor darkened. "Jeannetta, I do not claim to be a saint, and I'm starved damned near to death for you."

She sucked on her bottom lip and glanced at him from beneath lowered lashes.

"The guest room?"

He glared at her. "You're pitching hardball, honey; I'm going home."

"Of course you are. Tomorrow morning. Right now, you're going to eat a sandwich, drink a glass of milk, and get some sleep. What's so funny?" she asked when his booming laugh reverberated throughout the house.

"Just the right touch. As soon as you see reason, I'll let you tell me when to get up and when to go to bed; I may even eat oatmeal for you but, tonight, baby, I'm going back to New York."

"You're serious?"

"Does the sun rise in the east?" He got his medical bag, took out the sack of peanuts, and asked her. "Where can I warm these up?"

"You don't want a sandwich," she asked him, walking toward the kitchen.

"We will not discuss what I want, Jeannetta. I haven't had any hot roasted peanuts in ages, and this is a good time for them."

"You won't get to New York until after midnight." He dumped half of the nuts into the pan she gave him and put them in the oven.

"True. But I'll like myself when I get there."

"What about the sunrise?"

"There'll be others, plenty of them."

She watched his face bloom into a smile, as though reflecting a cherished idea.

He had, indeed, been thinking of the two of them, she knew,

when he said, "Ever since my parents died, I wanted to live in a big house high on a hill with the world visible from every direction." His smile slowly ebbed. "You could have your sunset, and I, my sunrise." In that second, she had a glimpse of him as the man she needed and wanted for herself, and she wouldn't settle for less. Go on, let it out, she wanted to shout at him when he concentrated on removing the nuts from the oven. She let her right hand cover his left one so he'd know that she understood his need, but he avoided her eyes, took her hand, sat down, and focused on the peanuts.

"What's that?" he whispered. Goose pimples broke out on her bare arms as she caught his tension. "Any wild animals around here? There it is again." He jumped up from the table and raced toward the front door.

"Mason, wait. That sounds like Casper." The low growl grew louder and more ominous.

"My Cougar is the only car out there. What do you think he's after?" He doused the lights in the living room and looked out of the window. The growling intensified and, when a loud yell rang out, she clamped her hand over her mouth.

"Steady, baby. Do you have a gun around here anywhere?" She shook her head.

"I don't know. I c...c...couldn't u...u...use it if th...there was one." She had never had a need for the big dog's protection, and needles pricked her whole body at the sound of his increasingly loud and angry growl.

"I'm going out there; he could kill somebody."

It had never occurred to Mason that Jeannetta could move with such speed. In a second, she was between him and the door, facing him with an expression of defiance that he would not have associated with her.

"You're not going out there. Period." He checked himself when he would have moved her aside and summoned control.

"I can take care of myself, and you, too, if necessary. So please step aside." She didn't budge.

"David said Casper won't mortally wound anybody unless the person tried to get in the house or attacks someone who lives here, but if you go out there..." The growling had ceased, and he thought he heard scratching and whimpering.

"Is that Casper?" She moved quickly, grabbing his hand, and he followed her to the back door. He opened the door, but the dog didn't enter.

"I think he wants us to follow him " he told her. "You stay behind me." They saw a youth dragging himself away from the house, and Casper ran ahead and stopped him.

"What were you up to?" Mason asked the boy.

"I didn't know he'd bite. I...I was going to take him home with me. I thought maybe he was a hunting dog. I wanted a pet."

"How old are you?" Jeannetta asked the boy, who was favoring his arm.

"Sixteen."

Mason looked at Casper to make certain that the dog trusted him. Satisfied, he told the boy, "I'd better look at your arm; come on inside." They started back to the house and Casper blocked the way.

"I can't let him go off like this; he could get an infection, gangrene. Try to get Casper to walk back to his house with you." He could see that Casper wouldn't cooperate, took the little phone hooked to his left side, and dialed nine-one-one.

"We'll stand here until we get help, because this dog has no intention of letting the boy in the house."

"He'll be in trouble," Jeannetta said.

Pity was not what the boy needed, he told her, as he recalled Skip's desperate efforts to avoid getting into trouble; this boy needed discipline. "Better now than later." He looked directly at the young man. "The next time you want a dog or anything else, find a job, go to work and, get it honestly." When the police arrived, along with an ambulance, Mason dressed the boy's shoulder wounds, gave him an antibiotic and a stern lecture, and stood with Jeannetta and Casper until their intruder and the others were out of sight. Casper wagged his tail, and Mason knew that morning would find him in West Tiana. Probably sleeping on the porch, he murmured to himself, fighting off the onset of an ill temper.

"It's definitely too late…" Jeannetta began. He looked at her, shrouded in bright moonlight and her come-hither dress. Not that the dress made a difference; she would have enticed him if she'd been draped in a sackcloth.

"Go to bed, Jeannetta," he told her, "that way, we'll both stay out of trouble."

"But where will…?"

He arched both brows and seared her with a libidinous stare, exposing his need for her.

"Alright. Alright," she said. "The guest room's upstairs to your left at the end of the hall. See you in the morning."

He watched as she wasted no time getting up the stairs. He took a coat from the hall closet, walked out on the screened-in side porch, pulled off his pants, shirt, and shoes, and stretched out on the chaise lounge. He threw David's coat over himself to ward off the cooling air. Not for money would he go up those stairs; he didn't think he'd ever walked in his sleep, but there was a first time for everything.

Jeannetta looked down at the dress pooled around her feet. Did she dare to walk back down those stairs? He'd welcome her; she didn't doubt that. But she also knew that he wouldn't hold her in high esteem if she seduced him into violating his principles. And he had made it clear that, where her health was concerned, the doctor ruled the man. She walked to the window and looked out at the moonlit garden, its plants already adjusting to the changing season. She ought to be grateful for what she had, and she was, but the man she loved was bunked downstairs somewhere while she prowled in her bedroom, hot enough to ignite a furnace. What she felt bore no relation to gratitude. She wondered if it would help to scream.

"Girl, you're getting yourself shook up," she muttered aloud, as she sat on the edge of the bed and pulled off the thongs. She stretched out on the coverlet, hoping he'd forget about honor and open her door.

She awoke with the thought that if Mason really had made love with her twice, the experience hadn't exactly blown his mind. She showered, dressed, and went downstairs. When she didn't see him in the den or the living room, she rushed to the window and let out a long breath. Thank God. His car was there. She found him in the kitchen, shirtless, stirring pancake batter. Her eyes rounded and her bottom lip dropped, before she could gather her composure, and she battled a wild urge to run her hands over his naked shoulders, biceps and every inch of flesh not hidden by his undershirt.

"Good morning." She knew he'd caught her ogling him, and ducked her head in embarrassment. "Where did you sleep?"

He looked up at her and grinned. "Hi. I slept on the porch. Do you know that's the first time I ever slept outdoors? The air was wonderful, and after a while all the night creatures went to sleep and you never heard such quiet…" His voice trailed off into a dark whisper. "Like what you see?" He set the cup of batter on the counter and started toward her, but she backed up and put the table between them.

"Oh, no, you don't. The next time you start a fire in this house," she pointed to herself, "you are going to put it out." Her pulse raced as he looked down at her and smiled, the slow, intimate beauty of it dulling her senses.

"You're the one who started that hot scene last night," he said, his smile broadening and lights dancing in his eyes. "All I was after was a kiss, but you pulled out the stops and, honey, I'm a hungry man."

She nodded toward the stove and the smoking frying pan. "Is that why you're making pancakes?"

He rounded the table, pulled her to him, and covered her lips in a quick, demanding kiss before releasing her and walking back to the stove.

"I'm making these things because I always eat breakfast, and that's all I could find, but pancakes and nothing else that goes in my stomach are going to satisfy the hunger I'm talking about.

So be a smart gal and stay away from the subject of my appetite. Where's the butter?"

"Butter? I'd think a doctor would be concerned about cholesterol."

"Absolutely. Where's the butter?" She got it for him, and her eyebrows arched at his practiced performance when he shook the pan and flipped over a cake.

"Where'd you learn how to do that?"

"Working in dozens of greasy spoons. I hope that stuff over there is maple syrup." He pointed toward a bottle.

"It is. Where'd you grow up?"

His head came up sharply. "San Francisco. Would you rather eat in here or on the patio? The sun'll be up in about half an hour, and I'd hoped we could watch the sunrise together."

"I love it out on the patio early in the morning; give me a minute to set the table." She went in the pantry for the linens and flatware and leaned against the doorjamb, certain that all she longed for had slipped through her fingers. Maybe she asked for more than he could give.

He took her hand as they walked down to the beach after breakfast with the early morning breeze whipping around them. Contentment, peace, enveloped him, and he let his right arm circle her waist and bring her closer to him.

"When I didn't see you in the living room or the den, I thought you'd left."

"That isn't my style. No offense meant, of course," he added, stopping and tweaking her nose. "Not like some people I know."

She showed no remorse for it, and he asked her whether she deserved some punishment for putting him through hell with her international escapades.

"I am not going to let you drag us into a fight and ruin this perfect morning."

They reached the beach, deserted but for them, pulled off their shoes, and walked along the water's edge as the sky welcomed the dazzling colors of the rising sun.

"If I wasn't dressed, I'd stretch out here." He pointed to a spot in the sand. "I love the feel of sand and cool breeze on my body."

Jeannetta picked up a handful of yellow grains and let them sift through her fingers, reminding him of other times he'd seen her do it. He wondered at its significance.

"You ought to burn your red bikini swim trunks—if you could call them that; they're indecent."

He stopped and gently turned her to face him. "You still think about that. Maybe you should have followed your instincts."

Her heavy lashes flew upward, and she looked into the distance. "Have you ever been…Has any woman ever…well…just *taken* you?"

"You mean have I ever been r aped?" He had to laugh at the idea. She nodded.

"Well, noooooo. Of course not. I'm rather big for that, don't you think?"

She looked out across the ocean, wet her lips with the tip of her tongue, and then met his gaze. "You came pretty close to it that morning on the Lido beach." He couldn't have moved if disaster had threatened them. If she'd wanted him a full two months before they made love, it was small wonder that she gave herself with such abandon.

"What stopped you?"

"I told you; I came to my senses. I still can't believe I got so close to committing such an awful crime." She stared, tongue-tied, as his laughter reverberated through the trees.

"*A crime?* We won't discuss what my reaction would have been, at least not so long as I'm still dealing with self-imposed celibacy."

Her gape of amazement was followed by a smile so dazzling that he had to believe she prized beyond measure his admission to wanting only her. He glanced at his watch. Seven-forty-five, and time he headed back to the city and checked out things in his office. They strolled arm in arm to the house, and as they reached the patio, the ringing of his phone jarred their quiet world.

"I've got to get back. Mabel is worse, and she wants to see

Skip and me. Come back with me. After what I saw last night, I don't see how I can leave you here."

"Please understand, Mason. I can't leave the house, Casper, my work. You saw that Casper will protect me, so don't worry."

"I need some tests on you, though that can wait a couple of weeks. But, honey, this place is deserted. Casper is a powerful dog, but could he handle two or three thugs, especially if they had guns?"

"The police were here within minutes after you called them last night. I have to stay, so please don't make me displease you."

"I don't want you out here alone where I can't protect you." What had he said to get her back up? He looked down at the fist propped on her hip and shook his head. If he lived to be a thousand, he'd never understand women.

"Now what?"

"You want to protect me, but it isn't protection that I need; I need you."

He frowned.

"What are you talking about? I've offered myself to you, and you've made it clear that you'll have me as a lover, but not as your husband. What does that make me in your estimation?"

"Oh, Mason, if only I could make you understand." He had to go; Mabel had about used up her resources, and time was of the essence. He phoned Laura and told her to send Skip to New York.

"I've got to go." He turned and looked at her. "You may wear your hair combed over that wound when you go out but, at other times, keep it uncovered." He grasped her hand. "Come on." She walked him to his car and stood on tiptoe for his kiss. She had to sense, to feel the pain that he couldn't hide from her. "I'll call you." As he drove off, he glanced at the rear-view mirror to see her white gauzy dress billowing in the breeze, and Casper standing close to her side, wagging his tail.

# Chapter 12

Jeannetta couldn't work; her mind clung to her tepid parting with Mason. She remembered how her parents had shared everything, had discussed problems, painful and pleasant, with Laura and herself. As far as she knew, they never argued and, with the wisdom of adulthood, she believed that their peace and congeniality sprang as much from knowledge of each other as from love. So she didn't think she had erred in holding out for the best of Mason. If she only knew why he wouldn't share himself with her, she'd know where to begin.

She walked out into the still, cool morning and released Casper. He stood obediently while she hooked a chain to his collar, and wagged his tail in anticipation of his morning frolic on the beach. If amazed her that the big dog didn't use his strength against her to force his will, but always waited patiently for her direction. After twenty minutes of chasing behind him, she brought him back to the house, took off the chain, fed him, and was about to put him in his house when his tail stood. She turned to see a Lincoln Town Car pull into the driveway.

A tall, well-dressed, and obviously furious man rushed from it, but Casper's angry growl brought him to a sudden halt. For the next half hour she dealt with a surly and indulgent parent who automatically took her for a maid. Upon learning that she wasn't, he demanded that she have the charges against his son dropped and his record cleared. It cheered her that Casper's presence tempered the man's belligerence. A bully, that's what he was, but not with Casper. He ranted and bellowed at her but, with each glance at Casper, he took a step backward.

"You ought to be thankful that my visitor was a surgeon who took care of your son's wounds. Your boy got a good lesson for trying to steal a dog. When my friends get back, you may speak to them about the charges; it's their house and their dog. Now, please leave."

"How dare you…"

"Do you intend to leave with or without Casper's help? You've got thirty seconds." After shaking his fist in the air, the man bolted for his car, got in, and rolled down the window.

"I hope I don't find out that you've bought the place because, if I do, you'll be looking for another one, and you'll have a hell of a time selling this." He backed out, and she wouldn't have been surprised if the speed with which he did it had split his tires. She went inside and called Laura.

"I'm sure glad you called, Hon, 'cause I was just about to ring you. Skip's shaken about Mabel—she passed away, you know. Mason's on his way here, and we just can't get the child settled down. You want to try calming him?"

"I thought he was supposed to meet Mason in New York. What happened?"

"Mason called back before Skip could leave and gave us the news. Here he is."

"Hi, Jeanny. I guess you know what happened. Aren't you coming up here with my Dad?"

She couldn't, and she knew he'd feel as though she had deserted him.

"If I leave here, Skip, there won't be anyone to take care of the dog, and he's too big for me to take with me."

"He is?"

She told him about Casper and promised that, if Mason didn't mind, he could visit her and the dog.

"Have you got a computer?" She offered to let him use hers when he visited.

He responded proudly. "That's okay; I can borrow my dad's

laptop. Aunt Laura and Mrs. Ames have been teaching me a lot of things."

"*Aunt* Laura?" She couldn't believe Laura let him call her that; if so, she didn't need any more evidence of Clayton's powers as a miracle worker.

"Yeah. She said I couldn't call her by her first name, and since she's going to be my aunt…you know, she's your sister…and all. Well, you know…"

She wondered at his sudden silence.

"You're gonna marry my dad, aren't you?" This wasn't the time to disappoint him, but how could she lie?

"Skip, I'm so sorry about your aunt. It hurts, I know, but now you have Mason and he'll look after you." She thought she heard a sniffle.

"I know, but I didn't have time to get there. When Dad gets here, do you mind if I ask him to let me stay with you one weekend? He'd been complaining that you shouldn't be out there by yourself."

This wasn't the time to give him the impression that he wasn't needed, so she let it slide, but she'd get around to divesting him of the notion that she couldn't look after herself. She hung up and wandered around the house, out of sorts and aware that the feeling enveloped her whenever Mason left her. She slapped her knee. *Something had to give!*

Working with her needles always gave her a sense of peace, so she took some materials out to the patio and began crocheting dolls. Lost in the rhythm of the needles, images of another scene in which she had sat on a veranda and gazed at a garden of flowers, butterflies, and bees swirled around in her mind. She knew it was real, but couldn't place it. Frustrated, she called Mason's travel office and left a request that he telephone her.

"Are you alright? I'm on my way to Pilgrim, and I just got your message."

Everything settled inside of her with the sound of his voice.

"Hi. I'm okay. But I just had a vision of a garden of flowers in some far-off place, and I can't figure out where it was. Were we together in a garden?"

"I don't think so, but nearly every private home and most hotels in Zimbabwe have flower gardens. What else did you recall?" She told him about the butterflies and bees.

"Where did you go when you left my room the morning after we made love that first time? In Zimbabwe."

She couldn't contain a gasp. "You're so insistent about this, Mason. You must have some proof, and I want to know what it is. Please tell me. I'm trying to remember, and if what you say is true, it must have been wonderful, and I don't want it to remain a mystery to me."

"It *was* wonderful. Both times. Since you ask, you've got two little red moles on the lower part of your left breast, one just above your belly button, and three almost where your left thigh joins your hip, pretty close to your venus mound. Right? And remember, as an ophthalmologist, I didn't look below your neck, when you were under anesthesia."

"Oh, Mason, I'm so sorry I don't remember."

"With your permission, madam, I should be honoured and pleased to joggle your memory."

Shivers danced all through her at the promise she heard in his low chuckle.

"I'll bet," she told him dryly.

"Don't push it; it will come back, and my considerable experience tells me it won't be long. Everything else there alright?"

With his uncanny ability to sense problems where she was concerned, she wouldn't be surprised if he suspected her morning encounter with the irate stranger.

"Casper and I are fine, thanks." Well, it wasn't a lie, and he didn't have to know everything, she told herself.

"I could use a kiss."

She couldn't help laughing. "Sure you could; you've got these wires for protection."

His laughter warmed her. Oh, what she wouldn't give to be with him.

"Go ahead, tease me. I'll haul you in here and get those tests and prove my suspicions."

Her heart skidded down a foot and into her belly. "What suspicions?"

"My suspicion that Dr. Fenwick can discharge you and leave you to the mercy of Fenwick the man."

"Really?" she blustered. "In that case, place the order with the hospital out here, and I'll get the test tomorrow."

"You're pretty anxious," he growled. "Challenging me again, are you? Alright. Call Dr. Betz there in about two hours, and be prepared to take the test tomorrow. No food or drink after seven this evening. I'll call you late tomorrow with your test results. Meantime, from the minute you leave the hospital, fill up on protein and carbohydrates; you're going to need them."

"You look after yourself, too, dear," she advised sweetly, "and if you have any doubts about what to do, get in touch with Michael Jordan, Carl Lewis, or one of those other sports fellows, and find out what keeps them going." The sound was that of tires screeching. But it couldn't have been; Mason was a level-headed man.

"Are you okay?" she asked him.

"Just wait 'til I get my hands on you."

Warming up to their bantering, she baited him with, "Tell me what you'll do," and held her breath for his response.

"Have you ever been hot and cold, wet and dry, crazy and sane, dying and bursting with life all at the same time?"

Shivers of anticipation raced down her spine, and goose pimples covered her arms.

"Not that I recall."

"I know you don't, but I intend to remind you; and I doubt it will ever slip your mind again, no matter what happens."

"Hmmm. Pretty big talk for a guy whose principles *always* rule his libido and who's never tempted to waver."

"Where'd you get that idea? Why do you think I slept on that chaise lounge on your back porch with my feet and half of my legs handing off of it? If I'd gone to that guest room, I'd have taken you with me. That was will power, and, if you want to test it, I'll keep you busy 'til you scream for mercy."

"Ho hum. Talk's easy done. I always heard that a man boasts of his feats because nobody else sees things his way." She couldn't help hugging herself when his deep warm laughter teased her ears.

"I've forgotten how we got into this conversation, but you have a habit of giving me a hard time when I'm not around to make you eat your words. I'll see you in a few days. Meanwhile, get plenty of rest, eat wholesome food, and conserve your energy." The dial tone terminated his joyous laughter.

"Oh, boy! I can't wait," she said aloud, and returned to her needlework, hoping for more revelations.

Mason pulled up in front of Rollins Hideaway and killed the motor. What would he say to Skip? The boy raced out of the building, ran up to him and stopped as though uncertain how to greet him. He put an arm around the child's shoulder and received a powerful hug; he wouldn't have thought Skip strong enough to embrace him so tightly.

"I know it hurts, son, but this is life. You have me now, and you are not alone. You understand that?" Skip nodded. "You and I have some business to attend to, and then we're going home."

"But my job still has a week to run, and Aunt Laura's depending on me. I can't leave her in a mess." They entered the Hideaway, and Geoffrey walked toward them.

"Lucy and I will be more than happy if Skip could visit with us for a few days before school starts. She says he can learn advanced math, and she wants to teach him." Mason fingered the keys in his pants pocket and made a decision.

"Thanks. I appreciate that, but Skip and I have to learn how to be a family, and the sooner we start, the better. I'll have less time next month when I resume my medical practice full time; after that, we won't see much of each other. He and I will be down to see you, though, and we'll always be in touch, Geoffrey."

The old man cocked his head to one side and looked Mason in the eye.

"Only a fool throws away a diamond, son, and Jeannetta Rollins is a rare one. Don't forget that. Give her our love."

Mason watched them get into the waiting taxi.

"Why didn't Laura or Clayton take them to the station?" he asked Skip.

"They offered, but Mrs. Ames said she wanted to ride around the lake and look at the mountains before she leaves Pilgrim. What kind of business do we have, Dad?"

"We have to get you relieved of your duties, and then we're going home." He explained to the boy while they walked up the stairs to their room that, in a few days, they'd have services for Mabel. He closed the door, kicked off his shoes and sat down, and, to his surprise, Skip brought him his house slippers. He looked at the boy and grinned.

"I see fatherhood has its rewards. Thanks."

"I told you," Skip said. "I'm going to take good care of you." Both of his eyebrows arched.

"Son, I'm only thirty-seven years old. You can take care of me when I'm eighty."

"Gee. Do I have to wait that long?" He couldn't help laughing; he didn't yet have Jeannetta, but this wonderful boy was his. His son. He gave silent thanks that they'd found each other.

Three days later, he and Skip began a new life. He took the boy to his office at the travel agency and introduced him to his staff, then to his medical office to meet his secretary and technician.

Edna had gone for the day, but he found her notes: Steve wants you to call him, and Dr. Betz said the tests are great and he's sending them by FedEx. He phoned Steve. He'd tell Jeannetta about the tests when he'd read them for himself.

"Mason, can you stop by here? I need to talk with you."

"Okay, but Skip is with me."

Steve's silence told him that the conversation would be personal.

"Uh...Okay. He can surf the Internet, and we'll talk in the living room."

* * *

"What's up, Steve?"

"Hi, Uncle Steve. Is it alright if I check out the Internet?" Steve nodded.

"What's this all about, man?"

Steve motioned to a big overstuffed chair. "Take a load off your feet." He went in the kitchen and returned with two cans of Pilsner. "Mason, a private investigator in one of the buildings that I service left a manila folder in the men's room, and when I opened it to see whose it was, I saw your name. So I stopped and read it. The next evening, I took it to the private investigator who'd left it there and confronted him. I refused to return it to him until he told me why he was investigating you. He had no choice but to level with me, because the folder also contained records of several of his current cases. Jeannetta Rollins ordered the report when she was considering taking the tour, so she knew everything about you. That guy is so good that he has his name on his door in brass, and he sits two doors from the company president. I'm sorry, Mason, but, from where I sit, this isn't squeaky clean."

Mason pushed his beer aside, and his right hand automatically went to the keys in his pocket. Another left hook to the belly. He looked up to see his brother's gaze locked firmly on him, but he didn't reply. He didn't want to react right then, because he needed to deal with his feelings in private. He loved his brother, but he couldn't help feeling some hostility toward the man who had pricked his balloon. With her test probably clean, he had planned to release her the next day and to see her within forty-eight hours. He rested his head against the back of the chair and told himself to be fair. Steve was doing as he always had; he put his brother's interests above everything else. Still, it wasn't Steve's place to judge her.

"I have to let this set a while; then, if you want to talk about it, okay. But not now." Steve nodded, but Mason knew that his brother wasn't remorseful for having told him; he'd thought it over well.

"How long have you known about this, Steve?"

"A couple of days. I did a lot of thinking about it, and you do the same. Our daddy used to say 'haste makes waste,' so don't do anything rash." At Mason's raised eyebrow, Steve corrected himself.

"I know that last comment was unnecessary; I'd trust your judgment any day."

"You said you wanted to meet her; I'm going to arrange that." Steve's head turned sharply toward Mason, and he looked hard at his brother, seemingly unable to utter a word. "By the way," Mason went on, ignoring his brother's state of mild shock. "I met a guy, a homeless fellow I'd like you to try out. I'm not certain, but you might be his one chance."

"What's special about this one?"

"He's an engineer who lost his business, his home, and his wife, in that order. He's only been on the street for about seven months, so there's hope for him. What do you say?"

"Okay, I'll give him a shot…if he wants it."

"I'm not sure he does, but he ought to have a chance. Thanks. I'll get in touch with him as soon as I can." A smile played around the corner of Steve's mouth, almost unwillingly, it seemed to Mason.

"I get a bang out of the way you tell a person to butt out of your business," Steve said, as much to himself as to Mason. "Not a single unpleasant word," he went on, as though bemused. "You merely change the topic. I can't help wondering what you'd do if some unfortunate guy insisted on pulling your strings. What *would* you do?"

"No telling. I need to think about what you said. Okay?"

"Sure. How you deal with it is your business; I thought you should know."

Mason got out of bed, turned off the air conditioner, opened a window, and let the cool night air soothe his body. She'd known him for over five months now, six if you counted their first meeting in March, and she'd had numerous opportunities

Forster

to tell him about it, to apologize, to say she wished she hadn't done it. Nothing. And how many times had he asked her why she'd decided to take the tour? Her answer each time was that she wanted to see the world. Granted that thirty thousand dollars was a lot of money, even for a two-month, first-class world tour, and a smart person would make certain of the sponsoring agency's integrity. But she investigated *him,* not the agency, and she did it because her sole reason for taking that tour was to get him to operate on her. He couldn't even blame her for that. But when she let him care for her, before she let him love her, she should have told him.

He threw on a robe and headed for Skip's room, needing the assurance that, at least, all was well with his boy. He blinked at the bright light.

"Why aren't you asleep?"

"I couldn't." He pointed his finger around the room. "I got my own room, my own closet and bathroom, even my own radio and computer. You're used to all this, but I always had to go out in the hall to the bathroom. I can't get over it. How do you expect me to sleep?"

He sat on the edge of the bed. "You'll get used to it, just as I did." He told him of the way in which he and Steve had struggled after losing their parents, and of his debt to his brother. "For a few months, a while back, I forgot where I came from but, once I remembered, I started to straighten out my life. Don't forget your roots, son; they're a part of who you are."

"Yes sir, Mas...Dad, you gonna marry Jeanny, aren't you?"

He thought for a bit and couldn't help being amazed that Skip could show so much patience, when the matter had become important to him.

"You and I aren't going to lie to each other, Skip. To be honest, I don't know." The boy sat forward in bed, his face crumpled with worry.

"But don't you want to?"

"Yes, I want to, but we have things to work out, and we don't seem to be getting anywhere."

"Want me to talk to her, tell her what a great guy you are?"

He couldn't help smiling. Innocence had its virtues; if nothing else, it allowed you to have hope.

"I'll take care of it, son. It's something that I, alone, can do. Now go to sleep, because you're getting up at seven o'clock." He went back to his room, got in bed, and stared at the ceiling.

Jeannetta raced to the phone, wondering who would call her so early in the morning. She'd just returned from a walk along the beach and had taken Casper with her. The ringing stopped about the time she picked it up, so she went back outside, fed the dog, gathered some orange and yellow marigolds, put them in the dining room, and sat down to work. Half an hour later, the phone's ring jarred the silence.

"Hi."

At the sound of his voice, her whole body came to life, and tiny needlelike pricks danced along her nerves. "Hi, yourself," she said, trying to sound casual.

"I thought I'd have to take a ride out there. I rang half a dozen times and, when you didn't answer...well, I didn't know what to think."

"Casper and I were on the beach."

"Oh, yes; let us not forget Casper."

She didn't see the need for sarcasm, and she wondered at it, because he didn't usually resort to that. "Have you seen my test?"

"I got a preliminary report. So far, so good. But that isn't why I'm calling. I'd prefer to discuss this face to face, but that isn't possible, and I need to talk about it right now."

She flinched at his cool and impersonal tone. "What is this about, Mason?"

His brief silence did nothing to allay her anxiety. "I can understand why you would have investigated the agency, and even why you hired a private detective investigator to scour my record and dig up whatever dirt he could find, but I do not understand and cannot accept your letting the relationship between us get to this point without telling me you did it. You didn't know me last March; I could have been a larcenous crook, so you were entitled to satisfaction that you were making a good investment. But that wasn't your purpose. You claimed that you only wanted to see the world, but what you wanted was certainty that I could do your operation and that I hadn't left medicine in disgrace. Fine. Suppose I say that, too, was your right. But you had no right to tell me you loved me, to make love with me, and to encourage my caring for you, without telling me you'd done this."

She released a deep sigh as she recalled Laura's prophesy. The piper had come to collect. "I can't deny what you're saying because all of it's true. My excuse for not telling you is that I was afraid of hearing you say no when I asked you to operate. I kept putting it off. Then, as I got to know you and learned to love you, I didn't want to hurt you by telling you about the investigation, so I kept quiet about it and prayed you'd never find out."

"As I think back, it's clear to me that I gave you plenty of chances to tell me about this *and* about your scheme to get me back into medicine. I've been sifting through this, and I don't much like what I see. I can't accept it, Jeannetta. I'm sorry."

Sheer black fright swept through her and pinion-like darts of panic knotted her belly. "What are you saying?"

"You said we're not suited to each other, that I don't meet your needs. Maybe some of your reasoning is subconsciously based on my humble background. Some of it could be more personal. Whatever. I'm accepting your judgment. I'll call tomorrow with a final report on your health. Take care."

She gazed at the phone, horrified. *"That's it?"*

"'Fraid so. Good-bye, Jeannetta."

She'd gambled and lost. Would he have reacted in this way if she had agreed to marry him? She supposed she'd never know. Calmly, she opened her computer, began chapter eighteen of her novel, typed five or six lines, and wiped the water from her face with the back of her hand. She typed faster and faster, then she looked at the screen and saw rows of nonsensical phrases, half-spelled words, sentences in which "Mason" appeared a dozen times. The water of her pain pooled in her lap, and some of it settled like brine on her tongue. She got up, washed her face, and went back to work but, within minutes, the tears that poured from her eyes obscured her vision. She wanted to ignore the phone, but the persistent caller won out. She moved slowly toward it; it could be anyone. Anyone but Mason.

"Yes." She spoke softly to hide the trembling she knew her voice would display.

"Jeanny, this is Laura. You alright?"

"I'm fine," she lied.

"Well, you won't be for long. Alma Williams has told everybody in town that Jethro left her for you. She says he's spent the last month with you."

Jeannetta imagined that her shriek could be heard for miles.

"I needed this. I've been leading a dull life out here with not a thing to occupy my mind. This is just the ticket."

"Jeannetta Rollins, you sure you're alright?" Jeannetta rolled her eyes toward the ceiling.

"Fine as French perfume. Anything else?" She looked around her at the house that wasn't hers, the furniture that wasn't her taste, the paintings she would not have chosen. If she had her car, she'd get in it and drive until it needed repair, no matter what Mason said. Laura's scolding got her attention.

"This isn't like you, Jeanny. You get on that train and come on back home. You hear?"

"I'll be back when Kay and David get here. Not before. Now for heaven's sake, calm down. I've had as much as I want to handle today." She regretted the words as they were leaving her mouth.

"What do you mean by that? Something's gone wrong between you and Mason. I just know it. I told Clayton that if you didn't stop stringing him along, you'd regret it."

"Laura," she began patiently, "does Mason strike you as a man anybody can dangle? Does he?"

"Oh, he can dangle, alright, but not the way you've been doing it. If you want the fish to bite, you got to know how to cast."

Her mouth dropped open; this new Laura became more amazing with the passing days.

"This fish bit."

"He sure did, but is he still on the line? Or was your reeling so fancy that he got loose? You come on home and deal with Alma. You hear? For all you know, that foolish Jethro will show up at your front door. Then what'll you do?"

"Let him. Casper could use a little exercise."

They said goodbye and she dropped the receiver into its cradle. One more hassle. Feeling miserable, and fighting a slowly rising tide of anger, she turned back to her computer, erased what she'd written after Mason's unsettling call and began the culmination of her novel. Anger, she realized, could be energizing. She had pitied Alma for her marriage to a man who didn't love her, though the woman had gone into it fraudulently, but she would have to put a stop to that vicious tongue. Pilgrim was as puritanical a town as its name, and she couldn't risk being the subject of every sermon preached there for the next month. And gossip was the fuel that kept the town's motor running.

She let the phone ring, but when she heard Skip's voice on the answering machine, she picked up.

"Hello, Skip, what a pleasant surprise."

"Hi, Jeanny. How you doing? My Dad told me last night he's not sure you're going to marry him. It's not because of me, is it?"

"Darling, I'd love to have you for a son, but this is between your dad and me." She understood his longing to be a part of a real family, to have a mother and father to love and who loved him, and she would have loved to help make his dream come true. But that gift was no longer hers to bestow.

"I don't think my dad wanted me to call you, so I better not say anything else. I'll ask him when I can go see you, okay?"

"Of course. I'd love to see you." Absentmindedly, she dropped the receiver towards its cradle and heard it bounce on the table top. She had put it in place and had started to the terrace when she heard Casper's growl and then the wheels of a car crunching the gravel. Her heart skipped wildly in her chest and then slowed. The postman. She should have known it wouldn't be

Mason, because he was not a wishy-washy man; if he said goodbye, he meant it. She talked aloud to herself, reaching deep inside for inner peace.

# *Chapter 13*

Jeannetta's fragile peace of mind deserted her the next day at noon when she heard the urgency and anger in Laura's voice. "Mason and Skip just got here, and Mason brought the *Morning Herald*. I told you to put a stop to Alma. You know Ed Wiggins; he publishes the paper. Well, she told him she's suing you for alienation of affection. I called him up and told him to get out of here with that nineteenth century stuff, but he says she can do that. Honey, Mason is pacing the floor like a caged tiger. You want to talk to him?"

She did. Oh, how she wanted to hear his voice utter a loving sound, but she declined.

"If he wants to talk, Laura, he'll call."

"There you go being clever again. Sometimes I'm glad I don't have your degrees; my uneducated way of doing things makes a lot of more sense. What are you going to do about Alma Williams?"

"I'll take care of it. Save me a copy of that paper, please, and don't worry about it."

Mason sat in the coffee shop with Laura and Clayton, while Skip broadened his mind on the Internet.

"Who is this Alma Williams?" Mason asked Laura. He listened to the story, strumming his fingers on his knee while Laura related it. "That's ridiculous."

Clayton sipped his cappuccino and leaned back in his chair. "You don't believe it?"

Mason knew he was releasing his own frustration when he eyed Clayton with a steel-like, unfriendly gaze. "Anybody who has spent any time with Jeannetta ought to know that such behavior is beneath her."

Clayton's loud laugher, unusual for him, told Mason that he'd just been tested. "How are you planning to help her?"

"Leave it to me, man; I'll think of something."

"Aren't you at least going to ask her whether it's true before you stick your hand in the fire?" Laura asked. "You know, let her know you're there for her."

The temptation to laugh at Clayton's stern glare at Laura was too great. Mason dropped his head in his hand and his shoulders shook. He had a mind to ask them if they knew how much like a long-married couple they appeared. Skip bounded into the room, ending that conversation.

"Dad, there's a hurricane watch for the East Coast, and it's supposed to hit Long Island. Jeanny's on Long Island. I found the place with my web crawler. Shouldn't you call her and tell her to come home or something?"

Apprehension gnawed at him, but he kept his expression neutral; Skip adored Jeannetta, and he didn't want to worry him.

"I'll call her; I was planning to do that anyway." He didn't bother to explain that his call wouldn't be a professional one. He hadn't wanted to come to the Hideaway; the sooner he got some distance between Jeannetta and himself, the quicker he'd get his life in order. But he had promised Skip that they would visit Laura and, if he did nothing else, he would keep his word to his son. He went up to their room and telephoned her.

"Hello." The soft, unsteady voice crept into him, shook him, its ability to clobber his senses taking him unaware.

"Hello, Jeannetta." His hand reached voluntarily for his chest as though to still his galloping heart. He was too old to be experiencing the kind of ache that tore through him. *He needed her.*

"Mason. How are you?" He couldn't let himself hurt her by using a professional tone, because no matter what she'd done, he loved her.

"Well enough. Skip tells me a storm's headed your way. Are you planning to come in?"

"I hadn't heard of it, but I'm in a protected cover, and Kay said this house never gets storm damage. I'll be alright."

"Don't be too sure; Skip said it's being projected to move right over you." He paused, unwilling to give her his news, because that would end their conversation, and he'd have to hang up. He made himself do it.

"You're free of me, Jeannetta. Your tests showed excellent results, and if you avoid stress, limit reading, writing, and TV hours to four hours a day for the next two weeks, you're home free."

"I see... I mean, thanks. Thank you for everything, Mason." She didn't want to hang up and neither did he. He switched the phone to his left hand, stuck his right one in his pocket and fingered the old keys. How on earth was he going to give her up? Her and all of his dreams.

"Don't forget to take care of yourself, Jeannetta," he managed, when the silence roared in his ears, broadcasting the extent to which their once warm and loving relationship had skidded.

"I... You, too, Mason. Mason, you may send your bill to me at Hideaway."

Sputtering wasn't something he did, but words nearly failed him. "Jeannetta, I hope that's the last time I hear you mention compensation to me. I should pay you for having led me back to my true calling, the life I love most. Consider us even. All the best."

"Good-bye, Mason." He looked out of the window at the autumn-hued mountain and wondered what his life would be like a year hence. Well, standing there wouldn't give him the answer, and he could at least get the rest of his life in order. He had to get back home and get ready to open his office after Labor Day. He called Skip as he ambled down the stairs.

"I'm ready to go. You stay with Laura for a few days and let Clayton help you finish building that chemistry lab."

"Okay. But you sure you won't need me for something?"

Mason ran his fingers over the boy's tight curls.

"I probably will, but I think it's best you stay here for two or three days. You'll know where I am." He looked down at Skip's hand tugging at his wrist.

"Are you going to West Tiana to look after Jeanny?"

Mason had promised never to lie to Skip, but he didn't know the answer to that himself.

"I don't know, Skip. I...I just can't say."

"She's real nice, Dad."

"I know, son. Believe me; I know."

He made it back to New York in an hour and a half.

"Any messages, Viv?" He wished he could have Viv at his medical office when he opened up in a couple of weeks, but she'd become indispensable to the travel agency and, if he persuaded Steve to manage it, his brother would need her.

"Steve called, and we had a nice long talk, but I couldn't get him to say he'd be my new boss. He did promise to stop by here, though." She winked at him. "How'm I doing?"

"Great. What about that storm? Heard anything?" She confirmed Skip's information that the storm would pass directly over Long Island. He twirled two pencils. No way could he leave her out there alone in a storm on that dead end street; if anything happened to her, he would never get over it. He picked up the phone and dialed Skip.

"You leave that place right now, you hear?"

Jeannetta wanted to cover her ears, but instead, she said, "Laura, you mean well, but even if I wanted to leave here, I'd have to take Casper with me, and I can't. The place is secure, so stop worrying."

"Well, if you won't listen to me, maybe you'll pay attention to Clayton," Laura told her.

Exasperated, Jeannetta released a sally. "Laura, I know Clayton has replaced the King James version of the Bible as your source of Gospel, but what he says isn't sacred to me, so give me a break. I can't use any of Clayton's wisdom right now. I have to get back to work. Goodbye." She finished taping the window panes and went outside to look at the clouds. Casper's whimpers alerted her to his precarious situation, and she decided to put him on the screened back porch. She remembered having seen a piece of oilcoth in the pantry, got it and nailed it over a section of the porch-screen to provide dry shelter for Casper. Then, she gathered as many candles as she could, found a portable radio, a flash light and some matches, made some sandwiches, and settled back to await whatever came. The black clouds soon released torrents of rain that pelted the house in an ominous rhythm. As she lighted the woodburning fireplace, Casper's low growl brought her upright. The growling increased, and she glanced toward the window just as the headlights illumined the driveway.

"Who on earth…?" She thought her heart slammed into her belly when she saw Mason's white Cougar. She had thought he was at the Hideaway. Casper growled furiously and she rushed to the porch to pat him and reassure him. She got an umbrella and opened the front door, but the rain and wind nearly knocked her backward, and drenched the marble foyer floor. She braced herself, stepped out, and attempted to open the umbrella, but within seconds she had no idea where the wind had taken it. Mason stepped into the foyer, drenched from the short run in the rain, pulled her from the door, and managed to close it.

She took his wet hand and walked them into the living room, pulled his jacket off of him and laid it in front of the fire. Then she brought several bath towels and wrapped one around his shoulders. She stood behind him trying to dry his trousers with a towel, and he turned and looked at her, seared her with the hot longing in his eyes. Her breathing quickened and deepened, and she knew he couldn't help noticing the sharp rise and fall of her bosom, and the way she longed for him.

"You're wet, too," he said, the first words spoken since he'd stopped the car in front of the house.

She shook her head vigorously. "It's okay. I don't care."

"I do."

She lost her battle to stop the trembling of her lips. "Do you?"

"Oh, sweetheart."

She was in his arms, and his mouth moved over her, plundering hungrily until she parted her lips and took his tongue into her mouth. He hadn't forgiven her, and she still needed something that he hadn't given her, but their bodies gave the lie to it as they clung to each other. She wanted to wrap herself around him, to know the limits of his virile power, and she held him as tightly as she could until he groaned and stepped away from her.

He answered her inquiring look with a rueful smile. "Walking away is easier said than done."

She didn't want to hope in vain, but she began to believe they had a chance. Maybe Laura was right about her fishing theory.

"I missed you, Mason. Oh, I know, all this happened yesterday, but it seems like years to me."

"Don't I know it. By the way, where's Casper?"

She was not going to let that hurt her. She'd try instead to understand him. "Do you want to change the subject?"

His half laugh was that of a person caught out. "Actually, no. I just wondered." His attention seemed to shift to the sounds of the storm, the rain that pelted the house, and the noise of the wind, giving the impression of someone anticipating danger. And she knew his thoughts focussed on the storm and their safety.

"I put Casper on the back porch. He's quiet, because he knows you." She went to the closet and got a robe. "I'm sure David wouldn't mind your borrowing this. I can put your clothes in the drier, and you won't catch a cold."

"Don't tempt me with that thing. If I pull off my clothes, it'll happen after I've taken yours off of you. I'll dry standing here, thanks."

She laughed. If he knew how good that sounded to her, he might regret having said it. She decided to test the water.

"You don't honestly think I have to lure you with a man's robe, do you? I always thought I had more beguiling assets. 'Course, if that's what lights your fuse, by all means put your arms in it." The lights flickered. Suddenly, she hoped they'd go out, hoped the storm would isolate them from the world until they'd resolved their differences. His steady, humorless gaze nearly unnerved her.

"*You* light my fuse."

Emboldened by the hunger in his eyes, she took recourse to daring. "Not recently, I haven't."

His hands gripped her forearms, and her body burned from the intensity of his hot gaze.

Rain pelted the roof, fire crackled in the big stone fireplace, the flames danced like frenzied sex partners, and the scent of half-green pine logs filled her nostrils. He was there. Big, masculine, handsome, and virile, the only man she had ever loved. Sparks shot through the grill that separated them from the roaring blaze, and another kind of spark shot through her body, lighting her passion.

She met him with raised arms and parted lips, and thrilled as his strong arms held her still for his plundering kiss. The evidence of his desire, strong, virile, and nestled near the portal of her womanhood, telegraphed a message to her brain, startling her. She knew what he'd do next, his lover's technique. The picture of his perfect body supine in yellow sand, almost every inch of him exposed to her in early morning sun rays, floated back to her, and the movement of her hips begged for his entrance. Dizzying sensations of long-awaited release streaked through her when his hand covered her breast, and damp warmth settled in her core. He stepped back and gazed intently into her eyes.

"Have you forgotten that you're no longer my patient?"

She didn't flinch from his stare.

"No. And neither have I forgotten that my doctor discharged me." Excitement hurtled through her when the telltale greenish-brown colored his irises and his lips parted. She tried to move closer to him, but he kept a safe foot of space between them.

"Nothing has changed; we're right where we were yesterday morning."

The wind howled, rain pelted the windows and roof, but things weren't the same, no matter what he said.

"It's changed for me, not completely maybe, but you're here because you needed to protect me in this storm when, yesterday morning, you'd told me goodbye and hung up."

"And you'll take me as I am? Offering nothing more than before?"

She sucked in her breath and willed her fingers to the buttons on her blouse.

"Aren't you doing the same?"

Her blouse hung open, exposing her bare breasts to him, and hot lights glittered in his eyes.

"Answer me, Jeannetta."

The urgency of his low guttural tones sent the heat of desire coursing through her. "No strings. I want you. I need you…"

He pulled the blouse from her shoulders, hooked his thumbs in the waistband of her skirt and panties, and peeled them from her body. Her busy fingers worked at his shirt until she could open it and touch her breasts to his hard chest. Frenzied with passion, she loosened his belt, unzipped him, and pressed herself to him as the remainder of his clothes dropped to his feet. He stepped out of them, fitted her to his body and held her there. Her whole self was a flaming torch as his lips claimed her mouth, his tongue dabbed at the pulse of her throat, and his hands alerted her body to its God-given potential.

He lifted her, and eased them to the floor, and carefully placed her on the thick brown carpet before the fire. Her arms opened to him as he knelt above her, and spread her legs for his loving entrance.

"Tell me, honey, can you remember being with me like this? Close your eyes and let it happen."

Her body twisted beneath him, inviting, urging.

"I don't and, right now, all I want is for you to love me, to show me what I don't remember, what I'm like with you." She brought him fully into her arms and lifted her body to him, but he took control. His fiery possession of her mouth erased thoughts of all but him, and she hooked her legs around his hips. When she couldn't hold back the need to move beneath him, he locked her hands above her head and pulled her hard nipple into his mouth.

"Mason, please…I…I can't stand this." He suckled her more vigorously until she cried out, "Honey, I'm going to explode." She didn't know whether rain and wind crashed through the window, if the door banged open, or if the storm only raged with intensity inside her, as his masterful strokes hurled her into ecstasy.

Mason looked down at Jeannetta asleep in his arms. The hurt from her lack of trust remained, and he didn't know how to rid himself of it. He did know that by making love with her again, he'd eliminated any chance of being happy without her. She suited him in every way that mattered. Her soft, sated purr sent frissons of heat through him and he felt the hunger grip him again. The wind had died down, but sheets of rain pelted the windows, and the storm in him raged anew. He reached for a towel, covered her with it, and let his eyes feast on her beloved face. Her lashes lifted and frowns creased her forehead. Then a smile spread over her face, and she raised herself up and kissed his mouth.

"Are you sorry, Mason?"

His heartbeat accelerated at the sight of the naked anxiety in her eyes. "I couldn't regret what I just experienced with you. No. I'm not sorry, and I'll never be."

"But does it change anything?"

He let his fingers trace her spine and tried not to let his mind dwell on how much he wanted her right that minute. "I don't know. I haven't begun to sort it out, so I'm as puzzled as you are that we could unite as we did with so much between us that isn't right. Excuse me, but if I don't put some wood on this fire, we'll freeze."

She wrapped a bath towel around her and, as she stood, her glance took in the ceiling-high window and the sheets of rain that cascaded down its length.

"Mason! *Mason!* Look at that. Look!"

"What? What is it?"

"That water. I've seen it in my dreams, falling down a mountain into a river. And that hotel lobby with the malachite columns, the jacaranda tree, the…the veranda of that hotel with the flowers and butterflies…the morning I…you had a nightmare…you were afraid your knife would slip when you operated on me…you were talking in your sleep, thrashing in bed and I…" her bottom lip dropped and her eyes widened as she stared into his anxious face.

"I remember…I remember that night, everything, and at my house in Pilgrim, when I could hardly make out your image. Thank God, I remember it all."

His arms went around her, and he smothered his face in the curve of her shoulder.

"Imagine not being able to remember something so wonderful as what we shared; I'd never had such feelings."

He raised his head and looked at her. "Why did you leave?"

"I had decided to go back with you and do whatever you recommended, but after I listened to you struggling with your subconscious, I couldn't be responsible for your turmoil if you failed."

"But you risked certain blindness, though it might have been reversible. Why?"

She tightened her arms around her body, walked to the window, turned, and faced him. "No matter what you believe, I loved you then. I love you now."

He looked down into the flames, and her pulse raced with her fear of rejection.

"It's best I don't respond. I won't say there's no hope for us, because I try to be honest about what I feel. But I have to come to terms with my reservations about you; if I don't, this resentment will harden, and that's no basis for a lasting relationship. I expect the same goes for you."

Her breath lodged in her throat, and she could only nod. He was saying that they had a chance.

"Can we still see each other? I mean, I need to know how you are, how Skip is."

"Alright. I'll touch base with you, and you can call me while we try to get a handle on this thing. We have to accept that we may not be able to work it out, and be ready to get on with our lives." She got the robe and handed it to him.

"That dark gray color doesn't do a thing for you, but then you're not a blue-eyed blond like David."

"Tell me what turns you on, and I'll stop by a store and order some of it." If he was serious, his sly grin and teasing tone belied it.

"Red string bikinis," she threw over her shoulder, as she headed up the stairs, to her bedroom. The other two times when they'd made love, he had drowned her in a vortex of ecstatic passion, but when he'd held her in his arms at the end of it, she had ached with unbelievable pain. The same deadening emptiness began to invade her.

When she had given Casper his morning run and finished her chores, Mason had already been driving for an hour. The south shore had been spared the brunt of the storm, and West Tiana hadn't sustained any damage. She had no inclination to work, but was tempted to daydream of her night and morning with him. He'd awakened her with loving that was tender, gentle, and caring, but he had been almost demonic in his drive to wring every semblance of passion from her, draw gesture after gesture of total submission from her, and to thrust her into orgasmic ecstasy time and time again. But she couldn't fault him; he'd been as honest as he was determined, and when he'd been lost in his own vortex of passion, he had let her see and feel his complete surrender. But he hadn't repeated his marriage proposal, and she didn't know what her response would have been if he had.

She got a rake and combed the debris from the lawn and hedges, well aware that if she didn't stop procrastinating, she wouldn't complete her novel by the Labor Day deadline. Nevertheless, she found other excuses. When his call finally came, late that evening, she understood the reason for her day-long mental vacation.

"Hi. This is Mason."

She fell backward across the bed, kicked off her shoes and rolled over on her belly.

"Hi."

"None the worse for your overnight activities, I trust?"

She glared at the phone and told herself to let only sweet words come out of her mouth if he started talking like a doctor.

"What activities, honey?" Excitement pervaded her, and she swung over on her back, as his rumbling laughter worked its magic on her.

"That's right; play dumb. You were there right along with me, sweetheart."

She rested both feet on the head of the four-poster bedstead and looked up at the ceiling.

"You must be talking about some other girl. I was here in this house all last evening.

He laughed aloud, and she wished she could see his face.

"Yeah, but whose boots were under your bed, baby?"

Laughter bubbled up in her, and she gave it full reign. "Search me."

"You don't know?" he growled.

"Well, from the look of this bite on my neck, it must have been Count Dracula, but he's supposed to be a myth, isn't he?"

"I'd laugh, but I'm not sure that's funny. Apply an antibiotic cream and a Band-Aid. That ought…"

"Cut it out." She yelled it, and she didn't care. "What would you do if you didn't have a cent?"

"Well, I don't know," he said, after obviously having thought about it. "I've never been flat broke. What would you do?"

"Me? I'd write Avon and tell them how much I love their toilet articles and inveigle them into sending me some free samples."

"Alright. I forgot you write jokes for comedians. Don't tell me anybody bought that one."

"I haven't tried to sell it, because I just made it up, but it already served the purpose of getting you off of your medical soap box. I didn't want Mason, the man, to get away from me."

"I'm not going any place. Sleep well." She blew him a kiss and waited.

"I kiss you, too. Good night, and be careful out there."

She sat up and tried to think. His mood had been intimate, but not his conversation. The job ahead of her would challenge any mortal woman: she had to teach him what it meant to love, and she had to earn his forgiveness.

Mason washed his pizza down with tomato juice, rinsed his plate and glass, and put them in the dishwasher. Skip usually rushed to do that. How could he miss the boy so badly when they'd been living together less than a month? He called him.

"Hi, Dad. Did you know Aunt Laura's worried about Jeanny? You want to talk to her?"

"Not right now. What's the problem?"

"Gee, I don't know. Uncle Clayton said it's just gossip. I'm ready to go home. When you coming up?"

"Tomorrow morning." He had to do something about getting Skip in Sunday school, but that would have to wait another week. He'd postponed it, because churchgoing wasn't one of his habits. Being a parent changed a lot of things; you not only had to know what was right, you had to do it. He hung up and took Steve's call.

"Thought I'd drop by for a minute, if you're not busy." Half an hour later Steve arrived with a quart of peach ice cream and a small coconut cake.

"I figured you'd already eaten dinner," he explained. They served themselves generous helpings of the desserts.

"Say, how'd you and Darlene Jones make out?"

Steve rested his spoon and seemed to pick his words. "So-so. I liked her alright, and I probably could've liked her a lot better, if I'd ever had a chance to say anything."

"What do you mean?" He watched Steve for signs of irritation, but saw none, and probed further. "She wouldn't talk with you? She always seemed pretty gregarious to me."

"The problem was that she talked *to* me. All the damned time. I couldn't get a word in edgeways. She acted as if I expected her to entertain me, and I couldn't get it across to her that I wanted a companion, someone to talk *with,* to share things with. I quit calling her; I didn't need the frustration."

"I'm sorry, Steve. I'd hoped the two of you would make it."

Steve helped himself to another slice of cake.

"How is it you never introduced me to Viv?"

Mason jerked forward. "Viv? I...it never occurred to me. You want to meet her?"

"Well," Steve began with uncustomary diffidence, "We've talked on the phone a lot since you got back from the tour; I'm either calling your travel office, or she's calling me trying to trace you, so she said to me one day that we'd been talking for ages but we'd never met, and maybe we ought to introduce ourselves. I told her I'd been thinking the same thing, so we agreed that I'd pick her up at the office after work and we'd get a drink, or go to dinner or the movies or something, whatever we felt like."

Mason stopped eating and stared at his brother. "What happened, man?"

"Well...I walked through the door, and this pretty woman sitting there looked up and saw me. Man, I stopped dead in my tracks; I couldn't have moved, if you'd pushed me."

Mason didn't bother to hide his disbelief; of all the scenarios he could have imagined, this wasn't one. "Are you serious?"

"Am I ever! She smiled like pure sunshine, got up from that desk, and came to meet me with her arms wide open. 'You're Steve,' was all she said, and I walked right into those arms." He shook his head as if he couldn't believe it. "Man, I haven't been the same since." Mason knew his mouth hung open but, in the circumstances, not even Steve would consider that bad manners.

He stared at Steve. "You fell for Viv?"

"Hook, line and sinker, and if that makes me stupid, it's too late to tell me."

"Stupid? Man, that's a stroke of brilliance. Viv's wonderful. Is it working?"

"It's working."

What would Steve say to the idea forming in his mind? "You two would make a great business team."

"That's what she says, but it's...I don't want to louse this up by working with her."

He had never discussed Steve's personal life with him, and

he wasn't sure how far to go, but he'd had his share of lectures, so he was entitled. "Some of the best partnerships are husband-wife teams."

"You think so? I haven't gone quite that far."

"You headed that way?"

"Looks like it."

Mason got up and slapped Steve's back. "Right on man."

Steve cut his third slice of cake, put a forkful of it in his mouth and allowed Mason to wait until he chewed and swallowed it. "I've been aiming to ask what's going on with you and Jeannetta."

"We're in limbo. I'm not what she needs, or so she says, and I've wondered whether that's a ruse, a cover to hide the fact that all she ever wanted from me was…"

"Don't finish it, Mason. Don't say it."

Mason shook his head in wonder. Nothing and no one had perplexed him so much as Jeannetta.

"Yeah. I know. When I start to think, to remember some things about her, I know I'm being unfair."

Steve finished the cake, stashed their dishes in the sink, and leaned against a wall, facing his brother. "You mind if I meet her?" At Mason's startled look, he added, "Skip's crazy about her and, when it comes to people, kids have good antennas. What do you say?"

Mason shrugged both shoulders and resisted reaching for his old keys.

"Alright with me. I'll arrange it."

Steve shook his head as though displeased. "Mason, I'm asking you to bring her to my apartment to see me." Their gazes locked, and Mason understood that Steve was demanding respect.

"Okay. I'll speak to her."

He parked a few feet from the Hideaway's front door, because he intended to stay just long enough to get Skip, but Laura rushed to him waving a subpoena and clutching a legal-size envelope in her other hand.

"I got a court summons to witness against my own sister, and I know this letter contains one for Jeannetta. Alma Williams has gone too far with her lies. This will be the talk of Pilgrim."

He couldn't believe it. "Let me see that." He looked at the claim that Jethro Williams currently resided with Jeannetta Rollins in West Tiana, Long Island, and that the claimant demanded restitution from Jeannetta and a divorce from Jethro.

"What are we going to do?" wailed a distraught Laura.

Mason examined the document closely and shrugged. "Forget it. Didn't you notice the dates between which they're supposed to have been living there? According to this, it began before I put Jeannetta in the hospital. Do you want me to stop it now, or do you think Jeannetta would like to see Alma Williams eat crow?" He walked to the phone as the last words fell from his lips.

"Hello, Jeannetta." He told her of the court orders.

"Would you like me to call the judge, have the hospital send the record, or what? It would serve her plenty if you let the town know what she's like." He listened to Jeannetta's story of how it had begun and her culpability in not having denied it, for the sake of vengeance.

"Alright. I'll speak with the judge." He did, and received the judge's agreement that Alma would be penalized if she mentioned the accusation again. That done, he stopped by the Hideaway, collected his son, and headed for home.

Jeannetta sat on the porch in the late afternoon autumn sun reading through her novel and making minor corrections. She loved the story and what she'd done with it, but it saddened her. She was glad for the telephone interruption.

"Hello."

"Hi, Jeanny. Whatcha doing?" A smile eclipsed her face at the sound of Skip's eager voice, and she told him she'd been working.

"I think you ought to come here with me and Dad, Jeanny. I don't like this woman who keeps calling Dad."

She didn't know what to say. "How's your father?" seemed a safe thing.

"He's okay, Jeanny, but some woman named Betty calls here every day, some time three or four times. I'm not saying she's Dad's bird. That's you. But, like, I don't want this chick to be my mother." She couldn't help smiling, though twinges of anxiety stole through her.

"Skip. I'm not sure you should be telling me this. Your father is entitled to privacy, and…"

"Yeah. I know. I'm squealing on him, but she ain't no good for him. She don't even like me, Jeanny. And I sure as…I don't like her."

"I'm sorry, Skip, but if your father wants to see her and talk with her, there's nothing I can do." His words hit her like sharp darts in her chest, but she controlled her voice. If she cried, Mason would hear of it. She managed to conclude the conversation. What she wanted most right then was to hear Mason's voice, but she couldn't make herself call him. She had to talk with *someone,* so she called Laura. And wished she hadn't.

"I was just going to call you, hon," Laura began. "I suppose you know one of Mason's old flames is helping Clayton with his lawsuit. Clayton says she's given him some useful information, but I tell you I'm not sold on her. She's calling him all the time, and now she's taken to coming up here, claiming it's 'such a relief from New York.'"

Jeannetta laughed at her sister mimicking the woman. "Don't think of her as competition, Laura; Clayton has eyes only for you."

"Humph," Laura snorted. "You know that, and I know that, but I'm not sure about this hussy, walking around here all day dressed up with her pants so tight I think they'll split, and a pound of make-up. I can take care of her, though," she seemed to assure herself. "Clayton said she used to be Mason's girl, and maybe she's really after *him*. Clayton said she's typical of those New York women."

"Laura, I'm sorry, but my pot's boiling over. I have to go." Jeannetta hung up, looked toward the ceiling and sucked her teeth.

"Clayton said. Clayton said." Didn't the man ever do anything but talk? She hadn't lied to Laura; she'd used an apt figure of speech. And she liked Clayton, even admired him in many respects but, for heaven's sake, he wasn't *the* latter-day oracle of truth, no matter how hard Laura tried to make him into one. She returned to her reading, but couldn't muster an interest in it. Had she been foolish in rejecting Mason's proposal? Could she have taught him the meaning of love once they'd married? Too late now, she reminded herself; he has grievances of his own.

# Chapter 14

Mason walked into Skip's room. "I didn't hear the phone ring; who were you calling?" The boy gazed at him, eyeball to eyeball, and refused to back down. Without being told, he knew Skip had called Jeannetta, and that he wouldn't apologize for having done it.

"Well?"

"I called Jeanny. You're not planning to marry Betty, are you?"

"*What?* What gives you that idea?"

The boy's belligerence had vanished, to be replaced by a sad, worried look. "'Cause she's always calling you, and you always talk to her."

Mason sat down, because he didn't want to seem threatening. "I'm your father. You look at me when you speak, but you don't stare me down as you would a roughneck kid. Don't ever do that again."

"I'm sorry, sir."

"Alright. Now, Skip, I won't always run my personal life to suit you, but you can be sure that I'll take your interests into account. You do not have to worry about my marrying Betty. Okay?"

"Okay." From the boy's release of breath, he imagined that he'd been deeply worried.

"But what about Jeanny, Dad? She…I like her so much, and she likes me a lot. I know she does." He looked at Skip's worried face, at the moisture pooling in his eyes. He didn't want to see him cry, and he knew that, if one drop fell, Skip would be mortified. He walked over to him and knelt in front of him.

"I love her, Skip, and I'm trying to straighten things out; I can't promise more. I have some errands to do, and I've decided it'll do you good to go with me."

They walked down to Bloomingdale's and Mason bought two pair of jeans, three dress shirts, two ties, two crew-neck sweaters, and overcoat, and a pair of leather gloves, all in medium size. He and Skip took the bus to One hundred and eight Street and Third Avenue and walked over to Park. Mason found the homeless engineer at once and called him aside.

"This is my son, Benjamin Fenwick; you didn't tell me your name.

The man didn't bother to contain his surprise; with eyebrows raised, he cocked his head to one side and rubbed his chin.

"Ralph Harper." He looked at Skip. "How do you do?" To Mason's amazement Skip replied, "Cool, how 'bout you?" and extended his hand.

Mason handed the man the package of clothing. "I'm Mason Fenwick. My brother has a job for you repairing office machines. Don't worry; he'll teach you. It's night work in office buildings around the city. Here's his phone number, and fifty dollars for whatever you need that isn't in this package. You said you couldn't look for work because you couldn't make yourself presentable. Now you can."

The speechless man managed to mutter his thanks, turned to his friends, and waved.

"Where're you going now, Mr. Harper?" Skip asked him.

Ralph Harper's startled glance at Skip telegraphed his surprise at being addressed in such a manner. "To the shelter, man. This time when I get a shower, I can put on clean clothes. Make sure you don't ever need one of those places. They're the pits."

"You think he'll do it, Dad?"

Mason was making up his mind about some other unfinished business.

"I don't know, son. I gave him his chance, and he has to do the rest. What did you learn today?"

"Not to get homeless and to help the ones I see." Mason knew a sense of joy that came from loving his son, and he had no doubt that he would give his life for the boy. He grasped Skip's hand.

"Let's go out on Long Island to see Jeannetta."

The smile on Skip's face and the added bounce to his step confirmed the boy's excitement and eagerness to see her. Mason stopped short. In his happiness, he had momentarily forgotten that a deep chasm separated the woman he loved from himself. He didn't want to disappoint Skip, but he doubted the wisdom of an impromptu visit to Jeannetta.

"I think we'd better call first, son; she may not be home."

Mason closed his bedroom door and phoned Jeannetta. His pulse pounded when he heard her voice. Soft. Feminine.

"Jeannetta, this is Mason. How are you?"

"Fine. Which Mason is this?"

In spite of the annoyance that he wanted to summon, he laughed. "Which one do you want?" He hoped the noise he heard was a giggle.

"That's below the belt and ungentlemanly. Either answer will incriminate me."

"Gentlemen seldom win this kind of battle, sweetheart. Go ahead and incriminate yourself; it may prove beneficial."

"To whom?"

"To both of us. Since you don't plan to give quarter, I'll take the heat. How about Skip and I drive out to get you? My older brother, Steve, has practically demanded that I bring you to meet him. We'll drive you back out there. What do you say?" He held his breath, certain that she would deny him this chance to see her.

"That would mean ten hours of driving for you in one day, because I can't leave Casper overnight. Today's Saturday. So why don't I take the train in to New York tomorrow morning; you and Skip meet me; we go see Steve; eat lunch or something; and you drive me back? I think that's a better plan."

His heat slowed to its normal pace and he let out a long breath. What had happened to make her agreeable to seeing him and, especially, to meeting his brother?

"What time will your train get in to Penn Station?"

"Ten-twenty."

"Good. We'll be there."

"Who'll be with Skip? The doctor or the man?"

Relief. He laughed for the joy of it. "Woman, you don't give up easily, do you? Well, neither do I. Which one do you want?"

Her laughter rang like bells, warming him long after he replaced the receiver.

Jeannetta stepped off the near-empty train with one thought; if he hadn't forgiven her, why was he taking her to meet his brother? She had agreed because she meant to earn that forgiveness if she could, and she wanted the chance to teach him what love meant. She saw Skip running to her, his face shining with pleasure, and quickened her steps.

"Jeanny! Here she is, Dad." She hugged him, surprised that a boy his age would welcome an outward display of affection. She looked up into Mason's glittering eyes. Eyes that invited her to drown in them.

"Hi."

"Hi." From the corner of her eye, she saw Skip elbow Mason in the ribs. He looked down at his son.

"Aren't you supposed to kiss her or something? Like, this ain't cool."

She watched for Mason's reaction and relaxed when he grinned and said, "Kissing should be done in private. And don't forget: you're still twelve; you don't run my private life; and don't use street language. Right?"

"Right. But you *are* going to kiss her, aren't you?"

Mason looked up and tortured her with the hot gleam in his eyes. "Trust me, son."

Her heart galloped throughout the ten-minute ride to Steve's apartment.

She liked Steve at first sight. A big, handsome man, he wore the same demeanor of competence and strength as his brother.

"I've wanted to meet you for a long time, Jeannetta, and I appreciate your coming all the way from Long Island to see me." They entered the living room, and her heart seemed to drop to her stomach. The elegant woman sitting on the sofa fitted Betty's description; surely Mason wouldn't...

Steve introduced her. "Jeannetta Rollins, this is Vivian Allen; Viv is what we call her."

Mason's secretary. She acknowledged the introduction, not surprised to learn that Viv knew about her. But why was she there, and why wasn't Mason surprised at her presence?

Skip quickly put an end to her puzzlement. With an arm slung around her shoulder, he whispered, "Don't sweat it, Jeanny; I think she's Uncle Steve's new uh...girl."

She couldn't help smiling, both at his familiarity and at his words.

"Yeah," came his smug confirmation, "that's exactly who she is." I could love this kid, she thought, as the realization struck her that he was exactly her height.

"Jeannetta how about helping me in the kitchen while we get acquainted," Steve said. "Mason wanted to take us all out to lunch, but I can cook as well as the next guy. Come on." She followed him in the kitchen, took a towel from the rack and secured it around her waist.

"What can I do to help?"

He pointed to a high stool. "Sit over there. Don't get it in your head that I'm meddling; I'm not. I looked after Mason from the time he was seven and I was twelve until he graduated from medical school. What happens to him is my business. *Are you in love with him?*"

Her mouth opened and her breasts heaved sharply; he had to see that he'd stunned her.

"I believe in cutting to the chase, Jeannetta. There's a lot at stake here."

Might as well go for broke, she decided, when she could get her breath. "Yes. I'm in love with Mason, and I have been since shortly after we began that tour."

His stare, so much like his brother's, but harder, nearly unnerved her.

"But you don't want to marry him."

Don't let him see that you're perturbed, she cautioned herself. "I don't want to settle for what he's giving me, when I know that we both would be so much happier if he could share himself fully with me. I've tried to explain this to him, but he doesn't understand. Steve, I have no idea what pains him, and I wouldn't have dreamed that he would adopt a young boy. I love him, but I don't truly know him."

"I expect you never know a person until after you're married."

Her withering look didn't seem to bother him.

"I at least ought to know what makes him angry."

Both of his eyebrows arched sharply. "In this case, you sure oughta. It doesn't happen often, but when it does, it's something to deal with."

She decided to voice her own problems. "Mason has reservations about me, as I'm sure you know. The way I see it, my error was in not telling him the truth about why I took the tour and that I'd had a PI investigate him. I did both before I ever saw him, and I didn't tell him because I feared he'd walk away from me and sentence me to blindness. I don't know how to earn his forgiveness."

Steve propped his foot on the rung of the nearest chair and studied her for a long time. She let him. At last he asked, "What about Skip?"

"I could love Skip as dearly as if I had given birth to him. He's already in my heart."

Steve nodded, topped the eggplant Parmesan with mozzarella cheese, shoved it in the oven and sat down.

"I can't advise you, because there's so much I can't know in this case. But I will tell you not to let it slip through your fingers. It's too precious."

"But it isn't up to me."

He smiled. "Love him. That's all you need to do." She must have seemed uncertain, because he stressed it. "You heard me. Just love him."

"But I do love him." She watched Steve's frown fade into a grimace. Didn't he believe her?

"A couple of months ago, I might not have understood any of this, but I can tell you now that, if you love a person, you don't keep tabs on what you give each other. My brother hasn't known a woman's love since our mother died when he was seven. How do you expect him to peel off a thirty-year habit of shielding himself without some help? He loves Skip without reservation, and he can love you the same way if you guide him. But if you wait out there on Long Island until he sees the light, and he hangs tough in the city questioning your every motive, the two of you will squander what you have sure as heat melts ice." He took a pan of biscuits from the freezer, wrapped them in foil and put them in the oven, looked at her, and shook his head.

'You won't catch me doing that."

A cold soul-sickness settled over her. Had she failed him? Failed herself? Her own slice of love hadn't been oversized, she reflected; was she bargaining for a sure thing? She looked up into Steve's knowing gaze.

"Doesn't look good when you strip it down, does it?" he asked with merciless accuracy.

"No. It isn't easy to see one's own shortcomings." She slid off of the high stool, removed the towel from her waist, and asked him, "Sure I can't help with this?"

"I've got it under control. Thanks. And Jeannetta... They say Rome wasn't built in a day, but I hear it's one of the worlds' great beauties."

She put a smile on her face and walked back into the living room, and a strong sensation flowed through her when she looked into Mason's face. Expectant. Hopeful. But he quickly covered his feelings with a broad grin.

"Well," Mason said, "don't tell me you're a closet gourmet cook like Steve."

She didn't feel like meaningless banter, but now was not the time for seriousness.

"I'm not much of any kind of a cook, if you take my recipe books away from me."

That remark evidently didn't please Skip.

"You can't cook, either? Yuck. You oughta taste Uncle Steve's lasagna, and Viv says she can cook, too. I'm gonna stay over here a lot and let Uncle Steve teach me; one of us is gonna have to know how to cook."

Mason glanced down at him. "Who told you that I can't cook?"

"Well, you said you're going to do your best by me, and about all we eat is pizza, so I figured…" Mason interrupted him, laughing.

"When I asked what you like to eat, you said pizza."

Skip fidgeted uncomfortably. "That's right, but my mouth has been watering for some pork chops and some of that roast beef ojo that Uncle Steve makes."

They all stared at him for a second, until Mason corrected him. "You mean roast beef *au jus.*"

Jeannetta chuckled at the boy's look of incredulity.

"Whatever," he said with disdain. He sat on the sofa beside Mason with his legs stretched out, his feet wide apart and his hands in his pants pockets, his pose and gestures identical to his father's. She wanted to hug him.

Steve served a memorable lunch and, as the conversation flowed, Jeannetta thought she might find a new friend in Viv. She marvelled at Skip's easy acceptance of his new relationship with Mason; a stranger wouldn't know that they hadn't been father and son since the boy's birth. Somewhere in their loving connection lay a message for her, and for Mason. Mason asked Steve whether he and Viv would ride out to Long Island.

"Thanks, but there're only so many hours in the day, Mason, and I aim to spend as many of them as I can making my case with Viv. Wouldn't hurt you to think along those lines."

Jeannetta's gaze caught Mason's unflinching stare, and the silent movement of his lips told her that she might well do the same.

* * *

Two weeks later, Jeannetta mailed her manuscript to her editor and decided to take a vacation from work, to loll on the beach and enjoy the environment. She hadn't figured out how to approach Mason to tell him that she needed him and the terms didn't matter, and she knew that was because, in her heart, they did matter. At the least, she had to hear it from his lips that he loved and needed her. She dressed in woolen slacks and a bulky wool sweater for a walk on the beach and started out, just as the phone rang. Her hello was greeted by a distraught Skip.

"What is it? What's the matter?"

"My adoption and christening ceremonies are next Sunday, and my dad said he hasn't asked you to come. Can't you come, Jeanny?"

Cold chills streaked through her; Mason was moving on without her. "Honey," she began, as she struggled to control her voice, "I can't be there if your father doesn't invite me."

"But the only people I want there are you and Uncle Steve. I'm inviting you, so you have to be there."

She hurt for him and for herself, but she couldn't crash Mason's party. "Skip, I'm sorry, but I...I'll have to wait until I hear from your dad."

"If you won't come, I'm not having any christening."

*"Skip!"* He hung up. She checked the telephone directory, got Steve's number, and begged him to speak with Skip, not to let the boy hurt Mason.

"Mason didn't say you weren't invited; he said he hadn't done it, because you two had a breakdown in communications and he didn't know how to approach you."

"You won't speak with Skip?"

"What for? Skip wants a family. He's decided he wants you for his mother, and he refuses to have such an important experience without both of his parents."

"But I'm not his parent, and I may never be." She heard the deep breath that signaled his shortage of patience.

"Skip started out with nothing, not even parents, and he got where he is by setting goals and going hard after them. I refuse to interfere with his strategy."

She changed from the heavy sweater to a cotton shirt and tried to think. Her manuscript. Maybe if she sent it to Mason, he'd understand her misgivings, her needs. She put a copy in an envelope and called Federal Express.

Mason closed the door behind the last of his patients for the day. Noona Shepherd always made sure she had the last appointment, and her complaints always centered near her chest or her pelvis. He'd told her that he wasn't an internist or gynecologist, but she still pestered him. All five of his office rooms reeked with her perfume. She'd had her very last appointment; let her chase some other doctor. He opened the window wide, sat down at his desk, and glimpsed the red, white, and blue envelope. He slit it open and stared the first page: *The Naked Soul Of A Man In Love,* by Jeannetta Rollins. He read three pages and leaned back in his chair, perplexed as to where the story would lead. Then he put the manuscript in his briefcase, took that and his medical bag, and went home. Tension marked his dinner with Skip, as it had for the last three days, so he went to his room early, switched on the light beside his lounge chair and began to read. Sometime after midnight, he finished the story and laid the manuscript aside.

Is that what she wanted from him? He couldn't get the scene out of his mind. The hero, strong, competent, and seemingly invincible, had wept in his woman's arms when the man he'd defended was found guilty and sentenced to life in prison. He'd wet her body with his tears, but she had given herself to him with a passion that might have suggested their last opportunity to make love before an approaching Armageddon. He found the lines, reread them, and mused over their relevance. The woman had never loved the man so much as when he came to her stripped bare of his public persona. Vulnerable. Jeannetta had said she wanted *him.* Is this what she meant? And would she share his doubts, misgivings, and pain, his disappointments and uncertainties, and still love him, as her heroine had loved her man? He remembered her having told him that she had left him in Zimbabwe because of his nightmare, and because she hadn't wanted to be the source of his guilt. And he remembered the times right after that horrible accident when pain had nearly ripped him apart, and he hadn't been able to share it with anyone, not even his brother.

Sunrise found him reading the manuscript for a second time. At seven o'clock, he showered, dressed, and went to the kitchen, where he found Skip setting the breakfast table.

"Good morning."

"Hi. Dad. You gonna call her? Huh? If you ask her, she'll come. I know she will; she said so."

Mason rested the egg on the counter and turned to Skip. "You called her?"

"Yes, sir. I invited her, but she said you have to ask her. Something like she didn't want to go against your wishes. Will you ask her?"

"Yes. I'm going to call her." He'd known that Jeannetta's presence at the ceremonies was important to Skip, but he hadn't realized how much. The boy showed almost no emotion, but sat down, propped his elbows on his knees, and held his face in his hands.

"I just couldn't do it, Dad. I mean, it's a big thing, a preacher holding an adoption service for us and me getting christened and all that…I couldn't do that without Jeanny. Next to you, I love Jeanny the best." Mason laid a gentle hand on Skip's shoulder.

"I didn't want to do it without her either, son. Now, hurry and get ready for school. Breakfast will be ready in five minutes."

The door closed behind Skip, and he dialed her number. If only he could be sure that she was asking him to let her stand with him through every adversity, to dance the slow pieces as well as the fast ones, to sail with him and crash with him. To go to the wall with him. Was there such a woman *anywhere?* He had to find out if that was what she wanted to offer. But not now.

"Mason. I…I'm glad to hear from you. Did you get a chance to read my manuscript?"

"Yes, I did; you're a fine writer, but that isn't why I called. If you don't mind, we'll talk about that later. I'm calling about the adoption service for Skip and me and his christening. It's this coming Sunday, and we want you to stand up with us." She had to grab a chair and sit down. It hadn't occurred to her that he would give her an important role in their service.

"Jeannetta?"

She pulled herself out of her mild shock. "I'm honored, and I'll be happy to attend. You caught me by surprise. I hoped you would ask me to be there, but to stand up with you…well, I didn't dream of it. Of course, I will."

"Thanks. I'll send a car for you."

"Mason, it isn't…"

"I want to do it. The driver should be there at eight next Sunday morning."

She stopped short of protesting. If she wanted the whole man, she'd have to accept all that he offered.

"Alright. I'll be ready."

"Jeannetta, your novel impressed me, but I don't want to discuss it right now, because I have to go to work. We'll talk about it when we're together."

"Okay. I'll see you Sunday." She waited for an endless minute and, finally, he said, "I miss you. See you." She listened to the dial tone, bemused. He seemed to have been at a crossroads, and her hammering heart prayed that he was.

Jeannetta didn't own a hat, so she substituted an elegant bow of green satin that matched her wool crepe suit. Only Laura would complain that the skirt stopped too far above her knees, she surmised, and Laura wouldn't be there. But she was, and so was Clayton.

Jeannetta had to hold back the tears when, at the end of the adoption service, Skip squeezed her hand and looked at her with joy blazing on his face.

"I put your name down to be my godmother. Okay? Uncle Steve will be my godfather."

She nodded and glanced at Mason beside whom Steve stood with glowing pride, and she thought her heart would burst with joy when Mason smiled and winked. The minister beckoned to Viv, Clayton, and Laura to come forward for Skip's christening and, after the ceremony, Mason took them to lunch at the Plaza.

"Laura and I are getting married in a couple of weeks," Clayton announced. "She wants me to know that marrying me isn't contingent on whether I clear my name."

"Of course, it isn't," Laura put in, "thought I'm just tickled to death about your getting a retrial and that those seven women have agreed to witness for you. Betty helped a lot, so I guess she isn't such a bad egg."

"Who said she was?"

"Now, Clayton."

Jeannetta marveled at her sister's fashionable haircut, short-skirted designer suit, and the bloom that loving Clayton had put on her face. The old Laura had ceased to exist.

It amused Mason that Skip always managed to sit beside him, but had stopped sitting or standing *between* Jeannetta and him. The twelve-year-old was a master matchmaker, and an interesting study, too. He didn't believe he had ever seen such joy on a human face as on Skip's when Steve stood and welcomed him into the Fenwick family. His hand went of its own will to find and enfold Jeannetta's, and his heart bounded into a gallop when she squeezed his fingers, looked up at him, and smiled with love in her eyes.

"I've got something to tell, too," Steve announced. "I've asked Viv to be my wife, and this beautiful woman has done me the honor of accepting me." He touched her hand, and she stood up and brushed his mouth with her lips. Mason blinked rapidly in astonishment. He'd known that they had become close, but their engagement came as a surprise. He walked over to Steve and hugged him, then leaned down and brushed a kiss on Viv's cheek.

"I never dreamed that I'd be your sister-in-law," she said. "I hope you're happy for us."

"I am. If I had tried to stage this, you can bet it would have flopped. I've always wanted a sister, Viv, and I couldn't be more satisfied."

Steve beamed at her. "I've also decided to accept Mason's offer of a partnership in Fenwick Travel Agency, so now, Viv and I will be partners in every respect."

Ever business-minded, Skip sat forward. "What about your office-machine repair business, Uncle Steve? You're not gonna trash that, are you?"

"Thank goodness I don't have to. I've got a new man who can manage it. Mason, you remember Ralph Harper. That guy's the best thing to come along since air conditioning. He's one fast study, but of course, he should be; he's an engineer."

"That's the homeless man, Dad."

"Not anymore." Steve informed them. "In six weeks, he's acquired an apartment and a whole new life. He's going to train a couple of his old buddies, and I think they'll work out okay. He knew an opportunity when he saw it, grabbed it, and took off."

Skip smiled up at him and then frowned. Mason steeled himself against what he knew would follow, and Skip mumbled, "Everybody's got it together but us, Dad."

He patted Skip's knee. "I'll drop by home so you can get your books and pack an overnight bag. You're staying with Steve tonight."

"Okay, but where're you...?"

Mason didn't think he'd ever seen such a rapid change in anybody's facial expression. He would have laughed, but he couldn't afford to encourage him.

"Good. You're learning that some things aren't your business."

"Yeah." The boy's grin was downright beatific. "If she doesn't say yes, call me and I'll talk to her for you." He regained his composure and glanced down at the woman beside him, relaxed and serene, and wondered how much of that was real. They hadn't resolved their differences, and everybody around them appeared to have done that, so she shouldn't exude so damn much bliss. He told himself he'd soon know once and for all where they stood.

\* \* \*

Mason parked in front of the house and hoped Casper remembered him, as he got out of the car and walked around it to open the door for Jeannetta, who fumbled with her seat belt. He unhooked it for her and suggested, "Why don't you put on some comfortable shoes and let's walk along the shore."

"I'll just take these off," she replied. "You aren't the only one who likes the feel of sand. Turn around so I can take off my stockings."

He repeated the order in his mind and wished he understood the female psyche; he'd seen every inch of the woman, but she wouldn't let him watch her remove her stockings. With his shoes and socks in his hand and his pants legs rolled up, they strolled hand-in-hand along the water's edge with the cool waves lapping at their bare feet. She stooped down and got a handful of sand, opened her fingers and let the wind take it away. He watched, mesmerized, at the smile that claimed her face. Previously, when he'd seen her do that, her expression had been that of a deeply troubled person.

"What pleases you so much?"

"The sand. This time, when I watched it falling, sifting through my fingers, I didn't think that every minute that passed brought me closer to blindness. That's over, thanks to you."

So that was it. "Come over here," he said, leading her to a nest of large rocks. He dusted the boulders with his handkerchief, and they sat quietly for a long time, looking out at the ocean.

"Are you going to forgive me, Mason? Try to remember that I did those things before I ever saw you, and that my crime was in not telling you. I have relived my opportunities to tell you one thousand times; you can't know how sorry I am." She folded her hands in her lap to steady them.

"You're asking my forgiveness. Does this mean that you can accept me as I am?" She rose and held out her hand to him, and they walked back to the house. He had to be aware, as she was, that this might be their last chance. As she stood with her hand on the doorknob, his piercing gaze unnerved her.

"You haven't answered my question."

"I accept what I know of you; I admire what I know of you."

When he reached past her to push the door open, his forearm brushed the tips of her breasts, stunning them both and bringing a blaze to his eyes. He stared down at her.

"I don't want you to compromise; I need you to love me for who I am, as I am."

Her head jerked back, and she looked at him, breathless with anticipation. He'd never said that before. She grasped his hand, hopeful now for their future, and led him to the living room.

"I won't settle for less than I need; don't let that worry you. I'm after what's inside you that you never let me see. That's all. I want you to open up to me and let me love you without reservations. I want to know you as no other human being does and, until you let me, you won't want to know who *I* am."

"Oh, yes; I read your novel, and it riveted me. I thought about my own life, the hard knocks, raw bruises, disappointments and uncertainties. I never had many friends, because I was too busy making my way; Steve was the closest person to me. But I couldn't tell Steve when I had a setback or missed out on something I wanted badly, because he sacrificed his youth, his education, everything, for me, and I wanted him to know that his trust was well placed. So I locked everything in, kept my problems to myself."

She gave silent thanks; the tide had begun, and she hoped it would bring a flood.

"I'll never forget the day I walked away from medicine," he went on, as though oblivious to her presence. "I tried to tell Betty, whom I was seeing at the time, what I was going through, and I had never before attempted to reach a woman at that level. She threw a tantrum about my foolishness and reinforced what I'd suspected: she didn't care about me or my feelings; she wanted the doctor, the socialite, not Mason Fenwick. I remember the hollow, sickening feeling I had as I turned away from her. I still dislike the smell of lilac perfume, because she was wearing it, and the scent hung in my nostrils.

"Three weeks. Three agonizing weeks of waiting and watching beside Bianca Norris's bed after I'd done all I could for her, praying that she could come out of that coma. You can't imagine the loneliness."

Her heart swelled, and moisture clouded her vision. Hurting for him, she moved closer and laced her fingers through his, but didn't speak. She wanted him to let it all out.

"Would anyone have understood that, if it had been possible, I would have exchanged places with that woman? I couldn't dump that on my brother and, when I walked away, I couldn't make him understand, and he never accepted it."

She decided to risk a question. "Why did you leave it all?"

He leaned back on the sofa and propped his right ankle on his left knee, and she let herself relax when she saw that he would continue. "I had become a society doctor, treating the wealthy, squiring around rich women—black ones, white ones, Latin ones, foreign ones—all decked out in designer clothes, wearing designer perfume and starving themselves to death in New York's most expensive restaurants. I was in great demand, socially and professionally; doctors sent me their toughest cases, and I began to believe that I could do no wrong. In that operating room that morning, I got straightened out. I was not infallible. Later, I looked at myself and didn't like what I had become. I no longer had time for Steve; I'd stopped going to church, quit volunteer work, and had even begun to neglect myself. No surgeon can make it indefinitely on five or six hours sleep, sometimes less, each night. I was busy at everything but what I should have been doing. I wouldn't have noticed Skip, and I shudder to think what I would have missed."

Her heart bloomed, a rose unfolding its petals, hammering an erratic rhythm, and she squeezed his hand in an effort to communicate to him the love that swelled inside of her.

He didn't recall ever before having spilled his guts to anyone, and still more churned inside of him, struggling for release.

"I'm boring you with all this."

She had wanted to know him, and he had opened himself to her. He started to draw himself inward, to put some distance between them, but her arm slid around him and tightened.

"Oh, no, my darling. You're not boring me, you're loving me."

"What?"

Her other slid across his chest, and her head rested on his shoulder. "I said…I heard somewhere that to love is to give yourself, imperfections and all. And that's what I wanted, all I wanted. Assurance that you'd let me be there for you when you needed love and understanding, because if you'd do that, you'd accept who I am as well."

She was too good to be true, and he couldn't help stiffening. From where he sat, all the saints were above.

"Nothing I told you makes you anxious? You don't think less of me?"

Her soft hand caressed his face, and he leaned into it. "How could it? What I feel is sadness that, when you most needed someone who loved you, you had no one. Oh, you survived it; you'll always do that, but life is easier and sweeter when it's shared. Are you sorry you told me?" She watched his fingers dance on his knee as he strummed the way in which pianists exercise their fingers. Part of his thinking process, she realized.

"No. Oddly, I'm not sorry; I feel as though I've dropped a weight." She snuggled closer, and he voiced a belated thought.

"Do you realize you called me darling? That's a first. Why?"

"I feel closer to you."

His pulse raced, and he had to gasp for the breath that lodged in his throat. "You're saying nothing's changed your feelings for me, that you love me?"

"More than ever. I realize that I hurt you when I said I didn't know you and that you didn't meet my needs, but I didn't know any other way to express it." Tears pooled in her eyes and wet his hand.

"Honey, don't cry. It's alright. I understand a lot of things now. Don't… Ah, baby…it…there's nothing to forgive. Sweetheart, I just wanted you to love me."

"I do. Oh, I do. I..."

He covered her mouth and kissed her with all the passion that fermented inside of him, with love that screamed for his admittance.

"I need you," she whispered. "Mason, *I need you*. It's been so long. So long." Shudders racked him when she parted her lips for his possessive kiss and pressed his fingers to her breast.

"Is that door locked?" She nodded impatiently, and he rose and raced with her up the stairs to her room. In the heat of passion, they couldn't strip each other fast enough. Her fingers stumbled over the buttons on the front of his shirt, and he finally pulled it over his head. Her skirt zipper caught the woolen fabric, and she wanted him to tear it off of her. At last, he lay her on the bed.

"Let me," she whispered, when he reached for his bikini underwear. Hot arrows of desire sliced through him, and he jumped to full readiness when she hooked her arms around him, drew him to her and kissed him. And he could hardly withstand the torture of wanting her when she lay back and opened her arms to him. He eased into the heaven of her embrace, his body screaming for gratification inside of her, but he gazed into her trusting, loving face and brought himself under control.

Jeannetta lifted her body to accept him, but he denied her, worried her mouth with his lips and traced a hot frenzied path to her neck, while his fingers toyed with her breasts. Her body began to beg for what she wanted, undulating from side to side, but he stilled her and covered a nipple with his lips, blowing on it until she begged him to suckle her. She couldn't help crying aloud when at last his mouth began to pull on it, and his knowing fingers found the core of her passion and teased it until it released its love liquid.

"Mason, please...Honey, please. *Please*."

He didn't answer. His busy mouth found her other nipple and brought a keening cry from her. Frustrated, she hooked her leg over his thigh, reached for him, and tried to get what she wanted. He leaned over her and asked permission to enter.

"Yes, Yes. For God's sake, *yes!*" She tensed with anticipation as he gathered her in his arms, positioned himself at her love gate and thrust into her. She bucked beneath him, begging for immediate satisfaction, but he withdrew, held her still, and entered with a powerful surge. Slowly, he began the dance, and she caught his rhythm and let herself go.

"Are you with me, honey? Am I where you want me to be?"

She let her legs tighten around him. "Yes. Oh, yes. Mason, darling, I want to burst."

"And you will." Shower after shower of hot darts penetrated her feminine core as he began a lover's kiss that simulated the movement of his body and duplicated the wizardry of his fingers between them. She couldn't help crying out as the spasm began, and he accelerated his powerful strokes until her screams filled the room and she surrendered herself to him.

"Mason. Oh, Mason, love, I love you so."

Her body clutched at him, demanding his total capitulation, and he splintered in her arms with words that he had never uttered before. *"I love you, Jeannetta. I love you. Love you. You're my life. Everything."*

Sated. Enervated. Drained. Long minutes passed before they spoke.

"I thought we were perfect together, that we'd reached the pinnacle of ecstasy," he whispered, still secure within her, "but it was never like this. Never." He propped himself on his elbows, and hugged her to him.

"I know. I used to feel empty inside for a long time after you sent me flying practically out of this world, and that bothered me. But now I know what it means to be fulfilled." He pulled her closer.

"I...I love you, and I don't mind saying it. I've loved you since Istanbul, do you know that?"

She could fee the smile that spread over her face, a smile of contentment. "I thought you loved me, because you acted as if you did, but I didn't know whether you knew it."

"I knew it alright. You're a wise woman."

"How so?"

"That novel of yours, it set me to wondering."

"I'd hoped it would."

"And what a title! *The Naked Soul Of A Man In Love.* It's heavy stuff. Look. If I don't have anything good to tell Skip tomorrow, my credit with him's going to suffer. Do you know he actually offered to talk to you on my behalf if you turned me down? I ought to be as good at this as my twelve-year-old kid thinks he is."

"What would you like to tell him?"

"That you're going to be my wife and his mother."

She gazed into eyes that blazed with love, knew that he offered more than she'd ever dreamed of wanting, and snuggled closer to him. But he moved away as though to emphasize business before pleasure.

"Well?"

"Fine with me. You're just what I want and need. Both of you."

He reached down beside the bed, took the old keys out of his pants pocket and pressed them into her hand.

"What's this?"

"The keys to our home, the one we'll build on a hill where we'll see the sun rise in the morning and set in the evening." She closed her fingers around them, snuggled closer and smiled. He gazed at her for long minutes, then turned to the business at hand, and she opened to the sweet honey of his love.